SHAUN HUTSON OMNIBUS

Purity
Deadhead

SHAUN HUTSON OMNIBUS

Purity
Deadhead

SHAUN HUTSON

timewarner
paperbacks

A *Time Warner* Paperback

This omnibus edition first published in Great Britain by
Time Warner Paperbacks in 2004
Shaun Hutson Omnibus Copyright © Shaun Hutson 2004

Previously published separately:
Purity first published in Great Britain in 1998 by
Little, Brown and Company
Published by Warner Books in 1999
Reprinted 1999 (twice), 2000
Reprinted by Time Warner Paperbacks in 2002
Reprinted 2002
Copyright © Shaun Hutson 1998

Deadhead first published in Great Britain in 1993 by
Little, Brown and Company
Published by Warner Books in 1994
Reprinted 1994, 1995, 1998, 1999
Copyright © Shaun Hutson 1993

A CIP catalogue record for this book
is available from the British Library.

ISBN 0 7515 3646 6

Printed and bound in Great Britain by
Clays Ltd, St Ives plc

Time Warner Paperbacks
An imprint of
Time Warner Books UK
Brettenham House
Lancaster Place
London WC2E 7EN

www.TimeWarnerBooks.co.uk

Purity

'Life is an incurable disease.'
Abraham Cowley

This novel is dedicated to
Barbara Boote
A 'real book' with real thanks

One

'So, how easy do you think it would be to kill some-one?'

Amy Watson took a drag on her cigarette then blew out a long stream of smoke, watching it slowly dissipate in the air. She gently flicked the dead end into the already overflowing ashtray on the desk, glancing at a microphone in front of her, then at a small video screen to her left. In luminous green letters the words PAUL – MUSWELL HILL were blinking.

She sat forward in her seat, one carefully manicured hand moving slowly over her black Levi's, wiping away a piece of fluff and some stray ash. She took a sip from her coffee cup, aware of the impenetrable silence inside the studio, then leaned closer to the microphone.

'Come on, Paul,' she said softly. 'This is supposed to be a talk show. Talk to me. Answer the question. Would you kill someone if you got the chance? If you *knew* you could get away with it? Could you bring yourself to take another human life?'

'If that person had killed someone close to me, yes I could,' said Paul from Muswell Hill. 'If it was like my girlfriend or someone like that.'

'I don't believe you. I think that even if someone raped your girlfriend and murdered your parents and you caught that person, you wouldn't be able to kill them; you wouldn't be able to bring yourself to do it.'

'I bloody would,' Paul grunted.

'You'd get up close and knife them, would you?' Amy persisted. 'You'd stick that blade in and risk getting covered in their blood, or you'd press that gun barrel to their heads and blow their brains out, would you? I don't think so.' She reached for the pack of cigarettes lying close by, placed one between her lips and lit it. 'It isn't a pretty sight, Paul. It isn't like it is in films, you know. There's a lot of mess and pain and it smells too. It's not like Arnold Schwarzenegger mowing down the bad guys with a smile and a stupid joke. We're talking about *real* people.'

'You don't know enough about me to tell me I couldn't do it,' Paul of Muswell Hill said angrily.

'I think I do, Paul,' Amy told him and flicked a switch on the console in front of her.

Paul disappeared both from her headset and from the video screen.

She glanced at the next name. GEORGE – ESHER.

She waited a moment before connecting him.

'Crime, capital punishment, murder,' Amy said, smiling. 'That's what we're talking about at the moment. All good clean fun here on the radio. If you've got a view on those subjects or on any others, ring in now. You know the number.' She gave it out once more. 'If you've got views that you think are worth sharing, then share them with me. I might even agree with you. If I don't, then you're history.' She flicked the switch. 'Go ahead, George from Esher, you're on. Dazzle us with your views.'

'Hello,' said a faltering voice.

'Go ahead, George,' Amy said, taking another drag on her cigarette.

'Hello, can you hear me?'

'Loud and clear, George. The nation is waiting.'

'Well, what I wanted to say was that I agree with you.'

'Grovelling won't keep you on the air any longer, George. Agree with me about what?'

'I don't think the average man would be able to take a life even if it was done in revenge. That's why I think we should have capital punishment.'

'George, you know what that's called? It's called passing the buck. You let someone else murder for you.'

'Capital punishment is hardly murder, is it?'

'Strapping a man's wrists and ankles together, placing

a linen bag over his head, slipping a noose of rope around his neck, then sending him hurtling through a trapdoor to break his neck – *that* isn't murder?'

'If he's committed a murder then he's got it coming.'

'He's got it coming. Now there's the voice of a reasoned liberal-minded individual, George. And what if he's innocent? Would you be prepared to let the state snuff out the life of an innocent man?'

'The chances of an innocent man being hanged are very, very slim. I—'

Amy cut him short. 'Are they, George? Tell that to Timothy Evans and James Hanratty. What about the Guildford Four and the Birmingham Six? They'd have been executed if we still had capital punishment. People who were later found to be innocent. Would those innocent lives have been worth it, George? What if that innocent man was you, George? As you were about to go hurtling through the trap, would your last thought be "Well, never mind, at least I'm only one in a thousand; this doesn't happen very often"? I doubt it.'

'So I suppose you think that they should be let off, do you?' countered George from Esher haughtily. 'You think they should be *understood* or pitied?'

'No. I think murderers should get life but life should *be* life. They shouldn't be out in ten years.'

'Capital punishment is a greater deterrent.'

'No it isn't, George. How many states in America have the death penalty and look at their murder rates? Much higher than ours.'

'Prisons are like holiday camps now. Three square meals a day, television—'

Again she cut him short. 'What would you advocate then, George?' Amy said, blowing out another stream of smoke. 'Rat-infested cells, bread and water, floggings twice a day? You're history, George.' She flicked one of the switches on the console in front of her.

'On line four we have Wendy from Harrow. What can you add to this debate, Wendy?'

'What about child murderers?' said Wendy from Harrow. 'Would you execute them?'

'I have my own views on what we should do with child murderers, Wendy.'

'And what are they?'

'The same thing we should do with paedophiles. We should put them in a room with the parents of the child they've abused or killed, tie them to a chair, then let the parents loose on them with baseball bats and hammers. It might seem a little radical but I think it would do the job.'

'Men who kill children, and paedophiles too, they should be treated. The important thing is to find out why they do what they do. They need help.'

'And what sort of help would you give the parents of the children they had abused or killed, Wendy?'

'It would help them to cope with the loss better if they knew why it had happened.'

'Have you got any children, Wendy?'

'No, I . . .'

'Then don't get involved in arguments like this. How can you hope to understand the feelings of a parent who's lost a child if you have no children of your own?'

'I'm a social worker and—'

'Say no more. You're history.' Amy cut her off gleefully. 'Thank you for that contribution, Wendy from Harrow. I love social workers, don't you? People who actually get paid for having no comprehension of real life. Perhaps one of the few cases where capital punishment should be obligatory. So, any social workers out there, if you're listening, why not ring in and tell me why you shouldn't all be put in a boat, towed to the middle of the Atlantic and drowned. Just call the usual number. You should know it by now.' Again Amy gave out the number of the show. 'We've got to take a commercial break but when we come back we'll be talking about a subject even more dear to my own heart. The one subject guaranteed to provoke a completely irrational response from normally stable people. Yes, we'll be discussing smoking. So, while you all get your questions and comments ready, I'm going to light up. We'll be back in three minutes.'

Amy got to her feet, pulled off her headset and dropped it on the desk.

She looked at the microphone, a smiling face drawn on its yellow foam cover, etched there with a Biro by one of the station's other presenters. On the screen to her left half a dozen calls were already waiting to be answered.

As she headed for the studio door she glanced first at her watch then at the clock above the console.

12.02 a.m.

Two

'The lines are on fire tonight,' Mike Osborne commented as Amy hurried into the control room.

He had produced Amy's show since its inception nearly eighteen months ago, and was, at thirty-six, eight years older than her. He was a tall, powerfully built man, and was dressed in a denim jacket and faded jeans, with a small rose-shaped tattoo on the back of his left hand. He'd tried to have it removed on three separate occasions using laser treatment, but the tattoo's shape was still clearly visible. Osborne always wore the sleeves of his shirts buttoned in an effort to hide the mark, believing the tattoo was somehow inappropriate for someone in his position. Whether any of his superiors thought the same he didn't know. None had ever voiced an opinion one way or the other.

The other occupant of the control room was two years younger than Amy. Joanne Parker acted as a researcher, assistant and, more importantly, a close friend to Amy. The two women had known each other for three years, having met at a party at Planet Hollywood. At the time Jo had been working as PA to a director of a firm making soft drinks and Amy was just beginning her career in radio. They had hit it off immediately with that curious kind of spiritual kinship that so rarely comes along in life.

'Can you get me another coffee, please, Jo?' Amy asked. 'I'm just nipping to the loo.'

'Make it quick,' Osborne said, glancing at his watch. 'You're back on the air in two minutes.'

'There's some mail, Amy,' Jo told her. 'Do you want to wait until after the show?'

'No, leave it on my desk inside the studio,' Amy said,

hovering by the door. 'How does it sound from here, so far?'

'It sounds good. Now get a move on,' Osborne told her.

'Are you sure?' Amy persisted.

Osborne picked up an empty paper cup and threw it at her with a smile.

'Move it,' he shouted, then grinned.

Amy hurried along the short corridor to the Ladies, one eye on her watch. Ninety seconds left.

She flushed the toilet, ran her hands beneath the hot tap, and hurried back to the studio. Swinging herself into her seat and pulling on her headset, she listened to the commercials through one earpiece while she waited for the red light to flash on to tell her she was back on the air.

There were a small pile of letters and two small packages stacked neatly on the desk next to a steaming cup of coffee. She sipped at the coffee as she began ripping open the first of the letters.

She read them swiftly.

The abusive ones she dropped straight into her wastebin. They didn't usually vary in content no matter what their source or writer. The main difference was the lucidity used to attack her. Some of the letters were short and sweet. Words like 'mouthy bitch', 'loud-mouthed tart', occasionally eclipsed by such descriptions as 'self opinionated' or 'arrogant', dependent on the source of the letter. Every now and then correspondence praising her opinions or the show in general would arrive, but Amy tended to treat those with the same scepticism she treated the more derisory correspondence. There was a number of requests for her autograph, more for signed photos. Some even included their own photos. Others sent old pictures taken of her when she was a model years ago. Some of these were accompanied by insults. Every now and then there would be a threat.

The word 'whore' had been used in one of the letters

and attached to it, a photo taken from a spread she'd done for *Penthouse* two years ago.

Amy screwed up the photo and the letter into a ball and binned them.

Above the studio door the red light came on, glowing dully in the gloom of the room.

'Welcome back,' she said, swivelling round in her chair and pushing the other earpiece into position. 'I hope you enjoyed those clumsy attempts to get you to part with your money. Now back to business.' She lit a cigarette. 'Smoking.' Amy blew out a stream of smoke. 'What is the rule now? You can only smoke in your own bedroom, under the duvet after midnight? That would be about it, wouldn't it? After all, everyone knows that smokers are to blame for everything from cancer to the break-up of the Royal Family. Cigarettes are the greatest single threat to human life since bubonic plague, and anyone who actually dares to admit they enjoy the filthy weed is lower down the food chain than plankton.' She took another drag, careful to lean close enough to the microphone so that every sound was audible. 'That tastes good and if I want to kill myself by doing it, then that's *my* choice. All you non-smokers who are always ranting on about the dangers of passive smoking should thank people like me. With the money the government screws out of smokers, it stops you paying so much tax. So, all you self-righteous do-gooders who complain about smokers just remember that.' She glanced at the video screen where several calls were already flashing green.

'Harold from Chiswick, what do you think of smoking and smokers?'

'It's a filthy habit,' Harold from Chiswick snapped.

'Have you ever smoked, Harold?' Amy asked.

'No, I haven't. It's disgusting and it's dangerous. Passive smoking causes cancer.'

'Where's your proof?'

'Any doctor will tell you that.'

'Any doctor will tell you that drinking to excess is bad for you. Do you drink, Harold?'

'Yes. What's that got to do with it?'

'Well, if I get behind the wheel of a car smoking a cigarette the chances of me killing someone are small, but if *you* go out and have a drink, drive home and hit someone then does that make them a passive driver? There are more deaths on the road every year related to drinking than smoking aren't there, Harold?'

'That's a ridiculous argument.'

'Is it? Have you ever been drunk?'

'I don't drink that much, I—'

'Have you ever been drunk, it's a simple question, I've tried to use single syllables where possible. Have you in your life ever been drunk? Yes or no?'

'Yes, when I was younger.'

'How old are you now?'

'Forty. What's that got to do with it?'

'Okay, somewhere back in your dim and distant past, dim being the operative word, you have been drunk. Correct?'

'Yes.'

'Now what do you think most people find more obnoxious, a smoker blowing smoke near them or a drunk slobbering all over them trying to tell them his philosophy on life or, if they're really unlucky, throwing up on them? Which would *you* rather have, given the choice, Harold? If you were shut in a room for twenty-four hours with either a smoker or a drunk, which would you choose?'

'That's not an argument, it's—'

'You're history, Harold.' She flicked another switch.

'Line two,' she said. 'Sarah from Wapping. Sarah, are *you* a smoker?'

'Yes I am; I'm also a nurse.'

'It's a wonder you can afford fags on the pittance you get paid. Isn't there a little bit of a double standard there, Sarah? You're a part of the medical profession, a profession dedicated to preserving health, and yet you ally yourself with one of its greatest enemies, cigarettes. How many do you smoke a day?'

'Twenty. Sometimes more.'

'And what point would you like to make?'

'Smoking is an addiction, right, but smokers get no help from the government or the media. I've seen junkies brought into Casualty suffering from overdoses; I've seen drunks brought in who've done themselves or other people damage and yet everyone wants to help them. Junkies can get methadone on the NHS to help them with their addiction and drinkers can go to Alcoholics Anonymous, but it seems as if no one wants to help smokers. It's as if everyone thinks it's our fault that we smoke.'

'How do you feel about people with lung complaints being refused treatment if they smoke?'

'I don't agree with it. Drinkers with cirrhosis of the liver are treated; they aren't told they'll be denied treatment if they don't stop drinking. I think it's unfair.'

'So do I, Sarah, and I'll tell you something else that's unfair. It's only ever cigarette smokers who are criticised. Never cigar or pipe smokers and I think we'd all agree that those things give off more and far worse smoke than a good old fag. Right?'

'Right.'

'Thank you, Sarah. Let's see what Andy on line one has to say. Go ahead, Andy. By the way, where are you calling from? I can't quite make it out.'

'I'm on a mobile,' came the reply.

'And are you smoking?'

'No, and I wouldn't go out with a bird who did.'

'A bird. Now there's a phrase you don't hear very often, Andy. Political correctness passed you by with the same speed as freedom of choice obviously. Because that's what it comes down to in the end, isn't it? *Your* freedom not to go out with a woman who smokes and *my* choice to steer clear of Neanderthals like you.'

'You think you're clever, don't you?'

'Well, I haven't had an invite to the Mensa Christmas

party yet but I do my best. Do you think *you're* clever? But then again this is supposed to be a *serious* discussion, isn't it? I beg your pardon. Back to the cigarettes.'

'Fu—'

'That's it, Andy, just stick to the reasoned arguments. They seem to work better for you.' She turned off the line. 'Well, there goes Andy into the night. Take care women everywhere, if you want a smooth-talking devil like him to romance you, then ditch those Rothmans now.'

As she spoke, Amy glanced across at the two packages on her desk, wondering what could be inside.

One was about the shape and size of a shoe box, the other was flatter, a squashed Jiffy bag.

Both bore London postmarks.

'You never see people smoking on the television any more either – has anyone noticed that?' she continued. 'On old episodes of *Coronation Street* and on chat shows people used to come on puffing away, but not any more. It's a bad influence, you see. Obviously the people who run TV are afraid that the sight of a celebrity smoking will induce millions to run out and start chain-smoking.' She glanced at the monitor.

'David from Petts Wood, what have you got to say on this subject?' Amy said, flicking another switch.

'Well, I don't smoke,' David from Petts Wood said with a slow deliberation over each word that made it sound as if he was reading from a card.

'You should try it, David,' Amy insisted.

'My father died of lung cancer.'

'I'm sorry to hear that. Did he smoke?'

'No.'

Amy ran a hand through her hair.

'So, what you're trying to tell me is that even if you don't smoke you can still get cancer, David, is that right?' she said, realising that this caller was struggling.

No need to crucify the poor bastard.

'I think so, yes.'

'Quite right, David. You could smoke fifty fags a day

and never be ill. You could steer clear of cigarettes all your life and still get cancer. In fact, you could get hit by a bus tomorrow so you might as well go out and enjoy yourself. Don't you agree, David?'

'I've got cancer.'

Shit.

'I'm sorry to hear that, David,' Amy said quietly.

Don't let them hear you're shocked.

'Is it smoking related?' Amy asked.

'The doctor said it could have been hereditary, because of my father.'

Amy looked up towards the window of the control booth and saw Osborne frantically drawing his hand across his throat in a cutting motion.

Amy ignored him.

'Do you think it's wrong for people to smoke around you if they know you've got cancer?' she enquired.

'Well, it isn't going to make me any worse.'

Amy smiled. *Thank you, David from Petts Wood.*

'David, I want you to do something for me,' Amy said, leaning closer to the microphone. 'I want you to ring this show again in a week and let me know how you're getting on. Will you do that for me?'

'I'm having some more chemotherapy tomorrow.'

'Well, then you ring back tomorrow night if you feel up to it, but do me that favour, will you, David? You keep in touch with the show and let us all know how you're getting on.'

'All right.'

'You take care of yourself, David.'

She cut him off.

In the production booth Osborne shook his head and smiled.

Amy sipped at her coffee, scanned the flashing names and selected another.

'Frankie from Upton Park in the good old East End,' she said cheerily. 'How are you, Frankie, and what's your point?'

'That nurse, earlier, right. She was wrong about what she was saying about drugs, right?'

'Which part of what she said was wrong, Frankie?'

'If you let me finish, I'll tell you, won't I?'

'I beg your pardon. Please continue.'

'If you're on drugs, right, then you can't get help from people 'cos, like, it's against the law, right?'

'This is fascinating, Frankie, do go on. And on. And on.'

'Are you listening to me?'

'For about another five seconds unless you make your point.'

'Fags, drugs, drink. It's all the same. It's all a drug but it depends what you're taking, don't it? I mean, fags, right, they ain't like cocaine, are they?'

'No, it *is* easier to buy a packet of Superkings than a bag of cocaine at your corner shop, I'll give you that. Have you taken drugs, Frankie? You sound as if you might be on them at the moment.'

'I've dabbled.'

Frankie from Upton Park dissolved into fits of whooping laughter.

'You're history, Frankie. Ian from Kilburn,' she continued, taking the next call. 'Have you ever dabbled?'

'With drugs?' the caller asked. 'Just the odd spliff, you know. Nothing like cocaine or heroin.'

'Do I detect an Irish accent there, Ian?'

'Yes. Is it that obvious?'

'Fairly. Which part of Ireland are you from?'

'Cork.'

'How long have you lived in London?'

'About ten years.'

'And what were you phoning in about?'

'Well, it's the drugs thing really. I wanted to ask a question. I wanted to ask *you* a question.'

'Fire away, Ian, or maybe that's the wrong thing to say to an Irishman. What's your question?'

'You used to be a model and I read somewhere that

catwalk models and photographic models snort cocaine because it stops them feeling hungry. So if they don't feel hungry, they don't want to eat and that's what keeps them slim. Is that how you kept your figure when you were modelling?'

Amy looked up at the clock on the studio wall.

'Congratulations, Ian,' she said, grinning. 'You are the first caller on tonight's show to mention my modelling career. A mere one hour and seventeen minutes from the beginning of the show. I think that's a world record.'

'I didn't mean to be offensive, it's just that everyone knows you used to be a model and it's something I've always been curious about.'

'Ian, you flatter me. Perhaps everyone listening doesn't know that I was a model.'

'Ah, go on. You were a model for about six years, weren't you?'

'Seven actually.'

'So, did you take drugs to stay slim?'

'Drugs were available, most models will tell you that. I've always been lucky. I don't have to watch what I eat and it was a hectic career, lots of dashing about. There wasn't always *time* to eat. Anyway, enough about me—'

He interrupted her. 'Being on the go all the time, you must have got pretty horny with no boyfriend. Did you and any of the other girls ever—'

'Thank you, Ian,' said Amy, cutting him off. 'You're history, but I'll tell you something, that attempt at a question towards the end raises an interesting point for you guys listening out there. What is so fascinating about two women having sex? Why do you always want to watch? Why do you all think that a woman's secret fantasy is to sleep with another woman? Let me know.' She gave out the number to call.

Amy took another drag on her cigarette and selected one of the many waiting callers.

'Don from Southwark. Tell us about *your* fantasy.'

'I want to rape a woman.'

Three

'Why, Don?' Amy asked, her voice even.

'Because that's my fantasy. Some women fantasise about it too.'

'Do they? Which women?'

'Women say in magazines that they dream of being raped.'

'Some women fantasise about rough sex, Don, but there's a world of difference between fantasising about rough sex and actually doing it. Just like there's a difference between rough sex and rape. Have you ever been rough with a woman you've made love to, Don?'

'Not that rough.'

'What's your definition of rough then?'

'A couple of slaps, a bit of pulling. You know, ripping her clothes off and that.'

'And the women you did this with, they agreed?'

'Well, one of them got a bit uppity about it.'

'Was this one of the women you slapped?'

'It was only a bit of fun. I'd had a few to drink. It happens, doesn't it?'

'So, she didn't want sex with a drunken slob so you slapped her? Is that right?'

'She'd been giving me the come-on all night. She was dressed in this short black dress, her tits were hanging out nearly. She was begging for it.'

'Was this your girlfriend?'

'I'd known her for a few months, we went out for a meal, hit a couple of clubs and then went back to her place. When it got round to time to do the business she bottled it. Said she wanted me to go home. Well, I wasn't having that. She'd been giving me the green light ever since I picked her up.'

'So you slapped her and had sex with her?'

'Yeah.'

'You had sex with her against her will? You raped her.'

'No. She enjoyed it after a while. I didn't hurt her.'

'You hit her. You had sex with her when she didn't want it. Wake up, Don. That was rape.'

'She enjoyed it.'

'Did she tell you that?'

'She didn't have to *tell* me.'

'Oh, I see, your incredible prowess as a lover was enough to let you know that she was satisfied. Is that right? So, Don, if that wasn't rape, what would be in your limited view? Your fantasy is to rape a woman – how would that fantasy differ from what you did to your girlfriend? You tell me what is different about rape?'

'With rape you'd have to hold the woman down, wouldn't you? She'd be spitting at you and fighting you, wouldn't she?'

'Has a woman ever spat in your face, Don?'

'No way.'

'Perhaps one should. Perhaps they should spit in your face, kick you in the nuts then stamp on your head with their stilettos. How do you think that would feel, Don? Or perhaps having your testicles shut in a vice might be more appropriate. Do you think you'd still feel like sex after that? Because that's probably how much your girlfriend felt like sex after you'd slapped her and forced yourself on her.'

'That's the sort of thing I expected you to say. I bet you'd like it rough, wouldn't you? I've seen your pictures in magazines, showing off your tits and arse. I bet you can't get enough of it—'

'Well, I've certainly had enough of you, Don, you moron. Crawl back under your stone.' Amy shook her head.

Fucking arsehole.

'Well, there goes Don into the night,' she continued.

'A plain, old-fashioned kind of guy. None of your "new man" rubbish for Don. A straitjacket might be an idea though. Let's see what our next and, hopefully, sane caller has to say. Go ahead, Emma from Camden.'

'Hello,' said Emma from Camden. 'I'd like to say firstly that I thought you dealt with that last dickhead . . .'

There was an awkward silence.

'I'm sorry, is it all right to say that?' Emma from Camden asked.

'What? Dickhead?' said Amy, smiling. 'I don't think they'll take me off the air for that, Emma.'

'Oh, good, because I thought he was a complete prat. That's just typical of some men's attitudes to women, isn't it? I mean—'

'You can make your point any time you like, Emma.'

'Sorry, yes, I was ringing in about fantasies. You know, sexual fantasies.'

'They were the ones I had in mind.'

'Well, what you said about men imagining two women in bed together – I agree with you that it's predictable but I also agree that most women would do it given the chance.'

'You think that most women would sleep with another woman if they had the chance?'

'Well, I don't think there's anything wrong with it.'

'Have you ever slept with another woman, Emma?'

'No, but my boyfriend wants me to.'

'Your *boyfriend* wants you to? And how do you feel about it? Who does he want you to sleep with?'

'My best friend, Kim.'

'Does Kim know this?'

'Not yet. My boyfriend wants me to talk her into a threesome. He's always going on about it. He says we should experiment with our sex lives.'

'That's a good idea, Emma. What's your boyfriend's best friend called?'

'Tony.'

'Well, as soon as you've persuaded Kim to sleep with

you and your boyfriend then get your boyfriend to go and arrange a threesome with him, you and Tony. How would you like that? Or more to the point, see how *he* likes that. What's your boyfriend's name?'

'Paul.'

'Well, if Paul wants to watch you and Kim having sex, tell him that you'd like *him* to watch while you have sex with Tony. How about that?'

There was a silence on the other end of the line.

Amy sucked on her cigarette.

'He says that he *needs* to do it before we get married,' Emma from Camden said. 'He says that it's his fantasy, that he needs to get it out of his system or he might be tempted to do it some time in the future.'

'So, you're thinking of getting married, are you, Emma? Has Paul made any other demands like this? Does he feel he has to sleep with an entire women's football team to get it out of his system before he gets married? Does he feel the need to fly off to Spain with his mates for one last lads' holiday before the big day? Stuff like that?'

'No, just the threesome. Do you think it's wrong then?'

'I'm not an agony aunt, Emma, but can't you see he's holding you to ransom here? He's blackmailing you emotionally. Either you arrange a threesome or he's threatening you with an affair later in your marriage.'

'But I do quite fancy Kim myself.'

There was a giggle at the other end of the line.

'Then sleep with her and tell him about it afterwards or make him a video,' said Amy, stubbing out her cigarette. 'Better still, make him a video of you, Kim and Tony. That should keep him happy for hours.'

Amy flicked a switch and went to another call.

'Hi, there, Peter from Muswell Hill,' she said, cheerfully. 'I've had a few calls from Muswell Hill tonight. There—'

'Did you get the package?' The voice was low and even.

'I've got a couple of packages here, Peter,' Amy told him. 'How do I know which one's from you?'

'It's in brown paper,' said the monotone voice, 'inside the Jiffy bag.'

'Will I like what's in it?'

'Just open it and find out.'

In the production booth Mike Osborne was already on his feet. He moved towards the glass partition, peering in anxiously at Amy.

Without a second thought and, as yet, unable to see Osborne, she pulled the package towards her.

Four

'Go on, open it.'

The voice seemed to reverberate around the studio.

'This is when you wish you were on television instead of radio, isn't it?' said Amy. 'So everyone can share the excitement.' She looked up and saw Osborne standing at the production-room window. He was pointing to the package and shaking his head.

Amy merely shrugged and reached for a pair of scissors to cut through the masking tape that sealed the top of the bag.

Beneath the brown tape, staples had also been used to secure the package.

'Do you do your Christmas presents up like this, Peter?' Amy said humourlessly.

At the other end of the line she could hear faint breathing.

'Well, ladies and gentlemen, listening out there,' she said, pulling the last of the masking tape free, 'I have undone the first part of the package. Exciting, isn't it?'

Osborne was scribbling something on a piece of card using a marker pen.

He pressed it to the glass.

It read: IT COULD BE A BOMB.

Amy read it as she prepared to undo the staples.

'Give me a clue what's in it, Peter?' she said into the microphone.

'Something for *you*,' the voice said softly. 'I listen to your show every night. I agree with everything you say.'

'Now that's my kind of man,' Amy said and chuckled.

She started on the staples using a pair of scissors to prise the metal free.

Osborne banged on the glass again and gestured even more frantically towards the sign.

Amy found that she could focus on only one of the hastily scrawled words now – BOMB.

She removed another of the staples.

'I've been listening to you for the last year,' said the voice. 'I've got photos of you. I even tape the programmes every night. And when you're on television, I videotape you.'

'What do you do for a living, Peter?'

BOMB.

Leave it there now. Leave it on the desk top.

'I haven't got a job.'

Leave the fucking package alone.

She freed the final staple.

Amy looked up at Osborne then pulled open the package.

There was a pungent smell coming from inside the Jiffy bag. A musty, familiar odour.

'Have you got it open yet?' the voice asked.

Amy used a pencil to feel inside the bag.

There was something soft in there.

She reached in with the tip of a finger.

It felt like material.

Silk.

The smell was growing stronger.

She used the scissors to cut down the side of the bag, opening it carefully and slowly, aware of both Osborne and Jo now watching her through the glass.

Why the hell was that smell familiar?

She used the pencil to lift out the contents of the bag.

'Well, Peter, just what I always wanted,' she said quietly.

The silk camisole dangled harmlessly on the end of the pencil.

Osborne placed both hands on his cheeks, a look of relief spreading across his features.

'I thought about you when I was picking them out,'

the voice told her, a note of excitement creeping into it. 'I pictured you in them.'

There was a pair of grip-top stockings in the bag too.

Both the camisole and the stockings were spattered with semen.

'That's *my* fantasy,' said the voice.

A chuckle.

Amy dropped the camisole, the stink of stale ejaculate strong in her nostrils.

'You'd look beautiful in them,' the voice purred. 'You'd look beautiful in anything. I'd like to see you in them one day. Perhaps we could meet.'

'That's very kind, Peter,' Amy said, gazing at the semen-stained stockings. 'I think I'm busy until the year two thousand and twenty.'

Another chuckle at the other end of the line.

'I like a woman with a sense of humour.'

'That isn't your first criterion, is it, Peter? I would have thought a pulse might have been top of the list. Or maybe not in your case.'

Amy lifted one of the white-flecked stockings up on the tip of the pencil so that Osborne could see it, then, with her free hand, she made a circle with her thumb and forefinger and shook them in the air.

The producer nodded.

'I'd do anything for you,' said the voice, then hung up.

'Well, it's not often someone cuts *me* off,' Amy said, pushing the camisole and stockings off the desk on to the floor.

The smell still clogged her nostrils.

'We're coming up to the news in about twenty seconds,' Amy said, glancing down at the crumpled clothes. 'Perhaps there'll be something worth talking about after we've heard it. You know the number to call.'

'I'd do anything for you.'

When she looked up again, Mike Osborne was still standing at the window of the production booth. He was shaking his head slowly.

Amy waved him away then glanced at the second package on her desk.

'Here's the news,' she said into the microphone. 'Listen carefully, I'll be asking questions later.'

She switched off the microphone.

When she looked back towards the window of the production booth Osborne was gone.

She reached for the other package.

Five

'Don't open it.'

Amy turned to see Osborne entering the studio, pointing at the package. 'You don't know *what* could be inside.'

'Probably more of that,' said Amy, motioning towards the pile of semen-spattered clothes beneath the desk.

'Sick fucker,' Osborne said contemptuously. 'I'll get someone in to clean it up.'

He noticed that Amy had the other package in her hand now.

'Amy, put it down, I'll call Security,' he told her. 'Let them deal with it.'

'Stop panicking, Mike.'

'It could be a bomb or anything.'

'People might not like everything I have to say but I doubt if anyone hates me enough to send me a bomb.'

'You'd be surprised,' he said, raising an eyebrow.

'Thanks for the vote of confidence. Look, it's just weirdo mail, Mike, nothing else.'

Before he could stop her, Amy had ripped off the brown paper covering to reveal a cardboard box. She shot him a challenging glance then lifted the lid.

Osborne flinched involuntarily.

'You're getting paranoid in your old age, Mike,' said Amy, smiling.

She turned the box towards him so that he could see its contents.

There was a box of chocolates inside, complete with a red foil bow stuck carefully on at one end. A small note was attached, which she read aloud. 'I love the programme, I hope you like these chocolates, lots of love, Stuart Gardiner.'

She pushed the box towards him. 'Want one? I'll save you the nut cluster.'

'Don't eat any of those,' Osborne insisted. 'They could be injected with poison or anything.'

'Have you been reading too many Agatha Christie novels, Mike?'

'Just bin the fucking things, will you? Make me feel better. Christ almighty, clothes that have been wanked on, poisoned chocolates. Who knows what—'

'No one says they've been poisoned,' Amy interrupted. 'Jesus, you *are* paranoid. But don't worry, I won't eat them. Happy now?'

'I put a trace on that last call by the way,' Osborne told her. 'The bastard who sent *those*.' He pointed towards the soiled camisole and stockings.

'What for?'

'Because he's a fucking weirdo.'

'Half the people who call this programme are fucking weirdos, Mike, you know that. The guy is harmless, trust me.'

'How can you be so sure?'

'Because I've had calls like that before, dozens of them.'

'And how many times has someone sent you clothes he's shot his load over?'

'I've been threatened with beatings, rape and Christ knows what else since this show started, and yet tonight is the first time you've reacted like this. Just cool it, Mike. The guy isn't dangerous, I'd bet money on it.' She took a drag on her cigarette. 'How long have we been doing this programme now? Eighteen months?'

He nodded.

'Nothing's happened yet and it's not likely to,' she said with an air of assurance that Osborne didn't share.

He glanced up at the studio clock.

'You're back on in fifty seconds,' he said flatly, turning towards the door. 'Don't blame me for being concerned, Amy.'

'I appreciate it, but don't worry. I can look after myself. I'm a big girl now.'

He looked up at the clock again.

'Thirty seconds,' he said and left.

She was alone in the studio again.

Six

Amy rubbed her eyes as she sat back from the microphone, listening to the tirade of words in her headset. Reaching for her coffee she took a sip, wincing when she found it was cold.

It felt chilly inside the studio and she made a mental note to check the heating at the next break.

Meanwhile, John from Fulham forged on, his words sometimes faltering. There was passion in his sentiments, anger even, but, she decided, enough was enough.

'Okay, slow down, John, I get your point,' she said, in an effort to halt the verbal barrage. 'So, what kind of role models would you like to see for kids?'

'Well, I suppose it should be their parents ideally but it doesn't work like that, does it?'

'Did you look up to *your* father?'

'Yes, he had his own business. I used to go out drinking with him at the weekends. He was everything I wanted to be.'

'What kind of business did he have?'

'He was a baker. He worked hard six days a week then he used to go out drinking on Saturday and Sunday.'

'And you went with him? How old were you then?'

'In my early twenties.'

'Didn't you have friends you could have gone out drinking with? I mean, it's a bit odd a bloke of twenty-two or twenty-three going down the pub with his dad, isn't it? That would be like a teenage girl wanting to go clubbing with her middle-aged mum.'

'What are you implying?'

'I'm not implying anything, John, I'm just curious. Did any of the other blokes your age go drinking with their fathers?'

'I don't know what the others were doing. That was their business, not mine. I went down the pub with my dad and his friends, that was what I wanted, I—'

'Hold on, John, rewind for a second. You went down the pub with your dad and his friends. So there you were, in your early twenties, surrounded by all these middle-aged men who you couldn't possibly hope to have anything in common with.'

'We talked about football.'

'Not the most expansive topic, John. You should have been out with guys your own age, chasing women, stuff like that. Are you married?'

'Yes, I have been for thirty years.'

'Kids?'

'A boy.'

'And does he look up to you the way you looked up to your father?'

'I would imagine so.'

'John, how can you say that? What have you given him to look up to? What have you given him to aspire to? Are you a good role model for him?'

'I work hard, I'm honest. Why shouldn't he look up to me?'

'Does he live at home?'

'No, he moved out when he was twenty-two. He's married now.'

'What does he do for a living?'

'He's a musician.'

'Do I detect a note of sarcasm in your voice, John? What's wrong with that? He earns money doing it, doesn't he? He makes enough to look after his own life, doesn't he?'

'He's a dreamer. He thinks one day he'll be in a pop group or something.'

'And perhaps he will. Didn't *you* ever have dreams when you were his age? Or was your only ambition to be like your father?'

'At least my father had a trade and I wanted a trade. I

didn't daydream about some hairbrained thing like being a musician.'

'So you never had any dreams?'

'I was more practical.'

'There must have been something you always wanted. Everyone has dreams, John. Everyone has something that they secretly long to do. Very few of us ever manage it but we all have dreams. If you don't you might as well be dead.'

'That's pathetic.'

'It's true, John and, I'm afraid,' she flicked a switch, 'you're history.'

She chose line four and the next caller stuttered on to the airwaves.

'Am I on?' said a hesitant voice.

'Joe from Romford, yes, you're on. Anything to add to this debate?'

'Well, I agree with that last bloke about kids not having anyone to look up to – well, they have but the people they look up to aren't worth looking up to, if you know what I mean.'

'Well, it took a bit of deciphering but I think I get your drift, Joe. Have you got kids of your own?'

'Leave off.' A chuckle. 'I'm only twenty-three. I don't want kids yet, do I? No, I'm talking about my young brother and sister. They're eleven and twelve. The boy's older, you know.'

'And they look up to what kind of people, Joe?'

'Well, you know, like pop stars and celebrities and these bloody nobodies in soap operas, people on the telly, that kind of person. I mean, that can't be right, can it?'

'Why, Joe?'

'Well, they're nobodies, aren't they?'

'Who?'

'These soap actors and actresses. I mean, you can't open the bloody papers or turn on the telly without seeing their faces. Or the women in them are having babies and selling the pictures to newspapers and magazines for bloody fortunes. It's not right. Or then one of them comes out and says he had a drink or a drugs' problem and he sells his bloody story to the papers for a fortune too. I mean, who gives a toss?'

'The public, Joe. That's why they read newspapers. Do you know how many million people a week watch soap operas?'

'Yeah, lots, but that's not the point. What I'm saying is, they think they're big stars, don't they? But they're nobodies. I mean, if people ask them for their autographs then they have to sign the name of the character they act as, because no one knows who the bloody hell they are in real life. And they say they're fed up with being in soaps, so they chuck it in to go off to Hollywood to become big stars and then, six months later, they come crawling back wanting their old part back in the bloody soap opera because it's the only thing they can act in. They haven't got the talent to do anything else, they just think they're so high and bloody mighty when they're just nobodies. And they get paid a fortune too.'

'Do you watch soaps yourself, Joe?'

'Sometimes, but my brother and sister watch them all the time and those Australian ones are even worse and then what happens? Every Christmas, half a dozen of them come over here and do bloody pantomimes. I mean, that can't be right, can it? A bunch of bloody Aussies coming over here and their acting's worse than the prats in our own soaps.'

'What do you think of the soap stars who start singing careers?'

'Well, that's out of order, isn't it? I mean, any of these so-called celebrities who've been on telly for more than six weeks, they think they can do any bloody thing. Sing, dance, tell jokes and the biggest joke of all is they can't even bloody act. They can't even do the thing they're supposed to be good at. I mean good actors are people like that bloke out of *The Godfather*.'

'Marlon Brando?'

'No, the other one. The short bloke who was in *Heat*.'

'Al Pacino.'

'Yeah, him. I mean, he was brilliant in that *Scarface* too. He's what you call an actor, not some bloody nobody in a soap opera.'

'I think your chances of seeing Al Pacino in *Eastenders* is pretty slim, Joe.'

'I *know* that.'

'What about Robert de Niro in *Coronation Street*?'

A laugh on the other end of the line. 'Yeah, or Tom Cruise in *Brookside*. That'd be a laugh.'

'Thanks for your call, Joe,' Amy said. 'How about any other suggestions for superstars in soaps? Stallone in *Home and Away*? Mel Gibson in *Neighbours*?' She glanced at the list of callers. 'Wendy from Peckham, what do *you* think?'

'I think you've got a bloody nerve,' said Wendy from Peckham. 'I mean, you got where you are today by putting it about with showbiz types, didn't you?'

'Would you like to be more specific, Wendy,' said Amy, lighting another cigarette.

'You were a model, weren't you?'

'That's right. I'm not ashamed of it. Why should I be?'

'I didn't say you should. I'm just saying. You were a model, you met lots of famous people, you went out with a drummer in a rock band, some famous writer, a TV producer. Next thing you know, you've got your own radio show. Still, they say it's not what you know but who you know, don't they?'

'And where did you pick up all these penetrating details about my private life, Wendy?'

'From the newspapers.'

'And you believe everything you read in newspapers, do you?'

'It was true though, wasn't it?'

'I did go out with a drummer and a writer, yes.'

'And he was married, wasn't he?'

'Separated actually. We were both unattached, it wasn't an affair despite what the papers said.'

'Whatever. You slept around with people in showbiz and now you've got your own radio show.'

Amy laughed. 'I wish it had been that easy, Wendy, I'd have done it years ago. Either that or I'd have slept with an executive from Warner Brothers and I'd be in charge of a film studio now.' She blew out a stream of smoke. 'When I finished modelling I was invited on a television show as a fashion consultant, I also did a number of radio interviews and I was offered a nightly spot on one of them to talk about fashion and the fashion business. It turned into a phone-in because it was so popular and after that I was offered *this* show. I feel I worked for this, Wendy; I'm sorry you don't but you're entitled to your opinion. Just as I'm entitled to the opinion that you're jealous of what I do.'

'Jealous of taking my clothes off so that men can stare at me – I don't think so.'

'Why, is your body that awful, Wendy?'

'There's nothing wrong with my body. I just don't want the whole world seeing it. I mean, you can't have much self-respect to do a thing like that and it's hardly a difficult job, is it, nor is sitting in a radio studio talking to people.'

'What do you do for a living, Wendy?'

'I'm a hairdresser.'

'So what would you do if someone offered you fifty thousand pounds to strip off for a magazine?'

'I'd tell them to stuff the money, because I've got too much self-respect. The only person who sees *me* naked is my boyfriend, and *he* never complains. He thinks I've got a great body and I didn't sleep with him just because he's got lots of money.'

'Meaning what, Wendy?'

'Well, when women like you sleep with men, it's always the rich ones, isn't it?'

'Hey, hey, hey, what do you mean? Women like me. What kind of woman would that be?'

'Well, you knew it would further your career by sleeping with rich men.'

'I had enough money of my own, Wendy, I didn't need a rich man to pay my bills.'

'That drummer you slept with, you wouldn't have looked at him twice if he'd been a plumber. Or that writer, if he hadn't been well known, you wouldn't have gone near him. You slept with them because of what they had, not what they were. All you were interested in was the money and the fame.'

'Wendy, how is it possible to be bitter, jealous, vindictive and stupid all at the same time? I'd love you to tell me.'

'I'm not jealous!'

The words were shouted with such vehemence that Amy sat back and slipped one earpiece off.

'Okay, I'll make do with vindictive,' Amy persisted.

'You people are all the same – it's like the man before said – all these so-called celebrities, they get paid hundreds of thousands a year and then they moan because they've got a hard life. Well, if they don't like it why don't they go and do a job in Tesco's or something. They complain when they're photographed coming out of restaurants – well then, why do they always go to restaurants where they know the photographers will be? They'd be more upset if they *didn't* get photographed. They *want* people to see them. And the men are even worse. These ugly men always have beautiful women around them because they've got money, not because of who they are. If they had nothing then none of these beautiful women would want to know them. But they're too stupid or big-headed to realise that. They've got no personality, they don't need one because they've got money. Not like ordinary people.'

'So if you won the lottery and loads of men started hanging around you, wouldn't you think it was a little bit suspicious, Wendy? Wouldn't they be after you for your money?'

'But I'd have my boyfriend. I wouldn't want any other men.'

'And what if your boyfriend only stayed with you because you had money? What if he secretly despised you? He might not think that much of you now. He might just be with you because you're good in bed, or good looking. He might just be using you until another better-looking alternative comes along. How do you know he's not cheating on you as we speak?'

'He wouldn't do that.'

'Is your knowledge of men as specialised as your knowledge of showbiz, Wendy? Most men will stray given the chance.'

'Not *my* boyfriend.'

'That's very naive, Wendy. What makes your boyfriend so special?'

'He agrees with me on everything. We never argue.'

'Perhaps your lives are so empty you have nothing to argue about. Is your life lacking passion so badly, Wendy? If it is I feel sorry for you.'

'I don't want you to feel sorry for me,' Wendy from Peckham shouted angrily. 'Not you or any of your showbiz friends, those overpaid, overrated bastards. All they want to do is get their faces on television and in the papers. They take so much and give nothing back. When I have kids I don't want them looking up to scum like that. I want them to look up to nurses and doctors and teachers. People who *give* something to society instead of sucking it dry.'

The line went dead.

Amy looked towards the production booth and shrugged.

Osborne was standing close to the glass looking at her, shaking his head slowly.

She connected another caller.

'Peter from Muswell Hill,' Amy said, again looking towards the production booth, and this time her brow was furrowed. 'Twice in one night. I *am* privileged.'

'That whore who just insulted you,' the voice said flatly. 'Someone should do something about her.'

'Like what, Peter,' Amy said, smiling.

'Kill her.'

Click. The line went dead.

Seven

'Perhaps I should get a job reading the fucking weather,' said Amy, pushing the door of the production booth closed and slumping against it. She blew out her cheeks and stood motionless for a moment. Then she crossed to a table at the rear of the small room where a pot of coffee, one of tea, some milk and a plate of biscuits stood. She poured herself a coffee and flopped into one of the high-backed swivel chairs next to the table, reaching for a bourbon, which she pushed into her mouth piece by piece.

Jo Parker joined her and poured herself a coffee.

'If you can't stand the heat . . .' Mike Osborne called from behind the mixing desk where he was scribbling something furiously on to a pad.

'Up yours, Mike,' Amy called back, reaching for another biscuit.

'Another witty comeback from the queen of the air-waves,' Osborne chuckled. 'What's wrong, anyway? It was a good show tonight.'

'Yeah, after all, it's not every night I get sent some underwear, is it? Even if the bloke has wiped his knob on it first,' Amy said, lighting a cigarette.

'The bloke who sent those things must be really sick,' said Jo quietly.

'It could have been worse, Jo.' She turned towards Osborne. 'It could have been a bomb, couldn't it, Mike?' She grinned.

Carrying a sheaf of papers, Osborne joined them, topping up his own cup of coffee.

'You can laugh,' he said, pointing a finger at her. 'You had no way of knowing what was in that package. Some of the nutters who ring this show – I wouldn't put *anything* past them.'

'I'd have been sick,' said Jo, shuddering. 'I mean, fancy wanking over them.'

'He must have money to burn, the camisole looked decent quality,' Amy mused. 'Perhaps I ought to get it back from Security and get it cleaned.'

'Now that *is* sick,' said Osborne, smiling. He took a sip of his coffee and headed for the door. 'I'll be back in a minute. Jo, order cabs all round, will you?'

And he was gone.

'He says that every night,' Jo muttered. 'And every night he knows I do it before the show even starts. What does he think I am, stupid?'

Amy regarded her warily for a moment then leaned forward.

'I don't think it was a trick question, Jo,' she said quietly, a smile playing on her lips.

'Sorry, I didn't mean to snap but sometimes I think Mike gets the impression I'm some bloody YTS trainee. I have been here for nearly two years.'

'Well, *I* appreciate you.'

Jo managed a smile.

'Do you fancy going on to a club or something?' Amy asked. 'I could murder a drink.'

'No thanks, Amy. You go. I'm not in the mood. Another time perhaps.'

'Are you okay, Jo?'

'I'm fine, why do you ask?'

'Just curious. No, make that concerned. You've been quiet for the past three or four days. It's not like you.'

'Thanks a lot,' Jo said, smiling.

'You know what I mean. Is something wrong?'

Jo shook her head.

'I'm tired, that's all,' she said. 'I've got a few things on my mind.'

'But nothing you want to talk about?'

'No, but thanks for asking. I didn't know I was making it that obvious there was something wrong.'

'Like I say, if you want to talk.'

The door of the production office opened and Osborne walked back in.

He pulled on his coat.

'Come on then, you two,' he urged. 'Unless you want to spend all night here.'

'No thanks, three hours is quite enough for me,' Amy insisted, pulling on her own jacket.

Jo snatched up her handbag and coat and the three of them headed for the lift, passing framed photos of some of the station's other presenters as they made their way down the corridor. The sightless eyes followed their passage.

Amy looked at her own picture as they waited for the lift to arrive. Her hair was shorter in the photo, cut into a bob that brushed her collar. Now her blond locks reached well past her shoulders.

'Christ, I look so young in that picture,' she said. 'It's depressing.'

'You're not exactly ready to draw your pension, Amy,' Jo said, smiling.

'You look angelic,' said Osborne, chuckling. 'Almost untouched.' He cracked out laughing.

Amy punched him playfully on the arm as the lift arrived.

They rode it to the ground floor.

The security guard who sat behind the desk in the marbled foyer was reading a well-thumbed copy of *Maxim* magazine. He looked up and nodded, hitting a button on the control panel to open the electronic main door of the building.

There were three cabs parked outside.

Amy pulled up the collar of her jacket against a sudden icy blast of wind that swept across Bedford Square.

'Are you sure you don't fancy that drink?' she said to Jo but the younger woman shook her head.

'I'll see you tomorrow,' she said and scurried across to one of the waiting taxis.

'What drink?' said Osborne, watching as Jo clambered into the cab. He and Amy watched it pull away.

'I was going to drop into a club before I went home,' Amy told him. 'I fancied a drink.'

'Do you want some company then?' he asked, still not looking at her.

'Jo wanted to get home.'

'Good for Jo. Do you still want that drink?'

'I'll have one when I get home.'

'Is that a "no", Amy?'

'I didn't hear you ask, Mike.'

'Do you fancy a drink with me?'

'Not tonight.'

She squeezed his arm gently and took a step towards her waiting cab.

'You wouldn't have said "no" a year ago,' he told her.

She turned, one hand on the cab's door handle.

'A year is a long time,' she reminded him, smiling.

He watched as she climbed into the cab, watched as it pulled away, its brake lights flaring red as it turned a corner out of sight.

Osborne walked to his own cab.

Another blast of cold air swept across Bedford Square.

Eight

The first thing that struck Amy Watson was the silence. *It was always the silence.* And she hated it.

She locked the door of her first-floor flat and hung up her coat, the silence closing around her like an oppressive, invisible fist. Even before she flicked on any lights she crossed first to the television set then to the stack system and switched them both on.

She pressed the Mute button on the TV remote, glancing at the silent screen for a moment, the sound of music from the hi-fi floating on the air. Only then did she seek out the lamps dotted around the room and begin turning them on, each one making its own pool of soft light in the darkness.

Amy kicked off her boots and padded over to the small drinks' cabinet where she poured herself a measure of Jim Beam. She sipped at it, feeling the amber liquid burn its way to her stomach. It was cold outside but her central heating was timed to come on at midnight. The flat was warm and cosy.

What about welcoming?

Amy took another sip of the drink.

It would have been more welcoming with the presence of someone else.

She glanced at the television, at some cookery programme, (*who the hell would be learning to cook at 2.45 in the morning?*) then at the stack system. She crossed to it and changed the CD, slipping the latest Clannad album in. Amy lowered the volume then wandered into the kitchen, still clutching her drink. She could still hear the music in the other room but she felt sure that it would not disturb the other residents of the building.

There were five other flats in the large building in

Northampton Square. One on the same floor. Two above her and two below. She saw little of the other residents, due in part to the unusual (or ungodly, she sometimes thought) hours she worked. The flat on the same floor as hers was occupied by a divorced man in his fifties who, as far as she could remember, worked at Lincoln's Inn in some legal capacity. He was a slim, grey-haired individual she knew only as Mr Greaves. He was the longest serving resident and he'd been there when she bought the flat five years earlier.

Immediately above her were a couple in their thirties who she'd spoken to a few times. Michael and Patricia. She hadn't a clue what either of them did for a living, only that they weren't married and that Patricia had moved out for three weeks about nine months ago, presumably over some row Amy had been fortunate enough to miss.

The other flat on the second floor was occupied by one Karen Walsh, who was a year or two older than Amy. She was the marketing manager for a large cosmetics firm and was hardly ever there. The two women had spoken a handful of times, even had coffee together in Karen's flat but, apart from that perfunctory attempt at community spirit, they had seen little of each other since then.

Below her were George and Vanessa Seaton, both in their forties. They had a son who occasionally stayed with them but, as with Michael and Patricia above her, Amy hadn't a clue what the Seatons did for a living. Meetings with them had been even rarer.

The other flat, directly below her, was empty. It had been for about a year now. Previously occupied by a freelance journalist whose name she'd forgotten. Amy had discovered that the man had done a runner one night, taking all he could carry with him. Exactly why, she never did discover. She didn't really care either.

The residents of the flats, like so many in London, were living proof of how easy it was to live in close proximity to others while remaining blissfully ignorant of the details of their lives. Her fellow tenants, she assumed, were as uninformed about *her* as she was about *them*. It was a situation that suited everyone. People tended to keep themselves to themselves. Cocooned within their own little worlds, very few found the need to venture beyond.

And Amy was content to be on nodding terms with her fellow residents. She wanted no more. She *needed* no more.

So what about the loneliness?

She took another sip of Jim Beam. She was alone. Not lonely, she told herself.

Are you fooling yourself?

There had been men in the past. Too many, she sometimes thought in her more prudish moments. She'd fallen in love before. How many times? Twice? Three times?

Four long-term relationships and quite a few – *how many was 'quite a few'? It was a convenient euphemism –* liaisons.

Good word.

The surroundings, the people, the business had all contributed to her enthusiasm – *another euphemism?* – with the men she'd shared beds with over the years.

There had been no one in her life for over a year now. Certainly not on a regular basis. It was a complication she was happy without.

Wasn't it?

What the hell. She wasn't looking, but if the right man came along then . . .

She smiled to herself and moved through the kitchen without turning on the fluorescent lights. She fumbled in the fridge for the remnants of a fruit salad she'd bought the day before.

There was a Danish pastry on the top shelf but, other than that, the fridge was full of salad stuff, low calorie drinks, mineral water, low-fat cheese and lean meat. It was a culinary legacy of her modelling days. The Jim Beam hadn't always been on the menu then but Amy had always enjoyed a drink. She finished it and set the glass down on the draining board, before making her way back through the sitting room clutching a chicken leg she'd taken from the fridge. She nibbled at it as she passed the silent, flickering television, heading for the bathroom.

She turned on the shower, finished the chicken leg and dropped the remains into a small bin beside the toilet, then she quickly undressed and stepped beneath the cleansing jets of water, enjoying the feel of the stinging water against her skin.

Amy thought that she might sit and watch television or listen to some music when she'd finished in the shower. She needed something to help her sleep. She felt like this every night after the show. It was difficult to switch off. The adrenaline that flowed so quickly during the programme still coursed through her veins.

Perhaps she would read. The flat was full of books, mostly paperbacks. Most unread. She bought a lot of them but read very few. There were some in her bedroom that she tended to scan over and over again. She was comfortable with them.

One in particular. It was signed and dated. That date now four years old. He'd signed it for her one night as they lay in his bed in the hotel in Mayfair. Their love-making over for that night they had talked into the small hours and she had asked him to sign a book for her. It had amused him but he'd done it, written something special on the title page for her in that sweeping scrawl of his.

The affair had lasted three years, then just petered out like the dying embers of an untended fire. One day they had lunch together, the next he was gone. She hadn't seen him, other than on television or in magazines, for eighteen months but there wasn't a day that passed that she didn't think of him.

And sometimes those thoughts were tinged with anger. She wondered *why* he'd allowed their relationship to disintegrate so rapidly. Why he couldn't at least have called her once or twice. After all, he had been the one who had pursued her so single-mindedly when the affair had begun.

When she stopped to think about it, the situation was maddening. And yet pride had prevented her from contacting him.

On two occasions she'd written to him via his publishers, never sure whether the letters had reached him or whether he'd merely chosen to ignore them. She'd even phoned there once and asked for his number. Just the sound of his voice would have been enough for her.

Wouldn't it?

She closed her eyes tightly as she felt the shower spray splashing her face.

No, it wouldn't have been enough, would it?

If she'd spoken to him again she would have wanted to see him again, wanted to touch him.

To love him again?

He had a book out at the moment; she'd seen it in a book shop a week ago. It was dedicated to his new-born son. She hadn't bought it.

Amy switched off the shower, slipped on a bathrobe and padded back into the sitting room.

The news was on television so she turned up the volume, drew her slender legs up beneath her on the sofa and watched as the stories unfolded. A child abuse ring in North London. A plane crash.

It was the final story that made her sit up.

Nine

Jo Parker sat bolt upright as she heard the sound of a key in the door. It took her a couple of seconds to realise that it wasn't *her* door but the flat across the landing. She heard muffled voices, a muted chuckle then a loud bang as the door was closed once more.

She exhaled wearily and lay back down, rolling over on to first one side then the other, eyes clamped tightly shut in the hope that this would hasten the onset of sleep.

It didn't.

She rolled on to her back, eyes now open and gazing at the ceiling, her glance alighting on a crack in the artex. She traced the black blemish as if it were a river on a map. There were other cracks in the ceiling. The room needed redecorating, she thought. In fact, the entire flat needed redecorating. She'd been meaning to do the job ever since she moved in ten months ago, but she seemed to have neither time nor inclination lately.

Jo rolled over on to her side and looked at her wardrobe, one door slightly open where a hinge was broken. Something else that needed fixing. *Everything needed bloody fixing.*

She remembered, as a child, she had had a wardrobe in her room. A big wooden antique piece of furniture that seemed to be more like an heirloom than a place to store clothes. It had, her mother told her, been in the family for eighty years. A little bit different to the flimsy IKEA structure that held most of her clothes at the moment. The only thing the two pieces of furniture had in common was that they had faulty hinges. The doors of both would not close properly and, at night, when she'd been a child, she had stared in fear at that heavy wooden door, convinced that some unspeakable creature lived within its black depths. Lurking behind the coats and dresses.

She believed it because her older brother had told her that every wardrobe had a monster inside it, especially old ones like the one in her room. He didn't have to worry because he only had a small wardrobe and two chests of drawers, but she was in big trouble with that old antique in her room.

She smiled as she recalled his words, the smile fading quickly. Danny had left home when she was eighteen, intent, as he'd put it, on seeing the world. Her parents had tried to stop him but he had saved enough money from his two weekend jobs to be able to go. He and his friend he was travelling with would find work in the places they visited. There was nothing for anyone to worry about. He'd be back in a year or two unless he settled in one of those fabulous far-off places.

Jo could remember waving him off from the airport as he and his friend caught the flight to the South of France. She had cried and he had teased her for it, then he had hugged her, told her he loved her and disappeared out of her life. Postcards had arrived with surprising regularity for the first five months from locations as exotic and far flung as Egypt, Turkey, Greece and several parts of the United States. Jo, then just fifteen, had taken them into school to show her friends. Then they'd stopped.

The next communication to arrive was an official one. It was postmarked Bangkok. Her brother was dead. He'd been working as a barman in a nightclub and been involved in a fight. His hand had been badly gashed with a broken bottle. Somehow, the communique didn't say how, the wound had become infected and Danny had been rushed into a Bangkok hospital. The treatment he'd been given had not worked. His condition had grown steadily worse.

It had taken him two months to die.

She could still remember her mother crying late into the night on most nights, while she herself sobbed in her own room, glaring at the half-open wardrobe door, thinking that whatever lurked within couldn't be anywhere near as bad as the reality she and her family were living through.

His body arrived back in England in a metal coffin.

Her younger brother, Billy, seemed less affected by the tragedy, even though it intensified an introversion that he had already displayed from an early age. Her parents gave up on him, too concerned with their own grief. Jo tried to offer her own comfort but he seemed to dismiss it. Isolated, even within the confines of such a tightly knit family, he became secretive. Self-obsessed.

Jo left home shortly after finishing college and walked straight into a job at a publisher's. She rose quickly through various positions, moved to a record company for a few months, then returned to publishing briefly before taking a job as a PA.

The job was good. The money was excellent. The opportunities for travel superb. However, when her boss told her that she should book double rooms for them for all their foreign trips, and that if she didn't follow instructions she'd be looking for another job, the offer to work with Amy Watson was one to be grabbed with both hands. The money was less but the work was enjoyable and she'd become close friends with Amy.

Everything seemed fine in her life.

Except it wasn't. Like that bloody hinge, it needed fixing.

She finally gave up trying to sleep and swung herself out of bed.

She wandered through to the small kitchen and switched on the kettle, dropping a tea bag into a mug she took from the sink.

She ran a hand through her chestnut hair, waiting for the kettle to boil. The beginnings of a headache gnawed at her skull. Her eyes felt as if someone was trying to poke them out of her head from the inside.

She looked up at the wall clock. It was 3.56 a.m.

Again she heard a key in a lock. This time it was her door.

The kettle began to boil.

She walked through into the sitting room, her face set in hard lines.

'Where the hell have *you* been?' she snapped angrily at the newcomer.

Ten

Billy Parker pulled off his jacket and tossed it unceremoniously on to the back of the sofa.

He brushed past Jo, smiling mockingly at her as he slumped down in one of the chairs facing the television. He looked at the blank screen, as if expecting it to burst into life beneath his gaze and drummed agitatedly on one thigh with the thin fingers of his right hand.

'So, what are you doing up then?' he asked, cheerfully.

'I couldn't sleep,' she snapped. 'I was worrying about you and where you might be.'

Billy coughed and got to his feet.

'No need to worry about me,' he told her, making his way into the kitchen.

He saw that the kettle was boiling.

'I'll have a coffee with you, if you're making one,' he said, taking a slice of dry bread from the loaf that stood on the chopping board. He pulled it into pieces and began pushing them, one by one, into his mouth.

'So, where have you been, Billy?' Jo persisted.

'Just out.'

'Out where?' she snarled. 'Don't get funny with me.'

'I was seeing some friends. Any problem with that?'

'What kind of friends?'

'Oh, give it a fucking rest, Jo. What do you want? Names and addresses. Friends, right. That's it.'

'I've got a right to know where you've been, Billy. While you're living here, you abide by my rules.'

He saluted mockingly.

'Yes, madam,' he chided. 'Jesus, you sound more like my fucking mother than my sister. I met a few friends, we had some drinks, something to eat. We talked. Satisfied?'

'Where have you been drinking until four o'clock in the morning, Billy? And what *with*? You've got no money,' she reminded him. 'You've got no money because you've got no job. You've been sponging off me ever since you got here.'

He stood up, digging one hand in the pocket of his jeans.

Jo watched as he pulled out some notes. She glimpsed the purple of twenties, the pale red of a fifty.

He threw the untidy bundle at her.

'There, that's this week's fucking rent, right?' he rasped.

She looked down at the money strewn across the floor and the sofa. Slowly she picked up a crumpled twenty.

'Where did you get this?'

'What does it matter to you? Just take it.'

'It *does* matter. There's more than a hundred quid here. I want to know where you got it.'

'What difference does it make?'

'You're living under my roof. Now tell me, where did you get this money?' She took a step towards him, the twenty gripped in her fist.

He looked into her blazing eyes and chuckled. It was a mocking sound.

'Oh, you look sexy when you're angry,' he said softly, a sly grin on his face.

She stepped even closer. 'Listen, you little bastard, I want to know where you got this money,' she hissed angrily. 'Where did you steal it from?'

Billy took a step back, his grin fading, his eyes narrowing.

'That's just bloody typical of you, isn't it?' he snarled. 'Just because I've got some money in my pocket, you assume I must have nicked it. You don't think I could have worked for it.'

'I know you, Billy. You've always taken the easy option and stealing's easier than working, isn't it? Anyway, where's someone like you going to get a job. Who's going to employ *you*?'

'Plenty of people. Just because I didn't go to fucking college like *you* did doesn't mean I can't get a job. There're plenty of things I can do. Plenty of people who want my services.'

'What kind of services do you offer, Billy? Pimping? Drug pushing?'

'If you don't want the money then give it back,' he snapped, holding out his hand.

'I don't want this money,' she told him, pressing the twenty into his palm. 'I don't want any of your money unless I know where it's come from.'

He snatched the note away.

'You just stay out of my fucking life then,' he told her. 'It's none of your business anyway.'

'While you're here, it *is* my business. I didn't ask you to come here, Billy. You turned up on my doorstep, remember?'

'You didn't have to let me in.'

'What was I supposed to do? Turn you away? You are my brother.'

'Yeah, don't remind me. But if it had been Danny, you'd have been pleased to see him, wouldn't you?'

'Leave Danny out of this.'

'Why? Hit a nerve, have I?'

'Leave it, Billy,' she said, glaring at him menacingly.

'You'd have welcomed *him* into the flat, wouldn't you? Would you have shared your bed with him, Jo? It wouldn't have been the first time, would it?'

'You're sick,' she said dismissively.

'*I'm* sick?' he countered.

They regarded each other angrily for a moment, the silence finally broken by Billy.

'You were the same as Mum and Dad,' he said, his voice low. 'You all thought the sun shone out of Danny's arsehole. He couldn't do anything wrong, could he? Nobody ever cared about me.'

'It's a bit early in the morning for sob stories, Billy.'

'It's true. If it had have been me that was killed no one

would have cared. But because it was Danny everyone was gutted.' He leaned closer to her. 'Fuck him, I'm glad he's dead.'

Jo struck him hard across the cheek with the flat of her hand, the sound of the blow reverberating around the flat.

Billy rubbed his cheek gently, surprised by the power of her blow.

'I'm going to bed,' she told him.

'Good. Perhaps *I* can get some sleep. If you had a decent flat at least I'd have my own room to sleep in, instead of having to doss down on your fucking sofa.'

Jo spun round.

'If you don't like it, Billy,' she rasped. 'The door's there and the sooner you walk through it, the better.' She glared at him for a moment then turned back towards her bedroom door.

She slammed it behind her.

Billy looked at the door for long seconds then set about retrieving the money from the floor. He sat down on the sofa again, folding each note as he counted it.

He smiled. A good night's work. And there would be plenty more where that came from.

Eleven

Phillip Barclay removed the plastic sheet from the corpse with the flourish an artist might use to unveil his latest masterpiece. The pathologist laid the sheet on the adjacent slab then gestured towards the body which lay before him.

'Claire Glover, aged twenty-one,' he said evenly. 'Death by strangulation.' He pointed to a particularly raw, vivid striation mark just below the larynx.

The youngest of the three men in the room leaned closer to the body, his eyes fixed on the red mark on the victim's throat.

'What did he use?' Detective Inspector David Grant wanted to know.

'Thin flex or possibly nylon string. I found fibres in the wound,' said Barclay.

'It looks deep,' Grant observed.

'Nearly three and a half millimetres,' Barclay told him. 'The killer was strong.'

'Time of death?'

'Some time between eleven and one last night, possibly earlier. I can't be more specific yet.'

'Try,' said Grant, allowing his gaze to travel over the rest of the body.

Claire Glover had probably been fairly pretty in life but her swollen features, bloodshot eyes and gashed lips made it difficult to appreciate that now, Grant thought. She was about five-three, wide hipped but a little on the thin side. She looked as if she could have done with a few good meals. Not that it mattered any longer.

'The rigor mortis would seem to indicate the early hours,' Barclay continued. 'I'm going to do a vitreous humour test to try and pin it down more exactly.'

'What's that?' the third man in the room asked.

'The vitreous humour is the jelly-like substance behind the lens of the eye,' said Barclay. 'We take it out with a fine-needled syringe for examination. We then inject water back into the eye.'

'What for?' Detective Sergeant Stuart Lawrenson enquired.

'If we didn't, the eye would collapse,' Barclay told him. 'It's a purely cosmetic exercise before the body goes off to the coroner.'

Lawrenson nodded, his eyes scanning the body.

He was three years older than his superior but the thick moustache he sported made him look older than his thirty-seven years. The flecks of grey in it, as with those in his hair, didn't help either.

Lawrenson looked first at the corpse then at Grant, who was bent close to the body, inspecting every inch of the dead girl. She had a tattoo of a rose on her right shoulder, another of a heart enclosed in barbed wire on her left thigh. There were also several bruises on her thighs.

'What about these?' Grant asked, pointing to the purple blemishes.

'As far as I can tell she got them when she fell,' said Barclay. 'She must have been semi-conscious, trying to fight. The killer pushed her down and straddled her to get some leverage.'

'Any fibres?' the detective inspector continued.

The pathologist shook his head.

'Blood?' Grant persisted.

'Only hers,' Barclay observed. 'There wasn't much blood loss from the wound around the throat. Strangulation's a pretty clean killing method if you know what you're doing.'

'And our boy obviously did,' Grant murmured to himself, his gaze still travelling over the body.

'What about semen?' Lawrenson enquired.

Barclay raised an eyebrow. 'We did rectal, vaginal

and mouth swabs,' he said. 'We found semen present in all three.'

'Busy night,' Lawrenson said.

'Well, she was a working girl, wasn't she?' Grant added.

'There were traces of KY jelly on the rectal swab and lubricant on the vaginal one, the kind you find on a condom,' Barclay continued. 'At a rough guess I'd say she saw at least seven punters last night before she was murdered. Protected *and* unprotected sex.'

'Jesus,' grunted Lawrenson. 'I can't understand why they do it without a rubber, what with AIDS and all that shit.'

'Because they can get twice as much for doing it without one,' Grant told him. 'When I was on the vice squad I knew pros who could get fifty quid for a blow job without a johnny. It's only twenty if the geezer wears one. I mean, come on, Stuart, we're not looking at some Mayfair fanny here, are we?' He made an expansive gesture with his hand over the body. 'This is King's Cross fluff. No class. No looks.' He shook his head. 'No choice. She was probably selling it to finance a habit anyway.'

'We did find evidence of amphetamines in her bloodstream,' Barclay added. 'And alcohol too.'

'Fifty quid's worth of speed goes further than twenty quid's worth,' Grant mused.

'Could she have been raped?' Lawrenson wanted to know.

'There's no bruising around the vagina or anus to indicate that,' Barclay told him.

'Kinky punter,' Grant offered. 'He goes back to her flat, gets out the rope or flex or whatever, offers her fifty, maybe even a hundred to fuck her while he's got the noose round her neck. She says yes, he gets carried away. Scratch one pro.'

'But there was evidence that she was trying to fight off her killer,' Lawrenson protested.

Grant shrugged.

'It started off as a bit of business,' he offered. 'When she realised he was going too far she got scared.'

'As simple as that?' said Lawrenson.

'Either way, I think we're going to be pulling in some overtime,' Grant murmured.

The three men stood looking at the body for a moment longer then Barclay broke the silence.

'There's something else,' he said. 'It's not relevant to the case but I thought you might like to know.'

Grant looked at him expectantly.

'She had cervical cancer,' the pathologist said. 'It was very advanced. She was dying. She might even have known it.'

'AIDS or cancer,' murmured Lawrenson. 'That's a hell of a fucking choice.'

'It didn't matter in the end, did it?' Grant observed. 'Someone made a choice for her.'

'What do you reckon, Dave?' Lawrenson asked. 'Two in four days. There has to be a link, doesn't there?'

Grant continued to gaze at the lifeless body of Claire Glover, his attention riveted on the savage red mark around her neck.

'Let's have another look at the other victim,' he said to Barclay.

Twelve

'Claire Glover,' Grant said and banged the first photo stuck to the blackboard. 'And Tessa Carr.' He tapped the second one, gazing at the assembled throng of plainclothes and uniformed police gathered in the Incident Room at New Scotland Yard.

'Aged twenty-one and nineteen respectively. Both prostitutes. Both strangled within three days of each other. Bodies found within half a mile of each other. MO in each case is identical.' He continued looking around the room, as if allowing the information to sink in. 'We could be looking at a possible serial killer, although it's too early to tell. It could stop at two but I doubt it. Whichever way this goes I want results. Got it?'

There were a few murmurs inside the room; one of the plainclothes officers got up and moved closer to the blackboard, studying the array of photos of the two dead girls more closely. The snaps showed them in both life and death but most had been taken after their murders.

Grant lit up a cigarette and waited for the burble of chatter to die down.

'There's a lot of ground to cover on this,' he said, flicking ash on the floor. 'I want to know if they were working the same patch, if they had regular customers, if they had a pimp. If they *did* I want to know his name. I want to talk to him.'

He turned to the blackboard and pointed at a photo showing the crook of Tessa Carr's arm and the track marks on it. Thick purple scabs had formed over the bruised punctures.

'This one was on smack,' Grant said. 'That means she had a dealer. I want to know *his* name too.'

'What do we know about them, guv?' asked Detective

Constable Dennis Schofield. He was tapping a pen gently against the palm of one large hand.

'Claire Glover was from Coventry,' Grant told him. 'The usual shit with her. Didn't get on with her parents, thought the streets of London were paved with gold. Did a runner when she was sixteen. Couldn't get work and ended up going on the game about four years ago.'

'She was picked up four times by vice between then and her death,' Lawrenson added. 'She also had convictions for shoplifting.'

'Tessa Carr was from Croydon,' Grant continued. 'She spent most of her life in foster homes and children's homes. Her parents are being traced now, for what it's worth. She'd been on the game since she was fourteen. She did three months in Holloway for possession of pot when she was eighteen. She had a suspended for assault too. Some punter got a bit rough with her, she stuck a steel comb in his arse.'

A ripple of laughter ran around the room.

'Are you sure that wasn't a request, guv?' someone shouted from the back of the room.

More laughter.

'Well, whoever he was he didn't get as rough as the geezer who strangled her, did he?' Grant said flatly. 'Anyway, check him out.'

'Was the same weapon used in both murders?' Schofield wanted to know.

'No,' Grant told him. 'The MO was the same but Tessa was strangled with thin flex, possibly from a lamp or something like that. Claire was done with nylon string according to the pathologist.'

'Were either of them raped?' someone called.

'There's no evidence of it in either case,' said Grant. 'There is also no evidence of fingerprints at either crime scene. Not on the bodies at any rate. Any prints that were found are being processed at Hendon as we speak but we're not expecting much more than those belonging to the victims.'

'Where were they found, guv?' Detective Constable Keith Friel enquired.

'Tessa was found under Maiden Lane bridge behind King's Cross,' Grant informed him. 'There's a strong possibility that she was killed somewhere else then dumped there. Claire had a flat she used in Argyle Square. The rent was paid on time on that place every month, so it's my guess that someone else was paying it, I doubt if she had enough money to keep up the payments. This means either a pimp or a friend. Another girl working that area, maybe even a punter. Some of the silly bastards get that attached to a particular girl. Whoever it was, find them.' He took another drag on his cigarette and regarded the other occupants of the room challengingly.

'I've requested plainclothes *and* uniforms on this one,' Grant said. 'It's going to be a big job. Let's just hope it doesn't get any bigger.'

There was a heavy silence broken by Grant himself.

'On a personal note, I know there are some of you in this room who don't think I should be in charge of this case,' he said, drawing on his cigarette. 'Some of the – how shall I put it – more senior among you. Senior in years, I mean.' He looked slowly around the room. 'Well, that's tough shit I'm afraid. I got the promotion on merit and anyone who doesn't like being told what to do by a younger man can walk out of here now.' He gestured towards the door. 'This is my first big case as DI and I don't want anyone fucking it up, got that? Some of you might think I've got something to prove. Well, that's fine because I'm going to prove it by nailing this bastard. And I'm going to do it with your help. All of you. I couldn't give a fuck who does or doesn't like me. This investigation is all that matters. I'm going to push you all hard but I'm going to push myself even harder.' He dropped his cigarette and ground it out on the floor. 'Like I say, I want results and if *I* think someone's not pulling their weight then I'll have them off this fucking case like that.' He snapped his fingers.

Someone coughed but, other than that, his tirade was met with silence.

'I'm glad you all understand the position,' Grant said quietly. 'Are there any more questions?'

There weren't.

'Until we know about these girls in more detail,' Grant continued, 'or the people they mixed with at any rate, the motive for these killings is anyone's guess, but it might be worth checking out some of the local clap clinics because, according to the pathologist's report, Tessa Carr was suffering from non-specific urethritis *and* syphilis. The murderer could be a punter who caught a dose off her and decided to take it out on a few other pros as revenge.'

Grant glanced at his watch.

'Right, let's get moving on this,' he said. 'Like I said, I want this bastard and I'm going to get him, no matter what it takes.'

Thirteen

The imposing figure at the lectern stood motionless apart from barely perceptible movements of his head. All around him shouts of approval or disapproval resounded, reverberating off the oak-panelled walls of the House of Commons.

Home Secretary David Albury gazed around impassively, first at the opposition benches then back at his own party, many of whom were nodding their heads in a gesture of solidarity.

Albury waited for the noise to die down, brushing one sleeve of his Armani suit as he waited.

He was a tall, powerfully built man with greying hair and deep lines across his forehead and around his eyes. Although well into his forty-eighth year, the advance of time had brought to his appearance distinction rather than the weariness that seemed to reside in the features of so many of his colleagues of the same age. And, he noted, with a degree of smugness, some even younger.

He glanced down at his notes as the chamber was quiet once again.

'Despite the protestations of my learned colleagues opposite,' he continued. 'The decline in morals and standards in society is not attributable simply to lack of housing, bad schooling or shortage of jobs.'

There were more shouts, cheers and challenges.

Albury again waited patiently for the rumblings to subside.

When it finally did he looked around him again.

'There is a more insidious cause,' he continued. 'Insidious because it is so accessible and so powerful. I speak of course of the media. In particular of films and video. The constant diet of violence, sex and obscenity which we see paraded on cinema screens and, even worse, on our own television screens, is without doubt a contributory factor in this horrific decline in moral standards that we are experiencing not just in our own country but throughout the world.'

Another chorus of approval from behind him.

'All one needs to do is look at the list of top ten films showing around the country or the list of the ten most popular videos being rented or bought,' he continued. 'It is a catalogue of violence, sex, perversion, blasphemy and filth. No deviation is too foul. We have films and videos glorifying the taking of heroin, delighting in the after-effects of car crashes, showing in close-up the effects of violence. We are assaulted with images of sex, not just wholesome sex but perverted sex. Incest, child molesting, lesbianism. There seems to be no limit to the depths to which some film makers will stoop in an effort to shock us. And they call this entertainment.' He took a sip of water. 'Is it right that the public should be subjected to this constant barrage of horror and obscenity? Surely there is enough violence in the world already without having to portray it on screen.'

More cheers.

'But the ones I feel most for are the children,' said Albury, lowering his voice slightly until it had an almost reverential tone. 'I feel sorrow that their young lives are being blighted by these people who call themselves artists and entertainers. Because it is children who are most susceptible to the kind of filth which these film makers choose to pollute our screens with.'

There was a sustained round of applause.

Albury nodded, raising a hand to quiet his approving audience.

'When children see violence glorified on screen, is it any wonder they feel that it is right?' he persisted. 'Is it any wonder that they imitate it? And yet those film makers who continue to produce these kind of films choose to ignore the consequences of their actions. The only allegiance they have is to the god of money. They care nothing for what they are doing to young minds, they have just one interest. The pursuit of wealth and if innocence and morals are to be sacrificed in this quest for riches then their response would seem to be, so be it.'

He reached for a sheet of paper and held it up.

'The top ten films in the country at the moment,' Albury snapped, pointing to the list. 'Sex, violence, profanity and perversion in every one. Where is there a family film in this list? Where is the kind of good wholesome entertainment that we enjoyed years ago? Instead there are films here about bank robberies, murder, sexual perversion. They contain scenes of torture, nudity and crime, and every one is further blighted by gutter language. Do we want to hear the language of the terraces when we are sitting in a cinema? Do we want to see what should be reserved for the bedroom splashed across the screen before us? Is there any need to show us beatings and shootings in such lurid detail? The answer, I'm sure you'll agree, is no.'

There was another round of applause. A number of the members of the House stood up to add their support.

'And these film makers tell us that this is the *real* world,' Albury continued. 'This is supposed to be the world *we* live in. Well, I don't know about you but it's not like any world *I* am aware of. And, furthermore, I don't think the public wants to see this so-called reality on the screen when they visit the cinema or watch their televisions. I don't believe they want to see nudity or hear bad language. These have no place in what should be works of entertainment.'

He took another sip of his water.

'Many cases can be cited of individuals imitating what they have seen on the screen, be it a cinema or video screen,' Albury insisted. 'And yet still the defenders of these vile films cry that they are not to blame. I say that is rubbish. I say that the public must be protected from this kind of corruption. The public in general but, in particular, children. Video reaches all too easily inside homes these days, children have access to material they should never see but these film makers and those who defend them, don't consider that or, if they do, they choose to ignore the implications. Well, *I* will not ignore the implications. *I* will not stand by and watch while these films contribute even more to the breakdown of our society. *I* will not look on dispassionately while the public is subjected to this continuing stream of filth and corruption. That is why I believe this Bill that I propose must become law as quickly as possible. That is why I propose a complete re-think on the obscenity laws and how they are applied to films and video. A new form of classification must be introduced and these vile films must be controlled and, if necessary, banned. A committee must be set up immediately to look into this. For the sake not just of the children of this country but for all right-minded people everywhere. It is our duty to protect and that is what we must do.'

The applause was deafening.

Fourteen

Anita Bishop reached for the remote control and hit Mute so that all she could see was the picture of the House of Commons. The camera had zoomed in on the face of David Albury. She could see the triumphant look on his face as he took the applause of colleagues and opponents. She was sure she could detect the vaguest hint of a smirk on his thin lips. During the nine months she had worked as his secretary, she had come to know that expression well. Of course, those not so familiar with him would not notice such a minor muscular mannerism, but she prided herself on her powers of observation. That was one of the many things Albury himself had taught her.

She had first met him while working for a local paper in her home town of Brighton. The death of the local MP had threatened to cut the government's majority and Albury had decided to contest the seat on behalf of his party. They had crossed paths at a series of press junkets and then later in more intimate circumstances when she had interviewed him for a feature her paper was running on the forthcoming by-election.

From the first meeting she had found him to be charming and, unusually for a politician, relatively sincere. Either that or he was even more practised at duplicity than the rest of his colleagues. However, Anita had given him the benefit of the doubt and she'd found him to be a witty and warm man. Despite his wealth he seemed at ease amongst those less privileged than himself. Something else few of his colleagues were very adept at faking.

Anita was no stranger to wealth herself. Her father had owned a chain of greetings' card shops before he retired to live on the Côte d'Azur with her stepmother. That had been six years ago, two weeks after Anita's twenty-third birthday. She heard from her father every three or four months, occasionally she flew out for a few days holiday when work permitted but, they had never been a close family, even when her real mother was alive.

Despite representing his Brighton constituency, Albury spent most of his time in London where he had a flat in Kensington. His family home was in Sussex. She'd visited it once and met his wife and daughter.

She'd visited the flat in Kensington too on more than one occasion.

Since starting work for Albury as a secretary-cum-PA, she had discovered that he was something of a workaholic and, when he didn't feel like working in the confines of his office at the Houses of Parliament, he was just as likely to suggest they continue their work at the Kensington flat. The dwelling reeked of good taste and money. A little like Albury himself.

When he'd offered her the job as secretary she had accepted without a second thought. She had never held particularly strong political views, even as a student, but she had been captivated more by Albury the man than by the politician. She admired his determination. She envied his passion and she was more than a little in awe of his power. Besides that, for a man twenty years her senior, he was extremely attractive. Power and wealth were potent enough attributes in themselves but combined with his physical appearance, they were positively dynamic.

She knew that his ambition was to be Prime Minister before he was fifty, and such was his self-belief he had convinced her that it was only a matter of time until that happened. That ambition, however, was something he only ever spoke about when they were alone. Even Albury didn't intend letting personal goals interfere with the overall well-being of the Party. It was something else she respected about him.

Anita continued looking at the screen, noticing that Albury had stepped away from the lectern. She could see him seated in his familiar position on the front bench, pulling at one cuff and smiling as the Prime Minister leaned close and said something to him.

She switched off the set and turned her attention back to her work. There were some dates to be fitted into his diary. Rumours were rife that an election was due in less than six months. There weren't many empty spaces left in that diary.

She smiled then scribbled a note on one of the pads on her desk. When he returned to the office there was something she wanted to ask him.

Fifteen

Amy Watson drove her foot into the punch bag, her teeth gritted as she felt the impact. It felt good.

She stretched, took a step back then drove another powerful kick into the hanging bag, shouting as she did. *Christ, that felt good.*

She twisted around on her shapely legs and kicked twice with her right foot, the shuddering impacts both creating harsh thuds as they connected with the leather. Her red leotard was already dark with sweat, her blond hair hanging like snakes' tails from so much exertion. Her bare feet were taped across the insteps, around the ankles and under the arches and she paused momentarily to fasten some of the tape, massaging the toes of her right foot as she did so.

Close by, clad in a black leotard and white leggings, Jo Parker was lifting some five-kilo weights, inhaling and exhaling, gazing at her own reflection in the huge mirror that ran the full length of the rear wall. She could see her biceps bulging as she lifted each weight up to her chest then lowering it again in repetitions of ten, pausing only briefly between each set to reposition herself.

The gym smelled of sweat and damp hair.

The two women had been coming to the place together for the last six months, Amy for even longer. She had always worked out whenever she found the time when she was modelling, now she found she did it because she wanted to. Kick-boxing particularly was something both she and Jo had taken to immediately. The other attraction of this gym, run by an ex-boxer who was known to all and sundry only as Gus, was that it was rarely busy at the time Amy and Jo wanted to use it. Indeed, on this particular day, there were only three other people using the facilities.

A man in his fifties was pedalling happily on one of the exercise bikes on the far side of the room, a Walkman clipped to his shorts.

A man in his thirties, dressed in an immaculately clean adidas tracksuit was using one of the three stairmasters in the gym while a third man, in his late twenties, sat about ten yards away, dressed only in shorts and trainers, lifting weights Amy guessed must be close to twenty pounds each. He'd obviously been doing it for some time too because his entire upper body was bulging with overdeveloped muscle. There was no careful body sculpture going on, she mused. He had set out to build huge muscles and he'd succeeded. He looked ungainly, his head appearing too small for his body.

Perspiration was running in rivulets between his huge pectoral muscles. Every now and then he would cast a furtive glance at Amy and Jo. His appreciative gaze travelled over the sweat-stained women, pausing to enjoy the sight of Amy's slender legs and taut buttocks constrained so exquisitely by Lycra leggings or of Jo's breasts pressing against her leotard. He watched as Amy drove several more kicks into the punchbag, hurriedly averting his gaze as she turned towards the bottle of Evian she'd left propped beside the mat. She took a large swig and offered some to Jo, who shook her head and continued lifting, sweat trickling down her face.

Amy stood there with her hands on her hips watching her companion, seeing the muscles bulge on her forearms and biceps.

'If you don't watch it, Jo,' Amy said, smiling, 'you'll end up looking like Hercules over there.'

She made a movement with her eyes in the direction of the musclebound man who was busily fixing another five kilos to each of the weights he was lifting.

'He's watching us,' said Jo, still lifting steadily.

'What?' Amy said and chuckled.

'He's been watching us ever since we got here,' Jo went on, gritting her teeth as she continued lifting.

'There's no law against him looking, Jo,' Amy told her, running a hand through her hair.

'He was watching us while we were on the bikes and he's been watching us ever since we came over here.'

Jo dropped the weights, the loud clang reverberating around the gym.

'I've had enough of this,' she hissed. 'I'm going. I've got things to do anyway and I can do without that fucking idiot staring at me all the time.'

As she spoke she turned the full fury of her gaze in the direction of the musclebound man, who saw the malevolence in her eyes and wondered what had provoked it.

'What the fuck are you looking at?' Jo rasped at him.

'Jo, for Christ's sake,' said Amy, stepping in front of her. 'Just leave it, will you?'

'What's wrong with you?' the man asked innocently, his voice shaky, unprepared for the verbal onslaught aimed at him.

Jo stepped towards him. 'Had a good look at us, have you?' she snapped.

'I don't know what you're talking about,' said the man, continuing to lift the weights, looking away from Jo now. His face was flushed and not all of it was from the effort of lifting.

'Are you coming?' Jo said, looking at Amy who merely shook her head.

Jo spun away, heading for the changing rooms. 'I've got things to do, I've got to go,' she said.

'Jo, we've got to talk,' Amy said, gripping Jo's wrist. 'What's wrong?'

Jo shook loose.

'Not now, Amy,' she said, the knot of muscles at the side of her jaw pulsing angrily. 'I'll see you tonight.'

She turned and stalked away.

Jo watched her go then turned back towards the punchbag.

'What's wrong with your bloody friend?' said the musclebound man. 'Time of the month or something?' He smiled crookedly.

Amy looked at him disdainfully.

'She should be *grateful* people are looking at her,' the man continued. 'She's got a good body – she can't expect people not to look. Touchy cow.'

'Well, at least she's given you an excuse to exercise your *right* arm a little more now, hasn't she?' Amy said dismissively, watching as the smile slipped from the man's face.

Amy spun round and drove three powerful kicks into the punchbag.

It swung gently back and forth on its chain, the imprint of her last kick still visible on the leather.

Sixteen

Jo Parker dropped the sports bag in the hallway of the flat then turned to lock the flat door. She stood with her back against it then she sucked in a deep breath, held it a moment and let it out in a long sigh. She could hear music coming from the sitting room and she sighed again when she heard how loud it was.

As she strode into the room the sound seemed to envelop her. There were CD cases strewn over the carpet in front of the stack system, some of the discs out of their cases.

She picked her way through the debris and immediately switched off the thumping sound system.

'I was listening to that,' said Billy Parker who was seated at one end of the sofa, a cigarette jammed between his lips.

He used the remote control to reactivate the hi-fi, the sound filling the room once more.

Jo jabbed the Off button once again and stood with her back to the player, glaring at her brother.

'You're home early, aren't you?' Billy asked, flicking ash into an overflowing ashtray.

'Is this what you've been doing since I left?' Jo demanded. 'Sitting around on your arse wasting time?'

'I went out to get a sandwich. You didn't have fuck all worth eating.'

She saw three empty cans of Stella by the sofa.

'Is that when you got those?' she demanded, pointing at the cans.

'Man cannot live by bread alone,' he said and cracked out laughing.

Jo glared at him. 'You were supposed to be out looking for a job,' she reminded him.

'I had other business.'

'Yeah, I bet you did.'

He sniffed the air exaggeratedly. 'Good work-out?' he asked. 'It smells like it.' He grinned. 'What's wrong, were the showers broken?'

He stubbed out his cigarette and reached for another can of Stella.

'Did you make the appointment?' Jo asked.

'What for?'

'Did you?'

'What's the fucking point? No one cares anyway.'

'Don't start with the sob stories again, Billy, I'm not in the mood.'

'Don't pretend you care, Jo. You don't care and neither do Mum and Dad.'

'If I didn't care I wouldn't have let you stay here, would I?'

'Do Mum and Dad know I'm here?'

'I spoke to Mum about a week ago. She knows.'

'Did she send her love?' he asked, his voice heavy with scorn. 'I bet she didn't even ask how I was, did she? If they cared that much they wouldn't have thrown me out in the first place.'

'You didn't help yourself, Billy.'

'It's not my fault, the way I am.'

'Nobody said it was.'

'They blame me and do you know why? Because it doesn't go down well with their friends at the Rotary Club or the fucking Round Table. They lost points when the truth came out.'

'What the hell are you talking about?'

'They've been doing it all their lives, Jo. Scoring points off their friends and using us to do it. Their life is one big competition. All their friends' kids went to grammer school so we had to go to *private* school. It put them in front on points.'

'You're being ridiculous.'

'Am I? Why do you think they pushed you to go to college? Because all their friends' kids were going to college.

They couldn't be left out of the game. That would have killed them. So, when you went they got more points. When Danny was killed it was like rolling a double six. All that fucking sympathy. None of their friends could hope to compete with that, could they? They were in front. They had an unassailable lead, but then it all went wrong with *me*, didn't it?' He took a swig from the can. 'When I told them I was gay, that was it, and once their friends found out, it was all over for them. Slide down the biggest ladder back to square one and miss a turn.'

Jo sat down opposite him.

She was the one who broke the silence.

'Please make the appointment, Billy,' she said quietly. 'I'll come with you.'

'To hold my hand? No thanks.'

'You've got to know.'

'Why? There's a better-than-average chance I'll be positive.'

'You can't be sure but even if you *are*, you can get help.'

Billy laughed mockingly.

'The experts always say that, don't they?' he chided. 'Take an AIDS' test, put your mind at rest. What a fucking joke. If you take it and you're positive then all that tells you is that you're going to die soon. Who wants to know *that*?'

'But there are drugs that could help you, Billy.'

'Help, not *cure*, Jo. Do you know what ZCT and all those other fucking pills are? They're not help, they're a stay of execution. Well, if I've got it, I don't want to know.'

He took a last swig from the can and crushed it in one fist.

'But I'll tell you something,' he continued. 'If I *am* positive, if I have got AIDS, then I'll make sure I'm not the only one. I'll take as many with me as I can. If *I'm* going to die, then so are a lot of other people.'

Seventeen

Detective Inspector David Grant switched off the engine of the Montego and sat in silence for a moment gazing at the house ahead of him. The house in Paddock Road was similar to many in this and other roads like it in Dollis Hill. Modest but comfortable the estate agent had called it. For some reason Grant could still remember his words but then again, he mused, remembering things was part of the job after all. The ability to recall the smallest and seemingly most insignificant detail was a prerequisite in his work as a detective. It was normally something he prided himself on but it occasionally irritated him that his capacity for recall extended not just to things of importance but also to bullshit.

'Modest but comfortable.' That was in the file marked bullshit.

He picked up his briefcase from the passenger seat, locked the car and made his way to the front door. A light was on in the sitting room and another upstairs. Tina was home.

He let himself in and when he heard the television headed straight for the sitting room, but as he entered the room, he found it was empty. A comedy programme was on, the canned laughter loud in the background. He switched channels and found the news before heading into the kitchen to get a cup of water, which he gulped down like a man who has just emerged from a trek in the desert.

The air smelled of cooked food. The table was laid for one. He assumed she'd already eaten.

Grant wandered back into the sitting room and flopped into one of the armchairs.

'Hey, you.'

He looked up as he heard her voice, managing a weary smile as Tina padded into the room wearing just a pair of jeans and a baggy white sweater.

She crossed to him and sat on his lap, kissing him, and he inhaled deeply, savouring her scent.

It was warmth and freshness. She always smelled as if she'd just bathed.

He slid one hand up inside her sweater, feeling how smooth her skin was. She giggled and writhed on his lap as he closed one hand around her unfettered right breast.

Tina pulled free of him and retreated to the kitchen.

'Calm down, Tiger,' she called, the merest trace of a northern accent in her voice. It had been stronger when they'd first met, the Yorkshire twang having softened during the intervening five years. For three of those five years they had been married.

He followed her out to the kitchen where she was pulling a cottage pie from the oven, spooning some on to a plate for him.

'I'm not hungry, babe,' he said apologetically. 'Sorry.'

'Eat something, Dave,' she advised. 'You'll be ill if you don't.'

'I've only been home two minutes and you're lecturing me already,' he said, smiling.

He sat down at the carefully laid place and picked dutifully at the food.

Tina got herself a Diet Coke from the fridge and sat down opposite him.

'What time did you get in?' he wanted to know.

'About eight. I got a Chinese on the way back.'

'You didn't cook this especially for me?' he said, jabbing the cottage pie with his fork.

'Took it from the freezer and heated it up with my own fair hand.'

'How did the show go today?' he asked.

'Well, apart from the bloody photographer being late it was fine. The usual thing – organised bedlam – but then fashion shows usually are. Still, we got some good shots, especially of the new Galliano and Conran stuff. We're running a big feature on those in the next issue.'

He nodded dutifully.

'I'm pleased *somebody* had a good day,' he said wearily.

'I wasn't too impressed with some of the new Versace dresses,' Tina continued, oblivious to his remark. 'But they showed us some trouser suits and they were gorgeous. I wish I could afford their prices.'

Grant pushed food slowly into his mouth, watching her as she swigged from the Diet Coke can.

'Another girl was found dead this morning,' he said quietly. 'Another prostitute.'

'Well, they ask for it, don't they? Doing a thing like that, I mean, they don't know what kind of weirdos they're picking up, do they?'

'That's two he's killed in a week. I think it's the same guy.'

'Do you want a drink with that?' she asked, getting to her feet and crossing to the fridge.

Grant exhaled deeply. 'I'll have a beer.'

She put down the can beside him and sat again, watching as he continued to prod at his food.

'If you don't want it, don't eat it,' she said finally.

He dropped the knife and fork on to the plate and pulled open the ring pull on the can, taking several deep swallows. With the back of his hand he wiped his mouth and shook his head.

'You couldn't give a shit about my work, could you?' he said, looking directly at her.

Tina picked up his plate and began scraping the leftovers into the nearby pedal bin.

'I don't particularly want to hear about it over the dinner table.'

'You don't want to hear about it *anywhere*, Tina.'

'Don't start, Dave.'

She dropped the plate into the bowl and ran hot water on it.

'I'm not starting,' he protested. 'But it's true, isn't it? You're not interested.'

'I don't want to hear about people who've been shot or cut up or beaten to death.'

'But it happens and I have to deal with it. It's my work.'

'Then leave it in the office at New Scotland Yard, Dave.'

'Jesus Christ. I wish it was as easy as that.' He sucked in an angry breath. 'I can't "leave it at the office", Tina. I carry it with me all the time. Twenty-four hours a fucking day it's here.' He tapped his forehead.

She took the plate and cutlery from the bowl and began drying them up.

'Leave the bloody drying up, will you?' he shouted. 'Just for once stop with your tidying and cleaning.'

'Look, just because you've had a shitty day, don't come home and start taking it out on me.'

'Sometimes I just want to talk. That's all. But you don't want to listen, do you?'

She was standing at the sink staring at him.

'Sometimes I need to get things off my chest,' he continued. 'But you're not interested, are you? And yet I have to sit here and listen when you talk about *your* job.'

'Sorry if I bore you, Dave.'

'You know what I mean,' he hissed. 'You'd be interested if I was talking about kids, wouldn't you?'

'Yes I would,' she snapped. 'If you were to come home one night and say "Tina, I've changed my mind, I *do* want kids" I'd be *very* interested. But that's not likely to happen, is it, Dave?'

'We've been over this time and time again. What's the point?'

He got to his feet and wandered into the sitting room.

Tina followed him.

'What's the point?' she repeated angrily. 'I'll tell you what the bloody point is. You're being selfish. *You* don't want kids. You never stopped to consider how I might feel.'

He flopped into one of the armchairs, his eyes on the television.

'We've been through this.'

'So that's it? We've discussed it a couple of times so you've had enough? Well there are still things we *haven't* talked about.'

'A couple of times? Christ, it's all we *ever* talk about. We agreed at the beginning that our careers should come first.'

'No, Dave, you wanted *your* career to come first and it has. I've always respected that. All I'm asking now is that you consider *my* feelings.'

'I can't understand you, Tina. You've got a bloody good job with that fashion magazine. You've got a career. But you'd be willing to give all that up to be up to your knees in shit and nappies twenty-four hours a day. It doesn't make sense.'

'It doesn't make sense to you,' she snapped. 'Because you can't see any further than the next promotion.'

'So now you're pissed off because I want to get on?'

'You're a detective inspector. How much further do you want to go? When is this obsessive desire to better yourself going to stop, Dave? When you've got the bloody commissioner's job? Who the hell are you trying to impress? You've done what you set out to do. You're at the top of your profession. Why are you still so resistant to having kids?'

'We've got a good life together, Tina. We live well. We're both successful at what we do. Why let a kid spoil that?'

'Why do you always see a child as an obstacle? You never even consider what it could give us, do you?'

'I see it disrupting our lives, making demands on us. I'm not ready for that, Tina.'

'How can it disrupt *your* life, Dave, you're never bloody here. I never know what time you're going to walk in at night. I don't even know *if* you're going to walk in. Take a close look at us. What life have we got for a child to spoil? We haven't even got a life together. We don't go anywhere because of your work and if we do then you're always on call. We spend most of our time apart. You're working or I'm working. We're like two lodgers sharing the same house.'

'And a baby would change all that, would it?'

'Probably not,' she said wearily. 'Perhaps it's too late for that. Perhaps it's too late for anything to save this marriage.'

Eighteen

'Who does this sanctimonious bastard think he is?'

Amy sat back in her seat, a copy of *The Standard* open in front of her.

David Albury's speech had been well reported and the paper had even run an editorial that, for the most part, backed the views of the Home Secretary. There was a photo of Albury with his wife and daughter on one page and another of him in the House of Commons on the other. On the opposite page in a column headed THE DIRTY DOZEN were twelve films or videos that Albury had singled out for attention during the speech.

Natural Born Killers
Lethal Weapon IV
Man Bites Dog

Amy continued down the list, shaking her head.

The Last Temptation of Christ

'He's a bit out of date on most of these, isn't he?' she said mockingly.

'You're back on air in ten seconds, Amy,' said Mike Osborne from the production booth, his voice sounding robotic over the microphone.

Amy took a sip of coffee and fumbled for a cigarette, one eye on the studio clock.

'Five seconds.'

Amy lit up and took a long drag.

The red ON AIR sign flashed on.

'Welcome back,' she said. 'For those of you just joining

us we're talking about free speech and censorship. I don't know about you but I think we have far too little of the former and far too much of the latter in society today. But today, Mr David Albury, who you may or may not know is Home Secretary, proposed plans for an all party committee to look into the – as he put it – "appalling and ceaseless stream of filth that we are all subjected to every time we visit the cinema, switch on our television sets or rent a video." His words, not mine.'

She hit a button and connected one of the waiting callers.

'Sarah from Richmond. Have you been exposed to any streams of filth lately, Sarah?' Amy asked, smiling.

'I do agree that there's too much violence on television now.'

'Do you watch violent programmes, Sarah?'

'Well, you don't always know they're going to be violent when they start, do you?'

'What sort of TV do you watch then?'

'Soaps, costume dramas, stuff like that.'

'They're violent, aren't they? Soaps have wife beating and car crashes and vandalism. That's violent, isn't it?'

'Yeah, but it's not guns, is it?'

'Oh, I see, so violence only counts if it entails guns. What about knives? Axes? Chainsaws? Rocket launchers? Don't they count as violent? Or how about good old-fashioned fists. They can be pretty lethal sometimes.'

'I don't think people want to see violence on television all the time.'

'Do you watch the news, Sarah?'

'Yeah.'

'Well, there isn't a more violent programme on the TV than the news and that's all *real*. Isn't that worse?'

'But that's real life. They're just showing you what goes on, aren't they? I mean, in films, it's not realistic.'

'Have you ever seen anyone shot, Sarah?'

'No.'

'Then how do you know it's not realistic?'

'Well, they do it to make the heroes look good, don't they?'

Amy shook her head despairingly.

'What do you do if a violent scene comes on the TV, Sarah? Do you watch it?'

'I suppose so.'

'Why don't you turn the TV off? If you hate violence that much, why not exercise your right to freedom and switch off?'

She smiled.

'Because that's what I'm going to do to you right now, Sarah,' Amy said. 'You're history.' She cut the connection and flicked another switch.

'Alan from Notting Hill. What do you think? Are violent films and videos to blame for the ills of our society?'

'Well, no, and I'll tell you what really pisses me . . .'

There was a momentary pause.

'Hello, Alan,' said Amy.

'Hello, am I still on?'

'You're still on. The world is waiting for your pearls of wisdom.'

'Like I said, what really . . . gets to me is all these bloody do-gooders trying to tell people what they should and shouldn't watch. Like you said, it's supposed to be a free country.'

'So you don't agree with the Home Secretary's plans?'

'What plans?'

'He wants to re-classify films, bring in stricter censorship. What do you think of that, Alan?'

'I think he should mind his own business. They should all mind their own business. All these old gits are so out of touch with everyday life they don't know what goes on anyway. You get these do-gooders telling people to stop watching violent films and then one of them . . . that old prat with the bald head. What's his name? You know? The one that's always visiting murderers in prison and saying they should be let out.'

'I think I know who you mean, Alan.'

'People like him, or that stupid old cow who's always complaining about stuff on the telly. What's her name? You know? They should just shut up and let people live their own lives. I mean, they wouldn't like it if people started coming round their houses and telling them what to do.'

'Quite right, Alan. Thanks for your comments,' said Amy. 'I think the real problem is that these self-appointed guardians of our morals aren't even elected by members of the public. No one voted them into a position where they have any right to speak for anyone other than themselves. They are expressing their own views, not the views of the vast majority.'

She glanced across at the screen and saw half a dozen more callers' names flashing.

'I read the Home Secretary's speech as it was reported in the paper,' said Brian from Southwark. 'And I have to say, I agree with what he said. I have children and I don't want them exposed to this kind of thing.'

'How old are your children, Brian?'

'I've got a boy of twelve and a girl of ten.'

'Well, then they're not going to be exposed to any of the films David Albury mentioned, are they, because all of those films had "eighteen" certificates.'

'They could get them from a video shop.'

'Any video shop renting "eighteen" certificate films to kids under age is liable to be fined. Besides, Brian, what happened to parental responsibility? Isn't it *your* job to make sure they don't see material you feel is unsuitable.'

'I can control my children when I'm with them. I don't know what they're up to when they're round friends' houses. Perhaps not all parents are as conscientious as I am.'

'So you're blaming the *parents* of your kids' friends if your kids get to see these films?'

'If these films were banned in the first place then they wouldn't be able to see them, would they?'

'Have you actually seen any of the films that the Home Secretary listed as those he wanted banned, Brian?'

There was a moment's silence.

'No I haven't seen them,' said Brian of Southwark.

'Then how can you comment on them?' Amy asked.

'I've read reviews of them, I know what they're about.'

'I've seen photos of Adolf Hitler, it doesn't make me a fascist. You can't comment on something you haven't seen, Brian.'

'I've spoken to people who've seen them.'

'Is all your information on every subject secondhand, Brian? Do you watch television?'

'Not often.'

'Do you read?'

'Yes, I read a lot.'

'Then presumably you'd like violent books banned as well? Because they'll probably be the next target of someone like David Albury. He'll start with films and videos, move on to TV then books. If these new laws of his are as Draconian as he would like, then no branch of the entertainment business will be safe.'

'I don't see it as a bad thing. I'd ban violent books too, I mean, they're even easier for children to get hold of.'

'So what would you start with, Brian? Which books? The Bible? The complete works of Shakespeare? *The Iliad*?'

'That's ridiculous.'

'No, it isn't. There are few books in print more violent than the Bible or Shakespeare. Surely they should be amongst the first banned?'

'The works of Shakespeare are art. You can't ban art.'

'Anything creative, to a degree, is art, Brian. Art and creativity should not be banned, no matter what their subject matter. Do you feel the same about sex as you do about violence?'

'What do you mean?'

'Would you ban sexually explicit material as well as violent material?'

'I think sex is a different matter.'

'So, in your opinion, it's fine for children to watch two people having sex but not to watch two people shooting at each other? Don't you realise that *your* life is being controlled too by these self-appointed moral guardians, Brian. Doesn't it bother you that you have no control over your own life?'

'I'm perfectly in control of my own life.'

'No you're not. There is censorship in every walk of life. Things that you are told you cannot do because the law says you cannot do them. That is a form of censorship, Brian. But perhaps that suits you because it means *you* don't have to make responsible decisions. *You* don't have to make choices because those choices are made for you by faceless bureaucrats and self-important people more concerned with voicing their own opinions than caring about those of others.' She took a drag on her cigarette. 'I just wondered if I was the only one to have remembered that there's an election due soon. The kind of public hysteria David Albury is trying to whip up is useful for vote-catching. It deflects public attention away from things like government policy failures. Basically, a campaign like this is using films as a scapegoat. Films are blamed for problems that have already been created by the state of our society – with its poor housing, joblessness, domestic violence and a general sense of hopelessness felt by a large majority of the population. It's a bandwagon to jump on and Albury's inviting anyone who wants to jump up there with him.'

She glanced up at the studio clock.

'We're going to take a break for the news,' said Amy. 'Then we'll carry on with this fascinating topic. I want to hear from all the do-gooders and those who hate them. Let's have a balanced view. And, if you're out there listening, David Albury or any of your cronies, give me a call. If you've got the guts.'

She flicked off a switch and the music that introduced

the News began to fill her headset. She pulled it off and glanced at the screen. At the flashing names.

One of them looked familiar. *Why?*

She frowned as she gazed at it.

PETER FROM MUSWELL HILL

There was something . . .

'Amy.'

She heard Mike Osborne's voice from the production room.

'That next call,' he said, a note of concern in his voice. 'Don't take it.'

Again she looked at the screen. At the name.

'Can you hear me, Amy?' he persisted. 'Don't take that call.'

Nineteen

'Peter, we're going to have to stop meeting like this.'

Amy leaned close to the microphone and blew out a stream of smoke. Then she glanced up and saw Osborne standing at the large window that separated the studio from the production room. His arms were folded, his face set in hard lines. Amy thought that she could see him shaking his head gently.

'I bet you don't agree with censorship, do you, Peter?'

'No,' said Peter from Muswell Hill. 'I agree with what you said.'

'About everyone having the right to watch what they want to watch?'

'About everything you said.'

'What kind of films do you watch, Peter?'

Silence.

'Peter,' she persisted. 'Can you hear me?'

'There's nothing wrong with violent films,' he said quietly.

'Do you watch violent films, Peter?'

'I watch all kinds of things. I'm not prudish.'

Osborne was still standing sentinel at the glass partition. Amy watched him for a moment as she listened to the caller.

'I find them liberating,' Peter continued.

'In what way, Peter?'

'Violence happens in everyday life, you can't hide from it. Sometimes it's necessary.'

Amy blew out a long stream of smoke.

'In what circumstances is violence necessary, Peter?' she asked.

Silence.

'Have you ever been violent to anyone, Peter?' Amy asked.

'Sometimes you have to hurt people,' he told her.

'What would make you *want* to hurt someone, Peter?'

Silence.

Amy looked across at Osborne who was imitating a cutting action across his throat.

Amy shook her head and leaned closer to the microphone.

'What I do, I do for you,' Peter said suddenly.

'What *do* you do for me, Peter?'

'I tell people about you. I tell them to listen to you, to what you have to say.'

'Thank you very much, Peter, I appreciate that.'

'Did you get the present I sent you?'

'Yes, I told you that last time you called the show.'

'No. This is something else. Something new. It's a surprise.'

'What is it?'

'If I told you that it wouldn't be a surprise, would it?'

The laughter which she heard raised the hairs on the back of her neck.

'I like to give surprises,' he continued.

More laughter.

Again she felt those icy fingers at the back of her neck.

'How will I know it's from you if you don't tell me what it is?' said Amy.

'You'll know,' he said flatly.

'Will I like it?'

'Wait and see.'

He hung up.

'The guy is a fucking nutter,' said Mike Osborne. 'He should be reported to the police.'

Amy stretched in her chair and took a sip of her coffee.

'He's harmless,' she said dismissively.

'How the hell do you know that?' Osborne protested.

'Jesus, you don't know what's going through his mind. He's fixated on you. Obsessed.'

'What do you think, Jo?' Amy asked, looking across the production room at the younger woman.

Jo shrugged. 'I'm no psychiatrist, Amy, but I think Mike's right about him being obsessed with you.'

'What's your problem, Mike?' Amy said. 'He hasn't made any threats against me, he hasn't said he's going to kill me.'

'That might just be a matter of time,' Osborne insisted. 'What if you reject him? What if he turns against you?'

'How can I reject him? I haven't even met him and I'm not likely to either.'

'And what if he turns up at the station one night? What then?' Osborne demanded. 'I'm telling you, Amy, the police should know about this guy. Before it's too late.'

Amy shook her head and got to her feet.

'You worry too much, Mike,' she said, pulling on her coat.

'And maybe you don't worry enough,' he snapped irritably.

Amy held his gaze for a moment then headed for the door, Jo close behind.

The two women walked to the lift in silence, Amy jabbing the Call button. When it arrived they rode it to the ground floor.

'What if Mike's right about this bloke being crazy?' Jo said, as the doors slid open.

'Don't you start too.'

They walked to the main entrance, Amy raising a hand to the nightwatchman who nodded back in acknowledgement, watching as the women stood on the pavement outside chatting for a moment. Then he returned to his magazine.

Amy looked across at her waiting cab then glanced at her watch. Before she could speak, Jo was already heading towards her own taxi.

'I'll speak to you tomorrow,' said the younger woman, as she slid on to the back seat of the vehicle.

Amy nodded and looked around Bedford Square. Tall buildings towered over her from all four sides, only the odd light burning in windows here and there.

She shuddered slightly and walked to the cab, clambering in.

As the vehicle moved away from the kerb a dark shape moved in the shadows thrown by the building behind.

A form that seemed to be a part of the blackness itself.

The figure watched the taxi disappear around a corner then melted back into the gloom as soundlessly as it had emerged.

Twenty

Christ, it was cold.

Even inside the Montego with the heating on, Detective Inspector David Grant shivered as he brought the vehicle to a halt outside number six Wenlock Road. The wind was whipping wildly around the car and the street, sending spilled rubbish flying from a nearby dustbin. A crisp packet stuck to the windscreen momentarily before another gust of wind sent it spinning into the air.

Grant switched off the engine and glanced out. The sky filled with huge, bruised clouds threatening to unleash a downpour any second. Not all the streetlights were working but the slowly turning, blue lights of the ambulance parked across the pavement outside number six illuminated the early morning somewhat.

In addition to the emergency vehicle, there were also two marked police cars parked nearby and a blue Saab, which he recognised as belonging to Detective Sergeant Lawrenson. It had been Lawrenson who had called him about fifty minutes ago.

Grant swung himself out of the car and headed towards number six. He flipped his ID at the uniformed man standing at the top of the narrow staircase that led down to the basement flat, noticing how red the man's face was. The uniformed man was shivering. He stepped aside to let the detective inspector through.

As he reached the front door, the paint chipped and peeling, Grant noticed that there was a window-box on the sill but it seemed to consist only of dried earth. Any flowers that may have flourished there were long dead. Cat shit lay in one corner of the paved area at the bottom of the steps.

Grant wandered into the hallway, and could hear

voices inside the flat. As he entered, he noticed that the walls were bare; no posters or prints brightened up what was a distinctly dismal abode. Two pairs of dirty trainers lay discarded close to the door, and a leather jacket was hanging from a coat hook to his right, the material worn and scuffed in places. He turned and glanced at the door. The hinges were intact. The lock didn't seem to have been smashed.

'No signs of forced entry, guv.'

He recognised the voice immediately as belonging to Lawrenson.

The detective sergeant was smoking a cigarette, flicking ash on to the worn carpet.

'I've already checked the doors and windows,' Lawrenson continued.

Grant nodded. 'Let me see what we've got,' he muttered, following his companion through into the sitting room.

It was small anyway but the presence of three men made it look even more cramped. As in the hallway, the walls were bare. A single light hung from the ceiling, its bulb illuminating the scene below. The fact that the shade which surrounded it bore pictures of Marilyn Monroe made it seem all the more bizarre. A two-seater sofa had been overturned and lay on its side close to a chair and a small portable television which, Grant noticed, for some reason had no plug on.

There was a fireplace housing a two-bar electric fire and, on the mantelpiece above, a radio. He saw a stack system, which had only one of the speakers attached.

And he saw blood. Splashes of it littered the carpet and fireplace and, as Lawrenson stepped aside, Grant saw where it had come from.

The body sat in the chair was a man in his late twenties. He was naked apart from a pair of underpants, his long legs stretched out in front of him as if he was warming his feet in front of the fire. His face was tinged blue, his eyes open and bulging in their sockets, the whites spattered

red. A dark patch stained the front of his pants. As Grant stepped closer he could smell urine and the stronger, more pungent odour of faeces. As well as these odours, the coppery smell of blood filled the room.

It was everywhere. The red fluid covered most of the dead man's upper torso and it looked as if his arms, from the elbows down, had been dipped in the stuff. There was more of it around his mouth, some having congealed on his lips and chin. Several vivid striation marks ran around his throat as though someone had drawn on his flesh with a red Biro.

On the other side of the chair, the pathologist Phillip Barclay leaned close to the body, running expert eyes over each injury in turn.

'How long's he been dead?' Grant wanted to know.

'I'd say about seven hours,' Barclay told him.

'Cause of death?'

'Strangulation.' The pathologist pointed to the marks around the throat. 'Performed with thin flex or string.'

'Like the other two?' Grant murmured.

Barclay nodded.

'From the nature of the wounds and the pressure exerted, coupled with the angle of the attack, I'd say—'

'Same killer,' Grant finished the sentence.

Barclay nodded.

'So who's our boy?' Grant nodded towards the corpse.

'His name's Harvey Dwyer,' Lawrenson filled him in.

'What do we know about him?'

'More form than Desert Orchid. Robbery, aggravated assault and he ran a little sideline too.' The detective sergeant produced a small plastic bag from his jacket pocket and held it up. 'We found this in the kitchen.'

Grant looked at the brownish-white powder. 'Heroin.'

Lawrenson nodded. 'There are syringes in there too. We found more in the bathroom and there was other stuff in the bedroom. Coke, Es, speed. He was a walking pharmacy.'

'There are track marks on his arms and thighs,' Barclay added.

'You say there was no forced entry, Stuart?' Grant said, still peering at the body.

'No, and as far as we can tell, nothing was taken. No personal effects, not the drugs. There was still money in his wallet.' Lawrenson nodded towards the mantelpiece, where a black leather wallet lay untouched.

'No forced entry means he could have known his killer,' said Grant.

'He was dealing as well as using,' Lawrenson offered. 'Maybe someone didn't like the prices he was charging.'

'Then why not take the drugs too?' Grant said. 'Robbery's not the motive. Someone wanted him dead, it's as simple as that.' He pointed to the blood-drenched arms of the corpse. 'What happened there?'

Barclay raised an eyebrow.

'Something *I've* never seen before,' the pathologist said. 'The wrists were cut after strangulation using a *very* sharp knife. A Stanley knife or something similar. Look—' He pointed to a cross-shaped incision on each wrist. Both were gaping open like gasping mouths. '—The ulnar and radial arteries were then pulled out. Not just cut. The killer literally ripped them out of Dwyer's arms.'

Twenty-One

'Perhaps it was symbolic,' said Detective Constable Keith Friel, 'ripping the veins out. Perhaps it was meant to mean something.'

'Like what?' Grant challenged.

His words echoed in his office as he looked around at his colleagues, searching their expressions.

Lawrenson stifled a yawn and ran both hands through his hair.

Friel lit up a cigarette and puffed anxiously on it.

Detective Constable Dennis Schofield was glancing at the photos of the dead man and shaking his head.

'Come on, for fuck's sake,' hissed Grant. 'Somebody give me *something*. Why has he changed his MO?'

'The pathologist's report says that all three victims were strangled the same way, guv,' Lawrenson offered. 'Who says he has changed it?'

'This business with the veins, it might just be some kind of sick joke to put us off the scent,' Friel added.

'What fucking scent?' snapped Grant. 'We haven't got a scent yet. We've got three bodies, all strangled and no motive. That's all we've got. No motive, no links.'

'It's going to take a bit of time,' offered Schofield.

'We haven't *got* time,' rasped Grant.

'Two pros and a drug pusher,' said Lawrenson. 'Perhaps the killer is wiping out low-lifes.'

Grant shrugged.

'We do know that Claire Glover bought drugs from Dwyer,' said Friel. '*That's* a link.'

'What's the word on the street?' Grant asked. 'Is anyone talking?'

'*Everyone's* talking,' Schofield informed him. 'It's just

that what they're saying isn't helping much. They're scared but they're *more* scared of us.'

'You're not talking to the right people,' Grant snapped.

'We just need some luck,' Schofield protested.

'Then get some,' Grant demanded.

A heavy silence descended on the room, finally broken by Grant.

'All right, this business of him pulling the veins out of Dwyer's arms, perhaps it *does* mean something,' he mused. 'But what?'

'It was done after Dwyer was killed,' Friel said, 'so the killer wasn't torturing him. It has to have a meaning.'

'It doesn't *have* to,' Grant said. 'The killer was just making sure.'

'If he wanted to be sure he could have cut Dwyer's throat, stabbed him through the heart – anything,' Lawrenson said. 'This business with the veins is a bit elaborate, isn't it?'

'So,' Grant conceded, 'the *act* itself probably does have meaning. But who is it sending a message to? Us or to other people like Dwyer?' He flipped through the pile of papers on his desk. 'By the way, who found the body?'

'Dwyer's landlord,' said Lawrenson. 'His statement's on your desk. He heard raised voices about eleven; he said it sounded like an argument.'

'But he didn't go down to the flat until nearly five hours later,' Grant observed. 'He didn't intend getting involved, did he? Have we eliminated him as a suspect?'

'His wife was with him all night; besides, he had no hassle with Dwyer. He said his rent was paid on time every month. He hardly saw him,' Lawrenson continued.

'So, other possible suspects?' Grant mused. 'Another drug dealer trying to muscle in on Dwyer's customers?'

Friel nodded. 'That's *my* bet.'

'That explains his death but not the other two,' Grant reminded the younger man.

'Maybe he was into pimping too,' Schofield offered.

'There's nothing in his past form to indicate that,' Grant said. 'But I'm inclined to think it was someone who knew all three victims.'

'Why?' Friel asked.

'Because at all three murder scenes there was very little or no sign of a struggle. There was no forced entry into Dwyer's place last night.'

'Perhaps it was one of his customers,' Schofield suggested. 'The deal could have cut up rough and the buyer topped him.'

'Then why not take the gear that was lying around the flat? Another user would have taken the coke and smack we found and used it or sold it on. But nothing was taken. Christ, whoever killed him didn't even bother going through his fucking wallet.' He sat back in his chair, hands behind his head.

Another heavy silence fell upon the four men.

'What I can't understand is why Dwyer didn't fight back. He was a big geezer, he should have put up a decent fight,' Lawrenson said.

'Perhaps he was already out of his head on smack when the killer attacked him and took him by surprise,' Grant surmised. 'The pathologist's report shows traces of heroin in his bloodstream.'

Lawrenson reached for the report and ran a finger down the carefully typed sheet. 'It also says he was suffering from septicaemia and hepatitis B. He was a sick man.'

Grant nodded. 'And now,' he said quietly. 'He's a *dead* man.'

Twenty-Two

Amy heard the shout before she heard the crash. An angry yell followed by a loud bang and then a voice once again, muttering.

She locked the door of her flat and peered over the banister, spotting several wooden crates in the hallway.

She could still hear the voice but, as yet, she couldn't pinpoint its owner.

Amy dropped her keys into her jacket pocket and made her way unhurriedly down the stairs, glancing over the banister as she went.

She saw the back of the man's head first. He was kneeling in the hallway picking up saucepans, and was muttering to himself as he dropped the pans back into a packing crate.

He was wearing a leather jacket and jeans; his hair, an inch or two over his collar, was thick and lustrous.

As Amy approached the bottom of the stairs she saw another half a dozen or so crates and boxes of various shapes and sizes piled outside the door of flat number one. The door was slightly ajar but she couldn't see into the flat.

The man dropped the last saucepan into the box, straightened up and turned just as she reached the bottom step.

'Having trouble?' said Amy, smiling as he looked at her.

His own smile was immediate and welcoming and she found herself momentarily gazing into his steel-grey eyes.

'You could say that,' he said and chuckled. 'I suppose that's what I get for being cheap and moving myself. I should have hired Pickfords.'

'Are you moving in to number one?'

Again he nodded. 'You might not have known if I hadn't dropped those bloody saucepans,' he said and grinned. 'Sorry if I disturbed you.'

'You didn't. Besides, it looks as if we're going to be neighbours; I live in the flat above.' She extended her right hand. 'Amy Watson.'

He shook the offered hand and she felt the strength in his grip.

'Jake Webber,' he replied, holding on to her hand a fraction of a second longer than necessary. Long enough to look into her green eyes. 'Nice to meet you.'

'I had no idea anyone was moving in. I hadn't seen or heard anyone looking round. No estate agents or anything like that.'

He shrugged then bent down to pick up one of the boxes. 'Well, I'd better get on.'

'Look, I was just going to get some shopping. Is there anything you want? You seem to have your hands full, if you'll excuse the pun, moving in.'

'Actually, could you get me a sandwich and some teabags if you're going anywhere near a supermarket. I haven't eaten since seven this morning. I'm starving.'

Amy smiled broadly. 'No problem. Do you want me to help you carry this stuff into the flat?' She moved towards one of the crates.

Webber spun round, his eyes blazing. 'Leave it!' he snapped.

Amy took a step back, stunned by the vehemence of his tone.

Immediately his smile returned. 'They're heavy,' he explained. 'Thanks anyway.'

'Okay, I'll go and get the provisions then.' She paused as she got to the main door. 'Don't drop anything else, will you. You might disturb the neighbours.' She grinned, then was gone.

He too smiled broadly, watching her as she left.

As soon as he turned around the smile disappeared.

He lifted the box with ease, despite its weight, pushed his way into the flat, then returned for another. He wanted them all inside before she returned.

Amy checked her watch as she opened the door into the hallway. It was 2.30 p.m. She'd been gone less than an hour.

The hallway was empty of boxes, the door of flat number one firmly closed.

She hadn't bought too much food for herself, just enough to last until the weekend when she would spend up to three hours in the supermarket replenishing her depleted fridge and cupboards. She actually enjoyed the trek up and down the aisles. For now, she had only two carrier bags. Inside one were two packs of sandwiches.

She knocked on the door of number one and waited.

Webber opened it almost immediately and she held up the bags in front of him.

'Meals on wheels,' she said chuckling, and handed him the sandwiches. 'I didn't know what you wanted, so I got a mixture.'

'How much do I owe you?' he asked.

'Call it a house-warming present.'

They both smiled. She gave him the teabags too. Still he was standing in the doorway, leaning against the frame.

'Look, I would ask you in, but the place is a tip.'

'So is mine and I've lived there five years.'

'I haven't had time to unpack much yet and . . .'

She held up a hand to silence him. 'Don't worry about it.'

'Some other time perhaps?'

She nodded.

'I'll leave you to get on then,' Amy said, again looking into his eyes. 'If you want anything, like I said, I'm in the flat directly above.'

'Before you go, I've got a confession to make,' he said, that faint smile still creasing his lips. 'When you introduced yourself earlier, I knew you were Amy Watson.

You've probably heard this so many times but I used to collect your photos when you modelled. I even had one of your calendars. Sorry if that embarrasses you.'

'I'm very flattered.'

'You did a spread for *Penthouse*, didn't you? A couple of years ago.'

She nodded.

'I've still got it,' he said almost guiltily.

She smiled broadly. 'Well, you've got me at a disadvantage, Jake,' she said. 'All I know about you is your name. You even know where my birthmark is.'

Webber cracked out laughing.

'I feel like some teenager who's been caught wanking,' he said, feeling his cheeks colour. 'I listen to your radio show too.'

'Now you're grovelling.'

'Look, thanks for these,' he said, holding up the sandwiches. 'Next time, *I'll* buy.'

'I'll hold you to that,' said Amy and turned towards the stairs. 'See you around, Jake.'

He waited until she was halfway up the stairs then closed the door.

Amy was on the top step when she heard a low clunk.

The door of number one had been bolted.

Twenty-Three

The only sound in the incident room was the low hum of the air-conditioning. David Grant walked slowly around the deserted room, drawing on his cigarette, glancing at the array of photos tacked to the noticeboards at one end of the room.

Claire Glover.

Tessa Carr.

Harvey Dwyer.

There were half-a-dozen photos of each victim. One taken in life, the others in death.

Was this it? The existence of three people reduced to black and white ten-by-eights and a handful of files.

They all had families somewhere. People to grieve for them. People who loved them.

Didn't they?

Each one a son or daughter.

Each one now a statistic.

Nothing more.

For Grant they were a means to an end. In death they would tell him much more than they ever could while they'd lived. The examinations, the post-mortems should give some clues as to who had snuffed out their lives so brutally.

But *why* had those lives been snuffed out?

Come on, think.

He moved closer to the pictures and gazed into the blank, monochrome eyes. *What can you tell me?*

He stared at the pictures of Claire Glover. Stared into those eyes. At the livid complexion. At the deep gouges around the neck and the bruises on the face.

Who did this to you?

In the post-mortem photos of Tessa Carr her eyelids were open wide enough for him to be able to see her glazed eyes. Like those of a fish on a skillet. People used to believe that the last thing imprinted upon the eye of a murder victim was the identity of the killer.

Grant smiled.

Look into those eyes.

There was bruising around the left one. A slight tear in the lower lid of the right.

What did you see?

He peered at those of Harvey Dwyer.

As the life was being throttled from you, did you look into the face of your killer?

Grant examined a separate set of photos that showed just Dwyer's forearms, the veins and arteries torn out.

He exhaled wearily and turned his back on the pictures. A headache was beginning at the base of his skull and he used one hand to massage the tight knot of muscles there. A glance at his watch told him that it was 10.56 p.m.

Time to go home?

He'd rung home two hours ago to tell Tina he'd be late. He'd left a message on the answerphone just like he'd done so many times before, and he knew that she'd listen to it with the same weary resignation she had listened to other similar messages he'd left.

Time to go home?

There were files on the desks in the incident room. Statements. Medical reports. Post-mortem notes. He picked up the first of the manilla files and sat down at one of the desks.

He lit another cigarette and began reading.

She knew as soon as she closed the front door behind her that he wasn't home. As soon as she saw the red message light flashing on the answering machine she knew that he had called.

Tina Grant didn't even bother to check the message. She kicked off her shoes and left them in the hall, before heading upstairs, switching on the lamp at the bottom of the staircase as she passed.

She made her way up to their bedroom and undressed

quickly, slipping on a T-shirt. Then she wandered into the bathroom, brushed her teeth and headed back to bed.

Back to *their* bed.

It was cold beneath the sheets. It was always cold these days, she thought.

She stretched, realising how tired she was. She didn't know what time he'd be home. Even if he would be home.

She glanced at the clock then set the alarm, settling herself once more.

Rolling on to her side, one hand almost unconsciously strayed to the empty side of the bed where her husband should be lying.

It felt so cold.

She closed her eyes and sleep was upon her in minutes.

Amy sat up in bed, muttering irritably to herself. *Jesus Christ. Was it too much to ask for a few hours sleep?*

She sat in the gloom for long seconds before finally reaching across and flicking on one of the bedside lamps. She hated the darkness when she was alone.

She yawned. *You're tired. Why can't you sleep?*

For the last eighteen months she had found it difficult to sleep at night. A few hours here and there. She'd always been able to function on a surprisingly small amount of sleep but, lately, it was becoming more of a hindrance. She rarely rose in the mornings feeling refreshed.

The sleepless nights had begun when the affair had finished. Whichever way she chose to look at it, she was faced with the inescapable fact. She missed him.

Missed having him close to her at night.

Missed the knowledge that they would meet, however infrequently.

Him. Him.

Can't you even bring yourself to say his name?

She looked across to one of the bookshelves on the far side of the room. Several of his books were displayed there.

John Howard.

She'd felt safe with him.

There had been a time during their affair when she'd confided in him that she'd been suffering bad dreams on an almost nightly basis. One night, as they'd drifted off to sleep, he'd whispered to her to wake him if those bad dreams returned.

She had slept soundly in his arms that night and on every occasion she'd seen him. Usually exhausted by the intensity of their lovemaking, she had rested safely with him and the dreams had not returned.

He had driven them away. She'd convinced herself of that.

And where was he now? Lying in bed with his wife? Or with another woman perhaps?

He'd cheated with *her*, why should he stop?

Amy wondered what he was doing and she was angry with herself for even entertaining those thoughts.

Angry with *him* because she could not rid herself of them.

Of his image.

Of the memories. Because now memories were all she had.

She ran a hand through her hair and exhaled deeply.

The bang came from below her. A loud impact of wood on wood.

A door being slammed?

Amy swung herself out of bed as she heard the sound of a key in a lock, the silence of the night acting as an amplifier for the smallest noise.

She crossed to one of her windows and peered out into the street. There was a lamp directly opposite, the sodium glare casting deep shadows. Someone had emerged from the flats and was making their way across to the other side of the street, walking swiftly, hands dug into their pockets. The figure was unmistakable.

Amy glanced at her bedside clock then back out into the street to see the figure being swallowed up by the gloom.

She frowned. Where the hell was Jake Webber going at 3.22 in the morning?

Twenty-Four

'Dirty bastard,' muttered Nancy Kendall, bending low over the sink.

She coughed loudly, hawked and spat into the dirty basin, spinning both taps afterwards. She watched the mixture of phlegm, semen and water swirling around the plughole, as if mesmerised by it, then she straightened up and inspected her reflection in the cracked mirror.

She leaned closer and put out her tongue. God, she hated it when they came in her mouth.

'Dirty bastard,' she said again, reaching inside her handbag for a small jar of Listerine. She swilled a capful of the liquid around her mouth and spat again. Then she splashed her face with water and smoothed her hair away from her forehead. She had a spot just above her right eyebrow. It looked red and angry against the paleness of her complexion. She prodded it with her index finger before swigging more of the Listerine.

The taste was beginning to fade now. That horribly familiar salty, oily flavour, which she had come to know only too well during the last four years. The first time a punter had come in her mouth she'd nearly vomited, spitting out most of the ejaculate, much to the man's fury. She'd spattered his trousers with it.

Nancy grinned as she remembered the incident, the grin fading slightly as she remembered too how hard he'd hit her. He'd knocked out one of her teeth.

Bastard.

That was how she'd met Simon. Both of them had been sitting in Casualty at The Royal North Hospital that Saturday night – she, wondering if her jaw had been broken and he, awaiting stitches for a cut hand.

He'd started talking to her, even introduced her to the

girl he was with. She'd been fifteen then. She'd guessed he was in his early twenties.

They'd become lovers a week later.

Two days after that he was pimping for her. But he was doing it, he kept reminding her, because he loved her and he didn't want any harm to come to her on the streets. She would be safe with him because he was careful. He only worked with three other girls and he didn't allow them to get into trouble. He looked out for them. Just like he'd look out for her.

She looked at her reflection once more and, running a comb through her long dark hair, smiled as she thought of him. It was only a short walk to their flat from where the punter had dropped her off. She'd taken the money from him then headed for the all-night café near St Pancras Station to wash out her mouth. To swill the taste of him away. It was in that toilet she now stood.

It had been a good night. She'd made over seventy pounds. Simon would be pleased.

She took a five-pound note from the wad in her purse and gazed at it for a moment before slipping it beneath her right foot, and pressing it into the high-heeled shoe she wore. She'd tell him she used some money to get a taxi home. He wouldn't mind. He wanted her to be safe. He cared about her.

She walked out of the café toilet, through the clutter of tables, where two or three taxi drivers sat talking and drinking coffee, and out into the night.

The wind was whipping along Euston Road, hurling rubbish before it. A discarded McDonald's container tumbled past her, propelled by the breeze. Nancy pulled up the collar of her jacket and began walking, grateful that she hadn't got far to go.

She passed St Pancras town hall and headed down Judd Street, noticing that one of the doorways contained what looked like a discarded bundle of clothes.

As she drew alongside the bundle moved and an unwashed face glared out at her. A man in his twenties?

It was hard to tell his age. He muttered something under his breath, annoyed at being woken by the clicking of her heels on the pavement, then he rolled over, pulled his filthy sleeping bag more tightly around him and tried to sleep again. Nancy could smell the acrid stench of urine emanating from the man, wafting on the breeze like an invisible cloud.

She walked on, turning into Cromer Street. Several of the streetlights were out and the thoroughfare was in virtual darkness.

A car parked close to the kerb suddenly started up, the sound of the engine making her jump. She peered into the gloom inside the car but couldn't make out the face of the driver. The engine spluttered and died and she heard grunts of anger from inside as the occupant tried once more to get the car going. As she crossed the road she could still hear the whining of the engine behind her.

The church opposite towered above her, its spire thrusting up into the dark sky. The building was dark and it appeared as if it had been hewn from the blackness itself, part of the deep gloom that covered the street.

She could hear creaking and, as she drew nearer, realised that the wrought-iron gate that led up to the main door of the church was moving in the breeze, the hinges groaning.

She reached into her handbag and pulled out a key, happy that she'd reached her destination.

Simon would be glad she was back.

She pushed the key into the door and stepped into the tiny hallway.

Nancy heard laughter coming from the sitting room. The door was slightly ajar and she realised that he had the television on. That was where the laughter was coming from.

She smiled. He'd waited up for her. God bless him. He must have missed her.

She pushed open the door, a smile spreading across her face.

It vanished rapidly as she began to scream.

Twenty-Five

In her dream someone was knocking on a door. Banging insistently. Someone she couldn't see.

The knocking was getting louder.

Inside her head it was deafening.

Amy wanted to clap her hands to her ears, to shut out the sound, to stop the dream.

She sat bolt upright. The banging continued.

She blinked myopically, looked around her.

The banging?

She was awake and yet the noise continued. She sat in bed listening, gradually realising that the sound wasn't part of a dream but was happening below her.

It wasn't banging. There was no one banging on a door.

She had heard the door to number one being opened and closed. There was movement below. Amy could hear someone moving around.

She shook her head as if to clear the lethargy. An attempt to separate dream from reality.

Amy rubbed her eyes and looked at the bedside clock. 4.36 a.m.

Jesus Christ.

It was still dark outside. Dawn was another hour or more away. And yet, below her, Jake Webber was moving about as if it was midday. It had been *his* door she had heard. Not some imagined, dreamlike intrusion. As she slowly lay back down she heard the sound of his shower running.

Amy closed her eyes, surprised at how tired she was, at how easily the drowsiness washed over her as she rolled on to her back.

Below her, the hiss of Webber's shower continued.

She glanced again at her clock and pulled the duvet up more tightly around her neck to keep out the cold.

Her eyelids began to close. Sleep was a welcome invader. She felt herself drifting off.

Where had Webber been?

She exhaled deeply.

Where?

She stretched, luxuriating in the warmth of her bed.

What kept him out in the early hours?

Perhaps she'd ask him.

'Jake. Where were you . . .'

Outside the wind was growing stronger. Amy slept.

Twenty-Six

The lift bumped to a halt and the doors slid open with a soft whirr.

Detective Sergeant Lawrenson shuddered involuntarily.

'It's always so bloody cold down here,' he said as he and Grant set off along the corridor.

Grant chose to ignore his colleague's remark.

He reached the door marked PATHOLOGY and pushed it open. The strong smell of chemicals swept over the two men like a wave. It was a smell both of them were well acquainted with.

A man was seated at a desk inside the outer office. He looked up and nodded cursorily at the two detectives as they passed.

'He's just finished,' he commented, watching as the men headed through another door.

'How long had Costello been pimping?' asked Grant without looking at his companion.

'Seven or eight years,' Lawrenson told him. 'He started young.'

'He finished young too, didn't he?'

Grant pushed open a set of double doors and the two men entered the main pathology lab.

Banks of fluorescents set into the high ceiling reflected their cold light off the white-tiled walls and floor and also on the cold steel surfaces of six worktops inside the lab. Only one of these was occupied.

The two men crossed to it immediately.

Phillip Barclay looked up from the corpse, wiping his hands on his apron which was already flecked with blood. Simon Costello's body was naked. Exposed to any prying eyes that cared to look.

Grant pointed at the throat. At marks that were becoming all too familiar.

There was a deep, angry crevice about half a centimetre thick in the flesh of the neck. Just above the larynx. There was dried blood around the mouth and, Grant noticed, at the base of a nostril. Several dark bruises showed up vividly against the pallid skin, most of them around the tops of the arms and the shoulders.

Lawrenson looked on with similar interest, trying to avoid looking at the huge Y-shaped cut that ran from Costello's sternum to his pelvis. The flesh had been folded back and the internal organs were exposed.

A set of scales hung above the autopsy table and, in one of the dishes, Lawrenson noticed two huge reddish-pink lumps of tissue, which he recognised as lungs. Close to Barclay, alongside a trolley that bore his implements, was a smaller dish also containing some human offal. A more shapeless discoloured object glistened beneath the bright lights. He had no idea what it was. The smell coming from the lungs and the open abdominal cavity of the corpse threatened to overpower him, and combined with the smell of chemicals, was almost intolerable.

'Go on then, Phil,' said Grant, looking at the pathologist. 'Surprise me. What did you find?'

'It's the same MO as the other three.'

Grant smiled and nodded. 'Murder weapon?'

'The lead of a lamp inside Costello's flat.'

'Why is there so much blood around the mouth?' Lawrenson enquired.

'There's always a certain amount of internal bleeding within the windpipe itself during a strangulation,' Barclay explained. 'The rupturing of blood vessels due to pressure, that kind of thing. In this case he bit his own tongue off too.'

'What about the bruising?' Grant asked.

'It's where he fell or was dragged by the killer. As I told you when we found the first two victims, this killer is very strong. However, in this case, he might have found the job a little easier.'

Grant looked puzzled.

Barclay pointed at the lungs dangling in their metal dish above the body.

'The lungs are diseased,' he said flatly. 'Costello had a chronic bronchial condition. At the time of his death he was in the early stages of emphysema. He was using an inhaler most of the time. It was found in his flat, as I'm sure you know.'

Grant nodded.

'It's not so difficult choking to death a man who can hardly breathe anyway,' Barclay added.

'There were no signs of forced entry, just like the last one,' said Grant. 'So, again, I'm wondering if he knew his killer.'

'Pissed-off punter again?' Lawrenson offered.

'Did Costello know any of the other victims?' Grant asked, his gaze still riveted on the corpse.

'Some tart we spoke to thinks he used to pimp for Claire Glover at one time,' Lawrenson informed his superior. 'But that was a while ago. He had a small stable. Three, four girls tops, including his own bird, the one who found him.'

'Time of death?'

'Early morning,' Barclay informed him. 'I'd say between two and five.'

'What kind of person would know a drug pusher *and* a pimp well enough to be able to walk into their flats and attack them without arousing their suspicions,' Grant mused. 'It had to be someone they trusted. Someone they'd both dealt with before. Either that or the entry *was* forced.'

'There was no sign of that at Dwyer's place or Costello's,' said Lawrenson.

'I don't mean he kicked the fucking door down,' Grant snapped. 'I mean, what if they had no choice but to let him in. There's a knock on the door, they answer it and someone's standing there pointing a gun at them. Open the door or I'll blow your head off. It's not out of the question.'

'Then why go to the bother of strangling them once they were inside?' Lawrenson insisted. 'If the killer used a shooter to gain entry then why not just use it on them?'

'Because guns are easier to trace than ropes or flex. And they're noisier. If the killer had shot them, Christ knows who might have heard. He could have been spotted leaving the scene. But if he only used a gun to get *into* the flats then he could have taken his time, chosen how he did them. Neither of them were going to fight back with a gun stuck in their face, were they?'

Lawrenson stroked his chin thoughtfully.

'Come on,' snapped Grant. 'At least admit the *possibility*.'

'Fair enough, guv,' said Lawrenson. 'But that still doesn't give us a motive, does it?'

'How many statements have been taken regarding this case?' Grant wanted to know.

'So far, nearly seventy and we've still got fuck all. We've had men out round the clock, like you said. We've tried all the usual sources.'

'Then try them again.'

'We're stretched to the limit already.'

'Bollocks,' Grant hissed. 'Someone somewhere knows something. And I want them found. If we don't stop this bastard soon we'll be up to our necks in corpses. He's on a roll and I'll tell you something, he's not going to stop until we get him.'

Twenty-Seven

David Albury sat back in his seat and pulled gently at his cuffs, a smile hovering on his lips as he listened to the tirade of words being flung at him from a member of the audience. Albury looked directly at the man, who was now on his feet, pointing angrily at the Home Secretary. He thought how grubby the man looked, dressed in his cheap shirt and jeans.

Judith Maddison, presenter and host of *Late-Night London*, moved closer to the furious man, trying to ensure that his words were heard through her microphone while at the same time not allowing him to rip the implement out of her hands.

The rest of the audience were either gazing at the speaker or looking at the stage area where Albury sat. Opposite Albury were two men in their twenties, one of whom was dressed in a suede jacket and black cords, the other looking somewhat ridiculous in a waistcoat and black trousers, a key-fob hanging from the pocket of the waistcoat. His greying hair was pulled back in a ponytail and, when he looked at Albury, it was through thick bi-focals.

The man in the audience finally sat down and Judith Maddison hurried towards Albury. 'How do you respond to that, David?' she asked the politician. 'How do you justify your new Bill to limit the availability of violent or pornographic films and videos? Isn't it an infringement of freedom?'

Albury waited a moment then adopted his much-practised and patronising tone.

'Judith, this isn't about freedom of speech,' he said earnestly. 'My Bill is to prevent the kind of so-called freedom granted to film makers and video distributors who are more concerned with making a fast buck with sensationalism than trying to use their medium for more useful purposes.'

'So what kind of films would *you* like to see being made?' Judith asked him.

'That isn't the issue here, my personal opinion isn't important. What I care about is ordinary people, families and, more particularly, children.'

There was a muted round of applause from some audience members.

'We've already seen the damage some of these videos can do,' the Home Secretary continued. 'For instance, if *Child's Play 3* had never been made then perhaps a little boy would still be alive today in Liverpool. His killers admitted committing their crime after seeing that film.'

'That was never proved,' said the man with the ponytail.

'The killers themselves said it,' Albury countered. 'Are you prepared to see more innocent lives affected by the kind of mindless horror which brought about the death of Jamie Bulger?'

'What do you say to that, Tim Newton?' Judith asked the man with the ponytail. 'Would there be less crime if this kind of film was banned?'

'There is no empirical evidence that violence in films is linked to violence in real life,' said Newton, shifting in his seat.

'I wonder if you could look the mother of that mur-dered child in the eye and say that,' Albury said, leaning towards Newton. 'Could you comfort that woman by telling her that?'

There was more applause from the audience.

Albury realised he was in a stronger position now and he pressed on, raising a hand to silence Newton when he tried to speak.

'I must say, Judith,' said the MP wearily, 'I feel something close to pity for Mr Newton if he refuses to see the effects of this kind of film. Do you have children, Mr Newton?'

'I don't think that's relevant.'

'*Do* you?' Albury persisted.

'No, but—'

'Well, one day you might and then perhaps you will understand the fear which so many parents in this audience feel,' the Home Secretary continued. 'We all want the best for our children and I don't feel that subjecting them to an endless diet of violence and sex on film and video is the best we can offer them. Do you?' He smiled condescendingly, the smile broadening as a loud round of applause swept from the audience.

Newton twisted in his seat again, his face darkening.

'But children don't see violent films or sexually explicit films because of our certification standards, they—'

Albury interrupted him again. 'That's rather naive, isn't it?' he said, his head on one side as if he was addressing a naughty child. 'As long as these films are freely available then children will find some way of seeing them. Violence begets violence. What people *see* they will copy.'

Another round of applause.

'But people have a right to see what they choose to see,' Newton responded angrily.

'And you would give them that freedom irrespective of the risks, would you?' Albury smiled that patronising smile again.

Newton opened his mouth to say something but it was drowned beneath another round of applause.

The Home Secretary pulled at his cuffs once more.

'You're talking about bringing in tougher ratings for films,' said Newton irritably. 'This has nothing to do with kids, you'll be depriving *adults* of the right to see films they want to see if you try to ban everything.'

Albury shook his head wearily. 'The Bill I am proposing,' he said disdainfully, 'will ensure that the kind of violent and pornographic film I am opposed to, I and the vast majority of right-thinking members of the public, will not be so widely released. This kind of film will be cut more heavily to make it more acceptable, although how anyone can find violence acceptable I really don't know.'

Judith Maddison stepped forward towards the man sitting on Newton's right.

'Stephen James,' she said. 'You run film festivals that specialise in showing horror films and violent films, don't you?'

James looked perplexed by his sudden inclusion in the debate. He swallowed hard and managed to nod.

'What kind of films do you show at these festivals?' Judith Maddison persisted.

'Zombie movies,' James began. 'Cult horror stuff.'

'Such as?'

'*The Texas Chainsaw Massacre, Suspiria, Cannibal Ferox,* that kind of thing.'

'And are these festivals popular?' the interviewer asked.

'Yes, very popular,' said James. 'We've been doing them for about five years now.'

'And what kind of people come to see films like that?' Judith enquired.

'Just normal people,' James said.

'What is your definition of normal,' Albury interjected scathingly. 'I think that people who would pay good money to watch that kind of garbage must be rather pathetic and possibly dangerous.'

There was laughter from the audience.

Newton and James squirmed angrily in their seats.

James shouted something at the Home Secretary and gestured furiously at him but Albury merely turned away, smiling evenly at the audience.

People were standing up in the audience now, anxious to make their point.

Hidden from the prying eye of the four cameras, standing in the gloom at one side of the set, the producer smiled and looked at Albury.

'He's very good, isn't he?' he said, nodding in the Home Secretary's direction.

'Yes, he is,' Anita Bishop agreed, smiling. '*Very* good.'

Twenty-Eight

As Amy stepped from the cab she dropped her Puma sportsbag on the pavement and fumbled in her handbag, reaching for her purse.

She glanced at the meter and handed the driver a ten-pound note.

'Keep a couple for yourself,' she said, watching as he counted out the change.

He gave her one last appraising look then pulled away.

'Carry your bag, miss?'

The voice startled her and she spun round. Jake Webber was standing behind her, grinning broadly.

Amy smiled. 'You scared me,' she said, laughing.

She thought how fresh he looked considering how late he'd returned home. Apart from some stubble he looked as if he'd had more sleep than *she* had.

'I saw you arrive,' he told her, allowing his gaze to travel swiftly over her – the trainers, tracksuit bottoms and the white T-shirt covered by a leather jacket.

'Spying on me, eh?' she said, smiling. 'I've been to the gym.'

'And now?' he asked, picking up her bag.

'Now what?'

'Any plans?'

'No. Why?'

'I was just about to get some lunch. I wondered if you'd join me?'

'Sandwiches?'

'I can run to beans on toast.'

She laughed, looking deeply into his eyes. 'Thanks, Jake.'

'Let's go,' he said and they started walking.

*　　*　　*

DEE-DEE TEAS was a small café on the corner of Percival Street. Immaculately clean, it was more a miniature restaurant than a café, the menu boasting everything from sausage, beans and chips to cannelloni.

'I've lived here for four years and I never knew this place was here,' said Amy pushing a forkful of pasta into her mouth.

Webber smiled.

'How did you find out about it? You're not from around here, are you?'

He shook his head. 'I hear things.'

'Where *are* you from, Jake?'

'Originally? Hertfordshire. Hatfield, that way. What about you?'

'I was born in London. Hackney.'

'It's not a very strong accent.'

'It's still there sometimes. You know what they say? You can take the girl out of Hackney but you can't take Hackney out of the girl.'

They both laughed.

'I suppose jetting around the world modelling helped lose that accent,' he observed, sipping his coffee.

'Maybe.'

'Why did you give it up?'

'I was getting too old for it. It's a bit depressing when you're sharing a changing room with girls young enough to be your . . .' she shrugged. 'Younger sisters.'

She smiled and found the gesture returned.

'*How* young?' he enquired.

'Thirteen or fourteen sometimes.'

'That's disgusting. They're still kids.'

'That's the kind of model designers want to use. No curves. No shape. Skinny. They say most male fashion designers are gay, the clothes they design would look fine on young boys, so they choose girls with no waists and no tits. Girls who have bodies like boys. Boobs can be a handicap with some designers.'

'So who did you model for?'

'Most of the big names. Versace. Westwood. Calvin Klein. Are you impressed?' She grinned.

'Very. Why did you pack it in?'

'You just asked me that. I told you, I was getting too old.'

'Bullshit.'

'Jake, in case you hadn't noticed, once you hit twenty-five, everything starts heading south. Boobs, bum, the lot. I got sick of fighting gravity.'

'Don't you miss it?'

'Sometimes. I met some good people. Had some laughs. I met some arseholes too though.'

'Go on then, spill the beans. Give me the gossip.'

'Oh, photographers were the worst. If I had a pound for every one who's tried to get me into bed I could retire.'

'I can sympathise with them.'

She grinned. 'I think that's a compliment, isn't it?'

He nodded.

'Didn't you want to become an actress or a writer?' he asked. 'Most of these bloody models seem to think they've got gifts in those directions.'

'Do I detect a hint of cynicism there?'

'Sorry.'

'Don't be. I agree with you. No, I enjoy doing the show. That's enough for me.'

She sipped her Perrier and regarded him over the rim of the glass.

'Well, that's *my* life story,' she quipped. 'Your turn.'

He smiled.

'I don't even know what you do for a living,' she told him.

'As little as I can get away with,' he said, holding her gaze.

'Is it such a big secret, Jake?'

'I didn't offer to buy you lunch so I could talk about myself for two hours.'

'You're a very unusual man then. Most I've met can't

wait to talk about themselves. This is like having lunch with a spy.'

He chuckled. 'Perhaps I'm just a good listener. And it helps because you're a good talker.'

She punched him playfully on the arm.

'Hey,' he said, feigning annoyance. 'That was a compliment too.'

'You're full of compliments, Jake. Or full of shit.'

'Now who's being cynical?'

'How are you settling in?'

'Fine. I haven't seen much of the other tenants though. What are they like?'

'To tell you the truth, I haven't seen much of them either. Fortunately no one's suggested a residents' committee yet.'

They ate in silence for a moment, Amy occasionally looking at her companion. He was an attractive man, she had to admit. As she studied his features she saw a scar running from the corner of one eye across towards his ear.

'Where did you get that?' she asked, boldly tracing the outline of the scar with her finger.

He looked up as he felt the smooth flesh against his skin.

They looked deeply into one another's eyes, her finger still brushing against his face.

'Does it matter?' he asked.

'I was just curious.'

'You seem to be curious about a lot of things, Amy.'

'If you told me more about yourself I wouldn't need to keep asking.'

'There's not much to tell. There's a lot less to me than meets the eye.'

'I find that hard to believe.'

'Trust me.' He winked at her.

Amy laughed. 'That is so corny, Jake.'

Webber looked at her. The smile illuminated her features.

'You're very beautiful,' he told her.

'And *that* sounds even cornier but thanks anyway. Listen, are you doing anything tonight? I was wondering if you'd let me cook you dinner. I know that sounds a bit forward, doesn't it?'

'I'm not complaining, am I? I'd like that. Promise not to rag me if I don't spend the whole evening talking about myself. What time do you want me?'

'About eight? But don't expect anything fancy, will you?'

'Formal dress? Casual?' he said, grinning.

'Whatever you want.'

'I'll get the bill,' he said, reaching into his pocket for his wallet. Flipping it open, he pulled a couple of notes free.

Amy saw pictures inside the leather container. There were two of a young child.

She sipped at her drink, trying not to make it obvious that she'd spotted the snaps.

Another mystery?

He snapped the wallet shut and re-pocketed it.

Who was the child?

Webber was looking at her and smiling.

Amy returned the gesture, her eyes never leaving his.

Only when she finally glanced down did his smile fade.

Twenty-Nine

Jo Parker pushed the flat door shut with her back and dropped the four plastic carrier bags.

She ran a hand through her hair, wincing as she inspected the red marks across her palms where she'd been lugging the weight of the shopping. She hadn't been able to get a taxi from the supermarket and she'd got sick of waiting for a bus so, despite the weight of her load, she'd walked and now, as she rubbed her hands, she was regreting that decision.

The flat seemed almost unnaturally quiet as she headed towards the kitchen with the shopping.

No television. No hi-fi.

'Billy,' she called.

No answer.

She passed through the sitting room and saw a couple of T-shirts and a pair of jeans scattered wantonly on the sofa and the floor. One sock had also been tossed unceremoniously into a nearby armchair.

Jo exhaled wearily as she saw the scattered clothing.

There was a duffel bag beside the sofa, more clothes spilling from it like stuffing from a ripped toy.

Lazy bastard, she thought as she glanced irritably at the discarded clothes.

She could only guess where her brother was. He'd been sitting watching a video when she'd left nearly two hours ago. She'd asked him to clear away the clothes then, on her way out.

She shook her head in dismay, wondering whether or not to leave them and let *him* tidy them up when he returned. Whenever that might be. But one more glance at the untidy, dirty garments and she decided she'd clear them up herself.

But first the shopping had to be attended to.

She took it from the bags and began placing it in cupboards or freezer or fridge, moving with practised, almost robotic movements.

Since Billy had been staying with her, the bills had almost doubled. She earned a decent salary but Billy would prove to be an even more considerable drain on her resources if he stayed much longer. And not just on her financial reserves. His constant presence or, more particularly, his attitude were pushing her close to breaking point.

She tried to tell herself that blood was thicker than water and that, in his condition, he needed her, needed someone close. But, even the string of clichés she presented herself with didn't seem to justify having him stay with her indefinitely. At times like this, as much as she disliked admitting it to herself, she found it easy to understand how her parents could have rejected him so easily. She didn't blame them for not wanting him around if he behaved the same way he'd behaved since he arrived unannounced on her doorstep.

Would it have been different if it had been Danny?

She knew the answer without asking the question. Billy had been right. She would have welcomed her older brother with open arms. Told him he could have stayed as long as he wanted.

But that was not to be.

It was *never* to be. Not any more.

She stopped what she was doing for a moment, the thought of Danny catching her unawares, the momentary vision of his face flashing into her mind making her feel disorientated.

Jo swallowed hard and the image vanished. She finished unpacking the shopping and headed back into the sitting room.

Angrily, she snatched up the clothes from the sofa and floor. She'd give him another week then he was out.

You won't throw him out.

She'd help him look for a place if he'd let her or perhaps even have a word with her parents and see if they'd take him back.

They don't want him. No one wants him around. Not even you.

The T-shirts needed cleaning; she wrinkled her nose as she smelled perspiration. She balled them up.

One minute you're talking about throwing him out, the next you're getting ready to do his washing.

She picked up the sock and jammed it, along with the T-shirts, into the duffel bag before reaching for the jeans.

As she picked them up something fell from one of the pockets.

Jo knelt and inspected the object. It was a bottle with a child-proof lid. A bottle for pills.

The label had been scratched off. Whatever this bottle contained, she suspected, was not a prescription drug.

She held the plastic container in the palm of her hand for a second longer then pushed it back into the pocket of the jeans before checking the other pockets.

In one back pocket there was a piece of paper.

She unfolded it and scanned what was written there. It looked like a mobile number.

But whose?

She rummaged in the other pocket and found a handkerchief. It gave off a rank, familiar odour. Stale semen.

She winced and stuffed it back into the jeans.

She sucked in a weary breath.

She hurried across to the notepad next to the phone and wrote down the number on a sheet about halfway into the pad. Then she returned the slip of paper to her brother's jeans and jammed the whole lot into the duffel bag.

She made her way to the bathroom and washed her hands thoroughly, the smell of soap replacing the musty scent of semen.

Phone numbers. Pill bottles. What the hell was Billy up to?

One part of her wanted to confront him, to force the truth from him. Another told her to wait.

It could be innocent.

Could be?

She studied her own reflection in the bathroom mirror.

She would wait.

For now.

Thirty

Jake Webber watched the candle burning lower, its flame wavering as a draught caught it.

Amy watched him across the table, the dull yellow glow of the flame casting deep shadows.

'Penny for them,' she finally said.

Webber looked up and smiled, shaken from his aimless gazing by the sound of her voice.

'I'm sorry,' he said quietly. 'I was miles away.'

'Charming.'

He grinned broadly. 'I was just thinking what a beautiful meal that was. Thank you very much. It beats the shit out of a Birds Eye Ready Meal For One.'

'You sound like an expert, Jake. Do you eat a lot of them?'

'You know what it's like. When you're on your own you don't always bother cooking for yourself, do you? I usually end up with a take-away or a microwave dinner.'

'Didn't your mother ever tell you how important it is to eat properly?' she said, smiling.

He raised an eyebrow. 'She didn't tell me much about anything really.'

'Do you still see her?'

'She died twelve years ago. A stroke.'

'I'm sorry.'

'Don't be. It happens, doesn't it. My old man was killed in a work accident two years later.'

'What kind of accident?'

'He was a roofer by trade. Him and some other bloke were working on a church roof in Kentish Town. The bloody thing collapsed under them. The other bloke broke his back, he's been paralysed ever since. My dad was killed.'

'Were you close?'

'You're doing it again.'

'Doing what?'

'Asking questions.'

'I'm trying to find out about you, Jake, that's all. There's nothing sinister to it, you know.'

'I thought I'd done well, we got through most of the meal without you probing.'

'If it bothers you . . .'

He raised a hand. 'Like I told you this afternoon,' he said softly, 'there's not much worth knowing.'

'We've spent over three hours sitting and talking and eating and I still don't know any more about you apart from the fact that your parents are both dead. All we've done is talk about *me*. My life. What I've done.'

'It's more interesting.'

'Are you always this secretive with women?'

He laughed. 'Why do you think I'm being secretive just because I'm not rabbiting on about myself all the time?'

'Are you always this mysterious with your girlfriends?' she enquired, pushing her wine glass towards him.

He refilled it then repeated the procedure with his own.

'What makes you think I had any?' he said flatly.

'Jake, you're a good-looking guy. I think I'd be pretty safe in assuming you'd had some kind of contact with the opposite sex.' She raised her glass and sipped from it.

'I could be gay,' he said, grinning.

She shook her head.

Webber laughed again.

'Look, you're the model. How come there's no man in your life? I'd have thought there'd have been blokes queuing up to take you out.'

'Did you pass them on the stairs?'

'So, what's your secret? Why no man?'

'I'm a dyke.'

'Got any pictures,' he said, chuckling.

She picked up her discarded napkin and threw it at him.

'You went out with a drummer from a rock band,' he told her. 'I remember seeing it in the paper and then some writer. What was his name? Howard, that was it. John Howard.'

She nodded slowly, the brightness fading from her face. She took another sip of her wine.

Yes. John fucking Howard.

He watched her intently, aware that mention of the name had struck a nerve of some kind.

'No one on the scene at the moment?' he continued.

She shook her head. 'What about you. Anyone "on the scene"?' There was a hint of scorn in her voice which she tried, but failed, to conceal.

They looked at each other across the table, the flames of the candles still flickering.

'Come on, Jake,' she said, 'you know all about *me*. Tell me something about yourself.'

'Like what?'

'Like who's the kid?'

He looked surprised.

'At lunchtime, when you were paying for the food, I saw some photos in your wallet of a kid,' she told him. 'I assumed it was yours.'

'Yes,' he said sternly. 'She was mine.'

'So, is there a wife somewhere too? Is that why you're so secretive? What's going on? Let me guess. You're going through a divorce, she's kept the house, kicked you out and you see your kid only occasionally. Right?'

'I'm not on your fucking show, Amy,' he snapped. 'I'm not one of those sad bastards who call you asking for advice or spilling their fucking problems for the whole world to hear and laugh at, so don't treat me like one of them.'

The vehemence in his tone shook her.

'Am I right?' she persisted, her voice softer.

'Would it matter if you were?'

'I'm interested in you, Jake. Is that such a crime?'

He swallowed what was left in his glass and refilled it.

'There's no wife,' he finally said. 'There never has been. There've been women. Enough of them.'

'And the child?'

'She was mine,' he said, his voice cracking slightly. He cleared his throat, reaching into his pocket for his wallet. He flipped it open and pulled the two photos free, pushing them towards Amy.

'She's beautiful,' said Amy, inspecting the snaps. 'How old is she?'

Webber swallowed hard. 'Eighteen months when those were taken,' he said quietly, filling his glass again. 'Her name was Samantha.'

'So, where is she?'

'She's dead.'

Amy looked first at the snaps then at Webber who was staring blankly ahead.

'Those were taken about a month before it happened.' Again his voice cracked.

'How?' Amy asked.

He took the pictures back, cradling one in the palm of his hand, gazing at the tiny smiling little face captured there.

'I was living with someone,' he began, not taking his eyes from the picture of his child. 'Her name was Kim, she worked for a cosmetics firm. It was a good job, good prospects. She was very career-minded. She never wanted kids.'

'Did you?' Amy asked softly.

'They were all I ever wanted,' he confessed. 'I suppose after my parents died it got worse. Some fucking shrink would have a field day with the Freudian implications no doubt.'

'What about your girlfriend? Did *she* know how badly you wanted kids?'

'We never really talked about it. She was on the pill, she had no intention of coming off it, no thoughts of giving up her career to become a mother.' He gazed more intently at the photos of the child.

'So, what happened?'

'Kim had a bout of food poisoning. She was sick a lot. The pill never worked. She got pregnant. It was an accident, as simple as that.' He took a sip of his wine. 'I was fucking ecstatic when I found out.' A smile hovered briefly on his lips. 'Kim was pissed off. All she could think about was how having a baby would ruin her career.'

'Didn't she think about an abortion?'

'She might have thought about it but she never mentioned it to me. That was never an option as far as I was concerned.' He shrugged. 'So she had the baby. I was there for the birth. I was the first one to hold Sam. She was premature. Christ, she was tiny.' He took a sip of his wine. 'I took them home three days later. Within the space of a week, Kim was looking for child-minders. She just wanted to get back to work. She couldn't get on with breast-feeding or the sleepless nights. I think she started to hate Sam. I did everything I could to help but, as far as Kim was concerned, it was never enough.'

'Did she go back to work?'

'Part-time. She missed out on a promotion because of that. She started taking it out on Sam.'

'Did she hit her?'

'Not as far as I know but she was sharp with her, she had no patience with her. I think every time she looked at Sam she resented her.'

'How did she die?' Amy asked, reaching out with one hand to gently touch Webber's arm.

'She was crawling around on the landing one day and she fell down the stairs. Broke her neck.' He clenched his teeth.

Amy saw the tears welling in his eyes.

'The fucking stair-gate was open, Kim should have shut it, she should have been watching her,' Webber rasped. 'Sam was dead before we got her to the hospital.'

'Jake, I'm so sorry.'

'Yeah, so am I,' he hissed, the knot of muscles at the side of his jaw throbbing angrily. He had one fist clenched tightly and was bumping it gently against his chin. 'At the funeral, Sam's coffin was so small I carried it on my own. It was like a little white shoebox and it had a white bouquet on top with a silk bow; as if she'd been gift-wrapped.'

He lowered his head.

'Kim and I split up a month later,' he said. 'I'll never forgive her for what happened.' He looked directly into Amy's eyes and the rage and sadness burning there transfixed her. '*She* deserved to die too,' Webber snarled. 'I should have done it then. I should have put her in the fucking ground next to Sam.'

Thirty-One

They sat in silence, either unable or unwilling to speak, as if any utterance would be an intrusion. Then Webber carefully slid the photos back into his wallet. It was he who broke the silence.

'I haven't been back to the grave since Sam was buried,' he said in a quiet voice.

'Why?'

'Because I can't face it,' he snapped. 'I can't face *her*.'

'You *need* to go back, Jake.'

'Why? So I can relive all the memories again? So I can go through all that pain again?'

'You'll never cope with her death if you don't face it.'

'Don't patronise me, Amy. I cope with it, in my own way.'

'It's tearing you apart. Don't tell me you don't want to go to see her grave because I won't believe you.'

He eyed her warily.

'Very professional,' he said, scathingly.

'Oh, for Christ's sake, I'm not trying to psychoanalyse you, I'm trying to help you. Stop being so bloody defensive, Jake.'

'How much more do you want to know about me, then? Isn't what I've told you enough?' He finished what was left in his glass and banged it down hard on the table. 'Perhaps I'm scared. There, I've said it. Satisfied? Perhaps you're right, perhaps I can't cope with it. How the hell would you know what it feels like? No one can unless they've been through it.'

'What are you scared of?'

'I let her down too, Amy,' he said, his voice quivering. 'I blame Kim for Sam's death but perhaps I was as much to blame. I was there when it happened and I couldn't stop it.'

'It was an accident, Jake, how could you have stopped it?'

'I knew Kim didn't give a shit, I should have kept a closer eye on Sam myself. Maybe that's why I don't want to go to visit the grave. Because it would make me confront my own guilt, my own part in her death.'

'Would you go if I came with you?'

Webber looked fixedly at Amy.

'Why would you do that for me?'

She shrugged. 'I'm just trying to help.' She got up, walked around the table, and sat beside him, squeezing his hand, feeling him respond, feeling the strength in his grip.

Almost without thinking, she leaned forward, her face close to his.

'If I go with you, will you go?' she whispered, one slender finger tracing a pattern across his cheek.

He slid a hand around her shoulders and pulled her closer and their lips brushed. Lightly at first, then with more urgency. She snaked her own arms around his neck and, as she did, she felt his tongue pushing urgently against her lips, then her teeth. She responded fiercely, sliding her own tongue into his mouth.

They remained locked together for seconds that seemed to stretch into an eternity.

Amy allowed one hand to drop to his thigh, her fingers trailing across the material of his trousers, feeling the muscles beneath. He gripped her arm, his strong fingers digging into her soft flesh, but in that strength there was tenderness. The strength was replaced by a feather-light gentleness as his hand moved slowly across to first brush then cup her right breast, and then his thumb brushed one swollen nipple.

She shuddered.

They broke the kiss and sat looking intently at each other, both of them sucking in deep breaths.

He touched her lips with a finger and she flicked out her tongue to moisten the end of the digit. Webber drew that slippery finger across her bottom lip with excruciating slowness, her own saliva glistening in the candlelight. Then he repeated the process on her top lip, feeling her ever-willing tongue once again slide around the probing fingertip. She kissed it lightly.

She was stroking his thigh gently, rhythmically, and still they continued to gaze into each other's eyes.

'I've got to go,' he said, leaning forward, kissing her lightly on the lips.

'Why, Jake?' Her voice was low and shaking.

She kissed him again and this time she felt his hand on her thigh. Stroking. Kneading the smooth flesh just below the hem of her short dress.

'You don't have to go,' she told him breathlessly.

He got to his feet and she rose with him.

'I know I don't,' he whispered, leaning forward so that his mouth was pressed right against her ear.

She felt the warm breath against her tender lobe.

'This seems so pointless, Jake,' Amy said. 'You leaving.'

'There'll be other times.' He raised an eyebrow. 'Won't there?'

She smiled and nodded.

He paused at the front door, turned and they kissed again.

'I'll see you tomorrow,' he said.

'Think about what I said,' she told him. 'About Sam.'

He nodded then headed for the stairs.

As she closed her door she heard his footsteps receding away, heard his own door open and close.

Amy stood against her door, her breath coming in shallow gasps.

Things moving a little fast aren't they?

She sighed then walked back into the sitting room, glancing across towards the dining area. To hell with it, she'd clear up in the morning.

You hardly know the bloke and you are trying to seduce him.

There was half a glass of wine left and she picked it up, sipping at it.

Time for a cold shower before bed?

She smiled to herself and crossed to the window of the flat, looking out into the street. It was deserted out there. People were either out partying or tucked up in bed.

Lucky bastards.

She could still taste him on her lips.

Frightening, isn't it, how quickly feelings overtake you?

The streetlight opposite was flickering again, threatening to die completely. Amy wondered if anyone had reported it to the relevant authority. For what it was worth.

She finished her wine and was about to move away from the window when she saw him. Crossing the street, hands dug in his pockets in that familiar stance.

It was Webber.

He had changed into jeans and a leather jacket.

Going where?

She glanced at her watch.

1.23 a.m.

By the time she looked back he'd disappeared into the night.

Thirty-Two

Ralph Harker knew there was going to be trouble. It might just be an argument, a few threatening words hurled back and forth but, whatever the final outcome, he was sure that there was going to be trouble.

He fumbled in one pocket of the dirty overcoat he wore and felt the short-bladed knife he always carried. It felt reassuringly sharp against the pad of his thumb. In his other pocket was a half-bottle of White Horse. He patted that lovingly. He'd stolen it only hours earlier from an off-licence in Shaftesbury Avenue. Some he'd already drunk but he still had three-quarters of a bottle left, and now all he wanted to do was drink it in peace. Drink it and sleep, if he could in the chill wind. Sleep in his usual spot but, at present, someone was occupying his usual spot.

That was why Ralph was convinced there was going to be trouble.

He'd lived on the streets of London for the past eighteen months and that nomadic existence had taken its toll on his body both internally and externally. His face bore lines and creases that made him look older than his forty-two years. His body was thin and undernourished. Every few days he took a trip to the Centre Point Hostel and got what passed for a square meal but, most of the time, he did as others like him did. He scavenged in wastebinds and skips, he begged and, when necessary, he stole.

There had been nowhere for him to go when he'd finished his latest five-stretch in Wandsworth. No home to return to. No family to shelter him. One of his sisters had written to him on a regular basis while he'd been inside but she'd made it clear that she didn't want him knocking on her door when he was released.

One of the screws had said 'See you soon' as he'd walked free and, at times, Ralph wondered if there was not only an inevitability about those words but also a kind of salvation. At least inside he was warm, well fed and reliant only on the screws. Outside it was more difficult.

He'd tried to get jobs but who the hell was going to employ him with his form? His parole officer had offered to help but he'd done nothing. No one wanted to offer Ralph anything, not even washing up in some greasy fucking café.

Bollocks to them.

He'd manage. It wouldn't be the first time he'd been on the streets.

He coughed and rubbed his chest. The fucking pain was worse now. It always hurt more when he coughed. The quack inside had said something about a bronchial condition, and possible liver damage. He'd said that Ralph should drink less when he got out.

Fat fucking chance. He patted the bottle of White Horse once again and advanced steadily towards the figure sleeping in his spot.

The lights that usually illuminated the canopy of the Phoenix Theatre in Charing Cross Road were off. It was darker than normal in the small passageway that ran alongside. There was a dry riser inlet close to the stage door. That was Ralph's spot. It had been for the last six months and now there was someone in it. Cheeky fucker.

Ralph looked down at the dark shape covered with blankets, and coughed.

The shape didn't stir.

He prodded it with his toe.

'Oi,' he said, his hand closing around the knife.

One of the dirty blankets was pulled down to reveal the face of a youth in his early twenties, his face pale, his eyes heavy with sleep.

'Move,' said Ralph. 'This is my fucking patch.'

The youth rubbed his eyes and blinked myopically at Ralph.

'Come on,' Ralph insisted more loudly.

The youth looked him up and down. 'I'd just got to sleep,' he complained.

'I couldn't give a fuck, move it or I'll move you,' Ralph hissed.

'I don't want to fight about it—'

'Then move.'

The youth gathered the blankets around him and got to his feet.

'Go on, fuck off!' said Ralph dismissively.

The youth stood there for a moment longer gazing at Ralph.

The older man pulled the knife free and brandished it before him. 'You want a bed for the night?' he snapped. 'I'll put you in a fucking hospital bed. Now piss off.'

The youth turned and walked away briskly.

Ralph settled into his space over the dry riser and wrapped his coat more tightly around him, digging the whisky out of his pocket. He couldn't carry on living like this. He'd go and see some of his old contacts tomorrow, see if there were any jobs he could do. It didn't matter what he had to do, he had to get off the streets. Someone might even have a job lined up. He hadn't lost his touch, he was sure of that. If they needed a little muscle he could help. If they wanted someone to keep an eye open he could do that. He could even drive if they'd let him. Ralph took a swig from the bottle. Maybe crime didn't pay but it was better than sleeping on the fucking streets.

He never saw the figure approaching him from behind.

Never heard the footsteps.

All he felt was something being slipped around his neck but he had no time to protest.

The wire was jerked hard.

So hard it lifted him off his feet.

The whisky bottle fell from his grip and shattered at his feet, the amber fluid racing away into a drain.

Ralph's eyes bulged in their sockets as the wire was tugged more tightly. It felt as if his head was swelling, threatening to burst like a balloon.

Then, nothing mattered any more.

Thirty-Three

David Grant slammed the newspaper down on the desk top and looked around at his companions. The other men in the Incident Room looked on impassively as Grant held up another of the papers lying close by, pointing to the headline.

SERIAL KILLER ON THE LOOSE?

it screamed.

'See it?' he snarled, reaching for another.

POLICE BAFFLED BY LATEST KILLING

He hurled that one across the room.

'There are details in all of these fucking papers about the murders,' Grant rasped. 'Details I have gone to great lengths to suppress.'

He picked up another of the tabloids. 'There are even details of the killing method,' he said angrily.

He eyed the men in the room challengingly. 'Now what I want to know is who leaked this information? Who gave the press this story?'

Silence.

'It had to be someone on this team,' Grant persisted. 'Only the officers working on this case knew the kind of details printed in these fucking rags. I've had reporters on the phone all morning asking me to confirm whether or not there is a serial killer at large in London. A serial killer who is strangling his victims. Something they couldn't possibly have known without inside information and I want to know where they got that information.'

'Why would anyone on this team release those details?' asked a voice from the back of the room.

Grant looked up to see that the question had been asked by Detective Constable Friel.

'You tell me,' snapped Grant. 'My guess is this is personal. Someone wants me to fuck up this case. Someone wants me to look like a idiot in front of the press and the Commissioner. Somebody's got a grudge and I'd lay money it's someone in this room.'

Again he scanned the rows of faces.

'Why would anyone want you to fail, guv?' Lawrenson wondered, puffing on his cigarette.

'Jealousy,' Grant told him. 'I knew when I got this promotion that there were some people who resented me for it. Well fuck them. I can put up with envy but what I won't tolerate is this.' He reached for one of the papers and held it up, waving it accusingly in the air. After a moment he threw it down again. 'This investigation isn't just about me, it's about this entire department. Whoever's leaking this stuff to the press isn't just making *me* look bad, they're making all of *you* look bad too.' He pointed at the watching officers.

'I think your paranoia's showing, Dave,' said a voice from the back.

'Leech. I should have expected that from you,' said Grant, aiming his ferocious gaze at an older man seated on a chair towards the rear of the room. Ronald Leech was in his late forties. A powerfully built man with a full head of almost pure white hair.

'You're looking for someone with a grudge?' Leech said defiantly. 'You might as well get the fucking phone book out and work your way through.'

'Perhaps I don't need to look any further than you, you bitter, twisted old bastard,' Grant snapped. 'I know you wanted this position. You'd been suck-holing the Commissioner long enough before he gave it to me.'

Leech got to his feet. 'I don't have to listen to this.'

Grant stepped in front of him. 'Yes, you do,' he rasped. 'Remember who's in charge here, Ronnie. Now sit down.'

The two men glared at each other for long seconds then the older man returned to his seat.

'If I find out you were behind these leaks I'll see to it you're back on a fucking beat in a month,' Grant threatened.

'What would I have to gain by going to the press?' Leech demanded.

'What would any of us have to gain, guv?' Schofield added.

'I told you, it discredits *me*.'

'But it makes us all look bad, like you said. It makes no sense,' Schofield persisted.

'I told you when I took over this investigation that there were people in this department who wanted to see me fail,' said Grant.

'I can't believe that,' Lawrenson added.

'Believe what you like, *I* know it's true and I'll tell you something else, the way this fucking investigation is going at the moment they must think they're on to a good thing.'

'There's nothing out there, guv,' Schofield said, puffing on a cigarette.

'There's a fucking murderer out there who's killed five people,' snapped Grant angrily. 'Five killings and we still haven't got shit. Who the hell have you been interviewing?'

'We've been working round the clock on this one, guv,' Lawrenson said. 'You know that.'

'Then where are the results?'

'We've asked all the usual,' said a voice from the back.

'Then ask the *unusual*,' Grant said. 'The media think we don't know what we're doing and I'm beginning to think that some of you *don't*.'

'So what's your theory?' Leech asked.

'I still think the killer knew his victims,' Grant said.

'We have to find out how he knew them, how he *found* them because when we find out how he found them, we find him.'

'Just like that?' said Leech disdainfully.

'Do whatever it takes,' Grant snarled. 'But I want someone and I want them quick.' He turned to the blackboard behind him where the photos of the murder victims hung. 'Otherwise this lot are going to have company.'

Thirty-Four

Amy Watson puffed on her cigarette, listening to the rantings of the latest caller, occasionally looking towards the window of the control booth where Mike Osborne was standing. He was sipping from a mug of coffee, watching Amy intently.

'I blame the police for these killings,' said the caller indignantly. 'Things like this didn't happen years ago. There used to be bobbies on the beat, you could talk to them, they knew everyone by name but—'

'Does the name Jack the Ripper ring a bell?' Amy interrupted.

'What?' the caller asked, bemused.

'You said things like this didn't happen years ago. I mentioned Jack the Ripper. And what about Haigh, the acid-bath murderer. Christie. Crippen. Peter Manual. George Joseph Smith. These are men who've gone down in criminal history. Don't try to say that the serial killer is just a *modern* phenomenon.'

'But all those men were caught.'

'That wasn't much help to their victims, was it? Are you suggesting that this murderer won't be caught, then?' She looked at the name flashing on her screen. 'Is that what you're saying, Maurice?'

'They might get him but they haven't done much so far, have they?' Maurice from Enfield continued. 'He's killed five people and they haven't even arrested anyone.'

'Do you work for the police?'

'No? What's that got to do with it?'

'Then how do you know they haven't arrested anyone yet?'

'It would have been in the papers and on the television.'

'So where do *you* think the police are going wrong then, Maurice?'

'There aren't enough of them walking a beat now. They sit around in those cars, none of them want to get cold by getting out. The policemen these days are lazy, and even when they do catch criminals they're out of prison in no time.'

'The sentencing isn't the fault of the police, Maurice, it's the judicial system that's to blame.'

'Well, I still think the police are—'

She flicked a switch. 'You're history, Maurice,' Amy said, smiling, taking another call.

'Bob from Lewisham,' she said. 'What do you think about these killings? Do you think the police will get their man?'

'I read somewhere that the conviction rate is ninety per cent,' said Bob. 'So they probably will.'

'Do you think they do a good job?'

'On this case or in general?'

'Both.'

'I've got no gripe with the police. I think they do all right. I mean, they're undermanned and all that, aren't they? I reckon they'll get this bloke, but I just reckon he'll kill a few more before they do.'

'What makes you think that, Bob?'

'Well, I've read books about these serial killers, blokes like that Sutcliffe geezer and the other one who buried them under the floorboards, you know, Nelson.'

'Nilsen,' she corrected him. 'Denis Nilsen.'

'Yeah, him. Well, they get sort of addicted to the killing, don't they? They get a buzz out of it. A sexual thing. If this bloke's killed five already then he must be enjoying it. He's not just going to stop, is he?'

'But you think the police are doing their best to catch him?'

'Yeah. I think that last bloke was out of order trying to blame them for not having got him yet. I don't blame the police. I blame the media.'

'For not catching the killer?'

'No. For making someone like that in the first place.'

'I'm not with you, Bob.'

'Well, these geezers are a bit funny in the head, aren't they? I mean, that bastard who shot those kids at Dunblane, that Hamilton bloke. I mean, he was weird, wasn't he? But he knew that if he shot loads of kids that his name would become famous. Like the geezer at Hungerford. Ryan. They knew that their names would be all over the media, and ever since it happened the press haven't let it drop, have they? I mean, there's things in the papers saying we mustn't forget what happened but some nutter reading that could think "Hold on, if I kill a few people, I'll get my name in the papers. I'll be famous." If the media dropped the coverage I reckon there'd be less of these serial killers around.'

'That's an interesting thought, Bob,' said Amy, blowing out a stream of smoke. 'Do you think that's why *this* killer is doing what he's doing? For fame?'

'You can never tell with these nutters, can you?'

'Quite true, Bob,' she said, smiling. 'Let's see if our next caller agrees with you.' She hit a button. 'Roy from . . .' She could see no location on the screen. 'Where are you from, Roy?'

'I'm speaking on a mobile,' the voice told her softly.

'Do you agree with what Bob just said? Is this killer in it for the fame? Should the police have caught him by now?'

Silence.

'Can you hear me, Roy?'

'I don't care why he's doing it,' said the caller quietly. 'Those he's killed deserved to die and there will be more deaths. There are plenty more scum out there to be removed.'

Thirty-Five

Amy looked at the screen where the name was flashing, the caller's words still echoing in her ears, his low breathing audible over the phone lines.

'Why do they deserve to die, Roy?' she asked, glancing up to see Osborne had again come to the window of the production booth.

There was silence on the other end of the line.

'Roy. Can you hear me?' she persisted.

'You need to ask me that?' he said scornfully. 'But then I suppose you would, wouldn't you? You weren't that different to *them*, were you?'

'I'm sure you're making a very interesting point here, Roy. I just wish I could understand what you're on about.'

'The ones who died. They had no self-respect, no morals, no shame. They didn't deserve to live. Prostitutes. Pimps. Drunks. Drug pushers. They're all scum.'

'Why do you include me with *them*, Roy?'

'You have no morals either. You take your clothes off. You flaunt yourself.'

'Not any more, Roy.'

'You *did*,' he roared. 'You tempted men with your body. You exposed your body for everyone to see. You had no shame.'

'Did I tempt *you*, Roy?'

Silence.

Osborne was standing waving frantically at Amy now, trying to attract her attention.

'Did you find the pictures of my body exciting, Roy?' she persisted.

Osborne was drawing his hand across his throat in a cutting motion but Amy merely shook her head.

'Do you think there's something wrong with the human body, Roy?' she continued. 'Do you think it's dirty?'

'What *you* did was filth,' the voice rasped.

'I was a model, Roy. That's all. Do you think that all models are like me?'

'Others show their bodies too. They're whores. *They* deserve to die.'

'Are you married, Roy?'

Silence.

'I thought not,' Amy murmured.

'I don't trust women,' he told her.

'Have you been hurt by a woman in the past, Roy? Is that why you don't trust us?'

'Whores. I see them on television, in the streets, in magazines. Flaunting themselves.'

'And because of that they deserve to die?'

There was a hiss of static on the line.

'You said that *all* the murder victims deserved to die,' Amy continued. 'Three of them were men.'

'Scum.'

'We quibble over terms,' she said, chuckling.

'Don't laugh at me, you bitch,' he hissed, the vehemence in his tone enough to raise the hairs on the back of her neck. 'I'll call you again, after the next one dies.'

He hung up.

Amy was momentarily stunned but she sucked in a deep breath, composing herself.

'I'll be back after the news,' she said. 'So, pay attention.'

She pulled off her headset and slumped back in her seat. 'Fuck,' she murmured under her breath.

Osborne appeared in the doorway of the studio, his face set in stern lines.

'I'm going to call the police,' he told her.

'And tell them what, Mike? That another nutter called the show? They're hardly likely to be surprised, are they?'

'He made threats, Amy,' Osborne insisted.

'It was some arsehole having a laugh.'

'Well it didn't sound very funny from where *I* was,' Osborne snapped. 'This could be important.'

She held up her hands in supplication.

'If you want to call the police, Mike, then call them,' Amy said irritably. 'Do what you like.'

'What the hell's wrong with you? What if he's serious? What if that *is* the killer? You heard what he said before he rang off. He'd call you back after the next one. The police should know about that call.'

'You couldn't trace it – what good will it be to them now?'

'He threatened you.'

Amy shrugged. 'He wouldn't be the first,' she said quietly, sipping at her coffee. She inhaled wearily. 'Look, if you call the police in you might scare him off. If he calls again, perhaps I can get some information out of him.'

'Calls again?' Osborne murmured. 'After someone else has died?'

They locked stares then Osborne shook his head gently, reaching for the door handle.

'This is a hell of a fucking game you're playing, Amy,' he said angrily. 'I hope to Christ you know what you're doing.'

And he was gone.

Amy reached for her cigarettes and lit up another.

'So do I,' she murmured.

Amy stepped from the cab and thanked the driver, shivering as a breeze swept down the street. She hadn't realised how cold it had become. Emerging from the warmth of the studios into the chilly clutches of the night, she pulled her collar up as she headed for the front door of her building.

She fumbled for her key as she drew closer, glancing up to see that there were lights burning in Webber's flat.

She looked at her watch.

2.03 a.m.

Perhaps he couldn't sleep.

She found her key and let herself in, ensuring that the front door was securely locked again, then she glanced across at Webber's door.

From inside she could hear movement.

She felt like talking and wondered if Jake would too. Besides, apart from a brief meeting that morning, she hadn't spoken to him all day.

Missing him?

She smiled to herself and crossed to his door, knocking lightly. There were still sounds of movement from inside.

She knocked again. No response.

Again she tapped, a little more urgently now.

'Jake,' she called.

The door remained firmly closed. And yet, inside, she could hear his voice.

His voice.

She heard only a low droning sound, she couldn't pick out words. Maybe he was on the phone.

She knocked again.

Silence.

She pressed her ear to the wood but his voice was silent now.

'Jake,' she called again, her face close to the frame of the door. 'It's me.'

Nothing.

She waited a moment or two then began to climb the stairs, looking back towards his door.

She could hear the muffled sound of him speaking again but, as before, she was unable to pick out individual words. Only his tone. It was angry.

Thirty-Six

David Grant heard the door behind him open and he turned slightly, taking his eyes from the pile of papers on the coffee table.

Tina Grant padded into the room dressed in just a T-shirt, her hair unkempt. She crossed to the chair opposite her husband and sat in it, drawing her legs up beneath her, folding the hem of the T-shirt over her toes.

'Sorry if I disturbed you,' said Grant.

'I wasn't sure if you were coming home tonight.'

He ran both hands through his hair and sat back on the sofa.

'I got sick of staring at the office walls,' he told her. 'I thought a change of scenery might mean a change of luck. A flash of inspiration.'

She eyed the documents disinterestedly.

'I didn't get in myself until ten,' Tina said. 'A few of us went out for a drink when we left the office.'

He nodded.

'One of the photographers is off to the Maldives tomorrow on a shoot,' she continued. 'It was a kind of farewell drink. His name's Carlo.'

'Carlo. He sounds like an Italian waiter.'

'Actually he's very good at what he does,' she said, defensively.

'I'm happy for him,' Grant said scornfully.

'And he's very attractive – most of the girls in the office fancy him.'

'And what about *you*? Do you fancy him?'

'Dave, I didn't come down here to pick a fight.'

'Then don't tell me about this good-looking wop waiter. I'm not interested.'

'Interested? You sound jealous.'

'Do you *want* me to be?'

She eyed him malevolently.

'I don't expect anything to distract you from your work,' she sneered. 'I wouldn't want it to. Even if I told you I was fucking him I doubt if that would make much of an impression, would it?'

'Are you?'

'I might as well be. When was the last time *we* had sex?'

'I don't keep a fucking diary, Tina and, quite frankly, at the moment, I've got more important things to think about.'

'Like your case?' she said mockingly. 'You can't let anything get in the way of that, can you? Especially not your marriage.'

'Give it a rest, I've got work to do.'

He turned his attention to the papers in front of him. Statements. Pathologists' reports.

'You've always got work to do,' she snapped, getting to her feet.

She crossed to the video and pushed a tape into the machine.

'Well,' she said, handing him the remote control. 'If you can find time away from your work perhaps you'd better look at this.' She pressed the Play button while he held the control in his hand. 'It looks like someone else is taking an interest in your work.'

'What the hell is this?' he said, looking at the screen.

'It was on the news, I taped it for you. I thought you might be interested. After all, it is to do with your work.'

She slammed the sitting-room door behind her.

The picture on the video screen flickered slightly then settled and Grant leaned forward, raising the volume on the set simultaneously.

'. . . claimed five victims and yet there has still been no official word from New Scotland Yard . . .'

Grant frowned as he saw that the source of the words

was a well-dressed, attractive woman in her mid-forties. She was sitting in a large office, the camera pointing at her while a reporter, out of shot, listened to her speak and fed her more questions.

'I realise the difficulties facing the police in a case such as this,' the woman continued, and Grant now saw that a caption at the bottom of the screen had identified her as Charlotte Kilbride.

He wrote her name on a piece of paper.

'That's why I think they should accept my offer,' she continued.

'What exactly *are* you offering the police?' the reporter asked.

'My help,' Charlotte Kilbride said smugly. 'I've had my own practice here in Harley Street for over ten years now. I feel that my insights as a psychiatrist would be invaluable to the officer in charge of this investigation. I think his name is Detective Inspector Grant . . .'

'You fucking bitch,' whispered Grant, his gaze fixed on the screen.

'. . . Furthermore, I think that Detective Inspector Grant and his team would be foolish to ignore the help I can offer as they are obviously having problems catching this killer.'

'Fucking bitch!'

He rewound the tape, the picture spinning backwards, then he hit Play again.

'. . . obviously having problems catching this killer.'

He studied her every feature.

Rewind. Hit Play.

'. . . problems catching this killer.'

Rewind. Play.

'. . . problems catching this killer.'

He hurled the remote furiously across the room.

Thirty-Seven

Jake Webber slumped into the passenger seat of the black Vectra and gazed blankly through the windscreen.

Amy slid the key into the ignition and looked across at him.

'Are you okay, Jake?' she asked, starting the engine.

Webber nodded slowly, his eyes still fixed ahead, drawn for some inexplicable reason to a slick of bird shit on the glass.

'I don't know why I'm doing this. I don't know if I *can* do it.'

For the first time he looked at her and she saw something behind his eyes.

Anguish?

Fear?

He hadn't spoken more than half-a-dozen words since she'd knocked on his door five minutes earlier. She'd stood there and watched as he'd muttered to himself, snatching up first a denim jacket, then discarding it in favour of a leather one, pulling the jacket on and shrugging at her that he was reluctantly ready. His hand had shaken as he'd locked the door.

Now she guided the car skilfully through traffic, glancing at him occasionally, reaching across once to stroke his thigh with her left hand.

Webber looked down at the hand and for fleeting seconds he gripped it tightly. Again she saw that look in his eyes.

Fear?

'Thanks,' he said quietly.

'For what?'

'For coming with me.'

'You would never have gone if I hadn't.'

'Do you blame me?'

'You can't hide from it for ever, Jake. You shouldn't try to shut it out. What happened, happened, and God knows I can never even imagine what it must feel like to lose a child, but not visiting her grave isn't going to solve anything. It isn't going to change the way you feel.'

'You don't know *how* I feel,' he snapped.

An oppresive silence followed before Jake continued.

'I don't even know if Kim visits the grave. I don't know if *anyone* does. That was why I changed my mind, I'd never thought before that no one might go to visit Samantha's grave. I couldn't bear to think of her being so alone there. Does that sound stupid?'

Amy shook her head.

She glanced across at him and saw something else mixed with the fear in his expression. It was a vulnerability that touched her deeply. A facet of his character which she realised he was always careful to hide both from others and, she guessed, from himself.

You've known the bloke less than a week.

She noticed he was gazing blankly out of the side window.

How can you hope to know what he's thinking. Jesus, you don't even know what he does for a living let alone how his mind works.

Webber shifted uncomfortably in his seat, tapping on his right knee with an index finger.

'What about her Grandparents on her mother's side?' Amy asked. 'Wouldn't *they* visit?'

He could only shrug.

'I just don't know, Amy,' he said a little irritably. 'For all I know, I might have been the last person to see her grave the day we buried her.'

She drove for the next few miles in silence, unable to find the right words to comfort him, Webber unwilling or unable to speak. If he was feeling something other than what showed in his troubled gaze then he was keeping it to himself.

Thirty minutes stretched into forty-five then into sixty.

She thought about turning on the radio to break the increasingly heavy solitude, but contented herself with concentrating on driving and looking at her companion every now and then.

Just leave him alone.

He lit up a cigarette and wound down the window slightly to let the smoke escape.

Alone with his thoughts?

'Mind if I join you?' she said finally, nodding towards the Marlboro.

He lit one for her and pressed it to her lips. She took a drag then exhaled.

'I've got to get petrol,' she said, spotting a Texaco station up ahead.

She swung the Vectra into the forecourt, stubbed out the cigarette and hauled herself out of the car.

A moment or two later Webber also clambered out. She watched as he walked across the forecourt towards the small shop. Along with a rack of newspapers, there was an array of Cellophane-wrapped flowers. Small bunches from which Webber selected two. She watched as he went inside and paid, striding back towards the car with his purchases.

He brandished them over the roof of the car.

'I knew there was something I'd forgotten,' he said, attempting a smile.

He climbed back into the Vectra.

Amy continued filling the tank.

They should be at the cemetery in another fifteen minutes.

Thirty-Eight

Grant looked fixedly at the house in Harley Street, his face set in firm lines. He took a drag on his cigarette and blew out a long stream of smoke.

'Is that the one?' asked Lawrenson, nodding towards the three-storey Georgian building. It was indentical in numerous ways to so many of the other dwellings along the street. Large edifices that had been homes to the wealthiest families in London in an earlier century were now host to a similarly affluent financial group. The doctors, psychiatrists, psychoanalysts and consultants who worked in this famous centre of healing plied their trades for considerable reward.

Grant looked at the array of expensive cars parked up and down the street and wondered which belonged to patients and which to practitioners. He also wondered which one belonged to Charlotte Kilbride.

Fucking bitch.

He took another drag.

Interfering fucking jumped-up bitch.

'Guv, I said is that—'

Grant cut his colleague short. 'I heard what you said,' he muttered, nodding. 'That's the one.'

Lawrenson prepared to swing himself out of the car but Grant shot out a hand and gripped his shoulder.

'You wait here. I'll deal with this.'

The detective sergeant watched as his superior clambered out of the vehicle and strode across the pavement and up the four stone steps that led to the ornate front door of the building.

Grant noticed several buzzers on a panel, each one accompanied by a name.

'Doctor Charlotte D. Kilbride,' he read aloud, pressing his finger on the buzzer and keeping it there.

After a second or two there was a metallic crackle and the intercom spat into life.

'Hello.'

'I'm here to see Doctor Kilbride.'

'Do you have an appointment?'

'Just open the door, I want to speak to her.'

'She has appointments all—'

'Open the door, I'm a police officer, this is important.'

The intercom went dead and Grant peered through the small window in the door and saw a middle-aged woman making her way down a narrow hallway.

As she opened the door he stepped through without waiting for an invitation, pulling his ID from his pocket and pushing it towards her for inspection.

'I want to see her now,' he demanded, making his way up the hallway.

The secretary or receptionist (*whatever the hell she was*) scurried along behind him, her face flushed.

To his right was a waiting room and he peered in quizzically. The room was huge, its centre-piece an enormous marble fireplace and an open fire which was crackling away merrily, sparks jumping from the coal. Decorated in a soft green and beige, the room possessed a high-vaulted ceiling and was immaculately furnished with leather chairs and a couple of two-seater sofas. In the centre of the room was a large oak coffee table, magazines lying in rows of almost unnatural neatness on its highly polished surface. He saw the latest copies of *Go, Sight and Sound, Four Four Two* and *Time Out* amongst others. No dog-eared, out-of-date copies of fucking *Reader's Digest* here, thought Grant.

Paintings hung on the walls. Copies in most cases.

He recognised a couple. *When Did You Last See Your Father?* by Yeames. *1814* by Meissonnier.

No AIDS posters plastered to cracked and peeling walls. Money bought better medical care and also better waiting rooms it seemed.

Two people were inside the waiting room, both in their

late thirties. A man in an Armani suit who was doing his best to hide behind a copy of *The Times* and a woman with a pinched face and sad eyes who looked blankly at Grant then returned to her laptop computer.

Grant stepped back out of the waiting room and glared directly at the receptionist. 'I want to see Doctor Kilbride now.'

'That isn't possible,' the woman told him. 'I've already told you that. She has appointments and—'

'Is she with a patient now?' he demanded.

The woman shook her head.

There was a white-painted door at the end of the hall and Grant headed towards it.

'She's on the first floor,' said the woman wearily. 'First door on your right. I'll tell her you're coming up.'

'Don't bother, I'll surprise her.'

He gripped the handrail and began to ascend. As he reached the top of the stairs he glanced back and saw the receptionist was still standing at the bottom looking up at him, her face still flushed. He held her gaze until she retreated back towards her desk out of sight.

There was a window on the landing that looked out into the street and Grant crossed to it, peering out at the scene beyond. Lawrenson was now out of the car, leaning against the driver's door, puffing agitatedly on a cigarette and glancing occasionally at his watch. Waiting.

Grant waited a second longer then spun round, knocked once on the door to his right and walked in without invitation.

Dr Charlotte Kilbride was seated behind her desk. If she was surprised by the sudden intrusion, it barely registered on her face.

'Can I help you?' she asked.

Grant ran appraising eyes over her. Early forties, shoulder-length brown hair cut in a bob. She was wearing an immaculately pressed black jacket and skirt over a white blouse. She looked better in the flesh than she did on the tape last night, thought Grant.

That fucking tape.

He produced his ID once more and pushed it towards her.

'Detective Inspector David Grant, Murder Squad,' he announced. 'I want to talk to you.'

'How can I help you?' she asked, a slight smile on her lips.

'You *can't* help me, that's what I'm here to tell you.'

She nodded. 'You saw the interview last night?'

'Yeah, I saw it and like I said, you can't help me. I don't *want* your help, I don't *need* your help.'

'At least have a seat.' She gestured to one of the leather chairs in front of her desk.

'This isn't a social call,' he reminded her. '*Or* a consultation.' He looked around the room at the shelves lined with books, the brass lamps, the leather furniture.

'Then what can I do for you?'

'I'm here to tell you to keep your nose out of police business.'

'I wasn't aware I was interfering with police business, Inspector.'

'*Detective* Inspector,' he reminded her. 'I'm talking about that bullshit interview you gave last night.'

'I was asked for my views, I gave them, I'm sorry if they caused you any offence.' She turned in her chair to face him, uncrossing her slender legs, brushing a fleck of dust from one thigh.

'You tried to make me look stupid,' he snapped.

'I merely spoke my mind. I offered help, I offered my expertise. If you don't want it—'

'I don't,' he snapped.

'If you think it undermines your authority, then perhaps you have a different kind of problem.'

'Don't try to psychoanalyse me,' he sneered. 'I'm not one of your fee-paying nutcases.' He crossed to a filing cabinet beside her desk. 'Perhaps they're the ones I should be checking up on. You treat nutters, don't you? How do I know one of *them* isn't the killer?'

'My patients are suffering from various psychological problems,' she said calmly.

'So let me check some of their files.'

'Those files are confidential.'

'Not if I come back with a warrant they're not. How do I know you're not protecting one of them?'

'What goes on between myself and my patients is my business,' she said irritably.

'And this murder case is *mine*,' Grant rasped. 'So keep your nose out of it otherwise I'll be back with a warrant and I'll grill every one of your *patients*.' He slapped the filing cabinet.

'Are you frightened of my offer of help, Detective Inspector? Afraid I might be useful to you? Worried that I *could* help you catch this killer?'

He turned towards the door.

'Stay out of it,' he warned. 'I'll get him and I don't need help from *you* or anyone else.'

As he reached the door he paused again, pointing an accusatory finger at her. 'And stay away from the press and television.'

'Is that a warning, Detective Inspector?' she asked, getting to her feet.

Again he ran his gaze over her figure.

'Just do what I said,' he snapped. 'Keep out of it.'

And he was gone, slamming the door behind him.

She heard his footsteps receding down the stairs then, a moment later, the front door banging shut.

Charlotte Kilbride crossed to the large picture window close to her desk and watched as Grant climbed into the waiting Montego, which pulled away rapidly.

For a moment longer she stood there gazing out into the street then she turned to the filing cabinet closest to her and, carefully, pulled out the file she sought.

Thirty-Nine

As Jake Webber pulled himself reluctantly from the Vectra, he glanced up at the sky. A watery sun hung against the cloud-smeared heavens, offering little warmth.

'I'm cold,' he said under his breath.

Amy walked around the car and took a firm grip of his free hand.

'Ready?' she asked softly, squeezing his hand.

He nodded none too convincingly and they began walking, the gravel path crunching beneath their feet.

The vast necropolis that was Norwood Cemetery stretched out before them, lines of headstones and stone markers standing like frozen sentinels. In some places they were in arrow-straight lines, in others, in irregular configurations. There was a wide central walkway and dozens of smaller paths leading off it, some man-made, others merely tracks worn in the grass by the passage of so many weary and sorrowful feet.

A single sparrow was singing cheerfully in the lower branches of one of the nearby trees but as Amy and Webber approached it flew off and Amy became aware again of the heavy silence that enveloped the resting place. The only sound was that of their feet on the pathway.

Webber paused for a moment and looked around, his already strained expression showing signs of increased distress.

'I'm not sure where it is,' he said quietly.

'Take your time, Jake,' Amy told him softly.

'I should be able to remember where my own fucking daughter is buried,' he snapped, his tone hardening.

He shifted the bunches of Cellophane-wrapped flowers from hand to hand, the wrapping crackling in the stillness.

Ahead of them was a small ridge topped by a carefully tended privet hedge and a row of small conifers. Webber headed up the incline, Amy trailing in his wake.

Something here looked familiar to him.

Amy hurried along behind him, reaching the top of the incline. More graves stretched away before them. To the left, about twenty yards away, a woman in her fifties was filling a watering can from one of the many taps dotted about the cemetery. To the right was a small willow tree, its lower branches draping over the ground like a net.

Amy noticed a number of graves close to the tree. The grass around them was uncut. Long and untended.

Webber had frozen and was standing still, staring towards the willow tree and the overgrown plots.

Amy saw how pale his face was and she reached out and gripped his arm.

'Jake,' she whispered.

'I can't do this, Amy,' he said, turning to look at her and she saw that there were tears in his eyes.

'Is she over there?'

He swallowed hard.

'Is Sam buried there?' Amy persisted gently, nodding towards the weed-infested graves.

One single tear rolled from the corner of his eye and trickled slowly down his cheek.

He wiped it away angrily. 'Let's go. I should never have listened to you in the first place.'

'Jake, you're here now. You've come this far.' She kept a firm grip on his arm.

She saw the knot of muscles pulsing at the side of his jaw.

'Do it for *her* sake, for Samantha,' Amy continued.

He looked at Amy then at the bunches of flowers he was gripping tightly in his powerful fist, almost crushing the stalks. He closed his eyes for a moment. Jesus. Had it really been so long since he'd been back here?

Ten yards. You only have to walk ten yards.

He looked into Amy's eyes again.

Ten lousy stinking yards.

He felt as if someone had opened a hole in his stomach.
The feeling of emptiness there seemed to be spreading until it filled every limb, every fibre of his body,
every pore.

Turn and walk.

Amy wanted to say something, to tell him that it would
be all right, that she was with him, but whenever she tried
to speak the words wouldn't come.

What the hell do you say to him?

She saw the pain in his expression. A deep-rooted
torment the like of which she could never remember
seeing before. As if, before her eyes, she was seeing a
man having his soul ripped apart. Then he turned and
headed towards the grave and she walked beside him,
holding his arm as he moved inexorably closer to the plot
he sought.

So small.

The grave was less than three feet long, the grass and
weeds having covered it like unruly invaders. Leaves
that had fallen from the willow were also scattered
across it. A metal plaque was set in a small square of
marble at the head of the grave. Amy tried to read it
through the overgrown grass and the grime that stained
the brass.

She watched as Webber knelt, pulled a handkerchief
from his pocket and wiped the plaque clean.

Finally, she could read it.

SAMANTHA JOANNE WEBBER
AGED EIGHTEEN MONTHS
ASLEEP IN THE ARMS OF GOD.

Amy felt tears welling up in her eyes as she watched
Webber looking helplessly down at the grave.

'Hello, babe,' he said softly, his voice cracking. 'It's
Dad.'

He wiped his nose with the back of his hand and began

pulling at the weeds covering the grave, hurling them angrily to one side.

Amy waited a moment then began helping him. She could see the tears rolling down his cheeks as he tore at the intruding weeds, ripping them free furiously.

'It doesn't look as if it's been touched since she was buried,' he said angrily, sitting back on his haunches for a moment and regarding the plot, taking every detail in.

'What about the plaque?' Amy asked, still pulling weeds and grass away. 'Who would have put that there?'

He could only shrug.

'Kim maybe. That's probably why my name is there – she didn't even want to be associated with Sam when she was gone,' he said bitterly. 'Well that's fine. I'd rather people knew she was *my* daughter.'

He continued to stare down at the plaque.

'When she was buried,' he said, his tone more even now, 'she was buried with one of her toys. Some kind of little dog. She loved that. She always had it in her pram or her cot. I thought she should have it with her for ever.'

Amy moved towards him as his head dropped forward and tears ran down his cheeks.

Amy felt helpless to stem this tide of grief, angry with herself that she could offer no comfort. She merely snaked her arm around his waist and pulled him close, wiping a tear from her own cheek.

'Oh Christ, Amy,' he said, the desolation in his voice making her shudder. 'Why her? Why my baby? She didn't deserve to die. There are so many in this fucking world who should be lying there instead of her.'

He shook loose of Amy's comforting grip and continued clearing the grass and weeds away.

Amy stepped back and watched him, watching until the plot was exposed, the plaque clean and gleaming for all to see.

She didn't move towards him, merely watched as he wiped his dirty hands on his handkerchief then gently laid the flowers on the grave. Amy was reluctant to intrude upon his grief. She stood with her hands clasped in front of her.

The slight breeze that had sprung up rustled the Cellophane that encased the flowers.

'Dad's got to go now, babe,' Webber said, gazing down at the grave, wiping away another tear with a muddy hand. 'Sleep tight.'

He sobbed uncontrollably, his entire body shaking as he stood at the graveside.

Amy bowed her head, warm tears flowing from her eyes. She felt his pain but she knew that nothing she could do or say would ease it and that realisation brought only fresh tears.

A bird which had been sitting in the branches of the willow took flight, rising into the sky, heading away from the two distraught figures below as if it could no longer bear the sight of such devastating sorrow.

Forty

Amy had turned to glance at Webber a number of times and, on every occasion, she had found him staring blankly out of the side window. Once or twice she thought about speaking but couldn't find the words.

What the hell could she say to him?

They sat in traffic, the silence inside the Vectra growing more oppressive by the minute.

Webber allowed his head to loll back against the headrest, his eyes closed.

Amy wondered if he was trying to sleep. Perhaps with sleep would come the chance to blot out the memories.

Perhaps.

'Do you believe in God?'

The words took her by surprise. He hadn't spoken for more than thirty minutes and she hadn't expected him to utter a sound perhaps until they reached home.

She looked across at Webber and saw that his eyes were still closed.

'Did you hear me? I asked if you believed in God.'

'I've never really thought too much about it, Jake,' she confessed. 'I believe there's *something* but I don't know whether I'd call it God.'

'Someone once said that God is a sadist but probably doesn't even know it.' A bitter smile creased his lips. 'I don't believe. Not any more.'

'I think lots of people who've lost relatives think like that, they—'

'I'll tell you why I don't believe,' he interrupted. 'Because none of it makes any fucking sense. It isn't logical.'

'What isn't?'

'Life. Death. God. None of it makes sense. Why did

my little girl have to die when there are all kinds of fucking scumbags walking the streets?' he rasped. 'They're the ones that deserve to die, not her. The pimps, the pushers, the slags, the fucking junkies. The garbage. They're the ones who should have died, not *her*.' He exhaled deeply. 'Eighteen months old,' he murmured. 'It's not fair.'

'I'm sure the parents of other children feel the same as you,' Amy offered. 'Those who lose kids must think it's unfair too.'

'What do *you* think?'

She looked puzzled.

'Do you think it's fair that there's so much scum walking the streets when my child is dead?'

Amy felt helpless, unsure of what to say.

'Jake, I feel sorry for you, you know that.'

'I don't want your fucking pity,' he hissed. 'I asked if you thought it was fair.'

'No,' she admitted. 'All right, it's not fair, is that what you want to hear? It's not fair that people die in wars or famines or floods or plane crashes.'

'Because it's always the *wrong* people. It's always *decent* people,' he told her angrily. 'Do you know what would be fair? If a plane load of junkies crashed. Five hundred of the bastards packed into a 747 going down in flames. Now *that* would be justice. If that happened, even *I* might start believing in God.'

There was a vehemence in his tone that unsettled her and yet, deep down, she told herself she could forgive his bitterness and his rage. To have a life he cherished so much snatched from him so cruelly, she believed, at least gave him the right to his anger.

They drove some way in silence then she placed a hand on his knee, wondering what kind of response it might elicit.

'Why don't you come to the show with me tonight, Jake?' she asked.

He looked at her blankly.

'Come to the studios with me. We'll have a meal first and—'

'No,' he said, interrupting her, some of the anger having left his voice. 'I think I'm better off on my own tonight.' He managed a wan smile.

'You'll sit around brooding.' You shouldn't be on your own tonight.'

'I think that's *exactly* what I should do. I'm not going to be very good company.' He squeezed her hand. 'Besides, I've got things to do.'

'Such as?'

He didn't answer, merely squeezed her hand more tightly.

'Jake, what's so important?' she persisted.

'Leave it, Amy,' he said, fixing her in a cold stare. 'I'm better off alone.'

She held his gaze a second longer then returned her concentration to the road.

Webber fumbled in his jacket pocket for his key and let himself in, turning to face Amy, who was standing on the threshold.

'Are you sure you're going to be okay?' she asked him.

He nodded. 'I'll be fine.'

He stepped forward and kissed her gently on the lips. 'Thanks for coming with me,' he said quietly. 'For making me go in the first place. Thanks, Amy.'

They kissed again, more urgently this time, their tongues slipping and sliding against each other as they pressed their bodies hard together. She draped her arms around his neck and felt his strong hands gripping her waist.

When they finally parted, Amy was breathing heavily.

She touched one of his cheeks gently. 'I'll be home about two. If you're still up, what about a night cap?'

'Sounds good to me.'

'Just come up when you're ready.'

He nodded and pushed the door a little. 'I'd better let you go,' he said.

Why did she feel he was pushing her out?

'See you later?' she said but it sounded more like a question.

'Yeah, more than likely,' he told her, his smile looking a little strained.

She stepped back.

'Thanks again, Amy,' he said, and he pushed the door shut.

She was left staring at the wooden partition.

Shut out.

She stood staring at the door then turned and slowly, almost sadly, made her way up the stairs towards her own flat.

Inside his flat, back pressed to the front door, Webber heard her ascend.

Only when he heard her key in her lock did he move.

Forty-One

She rarely thought about death. Despite the fact that she'd been working in St Angela's Hospice in Camden for the past six years, confronted by the dark spectre on a daily basis, Valerie Hardy seldom stopped to consider either her own mortality or that of those she cared for.

Those who knew her found it strange that such an environment did not precipitate feelings of fear within her; the constant closeness to death that she experienced so often seemed to negate rather than reinforce any contemplation of her own life and death.

Valerie had found the first year something of a struggle, the inevitability of losing so many patients had been hard to bear to begin with but she had gradually come to terms with it. There was sadness, she didn't deny that and, in the small hours, when she was doing her rounds, she sometimes shed tears for a particular patient who had died. But the overwhelming feeling she had from working at St Angela's was one of satisfaction. She rejoiced in the knowledge that the care administered by herself and her colleagues to those within the walls was first class and helped to make the last few months or days of a patient's life not just bearable but almost enjoyable.

The hospice wasn't a place of sadness and depression. The staff did their best to see that it was one of good spirit. Val never ceased to be amazed at the fortitude with which some of the residents faced their predicaments. It was humbling. She felt privileged to tend to their needs, proud to be their friend.

Prior to joining St Angela's she had worked in the Intensive Care Unit at St Barts. A job that required a completely different frame of mind and was, in its own way, perhaps even more depressing than working with those she knew were going to die. In ICU there was the distant hope that a patient would survive, would recover from some horrendous injury, or wake from some deep coma. And often that happened but when death struck, to the nurses working in the unit, the blow was somehow harder to take than the inevitability of death she faced at St Angela's. Here she was working with men and women who *knew* there would be no miracle recovery, no unexpected cure. There were no false hopes here, just the unavoidable conclusion both patient and staff could only wait for.

Val found it curiously reassuring.

The hospice (although she hated the word and the connotations it carried) held about fifteen patients at any one time, mostly in their late sixties and upwards. She knew them all. Knew their lives as well as she would know their deaths.

Val and five other nurses, plus three doctors, were on constant call to tend to the needs of these special people who lived what little life they had left with a zest that sometimes put others to shame.

She checked her watch and continued with her rounds. The night shift was easier as far as work load was concerned. Walk the corridors, check on each patient, ensure they were comfortable. She would administer some sleeping pills to those who had difficulty sleeping if they requested them or, sometimes, she would just talk to them. That was all they wanted at times. To talk.

The silence inside the building was one not of oppression but of overwhelming peacefulness.

Val checked on three patients. Two stricken with cancer, the other with advanced multiple sclerosis. All three were sleeping soundly. Val stood looking at them with the same love in her eyes that a mother reserves for her sleeping child.

She moved around the hospice assuredly and swiftly, shivering as she felt a chill sweeping down one corridor. She checked the central heating and saw that it was set at Normal. Val pressed one hand to a nearby radiator and found it was warm.

She eased the temperature up a few notches and then crossed to the first room, easing the door open and entering.

Mrs Bridgeman was snoring quietly.

Val tucked in the corner of a blanket that had come loose on the woman's bed then glanced around her room. There were two vases of flowers in the room, one of which smelled a little rank. Val made a mental note to change the water in the morning before she went off duty.

Photos were scattered all around the room. Mrs Bridgeman's son. Her granddaughter. A sepia tinted one of her husband.

Val leaned forward and gently slipped the Mills and Boon from the sleeping woman's hands, sliding her bookmark into the appointed pages and placing the paperback on the bedside unit. Then she backed out of the room quietly and closed the door, moving across to the next patient.

Mr Cross was in his late sixties. The cancer had spread rapidly from his lymph glands to virtually every other part of his body. No one gave him more than a month but he was almost unbearably cheerful, and again Val found herself overwhelmed with love. None of the patients, in fact none that she could remember during her six years at St Angela's, had ever expressed the slightest hint of bitterness or self-pity at their condition.

Humbling, indeed.

He stirred slightly as she wandered around the room. She waited, ensuring that she hadn't disturbed him but realising that the high dose of morphine he was given every night would secure his uninterrupted night's rest.

She moved out into the corridor once more. Again she felt the cold breeze and, this time, she saw that it was coming from the end of the corridor. The sash window was open five or six inches, allowing a chill wind through. Who had opened that?

Val headed towards it, shaking her head irritably. The window should be kept closed.

Only as she drew closer did she realise that the floor was slick with moisture. No, not slick. It was *swimming* with fluid. Thick, dark fluid that gave off a pungent and immediately recognisable smell. The entire corridor was filled with it, as if it had seeped through the open window. In places it had run beneath the doors of patients' rooms.

That fluid.

That smell.

She recognised it so well and yet her mind told her that it was impossible.

And then she was standing in it. Standing in the great, thick tide of it, watching it creep further down the corridor like a living organism.

No, this couldn't be.

But she knew that smell.

But why . . . ?

Why the open window? Where had the thick fluid come from?

She looked down at her feet, at the liquid lapping around them. The stench was starting to make her dizzy. That unmistakable odour. Cloying. Choking. The corridor was awash with it.

She was standing in petrol.

Val turned back towards the window, her eye drawn to something moving in the darkness beyond, outside. Something tiny. Something glowing red.

The match hit the petrol, spinning through the air as if in slow motion before it landed and Val opened her mouth to scream but could not force the sound out.

The petrol exploded.

The world turned a bright, searing red.

Forty-Two

Amy knew immediately that it was Webber heading across the street. From her position in her bedroom window she saw him approaching the flats, hands dug deep into his pockets.

She looked at the clock. It was 3.17 a.m.

She'd knocked on his door as she returned that morning but had received no answer. In fact, she had convinced herself, even as she stepped from the taxi that there would be no one home when she banged the door.

'Things to do.' That was what he'd said, wasn't it? He had 'things to do'.

Until this time?

As she watched him drawing closer she tried to see his face in the gloom, through the deep shadows, but she couldn't. As usual she could only guess at what was going on behind his eyes.

She had seen his pain that afternoon and she had felt unbearably, infuriatingly helpless to ease that pain. If only she could have found some words, no matter how clichéd or bland, to say to him as he'd stood at his daughter's graveside. But instead all she had been able to do was stand there impotently while he gave vent to so much pent-up emotion.

Amy had been surprised at how deeply his display of grief had affected her. She couldn't remember the last time something had touched her so profoundly.

And why? You've known the bloke a week.

She exhaled deeply and reached down for another cigarette, lighting it up, the lighter flame dancing in the gloom of the bedroom.

Only a week. You know nothing about him except that he lost a daughter.

She heard his key in the front door, then in the lock of his flat. The door was closed and then there was only silence.

Amy waited a moment then got to her feet, slipping on a pair of Reeboks, not bothering to fasten the laces. She brushed some ash from her jeans then walked through the sitting room towards her own door.

She hesitated a moment. Should she go down and see him now? Probably all he wanted was to be alone with his thoughts. The last thing he needed was company.

She looked at the door. Wondering.

Go to him.

She left her blouse untucked, slipped the latch, pocketed her key, then she made her way quickly and quietly down the stairs towards the door of flat number one.

She felt nervous. A stupid almost adolescent anxiety.

Frightened he's going to turn you away?

She tapped softly on the door and waited.

No answer.

He doesn't want to know.

Again she knocked.

The door opened almost immediately and she found herself looking into his eyes.

'Did I wake you?' he asked, a note of weariness in his voice.

She shook her head.

'I was waiting for you,' she told him. 'I heard you come in.'

He smiled weakly, as if the gesture was forced.

'If you want me to go I will, Jake,' Amy told him.

'No. Come in.'

He stepped back, ushering her inside.

Amy hesitated a moment longer, almost surprised at the invitation then she stepped past him and wandered through towards the sitting room, hearing the door close behind her.

He followed her in.

'Have a seat,' he told her, motioning towards the sofa.

She did so, glancing around the room surreptitiously, anxious not to make it too obvious that she was inspecting its contents. Christ, the place was almost spartan. A sofa, one chair, a small coffee table, a television, a portable music system and a couple of cabinets. And that was it. No pictures on the walls. No ornaments. Just what she saw.

He emptied his jacket pockets and she saw him lay some loose change, some keys, a pack of Rothmans and a box of matches on the coffee table.

'Is vodka okay?' he asked her.

'It's fine.'

'I've got some lemonade in the fridge, and some ice if you like.'

'It's fine as it comes, Jake,' she assured him, taking the tumbler from him and sipping the clear liquor.

He took a swallow from his own glass and refilled it immediately.

'How did the show go tonight?' he asked.

'It went well, you should have come.'

'I told you before, I don't think I'd have been very good company.' He swigged more vodka. 'Look, I need to have a shower, make yourself comfortable. I won't be long.'

He headed off towards the bedroom and through into the bathroom. After a moment or two, Amy heard the sound of running water.

She got to her feet almost immediately, walking slowly around the sitting room.

She pulled open the cabinet that supported the television and found a video inside and a handful of CDs which she flicked through. Nine Inch Nails. Metallica. Enya. Garbage. Roxette.

She smiled.

Eclectic tastes to say the least.

She moved across to the cabinet where the bottle of vodka was standing and pulled it open. It contained half-a-dozen glasses, some cocktail sticks and a cork-screw.

The sound of running water was still coming from the bathroom.

She moved into the kitchen. A table and two chairs. An electric kettle on one of the work tops. Tea and coffee caddies. She checked the cupboards in there too, not really sure what she was looking for. There were some tins of food, a couple of Pot Noodles, some instant milk and more teabags but not much else. The fridge was similarly bare. Half a carton of milk, some out-of-date sausage rolls. A couple of microwave pizzas. The flat might be home to Webber but it seemed more like a place to stop off rather than one to settle in. It was hardly welcoming.

She moved into the bedroom. Again it was sparsely furnished, only a chest of drawers and a small MFI wardrobe occupying any space near the bed. The bed was unmade from the morning.

Amy crossed to it and pulled up the duvet.

What the hell are you doing?

She smiled at her own actions.

What are you looking for? Why are you prying?

As she held the duvet she could smell him on it.

His jeans lay discarded close to the bathroom door, which was ajar. She crossed to it, carrying her drink and paused there, listening to the sound of running water. Then, slowly, she pushed it open and stepped in.

She could see the outline of his body through the shower curtain and for a while she watched him as he stood beneath the spray.

A small stool stood just inside the door. On the wall there was a medicine cabinet with mirrored doors and she caught sight of her own reflection briefly.

'How do you feel now?' she asked, raising her voice above the gushing water.

There was silence for a moment then Webber pulled

back the shower curtain slightly and looked at her with an expression of surprise and delight.

'Sorry to barge in.'

'Feel free,' he told her and let the curtain slip back again.

She sipped at the vodka, still studying his shape through the almost transparent plastic curtain.

'I hope you didn't feel as if I pushed you into visiting Sam's grave today.'

'I'm glad you did. If you hadn't, I would probably never have gone,' he admitted. 'I owe you for that.'

'I did it because I care,' she told him. 'I care about *you.*'

The shower curtain rings rattled as the flimsy divide was pulled open. Amy stood naked before Webber, her clothes discarded on the bathroom floor.

Without a word she stepped beneath the water with him and he pulled her to him, welcoming her into his arms, pressing her slender body against his.

She lifted her arms around his neck, their lips pressing together, tongues seeking each other almost frenziedly as the water bounced off them from the stinging spray. They were joined by the passion of their kisses until she pulled away slightly, her breath coming in low gasps.

He traced a rivulet of water as it coursed down her chest towards her nipple, using his thumb to further tease the already stiff bud, then he bent his head and flicked his tongue around the sensitive flesh, allowing it to swirl around the puckered skin. His saliva mingled with the water as he drew his head away and repeated his actions on her other breast. With his free hand he gently cupped first one buttock then the other, allowing one index finger to probe tentatively towards the top of her legs.

Amy felt his penis stiffen as her hand closed around it, coaxing it to full erection with firm caresses. She rubbed her thumb over his glans and felt him shudder.

They kissed again and she allowed herself to be pushed

back against the wall of the shower, his stiffness now nudging against her belly.

She pulled him harder against her, enjoying the feel of that rigid shaft, knowing that his excitement was as great as her own.

He broke the kiss and nibbled at her earlobe, then her neck, then slid down towards her breasts taking each nipple in his mouth in turn before allowing his tongue to trace a pattern across her belly, through the water, which still lashed them. Finally, he was on his knees in front of her, his tongue stirring the soft downy hair of her pubis.

She thrust her pelvis towards him as the pleasure grew and stroked his wet hair. She felt his tongue slide over her throbbing clitoris before trailing gently over her distended and slippery outer lips.

He tasted her moisture there and savoured it, using both hands to massage the flesh of her slim thighs, his tongue now working expertly around her swollen clitoris, pausing every so often to probe her wet cleft.

Amy pressed her back harder against the shower wall as he kept up this exquisite action, pushing her closer to ecstasy. She opened her legs a little wider, allowing him better access to her most sensitive areas and she shuddered as he used his tongue and fingers so expertly. She could feel the pleasure building to a crescendo and she gripped his shoulders hard, circling her hips as he concentrated his efforts. Clenching her teeth, she felt his expertise driving her closer to orgasm.

When he pulled away for a moment she almost cried out with disappointment, but the feeling was only temporary and a second later she felt his tongue between her legs again. He moved more urgently now as he sensed her release was near – but, despite her pleasure, she wanted him more fully. Wanted to feel that stiffness inside her – wanted his liquid pleasure deep within her – but then she surrendered to the feelings enveloping her. A warmth started to spread from between her legs and across her belly then up to her breasts until the skin there and across her chest flushed pink.

His tongue flicked incessantly across her swollen clitoris and she cried out as the first wave of orgasm swept through her, her whole body shuddering.

She felt him gripping her hips, her thighs. Jesus, there was such strength in those hands. She held him there as the sensations swept through her. The water bounced off her hardened nipples and ran down her quivering body as she gasped out her pleasure, and her own moisture glistened on his chin as surely as the shower spray.

She kept her eyes closed, wanting the ecstasy to continue.

And it did.

Forty-Three

When Amy woke she could hear Webber's low breathing beside her, feel the gentle rise and fall of his chest beneath her arm. She moved closer to him for a moment, pressing herself against him, allowing one hand to trail up his thigh.

Webber stirred slightly and Amy smiled to herself as she propped herself up on one elbow and looked down at his sleeping form.

The intensity of their lovemaking had exhausted them both and, as she moved, she felt the residue of his liquid between her legs. He had carried her from the shower, wrapping her in a towel as easily as a parent wraps a child and she had been amazed at the strength in his arms.

He had made love frantically, almost frenziedly, but that had served only to heighten her own pleasure and she had responded with equal passion. Within that fury there had been tenderness that was almost incongruous. A selflessness on his part that did not seem to sit naturally with the intensity of his lovemaking.

Was this to be the first of many such nights?

Was it to be as it had been with John Howard?

She closed her eyes briefly, as if to banish the image of the writer. The lover. She had never felt anything the way she had felt it with Howard.

Until tonight?

And yet, as she kept telling herself, what did she know of this man whose bed she now shared? Other than his anguish at losing his only child, she knew nothing of his character and yet she still felt strangely drawn to him, and she knew the feeling was reciprocated. There had been other men in the past she had shared a bed with and known nothing about, but they had not mattered.

She had been with them for one or two nights as *she* chose but they had meant nothing to her.

Webber *mattered*. This man, who was still so much a mystery to her, mattered.

She brushed a hair from his face then swung herself carefully out of bed, anxious not to wake him. It was warm inside the flat so, still naked, she padded through into the kitchen to the fridge and retrieved a carton of milk. Then she went to the cupboard where she remembered he kept some glasses, blew the dust from the bottom of one and filled it with the white liquid.

She drank deeply, illuminated only by the dull light from within the fridge.

She pushed the door shut and padded back towards the bedroom carrying the rest of the milk.

She paused at the bathroom and decided to relieve herself. Tugging the light cord, she was about to sit down when she noticed that the mirrored doors of the medicine cabinet were slightly open.

She pushed them shut but one swung open again and, when she couldn't shut it the second time, she opened the door fully to see what was blocking it.

There was a plastic bag full of cotton wool jutting out half an inch or so, preventing the door from closing.

She lifted it out, intent on shutting the cupboard. A box was behind the cotton wool. It was plain brown cardboard. About five inches long, half that across. There was black stencilled writing on the front:

50 CARTRIDGES
9mm BALL NATO M882 LOT WCC92D043 – 002
OLIN CORPORATION

Amy swallowed hard and reached for the box, hefting it before her.

She turned it over and read the back: WARNING: These cartridges are loaded to military velocity and pressure . . .

'My God,' she murmured, undoing one end of the box.

There was a piece of Styrofoam inside and, within each segment of it was a gleaming, brass-cased 9 m.m. round.

She looked down at the bullets uncomprehendingly.

Bullets. Dear God, do you realise what you're holding?

She took out one of the shells and turned it slowly between her thumb and forefinger.

Bullets. Real live, fire from a gun, fucking bullets.

She hurriedly replaced it in the Styrofoam, pushed the container back inside the box and replaced it in the medicine cabinet, her hand quivering slightly as she did so.

Bullets. What the hell was Webber doing with a box of bullets? And if there were bullets wouldn't there be a gun?

'Shit,' she said, her voice quivering. 'Shit.'

Her head was spinning. What did this mean? What the hell was she getting herself into? The rational part of her mind told her that there was a good reason for this unexpected find. That if she asked Webber he would explain why he had a box of 9 m.m. ammunition in his medicine cabinet.

But should she ask?

What if there *wasn't* a rational explanation?

This man, who you don't know, has live ammunition in his flat.

Why?

She swallowed hard.

Ask him.

'Amy.'

She heard him calling her.

Amy closed the cabinet door hurriedly, startled by the sound.

'I'm coming, Jake,' she said, trying to mask the confusion in her voice. 'I won't be a minute.'

He was sitting on the edge of the bed when she re-entered the bedroom.

'Are you okay?' he asked.

She nodded.

Come on, be convincing.

'I was thirsty,' she told him, holding up the glass of milk.

He lay back, patting the mattress beside him. A signal for her to join him which she did, allowing herself to be enveloped in his broad arms.

Ask him.

'I thought you'd walked out on me,' he said, grinning, and she felt one of those strong hands stroking her hair tenderly.

Ask him about the fucking bullets.

'Why should I?' she murmured as he pulled her closer, kissing her forehead. She felt his free hand slide down her back and cup one of her buttocks, kneading the smooth flesh. His penis was stiffening against her belly as he felt her warmth.

'Just hold me,' she said softly, kissing him tenderly on the lips.

He did and in a few moments he'd drifted off to sleep again, his low breathing stirring her blond hair as he exhaled.

Amy felt the strength of his embrace and she closed her eyes.

The bullets.

She would ask him when the time was right.

And when would that be?

It was a long time before she slept.

Forty-Four

Grant had smelled burned human flesh before but never as powerfully as this. That unmistakable sickly sweet odour of charred skin and scorched bone seemed to fill the air, clogging in his nostrils, even at the back of his throat. Twice he coughed, hawked and spat into his handkerchief while other officers around him also toiled amidst the vile stench.

Lawrenson actually had a handkerchief tied around his nose as he moved amongst the blackened debris that was once St Angela's Hospice. The smell of burned flesh mingled with the equally pungent stink of scorched wood and incinerated plaster. There was a gaping hole in the roof where the flames had roared upwards through the building, finally escaping through the tiles, blowing them aside.

At least half of the building had been reduced to a shell by the ferocity of the flames. Despite the fact that the fire brigade had responded so quickly, the fire had taken hold with a speed that surprised even those firemen still wandering through the wreckage. It had swept through St Angela's like some kind of blazing whirlwind, destroying everything it touched, incinerating both wood or flesh with the same ease and vehemence.

The floor which he walked on was swimming with water from the firemen's hoses. Filthy, blackened water that formed huge inky puddles on the remains of the scorched floor. He felt it splash around his feet, ducking to avoid a fallen beam, which was still smouldering, still giving off some heat.

Grant paused, hands on his hips, and glanced around at the destruction. Away to his right, on a patch of grass, twelve black plastic body bags were lying in a neat row. All of them filled.

'Eleven patients and one member of staff,' said Lawrenson joining him, and glancing at the row of bodies.

'What about the rest?' Grant asked.

'Two more patients are suffering from slight burns. The other two have been taken to hospital – they're being treated for shock.'

'And the staff?'

'One nurse is badly burned – she's in Intensive Care at University College Hospital. A male nurse was hit by falling masonry, he's stable.'

'Are there men with them?'

Lawrenson nodded.

Grant continued walking along the corridor, its walls scorched black by the fire, its floor deep in filthy water. There was a watch lying on the debris-strewn floor in front of him. He knelt and retrieved it on the end of his pen. It was old, the gold yellowed and worn.

The back bore an inscription:

TO MY DARLING LILLIAN ON OUR ANNIVERSARY

He shook his head. 'Lillian,' he repeated slowly, softly.

'Mrs Lillian Potter, she's over there,' said Lawrenson nodding towards the line of body bags.

The watch had no winder, probably hadn't worked for years.

Grant laid it carefully on top of a nearby radiator that had been stripped of paint by the searing flames.

'The response time of the fire brigade was less than five minutes once they'd got the call,' said Lawrenson. 'The call was logged at just after two this morning.'

'Who made it?'

'One of the staff, just before they got out.'

Grant walked on, passing firemen pulling the remains of a burned bed from the shell of a bedroom. In what was left of the bedroom there was a large wooden wardrobe, most of which had been incinerated in the blaze. But, still hanging inside it were a selection of suits, strangely undamaged by the raging flames. On the wall, also untouched by the fire, was a small metal crucifix. There were scorch marks all around the icon but it remained untarnished.

'What about the physical evidence?' Grant wanted to know.

'A petrol can, found outside one of the windows,' Lawrenson told him.

'Any prints?'

Lawrenson shook his head. 'Whoever it was wore gloves,' he informed his superior.

'What about footprints?'

'The paths around the hospice are all gravel. Even if the fire brigade *hadn't* been stomping all over them we'd have had trouble finding anything, as it is . . .' He allowed the sentence to trail off, shrugging his shoulders.

'So the petrol was poured in through a window and then ignited,' Grant mused.

'That's about the size of it, guv.'

'I want a full report from forensics within the hour – I'm going back to the Yard.'

'Who the fuck would want to torch a hospice?' Lawrenson shaking his head in bewilderment.

'You tell me.'

'As if it isn't bad enough that we've already got *one* nutter out there, now *this*.'

'What makes you think it isn't the same killer?'

'Where the hell's the motive *this* time?' Lawrenson protested. 'How the fuck can there be a link between this and the other murders?'

'I think there is,' murmured Grant. 'And what's more, I think I know *what* it is.'

Forty-Five

'This fire wasn't started to destroy property,' Grant began. 'It was intended to kill. We're lucky it didn't kill more people than it did.'

'Twelve's enough, isn't it?' called a voice from the middle of the incident room.

Grant looked around the group of weary, bleary-eyed policemen gathered before him and saw that the comment had come from Leech. The older man was seated on a desk puffing on a cigarette.

'Someone carried, or dragged, a three-gallon can of petrol to that hospice and emptied it through one of the windows,' Grant continued.

'Somebody bloody strong must have done it then,' said Friel. 'Those things are heavy.'

'Someone strong,' Grant repeated. 'That would be consistent with what we've got on the other murders, right?'

'What the hell has this got to do with the other murders?' Leech demanded. 'This can't be related. It—'

Grant didn't let him finish his sentence. 'Someone drove to the hospice, carried that petrol through the grounds without even leaving a fucking footprint, emptied the contents through a window then set fire to it.'

'What physical evidence have we got?' Schofield asked.

'Sod all. Not a fucking light, if you'll excuse the pun . . . The killer wore smooth gloves. There are no prints. Forensics say that any fibres left behind were burned up in the fire. So, we're even further up shit creek and no bastard is chucking us a paddle yet.'

'I still don't see the link between this fire and the other killings,' Leech persisted. 'The other victims were low-lifes. These victims were . . .' He struggled for the word.

'Normal?' Grant offered.

'Somebody kills a couple of pros, a pimp, a druggie and some dead-beat on the streets – fair enough,' said Leech. 'But why would the same geezer burn down a hospice? It doesn't make any sense.'

'It depends on motive,' Grant said. 'And I reckon we might have one at last.'

A heavy silence fell upon the room, all eyes riveted on Grant as he turned towards the blackboard behind him.

'The victims so far,' he said, pointing at photos of each murdered soul. 'Leech is right – at first this looked like a clean-up campaign – that's what I thought too. The killer was wiping out scumbags. As simple as that.'

'So what made you change your mind, guv?' Friel asked.

'These killings tonight – but there was a note on the coroner's report about the last victim, Ralph Harker, that started me thinking too.' He tapped the photos. 'Two tarts, a drug pusher, a pimp and a small time criminal who happened to be an alky. MO identical in every case. Suspects? None.' He looked around the room at the questioning faces of his colleagues. 'The murderer's physical and psychological profile indicates a very strong man with possibly some kind of deluded moral motive. To clean up the streets.'

'So what's the link with what happened tonight?' Leech asked impatiently.

'Illness,' Grant told him.

'The killer's sick,' Leech persisted.

'Not the *killer*, the *victims*,' said Grant and again he turned to face the photos pinned to the blackboard, tapping each one in turn. 'Tessa Carr was suffering from cervical cancer when she was murdered. Claire Glover had syphilis and non-specific urethritis.' He drew on his cigarette. 'Harvey Dwyer – hepatitis B, septicaemia and arteritis. Simon Costello – emphysema and a bronchial condition so bad that he needed an inhaler. Ralph Harker – cirrhosis of the liver and an advanced form of Bright's disease. It damages the kidneys of heavy drinkers. And now tonight eleven residents of st Angela's Hospice, all terminally ill with cancer. There's your link, there's your motive.'

'So you're saying that these people have been killed because they're *ill*?' Leech queried.

'As far as the perpetrator is concerned, these aren't murders, they're mercy killings,' Grant continued.

His comment was again met by silence.

It was finally broken by Schofield. 'But how would the killer know that the victims were ill?' he asked.

'He wouldn't have to be a doctor to work it out, would he?' Grant snapped. 'Two King's Cross tarts, probably poxed up to the eyes. It's a reasonable assumption, most of them are. A drug user – a fair bet he's shared needles, infected his blood. The killer could have *seen* Simon Costello using an inhaler. An alky living on the streets, a more than fair chance he'd have a fucked-up liver at the very least, and as for the hospice patients . . .' Grant shrugged and allowed the sentence to trail off.

'So what kind of killer are we looking for now?' Friel asked.

'Someone whose family could have suffered from cancer or one of these other diseases possibly,' said Grant.

'So what do we do next?' Leech asked disdainfully. 'Put everyone with the flu, a stomachache or a fucking hangover under guard in case the murderer tries again?'

There were a number of ironic laughs inside the room, hastily silenced by a withering stare from Grant.

'This shifts the entire focus of the investigation,' he said. 'It gives us a whole new set of leads to follow.'

'It puts us right back at square one,' Friel said wearily.

'We hadn't got *past* square one, even before tonight,' Grant said.

'You still don't know if your idea about illness being the motive is right,' Leech said.

'Have you got a better suggestion?' Grant snapped.

Leech hadn't.

'What about the nurse that was killed tonight?' Schofield asked.

'She was in the wrong place at the wrong time,' Grant said. 'Simple as that. The killer was after the hospice residents, not the staff. They were just unlucky.'

'Maybe the killer is ill,' Friel offered. 'Perhaps *he's* got some kind of disease and he wants to take as many with him as possible.'

'Then why take out people who are going to die anyway?' Grant countered. 'No, like I said, this fucking maniac thinks he's doing his victims a favour by ending their suffering.'

'All the victims were dying, were they?' Schofield interjected. 'I mean, they all had terminal illnesses?'

'I think syphilis can be a killer if it isn't treated,' said Grant, looking at the picture of Claire Glover. 'What's your point?'

'So it's reasonably safe to assume he's not going to have a crack at someone with a cold?' Schofield continued.

Grant nodded.

'But there are so many diseases that are *potentially* fatal,' said Schofield. 'Meningitis – pneumonia – angina. How the hell do we know who's a potential victim?'

Grant had no answer. He looked around at the faces of his colleagues in the smoke-filled Incident Room and they all showed the same expression of bewilderment.

'No one is safe until we nail this fucking headcase,' Grant said flatly. 'No one.'

Forty-Six

'Why did you hit her?'

Charlotte Kilbride's words seemed to echo around her large, high-ceilinged office. Suspended there like the motes of dust that twisted and turned gently in the rays of sunlight poking intrusive fingers through the windows.

Andrew Chapman shifted uncomfortably in the antique leather chair, the worn material creaking beneath him. He was in his mid-forties. A tall, imposing-looking man with a round face that looked somewhat out of place atop his thin neck and wiry frame. He pressed his fingertips together then the flat of his hands as if in prayer. Perhaps seeking some divine inspiration in his search for an answer to the question she had asked him.

'I didn't *want* to hit her,' he said finally, hauling himself to his feet and wandering across to the closest window.

He gazed out into Harley Street, his eyes blank, his mind fixed on the recollection.

'She laughed at me,' he continued.

'Why did she laugh?'

'She was just some cheap little tart. Eighteen or nineteen. It annoyed me that she was laughing.'

'You haven't told me *why*?'

'I was in Leeds on business. There was some kind of conference. I had to go on behalf of the bank where I work. One of the barmen at the hotel told me that prostitutes used the hotel to pick up customers. He even pointed a couple out to me.'

'And you picked one up?'

'She was pretty. Brown hair, cut in a bob. She was only about five-two but she had really long, slim legs and she was wearing a short skirt and black high heels – suede ones. And she had this yellow jacket on – I remember it because it was so bright. And underneath she just wore a kind of body suit. A black one.'

'So you took her back to your room?'

He nodded.

'She asked me if I wanted a girlfriend for the night,' said Chapman, grinning crookedly. 'When we got back to my room she told me how much it would cost. Thirty pounds for straight sex with a condom. Fifty without. Twenty pounds for a blow-job with a condom. Forty without. If I wanted her to stay the night then it would be a hundred.'

'And what did you tell her?'

'I laid the magazines out on the bed.'

'The pornographic magazines?'

'They weren't really pornographic. Just *Club International*, *Men Only* and *Mayfair*. They only have pictures of girls in. I told her I wanted to look at the magazines while she masturbated me, that was all. That was when she laughed.'

'Why?'

'She asked why I needed a real woman when I could just have a wank myself. She said I was wasting her time, that she could earn more money with someone else. I offered her ten pounds but she laughed even more. That was when I hit her.'

'Did you hurt her?'

'I only used the back of my hand but she started shouting. She even took a swing at *me*.' He smiled again. 'I threw her out of the room.'

He turned away from the window, looked directly at Charlotte Kilbride. The psychiatrist saw his smile widen but it never touched his eyes.

'That's the trouble,' he continued. 'It's never the same as it is in my magazines or films. Real life is never like that.'

'What makes the women in the magazines and films better, Andrew?'

'They're fantasies, aren't they? They always do what you want them to do. You can control a fantasy. You can't control a real woman the same way.'

'Is that really what you want? To control them?'

He turned away, back to the window, as if his answer lay somewhere out there in the street.

'I just want to look at them. When I look at sex magazines or watch porno videos, it's like I own those women. They're mine. They do exactly what I tell them to do. They're all there for *me*.'

'How many magazines do you buy a month?'

'Six or seven, sometimes more.'

'And videos?'

'Three or four at a time.'

'Where from?'

'A shop in Soho. Always the same shop.'

'And you've never thought of mentioning them to your wife? Asking if she'd like to look at the magazines too, or watch the videos with you?'

'She wouldn't do that,' he snapped. 'She thinks they're disgusting. She'd think *I* was disgusting if she knew.'

'And would that bother you, if she thought that?'

'Of course it would. I've got a family too.'

'A boy and a girl, isn't it?'

He nodded.

'Perhaps my wife is right,' he murmured. 'Perhaps it *is* disgusting. But I can't do without it.'

'You will, in time,' Charlotte said confidently.

'I'm not so sure,' Chapman said. 'I've been coming here over a year now, spending eighty pounds an hour to tell you that I buy sex magazines and videos like other men buy cigarettes. And for what?'

'So I can help you. Why did you come in the first place?'

'I wanted to stop. I wanted to stop feeling so pathetic.' There was a note of anger in his voice. 'So *reliant* on these magazines and videos. It's like a day doesn't pass when I don't have to look at one. I sneak them into my office in the bank and look at them when everyone else is out at lunch. I lock my office door and I turn those pages and I masturbate while I imagine what I'd be doing to the girls on those pages. And I can't stop looking and then when I've come I feel angry. With *them* and with myself. *I* feel disgusted. That was why I hit that prostitute in Leeds. She made me feel disgusted with myself.' He began pacing back and forth across the room.

Charlotte watched his steady progress, smoothing her skirt, brushing fluff from it.

'You've been with other prostitutes, Andrew,' she said. 'Did you feel the same with them?'

'The others did as I told them but I still don't like them. I caught VD from one. Filthy slag. Disease-ridden bitch. She told me she was clean. I shouldn't have trusted her.'

'Did your wife find out about the venereal disease?'

'No, I took the antibiotics the doctor gave me and it cleared up quite quickly.'

'What do you think your wife would have done if she'd found out? Do you think she'd have left you?'

'Perhaps. Do you blame her? I could have brought that infection home, given it to *her*.'

'What about your magazines? Your videos? You take those home, don't you?'

'I hide them.'

'What do you think your wife would say if she found them?'

He shook his head.

'What would *you* do if she found them?'

Chapman continued to gaze out of the window, his eyes blank.

'She mustn't know, just as she mustn't know that I come here for help,' he said quietly. 'I'd die if she ever found out. I'd be humiliated – but perhaps that's what I deserve.'

'You shouldn't hate yourself, Andrew. At least you're looking for help. You've come a long way. You should give yourself some credit for that.'

'And how much longer is it going to take? How much longer before I'm *cured*.' There was scorn in his voice. 'Before I don't have to look at those magazines and those videos. Before I don't have to visit disease-ridden whores any longer? How long before I can look myself in the eye without feeling ashamed. Disgusted? You tell me. You're the expert.'

'If you want to help yourself then you will. I'm here to aid that process. It's like healing, Andrew. Like a pain that has to be soothed. It's just that I can't give you a bottle of pills to cure you. In the end you have to cure yourself. It's the same for all my clients, irrespective of what they feel is their problem.'

'Do you know what it's like to feel self-hatred?' he demanded. 'To feel repulsed by your own feelings. No, you don't and you never will. You should be grateful for that.'

She glanced surreptitiously at the clock on her desk. His time was nearly up.

'I know,' said Chapman, as if reading her mind. 'Time to make another appointment. Time to leave. Time for the next eighty-pound-an-hour meal ticket to come in.'

'It isn't like that, Andrew, and you know it,' she said serenely.

He turned back to the window and continued to stare out, his face set in hard lines.

Charlotte Kilbride watched him and noticed that his fists were clenched at his sides, the knuckles white. She knew there was so much rage inside him, so much fury. What bothered her was where that rage would manifest itself. And against whom. She wondered if it already had. Such self-loathing would require an explosive outlet.

She looked again at his clenched fists.

Forty-Seven

Amy glanced at her watch then at the clock on the wall of the studio. They both told her it was almost midnight.

She stifled a yawn as she listened to the latest caller droning on, nodding her head as he ranted and raved about how wrong it was that women had abortions so easily.

'So you'd allow hundreds, even thousands, more unwanted children into the world every year, would you, Mark?' Amy asked. 'You'd take away a woman's right to choose whether or not her life is wrecked by an unwanted child, would you? You'd play God if you had the chance?'

He was about to say something when Amy flicked a switch.

'You're history.'

There was a flatness, an indifference in her voice which she was all too aware of but also felt helpless to disguise.

She wasn't surprised when she looked up towards the production-booth window to see Osborne standing there first pointing at her then shrugging his shoulders. The producer looked a little angry and, Amy reasoned, he had a right to be.

But he doesn't know what's on your mind, does he?

She lit up another cigarette and took another call, listening with the same undisguised uninterest.

She had a pen on the desk in front of her and, as Karen of Tower Hamlets continued the debate about abortion, Amy began doodling. She wrote the word:

BULLETS

Then, beneath it:

GUN

Ask him about the bullets when you get home tonight.
She exhaled deeply.
If he's there.
'I had two abortions when I was at school,' said Karen from Tower Hamlets. 'I mean, if I'd had those kids who would have looked after them?'
'Have you got kids now, Carol?' Amy asked.
'Karen.'
'Sorry?'
'Karen. My name is Karen, not Carol.'
'Excuse me.'
Amy checked on the screen beside her.
Come on, get a grip.
She looked up to the production-booth window again and saw Osborne shaking his head irritably.
'I've got two kids,' Karen continued. 'But I had them when I wanted them. I don't think it's right for people to judge women who have abortions. Especially men.'
'I agree with you.'
'I mean, I know some kids use it like bloody contraception, don't they? They get pregnant and nip off down the clinic for an abortion. I don't agree with that but they should at least have the choice.'
'Life's all about choice. I agree with you, Karen. Thanks for your call.' Amy pressed a button then leaned closer to the microphone. 'We're taking a short break for the news now but join us again in fifteen minutes for more scintillating chat and stunning insights into the modern world with me, Amy Watson, your friendly neighbourhood insomniac. I hope there are plenty more of you out there.'
She pushed the microphone away and got to her feet, dropping her headset on to the console then heading for the studio door.
As she emerged into the corridor, Osborne stuck his head out of the production room and gestured to her.

'Have you got a minute, Amy?' he asked briskly.

She joined him in the control room.

'What the hell is wrong with you tonight?'

'What are you talking about?'

'You know bloody well what I'm talking about. This is a talk show, right? Well, you're not talking. The poor sods who are ringing in might as well be talking to a brick wall. Show some bloody interest, Amy. It's unprofessional.'

'It's not *that* bad.'

'It *is* that bad. If I was listening as a punter I wouldn't be wasting my time ringing in to some bitch who's not interested in what I've got to say.'

She regarded him balefully for a moment.

'Bitch, eh?' she said sarcastically. 'So, it's worse than unprofessional, is it? I'm a bitch too.'

'Just show some interest, will you,' he snapped.

'Bitch,' she repeated.

'You might be pissed off but there's no need to let the world know about it. What is it, time of the month?'

'Oh, fuck you, Mike.'

'Not for more than a year,' he said scathingly.

'Then get over it,' she told him. 'I'm going to the toilet.'

'That's where this fucking show's going if you don't get a grip.'

She barely heard the end of the sentence as she stepped back out into the corridor and headed for the Ladies.

What was she supposed to do? Tell him what was *really* on her mind? *Sorry if I'm not quite my usual perky self, Mike, but the guy I'm sleeping with happens to keep bullets in his medicine cabinet. Okay?*

She pushed the door of the Ladies and walked in.

Jo Parker turned from one of the sinks and faced her, and immediately Amy saw how wan her friend looked. The younger woman swiftly looked away as Amy headed for one of the cubicles.

'Couldn't you stand it either?' Amy said, shutting the door and seating herself.

'Stand what?' Jo asked, wiping her face.

'Osborne's moaning about the show. About me.'

Jo didn't answer.

'Are you all right, Jo?'

Still no answer.

Then Amy heard the unmistakable sound of crying. Soft, almost childlike weeping.

She dressed hastily and hurried out to find Jo wiping tears from her eyes.

Amy embraced her and felt Jo return the gesture.

'What is it?' Amy asked.

Jo shook her head. 'I'm sorry,' she said tearfully. 'I didn't want to say anything.' She stepped back, wiping her eyes with her fingers. 'I didn't want to bother you with my bloody problems.'

'What are friends for?' Amy said, smiling. 'You know I'd bother you with *mine*.' She attempted a grin but it was wasted, Jo was too distraught.

'It's my brother,' Jo began. 'He's been living with me for the last few weeks. I think he's in trouble.'

'What makes you think that?'

'I found a bottle of pills and some phone numbers in his clothes the other day.'

'What kind of pills?'

'Well, there weren't any in the bottle, it looked as if he was just using the bottle to store them.'

'But how do you know that, Jo?'

'Because I know *him*. He's used drugs before.'

'And you think he's using now?'

'Pills, needles. I don't know what he's on. He hardly ever comes back to my flat any more. He's out all the time. He stays out all night most nights, never tells me where he is or who he's with.'

'It might be innocent, Jo, you—'

'Not *him*. He's always got so much money too and he isn't working. How else could he be getting money, Amy, if he's not dealing?'

More tears began to flow.

Amy hugged her again.

'You don't know for sure, Jo,' she said softly. 'You might be jumping to conclusions.'

Just like you don't know for sure the significance of the bullets?

'I'm frightened of what he might do,' Jo continued. 'Or of what might happen to him. I don't want to lose another brother.'

Amy held her friend close.

'What the hell is he mixed up in?' Jo whimpered. 'I've got to know.'

Forty-Eight

12.31 a.m.

Amy sipped at her coffee and connected a caller named Roy.

'Where are you calling from, Roy?' she asked, noting that there was no location for the source of the call.

Roy. Why did that name ring a bell?

Silence.

'I asked where—'

'I told you I'd call again after the next murder.'

Amy felt a shiver run up her spine, icy fingers tickling the nape of her neck.

'Where are you calling from, Roy?' she persisted.

'You won't be able to trace this call – I won't be on long enough. You need twenty-nine seconds for a trace, don't you?'

'Very clever, Roy,' she said sardonically. 'What's your point?'

'I want to talk about death,' the voice said, and again Amy felt the skin of her neck puckering.

'Whose?'

'No one specific. Not yet.'

'Did you mean those people who were killed in that fire yesterday?'

Silence.

'Roy?'

'Time's up. I'll call you back.'

And he was gone.

Before Amy had time to react, his name flashed brightly on the screen again and she looked up to see both Osborne *and* Jo looking in at her.

She connected him again.

'Welcome back, Roy,' she said. 'Are you going to do this all night? Talk for twenty-odd seconds then hang up?'

'I'm on a mobile now. You can trace the signal but not pin down the location.'

'What makes you think I really *care* where you are, Roy?' Amy said defiantly.

'Because you care what I've got to say about these killings.'

'They're nothing to do with me and, for all I know, they're probably nothing to do with *you* either. You might be one of these nutters who gets his rocks off confessing to murders he hasn't committed. You just want to sound important, Roy.'

She puffed on her cigarette.

'Twelve bodies recovered from that fire,' he snapped.

'You could have read that in the newspapers. Am I supposed to be impressed?'

'Two prostitutes, a pimp, a drug pusher and a tramp before them,' he continued.

'*That* was in the papers too. Tell me something I don't know.'

'There'll be more.'

Icy fingers.

'That's a reasonable assumption – hardly privileged information though.'

Tracing chilly patterns over her neck and shoulders.

'One of them could be *you.*'

'Oh, yes, you disagreed with my work in the past, didn't you, Roy?'

'It wasn't work. Work is done by honest, clean-living people. You sold yourself. Sold your body. Sold your morality.'

'So, you're going to kill me because I've got no morals, Roy? That means you'll have to kill half the population of the country too.'

A long silence.

'Why were the people killed last night, Roy?' Amy continued. 'What kind of moral code had *they* broken? They were sick people, that was all.'

'Then they were released.'

'From what?'

'From suffering. From this world and its corruption – and it's been made corrupt by people like *you*. People with no sense of decency – no standards or concepts of morality.'

'You should have been a politician, Roy,' she said with a sneer. 'You like the sound of your own voice.'

'You don't like it because you know I'm telling the truth,' he countered angrily.

'I know you're a sad, self-important little man who thinks he's being profound but you're not. You should be pitied. But not by me, Roy. I just find you irritating. You're history.'

She severed the connection.

As she glanced across she could still see his name flashing madly on the screen but she went to the call below it.

'Dennis from Golders Green,' Amy said. 'You're not going to threaten to kill me, are you?'

'I couldn't believe what that bloke was going on about,' said Dennis from Golders Green. 'You should sue him for threatening behaviour.'

'Roy is too insignificant to waste time on, Dennis,' she said, still watching his name flashing on the screen. 'What point would *you* like to make?'

'Well, it is to do with these murders.'

Roy's name continued to flash.

'I wonder if they might be racially motivated,' Dennis mused.

'In what way, Dennis?'

'Well, all the victims have been white, haven't they?'

'So, what's your point?'

'Well, the blacks are always going on about how everyone is against them and that and, well, it might be a black killer trying to get back at us whites.'

'An interesting theory, Dennis. Not much evidence to back it up though.'

'Well, I mean, most blacks have got a chip on their

shoulder, haven't they? I mean, if they don't like the way they're treated then they should go home. Same with the bloody Pakis. I mean, they come over here by the boat-load and—'

'Have we got your location right, Dennis?' Amy interrupted. 'You are calling from Golders Green, aren't you?'

'Yes, why?'

'I thought you might be calling from Auschwitz. I think your kind of bigoted viewpoint belongs there.'

'I say these blacks are too powerful . . . they—'

'You're history, Dennis,' she hissed, dismissing him. 'Get back to your copy of *Mein Kampf*.'

On the screen the name ROY was still flashing.

Amy looked towards the control booth but there was no sign of Osborne.

She connected Roy again.

'Go ahead, Roy,' she said. 'Give us more pearls of wisdom.'

This time she saw Osborne standing there with his arms outstretched and his head back in an attitude of resignation.

Silence on the line.

'Come on then,' she chided. 'Gone shy on me?'

'You're dead, bitch,' he hissed. 'DEAD!'

The final word was roared with such ferocity that Amy was forced to slip one earpiece off.

The line went dead.

She watched as his name dimmed and faded on the screen. Empty screen. Dead line.

That icy caress moved once more over the back of her neck.

When she reached for her coffee her hand was shaking.

'Are you sure you're going to be okay?' asked Amy, placing one hand on Jo's shoulder.

The younger woman reached up and touched the hand softly.

'I'm not the one who was threatened,' Jo said. Then she nodded. 'Yeah, I'll be fine.'

'You can come and stay with me for a couple of nights if you like,' Amy persisted.

'Thanks for offering but I'm going to be thinking about Billy wherever I am and, who knows, he might even come home. I want to be there when he does.'

'It might not be what you think, Jo.'

The younger woman could only shrug as she headed for the waiting taxi.

'If you need me, call me. It doesn't matter what time,' Amy said, watching as her friend climbed into the cab.

The driver guided it out into traffic and it pulled away.

Amy pulled the collar of her jacket up, finished her cigarette, then, before she climbed into her own taxi, she glanced around, squinting in the gloom.

If there was anyone skulking around in the shadows she couldn't see them.

Skulking in the shadows? Imagination running away with you?

Who would be?

Roy's words echoed inside her head. *'You're dead, bitch.'*

The wind was getting stronger, it whipped her hair around her face as she stooped to get into the cab.

'You're dead, bitch.'

Forty-Nine

Despite the soothing warmth of the water she was lying in, Amy was irritated that the drowsiness that precedes sleep as yet eluded her. She rarely felt tired after a show, never felt like coming straight in and flopping exhausted on the bed. The adrenaline was always coursing too strongly through her veins. Particularly if it had been a good show and the callers had been challenging.

But tonight she felt that her unwanted alertness, even at such a godforsaken hour (it was approaching 2.35 a.m.) was due more to the thoughts tumbling through her mind than to any stimulating conversation she'd had with those who called her show.

Amy drew the flannel through the bathwater, wrung it out, then laid the cloth across her face. She wished that cutting out the light would also cut out her thoughts, and she cursed the fact that so much seemed to be tormenting her at present. Fragments of sentences. Of ideas. Of suspicions. They all whirled around inside her head, unwanted but so difficult to remove. Like stains on her consciousness.

Webber.

The bullets.

She had glanced at his door as she'd entered the building, thought about knocking, then decided against it.

Roy (if that was his real name) and his rantings. His threats against her. *Death* threats. Jo Parker's distress and fear for her brother. The entire twisted, unfathomable mess lodged in her mind like a splinter in soft skin.

She pulled the flannel from her face, exhaled deeply and raised one leg, washing it gently.

Webber. *What was he doing now?* Was *he* thinking about *her*? *What* was he thinking? Probably thinking about his dead daughter.

Amy remembered the soul-wrenching grief he'd shown

at the child's graveside, and her own feeling of help-lessness to ease his suffering at such a terrible loss. His gratitude to her for helping him overcome the pain, even though they both knew it would take a long time, perhaps longer than either of them could imagine.

Then she thought of the bullets. Bullets equal gun. It was a simple equation. Gun equals violence and possible death. Was that equation quite so cut and dried? She thought not.

Was Webber a killer? Having a gun doesn't make him a killer? Why would he want a gun?

'You don't even know he's got one,' she said aloud, answering her own unspoken question.

She washed the other leg.

And Roy? Was he a killer? *The* killer? A psychiatrist would call his maniacal rantings and threats a craving for attention. Threats to be treated with contempt or scorn? Or to be received with trepidation and fear?

'*You're dead, bitch.*'

Perhaps she should tell Webber about Roy's threats. So he can use his gun on him?

Amy shook her head, irritated with herself, with her own train of thought.

She soaped her hands and washed first one breast then the other. She sucked in a deep breath and decided she wouldn't mention the threats to Webber when . . .

She felt it to the right of her left nipple. Beneath the soft flesh she felt the lump.

Amy froze, her hand on her breast, her fingers probing the lump. The lump in her breast. The words screamed inside her head. The lump in her breast.

She probed it with shaking fingers, recoiling from the pain as she pushed too hard.

'Oh God,' she whispered, her throat already dry.

She looked down, trying to inspect the lump more fully.

The lump.

She was amazed at how quickly the panic spread through her, like a forest fire through dry timber it engulfed her, the word and its connotations hammering inside her brain like a jack-hammer.

The lump in her breast.

As she felt around it as calmly as she could, she realised it was about the width of a fifty-pence piece. The circumference was more difficult to gauge.

But what the hell did size matter? The size of a pea, the size of a grapefruit. She had a swelling there. A collection of cells that had formed into a firm and painful knot beneath the smooth flesh. Cells that could, even as she touched and probed, be cannabalising others. Growing.

The word seared through her consciousness. *Growth.*

Others followed it. Tumour. Cancer. Breast cancer. This was how it started, wasn't it?

She checked her nipple for any signs of discharge, any blood.

There was none. At least none she'd noticed. Had she just failed to see it in the past few days? How long had it been there?

Amy felt faint.

She hauled herself up and out of the bath, pulling her robe on, dripping water on the tiled floor. For a second she thought she was going to be sick but the sensation passed and she realised that the feelings were caused not by the (*The what? The growth? The tumour? The lump?*) knot of cells in her breast but by her own panic.

She sucked in several deep breaths, trying to calm herself, fighting to find reason in this madness of fear. Many women, most women, found lumps in their breasts, the vast majority of which were benign, harmless. They gave no pain, they . . .

But this lump hurts.

She caught sight of her face in the mirror as she passed it, her features strained, the colour gone from her cheeks.

She hurried into the sitting room and poured herself a brandy but, as she raised it to her lips she felt sick again. Sick with worry. She couldn't drink it.

Amy reached for the phone. She needed to tell someone.

Needed to hear some words of comfort. She was trapped alone in her flat with this lump in her breast and her thoughts of breast cancer and mastectomy and death and she felt as alone and frightened as she'd ever felt in her life.

She dialled Webber's number and waited. And waited. *Be there for me*. And waited. No answer.

She jabbed out the digits of Jo Parker's number.

Ringing.

Please, Jo, pick it up. Let me hear a voice.

No answer.

She *was* alone.

Amy put the phone back gently, her panic now receding slowly, her heart rate slowing somewhat.

She sat on her sofa, head back, gazing blankly at the ceiling. The voice of reason tried to batter its way through the wall of fear and riotous imagination.

'Call the doctor in the morning,' she said aloud, hoping that the sound of her own voice would drive away the terror.

She could feel herself becoming more calm and she sucked in several more deep breaths to speed the process. Her heart had stopped battering against her ribs.

She closed her eyes for a moment, almost meditatively.

That's it. Calm down.

Benign. She clung to the word like a drowning man clings to a lifebelt. Benign.

She used it to push away that other word. That word that sounded so terrifying in *any* context.

Malignant.

She fought to force that word from her mind but the battle was a mighty one and the malignancy of her fear clung as surely as the possible malignancy of that lump in her breast.

She ran a hand through her hair. See the doctor tomorrow. He'll tell you it's benign.

She nodded to herself, the initial panic over.

It was then that she started to cry.

Fifty

The limousine waited outside number six, Drayson Mews, its engine idling, its tinted windows occasionally reflecting some of the many faces outside the three-storey Georgian house.

The small thoroughfare, just two minutes from Kensington High Street, was normally quiet, but this particular morning there were up to a dozen journalists and at least three film crews arrayed along its length. Many of those present were looking around at the other dwellings around number six, and more than one comment was made about being able to 'smell the money'.

From some of the windows of other houses in Drayson Mews, faces appeared and looked out almost disdainfully at the clutch of media thronging around the front door of number six. Some residents objected to the intrusion, others accepted that this kind of invasion would happen periodically when they shared a street with the Home Secretary. One or two even welcomed the cameras and the jabbering horde. It gave them a feeling of importance themselves, as if living in the same street as a member of the cabinet somehow gave them a vicarious importance and re-emphasised the social heights to which they had risen.

David Albury had already seen the newsmen and women outside his house and he stood watching them from behind his curtains for a moment, before finally heading towards the front door.

'Who *are* those people, Daddy?' asked his daughter, Harriet, also looking out at the gathering throng. She was twelve years old, a tall, gangling child who looked, with her pinched features and large eyes, more like her mother than Albury.

When she spoke it was with a voice shaped at expensive

kindergarten, honed at Roedean and polished at St Paul's. But if she had her mother's looks, she had her father's manner. A slightly superior air that seemed to sit quite comfortably on such young shoulders.

'Why are they outside our house?' Harriet continued.

'They want to speak to your father,' said Louise Albury, emerging from the kitchen clutching a cup of tea. 'He's very popular at the moment.'

'Some of them look rather common,' Harriet observed. 'One of them is smoking.' She wrinkled her nose.

'Your father will handle them, won't you?' Louise said, turning her attention to her husband.

If Albury caught the edge in her tone he didn't react to it. Instead he headed for the front door, waited a second, then pulled it open.

Immediately, the reporters outside surged forward calling out questions, and a barrage of cameras went off.

'Mr Albury, over here.'

'What kind of impact do you think this Bill will have?'

'Are you glad that the legislation has been passed?'

Albury raised a hand, as if to force back the throng then he stood silently until the chorus of voices died away.

'I'll answer your questions,' he finally said. 'But keep them brief, I'm due at the House of Commons within the hour.'

More cameras snapped.

Microphones and mini-tape recorders were pushed closer to him. The cyclopean eye of a television camera fixed him in its unblinking stare.

'What exactly do you expect this Bill to achieve, Mr Albury?' asked one of the journalists.

'It will make it more difficult for children and other impressionable people to view offensive material,' Albury replied.

'What do you class as offensive?'

'That's a very difficult question to answer,' Albury said almost dismissively. 'I think most right-thinking people will be able to discern what gives offence and what doesn't.'

'Is it aimed specifically at violence in films and video?' asked another reporter.

'The measures included in the Bill also take into account the gratuitous amount of sex seen in films and on television. It is a very wide-reaching piece of legislation.'

'Someone said that the censorship laws were strict enough already. Why strengthen them?'

'You only have to look at society to realise that those laws were *not* sufficient,' Albury countered. 'The increase in violence and sex in films and on video has led to a steady decline of values in day-to-day life. Moral codes have been eroded by this particular branch of the media.'

'How do you respond to the suggestion that the measures proposed in your Bill aren't just strict but Draconian?' a television reporter challenged.

'Society has to be protected against this kind of thing. People have to be protected, for their own good,' Albury said condescendingly.

'What about freedom of expression? Doesn't that extend to film makers or artists of any kind?' someone else asked.

'This Bill doesn't attempt to stifle creativity,' Albury chided. 'It will ensure that the creativity of which you speak is kept within guidelines – moral guidelines.'

'Is it true that it extends to the closure of stripclubs and sex shops?' another reporter enquired.

'There is provision within the Bill for certain establishments to be closed if they are not working within the parameters outlined *in* the Bill,' Albury explained.

'Aren't you afraid you'll force the video industry underground?'

'Film makers, video distributors, publishers or anyone else affected by the Bill would have no need to fear it if they were making and producing suitable products for public viewing or consumption,' Albury stated.

'By that, do you mean films and books that *you* approve of?' asked the same journalist.

'I speak for a huge majority of people in this country who are sick and tired of being subjected to the filth served up to them by film makers, video distributors and other so-called artists,' Albury said with an air of superciliousness.

'Isn't this just a good vote-catcher with an election coming up? That's why it's being rushed through Parliament, isn't it?'

Albury ignored the question.

'For too long now this country has lost sight of family values.' He began to sound sanctimonious. 'It was my wish that this Bill would help to restore those values.'

'So, it's nothing to do with the election coming up, then?' the reporter persisted.

'Is it true that the Bill includes provision for the banning of certain films and videos that have already been released?' somebody called from the back of the throng.

'A number of films and videos will be withdrawn from circulation – yes,' Albury answered. 'Once again, in the public interest.'

'What's the point if these films have already been viewed?' the same journalist persisted.

'No more questions,' said Albury, raising both hands.

'When will the Bill become law?'

Albury merely waved, turned and headed back inside his house.

He emerged a moment later carrying a briefcase, with his wife and daughter on either side of him. They were both smiling fixedly as the cameras snapped away.

Albury bent and kissed his daughter on the cheek, then he moved through the throng of press towards the limousine.

The driver sprang from behind the wheel and opened the back door, standing between Albury and the press.

He slammed the door, the tinted windows making it impossible to see inside the vehicle.

Albury relaxed back into the leather seat and exhaled deeply. Sitting across from him, smiling, was Anita Bishop.

Albury returned the smile as the car pulled away.

Fifty-One

'I thought *I* was supposed to be the quiet one.'

Amy looked up from her plate, momentarily disorientated by the words. She saw Webber gazing at her, a slight smile on his lips.

Apart from a man who sat alone reading the *Telegraph*, they were the only ones in the small restaurant off Portland Street. Most of the other lunchtime customers had long since left. Staff had been clearing tables for about twenty minutes now and those that weren't busy were standing around the till or in the kitchen chatting, content to let their last patrons finish their meals in peace.

Outside, traffic rushed past in a noisy haze but inside the restaurant and particularly inside Amy's head the world seemed to be barely moving. It was as if time had been slowed, as if everything moved in slow motion. Including her own thoughts. Her world had narrowed to the tiny space she and Webber now occupied at the corner table.

And to the lump in her breast.

A cone seemed to have descended around them, shutting out the rest of the world, focusing their own problems in that one small area.

'Sorry, Jake,' she said, trying to shake herself from her thoughts.

'It's okay, I should be used to it by now, you've been like it all through lunch,' he said, still smiling. 'What's wrong?'

'Nothing,' she lied.

Apart from the fact I found a box of bullets in your medicine cabinet and, last night, while you were out at 3.30 in the morning, I discovered a lump in my breast, everything is just fine. Honest.

Webber raised an eyebrow.

'You know that expression about not bullshitting a bullshitter?' he said.

She nodded.

'I'm smelling bullshit. What's on your mind?'

She sipped her drink, watching the slice of lemon bobbing up and down in the Bacardi when she prodded it with the cocktail stick.

'If you want me to mind my own business I will,' he continued. 'If you don't want to talk about it, that's fine. I just wondered if I could help.'

'I wanted to talk last night, Jake,' she said a little too vehemently. 'But you weren't there.'

He eyed her warily.

'Just like you're not there most nights,' Amy continued. 'You're out somewhere in the small hours doing Christ knows what.'

'I thought this was about *you* not *me*,' he said evenly.

'It is,' she snapped.

'So tell me. What did you want to talk to me about last night that you can't talk to me about today.'

'It doesn't matter.'

'It matters to me,' he said through clenched teeth and she saw how his eyes blazed as he looked at her.

'I found a lump in my breast,' she blurted out.

His features softened and he reached across the table to touch her arm.

'Why didn't you tell me earlier?'

'It's taken me this long to tell you *now*.'

'And you called me last night?'

She nodded. 'I called you then I called Jo.'

He looked vague.

'Jo Parker, a friend of mine,' Amy elaborated.

'And what did *she* say?'

'She wasn't there either. I just wanted to talk to someone, Jake, to *tell* someone. It's not the sort of information you want to keep to yourself, believe me.'

He squeezed her hand.

'I wanted someone to talk to *me*, to tell me that every-thing was going to be all right,' she continued.

'I'm sorry I wasn't there when you needed me.'

'You weren't to know.'

'Listen to me, whatever I can do to help, just tell me.'

'I don't know *who* can help.'

'How bad is the lump? How big?'

'Big enough.'

'Have you seen a doctor yet?'

'I only found out last night.'

'You should have been at a doctor's first thing this morning.'

'I'm frightened. I know I've got to go, I know that's the only way they can help me, but I'm scared shitless, Jake. Do you blame me?'

He shook his head.

'You didn't say anything the night we spent together,' he observed. '*I* never felt anything.'

'Perhaps there was nothing there then. Perhaps this is some kind of quick-growing cancer that—'

'You don't know it's cancer – don't say that,' Webber said, cutting her short.

'What else could it be, doctor?' There was scorn in her voice.

He fixed her in an unblinking gaze, surprised at the anger in her voice.

'Don't you think I haven't considered every possible alternative?' she said challengingly. 'I spent all of last night doing that, Jake. It's called clutching at straws. Trying to talk myself into believing that whatever it is it isn't cancer. The trouble is, every time I come back to the same conclusion – breast cancer.'

'Listen, Amy. You make a fucking appointment and quick, got it? And no matter where or what time, I'll come with you.'

'Jake, you don't have to.'

'I know that. I *want* to. I want to help you the way

you helped me. Without you I'd never have gone to see Samantha's grave. I owe you for that at least.'

'Don't feel you have to repay me, Jake.'

'I care about you. I care about what happens to you. This isn't a fucking favour, Amy. Don't shut me out. Not now.'

He squeezed her hand more tightly and she saw the concern in his eyes.

She reached across the table and gently ran a finger over his stubbled cheek.

'Thank you,' she said, her voice almost a whisper.

'Make the appointment.'

Fifty-Two

Police Commissioner Alex Hayward sat back in his seat, fingertips pressed together meditatively. Every now and then he would nod sagely but, not once during the twenty minutes that David Grant had been in his spacious office, had the older man's face betrayed even a flicker of emotion.

For such a small man, Hayward had a commanding presence that seemed to inspire a combination of respect and foreboding amongst his bigger built subordinates. Few people had ever witnessed him losing his famed temper but those who had spoke of such an incident in almost reverential tones. And yet, Hayward was an approachable and personable character, as likely to be found in a patrol car with a couple of uniformed officers as at a high-level meeting. He usually travelled with a mobile unit once a month. He was fond of telling his companions that it kept him in touch with the streets. It also put the fear of Christ into which ever unit he picked to act as his escort that particular day. Even so, the men seemed to appreciate that someone in so lofty a position as the Commissioner should still be interested in the day-to-day workings of uniformed men. It didn't lessen their trepidation however.

Hayward had said little since Grant entered the office. Pleasantries had been exchanged, Grant had been congratulated on his promotion, quizzed on the nature of the current investigation and even asked about his family. He'd lied and said that everything was fine at home.

The family was another pet concern of the Commissioner. He preferred family men working close to him. He felt that the family gave a man stability and a sense of responsibility. These were things that his family had done for him; he felt it only natural the same should apply to his subordinates.

He had also asked Grant if he had any kids or *planned* to have any.

Grant lied about that too.

Grant sipped the tea he'd been offered upon entering the office, winced when he found it had gone cold and replaced the cup.

He was finished. He had said what he had to say.

Now he waited.

Hayward remained in that fixed position, fingertips pressed together, eyes looking through, not past, Grant.

Grant shifted uncomfortably in his seat, wondering for a moment if the little Scot had even heard what he'd said.

Finally Hayward spoke. 'No,' he said bluntly. 'I'm afraid I will have to deny your request for extra men on your investigation.'

'But, sir, the men I've got aren't enough.'

'Every officer on the force says that, Grant. I can't spare any more men.'

'But the investigation has taken a completely different turn since the burning of that hospice. The men I've got can't cover the ground quickly enough. They—'

'How many are you using?'

'Sixty, sir. In plainclothes, undercover and uniform.'

'And you can't crack a case with sixty men, Grant?'

'I'm trying my best, sir.'

'Then try harder.'

'With all due respect, sir, you tell me a more important investigation that's going on at the moment,' said Grant with barely suppressed anger. 'The press are having a pop at us every day for not getting results, the media are crucifying us.'

'Not *us*, Grant,' the Scot corrected him. 'They're crucifying *you*.'

The younger man glared at his superior.

'Do you know one of the things I don't like about my job, Grant?'

Grant shook his head.

'I have to delegate,' the Scot continued. 'I have to let other people do what I would rather be doing myself. That means I have to trust other people and I hate trusting anyone. Now I'm having to trust *you* to wrap up this investigation and I have faith in you to do that. So don't let me down.'

'So, no more men, sir?'

'You're lucky I'm not taking them away from you, never mind assigning you more.'

Grant looked vague.

'You asked me if there was a more important investigation going on at the moment,' Hayward said with a touch of weariness in his tone. 'I don't think there is. Unfortunately, the Home Secretary doesn't agree.'

'I'm not with you, sir.'

'Starting this morning – and this comes direct from the horse's mouth, or arse depending on your views – all available officers are to be used to implement the Albury Bill. The fax came through this morning just before *you* arrived.'

'What the hell has that got to do with *my* investigation, sir?'

'It means, Grant, that any spare men are going to be running around bloody stripclubs, clip joints, video shops, book stores and anywhere else our esteemed Home Secretary tells me to send them. Just so this Bill of his can be *seen* to be having some sort of effect.'

'And he thinks that takes precedence over a murder investigation?'

'It wouldn't matter to Albury if someone had shot the Queen and stabbed the Queen Mum. The only thing he cares about is this Bill of his. That's why you can't have the men you request. You take your orders from me. I take mine from him. Neither of us has any choice in this, Grant. We've both just got to get on with it. Like it or not.'

A heavy silence descended, finally broken by the Commissioner. 'Was there anything else?' he asked, glancing at his watch.

'No, sir,' said Grant, getting to his feet. 'Thanks for your time.'

He turned to go.

'Grant.'

Grant turned.

'I know it's not much consolation,' Hayward told him, 'but if it was down to me, you'd have the men you need.'

'Thank you, sir.'

'You get this bastard,' the Scot said. 'And you do it as quick as you can. If you don't get him, when the press crucify *you*, they might just decide to nail *me* up beside you. Understand?'

Fifty-Three

Amy Watson struck the punchbag with her right fist.

Bang.

The shock travelled up her arm but it felt good, she enjoyed the feeling of strength.

She struck again. And again.

Concentrate.

She took two steps back and swung her foot at the heavy bag.

Force every other thought from your mind.

The kicks she drove into it were of thunderous power and she could see the muscles in her thigh bulging with each impact. She shouted as she kicked, sweat pouring down her face, flying in salty droplets from her soaking hair. The sound echoed around the gym but was lost beneath the sound of pumping music.

It was later in the day than normal for her workout and more people were present than usual. One or two of them cast quizzical glances in her direction as she laid into the punchbag with renewed ferocity.

Force every other thought from your mind.

She kicked.

Every one.

And kicked again. Spun round, changed legs, kicked again. It was done now. There was no going back.

She gritted her teeth with the effort of working herself even harder.

Do it. Do it.

She sucked in another deep breath. The insteps of her feet were red from the continual pounding on the bag but she felt no pain. The adrenaline rush that such strenuous exercise brought nullified everything else.

Concentrate. Her mind seemed to be emptying.

Force the fear out.

She kept kicking. Another ten minutes, then she'd shower, drive home and prepare herself for the night's show.

Amy wiped sweat from her eyes and prowled around the swinging bag like a cat stalking a bird, waiting to strike.

She unfolded a slender leg and kicked with devastating power. The appointment with the doctor had been made. She had come to the gym directly after making it.

Amy kicked again. Shouted in anger. She would be at his surgery at ten the following morning.

'Rack them up again.'

David Grant watched as the black ball disappeared. He chalked the end of his cue as Lawrenson retrieved the pool balls and slotted them into position.

At a table close by two youths in their late teens sat watching, one of them sipping at a pint as if it was his first. He was watching the two policemen intently, occasionally glancing at his watch. Sometimes he would lean across and speak to his companion, shielding his mouth with the back of his hand as if he feared that Grant was some kind of lip-reader.

Grant saw the furtive whisperings and looked at the taller of the two youths dismissively.

All around them, the pub was a mass of noise. Voices and the non-stop cacophony of sound expelled by a number of fruit machines and electronic games and the steady soundtrack provided by the juke-box. The air was thick with cigarette smoke.

Grant watched as Lawrenson slammed the cue ball into the triangle and sent balls spinning in all directions.

'So, that's the story,' he said, bending down to take his own shot. 'We get no help and that's official.'

He dropped a colour.

The tall youth whispered something to his companion.

'We have to find this fucking maniac with the men we've got now,' Grant continued.

He potted another colour.

'I'm beginning to think we're pissing in the wind, guv,' Lawrenson told him. 'No leads. No suspects. Just seventeen corpses.'

'But we have an MO and we have a motive,' Grant reminded him, potting another colour. 'Perhaps we should be grateful for *that* much.'

Lawrenson was unimpressed. He watched as Grant potted the remaining balls then stepped back.

'Another one?' Grant said. '*I'm* in no rush to get home.'

'One more, double or quits,' Lawrenson said.

The taller of the two watching youths got to his feet and stepped towards Grant.

'Look, mate, we've got our name down for a game,' he said. 'How much longer are you going to be?'

Grant regarded him contemptuously.

'Patience is a virtue,' he said flatly, his eyes boring into the youth. 'You'll have to wait.'

'Well, speed it up a bit, will you, you've been on there an hour already.'

Grant took a step towards him and the youth backed away, suddenly alarmed by the look in the policeman's eyes.

'Don't bother me, sunshine,' Grant hissed. 'I've got enough on my mind already. Got it?'

The youth moved further back.

Lawrenson took a step towards his superior, glancing at the white-faced youth.

'Your break, guv,' Lawrenson said.

'Your fucking mate's off his head,' the youth said to Lawrenson as Grant got down to take his shot.

'You could be right,' Lawrenson told him, not a trace of emotion in his expression.

The white slammed into the other balls with a loud crack.

It reminded Grant of breaking bone.

David Albury reached for the mobile phone and pressed

the keys for the number he required. He sat back in the plush leather seat of the Jag and waited for his call to be answered.

The driver guided the vehicle expertly through the maze of traffic, glancing down every now and then to re-check his destination.

Albury was due to address a meeting of the National Viewer's and Listener's Association that evening and the driver was making sure his passenger wasn't late.

Every now and then he glanced at Albury in his rear-view mirror and saw him with the phone still pressed to his ear.

When it was finally picked up, Albury's expression didn't change.

'It's me,' he said. 'I'm on my way now.'

The driver tried not to make it obvious that he was eavesdropping by gazing out of the side window every time the car stopped at lights. Besides, he wasn't really interested in his passenger's conversation.

A taxi cut in front of him and he was forced to brake a little sharply.

He caught sight of Albury's disapproving glance in his rear-view mirror.

'I don't know what time I'll be finished,' Albury said. 'No. I'll get something to eat before I come home. Give Harriet a kiss for me. Okay.'

The Jag wound its way through the steady stream of traffic.

'See you later,' said Albury and switched off the signal.

He waited a moment then pressed more digits.

When he spoke again his voice was muted – whispering almost conspiratorially.

The driver noticed that he was smiling too.

'I'll pick you up at the same place tonight,' Albury said.

The driver glanced at him in the mirror, and saw his smile spreading wider.

'Business first,' Albury grinned. 'Yes. Same time too. See you later.'

He switched off.

Andrew Chapman parked the Audi in the multi-storey car park in Brewer Street. Same car park as usual. Almost the same space as usual. Second level, close to the exit ramp.

He made sure that the doors were locked and stood watching the blinking red eye of the immobiliser for a second before heading towards the narrow flight of steps that would lead him out into the street.

The night was aglow with neon. The whole street was ablaze with multi-coloured signs. Beckoning.

He looked at his watch.

9.46 p.m.

He pulled free his tie, rolled it up and stuffed it in the pocket of his jacket.

He stood on the pavement for a moment, glancing up at the sign that blazed above him. Then, reaching for his wallet, he headed into the first of the stripclubs.

'Are you going to be here when I get back?'

Jo Parker stood in the doorway of her flat staring back at her brother who was sprawled on the sofa watching television.

Billy didn't answer, but merely took another swig from a bottle of Becks.

'Did you hear what I said?'

'I don't know if I'll be here,' he told her. 'I doubt it.'

'Where are you going?'

'Where are *you* going?'

'I'm going to work.'

'So am I,' he countered, a grin spreading across his face.

Jo hesitated a moment knowing it was futile to continue pressing him for answers.

'Break a leg,' he called. 'Or what ever they say in showbiz.'

As she closed the door behind her she heard his hollow laughter.

Fifty-Four

As Amy slipped her blouse back on and tucked it into the top of her jeans she could hear the sound of running water.

She stepped from behind the screen to see Dr Alan Davidson washing his hands in the small sink on the far side of his room. It was a large room, made to look larger by the fact that there was so little furniture in it. A large desk, occupied by a computer and its printer, two chairs, a filing cabinet and a couch were the only objects to fill the space. The walls were similarly bare except for some photos behind Davidson's desk. One showed him and two small children; Amy guessed they were about three and four. The other showed him, his wife and his children all smiling beatifically for the camera.

Davidson dried his hands on a paper towel and returned to his desk where he sat down and began scribbling some notes on a piece of paper.

'Have a seat,' he said cheerfully, motioning to one of the two that stood before his desk.

'I'd rather have a cigarette,' said Amy.

Davidson looked up, a smile spreading across his face.

He was a good-looking man in his mid-thirties with, Amy had noticed, extraordinarily large but gentle hands. She'd been particularly grateful for his expert touch during the examination. The lump in her breast had been tender when his probing fingers had found it and it ached now as she sat down.

'Well, Miss Watson,' he said and began scratching his chin. 'You don't need me to tell you that there is some lumpy tissue present in your left breast as you indicated. Exactly what it is I don't know yet.'

'How soon before you do?'

Davidson shrugged. 'The quicker we get it biopsied, the quicker I'll be able to tell you what we're dealing with.'

'And how soon can you do that?'

'We can have you in before the end of the week.'

'What *could* it be, doctor?'

'It could be a lot of things.'

'Such as?'

'Mastitis. A build up of fatty tissue in one part of the breast.'

'Or cancer.'

'It's possible,' he told her honestly. 'I'd be lying to you if I said that wasn't one of the possibilities, but there are several harmless conditions that imitate the symptoms of breast cancer. Many lumps turn out to be fibromas or papillomas. Innocent tumours.'

Tumour. The word made her shudder.

'Can you cure it if it is cancer?' Amy persisted.

'Any kind of cancer can be treated if it's caught early enough.'

'What kind of treatment would be involved?'

'Miss Watson, we haven't even ascertained whether or not it *is* cancer yet.'

'Please tell me, doctor. What would you have to do if it *was*?'

He sighed wearily. 'If the tumour was found to be malignant it would be removed, depending upon its size.'

'What if it spreads.'

'Then a mastectomy might be necessary.'

She felt a cold chill spreading through her, as if someone had injected iced water into her veins.

'You mean I could lose a breast?' Amy said softly.

'If that was necessary to stop the spread of the disease, yes.'

Amy saw something behind his eyes but couldn't decide whether it was compassion or pity.

'What else would you have to do?' Amy continued.

'To ensure the disease had been removed – X-ray treatment, chemotherapy and a course of other drugs might be necessary.'

Amy nodded slowly.

'Look, this is all academic until we get the results of the biopsy,' Davidson said in his best optimistic voice. 'As soon as we do then we'll know where we are. I'm not going to say don't worry because I know you will anyway. It's a natural reaction but, as I said, even if it is cancer then we'll have caught it early.'

'Better a breast than my life, if I have to lose something, then?' she said quietly.

Davidson nodded.

'One woman in fourteen develops some kind of breast cancer during her life, Miss Watson,' said the doctor. 'I wish I could tell you different but you wanted the facts.'

'I appreciate your honesty, doctor.' She smiled weakly. 'I think.'

'We'll have you in on Friday, get that biopsy done.'

She got to her feet and ran a hand through her hair.

'I'll go and have a fag now, calm my nerves,' she told him, smiling.

'I should tell you off for even thinking about it,' Davidson said, a grin also flickering across his lips.

She thanked him again then stepped out into the corridor. One of the fluorescents in the ceiling was faulty and it kept flickering on and off. When it went off, the corridor seemed oddly dark and foreboding. Amy hurried up towards the welcoming light of the waiting room.

Webber got to his feet as he saw her and crossed to her immediately.

'I need a drink,' she said.

Fifty-Five

Amy gazed blankly out of the window while Webber fetched two coffees. Two young women, a little younger than herself, were passing the café, laughing and joking. Not a care in the world, thought Amy. For one fleeting second her self-pity overcame her and she envied those young women. Envied them their laughter, their lack of apparent worry.

How do you know what's going on in their lives? They could be worse off than you. Snap out of it.

Her own mental rebuke didn't seem to have the desired effect though. Clouds of depression hung over her as dark and threatening as they had been all morning.

Webber returned with the coffees and set them down. He'd even brought them a Danish pastry each.

A little comfort in a time of need?

She managed a smile at his gesture.

'When I said drink I was thinking of something stronger,' she said, looking into his eyes.

'How *much* stronger?' he asked, grinning. 'This coffee looks like creosote.'

She laughed. *Forced* a laugh. Manufactured a grin.

'He didn't say it *was* cancer, Amy?' Webber offered. 'You told me that yourself.'

As soon as they'd left the surgery she'd repeated, more or less verbatim, what the doctor had said to her and Webber had listened, one of his strong arms around her shoulders.

Now he watched as she spooned sugar into her coffee and stirred it.

'I'm trying to be realistic, Jake,' she told him. 'Trying to prepare myself.' She sipped the coffee. 'The big C.'

'You don't *know* that.'

'If it is,' she began, raising a hand to silence Webber as he opened his mouth to speak, 'there's a sort of horrible irony about it, don't you think?'

'What do you mean?'

'Well, I used to model, I used to make a living out of showing my breasts and now I might lose one. Perhaps it's fate. Perhaps it's some kind of payback.'

'Now you're talking shit.'

'A guy's been phoning the show lately and saying that I degraded myself, flaunted myself when I posed nude. Perhaps he's right. Perhaps this is God's way of paying me back for that.'

'For Christ's sake, Amy. That's bollocks and you know it.'

'Is it, Jake? They say what goes around comes around. God pays back in other ways, that sort of thing.'

'You didn't do anything wrong and that bastard phoning in was probably one of the ones wanking over your pictures. You shouldn't listen to shit like that.'

'So you don't think God's paying me back for flaunting my body?'

'God's got nothing to do with this because there is no fucking God.' He sipped his coffee. 'What kind of God would take an eighteen-month-old child? What kind of God would invent cancer and AIDS? Or meningitis or heart disease? God's an invention of the Church. That's it. End of story.'

Amy studied his grizzled features for a moment then reached out and touched his hand.

'Did you feel like this after Samantha died?' she asked gently.

He grunted.

'Who wouldn't?' he snapped. 'When you've just carried your own daughter's coffin through a fucking grave-yard and stuck her in the ground, wouldn't you begin to wonder if God was as wonderful as everybody tells you?'

Amy gripped his hand.

'I lost the only thing in this life that I ever cared about thanks to *God*,' he rasped, emphasising the last word with disgust.

She broke a portion of the Danish pastry off and nibbled at it.

Webber exhaled deeply then looked into her eyes once more, his expression softening.

'Who else knows about . . .' he said, the sentence trailing off.

'Jo, I told her last night, and Mike Osborne, my producer,' she said quietly. 'That's it.'

'What about your family?'

'My mother lives in Canada with her sister – I don't even know where my father is.'

'What happened?'

'He left home when I was fourteen. He was an alcoholic. It wasn't much of a loss. My mum left for Canada about eight years ago. I haven't seen her since she left.' Amy chewed more of the Danish. 'She never really approved of what I did anyway. I've had a couple of letters but that's it.'

'No brothers or sisters?'

'No.'

She reached for her cigarettes and lit one.

'To tell you the truth,' she said, 'I don't think my mum ever forgave me for having an abortion.'

'You had an abortion? When?'

'When I was eighteen. It's a long story, Jake.'

'I've got time.'

He pulled his hand away sharply.

'What's the matter?' she asked, surprised at his reaction.

'Tell me about it,' he demanded.

'I just did. I was eighteen. I got pregnant. I had an abortion.'

'Who was the father?'

'What the hell *is* this?'

'I asked you a question. I'm curious. I want to know.'

His expression had darkened. His eyes were boring into her.

'A guy I was going out with at the time,' she snapped. 'Satisfied?'

'Why did you get rid of the baby?'

'I couldn't have looked after a child when I was eighteen, Jake. Besides, there were other considerations too.'

'Like what?'

She met his gaze, decided she didn't like the vehemence in his eyes and looked down at her coffee cup.

'I'd just been offered a modelling contract with a magazine,' she said quietly. 'Steady work. Well paid. It was a big break for me. I had to think about my career too.'

'You killed a child because of your career.'

'Don't be so melodramatic, Jake. I had an abortion because I *had* to. For practical and financial reasons.'

'You killed a child for the sake of your career,' he repeated. 'Mine died, Amy.' He raised his voice suddenly, attracting the attention of one or two people in the café. '*I* had no choice whether she lived or died. You did. I would have done anything for my daughter. I'd do anything now to bring her back and you sit there and calmly tell me that you *could* have had a child but you didn't want it. It wasn't convenient.' He snarled the words furiously.

Amy regarded him warily as he continued to glare at her, one hand balled into a fist.

Fleetingly, she thought he might hit her.

'Jake, I'm sorry you feel this way,' she said evenly, trying to calm him. 'I understand why you're angry—'

'No you don't,' he rasped. 'No one does.'

Suddenly he got to his feet.

'Where are you going?'

'I think I'd better go,' he said. 'It might be best if I wasn't around you for a while.'

'I'll see you later,' she said, reaching out for his hand.

He shook loose and she turned in her seat to see him storm out of the café.

Curious eyes turned in her direction and she met them

defiantly for a moment before sipping at her coffee. Lying opposite her was Webber's disposable lighter. She reached across and picked it up, dropping it into her handbag. She remembered the look in his eyes. That furious rage. The way he had looked at her – as if he loathed her. She could think of one word to describe his venomous glance and it made her shudder.

He'd looked murderous.

Fifty-Six

There was more mail than usual, Anita Bishop thought, as she opened yet another envelope addressed to David Albury. Since the successful passing of his Bill, the Home Secretary's correspondence had doubled, as had demands on his time. Most of her day was now spent fielding media enquiries as well as the usual tasks she'd always performed so efficiently. It involved working longer hours; during the past week or so she'd only managed anything resembling a lunch hour once. But Anita seemed to revel in the increased work-load as much as her employer did in his heightened profile.

The passing of the Albury Bill had catapulted the man even more strongly into the public consciousness. Whether people liked him or despised him, they couldn't ignore him.

She continued to wade through the mail. An invitation to address the Oxford Students' Union. An offer to appear as a guest on a special edition of *Newsnight* that would discuss the Bill from all angles.

She expected Albury to accept the invitation from the Students Union but doubted if he'd take up the *Newsnight* offer. He'd had several run-ins with its presenter before. She put the letter to one side.

The phone had barely stopped ringing either. More requests for interviews with newspapers and magazines.

Some were calling the Bill the single most important piece of legislation for five years. Others had branded it the worst intrusion into freedom of choice and expression since the 'Spanish Inquisition'. Anita smiled at that particular recollection. The article had been sent from a small magazine that she'd never heard of, a film magazine specialising in horror films. They'd sent a petition with the issue. Four thousand names objecting to the Bill.

It had been consigned to the waste bin.

She was about to open the next pile of letters when the office door opened and Albury walked in.

Anita turned and smiled at him, noticing that, as usual, he looked immaculate. His Armani suit was pressed to perfection, the creases in his trousers razor sharp.

He returned the smile and crossed to her, glancing at the huge expanse of mail both opened and unopened.

'Fan mail?' he said, grinning.

She laughed.

'Anything important?' he asked, inspecting some of the correspondence she pushed his way.

She told him about the Oxford Union invitation. The requests for interviews.

'You've had a busy morning, Anita,' he said, still scanning the letters. 'You should let me buy you lunch. You need a break.'

She blushed slightly. 'That's very kind,' she said demurely.

'And I think you should leave early tonight,' he continued. 'It hasn't escaped me that you've been working long hours lately and I appreciate it. But, all work and no play, as they say.'

'It has been hectic lately,' she admitted.

He sat down at his desk.

'I'll deal with the interview requests as soon as you decide which you want to do,' Anita told him.

Albury nodded, still reading one of the letters.

'I've had a woman on the phone three times this morning from a radio show. They want you to appear.'

'What kind of show?'

'A chat show, a late-night phone-in. It's hosted by a woman called Amy Watson.'

'Never heard of her.'

'They want you to answer questions about the Bill.'

'Doesn't everyone?'

'I said I'd ask you.'

'I'll think about it. I did intend spending some time with my family for at least the next *two* evenings, so if anything else comes up don't call me at home unless it's important.'

She nodded.

'What will you do tonight, Anita?' he asked, looking at her over the envelopes and letters.

'Put my feet up,' she told him. 'Take it easy while I can. Have a bath. Read. Phone some friends.' She smiled.

'Am I prying?' he asked.

'Not at all.'

'I'm curious. It's a politician's way. That's *my* excuse anyway.'

She began to open more letters when he got to his feet.

'That's enough,' he told her, smiling. 'Lunch beckons.'

He picked up her jacket from the back of her chair and held it for her, watching as she slipped her arms in.

'Where would you like to eat?' he asked, holding the door open for her.

'I'm in your capable hands,' she said, smiling.

'I hope you trust me.'

'I should do by now,' she confided.

He pulled the office door shut behind her and locked it.

They walked down the corridor together, his hand brushing lightly against her arm.

As they waited for the lift she leaned forward and carefully removed a stray hair from the lapel of his jacket.

Albury smiled.

Fifty-Seven

Billy Parker rubbed one hand repeatedly up and down his left arm in an effort to generate some warmth. It wasn't the coldest of days but he felt an uncomfortable chill creeping through him and the thick flannel shirt he wore over his black T-shirt was doing little to help.

He fumbled in the top pocket of the shirt and pulled out a crumpled box of Rothmans, delighted to discover that there was one inside. He jammed it between his lips and looked to his companion.

Brian Healy was a year or two younger than Billy – a thin, lean-faced youth with pitted skin who looked as if he hadn't had a good meal in weeks. He was wearing a leather jacket that still smelled new – possibly something to do with the fact that it had only been stolen that morning.

He pulled a lighter from the pocket and flicked it, lighting Billy's cigarette. The two of them huddled in one of the doorways of the Piccadilly theatre, glancing up and down Sherwood Street occasionally.

Two American tourists passed and gave them desultory looks, one of them wrinkling his nose at the aroma that seemed to surround the two young men.

'What the fuck are you looking at?' Billy snapped as they passed, realising that the smell came from the bundle of clothes and rags curled up in the next doorway. Only an unkempt head poking out of the pile even marked it out as a man. He asked the tourists for change as they strode by but got nothing except a disdainful look.

'Can you trust this bastard?' Billy asked, puffing on his cigarette.

'He's cool, Billy, honest,' said Healy, the words spilling out quickly.

'Then where *is* he?'

'He'll be here, he said he'd be here,' Healy babbled, shifting constantly from one foot to the other.

Billy checked his watch.

'I can give him a call if you want me to,' jabbered Healy, reaching into his pocket and pulling out a mobile phone which had been stolen the day before.

'Leave it another five minutes,' Billy murmured.

'He's coming, look, he's coming.'

Healy was pointing up the street in the direction of Golden Square.

'That's him, there, look. See, I told you he'd be here.'

The rapidity of his speech seemed to have increased to the point where the stream of words almost became a continuous drone.

'I knew he'd come. I wouldn't mess you about, Billy, I wouldn't.'

The man heading towards them was in his mid-twenties. He walked as if he was trying to take strides longer than the length of his legs would allow.

Trying to look the hard man, thought Billy, puffing on his cigarette.

As the man reached them, he nodded towards Healy then gave Billy an appraising, almost contemptuous, look.

'All right, Elvis,' said Healy excitedly.

The older man nodded.

'What did you call him?' said Billy, a grin on his face.

'Elvis, I called him Elvis, you know,' Healy gushed.

'Elvis? Is he joking?' Billy asked.

'No, he's not fucking joking,' snapped the newcomer.

'Your name's Elvis?' Billy continued.

'Yeah.'

'What, as in—'

'Yeah, as in Elvis fucking Presley. You got a problem with that?'

'You poor sod, how did that happen?' Billy enquired.

'My dad was a fan, right.'

'Elvis what?' Billy persisted.

'Elvis Thorpe. Happy now?'

Billy couldn't suppress a chuckle.

'What is it with this bastard?' said Thorpe, glaring at Billy.

'I told him about you, Elvis,' Healy babbled. 'I said you were cool.'

'Fucking right, I'm cool,' Thorpe said, adjusting the sleeves of his jacket.

He looked at Billy.

'Now, are we doing business or not?' he said irritably.

'If you've got what I want,' Billy told him.

'You got money?'

Billy reached into the pocket of his jeans and pulled out a wad of notes half-an-inch thick.

'That enough for you?' he said defiantly.

'My man is loaded,' Thorpe said, grinning.

'So, what do you want, Billy?' Healy said. 'I mean, Elvis has got it all.'

'On you?' Billy wanted to know.

'What kind of bloke do you think I am?' Thorpe said. 'I've got it back at my place.'

'Where's that?'

'I've got a pad in Flaxman Court. You tell me what you want and I'll sell it to you.'

Billy took a final drag on his cigarette then dropped it, grinding out the butt.

'Let's go then,' he said, digging his hands into his pockets.

The three of them turned and set off back up Sherwood Street.

'I've known Elvis for years, Billy,' said Healy, trying to walk alongside the other two men but forced, instead, to scurry along in the gutter.

'I haven't seen you around before,' Thorpe told Billy.

'I'm new in town,' Billy said, grinning.

Billy walked along, his eyes scanning Thorpe. He pushed his hands deeper into his pockets and, as he did so, his right hand brushed against the hilt of a flick knife.

Fifty-Eight

As Andrew Chapman parked the Orion outside number fifteen Beverley Road he could see that lights were on in the sitting room and one of the rooms upstairs.

His stomach rumbled and he patted it soothingly. He hadn't eaten much that day. A sandwich at lunchtime and that had been about it. Not that he'd *felt* much like eating. A rumour about threatened redundancies had been circulating within the bank for a week or two now, gradually building momentum until the reaction had gone from one of mistrust and concern to almost outright hysteria. Twenty jobs were to go, someone had said. From top management, right down to cashiers. No one was safe. Everyone was worried.

Not least Chapman.

He sat in the car looking at the house and he felt his stomach contract. They'd bought it three years ago, just after his promotion. Property in Chiswick was never cheap but, with his increased salary, Chapman had felt more than confident about investing in a place that many had thought too expensive.

Investment. That was the word that kept cropping up while they were considering the move. 'A bigger house would be an investment.'

As long as you had a good job perhaps it was. At the moment, the word millstone sounded more appropriate to Andrew Chapman. What with the mortgage, the school fees for their two children and his consultations with Charlotte Kilbride (*thank God Laura didn't know about those*) and, not forgetting his little obsession (there was a porn video in his briefcase now, along with two magazines) the financial drain on his resources was becoming considerable.

The threat of redundancy was almost too terrifying to contemplate. He hadn't mentioned it to Laura. No sense in alarming her unnecessarily. Not yet anyway.

He locked the Orion and made his way towards the front door, pausing to check that the lock on his case was secure.

He could watch the film tomorrow morning.

Laura was going shopping and taking Joe with her. Fiona was playing netball for her school and would be gone all day. He should have at least three hours to sit and watch *Cum Sluts*.

Even the thought was beginning to give him an erection.

He let himself in and wandered into the hall, sticking his head around the sitting-room door.

'Another day, another dollar,' he said as cheerfully as he could.

His wife was sitting at one end of the sofa, a book open in front of her, a news programme on the television.

'You're late,' she said sympathetically.

He crossed to her and kissed the top of her head. Her hair smelled as if it had been freshly washed.

'Sorry, the meeting went on longer than I expected and then a couple of the others suggested we go and have a drink, so . . .' He allowed the sentence to trail off, satisfied that the lie had sounded convincing.

'Who went with you?' Laura asked, without looking up from her book.

'Oh, just a couple of guys from investment,' he said. 'Are the kids in bed?'

His attempt to change the subject seemed successful enough.

'Fiona said she was going to read for an hour,' Laura told him. 'I said it would be okay.'

'Her light's still on.'

'She's probably dropped off. I'll switch it off when we go up.'

He sat down on the sofa beside her, glancing at the television.

'What time are you leaving in the morning?' he asked without looking at her.

'About ten, like I always do. Why?'

'Just asking.'

He reached across and took the book from her, carefully replacing her bookmark.

'I hadn't finished that chapter,' she said in mock protest.

He slid one hand on to her thigh and up beneath the hem of her skirt.

'What's got into you?' she said, grinning, then noticing that his erection was straining against the material of his trousers.

Should he tell her that the bed show he watched less than an hour ago had excited him? He thought not. Best not to mention how he had paid five pounds to gain entry to the show in Dean Street, then another twenty for two of their overpriced drinks while he had watched two girls writhing around licking each other's bodies.

Some things were best left unsaid, weren't they?

'Fancy an early night?' he said, his hand still beneath her skirt, his finger gently stroking across the gusset of her knickers.

'Yes, I'm shattered,' she said, grinning.

He pulled his finger away, his expression darkening.

'Andy, what's wrong?' she asked, wearily.

He was sitting bolt upright staring at the television screen.

'Andy.'

She looked at him then at the television. The face that filled the screen was that of Charlotte Kilbride.

'You look as if you've seen a ghost,' Laura said. 'What's wrong?'

'Nothing,' he lied. 'That woman was talking about these murders. I thought there'd been another one.'

'No, she was on earlier, saying that the police should

have caught him by now. She's a psychiatrist or something.'

I know, I visit her.

'Since when did you get so interested in murderers?' Laura wanted to know, smiling.

'This one is important,' he said sternly, his eyes never leaving the screen where Charlotte Kilbride was still being interviewed.

He barely heard what she said though. Seeing her there was like being on the end of some kind of spiritual visitation. It was as if she had appeared to remind him of his guilt. His secret. As if she could see out of the television set and was looking directly at *him*.

Only when she had disappeared from view did he seem to emerge from his trance-like state.

Laura prodded his arm. 'Welcome back.' She swung herself off the sofa and headed for the kitchen. 'I'm going to make a cup of tea – do you want one?'

He shook his head.

'Andy?' she called.

He crossed to the drinks cabinet. He needed something stronger.

Fifty-Nine

David Albury read the article in the *Guardian*. Then the one in *The Times*. Both were lengthy pieces about his own Bill, and about him.

He smiled smugly as he folded the paper and pushed it to one side, reaching for the *Independent*.

'Aren't you sick of reading about yourself?'

The voice came from the other side of the sitting room.

From Louise Albury. She was sitting at the antique writing desk that occupied one corner of the large lounge, a notepad and several reference books spread out before her.

As Albury looked across he saw that her eyes were still on the law books. She was scribbling as she spoke, not even affording him a glance.

'Urgent case tomorrow?' he said sniffily.

'Just making some final notes,' she told him. 'I think it's important and so does my client. I know it's always been a bit of a joke to you though, hasn't it, David?'

'You handle clients on legal aid for God's sake.'

'What's so wrong about that?'

'You should be using your talents on *better* cases. Better paid anyway.'

'I like the people I work with.'

'Council-house thugs and drug dealers. How delightful.'

'They're still people, David. Not everyone is as lucky as we are.'

'It's a waste of talent.'

'I studied law because I wanted to help people and that's what I'm doing. I'm sorry it doesn't comply with *your* grand scheme of things.'

Albury began reading the article in the *Independent*.

'Perhaps it's a good job *both* of our careers aren't so newsworthy,' said Louise, still writing. 'You've certainly got your pound of flesh from the papers, haven't you?'

'What are you talking about?'

'You love this attention, David. Don't try to deny it.'

'If a Bill that I propose happens to make the news that's fine,' he said dismissively. 'But I didn't propose it for my *own* interests.'

'David, everything you *do* is for your own interests,' said Louise, finally looking at him with an expression close to distaste.

He looked at her silently for a moment, considered saying something but his thoughts were interrupted.

The telephone was ringing in the hallway.

Albury got to his feet and wandered through to answer it.

Louise watched him disappear out of the room then returned to her scribblings.

Albury reached the phone on its third ring, hoping that it hadn't disturbed Harriet, who was sleeping upstairs.

He glanced at his watch as he picked up the receiver.

11.14 p.m.

He frowned.

'David Albury.'

He recognised the voice at the other end immediately.

'What do you want at this time of night?' Albury said irritably, his voice dropping in volume. 'I told you not to call me here tonight.'

He leaned across and pushed the sitting-room door shut.

'I can't, not tonight,' he said, answering the caller's question. 'You'll have to wait,' he continued, lowering his voice further, his tone softening slightly. 'All right, when?' He waited a moment, listening to the caller, one eye on the sitting-room door. 'Yes, tomorrow then. Yes. We'll arrange something. Yes. Listen, I've got to go.'

He pressed his fingers down on the cradle and then

replaced the receiver, sucking in a deep breath before walking back into the sitting room.

'Who was it?' Louise asked, without looking up.

'Another reporter,' he lied.

'At this time of night?'

'Well, as you said, I appear to be newsworthy. The press are no respectors of time or privacy, you know that.'

She studied him silently for a moment, then returned to her work.

Behind his paper, Albury swallowed hard. His heart was thudding a little too hard against his ribs.

Sixty

The first spots of rain were striking the window panes. They beat out an irregular tattoo against the glass, the sound growing louder as the rain became heavier.

Within the stillness of the bedroom the sound was intensified, and Andrew Chapman rolled over on to his side to watch the droplets rolling down the glass. Far away he heard the first distant rumble of thunder. Perhaps it would clear the air. The night was unbearably muggy.

He moved uncomfortably beneath the thin sheet that covered him, grunting quietly as he did so. His erection throbbed between his legs. Uncomfortably stiff.

Two girls. One blond. One brunette.

Chapman tried to control his breathing.

In their mid-twenties. As they had been before.

He pushed the sheet down a little, his right hand sliding down his body, fingers playing gently over his shaft.

They were usually the same two girls at the bedshow he visited.

He couldn't get the vision out of his mind. Their slender bodies. Busy hands.

Lying on his back, he stared at the ceiling, the rain still bouncing off the windows, but there was a softer counterpoint to that sound. Next to him he could hear Laura's low even breathing as she slept.

He turned his head and looked at her. Her mouth was open slightly, lips parted.

Like the blond girl as she felt the tongue between her legs.

Chapman slid closer to his wife, feeling the warmth from her body. He moved his face to within inches of hers, studying her features in the gloom, inching nearer until he rested his right hand on her thigh.

She stirred slightly but didn't wake.

Chapman slid closer so that his erection was pressing against the top of her leg, his right hand now brushing through the soft down of her pubic hair.

He nuzzled her ear, then her neck, his fingers now probing more urgently. He pressed his finger against the fleshy outer lips of her vagina, moving his own body so that he was squashed close and tight to her.

Laura opened her eyes and blinked myopically.

'Oh, Andy,' she murmured, her voice thick with sleep.

He kissed her cheek.

'It's late,' Laura sighed, her eyes only half open.

He had his eyes closed.

The blond girl had her head thrown back in ecstasy now.

He took Laura's hand and placed it on his throbbing erection, feeling her fingers envelop his shaft a little half-heartedly.

Gently, he rubbed between her legs.

She let go of his penis and touched his cheek gently.

'Tomorrow,' she said sleepily.

He took her hand and replaced it on his erection.

'Andy,' she murmured, aware now that the pressure he was exerting between her legs was growing. As she looked at him she saw that his eyes were still closed. He was breathing heavily, pushing his body more insistently against hers.

'Andy, leave it, will you?' she said wearily, wincing slightly as his fingers scraped a little too hard across her most sensitive area.

His eyes snapped open. 'Why?' he demanded.

'I said it's late. Besides, we'll wake the kids.' She smiled.

'Fuck the kids,' he rasped, and she was surprised by the vehemence in his tone.

He pressed harder against her, his hand still rubbing furiously between her legs.

She grabbed the hand and tried to pull it away but he would not stop his persistent movements.

'Andy, please.' Her voice wavered slightly.

'Come on,' he insisted, looking down at her face.

Outside, a louder rumble of thunder was followed by a flash of sheet lightning, which lit the entire room and momentarily illuminated his features with cold, white light. His eyes were blazing.

'Not now, please,' she pleaded, swallowing hard.

He glared down at her.

The blond would have begged him for it.

He pulled his hand from between her legs and pressed his fingers to his mouth.

'Nothing,' he hissed.

She watched him in silence, her heart thumping a little harder. When she tried to swallow, it felt as though someone had filled her mouth with chalk.

'Don't I excite you any more?' he demanded, pushing the fingers against her own lips. 'Nothing.'

His breathing was harsh and guttural as he looked down upon her almost contemptuously.

'I'm just tired,' she whispered, glancing quickly towards their bedroom door. 'And I don't want to disturb the kids. Maybe another—'

'Forget it,' he said, swinging himself out of bed.

He pulled on his dressing gown and stalked out of the room. She heard his footsteps crossing the landing, heard the sound of the toilet door opening and closing.

Laura finally managed to swallow. She lay on her back, heart beating fast, her tiredness now replaced by something else. Fear? She had never known him like this before and she didn't like it.

Outside there was another angry rumble of thunder.

Laura closed her eyes but sleep eluded her, driven away by the recollection of his anger, the force of his hands on her.

She shuddered.

The rain continued to batter at the windows.

Sixty-One

Amy stood before the full-length mirror in her bedroom and gazed at her reflection. She ran her glance from head to toe but, each time, she found herself dwelling on her breasts. More particularly the left one. The one with the lump.

The lump.

She swallowed hard and closed her eyes, her stomach fluttering even at the thought of it. She would go for hours at a time without the problem forcing its way into her mind, or at least not into the forefront of her thoughts, then suddenly, all the fears and terrors would come rushing in like a river suddenly freed from the restraints of a dam. When that happened she found herself almost paralysed with terror. Nauseous and fearful of what consequences her awful discovery may hold. What was the ultimate conclusion that could be reached? What if the lump was malignant? What if it had already begun to spread? What if they could not treat her in time? What if?

The answer was a chilling one and one which again made her feel a little faint because it was so damning in its simplicity. So inescapably final. If they could not treat her, she would die.

That was it. As simple as that.

Amy sucked in a deep breath and tried, again, to push this most terrifying conclusion to the back of her mind.

Outside, the storm seemed to be reaching its height, sheet lightning illuminating the sky with savage regularity, the ever-present crashing of thunder like a constant artillery barrage.

Amy moved away from the mirror and looked out of her window, watching the heavens being torn apart by the lightning. The power of that great elemental force was awesome. Unstoppable.

Like cancer?

She closed her eyes tightly, angry that she'd allowed the thought to intrude, to force its way back into her consciousness.

Wait for the biopsy. Wait for the results.

'Get a grip,' she whispered to herself, her voice wavering a little.

As she turned she glanced across towards her book-shelves, her eyes focusing on a number of books there. *His* books. John Howard.

What would *he* say if he knew of her problem? How would he help her to cope with it? It didn't matter. Howard didn't know and never would.

She checked her watch. It would be time to leave to do the show soon. The prospect didn't fill her with joy. She had her own thoughts to contend with. The thoughts of those who phoned in were of little consequence to her at present.

The phone rang.

She looked again at her watch, frowning, then picked up the receiver.

'It's me,' the voice said. 'I need to talk to you, Amy. Now.' Webber sounded subdued.

Amy hadn't seen or heard him since he'd stormed out on her that morning.

'I'll come down,' she told him without hesitation.

When she reached the bottom of the stairs she saw that the door to flat number one was already open.

Come into my parlour, said the spider to the fly . . .

She hesitated at the entrance, the brief remembrance of that look in his eyes earlier in the day still fresh in her mind. Then she took a step inside and closed the door behind her.

'Jake,' she called quietly.

She found him in the sitting room, perched on the arm of one chair, a glass of Jamesons in his hand.

'I know you're off to do the show,' he said. 'But I had to talk to you.'

'What's wrong?' she asked.

'Me. *I'm* wrong.'

She looked vague.

'This morning,' he elucidated. 'I shouldn't have blown up at you like that. You must think I'm a fucking nut-case.'

She smiled weakly.

'I've been sitting here thinking about it,' Webber continued. 'It just seemed so . . . wrong. I can't think of any other way to describe it.'

'My abortion was wrong, you mean?'

'Not wrong but unjust, when you think about what happened to my own child, even though that wasn't *your* fault, I . . .' He raised his hands. 'Fuck it, I don't even know how to say what I'm trying to say.'

'I think what you're trying to say is sorry.'

She took a step towards him, watching as he put down the glass. They embraced, Webber holding her tight to him, Amy clutching at him almost frenziedly. She wanted his arms around her. Needed them.

'I'm sorry,' he whispered, kissing her forehead.

The loud knocking on the front door startled them both.

Webber looked puzzled, the lines across his forehead deepening.

He left her in the sitting room, wandered out to the hallway and heard the knocking again. Louder, more insistent.

He reached for the handle and opened it.

'What the hell do *you* want here?'

Amy heard his words from the sitting room and moved nearer the door, curious about his late-night visitor.

'I wasn't expecting you,' Webber said to the newcomer. 'You'd better come in.'

David Grant accepted the invitation.

Sixty-Two

As Grant walked into the sitting room, Amy ran appraising eyes over him. He did the same to her, a crooked smile touching his lips.

'I can see why you didn't want to answer the door,' Grant said as Webber joined them.

Amy looked at him then back at the stranger. Whoever he was, he was wearing what looked like an expensive suit, she thought.

'Aren't you going to introduce us, Jake?' Grant asked, never taking his eyes off Amy.

'Just tell me what you want, will you?' Webber said irritably.

Grant ignored the comment and extended his right hand in Amy's direction.

'Detective Inspector David Grant,' he said, smiling.

She shook the offered hand.

'Amy Watson.'

Again she looked at the two men. First one then the other.

Detective. What the hell was a policeman doing here at this time? She wondered if her fears about Webber had been right. Was this man here to arrest him?

And yet he'd used Webber's first name. She was puzzled.

'Does she know?' asked Grant, nodding towards Amy as if she couldn't hear him.

'Know what?' she demanded.

'She doesn't, does she?' Grant continued.

'I didn't think it was necessary,' said Webber.

Amy's bewilderment was turning to anger.

'Somebody tell me what's going on,' she demanded.

Webber looked sheepish. 'I should have told you,' he began. 'I'm sorry I didn't.'

'Told me what?' she said angrily.

'I'm a policeman,' he confessed.

She stared at him for a while, then at Grant, then back again at Webber.

'I know I should have told you, I'm sorry if it's a shock.'

'A shock,' she blurted. 'It's a relief.'

It was Webber's turn to look puzzled.

'I was beginning to think *you* were the killer,' Amy told him.

'Why?'

'Jake, you haven't exactly been up-front with me, have you? You wouldn't tell me what you did for a living, you were out most nights until the small hours, you never said where. And then I found bullets in your bathroom and I was terrified that you were the killer.'

'Why didn't you say something to me?'

'Like what "Excuse me, Jake, but could you explain where that box of ammunition in your medicine cabinet came from?"'

'If you thought I was the killer why did you carry on seeing me?'

'Because I wasn't sure. I didn't *want* to believe what my mind kept telling me. I had to know the truth.'

'And now you do.'

She nodded.

'Sorry to interrupt this little lovers' conversation,' said Grant sarcastically, 'but this isn't a social call, Jake.'

'So he's your boss?' Amy continued, pointing at Grant.

Grant smiled. 'Jake and I are more like brothers than colleagues, aren't we, Jake?'

'Yeah, most brothers hate each other,' Webber snapped.

'We went through basic training together,' Grant told her. 'We were even partners for six years in the Vice Squad. Until we both moved on.' He grinned.

'Until you fucked me over, you mean,' snapped Webber.

'You wouldn't have wanted the promotion anyway,

Jake. You were never the ambitious one out of us two, were you?'

'Some of the credit would have been nice.'

'Life's a bitch, isn't it?'

'What happened?' Amy enquired.

'Let *him* tell you,' Webber sneered.

Amy held up both hands.

'Wait a minute,' she said, looking at each man in turn. 'I still don't get this.' She turned her attention to Webber. 'Jake, you moved in here because of this killer?'

He nodded.

'At the time, most of the killings had happened within a five-or six-mile radius of here,' he told her. 'It was a good base to operate from. There are three or four other undercover men set up in different locations like me.'

'All at the taxpayer's expense,' Grant added. 'So you'd better hope it works. It's costing *you* money.'

Amy sat down.

'Jesus Christ,' she murmured. 'I don't believe this.'

Webber crossed to her and rested a hand on her shoulder. 'I'm sorry I couldn't tell you the truth,' he said quietly.

All she could do was nod.

'Everything clear now?' Grant said sarcastically. 'If you wouldn't mind, your boyfriend and I have got business to discuss.'

'The investigation's stalled,' said Webber. 'I know that.'

'This is police business, Webber. No one else's,' snapped Grant, nodding towards Amy.

'You can't catch the killer, can you?' Amy said flatly.

'That's nothing to do with you,' Grant told her.

'We've got no leads,' Webber said.

'I might be able to help,' Amy told them.

Both men looked at her in surprise.

'I think he might be calling my show,' Amy explained. 'I think he's been contacting *me*.'

Sixty-Three

Webber glanced at his watch.

12.36 a.m.

He took a sip of his coffee, then got to his feet and crossed to the glass partition that ran the length of the production booth. Through it he could see Amy sitting at her console, leaning forward towards her microphone as she chatted to another caller. The sound of their conversation was being relayed through two speakers inside the control room.

Amy was talking to a man called Wayne from Beckton who was rambling on about why private education was a bad thing.

Webber stood there for a moment longer then returned to his seat next to Jo Parker. He smiled at her as he sat down.

Mike Osborne watched him carefully, not for the first time since he'd arrived at the studio.

'So, they ring in, give their names and addresses and you put them through to Amy?' Webber repeated, watching the console in front of Jo flashing with a dozen red lights.

'They don't give their addresses,' she told him. 'Just the area they're calling from.'

'Does she get many crank calls?' Webber asked Osborne.

'It's that kind of show,' the producer said condescendingly. 'You have to expect the odd weirdo.'

'Or killer,' Webber murmured to himself.

He listened to a moment or two more of Wayne from Beckton's tirade then got to his feet again.

'This guy that rings in claiming to be the killer,' he said 'does he ring at the same time every night?'

'No, he doesn't ring every night.' Osborne said.

'But when he does? Is it at the same time?'

'No,' the producer explained. 'He's not *that* predictable.'

Webber caught the disdain in the other man's voice. Jumped-up little prick, he thought.

Webber turned and walked back to where Jo was sitting. He looked at the screen and saw the names flashing in luminous green. As a new call came through on her headset, she typed in the name and location. They would be relayed to Amy in the studio via her own screen.

'Is it mostly men or women who ring in?' Webber asked.

Jo shrugged. 'Mostly men,' she said. 'Guys on shifts. Someone with something to get off their chest. People who just want to talk. We get about thirty per cent women callers though. Look.' She pointed to the screen where the legend KAREN. QUEENSWAY was flashing.

Jo smiled up at Webber who returned the gesture.

She held his gaze for a second then returned to typing in the names of new callers.

'What exactly are you hoping to find here, Mr Webber?' Osborne asked him.

'A straw,' said Webber, gazing out of the production-room window at Amy.

Because that's what I'm clutching at.

Osborne looked puzzled and, again, looked the policeman up and down.

'Am I bothering you?' Webber asked without looking at the producer.

'What makes you think that?' Osborne said.

'Just curious,' Webber told him, lighting up a cigarette.

Osborne glared irritably at the policeman's broad back.

Amy raised a hand and waved when she saw Webber standing watching her.

He smiled back at her, listening to her conversation over the speakers in the production room.

'. . . I think it's bloody crazy, the amount these so-called stars get paid,' said Gary from Hanwell. 'I mean, you get five dozy tarts singing some crap song and the next thing they're making a bloody film or advertising drink. It's mental.'

'Do you think everyone in showbiz is overpaid, Gary?' Amy asked him.

'Most of them. I mean, you've got your real superstars like Madonna, people like that, I mean, they deserve their money and some of these actors too, they deserve it but most of them they just get a load of money dumped in their lap for doing sod all. I bet *you're* on a bloody good wage for just sitting there and talking every night.'

'Well, thanks for your concern, Gary. I do okay. There *is* a bit more to it than just talking, you know.'

'Yeah, but before that you used to get paid for taking your clothes off, didn't you? I mean, that's hardly difficult, is it?'

'No, taking your clothes off is easy but modelling is hard work.'

'Getting flown to all different parts of the world. Having all your hotels paid for, all your food bought for you. If that's hard work, I reckon *I* could do that.'

'So what's stopping you? If you think it's so easy, why not have a go yourself.'

'Don't be stupid, I couldn't do that.'

'You just said it was easy.'

'I've got a proper job.'

'What do you do?'

'I'm an electrician.'

'So, why is your job any more worthwhile than a model or a singer or any other kind of entertainer?'

'Because I work hard for mine. I support a wife and kid on my money. I have to watch every penny. I can't just run out and buy a ten-thousand-pound watch when I feel like it, like some of these bloody so-called celebrities do. They've got so much money it's obscene. There are ordinary people struggling to make a living and you've got these rich bastards pissing away money they don't even deserve. There's no justice in this world.'

He hung up.

Amy looked up at Webber who merely shrugged.

In agreement perhaps?

Amy took the next call.

'Holly from Tottenham,' she announced. 'Anything to add to what the last caller said or did you want to make a different point?'

In the production room Webber was smiling.

'They get pretty heated, don't they?' he said. 'What happens if anyone swears while they're talking to Amy? How do you cut it out?'

'There's a four-second delay on each call,' Osborne explained.

'I should think you'd need it with some of them,' Webber continued, puffing on his cigarette.

'Well, people get passionate about things they care about,' Osborne said. 'Isn't there anything *you're* passionate about?'

Webber opened his mouth to say something but Jo suddenly raised a hand to attract his attention.

'Detective,' she said. 'I think I've got him.'

Webber crossed to her and looked at the screen.

'Are you sure?'

'That's the only way he ever identifies himself,' Jo explained.

She typed in one word and they both watched it glowing on the screen:

ROY

'I'm sure it's him,' Jo said.

'All right,' Webber instructed her, 'put him on.'

Sixty-Four

'It's been a long time, Roy,' said Amy. 'Where have you been? I've missed you.'

'Don't lie to me,' said the voice that had become all too familiar.

'Sorry, I didn't mean to add lying to my list of crimes. What are they? Would you like to run through them again for the benefit of those listeners who didn't hear you ranting last time.'

Silence.

'Come on, Roy,' she chided. 'You reeled off a long list of things I'd done wrong. Tell me again what they were.'

'You know.'

'Oh yes, I remember now. I'm immoral, aren't I? I have no standards. I have no self-respect and now you're calling me a liar too.'

'Does he always use a mobile?' asked Webber, listening to the conversation over the speakers.

Jo nodded.

'No way of tracing it. Crafty bastard.'

He straightened up and looked through into the studio, watching Amy.

'So, why are you calling, Roy?' she asked him. 'Afraid we might have forgotten who you are?'

'You think you're so funny, don't you? You think you can humiliate me on your little show.'

'I wasn't trying to humiliate you, Roy. What gives you *that* idea?'

'I've been watching you,' Roy said flatly.

Amy shuddered involuntarily. Those icy fingers were playing across her neck again.

'And what have you seen?'

'I've seen you come and go.'

'Where do I live then, Roy?'

'A flat.'

Her flesh rose in goosebumps. 'Whereabouts?' she demanded.

'You wouldn't want me to tell *everyone*, would you?'

'Do you think he's bluffing?' Jo asked Webber.

'He could be,' Webber said.

'And if he's not?' Osborne added.

'Are you planning on killing anyone else then, Roy? That's what you usually ring up to tell us, isn't it? When you're going to kill someone.'

'You don't listen properly,' he said angrily. 'I've never said *when* I'm going to kill, only that I will.'

'So the murders are going to go on, are they, Roy?'

Silence.

'Come on, talk to me. Who are you going to kill next?'

'You.'

She swallowed hard.

'I told you I would,' he continued. 'That's why I've been watching you. Tracking you.'

The laugh that rolled down the phone line froze her blood.

'Can't you do anything?' Osborne said angrily.

'Like what?' Webber demanded.

'You can do voice prints, can't you?'

'Chances are he's using some kind of electronic scrambler to disguise his voice. A little bit more sophisticated than a hankie over the fucking mouthpiece,' snapped Webber. 'Besides, I don't think he's kosher.'

'How can you be sure?' Osborne demanded.

'Gut feeling.'

'Policeman's instinct?' chided the producer.

'Something like that,' Webber replied, trying to ignore the scorn in the other man's voice. 'Besides, Amy told me on the way here that she'd asked this geezer about the killings before but that he couldn't give her any details. Nothing specific. I'd bet money he's just trying to frighten her.' He spun round. 'How can I speak to her now, while she's got him on the line?'

'This microphone is connected to her headset,' Osborne told him, indicating a small mike close to his console. 'It works like an earpiece – she'll be able to hear you but the listeners won't.'

'Work it for me,' Webber said, leaning closer to the microphone.

Osborne looked indignant.

'Just do it,' Webber snapped.

The producer complied.

'Amy, it's Jake,' she heard in her headset. 'Ask him what colour hair the first prostitute he killed had.'

'Roy, those prostitutes you killed,' she began. 'Did you kill the first one the way you're going to kill me?'

In the booth, Webber frowned. *What the hell was she playing at?*

'That would spoil the surprise, wouldn't it?' Roy said.

'What colour hair did she have?' Amy persisted.

'Who knows? It could have been dyed. Everything about her was false. She deserved to die.'

'So you don't know?' Amy said disparagingly.

'Ask him whose wrists he cut,' Webber's voice persisted.

'Jesus,' murmured Osborne. 'I thought the victims were strangled.'

'They were. But one of them was cut too. Only the killer would know which one. The papers just mentioned mutilations.'

'Whose wrists did you cut?' Amy asked, doing as she was instructed.

Silence.

'He doesn't know,' murmured Webber.

'Roy, can you hear me?' Amy said more urgently.

'Details aren't important,' the voice said finally.

'Because *you* don't know them,' she said damningly.

'I'll cut *your* wrists,' he said.

He hung up.

'You're putting her at risk,' Osborne said angrily. 'Making her talk to this maniac.'

'She wouldn't do it if she didn't want to,' said Webber, watching Amy through the glass partition.

He noticed that she was reaching for another cigarette. What he couldn't see was that her hands were trembling.

Sixty-Five

'It's getting out of control.'

Andrew Chapman ran a hand through his hair in a gesture of near desperation. He sat in the leather chair for a moment, then stood up and began pacing Charlotte Kilbride's office, finally crossing to the window, peering out into Harley Street.

'I thought I was learning to get a grip on it out . . .'

The psychiatrist looked at him, noticing how pale his skin was. The dark rings beneath his eyes stood out even more starkly against the pallor.

'You *are* learning to control it, Andrew.'

He shook his head. 'I can't,' he said, a note of defeat in his voice. 'I'm weak, I know that.'

'It took a tremendous amount of strength for you to come here in the first place. Even more so to come here today. By admitting to yourself that you've got a problem you're showing strength, not weakness. Don't be ashamed.'

'I'm *not* ashamed,' he snarled angrily.

'How did you manage to get here today?'

'I called in sick.'

'Does your wife know?'

'She doesn't know I'm *here*. I've told you before, if she found out about me coming to you it would kill her.'

'Why? What's so bad about you seeking help?'

'You don't understand, do you?' He turned to face her. As he did, he found his eyes drawn to her legs. They were crossed, her skirt riding up towards her thigh.

Aware of his probing gaze, Charlotte shifted position, smoothing the material of the skirt, brushing a thread from it.

He's watching you.

'It's as if I live two lives,' he said wearily. 'As if I'm two people in here.' He tapped his forehead. 'Even *I'm* beginning to lose sight of who's the *real* one.'

He wandered back towards the leather chair and sat down.

'I can't think straight any more,' he said. 'I try to work, I function day-to-day but it's like it's a robot, not me. Like I'm looking at myself from the outside. Detatched from what I do. I feel as if I'm losing grip on what's real and what's not. There are so many things going round in my mind, I can't seem to focus on one thing for more than a few seconds at a time.'

She sat listening, watching, never taking her eyes from him as he spoke.

'And I'm frightened,' he told her.

'Of what?'

'What I might do.'

Charlotte scribbled something on the notepad before her, aware that he was following her every movement.

'Afraid that you might hurt someone? Yourself even?'

'I wouldn't hurt myself but I might hurt someone else.' He lowered his head slightly. 'It wouldn't be the first time, would it?'

Charlotte held his gaze, her heart beating a little faster.

'Who else have you hurt, Andrew?' she enquired, her tone softening.

'You know.'

'The prostitute you told me about?'

He was tracing patterns on the arm of the chair.

'There have been others too,' he said finally.

'Who?'

He looked straight at her, his eyes boring into her.

'Help me before I hurt anyone else,' he said. There was a note of pleading in his voice.

'Tell me about the others you've hurt, Andrew. I can't help you unless you do.'

She was trying to keep her voice calm, trying not to let the professional mask slip, but beneath her apparently relaxed exterior she felt as if every muscle in her body was knotted.

He sat there silently.

Charlotte wanted to grab him and shake it out of him, *force* him to tell her the truth.

Stay calm, let him speak in his own time.

'Andrew,' she prompted softly.

He looked at his watch. 'I can't talk, not now,' he said, getting to his feet.

She rose with him, unable to restrain herself any longer.

'Who else have you hurt?' she asked.

He would only shake his head, then he looked her directly in the eye again and she wilted beneath that stare.

He turned towards the door, anxious to be out of the room, as if the atmosphere was suffocating him.

'Thanks for your time,' he said, then he was gone.

Charlotte stood behind her desk gazing at the closed office door, listening to his footsteps receding down the stairs.

'Shit,' she murmured, looking down at his file. She sat down and began flicking slowly through it.

'Help me before I hurt anyone else.'

His words echoed inside her mind.

Sixty-Six

Blurred visions.

Dreams?

Some kind of waking nightmare?

Amy closed her eyes again and tried to roll over, tried to escape the dream. She felt pain in her chest, particularly around her left breast.

Oh God, had the cancer begun to spread more rapidly?

She tried to remember what had happened to her, more convinced now that this *wasn't* a dream. The smell of disinfectant was strong in her nostrils and she could feel linen beneath her fingers. She was in a bed. But where? The thoughts, the remembrance came with difficulty at first. Incidents, words and visions tumbled through her mind in a disordered stream.

She opened her eyes again, saw white walls, indistinct outlines.

She had arrived at the hospital at eight that morning carrying just an overnight bag containing a change of clothes, toothbrush and some make-up. That kind of thing. Everything had moved so quickly. She had been shown to her room. Then she changed into a surgical gown. She vaguely remembered talking with a doctor but she couldn't remember what about.

Amy blinked hard and tried to focus. *Still so tired.* She couldn't remember the doctor's face. *Why won't my head clear?*

She tried to swallow but her throat was dry. *Anaesthetic wearing off.*

Her eyes jerked open. *The operation. The biopsy.*

The moment of savage clarity passed and she closed her eyes again.

She lay on the bed, every muscle tight despite the after-effects of the anaesthetic because with the realisation of where she was came the fear of what might happen to her. She exhaled deeply and tried to clench her fists, to force herself from this immobility. She felt warm flesh against her own.

A hand closed over her forearm and squeezed gently.

She turned her head to one side and saw a blurred shape and, as she stared, it began to take on detail.

She rubbed her eyes with her free hand and looked towards the bedside.

'Hello, you,' said Jake Webber softly.

He reached forward and brushed some hair from her forehead, allowing his hand to stroke her cheek.

'How long . . .' The words disappeared in the dryness of her throat.

Webber reached across to the bedside cabinet and handed her a beaker filled with water. There was a straw sticking out of it and he pushed it towards her mouth. She sucked the fluid down, swallowed, then drank some more.

'Thanks,' she murmured as he took it away.

'How do you feel?'

'I don't know,' she said, managing a wan smile. 'How long have I been out?'

'Two hours.'

'And how long have *you* been here?'

'About two hours. I was here when they brought you back from surgery.' He smiled. 'I told them I was your boyfriend. They said it was okay for me to wait.'

'My boyfriend,' she said, squeezing his hand.

He watched her as she lay there.

'I'll go if you want to rest.'

She shook her head.

'I don't want you to go,' Amy reassured him, and Webber leaned forward and planted a kiss on her forehead. 'Unless you have to.'

'I rang Grant this morning, told him about that call last night,' he said.

'Do you still think Roy isn't the killer?'

'He didn't seem to know enough details about the murders. I've got a hunch he's just some sad bastard who's enjoying the attention. On the other hand he could be cleverer than any of us think. The calls might be some kind of double bluff. Make us believe he *doesn't* know anything.'

'What did Grant say?'

'He said to play it by ear, if you'll pardon the pun. Don't dismiss the bastard, just in case.'

'Just in case he really *is* going to try to kill me?'

'Grant said I should keep an eye on you.'

'So that's the only reason you're here,' she said sleepily.

He squeezed her hand more tightly then kissed her on the lips.

The door opened and they both looked over to see who had entered.

Dr Alan Davidson crossed to the bed, scribbled something on the clipboard he was carrying, then hung it on the end of the bed.

'So, what's the news, doctor?' Amy asked.

'The biopsy went without any problems, we took a sample of the tissue. The next step is to get it analysed. We'll take it from there once we know what we're dealing with.'

'How long will that be?'

'Three or four days,' Davidson said.

'So what do I do in the meantime?' she asked. 'Sit around and worry myself even sicker?'

'We can't do the tests any quicker, I wish we could,' said Davidson apologetically.

'When can I go home?'

'Tomorrow.'

'How about tonight?' she said, sitting up.

'If you insist but I wouldn't recommend it,' he told her. 'You've had surgery, you shouldn't risk splitting your stitches.'

'What if I promise not to carry any sacks of cement around? Can I go home then?'

Davidson smiled. 'I suppose so,' he relented. 'But be careful.'

'I'll make sure she is, doctor,' Webber added.

'I want to go back to work as soon as possible,' she said defiantly.

'I would recommend rest for two or three days,' Davidson said.

'If I have to sit around with nothing to think about except what might be wrong with me I'll go insane,' Amy insisted. 'My mind's working overtime now.'

Davidson exhaled wearily. 'Again, I can't say I approve, but if you feel capable.'

'I've got to go back. I told you why.'

The doctor could only nod. 'I'm not going to try to stop you,' he said. 'I get the feeling I'd be fighting a losing battle.'

He turned to leave.

'What are the odds on me being okay, doctor?' Amy asked as he reached the door. 'On it being cancer?'

Davidson held up his hands in a gesture of surrender.

'What can I say?' he said. 'The tissue is either benign or malignant. That's all anyone can tell you at the moment. I wish I could tell you more. You'll have to wait. I'm sorry.'

'Thanks,' she said, trying to force a smile.

Davidson nodded then left.

'I don't want to die, Jake.'

'You're not going to die,' he said, squeezing her hand reassuringly, the look in his eye almost convincing her.

'If Roy is the killer then it looks like I've got a choice,' she said humourlessly. 'Either *he* kills me or the cancer does.'

'I told you, Amy. You're not going to die. I won't let you. I've already lost one thing in my life I loved. I won't lose another.'

She squeezed his hand and, as she did so, a single tear trickled from the corner of her eye.

Sixty-Seven

As David Albury swung the Jag into the multi-storey in South Audley Street he glanced down at the dashboard clock. In the gloom the green digits glowed.

10.56 p.m.

He guided the car up the entry ramp, the wheels squealing slightly in the silence as he steered it up towards level two. The place was practically deserted. Barely a dozen cars could be seen on each level. He hadn't even spotted an attendant in the payment area when he'd entered.

Perfect.

Albury pressed a button and the driver's side window rolled down with an electronic whirr. Immediately the smell of oil and petrol spilled into the car, and he wrinkled his nose at the cloying odour. The sound of the engine reverberated off the cold concrete walls and low ceilings as he drove.

Finally, he brought the vehicle to a halt in one of the bays towards the rear of the level. There were four or five other cars parked there. Otherwise, the place was silent.

He looked down again at the dashboard clock, thinking that time seemed to be moving slowly. He'd agreed to meet at eleven and there were less than three minutes until that appointed time.

He looked at his watch, as if that simple act would accelerate time.

Finally, he swung himself out of the Jag, the bones in his knees cracking loudly in the process. He winced and stood up, massaging the back of his neck with one hand and scanning the darkened car park for any signs of movement.

Fluorescents were set into the low ceiling but they

burned with such a cold, faltering light that they seemed barely adequate for their task. All around the meagre puddles of vague luminosity they gave off were oceans of blackness.

Again Albury looked at his watch then scanned the level.

Below him he heard something. The sound of footsteps from the lower level seemed deafening in the stillness. He heard voices. Someone laughed. A high-pitched feminine laugh. He heard two doors slam then the sound of an engine being started.

He stood motionless beside the Jag, listening to the car on the lower level pull away, tyres whining. The sound gradually died away and Albury let out a somewhat shaky breath.

The figure emerged from behind one of the concrete pillars close to him.

Albury spun round as he heard footsteps, his heart racing momentarily. Then, gradually, a look of recognition spread across his face.

'You're late,' Albury said. 'Get in.' He motioned to the passenger side.

Both Albury and the newcomer slid into the leather seats and sat for a while, in the blackness and the silence. 'I told you not to call me at home.' Albury finally broke the silence. He was staring straight ahead, gazing out of the windscreen. 'I asked you not to use my private number unless it was important. I thought you understood that.'

He felt a hand on his thigh. Resting there.

At last he turned and looked at the newcomer, whose features were still partially obscured by the gloom inside the car park.

The hand on his thigh moved higher – fingers were stroking gently across his groin now.

'I have to be careful,' Albury whispered as the movements of the fingers became more urgent. 'You know that.'

The figure leaned across and Albury moved to meet the advance.

'I have to be careful,' he said again, aware now of his erection throbbing beneath the skilled fingers that continued to knead him through his trousers.

His protestations were stifled by a kiss.

Tender at first then more persuasive.

When Albury finally sat back his breath was coming in gasps.

'We'd better go,' he said, smiling as he started the engine.

The figure nodded and slid down further into the passenger seat.

Sixty-Eight

Amy Watson rolled over and stretched, suddenly aware of a slight pain in her left breast. *The stitches.*

She sat up, lifting up her T-shirt slightly, inspecting the dressing that covered the breast.

No blood.

She had wondered what might happen if the stitches split during the night but she was relieved to see that there had been no such mishap.

Beside her, Webber stirred and turned his head to see what she was doing.

'Are you okay?' he asked, his voice sleepy.

She nodded. 'Just panicking again,' she told him, attempting a smile.

He reached across and touched the smooth flesh of her thigh, smiling as Amy lay down again and moved closer to him. He felt the warmth of her body against his and they kissed gently.

'Thanks for staying last night,' she said.

'What did you think I was going to do, drive you home from the hospital and leave you?'

She laid her head on his chest and felt him stroking her hair gently. The slow, rhythmic rise and fall of his chest was somehow reassuring and she pulled herself closer, one leg draped over his thigh.

'Are you really going in to work tonight?' he asked.

'I've got to, Jake. If I sit around here I'll go mad. What about you? Are you coming with me?'

'It depends what Grant wants me to do.'

'What is it between you and him?'

'I don't like him.'

'I gathered that.'

'I don't like the bastard and I don't trust him.'

'When he was here the other night, you said he'd fucked you over. What did he do?'

Webber sighed. 'We worked together in the Vice Squad,' he said wearily. 'We were a pretty good team. We had the record for most arrests two years running. Most of it was just bullshit stuff, little things, but one success was breaking up a paedophile ring that was trading by computer. Fifteen guys went down for that and related incidents.' As he spoke he continued to stroke her hair.

'So what went wrong?'

'There was a club owner in Soho who'd been dealing in snuff videos. Grant and I had been after him for years but we couldn't nail the bastard on anything. Then we got a sniff that he was dealing drugs too. I went over to Amsterdam to check out his supplier. Grant stayed here and kept his eye on the club owner. While I was out there, I found out that they sent the drugs back *inside* the video cases. Inside the cassette itself. The cases are always empty anyway.'

'What do you mean?'

'When porn is shipped into this country from abroad it doesn't come in the way you get it from sex shops. The spools and the tape are separated and carried in cases. Customs can't nick somebody for being in possession of miles of half-inch tape and fifty spools. It's all re-set and spooled up when they get it into this country – that's why the picture and sound quality on a lot of porn is shit. The cassette cases are shipped separately.'

Amy listened intently, trailing her fingers across Webber's belly.

'I found out these cassettes were filled with heroin,' Webber continued. 'I notified Grant and he was waiting for them when they arrived in England. Case closed. The club owner got ten years. Grant got promoted to detective inspector and I got fuck all.' He chuckled.

'Didn't Grant tell anyone you'd tipped him off?'

'What do *you* think?'

'I can understand you being mad.'

'He was right, *I* didn't want the fucking promotion. It pissed me off more that he could take the credit without even mentioning *me*. I didn't want any bloody medals. I just wanted him to admit that he couldn't have cracked it without me.'

'Why did you leave the Vice Squad?'

'I moved over to Murder Squad when Grant moved.' He chuckled again. 'Perhaps I just can't bear to be away from him. I've been working undercover for the last two years.'

She looked up at him.

'Anything else you want to know?' he asked, smiling.

She was about to say something when the phone rang.

Amy rolled over and picked it up.

'Hello,' she said, feeling Webber's finger weave a pattern over the small of her back.

'Amy, it's Jo,' the voice at the other end said. 'I was just ringing to see how you were. I saw the papers. I didn't know it was that bad. I'm sorry.'

'Sorry, Jo, I've lost you. What are you talking about?'

'There's a half-page in the *Sun* saying that you underwent major surgery,' Jo told her. 'There's more in the *Star* and the *Mirror*. The *Star* mentions breast cancer.'

Amy swallowed hard. 'Today's papers?'

'I thought you knew.'

'I'll call you back, Jo. Thanks for letting me know.'

'Amy, if there's anything I can do . . .'

'I appreciate it.'

Amy replaced the receiver and sat motionless, staring ahead blankly.

'What is it?' Webber asked, sitting up.

'Jo says it's all over the papers about this,' she looked down at her breast. 'How could they know?'

'Amy, people know your face, anyone could have seen you going into hospital and called one of the papers. It might even have been one of the nurses or doctors.'

'What happened to confidentiality for the patient?' she

said, a note of distress in her voice. 'How can those bastards run stories about this?'

'You know what the press are like. They couldn't give a fuck. You're news, Amy. It's as simple as that.'

'But not about *this*, Jake,' she said, turning to face him. 'I don't want people to know what's wrong with me. Except that now it seems as if half the fucking country knows.'

The tears he saw forming in her eyes were of rage.

Sixty-Nine

'She's a target now.'

Webber lit up another cigarette and blew a stream of smoke in Grant's direction.

'If your theory's right, about the killer going after people with illness,' Webber continued, 'then she's prime material.'

Grant nodded.

'A celebrity. Not some fucking low-life wino or pro,' Webber continued. 'If he goes after *her* and he gets her, that's one hell of a scalp for him.'

'What if he hasn't seen the papers today?' said Lawrenson.

'Do me a favour, Stuart,' grunted Webber. 'Three tabloids ran stories on her, three of them printed topless pictures. Even the fucking *Independent* ran a couple of columns. He can't have missed it.'

'I agree with Webber,' said Grant, getting to his feet. 'He can't have missed it. He's no fool.' Grant looked at Webber. 'We need to get some surveillance into that studio, trace those calls from this geezer who keeps ringing in.'

'Roy,' Webber told him.

'It's not easy to trace a mobile,' Lawrenson interjected.

'I'm not saying it's going to be easy, but it can be done,' Grant insisted. 'I *want* it done.'

'I'm not sure he's the one,' said Webber. 'He's too vague about the killings.'

'Well it's the only fucking lead we've got and I want it followed up,' Grant snapped. 'Besides, I would have thought you'd have been anxious to protect your girlfriend, Jake.'

Webber glared back at him.

'Stuart, go and see about that surveillance, will you?' Grant said, looking at Lawrenson, who nodded and left the office.

When Grant looked back, Webber was still glaring at him.

'You've got good taste, Jake, I'll give you that. Used to be a model, didn't she? Topless. Full frontal. The full monty, wasn't it? You're a lucky man.' He grinned crookedly. 'She's slumming it a bit with you though. I heard she'd been out with rock musicians, writers and Christ knows what else. Did she fancy a bit of rough?'

'Fuck you, Grant.'

'No, fuck *you*, Jake. Remember who's the fucking boss here.'

'How could I forget, *Detective Inspector*.' He emphasised the last two words contemptuously.

'So, what happens when you move out?' Grant wanted to know. 'Are you going to carry on seeing her?'

'I came in here to talk about this murder case, not my fucking love-life.'

'I'm just curious, Jake. I mean, you see these models in the papers and in magazines. It just makes you wonder if they put it about like they say.'

'She hasn't modelled for over six years.'

'She still looks good though. I bet she knows her way around.'

Webber got to his feet.

'You worked vice too long, Grant,' he said dismissively.

'I bet she's great in bed, isn't she? Pity about the operation. I mean, if it *is* cancer, they'll have to take her tit off, won't they?'

Webber suddenly lunged forward across the desk, hands reaching for his superior.

Grant stepped back raising his fists.

'Any time, Jake,' he snapped.

'I'll see you when this is over,' Webber snarled and spun round, heading for the door. When he got there he paused. 'By the way, who's your missus fucking these days?'

And he was gone.

Seventy

Andrew Chapman walked briskly through the bustling hordes that thronged the pavements of Soho. He walked with purpose, unlike so many others who meandered along the narrow, neon-soaked thoroughfares gawping into the windows of shops, or peering almost guiltily through the doorways of peep shows or strip clubs. Some even parted the doors of hanging multi-coloured plastic strips, the only barrier between the outside world and the forbidden pleasures beyond.

Chapman saw three youths doing just that, laughing to themselves, anxious to enter but not finding the courage. One of them said something to a young woman standing close to the door of 'The Pirate Club' who was handing out fliers. She ignored him and his inane remarks, looking past him towards others who filed by.

A couple of Ann Summers' shops he passed had been forced to cover their windows with black tape or shutters (one of the more noticeable effects of the Albury Bill, he thought) but it didn't deter prying eyes.

He saw a couple looking intently at the rubber and latex wear on display in one window, the young man gently stroking his companion's buttocks as they stood watching, talking in hushed tones. He heard the girl laugh softly and saw her move closer to her boyfriend.

The sidestreets were darker than the main thoroughfares – like furred veins running from the main arteries of light. A tall man in a worn suit stood at the door of a club whose sign was flickering, threatening to go out permanently. He called out something out Chapman ignored it. He had no desire to visit *that* club. He remembered it as being dirty. The women who danced inside it were older. Past their best. Not what he wanted.

Music spilled from many of the doorways as he passed other shops and clubs. With so many restaurants and bars amongst them, the area was always busy, and the constant chatter of so many diners and drinkers mingled with the unceasing music to form one unholy din.

There was a loud argument going on between two men outside one pub on the corner of Old Compton Street and Wardour Street. Chapman saw fingers being pointed angrily and hurried past the scene. Others loitered close by, slowing their pace as if expecting or anticipating the possible violence that might come from the exchange.

Chapman had no interest in watching two men fight. He had other things on his mind.

He turned a corner, ignoring a man who was sitting on the pavement playing an accordion, a blanket between his legs with loose change scattered across it. He heard a call for change but dismissed it.

Up ahead he saw the place he sought.

The doorway was lit by flashing neon strips in the shape of a pair of pursed lips. Beside the entrance there were several framed but faded pictures of young women in varying stages of undress. They pouted alluringly at those who would look.

Beyond the main entrance there was a small desk, a little like the check-in desk at an airport. The man who sat behind it took Chapman's money without speaking and gave him a small ticket that looked as though it had been torn from a raffle book.

PRIVATE BOOTHS a sign to his left announced.

Chapman smiled and walked in.

Seventy-One

Charlotte Kilbride was halfway home when she realised she'd left her Filofax in the office.

At first she decided that it wasn't such a problem. She had no calls to make when she got home. It could wait until the morning. No harm would come to it locked up in her office. Then she realised she'd left her mobile phone there too.

She'd left later than usual, determined to write up some case notes that had been left untouched for a week. That, she told herself, was the reason for the aberration. She was normally so organised, so methodical. To forget one item was annoying, to forget two was simply stupid. She felt she had no choice but to go back.

Wearily, she turned the car as soon as she could and began driving back towards Harley Street. By the time she finally got home, she reasoned, it would be too late to eat. She wouldn't want food by that time. She decided to leave the car outside the office and dine out. It had been a while since she'd done that, and, besides, after the workload she'd got through that evening, she felt she deserved a little pampering. The prospect of being waited on, sitting in a bistro sipping wine and enjoying good pasta suddenly seemed to override her annoyance at having to turn back.

The traffic, she was delighted to find, wasn't as heavy heading back to the office and less than half an hour later she pulled up in front of the building again.

She pulled the keys from her jacket pocket, locked the car, then headed up the steps to the front door and let herself in.

Silence greeted her as she walked in, enveloping her

like an invisible hand. That was wrong. *Why wasn't the alarm going off?* Had she forgotten to set *that* too?

Charlotte hesitated in the long narrow hallway for a moment, thinking back to when she left the office. She was sure she had set it.

Positive?

She looked at the panel beside the door. No blinking red lights. Perhaps she *had* forgotten. Perhaps working so late and so hard was something to be avoided in the future, she thought, smiling to herself as she moved through the darkened hall towards the stairs.

Only at the bottom did she bother to slap on a light, then she ascended swiftly, the stairs creaking beneath her. Had she not been in such a hurry she might have noticed that one of the paintings that hung on the wall had been knocked askew. Even if she had seen it, she might have simply assumed that the cleaner had done it accidentally.

She reached the landing and flicked on the light switch there. It clicked but no light was illuminated. The landing remained in darkness. The bulb would have to be changed, she noted.

Charlotte selected the key to her office door and inserted it. The door swung open as she touched it.

She saw that paint had been scraped off around the lock, even pieces of wood were scattered across the threshold.

She took a step towards the partition, her heart thudding hard against her ribs.

Get out now.

The door swung further open to reveal what lay beyond.

Don't wait. Just get out. Call the police.

But she was transfixed by the sight before her. Her office had been ransacked. No, that was a barely adequate description. It had been demolished.

Her desk was overturned. Banks of filing cabinets had been toppled. Books swept from their shelves. Pictures had even been ripped from the walls, glass from their frames lay across the floor like crystal confetti. The scale of the destruction was breathtaking. It was as if every single item and object in the room had been either broken or disturbed in some way.

Get out.

She turned to leave.

Something hard struck her across the face. The impact lifted her off her feet and sent her toppling backwards into the ruined office, blood spilling from a cut on her cheek.

She raised a hand to protect herself and felt another thudding impact against her wrist. The pain and the accompanying crack told her that it had been broken. She tried to force out a scream but it seemed locked in her throat.

In the darkness of her office she found it difficult to focus on her assailant. A task made impossible as she was struck again across the bridge of the nose. A blow that shattered bone and sent blood spewing into the gloom.

She dropped to her knees and tried to lift her head. A thunderous blow hit the top of her skull and consciousness began to slip away. The room was becoming darker but somehow she clung to her senses and dragged herself to her feet, her head spinning, blood now pouring warmly from several cuts. Charlotte was gripped by a sudden and uncontrollable fear. A vice-like conviction that she was going to die, despite every effort to save herself. A powerful blow broke her jaw, smashed teeth and sent two of them tearing through her top lip.

She reeled, tears flowing as well as blood.

Then powerful hands gripped her wrist and she felt herself being swung round, helpless in the grasp of her attacker. Consciousness didn't desert her quickly enough now.

She realised she was being flung towards the window.

The glass came hurtling towards her as her assailant finally let her go.

She struck the window, crashed through it and seemed to hang in the air, suspended like a puppet on invisible strings. Then she plummeted towards the ground. The ground rushed up to meet her.

Below, spiked railings at the side of the pavement gleamed wickedly in the street light. She hit them first. Two of the points punctured her body, ripping through her heart and lungs, tearing the breath and life from her. Gouts of blood like crimson geysers rose into the air from the wounds. Glass from the broken window showered down over her and shattered into even tinier fragments as they struck the concrete. In the light of the street lamps they sparkled like tears, their lustre finally extinguished as several thick streams of blood covered them.

Inside her office, one floor up, a figure peered quickly out at her impaled body then turned and left as stealthily as it had entered.

Its work was done.

For now.

Seventy-Two

Amy slipped off her headphones and sat back in her chair. Across in the production-booth window Webber was standing, arms folded, cigarette dangling between his lips.

She shrugged.

'He's not going to call, is he?' Jo Parker commented, glancing at her watch.

Webber didn't answer, merely consulted his own time-piece.

1.06 a.m.

'He doesn't call at a specific time, does he?' said the detective, not taking his eyes from Amy.

'We're off the air in ten minutes,' Mike Osborne reminded him.

'Where are you, Roy?' murmured Webber, still gazing at Amy, who was preparing to take another call.

'She's got four callers left,' Jo told him. 'Then that's it.'

Webber nodded.

'It looks like all that surveillance equipment you had brought in was a waste of time,' Osborne observed.

'Perhaps he'll call tomorrow,' Webber said, ignoring the barbed comment.

'Maybe he knows that you were waiting for him,' Osborne said. 'He might be cleverer than you think. He might know you're waiting to trace him.'

Webber took another drag on his cigarette, blowing the smoke out slowly, watching it dissipate in the air, his eyes never leaving Amy.

'Yeah,' he whispered, his eyes narrowing, 'maybe he *does* know.'

Seventy-Three

Dear David,

This note probably won't come as a surprise to you. It probably won't even bother you that much. I've taken most of my clothes, I'll be back for the others in the next few days but I don't suppose I'll see you. I know you're busy. You're always busy. That's one of the reasons I'm leaving . . . There's a number on the back where you can reach me, if you want to. I hope you do.

Tina

David Grant read the note again, turning the paper over to check the number she'd mentioned. He gazed at it for a moment then crumpled up the paper and dropped it into a nearby ashtray.

He was about to pour himself another drink when the phone rang.

Seventy-Four

As Webber ducked beneath the red and yellow tape he saw the bloodstains. The dark blemishes on the pavement outside the house in Harley Street had been covered by what looked like cling-film to prevent them being contaminated. The railings above had been draped in a similar material and he saw that they too were spattered with crimson. A man in a dark suit worn at both elbows was inspecting the railings, taking samples of material and fibre from them with a pair of tweezers. Webber passed him and moved on into the house itself.

In the hallway there were more plainclothes officers, most of whom he took to be from Forensics.

As he drew level with the spacious waiting room he peered in and found two more men in there. One was dusting for fingerprints on the smooth surfaces.

'Where's Grant?' Webber asked the other man.

'Upstairs,' Schofield told him, then looked up and recognised Webber. 'How you doing, Jake?' he added, smiling broadly.

'I've been better, Den. What happened here?'

'He'll tell you,' Schofield answered, pointing towards the ceiling.

Webber made his way up the stairs, pausing to allow another Forensics man past him. He was carrying two small plastic bags.

He reached the landing and turned to his right, spotting more movement through the open door there. Grant was standing close to the window, watching as small pieces of glass were removed from the frame and bagged for examination.

He glanced around at the destruction that had been wrought in Charlotte Kilbride's office. And at the blood.

There were splashes of it in several places. A long slick near his feet, spreading across the expensive carpet. A splash on the wall close to the broken window. More on the desk top.

Grant finally turned and saw Webber looking around.

'Looks like a hell of a party, doesn't it?' Grant commented flatly.

'Who found her?'

'A taxi driver saw the body dangling from the railings. He called it in.'

'What time was she killed?'

'Barclay reckons somewhere between ten and twelve last night. He's doing the full autopsy down at the Yard now. The fall killed her.' Grant nodded towards the shattered window and Webber peered out, looking down at the railings.

'Did the killer give her a belting first?' Webber asked.

'Yeah, with a chair leg, Barclay reckons.'

'Not our man, then?'

'I don't know yet.'

'Come on, the MO couldn't be much more different, could it? Beating someone almost to death with a chair leg then slinging them out of a window doesn't quite have the finesse of strangulation, does it?' Webber muttered. He looked around the room, particularly at the paintings on the wall and some of the ornaments, many of which had been scattered in the struggle. Others, however, still remained in their original positions, including a pair of expensive-looking vases on a shelf near the door.

'The killer disabled the burglar alarm,' said Grant. 'Then he broke in through a ground-floor window at the back.'

'Any prints?'

'Smooth gloves. He knew what he was doing but . . .' Grant smiled '. . . the bastard cut himself on the glass getting in. We've got a sample, it's being typed.'

'Nothing taken by the look of it,' Webber noted. 'Do

you reckon he broke in to kill her and just made it *look* like a burglary?'

'No, something *was* taken.'

'Money? Jewellery?'

'Files.'

Grant walked across to one of the overturned filing cabinets.

'About twenty of them,' Grant continued. 'Patient files. Obviously there was something in one of them that he didn't want anyone to see. When she first contacted me and offered her help she must have thought that the killer might have been one of her patients. It looks like she was right.'

'Any way of finding out which files have gone missing?'

'Her secretary came in this morning, she said they keep copies of every file. The killer obviously didn't know that or else he had to leg it before he had the chance to look for them. Probably after he killed her.'

'So you reckon the geezer who killed Charlotte Kilbride is the one we're looking for?'

'I'd bet money on it,' Grant said smugly. 'As soon as we've got the list sorted out properly, I want to start interviewing them. I've already narrowed it down to eight. The rest are too old, too young or women. The ones I've eliminated don't match up to what we've got on our killer.'

'Which isn't very much'?' Webber reminded him. 'Who's left?'

'A cross section,' Grant said. 'But there is one *very* interesting file. It belongs to Mister, or should I say, the Right Honourable David Albury.'

'The fucking MP?'

Grant nodded.

'She treated him about six months ago for depression,' Grant continued. 'Only a couple of consultations but we'll follow it up anyway.'

'Christ, if the papers got hold of that he'd be a laughing stock,' Webber observed.

'Well, it wouldn't exactly help his public profile, I'll give you that, but I doubt if Albury's our man. I've got a pretty good idea who might be though. I'm going to see him when I leave here.'

Webber was about to ask who when he was interrupted by a shrill bleeping.

Grant dug into his jacket pocket and pulled out his mobile phone, pressing it to his ear.

'Yeah, go on, Phil, what have you got?' he said into the mouthpiece.

While Grant spoke, Webber wandered slowly through the wrecked office running his gaze over the destruction, pausing beside the overturned filing cabinets.

He looked up and saw a number of framed diplomas and certificates on the wall behind her desk. There was a splash of blood on one of them.

He heard Grant snap the mouthpiece of his phone shut and turned to face the other man.

'Barclay's finished the autopsy,' said Grant.

'Did he get a grouping on the blood from the killer?'

'Type O.'

'Great. The most common group. That narrows it down to forty-six per cent of the population. Shit.'

'It narrows it down a lot further than that,' Grant told him. 'Barclay said that there were traces of viral contamination in the blood.'

'What kind of virus?'

'AIDS.'

Seventy-Five

'Should you be doing this?'

Jo Parker glanced across at Amy Watson who was pedalling the exercise bike with steady and powerful strokes of her shapely legs.

Amy wiped perspiration from her face and looked at Jo. There were two other people in the gym, both men, both working with weights on the far side of the room. The only other sound, apart from the steady churning of the bike wheels, was the loud pop music crouching from the speakers set on the gym wall.

'Doing what, Jo?' Amy asked, still pedalling.

'You're not well,' Jo said. 'Wouldn't you be better off resting?'

'Sitting around worrying about how ill I might be, you mean? Moping around my flat thinking about cancer and Christ knows what else.'

Jo regarded her silently, pedalling herself. They had been at the gym for over an hour now and both were stained with perspiration from their exertions.

'I'm sick of people trying to wrap me in cotton wool,' Amy retorted angrily. 'First the doctor tells me I should rest, then Jake says I shouldn't work. Osborne wants me to take it easy and now *you*.'

Jo lowered her gaze. 'I didn't mean any harm,' she said apologetically. 'I asked because I care about you. Sorry if that bothers you.'

She swung herself off the exercise bike, pulled her towel from the handlebars and headed towards the changing rooms.

Amy exhaled wearily then followed her, catching her as she reached the gym exit.

'Jo, I'm sorry,' said Amy, following her friend into the

women's changing room. 'I just wish people would stop
treating me like some kind of invalid.'

'But you're ill, Amy,' Jo reminded her, sitting down on
one of the wooden benches, pulling off her trainers and
socks and dropping them into her sports bag.

Amy also began to undress.

'But I'm not a cripple,' she said gently. 'I appreciate
people's concern, but the more they go on about what
might be wrong with me the more it makes me think
about it.'

She slipped off her leotard and stood there in just a pair
of Lycra leggings, towelling the sweat from her torso.

Jo looked at her breasts, in particular the left one. It
was still bandaged but not so heavily.

'Does it hurt?' Jo dared to ask.

'Only when I think about it,' Amy smiled.

Jo slipped off her leggings and T-shirt and stood naked,
close to Amy. 'I ask because I care,' she said softly, taking
a step closer.

Her face was flushed, her hair plastered to her smooth
skin and Amy could feel the heat from her naked body.

Jo reached out and touched Amy's cheek with her
finger. The touch was electric.

Amy found herself gazing deeply into Jo's eyes.

She reached out and brushed a hair from her friend's
cheek, then stepped back slightly and slid off her leggings.

They stood naked, inches from one another.

'If there's anything I can do, you *will* tell me, won't
you?' Jo said quietly.

Amy nodded.

Jo leaned forward and kissed her friend tenderly on
the left cheek.

'I care, Amy,' she said again, then turned away and
began to pull on her clothes.

Amy blinked hard, as if awaking from a trance, aware
but unconcerned that she was standing naked in the
changing room. She looked at Jo for a moment longer

then she too reached for her clothes, slipping on her bra first, as if anxious to hide the diseased breast.

Diseased?

She shook her head and continued dressing.

'Shall we go and get a drink?' she said, pulling on her jeans. 'I *need* one.'

Seventy-Six

Andrew Chapman looked up as he heard the knock on his office door.

'Come in,' he called.

'There's someone to see you, Mr Chapman,' his secretary told him. 'A Detective Inspector Grant. He says it's important.'

Police.

Chapman's heart jumped several beats.

'Send him in,' he said, his voice cracking. He coughed.

Grant entered, a thin smile on his lips.

'Andrew Chapman,' he said and it came out as a statement rather than a question.

'Yes, please sit down,' Chapman said, gesticulating wildly towards the chair that faced his desk.

Grant ignored the invitation momentarily and crossed to the large picture window that ran the full length of Chapman's office. He looked through the blinds, gazing down on to a view of Piccadilly Circus. An open-top sightseeing bus was passing by, tourists were pointing cameras and camcorders enthusiastically.

Chapman turned in his seat to watch the policeman. The banker's heart had slowed a little but it was still pounding with such force he feared the detective would hear it.

'How can I help you, Detective Inspector?' he asked finally, trying to ensure that his voice sounded as even as he could make it.

Had they traced some of the pornographic videos he'd bought?

Grant turned away from the window and sat down opposite him.

Chapman blanched slightly beneath the inquisitive

gaze of the policeman and, despite efforts not to, he lowered his eyes slightly.

Grant looked across the banker's desk. He took in details like the half-drunk cup of tea, the computer screen filled with numbers, the pad and pen that lay in front of Chapman, numbers and names scrawled on the paper. Then, finally, he looked directly into the other man's eyes.

'Can I get you coffee?' Chapman asked.

Grant shook his head. 'I won't waste your time,' he said tersely. 'We're both busy men. I need you to answer some questions.'

'Whatever I can help you with.'

'How long have you been having psychiatric treatment?'

Chapman swallowed hard.

How did they know?

'You were being treated for, what was it, an addiction, a reliance on pornography. That's right, isn't it?'

Chapman's ability to control his breathing was vanishing rapidly. He sucked in several deep breaths, trying to calm himself.

'You were being treated by Charlotte Kilbride at her Harley Street practice, weren't you?'

'How do you know?'

'I *am* a detective, Mr Chapman. How long have you been seeing her?'

'A year. I can't remember exactly how long.'

'What made you go to her in the first place?'

'What do you mean?'

'Why seek psychiatric help? Looking at a few dirty books never hurt anybody. Did it?'

'There was more to it than that.'

'Like what?'

'I was spending a fortune every month on books and videos. Visiting peep shows.'

'And prostitutes?'

'Occasionally.'

'Did your wife know?'

'No. It would finish her if she did. It would finish *me* if anyone here found out. That was why I needed help.'

'Were you and Charlotte Kiloride close?'

'Meaning what?'

'Did you fancy her? She was an attractive woman. It would have been understandable.'

'I didn't notice.'

'Oh, come on, Mr Chapman. You saw her once a week for a year and you never noticed that she was attractive. You were being treated for a condition that meant your main obsession in life was staring at naked women, either on paper, in films or in the flesh, and you're trying to tell me you never noticed that Charlotte Kilbride was attractive?'

'I suppose she was, I mean, I *did* notice, yes.'

'Did you ever come on to her?'

'No. Never.'

'You never made a move on her? So she never rejected you? You weren't having an affair with her?'

'What the hell is all this about, Inspector?' snapped Chapman, his initial fear turning to confusion.

'Have you ever had an AIDS test?' Grant continued.

'Why would I?'

'You were sleeping with prostitutes.'

'I wasn't sleeping with them, I . . .'

'And you weren't sleeping with Charlotte Kilbride?'

'No, now could you please tell me what's going on?'

'Charlotte Kilbride was murdered last night. Some patient files were stolen from her office. One of them was yours.'

Grant watched as the colour drained from the banker's face. Chapman tried to swallow but it felt as if his throat was being constricted. His mouth opened and closed soundlessly for a second.

Got you, you bastard, thought Grant, glaring even more intently at his quarry.

'She was murdered between ten and twelve last night,

Mr Chapman,' he persisted. 'Can you account for your movements between that time?'

Chapman lowered his head even more.

'Could your wife supply you with an alibi?' Grant continued.

Turn that screw a little more.

'Please don't tell my wife,' Chapman blurted, his eyes bulging in their sockets.

'Don't tell her what? That you're a suspect in a murder case? She's going to find that out soon enough anyway.'

'She doesn't know about any of this. The therapy or my problem. Please don't tell her.'

For a second, Grant thought the other man was going to burst into tears.

'You're worried about your wife finding out that you read dirty books and *I'm* telling you you're a murder suspect. Which is worse?'

'I didn't kill Charlotte Kilbride? Why should I?'

'Because she was convinced that *you* were the killer who's been topping pimps, pushers, prostitutes and all the others. She wanted to crack the case herself.'

'How do you know that?'

'Because it's in your file. All her notes about you. Her thoughts. Her suspicions. Now, why would she think you were the sort of man who could kill seventeen people, Mr Chapman? Or is it eighteen now?'

'That's ridiculous,' Chapman said, his face milk-white.

'She was on to you so you killed her. You knew that all her theories were in your file so you stole it to protect yourself and you killed her. You just forgot that she kept duplicate files, didn't you?'

'Are you charging me?'

'I'm just talking to you.'

'I'm not sure I want to say anything else without a lawyer here.'

Grant got to his feet.

'Fair enough,' he said. 'I've said what I came to say

anyway. Where would you like to do the next interview? Here, at New Scotland Yard or at home?' Grant
smiled again.

'I didn't kill her,' Chapman said, also standing up.

'Well then, you won't mind if we talk again and there's
something else. I need you to take a blood test.'

'What for?'

'Just routine procedure,' Grant told him, opening the
office door.

As he stepped out he saw faces turned towards
Chapman's office. One of them, a tall man with grey
hair, ran curious eyes over the policeman.

Chapman followed Grant out and saw the grey-haired
man. He nodded hesitantly towards him, his mind spinning. Duncan Scott had been manager of the branch ever
since Chapman had worked there. Nothing happened in
the bank without him knowing.

Scott watched for a moment longer then wandered into
his own office further down the hall.

'I'll be in touch,' said Grant, and headed for the escalator that would take him back to street level.

Chapman was aware of the faces turned in his direction. Of cashiers watching him from behind their glass
partition. Of secretaries casting furtive glances from the
other side of their desks.

He retreated quickly back into his office and closed the
door, aware of the perspiration that had beaded on his
forehead.

He sat down, his hands shaking, his head reeling. He
stared blankly ahead, his mind unable to focus on any one
single thought. Fear enveloped him and crushed him like
a powerful fist. For fleeting seconds he thought he was
going to be sick.

His phone rang. An internal call.

He sucked in a couple of deep breaths then lifted the
receiver.

'Andrew Chapman,' he said, trying to sound unconcerned.

'Andrew, it's Duncan Scott,' said the voice at the other end of the line. 'Could you spare me a moment or two in my office now, please?'

'I'll be straight down, Mr Scott,' Chapman said, replacing the receiver.

What now? How much worse could it get?

'He's cracking already,' said Grant, sliding into the passenger seat of the car.

Stuart Lawrenson looked across at his superior.

'I want surveillance on him,' Grant continued. 'Assign two men, day and night, and let the bastard *know* they're there. I want him to know we're watching him. Get phone taps sorted out too. One for this office line and one for his home phone. If Chapman has a shit I want to know about it. We've got him and he knows it. I'll have him charged within three days, you'll see.'

Seventy-Seven

Amy stretched on the sofa and looked down at Webber, who was sitting on the floor with his back to her, poring over some paperwork.

She leaned forward and gently massaged his shoulders, feeling the stiffness there.

'You're tense,' she said softly, kissing his ear lightly.

'That's the story of my life,' said Webber, smiling at her. He looked back at the file he'd been reading.

'Do you think that this Chapman bloke is the killer?' she asked.

'You mean do I think Grant is right?'

'*Do* you?'

'He's convinced.'

'But you're not?'

'He wants *someone* for these killings. There's pressure on him from the top brass and the media. Everyone wants the geezer caught.'

'But?'

He picked up one of the other files.

'The killer, supposedly, picked his victims because they had some kind of disease, right. So, that would indicate someone with a pathological hatred or fear of illness and disease.'

She nodded in agreement. 'I'm with you so far, Sherlock,' said Amy, smiling.

'"James Cavernar,"' he read from the file. '"Aged forty-two. Single. Diagnosis: mysophobia and nosophobia. Clinical fear of dirt and disease."'

'You think it could be him?' Amy asked.

Webber dropped the file.

'Perhaps I just *want* it to be him,' he said wearily. 'Perhaps I just want it to be anyone except Andrew

Chapman. Because I want Grant to be wrong. Does that sound childish?'

She continued massaging his shoulders gently.

'The bastard's convinced it's Chapman,' Webber continued. 'He's had tails on him for the last forty-eight hours. Questioned him five times. He says he's waiting for him to crack.'

'Would it matter so much if he *was* right about Chapman?'

'Fuck him. Let him get his conviction if he wants it. I want this killer off the streets as much as he does.'

'So, you were right about Roy? His calls were fake.'

'I'm sure he's not the killer, whoever he is, but he still threatened *you*.'

'I haven't heard from him for three days. Do you think that Chapman could have called in as Roy?'

'It's possible but I doubt it. I tell you what though, the thing that puzzles me is why he killed Charlotte Kilbride the way he did. If Chapman *is* the killer, why didn't he just strangle her like the others? By battering her first he risked getting blood on his clothes or himself. Strangling her would have been easier. Cleaner. And taking the files was clumsy – he must have known it would point us in his direction. I don't get it.'

'Aren't all murderers supposed to secretly *want* to be caught? That's what the experts always say in films.' She smiled.

He chuckled. 'Maybe but, like the man said, if it don't gell it ain't aspic. And this ain't gelling.' He picked up another file, flicked through it and discarded it.

'I'm sorry,' he said.

'For what?'

'I've been going on about this fucking case when you've got other things on your mind. More important things.' He turned and kissed her gently on the lips.

'Jake, I'm grateful for anything that takes my mind off *my* problems.'

She rolled on to her back, arms folded behind her head, her gaze fixed on the ceiling.

'What will you do when this is all over?' she asked.

'What do you mean?'

'Once the investigation is finished. You'll be moving out, won't you?'

'I couldn't afford one of these flats on *my* salary, Amy. I'm just a humble copper. Like Grant said, it's the taxpayers who've paid for this.'

'So where will you go?'

'Back home. Where else am I going to go?'

'And what about us, Jake? When you pack up and put your stuff back in boxes, what do you do with our relationship? Pack that up and put it in a crate too?'

He turned to face her, kneeling beside the sofa, one hand resting on her thigh, the other gently caressing her cheek.

'Is that what you want?' he asked quietly.

'I want *you*,' she whispered and pulled him down to her, their lips meeting.

He responded fiercely.

When they broke the kiss they were both breathing heavily.

'You're not getting rid of me,' he said, smiling. 'I told you before, I lost one thing I loved. I won't lose another.'

She enfolded her arms around his neck and pulled him tightly to her.

From the coffee table close by, the photograph of Andrew Chapman fluttered to the floor, displaced by Webber's movements. Blind monochrome eyes gazed upwards.

Seventy-Eight

Jo Parker watched as her brother pulled on his leather jacket.

'Out again, Billy?' she said wearily.

'Looks like it.'

'Where to?'

'It's not important.'

'Do you really hate me that much?'

'What the fuck are you going on about?'

'You must hate me. You never talk to me. You never share things with me. Have I been *that* awful to you since you came to live with me?'

Billy laughed. 'I get it,' he said, 'we've had the "angry older sister demanding to know where her no good brother is going" routine and that didn't work. So now you're trying the softly, softly approach. Is that it?'

'This isn't any *routine*, Billy,' Jo told him angrily. 'I care about you. I'm sick of telling you that.'

'And I'm sick of hearing it. Get off my fucking back, will you?'

'Don't you know what's going on out there?' she demanded, pointing towards the window. 'There's a killer on the loose. How do you know you won't be next?'

'How do you know *you* won't?'

They faced each other for interminable seconds.

'What is your fucking problem, Jo?' he said finally. 'Have I been sponging off you since I got here? No. I've put money in your pocket.'

'I just want to know where that money's come from.'

'Where do you *think* it's come from?'

She had no answer as he took a step closer to her.

'Well, go on, tell me,' he persisted. 'Where do you think

it comes from?' He stuck his hand in the pocket of his jeans and pulled out a thick wad of ten-pound notes.

'Drugs,' she said flatly.

'You think I'm pushing?'

'How else could you earn *that* sort of money?'

'I'm a very resourceful lad,' he told her sneeringly.

'Tell me, Billy.'

He turned away, but Jo shot out a hand and gripped his wrist.

'Tell me,' she rasped.

'It doesn't matter,' he snarled, shaking loose. 'Nothing matters any more.' She saw his hand go to his inside pocket where he pulled a piece of paper free. 'Here, read this, you'll see what I mean.' He hurled it in her direction then turned and headed for the door, wrenching it open.

'Billy,' she called after him, stooping to pick up the paper. She heard his footsteps receding down the stairs.

Jo unfolded the carefully folded sheet and glanced at it. At the headed paper.

THE HOLMWOOD CLINIC

She skimmed the typed letter, only the odd word catching her attention.

'*Dear Mr Parker . . .*'

Jo found that she was quivering slightly.

'*HIV test . . .*'

She could not swallow.

'*. . . Regret to tell you . . .*'

She had to hold the paper in both hands now to steady it.

'*. . . Positive . . .*'

'Oh, God,' she murmured.

'*Test result was positive . . .*'

'Billy!' she shouted again.

Jo tossed the letter aside, snatched up a jacket and rushed out of the flat, slamming the door behind her.

She took the steps two at a time, almost stumbling near the bottom, but she hurtled out into the small hallway, then dashed on and out into the street.

Frantically she looked right and left, searching for any sign of Billy in the street.

'Billy,' she whispered under her breath.

She saw him. On the other side of the road, about to turn left.

Calm down. Don't get too close. Don't let him see you.

He made his way briskly down Corfield Street then turned right.

Jo was relieved to see that there were more people in Bethnal Green Road. It would give her more places to hide. Not that Billy would have any idea she was following him. She darted and weaved past fellow pedestrians as if she was competing in some kind of bizarre slalom, never taking her eyes from her brother. He was crossing the road again, heading into the tube station itself.

She scurried across the road, slowing her pace slightly, allowing him to put more distance between them. Using a concrete pillar as cover, she saw him feeding small change into a ticket machine.

As he passed through the barrier she scurried across to the machine herself, hand fumbling in her pocket. No change. She would lose him.

Her heart thudded even harder against her ribs. She tried the other pocket, found coins and fed them in, punched one of the buttons and grabbed the ticket.

When she reached the escalator there was no sign of him. She hesitated a moment, knowing that the Central Line ran through Bethnal Green. But which platform was he on?

She decided to try westbound. *A hunch? Desperation?*

As the escalator carried her down she heard the rumble of an approaching train; she hurried down the last few moving steps and through the archway that led her to the westbound platform. The train was just pulling in.

Again she looked right and left.

Where the hell was Billy?

People were spilling off the train from most carriages.

She took a few paces to her left, eyes scanning the many figures waiting to board, mingling with those leaving.

Jo spotted him. He stepped on three or four cars down to her right.

She pushed past a middle-aged man who muttered something at her as she barged through and jumped on to the carriage next to the one where Billy was seated.

Someone had left a copy of the *Evening Standard* on a seat opposite and she snatched it up, banking on it giving her at least a little cover should he look her way.

Her hands were quivering as she turned the pages, aware of the ludicrousness of this entire episode. For all she knew he might have known she was following. Even now he might be preparing to jump off and leave her stranded on the train.

She cast an anxious glance in his direction. He was still there in the next carriage, head tilted back, head resting against the window. Waiting.

Where are you going?

The automatic doors slid shut and the train moved off.

Seventy-Nine

As the taxi pulled up outside the studios in Bedford Square, Amy was surprised to see Mike Osborne standing in the reception area.

She walked across to the main entrance, her eyes never leaving the producer, who was standing, statue-like, arms folded across his chest, his face set in stern lines.

Amy was barely through the main doors when he began talking.

'Where the hell is she?' he demanded angrily.

'Who?' Amy asked, signing in.

'Your bloody friend, Jo.'

They walked to the lifts.

'Hasn't she come in?' Amy asked as the producer pressed the Call button.

'Why the fuck do you think I'm standing down here?' he snapped.

'Look, I'm her friend, not her keeper, Mike,' Amy said irritably, stepping into the lift behind the producer. 'Hasn't she rung in?'

'No. And she's not answering her phone either, I've been trying for the last half-hour.'

The lift bumped to a stop at the appointed floor and they both stepped out.

'*I'm* going to have to work the fucking calls tonight,' Osborne said angrily.

He pushed open the production-room door and barged his way in.

'She could have had an accident or anything and all you're worried about is having to answer the phone?' Amy said.

'Well if it *is* an accident, it better not be anything

trivial,' he said. 'I hope she realises the mess she's dropped us in.'

'It's nothing we can't handle. I just hope she's all right. I'll try her flat again.'

Amy reached for the phone.

'Well, get a move on, you're on the air in ten minutes.'

Amy waved away his protestations and jabbed the digits she wanted.

'I've told you, there's no one there,' he said.

Amy waited.

It was ringing.

'I'm telling you, Amy, she'd better have a bloody good explanation for this,' he continued.

Still ringing.

'Come on, Jo,' Amy murmured.

Ringing.

'Nothing,' Amy said finally, gently replacing the receiver.

'I've already told you that. It's probably something to do with her brother.'

'What did she say to *you* about her brother?'

'I overheard her talking to your boyfriend the other night about him. He sounds like a fucking waster to me.'

Amy was dialling another number.

'Eight minutes to show-time, Amy,' he reminded her.

She ignored him, waiting for the call to be answered.

When it was, she recognised Webber's voice immediately.

'Jake, it's me. Listen, Jo hasn't turned up for the show tonight and there's no reply from her flat. It's probably nothing but it's not like her. I just wanted to check she was okay.'

'I wouldn't worry,' Webber told her.

'That's exactly what I *am* doing, Jake. Please check it out for me, will you?'

'I'll meet you there after the show,' he said. 'I've got to go.'

'See you.'

She hung up.

'Jake's going to check she's all right,' Amy said, getting to her feet.

'Well then I'm sure everything will be fine if *Jake* is on the job.'

'Fuck you, Mike.'

'I'll have her job for this, Amy, unless she's got a good excuse,' he said threateningly.

'And I'll have *yours* if you fuck up those calls,' Amy snarled.

She made her way into the studio. Six lines were already lit up.

Eighty

Jo became more agitated with each successive station the train passed through.

Liverpool Street.

She glanced from behind her paper and saw that Billy hadn't moved.

Bank.

Still he remained in his seat.

Did he know she was in the next carriage?

St Paul's.

Two youths got on and stood by the door, talking loudly. They were blocking her view of the next carriage.

Jo thought about changing seats but, even if she sat on the seat opposite, her view would still be blocked. By now the youths had noticed she was constantly looking in their direction. One of them leaned close to his companion to whisper something.

The second youth laughed loudly and also looked at her, licking his lips.

Jo lowered her gaze, glancing at the paper again as if engrossed. It didn't seem to matter that she hadn't even turned a page for the last fifteen minutes.

The youths got out at Chancery Lane, still laughing loudly.

Jo chanced a look into the next carriage, checking to see if her brother was also there. He was.

Holborn came and went and he still hadn't moved, had barely shifted position in fact.

Glancing at the map opposite, she noticed that the next stop was Tottenham Court Road.

Here perhaps?

The train was getting busier with each stop, more

people spilling on and off as it penetrated deeper into the heart of the West End.

Again she chanced a look into the next carriage. He looked up.

For one frantic second, Jo thought that he'd seen her. She felt sure that their eyes had met.

And what if they had? What would he do?

He was still on the train as it pulled away, laden with yet more travellers, heading towards Oxford Circus.

Jo was gripped by the unshakeable feeling that Billy knew she was following him, that, at one stop or another he would simply weave in and out of the crowd, give her the slip and leave her stranded. What had made her think she could carry on this ridiculous behaviour anyway? Things like this only worked in spy films. This was real life. Uncomfortably real.

The train slowed down as it pulled into Oxford Circus and, at last, Billy got to his feet.

She swallowed hard.

What now? Get up and step off the train at the same instant? Walk straight into his arms?

She sat still and waited for the train to stop.

It juddered slightly and the doors slid open. Still she waited.

How long would the doors remain open? Ten seconds? Fifteen?

She saw Billy pass by on the platform.

The doors would be closing any second.

She had to get off now. If she didn't she'd be left on the train.

But was he far enough away not to see her?

She moved slightly, heart thumping madly.

Move now or you'll lose him.

She heard a metallic rumble.

Move.

The doors were beginning to close.

She leaped to her feet and managed to squeeze through

the narrowing gap just in time. She landed on the platform and spun round, eyes searching the crowd.

She took a few paces in the direction that he'd walked,
slipping past a couple of other travellers. No sign of
Billy.

Up ahead there were two archways, one of them an
exit the other leading to the Jubilee Line.

Which one to take?

She sped towards the one marked Exit, slowing her
pace slightly as she reached the bottom of the stairs.

He wasn't there. Surely he couldn't have climbed the
flight so quickly? She decided to try the connection to
the other line.

As she moved breathlessly through the throng of
people Jo continually scanned the bodies moving in
front of her, her anxiety building to a crescendo. She
had lost him she was sure of it. How could she ever
have hoped to catch him when . . .

Billy was ahead of her. About twenty yards away.
He was standing on an escalator glancing at the panels
advertising books, films, museums and art galleries that
flanked each moving stairway.

Jo stepped on to the escalator behind a tall man in
a dark suit and lowered her head slightly in case her
brother should look back.

Unless he already knows you're there.

She forced the thought aside. She had to believe that he
didn't know. Had to convince herself that this subterfuge
would be worth it. She began to worry about what she
might find when she reached his destination. Perhaps it
would be better to turn back now. Maybe she was better
off not knowing where he was going.

He stepped off the escalator and, moments later, so did
Jo.

Don't give up now.

Billy wandered through on to the southbound Jubilee
Line platform.

She loitered at the bottom of the escalator, pretending

to tie her trainer, giving him time to move down the platform.

She could hear a train coming. Only then did she scurry through on to the platform.

She spotted him as he stepped on to the waiting tube and, again, she boarded one carriage away from him. This time he stood, holding on to one of the overhead rails, looking around him at the other passengers.

If he was standing, she surmised, this leg of the journey must be a short one.

She was right. Billy got off at the first stop. Green Park.

Jo followed.

Eighty-One

Andrew Chapman sat at his desk, the silence around him total. Even the sound of traffic outside in Piccadilly sounded muted, unreal. Everything had seemed unreal for the last three days. Seventy-two hours in which he had seen his life collapse around him. That was all it had taken for his world to be destroyed, his existence to be shattered. The police interrogations. The confession to his wife about his psychiatric visits and their nature. The fact that he was suspected of murder. The recriminations. The tears.

And this very morning, the redundancy notice.

The final nail.

He sat at his desk looking at it. Something else to break to Laura when he got home. If she would listen to him. They'd barely spoken a dozen words in the last thirty-six hours. She had cried a lot. Her sobbing was her only communication at present. Even his children had not spoken to him since the first police visit to his house.

And, as if that wasn't bad enough, there was the surveillance.

The unmarked police car followed him everywhere he drove. It parked outside his house at night. It remained close to the bank all day. The men who occupied it made no secret of their presence. One had even nodded a greeting to him the day before.

He knew it was parked out there now. Somewhere, hidden in the gloom but waiting for him. When he drove away it would follow, keeping a none too discreet distance until he arrived home, then it would carefully park up opposite his house, just like it always did.

In the gloom of his office he looked at his watch.

12.04 a.m.

He was alone in the building.

He was alone in the world.

There was no rush to get home. Laura and the children would be in bed. She would be sleeping in the spare room. Anxious to be away from him. He would have to find some way of telling her about the redundancy notice. Some way of telling her that the house repayments could not be maintained unless he got another job quickly. And what chance of that with a possible court case hanging over his head?

True, he hadn't been charged yet but it seemed just a matter of time.

He'd stayed on at the bank ostensibly to finish some work but really because there was nowhere else for him to go. In this office he was not watched by prying eyes, not subject to whispered scandal as he passed, not stared at the way he was when he emerged periodically during the working day.

He had felt many emotions during his life but never anything like this, never a sense of such utter helplessness and worthlessness. It was intolerable and it was unrelenting.

He got to his feet, pushed the redundancy notice into his inside pocket then walked to the office door and locked it behind him.

The lift was to his left. He pressed the Call button and stepped in, hesitating for a moment. It was a small, private lift for employees' use only, barely large enough to carry two people.

He pressed 3 and the lift rose. He stood motionless, eyes gazing blankly ahead, finally stepping out at the appointed floor when the car bumped to a halt.

A long corridor stretched away in front of him and, at the end of it, a locked door.

He strode down the corridor and unlocked the door. Management had keys to this door and, at least until the end of the week, he was management.

The end of the week.

He opened it and ascended the narrow flight of stairs that led to the roof.

He moved purposefully, eyes fixed ahead, tears forming in his eyes as they scanned the neon skyscape of Piccadilly. Around Eros, dozens were gathered. Traffic passed through. The night was filled with the sound of beeping hooters, car engines, disembodied chatter. Laughter. It was an alien sound to him now.

The breeze up on the roof was strong, it ruffled his hair as he stood by the parapet, looking down into the street wondering where the police car was parked. The car that waited for him.

He stood there, eyes closed, a single tear rolling down one cheek.

One reason to go on living?

There wasn't one.

He jumped.

Eighty-Two

As Jo emerged from Green Park tube station into Piccadilly she heard the wail of sirens, but she was more concerned with keeping as close to Billy as she could. The thoroughfare was busy even for such a late hour, and for that she was grateful.

He crossed the road and walked along in front of The Ritz, illuminated by the lights that shone beneath its frontage.

Jo waited a second then hurried across behind him, narrowly avoiding an onrushing Nissan that sounded its hooter at her. She ignored it and settled into a more measured stride about twenty yards behind Billy.

He had both hands dug into his pockets and walked without obvious concern. If he knew she was following he certainly gave her no indication. And surely, if he had known, he would have confronted her by now.

Wouldn't he?

There would have been a loud row in the middle of the street and he would have run off, leaving her to ponder about his destination and the nature of his business at such a late hour.

But no, he kept on walking, turning right into St James's Street.

Jo followed at a more cautious distance. It was less crowded here and her only hope of avoiding being seen would be to sneak into a doorway. However, he didn't turn. Just kept walking.

He turned again. Into Park Place. A dead end.

What the hell was going on?

Jo hesitated, pausing on the corner of the street, watching as Billy walked further along the darkened cul-de-sac.

He *had* seen her, she was growing more certain of that by the second. He would wait until she followed him down this dimly lit place, then he would confront her and tell her that he'd known from the beginning that she'd been tailing him.

And yet he continued on.

Jo darted into a doorway, enveloped by the blackness, squinting to see Billy now.

She moved a few yards further down. Getting closer.

He had stopped beside a car.

Oh, no. He was going to steal it. That was where the money was coming from.

It suddenly became so clear. So . . .

No.

The car door opened, light from inside suddenly spilling into the street as the driver stepped out to talk to Billy.

Jo watched mesmerised, her gaze drawn to the driver of the vehicle. There was something familiar about him.

The driver embraced Billy. They kissed passionately. The man touched his cheek then kissed him again, more deeply this time.

And she understood.

Now she knew where the money came from and it thundered in her head like an explosion. The realisation was there before her.

'Rent boy,' she whispered to herself.

It felt as if every muscle in her stomach had knotted into a ball.

Rent boy.

She saw Billy slide into the passenger seat of the car and something else struck her. Struck her like a thunderbolt.

Seconds before the driver's door was closed, while the car's interior was still illuminated, she saw the man kiss Billy again. And in that split second she knew who the driver was.

David Albury.

Eighty-Three

Amy left the studio and headed straight for the lift. She didn't even wait to say goodbye to Osborne, who was shouting something incomprehensible at her.

She rode the lift to the ground floor and asked the security guard to call her a cab.

She glanced at her watch.

It should be here in less than ten minutes, he told her.

Amy nodded, reaching for a cigarette.

She waited.

'What time was he found?' Webber asked, peering at the pulped face of Andrew Chapman.

'About fifteen minutes ago,' a uniformed officer informed him, turning away from the bloodied mess that had once been Chapman's head. He had noticed, with a tremor in his belly, that portions of pinkish-white brain matter had spilled from the ruptured skull.

An ambulance, its lights turning silently, was blocking one end of the street, a police car the other. Officers, uniformed and plainclothes wandered around the scene, all presumably engaged in some kind of meaningful activity.

Webber saw Grant talking to the two men who had been tailing Chapman for the past forty-eight hours. Grant was nodding, even smiling occasionally as he spoke to the other policemen. Webber finally got to his feet, glancing back one last time at Chapman's corpse before the waiting ambulancemen covered it with a plastic sheet and carried it to the waiting emergency vehicle, leaving a pool of blood fully twelve feet across in the corpse's wake.

'I think we can close this case,' said Grant smugly.

Webber didn't answer, merely took a drag on his cigarette.

'I told you he'd crack,' Grant continued.

'I didn't think he'd kill himself,' Webber announced.

Grant could only shrug. 'Who gives a shit? One way or the other this is over. Done deal.'

'So you were right?'

'Looks like it, Jake. Why sound so surprised?'

'What about the blood test?'

'That'll be done when they get the body to pathology. A match with the blood on the glass at Charlotte Kilbride's place and bingo. I'll call a press conference in the morning and announce that the investigation is over. The killer is dead.'

Webber sucked on his cigarette, blowing a stream of smoke out into the air.

Grant was heading back to his waiting car.

'It's over, Jake,' he called, smiling.

'What if you'd been wrong?'

'I'd have resigned. But I *wasn't* wrong, was I?' He slid into the passenger seat. 'I win again, Jake.'

The car pulled away.

She could take no more.

The lies. The deceit.

The pain.

Jo wanted no more.

As she stuffed Billy's clothes into his duffel bag she had to force back the tears.

Tears of anguish?

She didn't *want* to throw him out. Not now. Not now he *knew* he was dying.

Tears of sorrow.

He was her brother. No matter what he had done, or what he was doing, he was still her flesh and blood. Except that flesh and blood was diseased.

Tears of disgust.

He knew that he had AIDS and yet he was prepared to spread the virus. His words echoed in her head.

'*I'll take as many with me as I can. If I'm going to die then so are a lot of other people too.*'

How many had he infected? How many men who had paid to use his body and he theirs? How many would die?

Jo had run back to Green Park tube, fighting back her tears caused lay the vision of her brother and Albury together.

Albury. That two-faced bastard.

She had returned to the flat and begun packing Billy's things up immediately. She could take no more.

As she pushed the sofa back to look for any stray socks that may be hidden beneath she saw the carrier bag. A simple grey HMV bag. Billy's.

She picked it up, ready to stuff it into the duffel bag with the rest of his things. Things she didn't want in her flat any longer.

She saw an envelope inside. Larger than A4 size and thick.

Jo took it out and saw that the top was undone. She pulled at what was inside. Files. Brown, manilla files. There were about twenty of them. Too many for the envelope to confortably hold.

She pulled one free and opened it. It was a psychiatric report. There were other notes inside it. Prescriptions. A case history. One of the letters inside was signed in a sweeping hand.

Charlotte Kilbride.

'Oh my God,' Jo murmured, the colour draining from her face.

She stood motionless, the file gripped in her shaking hand. It was then that she heard a key in the lock.

Eighty-Four

When Billy walked in he saw Jo standing transfixed, one of the files still held in her hand.

'What are you doing with that?' he asked, closing the door behind him.

'You killed her, didn't you?' said Jo flatly. 'You killed Charlotte Kilbride.'

'I didn't want to,' he said almost apologetically.

'Why, Billy?'

'Does it matter?'

'You murdered someone and you ask me if it *matters*?' She shouted the last word, flinging the file at him. 'And how many others have you killed?'

'What the fuck are you talking about?'

'I saw you tonight.'

He looked puzzled.

'I followed you. I know where your money's been coming from. Did they all pay you as well as David Albury? Are all your clients as generous? How many have there been, Billy?'

'I didn't keep a list. Thirty, forty, maybe more.'

'You infected them. You knew you had AIDS but you still went with them.'

'That's *their* problem. Anyone picking up rent boys knows they're taking risks. If they wanted to do it without condoms and pay me extra I wasn't going to refuse. What's that old saying about a fool and his money?'

'You murdered them.'

'Don't be so fucking stupid.'

'You might as well have put a gun to their heads.' She ran a hand through her hair. 'Why Charlotte Kilbride?'

'I was paid to do it.'

'Who by?'

'David Albury.'

'Why?'

'He didn't want anyone to know that he'd been treated by her. He thought it might fuck up his political career. When she started going on television and talking about the murderer and how she could help the police, Albury got nervous. He thought if the police investigated her then they'd find out about her patients.'

'So he hired you to kill her?'

'He paid me to break into her place and steal his file. But then she walked in while I was doing it. I didn't know what to do. I was out of my skull and desperate not to get caught. I panicked.'

'Why did Albury pay *you*?'

'He was a regular. He trusted me.' Billy laughed and it had a hollow, empty sound. 'The old tosser's got it bad. I think he's in love with me.'

'Does he know you've got AIDS?'

'Like I was going to fucking tell him. I'm not stupid, Jo. He pays too well. I'd have to get fucked by *ten* blokes to match the money he pays.'

'How much *does* he pay?'

'Two hundred a time. Easy money for sucking his limp old dick.'

They regarded each other in silence for a moment then Billy spoke again. 'What are you going to do, Jo? Shop me?'

She had no answer.

'You've already packed my stuff,' he continued. 'Let me have it. I'll walk away. I'll walk out of your life. There's no need for you to get involved in this.'

'I *am* involved,' she snarled. 'What am I supposed to do? Just forget about what I've seen and heard?'

'Give me my stuff, Jo. You'll never see me again, I promise.'

'I can't do that, Billy,' she said, tears forming.

'Why? You wanted me out anyway. I'm offering to go.'

He watched a single tear roll down her cheek.

'You're ill too,' she said, softly. 'I can't let you walk out in your condition, knowing you're going to suffer. I couldn't live with myself.'

'I'll manage. Give me the bag.' He held out a hand for the duffel bag.

'And these?' she said, indicating the files.

'I'll take those too.' He still had his hand outstretched.

Jo wiped tears from her face and passed him the bag. He took it and smiled wanly.

'Time to go,' Jo whispered, her voice cracking.

Eighty-Five

Amy paid the taxi driver, and while he was preparing to hand her some change she hurried from the car and disappeared into the main door, taking the stairs to Jo's first-floor flat. She didn't care that she'd given him ten pounds for a six-pound fare. She was probably worrying over nothing, she told herself, but it was unusual not only for Jo not to turn up, but also for her not to phone in a reason.

She reached the flat door and pressed the buzzer.

It was answered almost immediately.

'Jo! Are you okay?' A smile of relief spread across Amy's face.

'I'm fine, why?' Jo said flatly, ushering Amy inside.

'When you didn't turn up for the show and I couldn't get hold of you I thought there was something wrong.'

Jo didn't answer, just sat down on the sofa beside Amy, who could see that her eyes were red-rimmed and puffy.

'There *is* something wrong, isn't there?' Amy persisted. 'Please tell me, Jo.'

'It's Billy,' the younger woman said, swallowing hard. 'He found out that he has AIDS.'

'I'm sorry, Jo. Why didn't you say something?'

'I only found out myself tonight. That and a couple of other things,' Jo continued, smiling crookedly.

'Where is he?'

'In my room. Perhaps you'd like to see him.'

'If you think it would help.'

Jo got to her feet and walked across the sitting room to a narrow hallway.

Amy followed, moving slowly, almost reverentially, into the room that Jo indicated.

Billy Parker lay on the bed, legs splayed, arms stretched out on either side of him in a cruciform position. His eyes were still open, bulging in the sockets, some of the blood vessels having ruptured in the whites. The skin of his face had a bluish tinge, especially his lips. A swollen tongue protruded from his mouth, which was stretched in an awful rictus. Blood had spilled down his chin and on to his chest where he'd bitten the inside of his cheek.

There was a length of cord around his neck that, at first glance, appeared to have come from a bathrobe. It had cut so deeply into the flesh that Amy thought it might have severed the head if it had been drawn any tighter.

She stared, transfixed, at the corpse.

'He was dying anyway,' said Jo, also looking at the body, her head tilted to one side, her expression blank. 'I saved him from more pain. Just like the others.'

Amy suddenly snapped out of her hypnotic gazing.

'The others?' she said, her voice, barely a whisper, betraying her fear.

'Those two girls, the prostitutes. They were ill,' Jo continued, monosyllabically. 'So was the pimp *and* the drug pusher. I only had to look at them. And what kind of life did those people in the hospice have to look forward to? Just day after day of pain. I stopped their pain. All of them. I stopped their suffering. Just like I stopped Billy's suffering.'

'Oh God, Jo,' Amy murmured, the full realisation hitting her.

She could smell something pungent in the air and realised it was excrement, the odour rising from Billy Parker's corpse.

'My other brother, Danny. He died in pain but there was nothing I could do about that,' Jo said, looking directly at Amy. 'I wasn't going to let Billy suffer the same way. I did what I did because I loved him.'

'And what about the other people you killed?'

'I didn't kill them,' Jo hissed. 'I *helped* them. I read up on all kinds of diseases. AIDS, multiple sclerosis, cancer.

All of those that had no cure, all of those that caused suffering. I couldn't bear to think of people with those illnesses suffering the way my brother Danny suffered. The way Billy was suffering.' She looked directly at Amy. 'The way *you're* suffering.'

Amy took a step backwards.

'I can't let you suffer too, Amy,' Jo said. 'I think too much of you for that.'

She lunged at Amy.

The attack was sudden and unexpected and Amy couldn't avoid it. The two women crashed to the ground, Jo thrusting out her hands in an attempt to close her fingers around Amy's throat.

Amy knocked one of her hands away and drove her fist into Jo's face, striking hard against the other woman's cheek.

A livid mark appeared immediately.

Jo hissed and struck back, splitting Amy's lip.

Amy tasted blood in her mouth and the coppery tang seemed to galvanise her even more. Using all her strength, she grabbed on either side of Jo's head and hurled her to one side. Jo crashed into the bedside table.

Amy leaped to her feet and sprinted from the room but Jo rolled over with incredible speed and lashed out, catching Amy's ankle.

Amy went crashing to the floor, the wind momentarily knocked from her but, as Jo came at her, Amy managed to drive a foot hard into her stomach with enough force to double the younger woman up.

Amy took advantage of the respite and swung another foot, cracking it with tremendous power into Jo's face. One front tooth snapped and tore through Jo's upper lip.

Blood spilled down her face as she opened her mouth to vent her rage.

Again she launched herself at Amy, the impact knocking Amy backwards over the sofa.

This time it was Jo who was first on her feet, grabbing Amy's hair and lifting her bodily to her feet.

Amy screamed in pain as she felt a clump of hair torn from her scalp. She was both amazed and horrified at Jo's strength. The power in those hands and arms was colossal.

Jo lifted her by her throat now, raising Amy from the ground, thumbs pressing with incredible force into her windpipe.

Amy felt her head beginning to spin, it was as if someone was pumping it full of air. Spittle and blood flew into the air, some of it spattering Jo who continued to squeeze, her face contorted with the effort.

Amy struck out and drove two fingers into Jo's right eye, part of the eyelid ripping.

Amy fell to the ground as the pressure on her throat was relaxed.

She struggled to her feet and kicked twice at Jo. The first blow caught her in the side and Amy heard the crack of a snapping rib. The second struck her on the shoulder, the impact enough to unbalance her.

Amy staggered towards the door, desperate to get out.

Jo reached her as her hand was tightening on the lock.

The younger woman grabbed Amy by the wrist and used all her strength to swing her around, driving her into the wall with incredible power. Amy's head snapped backwards and slammed into the plaster. She felt her knees beginning to buckle.

Jo struck out at her, the punch catching her in the mouth, opening the gash in her lip even wider. Fresh blood spilled from it.

Amy fell sideways, dimly aware through a haze of pain, that Jo was locking the flat door.

She tried to rise but Jo grabbed for her again and the two women fell back into the kitchen, crashing against a work top. Half-a-dozen plates, a knife block and the electric kettle all went hurtling to the floor, two of the plates shattering, knives skittering across the lino.

Amy rolled over on to her belly, grabbing for one of the knives. She swung wildly with it and the razor-sharp blade sliced effortlessly through Jo's calf. Blood erupted from the wound, some of it spattering Amy, who tried to haul herself upright.

Jo grabbed for the knife, missed and hissed in pain as the blade laid her palm open. Lunging further, she picked up the kettle lead, wrenching it from the wall and, with one expert flick, she looped it around Amy's neck and grabbed the other end.

Amy felt incredible pressure around her throat and dropped the knife, trying to pull at the flex that was choking her. Her head was swimming and, with horror, she realised that Jo was straddling her, using her weight to keep her pinned down while she tugged ever-tighter on the flex.

Amy felt her head being tugged back even harder. Her eyes were throbbing in their sockets, her tongue lolling from her mouth as she gasped for air. She was beginning to lose consciousness.

Eighty-Six

Webber was at the bottom of the stairs when he heard the crash coming from the first floor. He hesitated a second then sprinted up the flight, taking the steps two at a time, the din growing louder as he drew closer to Jo's flat.

He stood beside the door for a moment, certain now that the murderous cacophony of sound was coming from within.

'Jo!' he shouted, banging on the door.

Nothing. Just the sound of shattering crockery.

He drove one foot against the door. Then another.

Inside there was another crash then a shout of pain.

He slid his hand inside his jacket and pulled the .459 Smith and Wesson automatic from its shoulder holster.

He kicked the door again, mustering every ounce of strength he had.

Still it wouldn't budge.

Through a haze of pain and a steadily rolling tide of blackness, Amy heard the thudding of something heavy against the flat's door.

It meant nothing.

All she was aware of was the incredible force being exerted on her throat as Jo tugged with greater ferocity on the kettle lead, digging one knee into Amy's back to provide more leverage.

Amy's hands flailed helplessly then towards the knives spilled across the carpet.

With what little strength she had left she managed to pull one towards her by the handle. At last she was able to close her fingers around it and then she struck backwards with a power born of desperation.

The blade tore through Jo's thigh, ripped a path

through the quadriceps muscle and, driven with such desperate force, it struck bone, rasping against the femur.

Jo shrieked, and Amy felt the excruciating pressure around her throat ease as her assailant toppled backwards, the knife jammed firmly into her leg.

She gripped the handle, made sticky by gouts of blood spurting from the wound, and tried to tug the razor-sharp blade free but it remained stuck, the muscles having contracted around it.

Amy coughed, spat blood and tried to call out but realised that something in her throat had ruptured. Blood was spilling over her lips, forming small pools as she crawled towards the sitting room. Towards the sound of the thudding against the door.

She rose up on to her knees, dragging herself up by pulling on the back of the sofa.

As she did, the door exploded inwards, finally succumbing to the ferocity of Webber's assault.

He burst in, gun levelled. Immediately he froze, transfixed by the sight before him. The wrecked room.

The blood.

Amy was on her knees looking at him, her face and clothes covered with the crimson fluid. Her eyes bulging wildly in their sockets.

She tried to speak, to warn him but all she could manage was a guttural sound deep in her throat.

He took a step towards her.

There was a banshee-like wail as Jo hurtled from the kitchen, hobbling on her injured leg.

Again he hesitated. Shocked by the vision that was charging towards him.

He saw her rip the blade from her thigh and raise it above her head.

Before he could react, she had driven the knife forward with all her strength.

The aim was appallingly accurate.

The steel tip pierced his wrist, cut the flexors to his hand and snapped the ulna bone.

The blade erupted a full three inches from the other side of his arm, pinning his arm to the wood of the door as surely as if it had been nailed there.

He lost all feeling in his hand and the gun dropped to the floor.

Amy reached for it but Jo got there first.

She swung it up with both hands, pressed the barrel hard against his forehead and for fleeting seconds they were gazing into each other's eyes, only inches apart.

Webber saw the madness in Jo's eyes.

Then she pulled the trigger.

Eighty-Seven

Webber roared something unintelligible, expecting the deafening blast of the weapon to take his life.

Jo smiled crookedly, blood smeared across her face.

The hammer slammed down.

Nothing happened.

Jo squeezed the trigger again. And again.

Amy hauled herself upright and aimed a kick at Jo's injured thigh, slamming her instep against the spouting wound.

Jo dropped the pistol and Webber realised why it hadn't gone off. The safety catch was still on.

Gritting his teeth, and using his other hand, he pulled the knife pinning his arm from the door, then pulled the knife out of his arm. He shrieked in agony but he was free of the impaling blade.

He fell to the floor, his right hand crumpling beneath him uselessly but with his left he grabbed the automatic as he saw Jo rising above him once again, her face contorted.

Webber swung the pistol up and fired.

From point-blank range he couldn't miss and squeezed off four rounds in quick succession.

The thunderous discharge was deafening in such a small room; with the smell of cordite filling the air, the bullets – travelling at over fifteen hundred feet per second – slammed into Jo.

Each impact jerked her body backwards a few inches, the first shot drilling through her chest and erupting from her back. The second hit her in the shoulder. The third powered into her midriff, just below the sternum and the fourth caught her in the forehead. It stoved in a portion of bone before tearing through her brain and exploding from the back of her head, carrying a flux of greyish-red material with it.

Jo dropped to the floor in a bloodied, untidy heap.

'Jesus,' gasped Webber, the pain in his right arm agonising.

He looked round to see Amy stumbling towards him, her face and blond hair spattered with blood.

'Jesus,' Webber repeated, pulling her close to him with his good arm.

She was weeping uncontrollably, even though no sound would escape her battered throat. They held each other tight, ears ringing from the thunderous blasts of the .459. Webber still had it drawn, gripped in his fist.

A door opened across the hallway and a terrified face peered out. A man in his twenties.

'Call the police and an ambulance,' Webber shouted to him, watching as the man stared fixedly at the scene of carnage.

The man disappeared back inside his flat again.

Webber helped Amy to her feet, supported her against him, his right arm dangling at his side. The entire limb felt numb and a steady stream of blood was flowing from the wound in his wrist, trailing down his fingers and dripping on the floor.

He made sure that Amy was comfortably settled on the sofa, then he perched beside her.

Amy gripped his good hand in a vice-like hold, clinging on as if she never wanted to let go.

Neither of them spoke. Webber merely stroked her hair gently. Reassuringly.

The room smelled of blood and sweat.

They waited patiently.

Eighty-Eight

It took time for everything to sink in.

Jo's death.

What she'd done.

What had happened at her flat that night.

Some of it had blurred into one waking nightmare for Amy. There were details she couldn't remember no matter how hard she tried. Perhaps, she told herself, she didn't *want* to remember them. Didn't want to think how close to death she had come at the hands of a woman she had always regarded as such a close friend.

A woman who had been a murderer.

It still seemed unbelievable.

Webber watched her as she paced the office, his right arm still heavily bandaged and in a sling. He saw the hard lines etched across her face and he knew what she was thinking about. He didn't have to ask. He'd seen that look many times during the past couple of days.

Amy looked at her watch. 'Where is he?' she said, her voice still a little hoarse.

As if in answer to her question, Dr Alan Davidson entered the room carrying several files, one of which he selected and laid on his desk.

'Sorry to have kept you,' he said cheerfully.

Amy wondered if the smile on his face was manufactured. An attempt to soften the news he was about to give her.

She sat down beside Webber, her hand seeking his.

'We got the biopsy result,' Davidson said at last.

Amy squeezed Webber's hand more tightly.

The doctor coughed.

'It was positive,' he said flatly. 'The cells we removed were malignant.'

Amy gripped even more tightly on to Webber's hand and he responded.

'However, the growth was very small and there doesn't appear to be any evidence of secondary tumours or any spread,' he continued.

'Will I need more surgery?' Amy asked.

'It's unlikely,' Davidson told her.

'A mastectomy?' she persisted.

'No,' the doctor said, smiling. 'I want to keep a close eye on you for the next six months but, all in all, I'd say the prognosis is very encouraging. We caught it early enough.'

Amy relaxed her grip slightly.

'So I'll be okay?' she said, wanting to hear him say it.

'Like I said, I'll need to monitor your progress closely for the next six months, perhaps longer, but you'll be fine. Drugs and a little radiotherapy will eradicate any cells that might be left.'

'I'm not going to lose my hair, am I?' Amy said.

'You're not going to lose anything,' Davidson said, smiling.

'Is that it, then?'

'Make an appointment for two weeks' time, and I'll see you then.'

Amy and Webber got to their feet.

'Thank you, doctor,' she said, still gripping Webber's hand.

They left the surgery together. Outside he embraced her, ignoring the pain from his injured arm.

'It would have been ironic, wouldn't it?' she said. 'You stopped me from being killed by Jo but you couldn't have stopped the cancer killing me.'

'Forget about that shit now,' he said. 'You heard what the doctor said – you're going to be fine.'

She kissed him.

'What was that for?' he asked, smiling.

'Do I need a reason?'

'No. Feel free any time.' He touched her cheek gently.

'Look, I've got to go. I've got to get back to the Yard. There's a press conference in an hour and there's something else I want to see.'

'What?'

'Grant's resigning today.' He winked at her.

'Are you in line for his job?'

'We'll see. I'll tell you later. See you.'

He stuck out his hand and hailed a cab that pulled over to the kerb.

'Jake,' she called.

He turned as he prepared to climb into the taxi.

'I love you,' she said, smiling.

'I love you too,' he told her. 'See you tonight.'

She watched as the taxi pulled away.

Eighty-Nine

Amy sipped at her coffee, wincing slightly as she swallowed. Her injured throat still burned a little but it was more discomfort than pain.

On more than one occasion she had seen Osborne standing in the window of the production booth watching her. Checking on her. Each time she saw him she raised a hand to signal that she was okay.

Until someone was found on a permanant basis to replace Jo they had hired a temp to work the switchboard and put through the calls. She was a bright, cheerful girl in her late twenties. Lorraine. Her friends, she had informed them, called her Loz.

Amy checked the screen next to her and saw a number of names glowing there.

Alison from Clapham.

Gary from Mile End.

Roy.

She shuddered involuntarily.

When she looked up she saw Osborne looking at her again. He was shaking his head.

Nonetheless Amy took the call.

'Roy,' she said. 'Where have you been hiding?'

Silence.

'Come on, you haven't gone bashful on me, have you?' Amy persisted. 'What have you been up to?'

'You must think you're a hero,' said Roy. 'Helping to catch the murderer.'

'I do my best.'

'So one is gone,' Roy said flatly.

'What do you mean, Roy?'

'Out with the old, in with the new.'

He chuckled and, again, the sound raised the hairs on the back of her neck.

'I'm not with you, Roy.'

'Now it's *my* turn.'

'Roy?'

'I'll call again after I've started. After the first one. My style will be different.'

'Are you trying to tell me that you're going to start killing people, Roy? Now come on—'

'You'll hear from me soon,' he said.

There was a buzz of static.

'Roy?' she called.

She could hear him breathing.

'Roy?' Amy said more urgently.

Click.

Dead line.

. . . And if I close my mind in fear,
please pry it open . . .'

Metallica

Deadhead

'Terrible experiences make one wonder whether he who experiences them is not something terrible.'

Nietzsche

Acknowledgements

What follows is a list of people or things who have either directly or indirectly helped in some way, either large or small, in the preparation and writing of this book either before during or after.

Extra special thanks to my manager, Mr Gary Farrow, the man whose socks cost more than my entire wardrobe and whose efforts to shove 'class' down my throat have failed miserably. Thanks, mate. Also thanks to Chris at 'the office' even though he persists in supporting the team he does. Also to Christina and Damian Pulle whose continued existence ensures that I've never got any fax paper . . .

Many thanks to all at my publishers Little, Brown/Warner, both here and in America. Especially to John 'Globetrotter' O'Connor, Dave 'on the fairway' Kent, Terry 'where's me Gibson' Jackson, Don 'whippet' Hughes and every single man (and woman) in my sales team. The best there is. Thanks, too, to Barbara Boote. Thank you all.

Very special thanks to Mr James Hale, my editor, who continues to work with me nearly as vigorously as he tries to get me to invest in a word processor.

Thanks also to Caroline Bishop. To 'Mad' Malcolm Dome and Jerry Ewing at 'MF' (two men whose ability to keep faith in lost causes never ceases to amaze me . . . Bluenoses of different persuasions . . .). To Brian

Pithers who I will never again call 'Big P' (not after *that* label anyway . . .), to Graham Rogers, Phil Alexander (another man with deplorable taste in football teams), Jo Bolsom, Howard Johnson, Tony Dillon, John Gullidge, John 'I'm not taping this' Martin, Nick 'I *am* taping this' Cairns, Gareth 'the hi-hat's too low, the stool's too low and the baby needs changing' James. Steve Hobbs at Bletchley library.

Bert and Anita at Broomhills Pistol Club, indeed to everyone who's offered me advice (or the chance to use their gun); Maurice and Trevor. Thank you.

Many thanks as ever to the Magnificent Margaret Daly who continues to amaze me with her efforts in Ireland. Thank you.

For different reasons I thank Steve, Bruce, Nicko, Dave and Janick, Rod Smallwood, and everyone at Sanctuary Music especially Merck 'sliced up even more horribly' Mercuriadis. Special thanks to my most valued friend, unsociable bastard, etiquette-seeking, garden centre scourge, Wally Grove.

Many thanks to all the staff and management at The Holiday Inn, Mayfair and the Adelphi, Liverpool. To Jack Taylor, Stuart Winton, Amin Saleh, Brian Howard and Lewis Bloch. To Dave Holmes, Ian Austin, Ted and Molly, Zena, Neil Leaver, Frank Healey of Cerebral Fix.

Indirect thanks to Metallica, Great White, Megadeth, Sam Peckinpah, Martin Scorsese and Oliver Stone.

Special thanks to Liverpool FC, my continued source of joy, pride, frustration and occasionally raised blood pressure. Thanks in particular to Sheila and Jenny and all in the Bob Paisley Suite for keeping us fed and to Jimmy for supplying us with extra strong mints (when it's really cold). Come on you reds.

Many thanks to Everite Stationery in Bletchley. This novel, as ever, was written on Croxley paper wearing Puma trainers and Wrangler jeans (look, I don't give up easily you know . . .). Numerous mental blocks were cleared by Yamaha Drums, Zildjian Cymbals, Pro-mark sticks and Remo heads. On that note, thanks to Rob, Steve, Andie and Nicola at Foote's in Golden Square and to Chappells in Milton Keynes.

Special thanks to Duncan Stripp, film critic *extraordinaire* (or would be if some bastard would give him the chance). Thanks also to The Point in Milton Keynes.

That's just about it other than to thank my mum and dad for *everything*, as usual, and also my wife, Belinda, without who none of this would be possible and who, in so many ways, but especially on freezing cold days at Anfield or ear-splitting nights at Hammersmith, makes me realize how lucky I am.

The final group of people to thank are you, my readers. The newest ride begins here for all of you. Enjoy it.

Shaun Hutson.

PART ONE

'Boys and girls come out to play,
the moon doth shine as bright as day . . .'
The Oxford Dictionary of Nursery Rhymes

'Men fear Death, as children fear to
go in the dark . . .'

Francis Bacon

One

Robert Slattery felt as if someone had wrapped him in hot bandages. The moisture trickled down his back, beading between his shoulder blades as he walked, coursing down his spine, soaking into his T-shirt.

Although he wore only a thin top, shorts and trainers, he found the heat almost unbearable. The onset of evening had brought a respite from the blazing sun, but the searing heat had been replaced by a cloying humidity that seemed to blanket everything like a heated shroud.

The ground was cracked and dry, the grass brown and dying. The earth itself had split and yawned in places. Wounds in the dirt gaped like thirsty mouths, waiting for the rain which showed no signs of falling.

The entire country had been gripped by the heatwave for more than a month now. Less than an inch of rain had fallen and most of that had been in one massive deluge three weeks ago. Since then there had been nothing but unrelenting heat.

Slattery hated the heat. It was so bloody undignified walking around in a shirt which stuck to your back after only a few minutes. He'd dug out every single black or white shirt he possessed since the heatwave began. To wear red or blue would have meant risking those dreaded dark rings of sweat beneath the arms. Even the strongest anti-perspirant seemed helpless against the onslaught. He drew a hand through his hair and felt perspiration on his forehead.

As he walked slowly across Clapham Common he glanced to his right and left at the other souls who had ventured out into the sickly humid evening.

There were kids kicking a football around, shouting and dashing back and forth as if unaware of the temperature.

On a park bench nearby a couple in their early twenties were kissing passionately, limbs entwined like mating squids. Slattery smiled to himself as he passed, trying not to look too closely but unable to ignore the fact that the girl was particularly attractive; her cut-off denim shorts displayed a fine pair of tanned legs.

He wandered on, glancing down at his dog. It was, after all, the reason he was on the Common this evening. Slattery tossed a small rubber ball he pulled from his pocket and watched as the smooth-haired mongrel went chasing after it. The ball bounced close to a man sitting on one of the wrought-iron benches. He glanced irritably across and Slattery raised a hand in apology. The dog scuttled beneath the bench to retrieve the ball, apparently oblivious of the seat's occupant, and loped back towards Bob, the ball held in its jaws.

Perhaps he was feeling the heat too, Slattery thought, as he pulled it from the dog's jaws and threw it again, this time towards the trees.

The dog set off and caught the ball, returning it once more.

Clouds of midges circled around the tops of bushes like millions of animated cinders stirred by an invisible breeze. He watched them for a moment as he strolled on, feeling the perspiration soaking even more deeply into his T-shirt.

His dog looked up at him as if it expected the ball to be thrown but didn't really relish the prospect of retrieving it. He exhaled deeply, then sucked in a lungful of the dry air. There wasn't a breath of wind. The sinking sun bled across the sky but, despite the dark blue clouds gathering, the approaching night promised no respite from the heat.

Slattery threw the ball again and the dog loped off after it, disappearing into the bushes.

While he waited for the animal to return, he leant against a water fountain that looked as cracked and dry as the parched earth. He pressed the knob but no water came out. All he heard was a low gurgling sound.

From behind him there was a shout; he turned to see the kids who'd been playing football jumping around excitedly. He smiled to himself. Obviously a goal had been scored. Either that or someone had heard there was going to be a rain shower. He grinned and looked towards the bushes, waiting for his dog to reappear.

'Come on, Sam,' he muttered to himself, wiping perspiration from his forehead.

Then he heard the barking.

He frowned and set off towards the bushes. Perhaps Sam had found a bitch in there, he mused. Dirty little sod.

The barking continued.

There were other dogs on the Common and one or two were looking in his direction. He just hoped he didn't find himself surrounded by a pack of them.

He pushed his way through the bushes and caught sight of his own dog standing a few feet away.

He muttered as stinging nettles prickled his calves. Flies and wasps buzzed around him irritably.

The dog was standing perfectly still, only its head moving as it barked loudly.

'What's wrong with you?' Slattery asked, brushing leaves from his T-shirt.

Then he noticed the stench, a smell like rotting meat

only more pungent. It was so strong he felt his stomach somersault.

'Shit,' he muttered, covering his mouth, glancing first at his dog then at the swarm of flies that hovered around the object in front of him.

It took him only a second to realize what it was.

'Oh, Jesus Ch . . .'

Slattery never managed the last word.

He turned away and vomited violently.

The dog continued to bark.

Two

'So you're satisfied that the woman in the photos *is* your wife?'

Nick Ryan took a final drag on his cigarette and ground it out in the ashtray on his desk. With the phone wedged between his shoulder and his ear he reached for the packet of Dunhill, took out another cigarette, and lit up again, drawing deeply.

The voice on the other end of the line was hesitant.

'I suppose so,' Eric Johnson told him.

'Either it is or it isn't, Mr Johnson,' Ryan said, blowing out a stream of smoke.

'This isn't easy for me, you know.'

Ryan raised his eyebrows and glanced at his watch.

'I'm sure it's not,' he said, trying to inject a note of sympathy into his voice. 'But you should recognise your own wife.' As he spoke, Ryan flicked through the dozen black-and-whites. They showed a woman in her

6

late thirties getting into and out of a car with a man. Others showed her walking with the same man. Some had been taken in a crowded street, others in a park.

In one of them the couple was kissing.

'It's a bit of a shock,' Johnson told him. 'I mean, I suspected her of having an affair, I know, but . . . ' The sentence trailed off.

'It's never pleasant finding out something like this, Mr Johnson,' Ryan told him, glancing again at his watch.

'When I hired you, I suppose I was angry. Now I know for sure, I don't know what to think.'

The other man's voice cracked slightly.

She was being shafted by another bloke, Ryan thought. End of story.

'The photos will be proof enough when the case goes to court. I wouldn't worry about the Judge finding for you. It's there in black and white, after all,' Ryan said coldly.

'I didn't really want it to come to this,' Johnson murmured.

Ryan exhaled wearily and reached for a pencil. He began drawing circles on his pad.

'I don't know what I should do, Mr Ryan.'

Ditch the bitch, Ryan thought, smiling thinly.

'Well, you've got the evidence, Mr Johnson. What you do with it is up to you.'

'Perhaps I was hoping that it was just my imagination.'

Get off the fucking line, for Christ's sake.

'Do you think I should confront her with it?' Johnson wanted to know.

Make her eat the photos for all I care, just get off the line.

'You suspected her of having an affair; you now know for sure that she was. You hired me to get you proof and I've done that. What happens now is your

7

responsibility, Mr Johnson.'

There was a long silence at the other end of the phone. Ryan glanced at his watch again.

He thought he heard sniffling.

On his pad he wrote PRAT then went back to drawing circles.

'Thank you for your help,' said Johnson, his voice quivering.

'My pleasure. If you could send the cheque as soon as possible, I'd appreciate it.'

Johnson sniffed.

'Yes, I will,' he said quietly. 'I suppose this is all in a day's work for you, isn't it?'

'Every day's different,' Ryan said conversationally. 'As I said, if you could forward the cheque I'd be very grateful.' He took another drag on his cigarette. He could hear Johnson crying softly at the other end of the phone.

'Nice doing business with you,' said Ryan and hung up.

Three

He patted the receiver and got to his feet, gathering up the black and white photos and pushing them into an envelope. He slipped it into a drawer in his desk and reached for the half dozen letters he'd picked up as he entered.

Ryan Investigations' offices were situated on the top floor of a five storey building in Old Compton Street. The premises consisted of the office itself, a kitchenette and a toilet. The walls of the office sported framed photos and posters, including a picture of Ryan himself just after he'd joined the police force nearly twenty years before. The fresh-faced eighteen-year-old who looked happily out on the office bore little resemblance to the thirty-seven-year-old man sitting on the leather sofa opposite the desk, opening the mail. The icy blue eyes were the same, but now they were surrounded by wrinkles and the expression Ryan usually sported was one of indifference – not the expectancy he'd showed as a trainee policeman.

He'd risen swiftly to the position of Detective, and had hoped to reach the position of Detective-Inspector. But that was not to be.

Despite his arrest record, and his part in breaking a particularly large drugs ring, he'd been repeatedly passed over for promotion.

The excuse had always been that he was more useful on the streets, but he'd known the real reason. His temperament.

More than once his superiors had referred to him as a hot-head. It had come to a climax when he'd broken the jaw of a suspect who'd taken a shot at him during a chase through Whiteley's shopping centre in Bayswater. Despite Ryan's protestations that the man was carrying a gun and could have killed innocent passers-by, as well as him, the incident was the last straw.

He had been officially reprimanded and suspended for two weeks.

On his return he tendered his resignation.

Within a year he'd set up Ryan Investigations. Now, four years later, business was booming.

Divorce, surveillance, serving writs. The scope of Ryan's work was enormous; it had grown to such proportions that he sometimes needed to use outside help for what he saw as the more mundane tasks associated with the job. He had friends at some of the biggest security firms in the capital; they were happy to supply him with men for the jobs that required a little muscle.

So successful had business been lately that Ryan was considering not only moving to larger premises but also getting himself a secretary. It was the administrational aspect of the job that he found tedious. He had a temp come in once a week to type up his letters. She told him how exciting she thought it was working for a private detective. Even if it was only one day a week.

Ryan smiled as he thought about her. He sifted through the mail and found some circulars, a cheque and a letter from a woman who suspected her husband of having an affair with another man. Ryan raised his eyebrows, re-folded the letter and placed it in a plastic tray on his desk.

Most of the work was divorce work. His job was to gather evidence for his clients, which would then be turned over to their lawyers. It wasn't spectacular work but it paid well. His usual charges were fifty pounds an hour plus expenses. It varied according to the job, naturally.

He still had friends at New Scotland Yard, useful contacts who could supply him with information if he needed it. Not once in the past four years had he regretted his decision to leave the force.

He got to his feet and glanced out of the window that looked out over Charing Cross Road.

The thoroughfare was busy, as usual; people moved back and forth beneath the blistering sun.

In the cloudless sky the searing orb blazed with even greater brilliance than on the day before. The heatwave showed no sign of relenting.

Ryan opened a window and the heat flooded in, carried on an invisible tide of carbon monoxide fumes from the hundreds of belching exhausts below. It was cooler inside the office, even though the mercury in the thermometer on the wall was nudging seventy-six fahrenheit.

He looked into the street for a moment longer, then wandered through into the kitchenette, where he filled the kettle and flicked the switch to set it boiling. He rinsed a mug beneath the tap and flipped open the cupboard above in search of the coffee jar.

He found an empty one and muttered under his breath, tossing it into the nearby rubbish bin.

He turned off the kettle and decided to walk round the corner into Charing Cross Road. There was a small café there where he often picked up a sandwich.

On the way out he picked his newspaper up from his desk.

As yet, he hadn't noticed the headline.

Four

If the heat outside was intense, inside the café was like an oven.

Ryan felt the warm air hit him like a wall. The small eatery smelled of frying bacon; it always did. Whether it was early morning, lunchtime or late at night the smell of frying bacon was ever-present. Sandwiches and pies were assembled behind the clean glass counter for inspection. Steam billowing from the large tea-urn at

11

one end of the counter only served to add to the sweltering heat.

Ryan removed his tie and unbuttoned the top two buttons of his shirt, feeling perspiration form at the back of his neck. He wiped it away with his handkerchief. A large man with a massive stomach was waiting to be served. He was sweating profusely despite the fact that he was only wearing shorts and a vest. A tattoo on his left shoulder in the shape of a snake disappeared inside his vest, the head emerging on his right shoulder. Droplets of sweat rolling down his back made it look as if the snake was shedding tears.

Ryan fanned himself with his rolled-up newspaper and studied the array of sandwiches and cakes. He glanced around at the other occupants of the cafe; apart from the large man and himself, there were only three other people.

Two youths dressed in leather jackets, apparently impervious to the horrendously high temperatures, were talking animatedly as they thumbed through a magazine. Ryan realized that there was a gig on at the Marquee next door that night. Obviously, he reasoned, these two were taking no chances about being late.

On one of the high stools beside the mirrored wall an old woman sat nursing a polystyrene mug of soup, staring down into it every now and then. She had a plastic bag with her; the sleeve of a sweater hung out of it. The woman looked at her reflection in the mirror tiles, averting her gaze quickly, as if displeased by the image. Ryan shook his head and returned his attention to the sandwiches.

The large man with the tattoo was ambling off towards a table, balancing a huge lump of pizza in one hand and a mug of tea in the other.

Ryan stepped forward to the counter.

'Morning, Frank,' he said, nodding affably to the little

12

man who beamed back at him and pushed his black hair away from his face. It looked as if someone had sprayed his face with water, so much perspiration sheathed it.

'What can I get you, Nick?' asked the little man, still smiling. Frank Scalini wiped his pudgy hands on his apron and leaned closer. 'You on a case?' he asked conspiratorially.

Ryan nodded and winked.

'The case of the empty coffee jar,' he said. 'Give me a cappucino, will you, and a bit of that gâteau.' He pointed to the cake.

'My wife made it fresh today,' Scalini announced.

'How is she?'

'She has the baby in about three weeks,' he told him proudly, handing him the piece of cake and the coffee.

'I'll be in for my cigar when she does,' Ryan said, and paid.

He wandered over to the nearest table and sat down, flipping open his paper, pushing a forkful of cake into his mouth. As he read the back page he rummaged in his pocket and found his cigarettes. He took a couple more mouthfuls of cake then lit up.

There was a loud crackle from behind the counter as a wasp flew into the insectocutor. It disappeared in a flash of blue sparks to be joined a second later by a large fly.

Ryan sipped at his coffee and turned to the front page. The headline glared back at him.

BODY FOUND ON CLAPHAM COMMON:
THE FIFTH VICTIM?

There was a photo of bushes and uniformed men standing around. Ryan read the beginning of the article.

The body of eighteen-year-old John Molloy was found on Clapham Common yesterday. The youngster is believed to be the fifth victim, in as many months, of the same killer.

13

His body had been mutilated and was partially decomposed.

Like the previous four victims, Molloy had been living rough on the streets of London for some time . . .

Ryan sat back in his chair and sipped at his coffee, glancing at the remainder of the article.

Details of the precise nature of the mutilations had been withheld, as had the names of two previous victims aged fifteen. In every case the youngsters had been sleeping rough.

Ryan wondered who was in charge of the investigation. Maybe the bastard whose job *he* should have had? He folded up the paper and, finishing his cake and coffee, glanced down at his watch.

He lit up another cigarette and decided he should make a move. He'd grab a taxi outside.

The insectocutor crackled as it claimed another victim and Ryan waved to Saclini as he hurried out onto the pavement.

The concrete was warm beneath his feet, the heat from the sun intense.

He saw a cab approaching and stuck out an arm, stepping back as the vehicle pulled in. Once more he looked at his watch.

He didn't want to be late.

Five

The air-conditioning inside the office was so efficient that Ryan felt cold after the scorching heat outside. He had replaced his tie during the taxi ride and also slipped on his jacket. Now he sat opposite the large oak desk, his eyes flickering first around the room then back and forth between the two people who faced him.

Both were, he guessed, in their early fifties. The man, Graham Witton, was tall and thin, his face pale and drawn to the point of being gaunt.

His companion was an elegant woman with pinched features and hair drawn back with daunting severity from her forehead. She fixed Ryan in an appraising gaze and regarded his rumpled shirt with distaste. He noticed her stare and looked at her legs, suppressing a smile when she crossed them self-consciously. Denise Shaw coloured slightly.

As General Manager of The Royalton Hotel, Graham Witton carried the necessary air of simpering civility and practised officiousness that men in his position usually mastered effortlessly. His clothes and his appearance were immaculate; Ryan had the feeling that if he walked out into the street and into the inferno of the city, he would not so much as perspire. Every inch of his body was stiffly efficient.

Ryan leant forward and picked up his tea cup, hearing it chink against the saucer.

Denise Shaw kept her eyes upon him, looking at the

cup as if fearing that Ryan might shatter the expensive china simply by his close proximity to it.

He took a sip and replaced the cup, reaching for his cigarettes.

As he lit up, Denise Shaw wrinkled her nose.

'How long do you think the robberies have been going on?' Ryan asked, blowing out a long stream of smoke in her direction.

'We've had guests reporting items missing for about a month now,' Witton told him. 'But when the money was stolen we thought it was time to act.'

'How much was taken?'

'Nearly three hundred pounds.'

'Why didn't you call the police?' Ryan wanted to know.

'The guest in question didn't want to. Besides, we do have the good name of the hotel to consider,' Witton told him.

'What else has gone missing?' Ryan wanted to know.

'Travellers' cheques, items of clothing; pieces of jewellery in one or two cases,' Denise Shaw told him.

'And you're sure it's a member of staff?'

'If we were sure we wouldn't have called you in, Mr Ryan,' Denise Shaw said contemptuously.

Ryan eyed her indifferently and turned his attention back to Witton.

'And none of the guests have asked you to call the police?' he asked. 'I find that a little strange.'

'We . . . how shall I put it . . . we *dissuaded* them. We replaced money if it was taken, or we gave them the value of other items that were stolen. As I said to you, we cannot have that kind of publicity in a hotel like this.' Witton smiled his superior smile and pressed the tips of his fingers together.

'I was thrown out of here once,' said Ryan. 'For wearing jeans.' He smiled.

'We do have a very strict policy on denim in the hotel,' Witton informed him.

'It isn't allowed in any part of the hotel,' Denise Shaw echoed.

Ryan nodded. 'So at least you know your thief isn't the one in the Levi's.' He chuckled.

'When can you start your investigation?' Witton asked.

Ryan got to his feet. 'Tomorrow, if I can get someone in.'

'What do you mean?' Denise Shaw wanted to know.

'I mean that I'm going to have to use someone on the premises, someone posing as a member of your staff so that they can get close to the thief.'

'Why can't you do the job yourself?' Denise Shaw asked indignantly.

'Because I've got more important things to do than wander around dressed like a bell-boy trying to find out who's lifting some rich bastard's wallet or ring. I'll have someone here tomorrow.' He turned and headed towards the office door. 'Oh, and don't worry. I'll make sure he doesn't wear jeans.'

Six

The uniformed doorman glanced briefly at Ryan as he stood on the pavement in front of the hotel, then the man hurried to open the door for another departing guest.

As he pulled his tie free and stuffed it into his pocket,

Ryan watched the old woman move as graciously as she could out into the sweltering heat of the street. Why she was wearing a fur coat in temperatures nudging eighty and in the middle of the day Ryan could only guess, but she swept past him in a wave of perfume and make-up, heading towards a Mercedes at the kerb.

The private detective watched her scramble in, both the car driver and the doorman fighting for the privilege of opening the door for her. Ryan shook his head and scurried across the road, the full force of the sun hitting him as he left the shade of the canopy.

Piccadilly was busy, choked with traffic as usual. The heat, combined with the noxious clouds of carbon monoxide spewing from countless exhausts, made him feel light-headed. The perspiration was soaking into his shirt. A couple passed him, both dressed in matching shorts and tops, the man badly sunburnt on his shoulders and arms. The woman was carrying a large map of Central London. Bloody tourists, Ryan thought, almost colliding with a flustered woman pushing a buggy with twins in it.

Ryan was about to apologise when the woman told him to look where he was going. He raised his eyebrows, glancing at her as she stalked off, pushing the buggy through the crowds of pedestrians, cutting a swathe like a latter-day Boadicea.

All around him he saw faces flushed by the heat.

He coughed and felt a pain in his chest. Muttering under his breath he continued walking, wondering why the feeling of light-headedness had not passed. Heading down Berkely Street, past the Holiday Inn, Ryan hesitated a moment then turned and walked towards the main entrance of the hotel. He cursed when he felt another twinge of pain. Perhaps he should sit down for a while, wait until he'd recovered his wits and got rid of the bloody thing. It wasn't the first time he'd experienced it in the last few weeks.

He strode through the lobby of the hotel, smiling at a particularly attractive receptionist. She returned the gesture, colouring slightly.

He walked on through into the bar and sat down at a table near the window, laying his jacket on the seat beside him.

It was pleasantly cool in the bar and also pleasingly quiet. Apart from Ryan himself, only two other people were present. They were engrossed in conversation.

He sat back in his seat and wiped a hand across his forehead, feeling the perspiration there. As he turned he caught sight of his reflection in the mirrored wall to his right and was surprised at how pale he looked. The pain still jabbed inside his chest; Ryan winced as he felt needle-like prickles within his ribcage. He took a few deep breaths, his actions interrupted by the arrival of the barman.

Ryan ordered an orange juice and reached into his jacket pocket for a cigarette, relieved that the pain seemed to be diminishing slightly. If only this bloody giddiness would leave him too.

When the drink arrived he gulped half of it down immediately and ordered another, sucking in deep breaths and closing his eyes. It had to be the heat, he reasoned. He'd only felt like this for the last couple of weeks, ever since the temperatures had started to soar.

Yes. It was the heat.

Ryan tried to push the thoughts of pain from his mind and concentrate on the job at the Royalton. Reaching into his inside pocket he pulled out a small black diary and flicked through it until he reached the back and some phone numbers. He ran his finger down a list of names and numbers. Each of the men had worked for him in the past on one job or more. There were a dozen names; they were men he trusted (God knew there were few enough of them). He began looking for a likely name to work at the hotel. They were ex-policemen, bailiffs and security men. Each had a full-time job but would work for Ryan on a temporary basis because he paid well. He found the one he sought and made a mental note to call the man when he got back to the office.

He was replacing the diary in his jacket when he was struck by another coughing fit.

'Shit,' he muttered, pressing his hand to his mouth.

The pain was there again, too.

And the dizziness.

He hauled himself to his feet and headed for the toilets, pushing the doors open and crossing to the white hand-basins. The lights reflected off the brilliant white tiles; Ryan felt dazzled. He leant against one of the sinks, head down, then spun the cold tap.

As he looked up he saw how pale his skin was; it looked waxen, corpse-like.

He cupped his hands together, scooped water into them and splashed his face. The cold water felt good on his hot skin.

Ryan coughed again as he straightened up, hawking loudly, tasting mucus in his mouth. He spat it out.

The globule that hit the sink was thick with blood.

He stared at the crimson lump, watching as it slid slowly down the white porcelain, leaving a red smear.

He turned on the other tap and washed it away, cupping cold water to his mouth and swallowing. He coughed again and propelled another gob of fluid into the sink.

There was no blood this time.

The dizziness was beginning to pass off too.

He exhaled deeply, using the roller-towel to dry his face.

Ryan stood before the mirror and ran both hands

through his hair, glancing at the dark rings beneath his eyes.

He thought of the blood.

'Fuck it,' he murmured, still studying his reflection. He switched off the taps, took a couple of deep breaths, then turned and headed for the door.

He'd finish his drink, then get a cab back to the office. There were things he had to do.

Seven

'I would have killed the bastard.'

Brian Webster sat back on his seat and ran his hands slowly up and down his thighs, aware of the other eyes on him but unconcerned.

'Every fucking night he used to come home pissed,' he continued. 'He never had a job but he always seemed to find enough money for drink. For as long as I can remember he drank. I hardly saw him when I was a kid. My mum used to put me and my brother to bed but he'd wake us up when he got home. I'd always hear him. Shouting and swearing and throwing things. Then, when he got fed up of breaking plates or cups, he'd start on my mum. I wondered why she put up with it. She knew other people used to talk about her, about my old man, but it didn't seem to bother her. I used to feel sorry for her but then, as I got older, I started to get angry with her. I told her to leave him.

'I remember, on my twelfth birthday, she made a cake. I had about ten friends round to the house, but my

21

old man came in pissed and he wrecked everything. Then he whacked my mum. She had a black eye for two weeks, he hit her so hard. I used to imagine what life would be like without him. I used to wish that he'd just fucking die. Anything, so that me and my mum and my brother would get some peace. Then, when I got to sixteen, he started picking on me, too. He said that I was a man and that I should know how to look after myself. When he hit my mum I wanted to hit him back. I can remember hating myself for being scared of him, for not helping my mum. But that annoyed me even more. I was fourteen, my brother was twelve. Mum could have left him. We'd have gone with her. We'd all have managed somehow. But she stayed with him. She never even fucking moaned about him. If I told her she should leave him, she used to say that it wasn't all his fault. I couldn't believe that. He'd come home every night and beat shit out of her and she was telling me it wasn't *his* fault. Nobody asked him to go down the fucking pub every night.

'He put her in hospital twice. He broke her jaw *and* her nose. And she still stayed with him. After a while I started to hate her too. I hated her for being so stupid, for not having the guts to leave him. He could have killed her and it wouldn't have bothered him. When he was pissed, he didn't know *what* he was doing. He didn't care *who* he hurt.

'I used to dread holidays most. Christmas, Easter, that sort of thing. We never had one Christmas without that bastard ruining it. Mum used to cook a big dinner and he'd fuck off down the pub, then he'd come home at closing time mouthing off, throwing his weight about. Smashing things.

'One Christmas, just a couple of years ago it was, we were sitting round waiting for him to come home so we could have our Christmas dinner. He rolled in, smashed

22

out of his head and, because the dinner wasn't on the table, he turned the fucking thing over. Wrecked everything. Plates, glasses, food. Everything ended up on the floor. Then he started hitting my mum and she just took it, like she always did. Never hit him back. Perhaps she was scared that if she did he'd lay into her even worse.

'There was a carving knife lying on the kitchen floor and I picked it up. I wanted to stick it in him. I wanted to kill the bastard but he saw me with it. He must have realized what I was thinking and he turned on me. And my mum tried to stop him so he knocked her down and, while she was lying there, he kicked her. I ran. I locked myself in my bedroom but he got in and he beat the fuck out of me. I couldn't go to school for a week, until the bruises went down and some of the cuts healed. But my mum didn't do anything even then. She just carried on, as if it was all part of life. Still, I suppose it was by that time. She was used to it.

'I knew after that, though, that I wanted him dead. If I'd stayed I know I'd have killed him. I wouldn't have put up with what my mum put up with. That's why I had to leave home.

'I would have killed the bastard.'

Eight

Because of the heat inside the room the windows were open. The smell of diesel fumes was strong in the air. Carried on the dry wind, the stink of hot oil and smoke mingled with the more pungent fuel odour to create a noxious cloud that seemed to hang over St Pancras Goods depot like a man-made blanket. The already stifling heat made the stench even more repulsive.

From his position on his bed inside Ossulston Street hostel, Brian Webster could see out of the window and over the Goods Yard. Shunters trundled slowly up and down the network of rusty rails, fumes belching from them.

Aware of the others' probing eyes he wound his hair around one index finger repeatedly, not looking at any one face in particular.

The others were all roughly his age, nineteen going on forty. The ravages of living rough had taken a toll on their features. Gone were the fresh, mischievous, expectant faces of youth; these bore the bone-weary expressions of people who had never even dreamed dreams, never mind had them dashed. It was as if someone had systematically sucked the life from every one of them, draining away hope and replacing it with despair.

Their ages ranged from fifteen to twenty; boys and girls.

Brian Webster had often heard the expression 'Shit Happens'. He knew it was true. It had happened to him, to him and everyone else in the hostel.

Now lost in his own thoughts, he watched another train move lethargically about its business, aware only of the cloying heat.

'What's the point of all this, anyway?' asked Suzi Gray. 'I mean, every week we sit around here and talk about why we left home or what we're supposed to do, and the next week we're all sitting here again talking about the same things. I don't see why we bother.'

Suzi was a year older than Webster and had probably, at one time, been a very pretty young woman. She still

24

had a good figure, even if poor nutrition had served to make her a little skinny. It was in her hair and skin that the deficiencies showed. Her face was pockmarked, her long hair lank and dull. She sat cross-legged on a chair, barefoot.

'What *is* the point?' she repeated.

Emma Powell was hard pressed to find an answer.

She'd worked in hostels like this one, both long- and short-stay, for the past eight years. In fact she'd begun work in her first the day before her twenty-second birthday. The hostel in Ossulston Street was just one of many emergency short-stay hostels set up by the DSS in a desperate attempt to keep youngsters or anyone who had no accommodation off the streets. It was a desperate gambit by a desperate government to keep down statistics. No one knew for sure how many people were without homes in London and those in power were intent on it staying that way. The short-stay hostels kept people off the streets for up to three months at a time. It was time enough to allow figures to be juggled and it sounded good for ministers to crow about what was being done for the less fortunate.

Emma Powell knew from bitter experience that the solution wasn't so much an insoluble one as an inconvenient one. London was like a gigantic rug; the homeless were swept beneath it into hostels like this to hide them from sight.

She shifted uncomfortably in her seat, aware that they were waiting for an answer to Suzi's question.

'If you all talk to each other,' Emma began, 'if you all find out why you left home, you might begin to understand your problems a bit better.'

'Bollocks,' said Alan Casey, his Glaswegian accent hard.

'Our problem is that we don't have anywhere to live,' Suzi echoed.

25

'This is all bullshit,' Casey continued. 'We sit around talking and where the fuck does it get us? All we know is that in three months' time we're going to be thrown out of here and we'll be back on the streets again.'

'Or in some other hostel,' added Webster, still twining his hair around his finger.

'You won't be *thrown* out of here after three months, Alan,' Emma Powell told him. 'It's regulations. I'm as sorry about it as you are, but I'm only doing my job.'

'So were the SS' Casey said, and laughed. 'Only obeying orders. Orders from above. From some cunt who's never had to worry about going without food or a bed. The fucking rules are made by people who don't live in the real world. How many fucking starving politicians do you ever see? How many of *their* kids will end up getting mugged or fucking raped or worse because they've got nowhere to live except in a cardboard box or a fucking doss-house like this? I'll tell you. None of them. Bastards.' He got to his feet and crossed to the window.

Casey was a big, powerfully built figure, his size and the heavy growth of whiskers he sported making him look older than his eighteen years.

'It's not Emma's fault,' a broad Liverpudlian accent interjected. 'She can't do anything about it. It's no good blaming other people for your own faults.' Janet Ferguson picked agitatedly at the side of one black varnished fingernail and shifted her considerable bulk on her chair. 'It's not her fault you're here.'

'I know it's not her fucking fault,' Casey said, spinning round angrily. 'I'm just making a point.'

'If you don't like it, go back home,' Janet persisted.

'Get real, for fuck's sake,' snapped Casey. 'If I wanted to be at home do you think I'd have left in the first place? Why the fuck don't *you* go home, too?'

Janet lowered her gaze, her cheeks colouring beneath

the coating of her pure white make-up. It was in marked contrast to the bright orange of her hair, swept up in a high cockscomb, held in place by enough hair lacquer to put another hole in the ozone layer.

'Isn't it time we called it a day?' said Webster wearily. 'This isn't getting any of us anywhere, is it?'

Emma Powell was forced to agree. She nodded and got to her feet, looking around at their faces.

She saw only blank expressions, tired resignation.

'*I've* got something to say,' Maria Jenkins interjected.

She was a pretty girl of sixteen, her dish-water blonde hair pulled back in a pony-tail.

One or two people looked at her. Casey was already walking towards the exit.

'I want to go to John's funeral. Do you know when it is, Emma?' asked Maria.

Emma Powell looked puzzled.

'I can find out,' she said.

'Why do you want to go?' Webster asked. 'Molloy was only here for about two weeks.'

'He was a nice guy. I liked him,' Maria said defensively. 'I think it's right that one of us should pay our respects.'

'I hardly spoke to him,' Webster said.

'You hardly speak to anyone,' Suzi commented, chuckling.

'There's another reason one of us ought to go,' Maria said. 'We shared this hostel with John until he was murdered. It could just as easily have been one of us.'

Nine

There wasn't much in the file. The cumulative experience of sixteen years added up to less than half a sheet of A4.

Emma Powell opened the plastic file and looked at the card marked JOHN MOLLOY.

It carried his date of birth, his home address, his height, weight and the other minor details which were all that remained now. She wondered if the police had studied a similar sheet after they'd found his mutilated body on Clapham Common.

The newspaper on her desk carried the story of the discovery of his body but Emma had glanced only briefly at it. He was dead. It was enough to know that. She knew that he'd been mutilated. She had no desire to know how.

Emma replaced the file and flicked through others in the cabinet jammed into one small corner of her tiny office. There was no air-conditioning in the small room; she had the one window open wide in an effort to counteract the intense heat. As the afternoon wore on the temperature approached eighty-five. There wasn't a breath of wind.

She looked through the remaining files. There were over two hundred of them, all arranged alphabetically. Each one contained details of those presently resident at the hostel and also those who had previously stayed for the regulation three months. Each file contained details not only of age and physical matters but also of backgrounds, home addresses (if there were any), families and friends. It seemed pointless keeping the files. Emma knew that no one who had passed through the hostel could return; but it made her feel as if she were running something other than a refuge. Everything there was to know about residents past and present had been neatly typed, the sum total of their lives contained in a few lines.

Emma closed the drawer and crossed back to her desk. She sat down, running a hand through her hair, feeling how wet it was where it touched her neck. She took a tissue and wiped away the perspiration.

The office door was open but the knock startled her. She looked up to see Maria Jenkins.

'Come in, Maria,' Emma said, motioning towards a chair but the young girl decided to stand. She glanced out of the window across the Goods Yard.

'Did you find out about John's funeral?' Maria asked.

'I rang his home but there was no reply.'

'What about the police? They'd know, wouldn't they?'

'They might not give out that information to someone who wasn't in the family.'

Maria sighed and finally sat down.

'It said in the paper he was mutilated,' she muttered, noticing the folded copy of the *Mirror* on the desk. 'Like the others.'

Emma merely nodded.

'It's very sad,' she said finally.

'Don't you ever get sick of all this?' Maria asked, making an expansive gesture with her hand. 'You must realize there's nothing you can do in the long run to help. You can only keep people off the streets for three months. After that, they're helpless again. Don't you ever feel like giving up?'

'I've never thought about it. Even a little help is better than none at all, isn't it?'

Maria nodded slowly.

'I wonder if John's parents are sorry now he's dead?' she mused. 'I mean, if it was their fault he left home, I wonder if they blame themselves for his death?'

'That's difficult to say, Maria. It was *his* choice to leave. He came to London because *he* wanted to. Just like nearly everyone else here or at any of the other hostels.'

'Nobody cares, do they?' said Maria, getting to her feet. 'People say they're concerned about the homeless, but no one really cares unless it's happening to them.' She made for the door. 'No one really cares that John's dead because he wasn't important. He just lived rough. No one knew him. No one cared. No one cares about any of us.'

Emma opened her mouth to say something, but merely ran her tongue across her lips. There was nothing to say.

'No one would care if we *all* died. At least we'd be out of the way for good then.'

As much as she wanted to, Emma found it difficult to disagree.

Ten

'Where will you go?'

Suzi Gray sat on the edge of the bed, watching as Maria Jenkins removed what few belongings she had from the locker. She stuffed them into a small nylon holdall: a couple of pairs of socks, a pair of leggings, some knickers. She accidentally dropped a T-shirt onto the floor. Janet Ferguson retrieved it and handed it to her. She smiled and pushed it into the holdall with everything else.

'There are other hostels around, aren't there?' Maria said. 'I could try one of them.'

'I wouldn't if I were you,' Suzi advised her. 'Most of them are useless.' She swept a hand through her hair. 'Especially the mixed ones.' She lowered her head slightly, the memories painful.

It had been less than two years ago, but Suzi could remember it with the same appalling clarity as if it had been yesterday.

There had been three of them. All in their early twenties. Two of them drunk or stoned – she had never found out which. It didn't matter much, either. All that mattered was that they had attacked her. Pulled the covers from her bed as she slept. While she was still recovering her wits two of them had held her down while the third had raped her. They had taken it in turns, covering her mouth with a piece of sheet to stop her making a noise. Then, when they'd finished, they had left her there and run from the hostel.

She had dragged herself into one of the bathrooms and scrubbed their filth away, but no matter how many times she washed she felt she would always carry their mark, like a glaring tattoo only she could see. She'd left the same night and had wandered the streets until daylight, her anger almost as strong as her disgust.

Two weeks later, in a shop doorway in Oxford Street, a couple of youths had lunged at her late one night.

The first she had almost blinded when she jabbed at his eyes with her fingers. The second had fared even worse. Suzi had laid his cheek open to the bone with a piece of broken glass she'd snatched up.

She had watched in triumph as they'd run.

Now she pulled her legs up beneath her and accepted a cigarette from Janet.

'What will you do for money?' the large girl asked.

Maria shrugged.

'Beg, I suppose,' she said, smiling bitterly.

'You could go on the game.' Janet chuckled. 'There's a lot of money in that.' She took a drag on her cigarette. 'A girl I met at King's Cross was doing it. She said she was getting fifty quid a fuck.'

'Fifty quid and Christ knows what kind of diseases,' Suzi added.

'Fifty quid's fifty quid, though, isn't it?' Janet countered. 'You'd only have to do it five or six times a week and you could *buy* a bloody hostel.' She chuckled again.

Maria ran a hand through her hair and sat down on the bed.

'When do you leave?' Suzi asked.

'In a couple of days.' She ran a hand over her pillow as if smoothing out the creases. 'I'd been thinking of going back home.'

'Why did you leave in the first place?' Suzi wanted to know.

'I had a row with my mum and dad.'

'Join the club,' giggled Janet.

'What was the row about?' Suzi enquired, drawing on her cigarette.

'My mum had been having an affair. Dad found out about it. They were always rowing. I tried to stop them one night, but it didn't help. I just couldn't stand seeing them fighting all the time.'

'How long ago was that?' Janet asked.

'Two years.'

'So what makes you think things are going to be any

different now?' said Suzi, flatly.

Maria could only shrug.

'Perhaps I was just hoping,' she said softly.

'What's hope?' Suzi exclaimed, her eyes cold.

'So what *are* you going to do?' Janet repeated.

'Keep away from the other hostels. I mean it. Especially the DSS ones,' said Suzi. 'No one knows what the insides of those places are like until they've seen them. *I've* seen them and I'm telling you, you're safer on the streets.'

Eleven

Ryan heard the shouts as he stepped out of the taxi.

He looked round as he dug in his pocket for change and saw two waiters from the restaurant opposite dragging a man to his feet.

The man was in his thirties, although it was difficult to be precise because of his unkempt appearance. He wore a long overcoat which was holed and filthy, stained in many places. His trousers bore a dark stain around the crotch. The two waiters were trying to lift him by hooking their arms beneath his, but the very act of touching him seemed distasteful. They pushed him away from the front of the restaurant.

Ryan looked on impassively then slipped the driver a tip, glancing one last time at the tableau across the street.

The sun was still high in the sky, beating down mercilessly on the city. It sent tempers as well as temperatures soaring. In New York they called these searing, heat-shrouded times Dog Days.

Ryan selected his key and was about to open the main door when it swung back and two young men emerged. They nodded briefly at the private detective, then headed off down the street. Ryan returned the terse greeting with an equally swift nod then entered, climbing the stairs towards his office.

The young men worked in the graphic design studio on the first floor. Like Ryan, they shared the building with a small advertising agency and a tiny film production company which specialized in making TV adverts. The owner of the company was a man in his mid-twenties who'd been to Los Angeles a few times and insisted on calling Ryan 'dude' whenever he saw him. Something which never failed to irritate the private detective, especially as the young man was from Wembley Park. Not exactly West Coast California.

Ryan climbed the stairs to his office, feeling breathless by the time he had reached the third landing. He coughed gently, relieved when he felt no pain in his chest. The lift was, as usual, out of order.

When he finally reached the top floor he paused for a moment, sucking in deep lungfuls of warm air, both angered and surprised by his inability to climb the flights without feeling this way. He exhaled wearily, then sucked in another breath which wheezed asthmatically in his lungs.

In his office heat and exhaust fumes poured in to greet him. He pulled his tie out of his pocket and tossed it across the room, looking over at the answering machine. The green message light was flashing. As he passed it, Ryan flicked it from 'Answer Set' to 'Incoming Message'. The tape rewound, voices speeded up in reverse squealing through the cloying stillness of the office.

He ran the cold water tap in the kitchenette and retrieved a glass from the cupboard. Blowing the dust from it, he held it under the flow of water. He drank two glasses as the machine rewound then began to replay the messages.

Ryan splashed his face with cold water, listening to the voices on the tape.

There was a message from the manager of the Royalton hotel, thanking him for his time.

Very courteous.

Could he call a Mr Goldman who ran a car hire firm in Paddington and suspected that three of his cars had been stolen.

More work.

One of his men was calling to let him know that the writ they'd been ordered to serve today *had* been.

The message ended.

Ryan rewound the tape and took down Goldman's address and phone number, then pulled open the top drawer of his desk and took out a letter which had arrived that morning with the other post.

It was from his bank, agreeing to let him have the mortgage on a larger office in Covent Garden.

Ryan smiled, read it again and dropped it back onto the desk.

He picked up the phone and wandered across the office with it, peering down towards the restaurant.

The drunk was now lying in the gutter. One of the waiters gesticulated angrily at him before turning and walking back into the restaurant. Ryan could see the man in the gutter moving slightly, lying helplessly on his back like a turned turtle. He finally scrambled to his feet and lurched off across the road, bumping into a young man in the process. The youth shoved him and the drunk ended up flat on his back again.

Passers-by moved swiftly, only casting cursory

glances at the drunk.

Ryan held the phone in one hand, jammed the receiver between his ear and shoulder and jabbed out the digits.

Then he waited.

Twelve

She was surprised to hear his voice but it didn't show in her face. She sat expressionless through the short conversation, only smiling as she replaced the receiver and stayed motionless on the bed.

'Who was that?' a voice called from the adjacent bathroom.

Kim Finlay kept her eyes on the receiver for a moment longer, then got to her feet and wandered through into the en-suite.

Her husband was standing in front of the bathroom mirror, running an electric razor over his cheeks and chin.

Kim sat down on the edge of the bath and watched him.

'Who was it?' he asked again.

'It was Nick,' she told him.

Joseph Finlay switched off the razor and studied his wife's reflection in the glass. He splashed aftershave on his face, patting it against his skin.

'What did he want?' he asked a little sharply.

'He had some news to tell me,' she said.

'Was it *that* important?'

'He didn't say.'

'Then why did he phone?'

'He phoned to ask me if I'd meet him tomorrow for lunch. He wants to tell me face to face.' She clasped her hands around one knee.

Her husband said nothing.

'Is it such a big deal?' she wanted to know.

'Go if you want to,' Finlay told her, re-adjusting his tie. Although I suppose you will, whatever I say.' He walked through into the bedroom and opened one of the large wardrobes, searching through it for a jacket.

'I didn't think I had to ask your permission, Joe,' said Kim.

'You *don't*,' he snapped. 'I just can't see why you have to see him. You've been divorced for three years.'

'Exactly. And I've been married to you for over a year. It's you I love. Why does it bother you if I see Nick for lunch?'

'Perhaps if the roles were reversed you'd feel the same way,' Finlay said acidly.

'I haven't seen him for over three months. It's not as if he's ringing or calling here all the time.'

'I should hope not. It is supposed to be over between you, after all.'

'What's that supposed to mean?' Kim said defensively.

Finlay exhaled and turned to face her.

'You might not think anything of Ryan any more, but who's to say whether or not *he* still loves *you*?'

'He didn't have enough time to love me when we were married,' she said, a hint of bitterness in her voice. She moved closer and put her arms around him. 'Even if he does still love me, I'm married to you now. That's all that matters.'

'And you can tell me that you don't feel anything for him?'

37

Kim sighed wearily.

'Joe, don't start that again. He's the father of my child. We were married for twelve years. I can't just wipe him out of my life and out of my mind. It wouldn't be fair to Kelly to do that. He cares for her.'

'Is that why he didn't even bother contesting custody? Because he *cares* so much?' There was an edge to Finlay's words that Kim was not slow to pick up.

'He knew there was no way he could look after her. He knew that the best way for her to be happy was by staying with me.'

She stepped away from Finlay, who regarded her coldly for a moment.

'You're defending him again,' he said quietly.

Kim lowered her gaze momentarily.

'Kelly's happy here and you know it,' she said.

'And she'd be even happier if Ryan didn't just turn up whenever he felt like it, wanting to take her out. She doesn't know from one month to the next if she's going to see him or even hear from him. When was the last time he phoned her, for Christ's sake?'

'Why do we always end up having an argument when Nick is mentioned?' she said, smiling thinly.

'Because he has the knack of bringing out the worst in people. You should know. That's one of the reasons you divorced him, isn't it?'

'He's still Kelly's father, Joe, and all the arguing in the world isn't going to change *that*.'

She sat down on the edge of the bed and ran a hand through her hair. She felt hot and flustered.

'I'd better go,' said Finlay, reaching for his jacket. He pulled it on and inspected his reflection in one of the full-length mirrors behind the door.

'Don't go off in a bad mood,' Kim said.

Finlay took a step towards her, leant forward and kissed her gently on the forehead.

'Go and have lunch with him,' he said. 'Find out what his news is.'

Kim smiled, taking a playful swipe at him as he left the bedroom. He strode across the large landing and down the staircase, which turned twice at right angles before reaching the polished wood floor of the hall.

'What time will you be back?' Kim called as he headed for the front door, briefcase in hand.

'The meeting isn't until three,' Finlay told her. 'I'll call you when I'm on my way home.' Then he was gone.

Kim stood by the banister listening to the sound of his Jag starting up in the driveway, then heard the tyres crunch the gravel of the drive as he pulled away. She turned and headed back into the bathroom, turned on the shower, testing the temperature with her fingers as she pulled off her clothes. When she was satisfied that it was cool enough she stepped in, allowing the refreshing jets to play over her body for some minutes before finally shutting off the conduit. She stepped out and wrapped herself in a bath towel. She caught sight of herself in the long mirror and she admired her own reflection. At thirty-three she still had an excellent figure. Nothing sagging yet, she thought, smiling. She padded through into the bedroom and pulled on fresh jeans and a denim shirt, the clean material feeling cool against her skin.

From across the room a wedding picture of herself and Finlay stared back. She crossed to it and touched the frame fondly, straightening it on the bedside table.

Then she slid open the bottom drawer of the cabinet and rummaged under the clothes.

She pulled out another photo. A small snap only two inches square, it was curling at the edges.

It showed herself, Ryan and their daughter. It had been taken about six years ago, when Kelly was just eight years old.

She looked at the photo for a moment, then carefully replaced it in the drawer and slid it shut.

Kim didn't want Finlay to know she had it.

It might cause arguments.

As she made her way downstairs she wondered what her ex-husband was so keen to tell her.

Thirteen

The bruises and cuts on his face gave him the appearance of a human jigsaw puzzle.

Great purple and blue welts and deep gashes, some of them stitched shut, covered every inch of skin. There were even some on his hands and arms.

Nick Ryan couldn't have looked much worse if a truck had reversed over his face.

His upper torso was exposed to reveal more contusions; tightly wound bandages held his broken ribs in place. There was a cast on one of his legs. The limb itself was suspended from a pulley in the ceiling of the hospital room.

Kim sat beside the bed, her eyes red-rimmed and hollow. Her first reaction had been one of horror. She wondered how anyone could survive such horrendous injuries. She was even more flabbergasted to learn that he had been conscious upon admittance. Now she sat gazing at him, reaching out to touch his hand, to run her own fingers over cut and bruised flesh. Over two fingers which had been dislocated.

His lips had been split, one of them gouged open

when a tooth had shattered and ripped through it. His nose was broken and there was cotton wool jammed into one nostril. She could see the blood soaking into it. Ryan was breathing through his mouth. Low, guttural inhalations brought pain from his smashed ribs. One of them had come within millimetres of puncturing a lung. The doctors had said he'd been lucky.

She dreaded to think what they classed as unlucky.

The police had already been in to question him and Ryan had croaked answers to their questions through his split and swollen lips, wincing every time he coughed. He hadn't seen the faces of the men who attacked him as he returned home, he told them. He'd counted three. Including the one who'd been carrying the baseball bat. He couldn't identify them; it could have been anyone. There were many people who had reason to want him in this condition. Husbands discovered in the throes of affairs by his investigations. Men cheating on their business partners. Those he served writs on.

It was an occupational hazard, being hated by those he exposed. Sometimes it was by those who hired him. The wives or husbands confronted by evidence he'd found to prove their spouses' infidelities often seemed to blame *him* for actually forcing them to face the truth.

It wasn't the first time someone had taken a swing at him. It was just that no one had done it so comprehensively until now.

'A hairline fracture of the skull, a depressed fracture of the left sphenoid bone,' the doctor began, reading the inventory of injuries from the clipboard he held. 'Three broken ribs, though thankfully no internal damage. A hairline fracture to the left radial bone. Broken tibia and fibula on the right leg. Severe bruising and lacerations over the entire body.'

The doctor leant closer, using a pen-light to look into

Ryan's eyes, a task made difficult by the amount of swelling round them.

'You're going to have quite a collection of scars, Mr Ryan,' he said, glancing at two nasty cuts on the private detective's chest.

Ryan looked at him impassively, then at Kim. She swallowed hard.

'Is he going to be all right, doctor?' she asked.

'There was no internal damage. The breaks will heal in good time,' she was told. The doctor turned and headed for the door, leaving them alone.

They sat in silence for a moment. Then Kim spoke softly.

'You saw who attacked you, didn't you, Nick?'

Ryan drew in a painful breath.

'Yes,' he said, wincing.

'Then why didn't you tell the police?'

'Because I'll take care of it myself when I get out of here.' He tried to shift position.

'Take care of it?' Kim snapped.

'He might have put me in hospital but I'll make sure that fucker walks with a limp for the rest of his life. Him *and* the two cunts with him.'

'Who was it?'

'I was investigating a firm called Allied Security,' he said. 'One of the partners hired me; he thought his mate was siphoning off money. It turned out he was right. I exposed him, he got the hump and did this.' He motioned to his battered frame.

'The police would have arrested him.'

'And done what? They'd never have proved it. The bastard would have walked. Well, not now. I'll see to him when I get out of here.'

'You always have to have the last word, don't you, Nick?' Kim said wearily.

He didn't answer.

42

'You were lucky this time,' she continued. 'They could have killed you. And if it wasn't them it might be someone else. You don't know what's going to happen to you from one day to the next. It might not be a baseball bat, next time; it might be a gun.'

'Occupational hazard,' he said, trying to move into a more comfortable position.

'Then maybe you're in the wrong profession,' she said angrily. 'Get out now, before it's too late.'

'I can't get out,' he told her. 'I've got a business to run.'

'You've also got a family to consider. Unless you've forgotten about me and Kelly.'

'Why do you think I work so bloody hard? It's *for* you and Kelly.'

'She doesn't see you for days on end, Nick, because you're working. That's all you ever do. Since you set up this bloody business it's the only thing that matters to you.'

'You haven't missed out on anything; you've never gone without.'

'I've gone without *you*,' Kim said exasperatedly. 'You never know when to stop, do you? You won't stop until someone kills you. Well, I don't want to be around when that happens.' Her voice cracked slightly.

'So don't be,' Ryan said flatly.

As she woke from the dream Kim found that her eyes were moist.

She sat up slowly, trying to re-orientate herself with her surroundings, blinking myopically in the gloom.

Beside her Joseph Finlay slept soundly.

There were no doctors. No hospital.

No Ryan.

She lay down again, feeling her hair matted against the nape of her neck.

43

Kim closed her eyes but it was a long time before sleep came.

Fourteen

'Spare some change, please?' Maria Jenkins asked as the group of middle-aged people passed by on the subway steps.

One of them, a man in a dark blue blazer, dug in his pocket and threw a coin towards Maria as if he were tossing scraps to a dog. She retrieved the coin, glad to see it was a pound. Out of the corner of her eye she saw the man's companion grab him by the arm and pull him away. The words drifted back towards her on the warm air:

'Why did you do that, John? She's probably got more money than we have.'

There was a chorus of laughter as the people disappeared up the steps.

Maria looked at the money she'd collected in the past hour, counting it with her finger like a Dickensian miser. She found that the collective generosity of her public amounted to £2.36. She pocketed the money and set off up the stairs from Piccadilly Circus tube, heading for the Regent Street exit. She emerged opposite a branch of 'Dunkin' Donuts' and went straight in and bought herself a cup of tea and two donuts. As she sat eating them she watched the crowds pass by outside, bathed in the neon light. All across Piccadilly the night was lit by a rainbow of colours from the signs.

It was her first night away from Ossulston Street hostel. She tried not to think too much about the place, concentrating instead on where she might spend the night. The city offered plenty of doorways and back-alleys, but she would have to be careful which she chose.

The Strand seemed to be her best bet, she thought. Piccadilly tended to attract junkies and rent boys, while Oxford Street was the domain of drunks. In the society of the homeless, even the unwanted knew where they were welcome. Maria decided to head for the Strand.

She finished her tea and donuts and set off across Piccadilly, moving through the crowds that thronged the hub of the West End, slipping in and out of the hordes of tourists and sightseers enjoying themselves. She carried her small holdall, apologising occasionally when she bumped people with it.

As she passed the Trocadero Maria looked across the street towards a restaurant and saw people eating. She felt a combination of envy and bitterness. Next to it there was a fast food restaurant; two young girls no older than herself were emerging, sharing a hamburger between them. *Kindred spirits, perhaps?*

In Leicester Square a man with dreadlocks and a long dirty overcoat rummaged through a dustbin, delighted when he found a drinks container. He took off the top, smelled the contents and, deciding they were drinkable, swigged thirstily from the container.

Watching him drink suddenly reminded Maria how hot the evening was.

The city smelled of cooking food and diesel fumes. Rubbish bins, filled to overflowing, added their own pungent stench to the jigsaw of odours heightened by the hot air.

Maria swept her long hair away from her neck, feeling the perspiration there. She walked on through

45

the crowds and through the heat, her mind turning constantly to the thoughts she'd had before leaving the hostel.

Should she return home?

Surely even the pain of seeing her parents' marriage break up around her was preferable to a life spent begging and sleeping rough?

She crossed Charing Cross Road into St Martin's Lane and continued on her way.

On the other side of the road a queue waited to enter Stringfellows. The poseurs and the rich bastards were milling about on the pavement, awaiting the decision of the neanderthals posing as doormen to allow them in. Maria saw two young men turned away. They shouted angrily at the doorman as he pushed them aside. It was a world of which she knew nothing and wanted no part. Just as well; it would never be within her experience. She felt a twinge of anger. There were girls standing there only a few years older than she was. *They* had never been forced to beg for money to buy a cup of tea. They probably did their own kind of begging once they were inside, but their kind was achieved with a low-cut dress or a short skirt.

There was a café up ahead; Maria fumbled in her pocket to see how much change she had left. She found that she had enough for a can of drink and got herself a Coke.

On the steps of St Martin-in-the-Fields she sat down and looked out over Trafalgar Square. Nelson's Column thrust skyward, puncturing the thin wisps of cloud that wafted across the firmament, blown by the warm breeze.

Perhaps she should phone home before she actually made that monumental step, thought Maria.

What if they didn't *want* her back?

For all she knew the marriage could have disintegrated by now. There might be nothing left to go back to.

She took a swig from her coke can and put down her holdall on the steps, using it as a pillow to rest on. Two people already slept close by the doors of the church, one of them bundled up in a sleeping bag despite the heat of the night.

Perhaps she should stay here for the night.

Stay here and go home tomorrow?

But how to get home? If she *was* going home, she'd need the train fare. Maria realized she had no alternative.

The first two people who passed hardly paid her any attention. The third tossed her a fifty-pence piece.

'Spare some change, please?' she said, beginning to sound like a stuck record.

'How much do you need?'

The voice startled her. She turned to see a tall man dressed in jeans and a white shirt looking down at her. He was in his early forties but wore his hair in a pony-tail. The rest of it was pulled back so severely from his face that it made his skin shine. He had both hands dug in the pockets of his jeans.

'How much do you need?' he repeated.

Maria eyed him warily.

'Is it for something to eat?' he continued.

Her stomach rumbled as if in answer to the question.

The man with the pony-tail smiled.

'I was trying to get home,' she told him. 'I need the train fare. It's twenty pounds, though.'

He took one hand from his pocket and pulled out a wallet. From it he took a brand new twenty-pound note.

Maria's face lit up momentarily, but the light in her eyes faded rapidly.

'I'm not a prostitute, you know,' she said quickly. 'Just because you give me twenty pounds . . .'

He cut her short.

'Take the money,' he said indignantly. 'I was trying to

47

help, that's all.'

'Why?'

'Because I've got a daughter about your age and I'd like to think that someone would help her if she was in *your* position.'

'Thank you,' said Maria quietly, holding out her hand for the money.

It was suddenly withdrawn.

'How do I know you'll use it for your train fare or for food?' he said sharply. 'You could be spinning me this story so you can get money for drugs.' He prepared to put the money away.

Maria got to her feet.

'I'm telling the truth, honestly,' she said. 'I need it to get home. Please believe me. I'll get something to eat, then I'll use it to get home.'

The man shook his head.

'I don't believe you,' he said slowly. 'But there's a way you can prove it.' His smile returned. 'Let me buy you something to eat. At least I'll know you've had food before you go.'

Maria smiled too.

'Deal?' he said, holding out the twenty again, like some kind of promise.

She nodded.

'Thank you,' she said as he handed her the note.

'Come on,' he said. 'There's a place just round the corner where we can get something.'

Maria walked alongside him, the twenty-pound note clutched in her hand. She thought of home.

The man occasionally looked down at her. He had both hands in his pockets again.

One of them gently touched the hilt of a flick knife.

Fifteen

The first time Nick Ryan had seen Tiddy Dol's restaurant in Shepherd Market he'd been chasing a suspect.

He'd been an Inspector at the time, working on a case involving the murder of a prostitute in Red Lion Yard. A high-class call-girl someone had decided would look better with her hands removed and both eyes cut out.

It turned out to be a pimp for whom the girl had once worked.

Ryan had tracked him to Shepherd Market and finally cornered him inside the restaurant itself.

He'd brought Kim to the place on their first date.

Now he sat close to the main entrance, a vodka and lemonade cradled in his hand, watching for her. Around him other lunchtime diners were busy eating and talking. The place was pleasantly cool compared to the stifling heat outside. Giant rotor fans in the ceiling turned gently like the upturned propellers of helicopters, spreading a pleasing breeze throughout the dining area. Constructed of bare stone as it was, the building seemed a more than adequate guard against the perpetually scorching sunshine. Even in his jacket and tie Ryan felt comfortable.

He saw Kim approaching the front door and smiled.

She was wearing a black trouser suit over a white blouse. A pair of sunglasses hid her eyes but she removed them as she entered the restaurant, spotting him immediately.

He took a step towards her, leaning forward to kiss her. She met his kiss with her lips but the gesture was one of friendship.

'Do you want a drink?' he asked.

She asked for a gin and tonic and sat down beside him.

He thought how gorgeous she looked.

She thought he looked like death warmed up.

There were dark rings beneath his eyes and his face looked waxen, but when he looked at her there was a vitality there.

Once she had her drink Ryan asked if they could be shown to their table. It was one of the more secluded ones, inside what looked like a railway tunnel entrance. They sat on wooden chairs and studied the menus.

All around, the babble of many conversations seemed to merge into one unintelligible buzz. Many of the accents were foreign, after all. Tiddy Dol's attracted tourists because it served Traditional English Food.

'You look great,' Ryan said, peering at his ex-wife over the rim of his glass.

'I wish I could say the same for you, Nick,' Kim told him. 'Are you feeling okay?'

'I've been a bit tired lately. I haven't been sleeping too well, that's all.'

'Too much work?'

'There's no such thing as too much work. More work means . . .'

'More money, I know,' she interjected.

They regarded each other in silence for a moment.

'How's Kelly?' he asked finally.

'She's fine. You should come and see her, find out for yourself.'

'I will soon, but things are really busy at the moment.'

'They're always busy, Nick.'

'That's the way I like it, Kim.'

'You don't have to remind me.'

She looked at the menu and made up her mind quickly. Ryan did the same, ordering them both another drink when the waiter took the order.

'So what's the news you had to tell me?' she asked, smiling.

He told her how the business was expanding. About the new premises in Covent Garden.

If anything, she thought, the job had become even more important to him.

'I'm very happy for you, Nick,' she said, smiling. 'It's great news.' She raised her glass. 'Let's drink to it.'

They touched glasses and drank.

'Did Joe say anything about you coming here today?' Ryan wanted to know.

'Why should he?' Kim asked.

'Did he?'

'It's really none of your business, Nick,' she said quietly.

Their food arrived, providing a momentary distraction before Ryan returned to the attack.

'And how *is* the millionaire property developer? Still buying up all the slums in London and re-selling them at twice the price?' There was an edge to Ryan's voice that Kim didn't care for.

'Joe's fine, if that's what you're trying to ask,' she snapped.

They locked stares for a moment.

Ryan coughed, put a hand to his mouth, felt pain in his chest. It passed quickly enough.

'Are you sure you're okay?' Kim asked.

'I'm fine, I told you.' He took a sip of his drink. 'Thanks for the concern, though.'

'Don't sound so surprised, Nick. Just because we're not married any more doesn't mean I don't give a shit about you now. We were married for twelve years, in case you've forgotten. The only trouble was, for most of that time you were married to the job.'

'Don't start, Kim,' Ryan said irritably. 'You knew how important it was to me, especially when I started up the agency.'

'Yes, and I never tried to stand in your way, did I? All I ever asked was that you should remember you had me and Kelly as well as your bloody agency. I didn't ask for much, Nick.'

'You left me over it.'

'It wasn't just the agency; it was the chances you used to take. I couldn't put up with that. With never knowing if a call to the hospital was going to be to identify your body.'

'So now you're married to Mr Dependable and you don't have to worry about things like that. Or where the next penny's coming from,' he said sardonically.

'I love Joe. He's kind and generous and he loves me and Kelly, too. But I don't love him the way I loved you, Nick.' She swallowed hard and lowered her head. 'You were unpredictable, exciting. I never knew how you would react to a situation. Maybe Joe is dependable, you might even call him boring, but I don't care. At least I know he'll be there when I need him. That was something I never knew when I was with you. And now, if you give me a choice between boring or dangerous, I'll take boring every time.'

Ryan shook his head and sighed.

'What's he done to you, Kim?' he said, an ironic smile on his face. 'Taken all the life out of you? What use is living without a few fucking risks?'

She looked at him and wanted to hate him for what he'd said but couldn't.

'I hope he doesn't do the same to Kelly,' Ryan added.

'If you took the time to see her more often you might find out,' Kim chided. 'See if *she's* changed, too.'

Ryan regarded her.

There was a fire in her eyes he knew well. It still burned as brightly.

'You haven't changed, Kim,' he said. 'You've just settled for something different.'

She didn't answer; didn't even look up from her food.

Afraid to look at him?

She took a sip of her drink.

Afraid he was right?

They ate the rest of the meal in virtual silence.

Sixteen

So many faces.

After too long they all began to look the same. Vincent Kiernan had to blink hard, to convince himself he wasn't in the middle of a science fiction film in which the world was populated by identical beings.

The concourse of King's Cross Station was a seething mass of people all moving apparently directionlessly.

Kiernan sipped at his drink and looked across at the departure board, at the numbers and places flicking across it. People hurrying to catch the trains also stared at the board, sometimes anxiously. He saw a man, sweat soaking through even the light jacket of his suit, dragging a large suitcase towards the trains. Behind him a woman with a trolley laden with cases ran headlong, using the trolley as a means to clear a path for herself.

Elsewhere a line of people filed slowly round the station, waiting to board a train to Leeds. Kiernan glanced at their faces as they passed. Taking another sip of his tea, he could feel the perspiration soaking into his shirt. It also glistened on his thick forearms, matting the hairs there.

He walked away from the Casey Jones stand and moved slowly through the throng of people, looking at each person he passed, but more particularly at each young girl. His glances were furtive; he kept his eyes low, ensuring they didn't see his surreptitious looks. Blonde girls, dark-haired girls, brown-haired girls, redheads. He looked at them all.

She'd been blonde the last time he'd seen her.

Now she could have dyed her hair any colour.

It had been long and curly, cascading over her shoulders.

What if she'd cut it?

There were any number of things she could have done to alter her appearance, but could she have changed so dramatically in five months as to prevent him recognising her?

Kiernan moved past W.H. Smith, glancing inside briefly, seeing more faces. He paused for a moment, draining the last dregs of his tea, then tossed the polystyrene cup into a rubbish bin. From the back pocket of his jeans he pulled out a thin red plastic wallet and flipped it open.

It bore a passport-type photo of a smiling girl with blonde curly hair. She was seventeen. The name on the card was Josephine Kiernan.

He looked around at the crowd again.

Talk about a needle in a haystack, he thought, making his way towards the ticket office. One girl mistook his appraisal for inspection, but smiled at him nonetheless. Kiernan smiled back and moved on.

No sign of her near the ticket office. He walked in, looked round, then emerged back onto the concourse again.

54

The public address system burst into life and station announcements reverberated through the huge, dome-like edifice of the station. They mingled with the rumble of arriving and departing trains and the constant babble of chatter.

Kiernan felt strangely detached from it all, a part of the horde but also able to concentrate on each likely face. He wondered what the mathematical probability was of finding his sister in a place like this; a place where over half a million people a day passed through.

He dismissed the thought as rapidly as it had come. Along that road lay despair.

No matter how long it took, he would find her. He had convinced himself of that.

Kiernan walked down towards the platforms, glancing at the boards beside each gate describing the trains' destinations. Leeds. Leicester. Scotland. So many places. So many people.

Over by the public phones two young girls stood talking. One of them leant against a wall. She was dressed in a short, tight mini skirt, teetering on high heels. A leather jacket was draped around her shoulders, despite the heat. She puffed on a cigarette and pushed her blonde hair away from her face as she chatted animatedly with her companion, a smaller girl with raven black hair wearing jeans and trainers.

Kiernan paused, looking more closely at the blonde.

He took a step forward, narrowing his eyes to see her features more clearly.

His heart began to thud against his ribs.

Could it be Jo?

After all this time, after all this searching? The days and nights of depression following fruitless searches.

Dare he even hope it was her?

He moved closer.

The public address system roared out another

message. The words drummed in Kiernan's ears as he approached. If he could just hear her speak. If he heard her Irish accent he'd know for sure.

She *had* changed. Her face looked pale, her eyes red-rimmed.

He was within feet of them now and they were aware of him; they were turning to face him.

And as he drew closer he knew.

It was not Jo.

Kiernan stood motionless for a moment, staring at the blonde, his heart slowing its frantic pace. He felt that all too familiar crushing feeling of defeat descend.

'What the fuck are you staring at?' the blonde snapped.

He merely shook his head and walked past her.

Jesus, how much fucking longer?

He headed towards the subway, wiping sweat from his forehead with two fingers.

She was ahead of him.

Twenty or thirty feet away.

Jo and two other girls were hurrying down the steps to the subway.

He shouted her name once but she didn't stop.

Kiernan set off after her.

Seventeen

He crashed into a couple struggling with their cases, almost knocking the man over in his haste.

As Kiernan reached the top of the steps leading down

to the subway he heard the man's angry shouts behind him but he ignored them, intent only on catching up with the blonde he was convinced was his sister.

He jumped the last three stairs, almost stumbled then hurried on, weaving in and out of other travellers.

Ahead of him, about fifteen feet, he could see her head through the crowd. She was turning left towards the ticket machines. He'd have to catch up with her before she got her ticket, before she descended into the subterranean depths. If he lost her now he'd never find her again.

His heart thudded hard against his ribs, more in anticipation than with the exertion of his movements. He was so close.

A man turned the corner and Kiernan collided with him.

The man shot out a hand to steady himself against the wall. Kiernan overbalanced and slipped.

'Sorry, mate,' said the man, extending a hand to help him. 'Never saw you coming.'

Kiernan leapt to his feet and pushed past into the crowded area that housed the ticket machines.

He looked round frantically.

He'd lost her.

'Jesus,' he hissed, his eyes darting back and forth over the sea of faces.

Which way?

For interminable seconds he stood motionless, panic beginning to grip him.

He spotted her off to the right, heading for the escalators. The other two girls were with her; all three were beginning to walk down the moving stairway.

Kiernan knew what to do.

He couldn't waste time getting a ticket; by the time he did she'd be gone. Perhaps this time forever.

He pushed past people trying to get through

the electronic barriers and vaulted the swinging gates.

A guard saw him and hurried over, shouting something, but Kiernan shook loose of his weak grip and ducked through a couple heading the same way.

The London Transport worker followed him for a few yards but gave up as he found his way blocked.

Kiernan glanced behind him once, saw that the guard had given up the chase and pressed on, heading down the escalator.

Once more he had lost sight of Jo.

Cursing, he began to walk slowly down the moving steps. Halfway down and he still hadn't found her. Another few seconds and he would have reached the bottom.

What then? Which direction would she go?

At the bottom his path was blocked by a woman with a suitcase which was taking up the whole of one step. Kiernan knew he had no choice but to wait until he reached the bottom; he couldn't climb over the case.

In front, he saw the trio of girls step off the escalator and head through an archway towards the Northern Line.

There was the loud rumble of a train approaching.

The escalator slid to the bottom of the shaft and he leapt over the suitcase and bolted through the arch.

The platform was crowded; again he had lost sight of her.

Sweat was pouring off him, soaking into his shirt, running down his face as he sucked in lungfuls of the stale air.

The rumbling grew louder and the train burst from the tunnel like a huge metallic worm breaking free of its burrow. The headlights blazed like white eyes and the sound filled the subterranean chamber. People moved towards the edge of the platform.

Kiernan walked quickly along looking for his sister, knowing that the doors would open soon and passengers would pour off. The crowd on the platform would swell.

He had to find her.

There was a loud hiss as the doors slid open.

Kiernan was breathing heavily, his breath coming in gasps.

She was up ahead, no more than fifteen feet away.

He saw her take a step into the train and he ran forward, shoving people aside in his haste.

'Jo,' he called, oblivious to the stares.

One of the girls with her saw the young Irishman lunge forward.

She stepped away, afraid of his frenzied attempts to reach her, of his flushed, sweat-drenched features and wild eyes.

He grabbed the arm of the blonde girl and spun her round.

'Jo,' he gasped.

The girl shook loose from his sweaty grip, frightened by his actions, puzzled when he let her go so easily. She stepped onto the train with her companions, wondering who the man was who had gripped her arm and stared into her face. Probably drunk, she reasoned.

She moved over to the other side of the train as the doors slid shut.

Kiernan saw the girl disappear behind the grey metal doors.

The girl he had been convinced was his sister.

He bowed his head and sighed defeatedly.

The train began to pull away, finally disappearing into the tunnel at the other end of the platform. A slight slipstream of warm, reeking air followed it, stirring paper lying on the tracks. A plastic cup rolled off the platform.

Kiernan wiped his face with both hands, his breath still coming in gasps.

He had been so sure it was Jo.

So sure.

He turned and headed back towards the exit.

Eighteen

Both men wore masks. Black leather hoods with zips where the mouths should have been and slits in place of eyes.

Apart from that they were naked.

The girl tied to the bed between them was also naked but for a black blindfold over her eyes.

She thrashed her head from side to side as the first of them, a big man with a tattoo on his right shoulder, drove his erection hard into her.

The other man, pale-skinned but powerfully built and with a shock of red hair protruding from beneath his hood, pushed his penis towards her mouth, shoving the bulbous tip against her lips. He forced it into her mouth and he began to thrust back and forth, her saliva coating his penis. The two men matched rhythms as the girl writhed beneath their combined attention.

The music playing in the background seemed to grow louder, the thunder of drums and the relentless roar of guitars building to correspond to the frenzied movements of the men.

Red Hair pushed harder into the girl's mouth, making her gag on his organ. He withdrew slightly, his glans slippery, tendrils of saliva hanging from it.

Tattoo stopped thrusting and moved up the girl's body, grasping her breasts roughly, kneading them together before sliding his penis between them.

Red Hair forced his organ back into her mouth.

The music thudded on.

The girl continued to writhe.

' . . .Say your prayers, little one . . . '

Any sounds the trio were making were drowned by the music. Their lips moved but no sounds could be heard. Just the relentless accompaniment.

' . . . Don't forget, my son, to include everyone . . . '

The girl's breasts were red and sore from being manhandled so roughly by Tattoo, who was heaving his hips back and forth with renewed vigour, cupping the smooth flesh of her breasts into a tunnel with which he enveloped his organ.

She was held firmly by the ropes around her wrists and ankles.

'Tuck you in, warm within, Keep you free from sin . . .'

The hemp had chafed flesh from her limbs. The skin around her left ankle in particular had been rubbed raw, as if someone had gone over it with a rasp.

Red Hair reached out and cupped his own testicles with one hand and the girl's face with the other, holding her steady as his strokes became more powerful.

Her nipples were bulging red; Tattoo's grip on her breasts was strong and unrelenting. He moved in time with his companion, whose face was contorted.

' . . . Till the Sandman he comes . . .'

Perspiration had formed on all three of them. It ran in rivulets down Tattoo's back and Red Hair's chest.

The girl retched as she gagged on the erection in her mouth.

' . . . Sleep with one eye open . . .'

Red Hair grabbed a handful of her hair and pulled her mouth even further onto his shaft, his face twisting into a grimace of pleasure.

' . . . *Gripping your pillow tight* . . . '

He nodded to Tattoo who was gasping loudly, pushing the tender flesh of the girl's breasts around his organ with powerful force.

'*Exit light, Enter night* . . . '

Red Hair closed his eyes tightly and released the first spurt of semen into the girl's mouth, pulling back slightly, holding the tip of his penis against her lips as more of the sticky white fluid jetted from his organ. It landed in thick gouts in her hair and on her cheek; some of it ran down her chin.

' . . . *Take My hand* . . . '

Tattoo thrust once more between her breasts, his body tensing as he too ejaculated.

The girl twisted beneath his weight, her mouth open to reveal the oily discharge of Red Hair on her tongue.

More semen spattered her face and neck and Tattoo kept on driving his penis back and forth until the last drops of fluid had coated the girl's face and body.

He moved off her and climbed off the mattress that had been laid on the floor.

Red Hair was smiling as he looked down at the girl. She was still moving within the restraints of the ropes, her face and upper body now flecked with white ejaculate.

Blood had begun to seep from the cut on her left ankle as the rope bit ever more deeply.

With the blindfold still firmly in place across her eyes, she could only hear as Tattoo moved towards her again.

Her screams were inaudible as the music swelled.

' . . . *We're off to Never-Never land* . . . '

Nineteen

'Do you need to see any more?' asked Edward Caton, leaning forward in his seat, one hand poised over the 'Pause' button of the video.

Charles Thornton smiled and shook his head.

'No,' he said. 'I can see you two have surpassed yourselves again.'

'Better than the last one?' asked Don Neville, smiling.

'I'm a business man, not a film critic,' Thornton told him. 'Just run me seventy-five copies off. That should be enough to start with.' He looked at the TV screen.

Caton had hit the 'Pause' button so that just the girl was in shot.

Thornton sipped at his drink. The heat inside the small second-storey room was quite intolerable. The fan on the wall was boosted by another on the desk but all they served to do was to circulate the dry air more quickly. Outside, the traffic in Beak Street filled the air with fumes.

Neville got to his feet and crossed to the window, pulling up the blinds, allowing sunshine to flood in. Motes of dust twisted in the searing rays.

'Are you sure seventy-five will be enough?' Neville asked. 'The last lot went well, didn't they?'

'Better than I thought they would,' Thornton admitted.

'Are you doubting the quality of our merchandise, Mr Thornton?' Caton said with exaggerated disdain. 'We're craftsmen, you know. Every one of these films is a labour of love.' He and Neville laughed.

'I couldn't give a toss about the *quality* of your merchandise,' Thornton told them. 'It sells, that's all that matters to me and my partner. Like I said, I'm not a connoisseur of this type of film.' He smiled again, a gold tooth glinting briefly. It matched the thick gold bracelet he wore, exposed because his sleeve was rolled up. A nasty scar ran from the wrist to the elbow, vividly white against his tan. It had taken more than thirty stitches to close the ragged edges of the wound when a carving knife had first laid the arm open. But that had been more than twenty years ago.

He'd received the wound protecting his boss. The same boss who, five years later, he'd personally shot. Thornton looked on those early years as a kind of apprenticeship. He'd left the army after six years in the Paras. Unable to find a job, his older brother had got him a place at a club in the West End as a bouncer. From there he joined a firm and worked his way up.

Now *he* had men to protect *him*.

It had been that way for the last fifteen years. Charles Thornton had ruled London's gangland almost without interference for all that time. There'd been the odd run-in every now and then with the Triads; the slit-eyed little bastards were always chiselling away at his businesses but they usually kept their distance. Thornton preferred co-operation. After all, he was a businessman, and there was business enough for himself and anyone else who wanted to make an honest or dishonest living in the Capital. Violence was always a last resort.

Unless someone was paying a good price for it, of course.

But Thornton's days of direct involvement had ended long ago. He looked upon himself as an entrepreneur, a supplier of commodities he knew the public needed. Clip joints, casinos, magazine and video shops, cinemas or restaurants. If there was money to be made from it, Thornton was interested. If the public suddenly began to express an interest in crapping in the street then Thornton would be able to offer them a nice line in commodes.

At the right price, naturally.

He lived well and it showed in his features. He was tanned and looked healthy, he rarely drank alcohol and he followed a rigorous exercise programme every day. One of the reasons, he was convinced, that he looked younger than his forty-three years.

Caton was three years his junior, Neville four, and they too had the physiques of men much younger.

They had been making videos like the one Thornton had watched for the past year and selling them at a huge profit to men like Thornton. They dealt with every other gang boss in the City and out of it; Thornton knew it and it didn't bother him. As he kept saying, there was enough money to go round.

'I'll send the cheque when the shipment's delivered, right?' Thornton said, sipping at his Perrier.

'It'll take us a couple of days to run off the copies,' Neville told him.

'No problem.'

'We'll let you know when the next one's ready,' Caton said.

Thornton nodded.

'As soon as you two have got your bloody strength back, I should think,' he said, grinning. 'How do you work the camera while you're filming?'

'We put it on automatic,' Neville said, smiling. 'If we want close-ups we just stop the action. We can edit everything together afterwards.'

'We always shoot two different endings,' Caton said.

'We have a different one for the copies that go to Germany and Italy.'

Thornton looked intrigued.

'What's the difference? Do you bring on a Doberman or an Alsatian?' He laughed.

'The krauts and the wops are into heavier stuff. It's not just sex with them,' Neville told him. 'At least not with the people *we* deal with.'

'We do something different with the girl or the bloke at the end,' Caton informed him.

'Like what?' Thornton wanted to know.

Neville smiled and pulled at his pony-tail.

'We kill them,' he said. 'Snuff movies are very big on the Continent.'

'Each to his own,' said Thornton matter-of-factly. 'I'll stick with the usual stuff. My punters are more discerning.' He looked at the screen where the screaming girl was still frozen in the freeze-frame.

'Run it on to the end, will you,' he asked, watching as the images sped by.

The last shot was of the girl's blindfold being ripped away.

Thornton nodded, thinking that she was pretty. A bit on the thin side for him, but still pretty. He studied the contours of her face. Pretty kid. This video should go well at eighty quid a throw. He smiled. A nice little bit of business.

From the frozen frame of the picture the semen-spattered face of Maria Jenkins screamed silently.

Twenty

The stench rising from the pile of rotting vegetables was almost intolerable. The rancid odour seemed to permeate the air throughout Berwick Street market.

Stall owners plied their trade surrounded by the invisible fog of putrescence, the smell aggravated by the unrelenting heat.

In a cloudless sky the sun hung mercilessly, covering the city in a fearsome blanket of radiance. As he walked slowly through the market, Vince Kiernan began to wonder how much hotter it was going to have to get before paving slabs began to crack like parched earth. He swigged from the can of coke in his hand, rolling the can across his forehead every so often, the droplets of condensation from the cool metal mingling with the beads of perspiration on his skin.

At one fruit and veg stall a customer was arguing animatedly with the owner about the quality of a watermelon, pushing an index finger through the green skin of the fruit. The vendor was shouting angrily.

A dog nosed through the piles of rubbish in search of food but seemed unable to find anything the heat had not putrefied. Flies and wasps swarmed over pieces of rotten fruit that had rolled into the gutters. Kiernan grunted as he trod in the remains of a rotten plum, slipping on the furred fruit. He wiped the worst of it from the sole of his trainer and walked on.

The market was busy, as it always was. Every day he

passed through and every day it was bustling. So frequent had been his passage through this area that several market traders now nodded cursory greetings to him as he passed.

It was part of his pattern.

From his earliest days in London Kiernan had set himself a search pattern he followed rigorously every day. He rarely deviated from it.

Upon arrival from Dublin he'd found a cheap hotel in Edith Road, Hammersmith. The Broadway wasn't exactly a five star residence but it served its purpose for the young Irishman. Of the twelve rooms it offered only two, apart from his own, were occupied; he could live there comfortably enough for about a hundred pounds a week. It had been his home for the last two weeks and, every day, he'd followed the same routine.

The quest to find his sister had been as relentless as the scorching sunshine.

He rose early every morning, ate breakfast, then walked to Hammersmith tube station where he caught a train which took him to King's Cross.

Kiernan would then spend thirty or forty minutes wandering around the station before venturing out into the neighbouring area. He would walk up the Caledonian road as far as Richmond Avenue. Here he would cut across until he reached Liverpool Road, then make his way back towards Pentonville Road and the station once more, where he would search again for twenty or thirty minutes.

A quick journey by tube to Euston and he patrolled that particular station's huge concourse for anything up to half an hour. He took another tube after that, this time to Tottenham Court Road; from there he'd walk through into Soho Square and then down Dean Street, across Flaxman Court and Wardour Street to Berwick Street. Brewer Street finally took him into Shaftesbury

Avenue, then down to Piccadilly Circus, up Coventry Street and through Leicester Square and down Charing Cross Road to Trafalgar Square.

After that he'd walk up the Strand as far as Burleigh Street and from there up into Covent Garden. Then he would retrace his steps, ending up back at The Broadway around eleven most nights.

There was a kind of monotonous routine to it all that Kiernan found unavoidable but also deeply depressing. He knew he was clutching at straws in his attempts to find one seventeen-year-old girl in a sprawling metropolis like London. But it was all he could think to do, and he had sworn not to give up until he found her, although he realized his task was all but impossible. Armed with just her bus pass and blind hope, he made his journey every day like a strange kind of pilgrimage.

He would stop and ask people if they recognised the photograph's smiling girl with the curly blonde hair, but none so far had been able to recall the face. They'd been unable or unwilling; Kiernan wasn't always sure which.

Every now and then he'd be seized by the icy conviction that he would *never* find her, but it was a thought he had to force to the back of his mind. His emotions were curiously muted. He had to believe that he could find her, yet his sense of logic told him that he could not. The size of his task, the impossibility of it simultaneously terrified him *and* drove him on.

He caught a glimpse of his own reflection in a shop window as he walked past but he looked away. He was beginning to look round-shouldered. *Weighed down by the burden of the search? Ha fucking ha.*

Perhaps he was a different man to the twenty-eight-year-old who'd left Dublin just over a fortnight ago. There was a light covering of whiskers on his cheeks and chin. Dark rings had begun to form beneath his piercing blue eyes. He'd lost a little weight, too.

He wondered how much weight Jo had lost.

He reached Piccadilly Circus and looked across at the statue of Eros perched above the heaving throng of people.

What have you seen? Have you seen my sister?

Kiernan glanced at his watch; it was almost 1.15 p.m. He ducked into a nearby Wimpey and ordered himself a hamburger and a milkshake. The young Irishman found a seat in the window opposite two young girls not much older than his sister. They were both dressed in shop uniforms of some kind, chatting and poring over a magazine.

Kiernan watched them for a moment, his face set in hard lines.

Then he glanced out of the window at the dozens of people passing.

So many people.

'Where are you, Jo?' he said quietly.

One of the girls opposite looked at him and nudged her friend. The two of them got up and left, chuckling to themselves.

So many people.

Kiernan bit into the hamburger.

Twenty-one

There was a delicate chink as the wine bottle brushed the lip of the crystal glass and the waiter steadied his hand as he poured.

Charles Thornton tasted the 1983 Bollinger and nodded to the waiter, who poured full glasses for both men. He then left the bottle in the ice-bucket and disappeared to deal with his other duties.

Morton's in Berkeley Square was relatively quiet for lunchtime. Only nine or ten of the tables upstairs were occupied, including the one that overlooked the square where Thornton now sipped his champagne. The windows were open but the breeze that blew in was warm. Thornton prodded his starter and began to eat.

'Why the champagne, Charles?' his companion asked. 'Are we celebrating?'

'I like the best of everything,' said Thornton. 'Why not have the best champagne? At eighty quid a bottle it ought to be good.' He chuckled. 'Besides, I get bored with Perrier.'

Joseph Finlay nodded in agreement and sipped his own drink.

'How are the family?' Thornton asked.

'They're fine. And yours?'

'My mum hasn't been too well lately, so I packed her off to the Canaries for three weeks. Poor old sod.' He smiled benignly.

'What about that young lady you were seeing?' Finlay enquired, hiding his sly smile as he sipped his drink. 'What was her name? Amanda, wasn't it?'

'We weren't compatible,' said Thornton, raising an eyebrow. 'She wasn't too keen on some of my business interests, if you get my drift.' He shrugged. 'Plenty more fish in the sea, Joe.'

'So why did you want lunch today?' Finlay asked. 'What's so important?'

'Do I have to have a reason? I hadn't seen you for a while and I thought it would be nice to have a civilized get-together. Do I need a better reason?' He smiled.

'You never do anything without a reason, Charles.

71

I've been doing business with you for ten years now, I know you well enough to know that.'

Thornton shrugged.

'As a matter of fact there *is* something,' he confessed. 'I've got plans for expansion.'

'You always have. And you want me to help you get planning permission, is that it?' Finlay asked.

'No,' Thornton said, shaking his head. 'I don't need it. I'm not looking to build, I'm looking at conversion. I know the place I want and I know what I want to do with it. I want to open another restaurant.'

'You own five already,' Finlay said.

'Six,' Thornton corrected him. 'Yes, I do, and they're all doing good business. But this next one will top them all.'

'What had you got in mind?'

'A Japanese place,' Thornton told him. 'A club and a restaurant all in one. This Karaoke shit is really big, and so is Japanese food. Sushi, stuff like that. I must say I've never been too keen on the idea of eating raw bloody fish but there's no accounting for taste, is there?' He smiled. 'I figure the two together will go down a treat, especially right in the middle of the West End.'

'Where had you been thinking of?' Finlay wanted to know.

'You know it well, Joe. In fact, you own it.' He sipped his champagne. 'That place in Cavendish Square. Three-storey building on the west side of the square. That *is* yours, isn't it?'

Finlay ran his index finger around the rim of his glass.

'Yes, it's mine,' he said flatly.

Thornton smiled.

'Thought so,' he beamed. 'No problem then. Name your price.'

'It's not for sale, Charles.'

'What do you mean, it's not for sale?' he chuckled. 'I just said, name your price.'

'And I just said it's not for sale.'

The two men eyed each other for a moment, the smile fading from Thornton's lips.

'I *need* that building, Joe. It's ideally situated for what I want,' Thornton said.

'There are plenty of other places in the West End you could buy.'

'I *want* that one,' Thornton insisted. 'What's so important about it? If it's the money . . .'

'The money's got nothing to do with it. I bought that place six years ago for peanuts. I could sell it now for ten times what I paid for it. I don't want to sell it, it's as simple as that.'

'How much do you want for it? You're embarrassed to say because you think I'll be offended; that's the reason, isn't it?'

'I'm not selling, not to you or to anyone else. End of story.'

'What the fuck are *you* going to do with it?' Thornton snapped, raising his voice a little. Heads at a nearby table turned. He leant closer to Finlay and lowered his voice. 'You've been sitting on it for six years with no tenants, no rent. What use is it to you? I'll give you whatever price you want.'

'Find somewhere else, Charles,' Finlay said flatly.

Thornton exhaled deeply and sat back in his chair.

'Right,' he said, holding up both his hands as if in surrender. 'We're both businessmen. If you don't want to sell then you must have your reasons. But when you change your mind . . .'

Finlay cut him short.

'I *won't*,' he said defiantly.

'Famous last words,' Thornton said, his smile not quite as broad. The lights glinted off his gold tooth. 'We'll talk about it again in a few days. Perhaps, by then . . .'

73

Again Finlay interrupted him.

'We can talk about it every day for the next five years,' he said calmly. 'My answer will be the same. The building isn't for sale.'

Thornton regarded his companion coldly.

Beneath the table one fist was clenched tightly.

Twenty-two

'Fucking bastard.'

At the sound of fury from the back seat of the Mercedes Colin Moran glanced into the rear-view mirror at his boss.

Charles Thornton was gazing out of a side window at the other cars, his eyes seemingly fixed on something.

'Sorry, boss, I can't go anywhere until the lights change,' said Moran.

'What?' Thornton said, turning to look at the back of Moran's head.

His driver was a powerfully built man with a thick neck and a short hair cut which made his head seem too small for his considerable body.

'I said I can't move the car until the lights change to green . . .'

'I'm not on about the bloody lights,' Thornton hissed, exhaling deeply. 'It's that cunt Finlay. I was trying to do some business with him at lunchtime but he's not having it.'

Moran slipped the car into Drive and pulled away.

'Is this that place in Cavendish Square you're after?'

he wanted to know.

'Yeah. I mean to say, I told him to name his price and he still won't sell the fucking thing. What more have I got to do?'

'It's important you have the building, right?' Moran said, as if he was telling his boss something he didn't know. 'But Finlay owns it and he don't want to sell, right?'

'Your grasp of the situation is breathtaking, Colin,' Thornton chided. 'But unfortunately it is of no help to me since Finlay won't fucking sell.'

'Blow him away,' said Moran flatly.

'What the fuck am I? A gangster?' Thornton shouted, indignantly.

Moran glanced into the rear-view mirror, as if considering his answer.

'I'm a businessman,' Thornton reminded him. 'Just because someone won't do a business deal with you, you don't go blowing their fucking heads off, do you?' He scratched his chin. 'Well, not unless it's *absolutely* necessary.' He sighed. 'Besides, I need him.'

'For what?' Moran wanted to know.

'He's important. He's got lots of contacts high up, architects, councillors. He's in with all of them. If it hadn't been for him a lot of my business over the last few years wouldn't have been done. He's pushed through planning permission, stopped trouble with builders, that sort of thing.' He shook his head. 'I don't want him blown away just because he won't sell me a fucking building, do I?'

'Then why don't you look for another building?'

'Because I want *that* one. It's in a prime position.'

'But you could buy one anywhere.'

'I *know* that. Fuck me, what's the good of trying to explain the niceties of economics to you?'

'I still think you should blow him away.'

'And *I* think *you* should concentrate on your driving.'

Thornton sat back in his seat, gazing abstractedly out of the window again. Why the hell *was* Finlay so insistent on holding onto the building? The two of them had been working together for years; Thornton couldn't understand the other man's reticence. Maybe in time he'd change his mind, but Thornton doubted it. He ran a hand through his hair. It *would* be simpler to find another building, but the one in Cavendish Square was what he wanted. And what Charles Thornton wanted he usually got.

Still, he had time. Finlay might reconsider. Thornton frowned. No, Finlay *would* reconsider. He smiled to himself. He'd make the property developer see sense. Business was sometimes a matter of psychology, he told himself. Finlay would be persuaded. Probably just holding out for a better price.

'Name your price'.

He must have his reasons for not wanting to sell.

He'd give him a couple of weeks, then speak to him again. They were both civilized men, both able to talk and reason.

Besides, thought Thornton, if the bastard didn't sell it to him eventually, he'd have his fucking legs broken.

Simple economics.

Twenty-three

At this hour of the morning the smell was tolerable. Only when the sun rose high in the sky did the stench become unbearable.

As Phillip Welsh gripped the black bin bag and heaved it onto his shoulder, some of the rubbish spilled out onto the pavement in the process. One of his colleagues trailing behind with a bag in each huge fist kicked the refuse into the gutter.

It was just after 6.15 a.m. and London was coming to life, stirring in the coolness of early morning, preparing for the onslaught that would surely come as the day wore on. Even now, with a faint nip in the air, Phillip could feel beads of perspiration forming on his back. He hurled the bag into the back of the truck and stood aside as his companion did likewise with his load. The big man wiped his forehead with the back of one filthy glove and rummaged in the overalls he wore, producing a packet of Marlboro. He lit one for himself and offered one to Phillip, who declined.

One of their other companions, a short, red-haired man with a profusion of freckles, joined them, tossing his own bag of rubbish in with the others.

'They always say you can tell more about people from their rubbish than you can by looking round their houses,' he said, nodding at the bag he'd just hurled into the dustcart.

There were half a dozen used condoms spilling from

77

a rent in the bag.

'Do you reckon the whole bag's full of them?' said Phillip, smiling.

'If it is then someone had a good night last night,' the freckle-faced man said, accepting a cigarette.

'A bloody exhausting one, too,' his large companion offered.

The three men laughed.

'I tell you, this lot,' the freckle-faced man made an expansive gesture with his hand designed to encompass the immaculately-kept façades of houses in Belgrave Square. 'The rich. They're the worst of them all. The richer they are, the kinkier they are. I bet they've all been to fucking public school, all these geezers.'

Phillip looked on in amusement as the man continued his diatribe.

'Breeding grounds for snobbery and perversion, that's what public schools are,' he said authoritatively. 'The only two things you get from a public school education are a top job in management and an interest in perverse sexual practices.'

The other two chuckled.

'That's why fucking British management's so ineffective. As soon as they get in the boardroom, they're all slamming each other's dicks in the door.'

The three men's laughter echoed around the square.

The driver peered out of the cab and tapped the face of his watch.

'Sorry to disturb you,' he called. 'But we have got other bins to empty.'

The freckle-faced man performed an exaggerated Nazi salute and the driver ducked back into the cab.

'Miserable bastard,' the freckle-faced man said. The three of them wandered off to collect more rubbish as the truck rolled along slowly.

Phillip moved towards three bags bundled together at the top of a flight of stairs leading down to a basement flat. He reached for the first and recoiled from the stench emanating from it. He coughed and took a step back; the smell was almost palpable. Flies buzzed around the bags and crawled inside. Phillip saw something white wriggling against the black plastic and realized it was a maggot. The bloody bags must have been out in the heat for a couple of days at least, he thought, lifting the first of them, blowing hard.

Further up the street his colleagues were collecting bags, waiting until the wagon drew nearer before hurling them inside. Phillip decided he needed help with these three.

Besides, the smell was appalling.

He reached for the third.

The top of the black bag tore as he pulled it, the plastic ripping, the bag toppling over.

Flies swarmed from inside, a cloud of parasites buzzing madly around Phillip and the stinking contents of the bag. There were more maggots, too, flooding out across the pavement.

In amongst it all was a shape Phillip did not instantly recognize.

It was bent double, the skin mottled blue and grey where it wasn't covered in blood.

He smelled an odour so rank, so fetid that it was all he could do not to vomit.

Then he saw the head as it sagged forward, cracking hard against the pavement. One sightless eye gazed up at him. The other had gone; the socket was now filled with hundreds of writhing maggots.

The body of Maria Jenkins lay at his feet.

Twenty-four

Dear Vince,

How the hell are you, big brother? I bet you thought you wouldn't be hearing from me again, didn't you? Well, here I am. I'm writing this letter at about twelve in the morning. I've just got up. I get up late most days because there isn't much to do until the night-time then me and some of the other girls go out together. There are girls from all over the place living around here. I met a girl from Swords last week, but I can't remember what her name was. She was very nice. I don't know where she went. We all hang around together as much as we can. None of us like what we do and we hate the men we go with but it's the only way to earn money. There are no jobs. It's better than being at home, though. I will never come back now and I don't suppose dad would want me back. If he knew what I was doing and some of the things I've done here in London he'd go mad. Ha Ha.

I can't give you an address to write back to because I move around quite a lot. I've been living in one place in Islington for about a week now, but we've got to move on again. Me and a friend of mine called Stevie are thinking of finding a squat.

I'll write again soon.

Love, Jo.

Vince Kiernan folded the letter and put it on the bed with the others. There were half a dozen, all written in the last year. The last one he'd received had been dated almost three months earlier. He'd heard nothing from his sister since that time. The postmarks on the letters showed that they'd been posted in many different parts of London: Paddington, Kensington, Islington.

A needle in a haystack.

All the letters had arrived not at his home in Dublin but at the health club which he and a partner ran on the outskirts of the city. His partner had agreed to take care of the business while Kiernan was in London. He phoned twice a week to make sure there weren't any problems, but he trusted his partner to keep things ticking over. Kiernan had more important things on his mind.

He hadn't bothered telling his parents or anyone else in the family that he was travelling to London in search of Jo. His parents wouldn't have cared and the rest of the family had always considered Jo something of a tearaway. Ever since she'd been arrested when she was fifteen for being in possession of a joint. Kiernan wished it was something so trivial now.

. . . We hate the men we go with . . .

He gritted his teeth as he re-read the letter. He felt a bead of perspiration trickle down his face but he didn't wipe it away. It hung from his chin for a second before dropping onto the mattress where it splashed one of the letters, smearing the ink like a tear. He dabbed at the wet spot with part of the sheet then got to his feet and crossed to the small basin. He spun the cold tap, bending low over the basin, wetting his face.

The water felt good against his hot skin. He didn't bother drying himself, merely allowed the water to drip down his face and chest.

In just a pair of jeans he sat cross-legged on the bed,

looking first at the letters then around him at the small room.

The walls were yellowed, the paint cracked around the coving. There was a green stain under the sink and the carpet and floorboards were rotten from constant drips. The bulky radiator that took up one wall was in need of a coat of paint. Its unwieldy frame was rusted in places, dented. It looked as though it would take just one firm tug to heave it clear of the wall.

Sunshine penetrated the windows with difficulty; the film of dirt on them was so thick as to make them appear opaque. Kiernan wondered how long it had been since they'd been washed. A pair of similarly grubby net curtains also hung there, yellowed slightly as if from constant exposure to cigarette smoke. He stubbed out his own cigarette in the ashtray, the smoke rising mournfully into the stale air.

On the battered wooden bedside table beside the phone there were a pile of magazines. Men Only, Club International, Mayfair and Escort. There were others, too, specifically contact magazines. It was the personal columns which interested Kiernan. In every one of the magazines there were hundreds, perhaps even thousands, of numbers prefixed by 0898. These, he knew, together with the 0836 numbers, were recorded messages. They promised such sanitized delights as *'Your hand on my crotch'*. Kiernan flipped open the copy of Club International, flicking quickly past the array of girls until he found the phone-lines.

The adverts screamed out:

WIVES CAUGHT TALKING DIRTY

LET ME STROKE IT

TRIPLE X TIGHT PULLED PANTIES

Kiernan glanced at the models who fronted each panel and flicked on a few more pages.

There were ads for videos.

EXTREMELY STRONG HARD IMPORTED VIDEO FILMS. All guaranteed not cut or softened-down copies.

Kiernan shook his head. He skipped past a *'genuine offer of 28 video films from Cindy Thrust'*, ignored the invitation to 'CREAM OVER MY STOCKINGS' or to listen to a 'THREE IN A BED RUBBER ROMP' and found the page he sought.

CLASSIFIED

The numbers were all prefixed by 071, 081 or other recognisable city codes. Kiernan had already rung dozens of them, tiring of hearing answerphones promising 'elegant massages'. A few were answered by real live women, something of an oddity in the world of recorded sex. He'd already crossed out fifteen or sixteen and had reached an entry which boasted:

KNIGHTSBRIDGE. Fun-filled massage guaranteed 7 days. Call Ruth.

He took his marker pen from the bedside table and underlined the number, then lifted the phone onto the bed and dialled.

After a couple of rings he heard a woman's voice.

'I saw your advert,' said Kiernan. 'Can you give me some information, please?'

He ran a hand through his hair as the woman reeled off what was obviously a well-rehearsed speech.

She asked if he'd been before.

'No,' he told her.

She told him that Ruth could be found near to Knightsbridge Tube, that she was blonde, petite and measured 38'' 26'' 38''. The price was twenty pounds for a basic massage but any other requirements could be discussed in private. He was welcome to call any day after one o'clock.

He put the phone down and crossed the number out, running his finger down the column.

There were numbers for Birmingham, Leeds, Manchester; there was even one for Milton Keynes.

All of those he ignored; it was only the London numbers he wanted. The others he crossed out.

Perspiration ran in salty rivulets down his face. He wiped it away, dialling with his free hand.

Emma's 'Lady' told him that his beautiful masseuse was very slim, five feet six and blonde. She reeled off some prices.

Kiernan hung up before she finished speaking. He scanned the numbers again.

Was the hope of finding his sister via one of these classified ads any more ridiculous than trying to hunt her down in Soho or King's Cross?

He didn't care. It was worth trying.

The next number he reached offered another stunning blonde. *Surprise, surprise.* She charged sixty-five pounds for half an hour, one hundred and fifty if she had to travel to his hotel. But he did get a choice of uniforms or fantasies.

Kiernan tried three more numbers before dropping the phone back onto the cradle. He sat in the sweltering heat of the bedroom for long moments, looking first at the collection of magazines and then at Jo's letters.

He reached for the next magazine, flipped it open at the classifieds and began dialling again.

Twenty-five

The glare of the late afternoon sunlight was dazzling. After the darkness of the cinema it seemed even more intense. Nick Ryan slipped a pair of sunglasses from his pocket and put them on.

As the remainder of the crowd poured out of the building Ryan looked around for his companion. He saw her a few feet away. Dressed in jeans and a T-shirt, her hair freshly washed and gleaming, she looked older than her thirteen years. He smiled, thinking how popular she was going to be with the boys in a few years' time. She glanced round, saw him and moved to him through the throng of people. They crossed the road together and then headed over the Bayswater Road towards Hyde Park. As they darted in front of oncoming traffic, she gripped his hand tightly. Ryan squeezed back, feeling the warmth in her touch. When they reached the other side his breath was sticking slightly in his lungs. He felt a twinge of pain but dismissed it.

'I would have thought you'd have wanted to have been out in the sun on a day like this,' he said, 'not stuck in a cinema.' He smiled at her.

'I wanted to see the film,' she said. 'Thanks for taking me, Dad.'

He reached out and put his arm around her shoulder as they walked, his hand brushing against her silky hair.

With his free hand he reached into his pocket and took out a packet of cigarettes, slipping one between his lips and lighting up.

'Do you have to smoke, Dad?' said Kelly, her tone a mixture of weariness and reproach.

He looked at her, raised his eyebrows, took the cigarette from his mouth and dropped it on the pavement, grinding it out beneath his foot.

She smiled.

'Happy now?' he asked.

Kelly nodded.

Christ, she looked like Kim, he thought. Some of her gestures and expressions made her look like a clone of his ex-wife. He realized how much he missed her.

They entered Hyde Park and set off across the expanse of green towards the Serpentine. All around them the grass was littered with people sunbathing, playing games, even picnicking. To Ryan it seemed as if there were children everywhere, from small babies to teenagers, shouting, laughing or crying. The warm breeze carried the sounds across the vast arena. Every now and then he heard a dog bark.

There was an ice-cream van parked close by and Kelly tugged his arm and began running towards it.

'Come on, Dad,' she called, looking back at Ryan. He set off after her, trying to ignore the pain growing in his chest. He gritted his teeth, angered that he was suffering now. He sucked in several deep breaths and it diminished slightly.

He caught up with Kelly in the queue for ice-creams.

They waited patiently until it was their turn, then Kelly ordered two 99's with nuts and juice, thrust one into Ryan's hand and wandered away while he paid.

The sun began to melt the ice-cream immediately and the private detective found it was dripping onto his hand. He licked it away and joined his daughter.

'If it stays this warm,' Kelly began, 'Mum says we won't *need* to go away on holiday. We could just stay at home.'

'Where are you going?' Ryan enquired.

'Joe wants to take us to Barbados for two weeks.'

'You don't sound very enthusiastic, Kelly,' Ryan told her as they walked.

She shrugged.

Ryan rubbed her shoulders with one hand.

'You'll enjoy it,' he said none too convincingly.

'I told Mum I didn't want to go.'

'What did she say?'

'She told me not to be silly. She's always telling me not to be silly. I can't help it if I don't like him much.'

Ryan looked surprised.

'Why not? What's wrong with him? He doesn't treat you badly, does he?' His voice took on a slight edge.

'No, he's very nice to me. He's always giving me money or buying me things. I suppose I'm being ungrateful, but no matter what he does for me . . . ' She allowed the sentence to trail off.

'What?' Ryan prompted.

'Well, he's not my dad, is he? *You* are. I didn't ask Mum to marry him. I didn't ask her to leave you. No one says I have to like what's happening.' She turned and looked up at him. 'Why did you and Mum stop loving each other?' There was a hint of bitterness in her voice; Ryan found he could only hold her reproachful gaze for a second or two.

'We never stopped loving each other, Kelly. It wasn't that,' he said, tossing the half-eaten ice-cream into a nearby dustbin.

'It was your job, wasn't it?'

'Did your Mum tell you that?'

'I can still remember you and her arguing, Dad. That was why we had to leave, wasn't it? Because of your job.'

'You didn't have to leave. I didn't *want* you to leave. You *or* your mum. That was never what I wanted.' He wandered across to one of the numerous benches in the park and sat down. Kelly joined him.

'Then why did it happen?' his daughter wanted to know.

'It *was* my work,' he snapped, immediately feeling angry with himself. 'What I was doing, the things I was getting involved with, some of them were bad. Your mum was worried about me; it got her down. She couldn't stand it. It was best for both of you that you left.'

'How could it be if you still loved each other?' Kelly asked, with the kind of devastating logic that only a youngster can deliver.

'But your mum loves Joe now. She's happy and she and I still get on. We're still friends. We always will be.'

'And you still love her?'

Ryan exhaled.

'Yes,' he said flatly. 'I love both of you.' He snaked out an arm and pulled her close, kissing the top of her head. 'Especially you.'

'Then why don't you come and see me more often?' she asked quietly.

Again that awful, inescapable logic.

'Whenever I'm not busy I try.'

'You're always busy, Dad,' she said coldly. 'You always will be.'

She got to her feet and walked on.

Ryan gritted his teeth. He hauled himself off the bench and headed off after her.

The truth hurts, doesn't it?

'Fuck it,' he rasped under his breath.

Twenty-six

The sunshine reflected harshly from the surface of the water. Kelly shielded her eyes as she tossed stones into the Serpentine, watching them splash and send rings sliding across the surface.

Ryan stood behind her, puffing on a cigarette and alternately glancing at his daughter and at a particularly gorgeous young woman who, clad in a skimpy yellow bikini, was stretched out on the grass close to the water enjoying the sunshine. The private detective could feel perspiration soaking into his shirt. Finally he joined Kelly by the waterside, squatting down beside her as she continued to throw the small pebbles into the waterway. He, too, watched the ripples spreading out.

'Kelly,' he began, 'do you blame me for what happened with your mum?'

Avoiding his eyes, she searched around for more pebbles and began tossing them in. They entered with a subdued plop.

'I don't know,' she said. 'You had to do your work, I suppose. I just wish . . . ' She threw another pebble.

'What?' he said hurriedly.

'I sometimes wish we could be together again,' she told him, turning to face him.

Ryan found himself looking into her deep blue eyes. He felt as if he was floating.

'I'll come and see you more often,' he said quietly. 'I promise. We'll go out together more. When I'm not so busy.' Immediately he wished he'd not uttered the last sentence.

She looked away from him and back to the water.

'Mum said you were ill,' Kelly said after a long silence.

Ryan looked puzzled.

'You look tired,' she added.

'I haven't been sleeping too well lately, that's all,' he explained. 'That and too much work, but other than that I'm fine.' The twinge of pain in his chest did much to contradict his argument. He smiled thinly, hoping she hadn't noticed his eyes narrow as he felt the discomfort intensifying. 'Your mum worries too much.'

He picked up a stone himself and threw it into the water.

'Are you going to come and see my new office when I've moved?' he asked.

Kelly nodded.

'You didn't buy it from Joe, did you?' Kelly asked. 'He sells buildings.'

Ryan laughed.

'No, I didn't buy it from Joe,' he chuckled.

'Some of the girls at school know who he is. Some of their dads work for him.'

'What's school like?' he wanted to know. 'Have you settled in now?'

She blew out her cheeks.

'I don't like being away from home when it's term time, but most of the girls are nice. I didn't like sleeping in a dorm at the beginning, but you get used to it. The other girls' parents are rich, too, so I don't feel left out.' She looked at Ryan. 'Joe's very rich, isn't he, Dad?'

Ryan nodded.

'There's a lot of money in property, Kelly.'

'I suppose Mum must love him,' she said philosophically. 'But they have rows, too.'

'Every couple has rows.'

Ryan felt a flicker of delight at the thought that Kim and Finlay's marriage wasn't all sweetness and light but he administered himself a swift mental rebuke for feeling pleasure at the thought.

'You still haven't told me why you don't like him,' he continued. 'You said he was nice to you. He's not nasty to Mum, is he?'

Because if he is I'll break the fucker's neck.

'No. I don't know what it is. Perhaps it's because he wanted to send me to boarding school in the first place. I thought he didn't like me when he did that. I thought he wanted me out of the way.'

'I'm sure that's not it, Kelly. He just wants you to have the best education you can get. Boarding school might be better for that.'

'It's all right for him, he doesn't have to go.'

'How does your mum feel about you going?'

'She says she misses me, but she agrees with Joe.'

She would.

Ryan looked at his daughter for a moment, then reached out with one hand and touched her cheek. He stroked it gently.

'Come on, princess,' he said finally. 'Let's go and get something to eat.'

She nodded and smiled.

'Pizza or hamburger?' he asked.

'Both,' she chuckled, laughing loudly as he swept her up into his arms and held her high above his head before setting her down on the grass again. They set off together across the park.

As they walked, Ryan glanced at his watch. 4.36 p.m.

He made a mental note to call in at his office before he took Kelly back, just to check on any late mail or see if there were any messages.

He was expecting one.

Twenty-seven

It was after eight by the time Ryan arrived at Finlay's house in Hampstead.

He sat behind the wheel looking at the large house, then glanced across at Kelly who'd fallen asleep in the passenger seat. A combination of the heat and the long drive had made her nod off.

Ryan watched her for what seemed like an eternity. Her chest rose and fell slowly as she breathed, her eyelids flickering occasionally to signal that she was dreaming. About what, he wondered? About her day with him? About her new stepfather?

About the break-up of her parents' marriage?

That was all in the past, now. Only the memories remained, etched a little more deeply on a thirteen-year-old's mind, he thought, than on his own, but then memories were little more than spiritual wounds and the young's healed more quickly.

Ryan reached over reluctantly and touched her shoulder to wake her.

Her eyes snapped open and she sat up, taking a moment to recover from the disorientation. Then she looked at him and smiled.

'You're home,' he said quietly.

Her smile faded slightly.

'Tell your mum I'm sorry I didn't get you back earlier,' Ryan instructed her.

'Why don't you come in and tell her yourself?' Kelly enquired.

He glanced towards the house again and saw the Jag parked outside. Finlay's Jag.

'You tell her,' he said, smiling.

She thanked him for the day out and he kissed her on the forehead then on the cheek, watching her as she clambered out of the car. She ran round to the driver's side and stuck her head through the window, kissing him again.

'I love you, Dad,' she said.

'I love you too,' he told her.

'When will you come again?'

Ryan swallowed hard.

'Soon,' he told her.

'You *will* come, won't you?' she asked anxiously.

'You try stopping me,' he said, smiling.

'When?'

'When I can.'

Her smile faded.

'When you're not working,' she said flatly. Then she turned and scurried up the path towards the front door.

Ryan, watching her go, saw her press the doorbell.

As the front door was opened he pulled away, not looking in his rear-view mirror.

He snapped on the radio, anxious to fill up the silence that seemed to have invaded the car.

A rock track was thundering out of the speakers:

' . . . *You never know what you've got, 'til it's gone . . .*' the singer intoned.

Ryan switched it off again.

Twenty-eight

She thought he'd been asleep, he'd been so quiet.

Kim glanced across at Joseph Finlay and the images from the television screen danced across the lenses of his glasses. As she looked more closely she saw that he was looking blankly at the screen, the book he'd been reading open on his chest.

He sat forward, putting the book on the coffee table beside him, removing his glasses and rubbing the bridge of his nose.

He reached for the glass of Glenfiddich and took a sip.

'Do you want a top-up?' he said, getting to his feet and walking across the room towards the drinks cabinet.

'No thanks, I'm fine,' she told him, lifting her own glass of bacardi and Coke.

Finlay re-filled his own glass and stood there for a moment.

'Ryan was late bringing Kelly back,' he said finally.

Kim turned to face him.

'Only an hour or so,' she said. 'I knew she was safe with him.'

'That's not the point.'

'He didn't do it deliberately, Joe.'

Finlay sipped at his drink.

'I've been thinking. It might be best for Kelly if she

94

didn't see so much of Ryan.' He crossed back to his seat and sat down.

Kim jabbed the mute button on the remote control, cutting off the noises coming from the TV.

'She only sees him half a dozen times a year *now*.'

'He's a disruptive influence on her, Kim.'

'For Christ's sake, Joe, he's her father. What kind of *disruption* can he cause?'

'I've said all this before, Kim, I don't want to keep repeating myself. You know my views on the subject.'

'And that's it, is it? End of story?' she snapped. 'I know that you don't want my daughter to see her father any more. Why?'

'She's *your* daughter now, is she?' said Finlay, acidly. 'Strange how every time we have this argument she's *your* daughter. At any other time she's *ours*.'

'You know what I mean.'

'I think you should remember who puts a roof over her head and clothes on her back. I think that makes her as much *my* daughter as yours.'

'Jesus Christ, Joe, this isn't a bloody competition. You can't buy her. Just because you support us doesn't mean you have any more claim to her than Nick.'

'And what does *he* contribute to her upbringing? A visit every few months if she's lucky. A phone call once in a blue moon. She needs more than that, Kim. You should know that.'

'I do know that. I also know that she likes to see him. She has a right to see him and he has a right to see *her*.'

'Perhaps we should ask Kelly what *she* thinks about this situation. She might be dissatisfied with it, too.'

'You're afraid of him, aren't you?' Kim said, challengingly.

'And *you* still love him, don't you?' he said flatly.

Kim didn't answer.

'Don't you?' he snapped.

95

'I loved him for twelve years,' she said. 'I can't just wipe it out, Joe. I've told you, I love *you*. Do you think I'd still be here if I didn't? Do you think I'd have married you in the first place if I hadn't? Use your common sense. If it can get through that barrier of self-pity and hatred you seem to live behind.'

He took a hefty swig of whisky and banged the glass down.

'I don't want her seeing so much of Ryan,' he said, angrily. 'That's all I've got to say about it.'

'I'm sorry you feel like that, Joe, but it isn't that easy,' Kim informed him. 'There's nothing you can do to stop him seeing her.'

'We'll see,' said Finlay angrily.

The phone rang.

Both of them looked at it. At last Finlay crossed to it and snatched it up.

'Hello,' he barked.

Kim saw his expression change from one of anger to one of surprise.

'What do you want?' he said to the caller. 'Now?' He looked at his watch. 'It's almost ten-thirty. Can't it wait?'

It couldn't.

'I'll be there in an hour,' he said and put the phone down. He turned to look at Kim. 'I've got to go out.'

'What for?'

'Business. It's important,' he told her.

'You sound like Nick,' she said sarcastically.

Finlay glared at her and headed for the door to the hall.

'What time will you be back?' she wanted to know.

'One, perhaps later. Don't sit up.'

'I wasn't going to,' she told him.

Finlay hesitated and then strode out into the hall, closing the sitting-room door behind him. He took a light jacket from the stand in the hallway, picked his car keys up from the table by the front door and walked out.

Kelly saw him go.

Crouched on the landing, she saw him snatch up the car keys and leave.

Just as she had heard most of the argument. The words had drifted up to her as she lay in bed. When she heard voices raised in anger she had climbed out of bed and tip-toed onto the landing, straining her ears to hear what was being said. From her position she had heard nearly everything.

Now, as Finlay slammed the front door behind him, she scuttled back to her room.

Tears were running down her cheeks.

She swung herself into bed and lay there motionless, staring through the darkness at the ceiling.

Outside she heard the Jag pull away.

Twenty-nine

The thief at the Royalton had been caught. At least, Ryan's operative had gathered enough evidence against him to ensure a conviction.

The private detective sat at his desk with only the small table lamp turned on. He tapped his pen against his pad, the lamp casting thick shadows round him. The message had been on his answerphone when he'd returned to the office earlier. He'd thought about ringing the manager of the hotel but had decided to leave it until the following morning. Now he sat in the curious half-light gazing out of the window towards the dark sky and the dozens of bright lights illuminating it from buildings along Charing Cross Road and Oxford Street.

He'd ring the operative in the morning too and congratulate him on his work.

Work.

He glanced at his watch. 11.26 p.m.

He ought to be thinking about heading home by now. He'd driven straight to the office after dropping Kelly off, checked his messages and then wandered around the corner to Scalini's for a coffee and a sandwich. He'd returned to the office about nine and completed some paperwork, including some from Southwark Council concerning a series of eviction orders they'd asked him to serve.

He felt a twinge of pain in his chest and winced, gritting his teeth until it diminished.

It didn't.

'Shit,' he hissed and got to his feet, crossing to the window as if the movement would somehow lessen the pain.

It had the opposite effect. Suddenly he felt as if someone had filled his lungs with iron filings and were drawing a magnet back and forth across his torso. He coughed and put one hand to his chest.

Still the pain persisted.

He gritted his teeth and turned to the small drinks cabinet. He took a bottle of vodka from it, unscrewed the cap and drank straight from the neck, relieved and a little surprised when the pain diminished. He waited a moment and drank another few gulps. Perspiration had beaded on his forehead. He felt dizzy and shot out a hand to steady himself against the window-sill.

As the pain retreated slightly he sucked in a deep

breath, as deep as he could without starting the agony afresh. He stood there panting, drawing in shallow breaths then expelling deep ones to pump the pain away.

Ryan took another slug from the bottle and closed his eyes, practically falling into the seat by the window. He sat there, mouth open, a mixture of vodka and sputum bubbling on his lips as he exhaled. He felt light-headed. He told himself it was the effects of the drink on an almost empty stomach.

Who are you kidding?

He wiped his mouth with the back of his hand, wincing as he saw a dark stain there.

Blood.

It appeared like black ink in the murkily lit office but he could smell its coppery odour.

Ryan coughed again and tasted it. He pulled a handkerchief from his pocket and propelled the lump of sputum into the material, opening it a second later to see a bloodied ball of phlegm nestling in the cotton. The pain in his chest grew more intense. He rose to his feet, putting down the vodka bottle, stumbling through into the small toilet.

He barely made it.

A wave of nausea hit him and he dropped to his knees, head over the bowl, his stomach contracting, forcing its contents up his throat and into his mouth. An evil-smelling flux of half-digested food and blood poured out, spattering noisily into the lavatory. The smell made him retch again, but when the contractions finally died away, Ryan sat back on his haunches, his eyes closed, streamers of dark sputum hanging from his lips like rancid ribbons. His head was still spinning, the pain in his chest ever-present.

He crouched on the floor for what seemed like an eternity before he got to his feet. He flushed the crimson vomit away, slapping on the light.

In the harsh brilliance of the hundred-watt bulb he glared at himself in the mirror.

His skin was the colour of sour milk, and shiny, as if someone had stretched it over the bones of his face. Beneath his eyes there were dark rings; he could see a streamer of blood running from one corner of his mouth. He wiped it away with the flannel on the side of the sink, spun the cold tap and splashed his face with cooling water.

From the small cabinet on the wall he took a bottle of aspirin and swallowed two. The bitter taste on his tongue almost made him retch again but he washed them down with two handfuls of water and stood supporting himself on the sink, staring into his own bloodshot eyes.

The pain in his chest persisted.

His reflection stared forlornly back at him. He coughed and spat blood into the sink.

'You're fucked,' he murmured to his reflection.

The blood disappeared down the plughole.

'Well and truly fucked.'

He waited a few moments then swallowed another couple of aspirins, shutting the cabinet door and leaving the lavatory.

He wandered back into the office, the pain lessening a little.

Another half an hour, he told himself. Just sit down. Take it easy.

He slumped in the chair beside the window, his eyes half-closed.

Half an hour.

Then he'd go home.

And call the doctor?

No way.

He was ill, he knew that. He didn't know what the

hell was wrong with him, but he didn't need a fucking doctor to tell him that all was not well.

He didn't *want* to know.

You're fucked. Well and truly fucked.

It was over an hour before he felt able to drive home.

Well and truly fucked.

Thirty

Finlay found a parking space without difficulty and brought the Jag to a halt. Switching off the engine, he sat in the warm stillness looking up at the building in Cavendish Square.

He sat behind the wheel for some minutes just looking up at the place. The windows were blank, like dozens of blind eyes. Some had shutters, others had been boarded up. It looked derelict. Parts of the facade were crumbling, but other than that, the building was suitably impressive when viewed against its neighbours. Two large stone columns supported a canopy over the small flight of steps that led up to the large front door.

Finlay fumbled in his pocket and found a bunch of keys, selecting the one he knew fitted the massive front door. He swung himself out of the car, locked it and set off towards the main door, slowing his pace slightly as he reached the steps.

He glanced around to see if there was anyone passing then hurried up the steps and pushed the key into the lock, shoving against the door which swung back on rusted hinges.

He stepped inside and shut the door, waving a hand in front of him to dispel the clouds of dust he seemed to have disturbed.

To his right and left were closed doors; he was standing in what had once been a massive hallway. Lengths of bare wire hung from holes in the ceiling where lights had once been. Cables dangled like the innards of some monolithic creature.

Spiders had made webs in most corners of the hallway. As Finlay watched, a particularly large one crept along the wall, its bloated body resembling an eight-legged furry boil.

Ahead of him was a staircase, still covered by a threadbare carpet.

The whole place reeked of neglect. Damp, despite the scorching temperatures, was beginning to creep up the walls. Black spores had forced their way up beneath the wallpaper, making it blister and peel.

As Finlay began to climb the stairs, a couple of them groaned protestingly under his weight. He touched the banister and felt the thick dust there, brushing his hands together to remove it. It was difficult to see inside the darkened building but two or three of the windows on the first floor were unboarded and the half-light of night filtered through.

He reached the first landing and looked around. More closed doors faced him, and there were places on the walls where, at one time, pictures had hung. The patches were slightly lighter than the dark paper, much of which was peeling off. It hung like leprous flesh, dried and brittle. As he passed, Finlay pulled a piece from the wall, feeling it crumble between his fingers.

Unperturbed, he continued his climb until he reached the next landing.

To his left a door was ajar.

Finlay moved towards it, pushing it open gently.

The beam of light struck him in the face, making him recoil as if he'd been hit by a tangible object.

He put up a hand to shield his eyes from the glare, gradually regaining his wits as the light was lowered slightly.

'Good of you to come,' said a voice from the shadows. Finlay heard a chuckle.

'You took your time though,' said Don Neville.

Thirty-one

'What the hell do you think you're doing?' snapped Finlay. 'Calling me at this time of night?'

'We needed to talk to you,' Neville told him, flicking the torch onto his face again before sitting down in an armchair.

Over by the boarded-up window Edward Caton was tapping gently on the metal cover of a halogen lamp.

The room looked as if it belonged in another house.

The floor was bare of carpet but also clean of dust. The walls, painted white, looked grey in the darkness. In the centre of the room was a bed and two armchairs. Dotted around them were arc lights and two halogen lamps. A bare bulb hung from a cord in the ceiling. A video camera had been set up on a tripod close to the bed. Neville turned it towards Finlay.

'And what's so bloody important that it couldn't wait until tomorrow?' Finlay wanted to know, keeping his distance from the two men.

'We hear a whisper that Charles Thornton wants this

'building,' Caton said. 'Is that true?'

'Where did you hear that?'

'We have ears everywhere,' chuckled Neville, pushing the camera on its tripod, allowing it to turn slowly.

'So,' Caton continued. '*Is* it true?'

'You do business with him, why don't you ask him?'

'We're asking *you*,' Neville hissed, angrily. 'Does he want the fucking building or not?'

'Yes,' Finlay told them. 'But don't worry about it. *I'll* take care of Thornton.'

'He's a powerful man, Joey boy,' Neville said, smiling. 'I hope you can.'

'What's the sp on Thornton?' Caton wanted to know. 'Why is this place so fucking important to him?'

Finlay explained about the club and restaurant.

'He knows I own the building,' he added. 'He thought it would be an easy purchase. He asked me to name my price.' He looked at the two men in the darkness. 'Perhaps I should have done.'

Neville shook his head slowly, mockingly.

'No, no, no,' he chided. 'You know that wouldn't have been good business. You're better off sticking with *us*.' He chuckled again, pulling his pony-tail away from the back of his neck. 'You know it makes sense.'

Caton lifted an attaché case into view and laid it on the bed, flipping it open.

Finlay took a step closer.

The case was stuffed with money, great thick wads of fifty-pound notes piled on top of each other, bound by elastic bands.

'We brought you a present,' Caton told him. 'Your cut.'

He pushed the case towards Finlay, who glanced at both men in the gloom and then shut the case.

'You don't want to count it?' Neville said.

'He trusts us,' Caton told him, and both men laughed.

Finlay felt a single droplet of perspiration trickle down the side of his face.

'Twenty per cent?' he said.

Neville nodded.

'As agreed,' he added.

'You'd better not get careless.'

'What the fuck are you talking about?' Caton said.

'Don't tell us how to run our business, Finlay,' Neville rasped. 'We know what we're doing. Besides, if we stop, then your little bonus dries up.' He nodded towards the attaché case. 'I don't hear you complaining about *that*.'

'We're supplying a commodity,' Caton added. 'And there's a big fucking market for it and that market's getting bigger all the time.'

'But if you want out, just say,' Neville told him. 'We can find somewhere else to make the films.'

'You should be grateful I let you use this place for nothing,' Finlay snapped. 'Anyone else would charge . . .'

'The *rent* is in the fucking case,' Neville interrupted angrily, pointing to the attaché case. 'You let us make the films here because we give you a good cut of the profits. Let's not make any mistakes about that. And maybe you should remember, Finlay, if we're caught, *you're* an accessory. You know what goes on here. If we go down we're taking *you* with us.'

Finlay picked up the attaché case and took a couple of steps back.

'Leaving so soon?' Neville said, smiling. 'I thought you might be interested to hear how good business is, especially the sales to our European customers. Snuff movies are very big on the continent.'

'Snuff movies?' Finlay said, surprised. 'What are you talking about?'

'Don't play dumb, Finlay. You know what we mean,' Caton insisted.

'You're killing people.' There was genuine shock in his voice. 'Is that what you're saying?'

'They're big business, these films, like I said,' Neville continued. 'And as long as there's a market there we'll carry on.'

Finlay swallowed hard, feeling perspiration on his face.

'I want no part of this,' he said, quietly, his voice wavering. 'It's filth. Murder, that's something else. Don't involve me in it.'

'Too late,' Neville told him. 'You *are* involved.' He nodded at the attaché case again.

'I want it to stop. I want you out of this building,' Finlay said. 'This has got to stop.'

Caton hawked loudly and spat on the floor, a glob of mucus landing only inches from Finlay's foot.

'You want us out, you move us,' Neville said challengingly.

Finlay hesitated a moment longer, then spun round and headed towards the door.

'Nice talking to you, Joe,' Neville said, smiling. 'We'll be in touch.'

They both heard Finlay's footsteps receding down the stairs.

'He's too jumpy,' Caton said. 'If he loses his bottle we're all fucked. I think he's going to drop us in it.'

'Don't worry about it. He's in too deep and he knows it. He won't give us any trouble.' He pulled the pony-tail away from the back of his neck, wiping sweat off with the back of his hand. 'We'll make *sure* he doesn't give us any trouble. We'll have to take ourselves a little insurance.'

Thirty-two

The door of the Brewer Street Buttery was open but that one concession to the continuous scorching heat did little to alleviate the discomfort of the half dozen patrons inside.

In one corner a man in a shirt and tie sat fanning himself with a copy of the *Financial Times*, perspiration rolling off his face. At the table next to him three Japanese tourists babbled excitedly to each other as they passed round thick wads of photographs.

Vince Kiernan sat at the table closest to the door, alternately glancing outside and at his newspaper. He took sips of his coffee and looked again at the front page of the paper which was folded over at the headline:

VICTIM NUMBER SIX DISCOVERED IN BELGRAVIA Beneath it was a photo of the pavement outside the house in Belgrave Square where the body of Maria Jenkins had been found. There were two detectives in the picture, both examining what was, apparently, evidence.

Kiernan had read the story three times, checking to see if the victim's name had been mentioned. It hadn't. All the paper would divulge was that the victim was female, about sixteen years old and that she'd been mutilated in the same way as the previous five victims. Like them she had been living rough for some time prior to her death, the paper said.

Like Jo?

Kiernan took a cigarette from his packet and lit one, blowing out a long stream of smoke into the warm air. He wondered how the latest girl had come to be living rough, what had driven her to seek an existence on the streets of London.

What drove any youngster to forsake home for that kind of life?

Every one of them probably had a different reason, Kiernan thought.

Like Jo?

He reached into the back pocket of his jeans and pulled out her bus pass, looking at the photo. Jesus, she looked so happy then. Not a care in the world. He wondered how she looked now. *Still smiling? Still carefree?*

He pushed the pass back into his pocket and reached for his coffee cup with his free hand.

A sudden wave of anger swept over him. It was a feeling he had grown used to since she'd left Dublin, more so since he'd discovered she'd come here to London's netherworld. But his anger had so many causes. He felt anger towards his parents for not stopping her, for not being more attentive to her. They had said she was too wilful.

What an archaic fucking word that was.

They didn't know how to handle her.

She had said she didn't want to spend the rest of her life in Dublin. There were no prospects for her there. The only things to look forward to were a dead-end job, marriage and a family by the time she was twenty. That was not for Jo. She'd spoken to him many times about leaving Ireland, and each time, he'd tried to talk her out of it. Tried to persuade her to at least wait until she was a little older. But, he'd thought often, it wasn't *his* job to be telling her. He was her elder brother and he loved her dearly but her own mother and father should have offered more guidance than they did.

His mother and father.

They'd effectively washed their hands of her when she'd left. As far as Kiernan was concerned, they'd abandoned her to her fate.

Whatever the hell that might be.

He glanced at the paper again.

Was it just a matter of time before he saw Jo's name printed beneath such a headline?

The thought made him shudder. He reached for his coffee cup and drained the last few dregs, getting to his feet. He paid and walked out into the street, into the heat.

He left the newspaper on the table. Forgotten.

Like Maria Jenkins?

Kiernan pulled a pair of shades from his pocket, and slipped them on as protection against the bright sunlight. Then he set off, continuing his daily search.

He had the awful feeling time was running out.

Thirty-three

The car had stalled.

Ryan leant out of his window and peered ahead, past the other stationary vehicles in the road, towards the source of the hold-up. A choking cloud of exhaust fumes seemed to envelope him, the stinking air heated by the scorching sun. The private detective had the ventilators full on but they were merely sucking in more of the rancid warm air, turning the Sapphire into a mobile sweat-box.

He saw BSM signs on the stalled Metro and watched as the helpless driver struggled to escape the wrath of the motorists behind.

The Metro had blocked the junction of Holland Park Avenue and Royal Crescent and all the banging of hooters and angry shouts in the world weren't going to speed its departure.

Ryan drummed on the wheel with one hand, taking the butt of his cigarette from his mouth with the other and tossing it into the road.

He sucked in a deep breath, wincing at the pain.

Fuck. That hurt.

He suppressed a cough, knowing it would only increase the discomfort he'd felt all night. It had been building steadily since he rose at seven that morning. He'd not had much sleep the night before. Swallowing four paracetamols with some brandy had ensured at least three hours uninterrupted sleep, but the pain had woken him intermittently throughout the night. At last, sick of trying to doze off, he'd hauled himself out of bed at about four and drunk more brandy. He'd fallen asleep on the sofa and felt like shit when he'd woken up three hours later.

Ryan glanced at his reflection in the rear-view mirror. His hair looked uncombed, his face was pale and the rings beneath his eyes looked as if he'd been the canvas for some kid with black crayons. He felt like shit and he looked like it too.

He coughed, wincing at the pain as it intensified.

Up ahead, the learner was still struggling to move the car. It refused to budge. Someone hit their hooter. They were joined by another. Like some ridiculous fanfare, half a dozen horns were sounded. The learner glanced round sheepishly.

Ryan coughed harder, pulling a handkerchief from his pocket, spitting bloody phlegm into the material and balling it up. He wiped the corners of his mouth; the coppery taste was still there.

'Come on,' he murmured, reaching to the glove compartment and pulling out a tape. He shoved it into the cassette and turned up the volume; the music competed with the symphony of protest coming from the other cars. '. . . *Hey, little sister, scene's sure getting old* . . .' He tapped his fingers in time as the tape rolled on.

The learner was now sitting almost motionless as the instructor clambered out and began pushing the vehicle aside. Immediately a big enough gap opened up, the closest car swung round and others followed.

'. . . *Don't you think it's time we got to go* . . .'

Ryan pressed down on his accelerator and eased away, casting a cursory glance at the stricken Metro which now had its bonnet up, steam rising mournfully into the warm air.

Ryan felt perspiration sticking to his shirt and shuffled uncomfortably in his seat as he drove. Each movement brought fresh pain and he was beginning to feel light-headed. He told himself it was the result of losing so much sleep the previous night. He'd get to bed early tonight, catch up.

The stream of traffic slowed again as traffic lights blinked onto red and, once more, he was left sitting in the unrelenting heat.

A particularly savage stab of pain made him gasp. He put one hand to his chest, trying to breathe in but finding it difficult.

'Shit,' he hissed under his breath.

Maybe a trip to the doctor's wouldn't be a bad idea.

No.

He'd just suggest two weeks' rest, or bollocks like

111

that. Tell Ryan not to work so hard, to take it easy for a while.

Fuck it. He couldn't afford to do that. Especially not when there was so much work around. He wouldn't turn anything down if it paid well enough. There were always others who would take his place. No. He couldn't be away from work. Besides, cooped up in his house alone twenty-four hours a day he'd go nuts.

Forget the doctor.

He drove on, wiping sweat from his forehead, feeling the pain worsening in his chest.

He gritted his teeth, feeling faint.

Come on, get a fucking grip.

He turned the volume up on the cassette, as if to shock himself back to normality, as if the thunderous music would somehow drive away his dizziness and pain.

He was driving up towards Notting Hill Gate now, trying to concentrate on driving, on the thought of the day's work ahead.

On anything except this fucking pain.

There was a zebra crossing ahead. No one in sight.

The young woman stepped onto it from behind two men and Ryan slammed on his brakes, barely stopping in time.

He glared at her through the windscreen, ignoring the shout from behind, from another driver who'd barely missed him.

The man banged his hooter.

Ryan leaned out of the window and looked at him. He was a middle-aged man with a bald head and a collar that looked too tight.

'What's your fucking problem?' hissed Ryan, eyes blazing.

The man looked past him, waiting for him to move on. He dutifully did.

The music pounded inside the car. Inside his head.

' . . . *Let's move it, time to say so long* . . .'

The pain throbbed in his chest.

He passed Notting Hill Gate tube. Ahead, a bus was slowing down.

Ryan swung out to pass it.

As he did so the pain seemed to reach intolerable proportions; it was as if someone had suddenly pumped his skull full of air. He felt his hands slipping on the wheel, felt the car going out of control.

He was blacking out.

Jesus fucking Christ.

The world swam in front of his eyes, colours suddenly flaring with incredible brilliance, like fireworks exploding.

The car swerved across the road.

There was a Range Rover coming the other way. Heading straight for him.

He heard hooters, tyres screaming.

The cassette roared.

Ryan felt his hands slip from the wheel. His feet pressed down for the brake but the car didn't seem to respond.

Blackness slipped over him.

The car hit the kerb, bounced up it and hurtled on, smashing into the window of a restaurant.

Ryan had the presence of mind to cover his face but his arms were like rubber. All he felt was the terrible fire in his chest.

He heard shattering glass, screams, hooters, music.

His head snapped forward and slammed against the steering wheel.

He was unconscious before his forehead struck it.

Darkness.

Thirty-four

At first he thought someone had sewn his eyelids together. Try as he might, Ryan couldn't seem to open his eyes.

Fuck it.

Perhaps he was dead, he thought.

The undertaker had stitched his lids closed with nylon thread.

That was it. He was dead.

It didn't seem so bad after all. Just a bastard not being able to see anything and . . .

He felt pain in his chest.

In his head.

His arms.

His whole body was one mass of suffering, his mind able only to comprehend discomfort. Yet the pain wasn't as appalling as he'd known it in the past. His chest was sore, very sore. But he couldn't feel the gnawing pain he'd come to know only too well.

If only he could open his eyes.

He felt dizzy. Light-headed and disorientated. Yet he was lying down.

But lying down where?

He made another effort to open his eyes, feeling the lids part slightly, as if some kind of film were being peeled back. Light forced its way through and dazzled him. Artificial light. The light of fluorescent tubes. And now he noticed the strong smell, of antiseptic.

Ryan tried to move, tried to raise one hand to push his eyelids apart, rubbing at them, wincing as he felt the pain. But at least now he could see. Images swam before him momentarily as his vision cleared.

He was in bed. Grey blankets were pulled tightly across him, as if to restrain him. Only his arms were outside the covers.

There were drips running from both of them.

Ryan swallowed hard as he saw the narrow tubes running from plastic containers suspended above him to the needles embedded in his arms, held in place by surgical tape. He could feel them prodding him as he moved.

The drips didn't prevent him from moving his arms, though, and he pushed at the covers, easing them down slightly to expose his upper body.

His chest and stomach were swathed in bandages. He reached down to touch his pectoral area and felt padding there, and gauze beneath the bandage. Ryan tried to suck in a deep breath but found the effort almost impossible.

He glanced up and saw the clear solution in one of the drips trickle from the container down the tube towards his arm, where it was swallowed by the open vein.

What the fuck were they pumping into him?

The skin *not* covered by bandages looked blackened in places where it was bruised. Some of the discolorations were already beginning to yellow at the extremities. He had several more abrasions on his shoulders, one or two of which were already beginning to scab over. He tried to kick the covers off, anxious to see whether or not his legs had been damaged, but the effort was too much. He sank back onto the pillows, feeling as if he'd just run a mile.

Ryan tried to remember what had happened but his

recollections were as fuzzy as his vision. It was as if his mind had been wrapped in cotton wool and thoughts were trapped inside. He blinked hard. He felt as if he could close his eyes and drift off to sleep again.

Despite the pain.

He pulled the covers back up to his neck and lay there, gazing around the room. Now sounds too began to filter through to him. He could hear footsteps outside the door, people passing back and forth. He heard a trolley being trundled past, one wheel squeaking loudly.

Somewhere in the distance he heard a siren.

The door of the room opened and a man with short dark hair strode in. He was tall, his features thin and he looked as if he could do with some sleep. His long white coat was flying open; beneath it he wore a shirt and trousers. His tie was loosened around his thick neck. He carried a clipboard in one hand.

The doctor looked apprehensively at Ryan for a moment, unsure whether or not the private detective's eyes were actually open. When he saw that they were, a slight smile touched his lips.

He moved across to the bed, reaching for Ryan's left wrist and jabbing two fingers against it to search for a pulse which he checked off against his wristwatch.

'How long have you been awake?' the doctor asked, still looking at his watch.

'A few minutes,' Ryan told him, his voice croaky. It felt as if someone had been scrubbing the back of his throat with sandpaper. When he tried to swallow, it took more effort than he would have liked. The doctor released his wrist and reached for the jug of water on the bedside cabinet. He poured Ryan a beaker full then supported his head while he took a few sips, wincing as he swallowed.

He nodded when he'd drunk enough and lay back.

'Where am I?' he wanted to know.

'St Mary's Hospital, Paddington,' the doctor told him,

jotting something down on the clipboard. He crossed to the first of the drips and peered at the fluid level.

'What happened to me?'

'We were hoping you were going to be able to tell *us* that, Mr Ryan.'

'I can't remember much, just blacking out. I remember the car going out of control, then nothing.' He shrugged. There was a stab of pain in his chest.

The doctor regarded him impassively for a moment and then began pulling back the covers.

'I think I'd better have a look,' he said, motioning towards the private detective's heavily bandaged torso.

'What's the damage?' Ryan wanted to know.

'A couple of cracked ribs, cuts and bruises. You've got a bang on the head, too.'

'How long have I been unconscious?'

The doctor looked at him impassively.

'Two days.'

Ryan looked incredulous.

'Two *days*?' he repeated, as if that would somehow lessen the shock. 'But you said my injuries were minor. I didn't bang my head *that* badly, did I?'

'You were unconscious when you were brought in. You did come round, but after the operation you slipped under. You've been in a coma for the past forty-two hours, Mr Ryan.'

'Coma?' Ryan blurted. 'What the hell are you talking about?'

'You were brought here with minor injuries, as I've said,' the doctor informed him. 'We did routine X-Rays to see whether there was any internal damage.'

'And?' Ryan interrupted, a note of fear now in his voice.

'When we checked the X-Rays we found a shadow on both lungs,' the doctor told him calmly. 'We opened you up and performed an operation. We did a biopsy

117

on part of a growth we took from one lung.'

Ryan was looking directly at him now, his eyes blazing.

'Yeah?'

The doctor licked his lips swiftly.

'You have cancer.'

Thirty-five

'Cancer.'

Ryan repeated the word as if it was the first time he'd ever heard it. His voice was even, his expression one of bemusement rather than concern. He looked down at his chest and took as deep a breath as the constricting bandages and the pain would allow.

Gerald Newman was beginning to wonder if Ryan had heard him correctly, so unresponsive were his reactions. The doctor had seen some people break down when they were given the news. Others fainted. Most just sat motionless as the realization dawned.

Ryan now lay silently, running one hand across his chin, perhaps grappling with the disclosure.

'In the lungs, you say?' Ryan finally added.

Newman nodded.

Ryan shook his head slowly.

Perhaps I *should* have gone to the doctor, he mused, a slight smile on his lips.

'You must have been in considerable pain for some time now,' Newman said.

Ryan didn't answer.

Fucking right.

'Didn't you tell anyone?' the doctor persisted. 'Your own doctor, perhaps?'

'No,' Ryan said flatly. 'I never got round to it.' He shrugged.

Newman regarded him impassively.

'How far advanced is it?' Ryan wanted to know.

'Well, as I said, we found large growths in both lungs and there are signs that it is beginning to spread to the pancreas and the spleen.'

Ryan nodded.

'What did you do to me when you opened me up?' he enquired.

'There wasn't much we *could* do,' Newman confessed. 'Initially it was an exploratory operation. We were surprised at how far advanced the cancer was.'

'You didn't attempt to remove it, then?'

'That wouldn't have been possible, Mr Ryan.'

'Why not?'

'It was too deeply embedded, too far advanced. In both lungs there are up to four tumours. One of them in the right lung is the size of my fist.'

Ryan's eyes narrowed slightly, but otherwise he seemed more intrigued than perturbed. Newman wondered if the full gravity of his words had reached the patient. When hearing particularly bad news, he had found, the human mind sometimes shuts out what it cannot countenance.

'So what now?' Ryan demanded.

Newman shrugged. It was a question he had been dreading.

'What can you do?' the private detective continued.

'There's nothing we can do, Mr Ryan. The cancer is inoperable and, as I've already told you, it's beginning to spread.'

'What about chemotherapy?'

Newman shook his head.

'It's too late for that,' he said bluntly.

Ryan smiled bitterly.

'In other words I'm fucked,' he said. 'You can't operate, you can't treat the cancer. Right?'

'That's correct.'

'Why don't you just come out and say it?' Ryan asked challengingly. 'Why don't you tell me it's terminal?'

'I would have thought that was more or less apparent without my having to say it, Mr Ryan. I'm very sorry.'

'Don't be,' Ryan hissed. 'How long have I got?'

'That's impossible to say,' Newman explained.

'Take a fucking guess,' Ryan rasped angrily.

'If the cancer continues to grow at the rate it's growing now, and if the spread accelerates, then perhaps six months.'

Ryan fixed him in an unwavering stare.

'You're telling me I'll be dead in six months?' he said quietly.

'It may not take that long,' Newman admitted. 'On the other hand, we could operate on the tumours in the pancreas and the spleen. We could remove those, but they're not the real problem. They're secondary cancers. The primary tumours in the lungs are inoperable. The cancer could be arrested but not cured.'

'A stay of execution,' Ryan quipped.

'There are drugs which will help relieve the pain and which will slow down the growth of the primary tumour. Unfortunately, they won't cure you either.'

'Which drugs?'

Newman shrugged.

'I have a right to know,' Ryan snapped. 'It's my fucking life.'

'Chlorambucil, triaziquone or cyclo-phosphamide,' the doctor told him. 'There are a number of others. Morphine to stop the pain, usually in liquid form, to be swallowed.'

'Thanks,' Ryan said quietly.

Newman looked down at the private detective, feeling the same sense of helplessness he had known far too many times throughout his career.

'There's something else I have to know,' Ryan said finally. 'The symptoms. How will the disease progress?'

'Why do you need to know?'

'Because I'm the one who's going to be living through it,' Ryan reminded him. 'I'm the one who's got to face it. Now tell me what'll happen to me.'

'The cancer cells will continue to divide, to grow,' the doctor began. 'Breathing will become difficult, more painful. Finally impossible. The lungs will simply cease to function. Effectively you'll suffocate.'

Ryan nodded.

'I'll be able to walk about, though? Live life more or less normally?' he wanted to know.

'As the lungs become more diseased it'll become almost impossible to move around. You simply won't have the strength. You won't be able to take in enough oxygen to aerate your blood supply. In a weakened state you'll also become more susceptible to germs, to other infections and viruses.'

'I'm not going to lie here and wait for it to kill me, Doctor,' Ryan said defiantly.

'You might not have any choice, Mr Ryan.'

'I *won't* wait for it to kill me,' the private detective said through clenched teeth. 'No way.'

Newman nodded, then re-checked the drips before moving towards the door.

'I'll send a nurse in,' he said, one hand on the handle. 'In the meantime, if there's anything you need just press that button beside your bed.' He turned to leave.

'There is one thing,' Ryan told him.

'What is it?'

'I could murder a cigarette.'

Thirty-six

He drifted in and out of sleep, never able to snatch more than thirty minutes at a time. The combination of his pain and the incessant heat made complete rest impossible.

As Ryan rolled over yet again he glanced at his watch on the bedside table.

The luminous hands glowed green in the gloom; it was almost 1.00 a.m. The rest of the hospital was silent. To Ryan, it seemed as if the sound of his own laboured breathing filled the night.

Every now and then he could hear footsteps passing by outside the door of his room, receding away into the distance, swallowed up by the cloying solitude.

Beads of perspiration had formed on his forehead and he wiped them away with the back of one hand, pushing down his covers with the other.

Christ, it was hot.

He surveyed the bandaged torso. The bruised limbs.

Cancer.

Fucking cancer.

Ryan felt suddenly cold, as if someone had injected him with ice water, as if the liquid in the drips had turned to freezing moisture. He momentarily forgot the heat inside the room. A stab of pain in his chest shocked

122

him out of his musings. He sucked in a breath, wincing in the process.

Six months.

'Shit,' he murmured.

People rarely contemplated their own deaths. Not even in quiet moments, he thought. Certainly he had never thought about his own until Newman had given him the news of its impending arrival. Certainly everyone at some time wondered what it would be like to die. *When* they were going to meet their end. But to be *told*, that was something different. To know of that awful finality was bad enough but to be told to expect it in a matter of months was intolerable.

To be helpless against it was even worse.

Ryan felt a curious mixture of rage and foreboding. He shifted uncomfortably in his bed, feeling the perspiration soaking into the sheets.

He had been told he would die in less than six months.

That, according to Newman, was a fact. And one which there was no escaping.

And they expected him to lie there helplessly waiting for the end?

Fuck that.

Ryan gritted his teeth.

He would fight it. Fight this fucking disease which was trying to kill him. Fight it like he'd fought everything else in his life. He wouldn't *allow* it to get the better of him. All his life he'd been competitive, in his job, in his relationships. Now he was being forced to face the most potent opponent ever. Death itself.

Well, he *would* fight.

He'd read of others who'd been diagnosed as having terminal illnesses, who'd been given a limited time. And they had fought and some had won. Some had kept death at bay.

If others could do it then so could he.

Try and take me, you cunt, and I'll fight you.

He gritted his teeth, as if faced by a tangible adversary.

He would not surrender. He would not lie here and give up his hold on something so precious.

No way.

His thoughts were interrupted as the door to the room opened and light flooded through, causing him to shield his eyes. A figure was silhouetted there for a second, and then the nurse slipped inside, closing the door behind her.

'Perhaps you should be carrying a fucking scythe,' said Ryan.

The nurse looked puzzled.

'Did I wake you up?' she wanted to know.

He shook his head.

'I can't sleep, anyway,' he told her.

'Would you like a sleeping pill?' she enquired, checking the drips and scribbling something on the clipboard which hung at the bottom of his bed. She crossed to him again and felt for his pulse, checking it against the watch which hung from her uniform.

Ryan eyed her through the gloom, noticing that she was in her mid-twenties, pretty. She smelled of newly washed linen.

She moved to pull the covers up again but Ryan held out a hand to stop her.

'It's too hot,' he said protestingly, wincing as he felt a stab of pain.

'Are you in pain?' she asked.

'You could say that,' he answered acidly.

'Do you want me to get you something for it?'

'Yeah, major fucking surgery,' he told her caustically.

'I'll get you a couple of Brufen. They'll help you sleep, too.'

'I don't want to sleep,' he snapped. His tone softened. 'I'll have plenty of time for that in six months.'

She regarded him through the gloom for a moment as his expression relaxed.

'Is this an occupational hazard?' he asked.

She looked puzzled.

'Having to deal with moaning bastards,' he continued.

She smiled.

'Yes. All the time,' she told him.

'Why do you do it? It's not the fucking money, that's for sure.'

'Someone has to,' she told him. 'Besides, I enjoy it. I like looking after people. My mum was a nurse too, then a midwife right up until she died.'

'How old was she?'

'Forty-eight. She had a stroke.'

She was lucky.

'What's your name?' he wanted to know.

'Debra White.'

'Pleased to meet you, Debra White.' He nodded at her, as if the gesture made the introduction formal.

'One of the interns told me you were a private detective,' she said sheepishly. 'Is that true?'

Did he tell you I was dying, too?

'Yes, it's true. So what?'

'It must be a glamorous job.'

'Does it look glamorous now? I can think of more exciting ways of spending my time.'

'But in films . . .'

He cut her short.

'Forget what you've seen in films,' Ryan said. 'The people who make films about private investigators usually haven't got a clue.'

'Do you carry a gun?'

'I own *two* but I don't carry one with me. The police

125

tend to object if you go around shooting people. Even when those people are threatening to take your fucking head off because you've found out they're having an affair or something like that.'

'My boyfriend will be interested when I tell him I've met a private detective,' the nurse said, smiling.

'Don't forget to tell him the truth,' Ryan said. *Perhaps he'd be less interested in a dying private detective.* 'What does he do?'

'He works here in the hospital. He's a porter.' She smiled again. 'Have you got any family?'

Ryan's face darkened.

'No,' he said sharply. 'No one.'

The nurse looked a little sad.

She glanced round towards the door.

'I'd better go, Sister will be after me,' she said. 'Are you sure there's nothing I can get you?'

Ryan shook his head.

She smiled again and left, closing the door behind her.

Ryan exhaled, the action causing renewed pain. He closed his eyes and waited for sleep, knowing it would not come. Not yet. He wiped perspiration from his face with his hand; the drip moved on its stand as the tube was pulled by his movement. Ryan felt the needle prick and cursed under his breath.

He could not take this, lying here like a helpless invalid.

Like a corpse?

He *would* not take it.

Thirty-seven

The lighter flared once then went out, briefly illuminating her face with the glow.

Stephanie Collins flicked at it again, the JPS bouncing up and down between her thin lips as she tried to get the lighter to raise a flame. Despite her efforts it produced only sparks. Muttering to herself, she rummaged in her small shoulder bag, searching for matches. There were none. She took the cigarette from her mouth and dropped it into the bottom of the bag along with the other debris. A couple of empty cigarette packets. Lipstick. Some condoms. A small pocket knife.

Despite the heat she shivered.

The gloom inside the multi-storey car park on Waverton Street was almost impenetrable and the thick concrete pillar she leant against was cold.

The stink of oil and petrol was strong in the cloying night air, even though the last car had long ago departed.

She shifted from one stilettoed foot to the other, occasionally running a skinny hand over her spandex-clad legs. The short black leather jacket draped around her shoulders did nothing to warm her. Dressed all in black, surrounded by darkness, she seemed to be a part of the umbra, a shadow distinguishable only by a shock of platinum blonde hair.

She picked briefly at a tiny spot on her chin, hoping it

was still adequately hidden by her thick make-up. Yet to reach her twentieth birthday, Stephanie looked ten years older. Her pale features were weary and drawn, her eyes dull and lifeless, like those of a fish on a skillet. Those same dull eyes which darted furtively back and forth in the blackness.

She heard footsteps; the sound echoed through the cavernous car park.

Instinctively she pressed herself up against the pillar. Peering in the direction of the sound, she realized it could have been someone walking past the car park. Sound carried at such a late hour.

It was almost 2.10 a.m.

The footsteps receded and Stephanie ran a hand through her hair, shuddering involuntarily. She tried to slow her breathing, and quieten it. Every sound seemed to be amplified, carried through the darkness with increased clarity.

As she shifted from one foot to the other the clicking of her heels on the concrete sounded deafening.

She tried standing still but found it almost impossible.

Through the gloom she squinted at her watch once again, tapping the face with one false nail when she saw that the second hand had stopped moving. She raised the time piece to her ear checking to see if it was still working. She heard the ticking.

And suddenly, from behind her, she heard a whirring sound.

The lift was rising from the basement level.

Stephanie pressed herself more tightly to the pillar, her eyes on the yellow floor lights above the lift doors.

The one marked 'G' flared.

The lift began to rise again.

She swallowed hard, watching as it reached the first level. This level.

Interminable seconds passed before the doors slid open.

The lift was empty.

Silence descended again, broken only by Stephanie's harsh breathing.

The lift doors remained open, revealing the empty car beyond.

She took a step forward, her eyes fixed on the lift.

The blood roared in her ears and she could feel her heart thudding hard against her ribs.

Conscious of the noise of her heels, she leant forward so that she was walking on her toes, almost silently.

The lift doors still yawned open.

She swallowed hard and took a step closer.

The hand closed over her shoulder.

Unable to help herself, Stephanie Collins screamed.

The sound reverberated off the concrete pillars and low ceiling of the car park, drumming in her own ears as she spun round.

Donald Neville released his grip on her shoulder and took a step back.

He was smiling thinly.

'Jesus Christ,' she panted. 'You scared the shit out of me.' She wiped one trembling hand across her face.

Neville pulled at his pony-tail and looked her up and down.

'Why all the creeping about?' Stephanie asked.

'We had to be sure you were on your own,' Neville told her.

'I've been waiting here for ages,' she protested. 'You said midnight.'

'We had other business to attend to,' Edward Caton told her. 'You're not too high on our list of priorities.'

'I've been standing here fucking freezing,' she said. 'You got a light?'

Neville reached into his pocket and pulled out a

129

zippo, striking it.

She leant closer, sticking the JPS between her lips, pushing the end into the flame.

In the sickly yellow light he saw the dark marks on the crook of her arm and on her wrist. Some of them had scabbed over; others were purple welts where the skin had started to heal, only to be broken again.

'What are you on?' Neville asked contemptuously. 'Stevie? That is what they call you, isn't it?'

She took a couple of drags on the cigarette.

'What's it to you what I'm on? What do you care?'

'I don't,' Neville said flatly.

'Have you got the money?' she wanted to know.

Neville nodded.

'Have you got what *we* want?' he asked.

'It's here,' she told him, motioning to a small cardboard box at her feet with BEANZ MEANZ HEINZ stencilled on it.

'How long you had it?' Caton wanted to know.

'Five weeks,' she told him.

He snapped his fingers and she bent and picked up the box, holding it to her chest.

'Two thousand,' she said.

'One thousand,' Neville said, reaching into the pocket of his jeans. 'That was the price we agreed.' He fixed her in an unflinching stare. 'Give.' He curled his finger at her.

'Bastard,' she muttered, shoving the box at Caton. He peered inside and looked at his colleague, nodding.

Neville began pushing fifty-pound notes into Stevie Collins' hand.

She took their money.

They took her baby.

Thirty-eight

'What the hell are you doing?'

Doctor Gerald Newman froze as he pushed open the door to Ryan's room.

The private detective was sitting on the edge of the bed pulling the second drip from his arm.

There was a trickle of blood from the vein as he pulled it free but he wiped it away with a tissue before turning to look directly at the doctor.

'Mr Ryan,' Newman continued, moving into the room hurriedly. 'What are you playing at?'

'I'm not *playing*, Doctor,' Ryan told him. 'I'm leaving.' He stood up, steadying himself against the edge of the bed.

'That's impossible. You're very ill, you're . . .'

'Yeah, I know, I'm dying.'

Ryan crossed to the wardrobe and pulled open the doors, searching for his clothes. He pulled on his shirt.

'You can't do this,' Newman said. 'You've undergone an operation. You're more susceptible to all kinds of infections now.'

'Oh, no! You mean I could catch a cold, or something serious like that?' Ryan continued buttoning his shirt.

'You know bloody well what I mean. I can't allow you to do this. I can't allow you to leave.'

'Try stopping me,' Ryan said, stepping into his trousers.

Newman moved towards the bed and perched on the

131

edge of it, watching as the private detective continued dressing.

'You need help, Mr Ryan,' he said, his tone softening.

'But, according to you, *no one* can help me. I'm going to die anyway, aren't I? Well, I'm fucked if I'm going to lie here in some hospital bed waiting for it. Counting off the days.' He shook his head. 'Not a chance.'

'What you're doing is madness, you realize that?' the doctor said in a last attempt to dissuade Ryan from his actions.

'I'd be even more crazy to stay here, knowing what I know,' the private detective told him. He winced slightly as he felt pain in his chest but he continued dressing. 'I'd go mad, stuck in here. I might as well be on fucking death row. I know it's going to happen in the next few months; it'd just be a matter of sitting around here waiting for it to happen. I won't go out like that.'

'But there's medication you need. Special care.'

'What's the fucking point? It's all going to be over in six months anyway, isn't it? If I need medication, then write me some prescriptions.' Ryan looked at him impassively. 'If you want to help me then let me out of here.'

'The hospital has responsibilities to its patients. *I* have responsibilities,' Newman protested.

'I'll sign a letter absolving you and the hospital of all blame for me leaving. Don't worry, Doc, no one's going to hit you with a law suit if I drop dead on the pavement outside.'

'There's no need for that,' Newman said quietly. 'I'm just sorry you won't let us help you.'

'Help me in what way? Get your nurses to bring me bed-pans when I'm too breathless to walk to the shithouse? Shove drips into my arms when I can't take solid food? Send someone in with cratefuls of pills

132

every day? I can do without that kind of help. Besides, there are people in this hospital who need that kind of help more than me. People who are going to get better.'

'Your concern for the other patients is touching, Mr Ryan,' said Newman, a note of sarcasm in his voice.

'Concern, bollocks. I'm just being realistic. I couldn't give a fuck about anyone else in here, but most of them have got a chance of leaving in one piece. If I stayed here the only way I could hope to leave would be in a wooden box.'

Newman reached into his pocket and pulled out a prescription pad. He began writing. He scribbled down several different medications in his neat hand.

Ryan looked at him as he held out the pieces of paper.

'Some of those drugs will stop the cancer growing so quickly, others are pain-killers. There are a couple of prescriptions there for morphine, when the pain becomes too much.'

Ryan nodded and took them, folding them up and slipping them into his jacket.

He gritted his teeth at the pain burning inside him, but thankfully the tremor passed. He extended his right hand and Newman shook it warmly.

'If you can't cope,' the doctor said, 'come back.'

'Why?' Ryan said, smiling.

He stepped past the doctor and headed for the door, closing it behind him as he left.

Newman shook his head and looked across at the discarded drips.

Saline was trickling from one of them. Droplets of it fell onto the floor like tears.

Thirty-nine

He caught a taxi straight to his office in Old Compton Street. From there, Ryan rang Hertz and rented a Nissan 200SX until his own car was repaired.

He checked the mail that had arrived in the past three days, and the messages on the answerphone, but none required urgent attention. More work had come in, he was pleased to note. That was what he wanted now. Plenty of work, plenty to occupy his mind. He didn't want any time to dwell on his predicament.

No time to think about death.

Ryan sat at his desk and sucked hard on the cigarette he'd just lit, glancing at the Health Warning on the packet. He almost laughed. Who was to say it had been the cigarettes that had caused his illness? There could be a dozen different reasons for it. He took another drag on the Superking, blowing out the smoke in a blue cloud.

STOPPING SMOKING REDUCES THE RISK OF SERIOUS DISEASES

He ran an index finger over the warning again.

Fuck it. He knew guys who smoked sixty Marlboro a day who were healthier than he was.

Fuck it.

He'd nipped out earlier and picked up two of the prescriptions Newman had written for him. One lot of pills were pain-killers, the others were for retarding the growth of the cancer. He had hung on to the morphine scripts; no sense in using them until it was absolutely necessary.

Ryan glanced at the phone, rested his hand on it then withdrew it again.

Soon.

He got to his feet and crossed the office, glancing out of the window at the bustling thoroughfare of Charing Cross Road. The clouds of exhaust fumes from so many vehicles rose in a noxious wave. In the cloudless sky the sun blazed unmercifully. Ryan wiped perspiration from his face with the back of his hand, noticing that he was quivering slightly.

As he turned he felt a twinge of pain in his chest but he gritted his teeth, intent on ignoring it – as a bullock will ignore a troublesome fly.

To his left there was a teak cabinet about two feet square. Fumbling in his jacket pocket Ryan selected a key, knelt and unlocked the cabinet.

Inside it, lying on separate shelves, both lined with black velvet, were two guns.

On the top shelf lay a Smith and Wesson 9mm Model 39 Automatic.

Below it, a .357 Colt Python revolver.

There were half a dozen boxes of ammunition in there too.

Ryan took the .357 and hefted it, feeling the weight, seeing the light reflect off the gleaming metal. He traced the barrel with his index finger, feeling the engraved maker's name and serial number.

He swung it up and squinted down the barrel.

Ryan had owned the guns for the last six years but had never fired them in anger. He practised regularly at a shooting club in Druid Street, south of the river, but he'd never shot at anything other than a target with either weapon. He'd carried one or both of the weapons on a number of jobs but had only had recourse to pull them on half a dozen occasions, always in self-defence. The sight of the weapons alone had always done the trick.

Now he held the pistol close, studying every contour of it.

Six months of suffering?

Ryan swallowed hard.

Did he want that?

Six months was better than nothing. *Wasn't it?*

He pressed the barrel of the .357 up under his chin, the steel comfortingly cool against his hot flesh.

So easy to end it all now.

No more suffering.

No more pain.

He pulled the trigger.

The hammer slammed down on an empty chamber, the metallic click loud in the silent office.

'Fuck,' hissed Ryan, lowering the gun. He pushed it back inside the cabinet and locked it. Then he crossed to his desk.

This time he didn't hesitate. He snatched up the receiver and dialled.

Forty

Kim wasn't very happy by the time she reached the door of Ryan's office.

The drive into Central London had taken longer than usual because of an accident and subsequent detour. Once in the centre she'd had trouble finding somewhere to park and now she had been forced to trek up five flights of stairs because the lift was out of order. Kim Finlay was more than a little irritated as she banged on the door, perspiration trickling down her back in the warmth of the evening.

'This had better be good, Nick,' she snapped as Ryan opened the door and stepped back to let her in. She breezed past him and stalked into the office, noticing how dark it was in there. Lit only by the desk lamp, the room was filled with deep, thick shadows.

He offered her a seat but she declined, preferring to pace back and forth.

'Do you realize the trouble your phone call caused me?' she asked. 'I had a row with Joe before I left.'

'Do you want a drink?' he asked, apparently unconcerned by the tribulations his call had precipitated.

She regaled him with the details of her tortuous journey to his office.

Ryan sat down behind his desk and poured vodka into his mug. He lit a cigarette and took a drag, coughing. He touched his chest briefly, feeling the all too familiar pain.

'Well,' she said angrily. 'I've come all this way, you could at least tell me why.'

'Just sit down, will you, Kim?' he said.

She pulled up a chair and plonked herself in it.

In the dim light she saw that his face looked even more pale, how the dark rings beneath his eyes seemed to combine with his heavy lids to form black holes where his eyes should have been. The hollows of his cheeks looked as if they'd been inked over. His hand was shaking slightly as he raised the mug to drink.

'If you have to call, can't you do it when Joe's not there?' she asked, her tone softening.

'I didn't know he was going to pick up the bloody

137

phone,' Ryan said. 'Anyway, he might not have to bother about my calls for much longer.'

She looked puzzled.

'There won't be any more calls,' he told her.

'Why? Are you going away?'

He grunted.

'You could say that.' He downed what was left in the mug and poured himself another refill.

'Nick, what's going on? Are you in some kind of trouble?'

'Big fucking trouble,' he said, a bitter smile on his lips.

'What's happening? Presumably you got me over here to tell me?'

'I can't think of an easy way to say this, Kim, so I won't even try. I'm dying.'

There, it was said. Quite easy, really.

'Terminal lung cancer. Well, to start with, anyway. My liver and spleen are fucked, too. Cancer. I've got six months, tops.'

She felt very cold, despite the warmth in the office. It was as if all the blood was draining quickly from her body.

He raised his mug.

'Cheers.'

Kim wanted to speak but found that no words would come. Her lips moved but she found it impossible to make any sound.

Ryan explained what had happened. The chest pains, the blood, the vomiting. He told her about the blackout and the car crash, the subsequent operation and the doctor's words. Throughout it all she sat in numbed silence.

Ryan lit another cigarette, noticing as she glanced at it.

'It's okay,' he said. 'I've cut down. The fucking things kill you.'

She got to her feet and walked around the desk.

Ryan saw the tears glistening on her cheeks.

'Could there be some mistake?' she asked, moving closer to him.

Ryan shook his head, standing up to embrace her as she threw her arms around him.

'Oh God, Nick,' she sobbed, hugging him tightly to her. 'What are you going to do?'

'There's not much I *can* do,' he said. 'That's the worst thing about it.'

'I'm so sorry,' she said, tears streaming down her face.

'It isn't your fault. It isn't anyone's fault. I can't even blame some other fucker for it.' He chuckled humourlessly.

'I'm sorry for *you*,' she said.

'I don't want your pity, Kim,' he said through gritted teeth.

'It isn't pity,' she snapped, pulling back from him slightly. 'I don't want anything to happen to you. I never did. I love you.'

The words took him by surprise; he pulled her close again.

'I love you,' she whispered.

Ryan screwed his eyes tightly shut, so tight that white stars danced behind the lids. He felt a curious mixture of emotions.

She held on to him for a little longer, then reached out and touched his face. He took her hand and pulled it away.

'Kelly will have to be told,' Kim said.

Ryan wiped a tear from her cheek.

'Not yet,' he said.

'She has a right to know, Nick, before it's too late.'

'You mean before I'm down to five stone, and all my fucking hair's fallen out and I need a respirator to breathe? Is that what you mean?'

'I'll tell her.'

'No. She mustn't know, Kim. Promise me that,' he said, a hard edge to his voice. '*Promise* me you won't tell her.'

Fresh sobs racked her body as he pulled her tightly to him.

The darkness inside the room seemed to swallow them up.

Forty-one

The child lay in a cardboard box about three feet by two. It was wrapped in blankets to keep it warm, but even so its skin was tinged red about the cheeks and upper body.

'What if it fucking dies?' Edward Caton said, looking down at the child.

'Stop worrying,' said Don Neville. 'It's only port I've given it. My mum used to swear by it for the smaller kids when they cried. We're probably taking better care of it than the slag who sold it to us. If it survived five weeks with her it'll stand another couple of days with us.' He wandered slowly around the room in the building in Cavendish Square, checking the video camera and the lights. Double-checking that everything was in position.

'Are you going to offer this one to Thornton?' Caton asked.

'I'm not sure,' Neville said, wiping sweat from the

back of his neck. 'I reckon we'll do better abroad with a film with a baby in it. Mind you, I'm sure Charles Thornton's got plenty of punters who'd go for this kind of thing, too.' He smiled.

'And the other member of the cast?' Caton said, grinning. 'Maybe we should use a geezer this time.'

'Maybe, but the baby's a boy, isn't it?'

Caton shrugged.

'I don't know,' he chuckled. 'I didn't look.' He leant forward and pulled the blankets away from the child to get a better view. 'Fuck me, you're right.'

He laughed and covered the baby again.

'Finlay was right, you know,' Caton said, his tone changing.

'About what?' Neville wanted to know.

'Well, we've done six now. The law have found four of them.'

'And where the fuck has it got them? They're no closer now than they were when we first started and they never *will* get any closer. Those kids we took were just names or numbers, sometimes not even that. No one gives a fuck about them. They're expendable, Eddie boy. The shit that fills the gutter of society.' He smiled at his own philosophical musings. 'We've just been cleaning up that gutter a bit. Removing some of the unwanted debris from it, you might say.'

Caton grinned crookedly.

'No,' Neville continued, 'the law don't know where to start.'

'What about that little slag who sold us the baby?'

'What's she going to tell them? We should have used *her* in the next video. Give it another nine months and she'll be trying to sell someone else *another* kid of hers, if she hasn't O.D.'d by then.' He looked at his companion. 'You're not going soft on me, are you, Eddie? Not losing your bottle?'

141

Caton shook his head.

'Never,' he said, flatly. 'I was just thinking about Finlay and what he'd said.' He ran a hand through his hair, wiping the perspiration off on his jeans. 'What the fuck do we do about that cunt? What's his fucking game?'

'The only game Finlay plays is with himself,' Neville said.

'But what if he blows the gaff on us?' Caton wanted to know.

'He can't. If he tips off the law there's no way we'd go down without implicating him. He knows that. He knows we've got him by the bollocks.'

'Have we? What proof have we got to tie him in to us? I don't know, Don, don't you think we might be better off abroad with this kind of thing?'

Neville thought for a moment and then smiled thinly. 'I can take care of all that,' he said quietly. 'Tying him into the business in a way he'd never have expected.'

Forty-two

The public bar of The Roebuck in Great Dover Street was empty but for three people. Two of them, men in their forties dressed in suits and looking decidedly uncomfortable in the heat, were standing at the bar.

One sipped mineral water; the other nursed a shandy in a large hand.

Nick Ryan stood in the doorway, looking at the two men. He glanced at his watch.

'Drink after the job's done,' he said acidly. '*You* might have time to waste but I haven't.'

The two men spun round, the taller of the two spilling some of his drink.

'Are you Ryan?' the taller man asked.

The private detective nodded.

'Malcolm Webber,' said the tall man, pressing a finger to his own chest. 'This is Peter Crane.' He nodded towards his shorter, stockier companion. 'We're from the Council. We've been waiting for you.'

'Then why the fuck weren't you waiting for me across the road at the flat of the bloke we're serving an eviction notice on? As far as I know he hasn't paid his rent. I didn't think you had to check out his local first. You're bailiffs, right? Not fucking Weights and Measures Inspectors.' Ryan walked out again and the two men followed, striding briskly across the road after him.

As he reached the flight of stone steps that led to the first floor, Ryan lit a cigarette, sucking hard on it.

'You got one to spare?' asked Crane hopefully.

'They had a fag machine in the pub, didn't they?' Ryan snapped. 'You should have bought some. Come on.'

He led the way and the other two men followed him up the steps, Crane raising two fingers at his back.

The trio reached the first landing and Ryan pulled a piece of paper from his pocket, checking the address. He noted the numbers of the other flats as they passed them. One. Three. Five.

The door to number seven opened and a woman stuck her head out, glancing warily at the three men. Behind her a small child shouted something Ryan couldn't hear. The boy was about five and pushed past his mother to get a better view. She made a perfunctory grab for him but the child slipped out and scurried onto the landing, watching the men until they reached the door of flat number fifteen. The woman too was watching, leaning against the frame of the door, her arms crossed.

'What are you looking at?' asked Crane. 'There's nothing to see.'

The woman didn't answer.

Ryan banged hard on the door, noticing that some of the red paint had flaked off. There was no answer so he knocked again.

Still nothing.

'Mr Hughes,' he called.

Silence.

'Mr Hughes, can you hear me?' he said, sucking on his cigarette. 'Open up. My name is Ryan; I'm here with an eviction order from Southwark Council. I'm not moving until you open this door.'

They heard the sounds of movement from behind the door.

'Fuck off,' a voice shouted.

Ryan banged again.

'I told you to fuck off,' Hughes shouted again.

The private detective continued banging.

'Get away from the door,' Hughes told him.

'Open it,' Ryan called back.

'Shall we handle this?' Webber asked, stepping forward.

Ryan glared at him and the bailiff hesitated.

Further down the landing other doors had opened now, other inquisitive occupants of the block peering out. The small child moved closer to get a better view.

Ryan dropped his cigarette butt and ground it out.

'I've got a gun in here,' Hughes shouted. 'You get

144

away and you won't get hurt.'

'Put the gun away, you old bastard,' Crane snapped. 'We'll have the police here in five minutes.'

'Shut it,' hissed Ryan.

'Either you open the door or I'll kick it in,' Ryan said, leaning against the frame.

'Didn't you hear me?' Hughes bellowed. 'I've got a gun. I'll fucking use it, too. The first cunt through that door gets both barrels.'

Ryan shook his head, stepped back and aimed a kick at the door.

The impact sent it hurtling back on its hinges, pieces of paint and wood flying into the air. As Ryan stepped into the narrow hallway he smelled the acrid stench of stale urine and sweat. But it was what he saw that caused him to slow his pace.

Donald Hughes was standing at the end of the hallway, a Viking 12 bore shotgun gripped firmly in his hands. The twin barrels yawned menacingly as Hughes raised the weapon.

Ryan looked from the barrels to the man's face. He looked pale and frightened.

Frightened men were unpredictable, Ryan thought. Especially when they were pointing a shotgun at you.

'Put the gun down,' Ryan said, advancing a couple of steps.

Hughes backed off.

'Stay back or I'll fire, I'm telling you. I'll fucking do it,' he rasped.

Ryan continued to advance.

'Put it down,' he said through clenched teeth, his eyes locked on the older man's.

'I'll get the police,' Crane called.

Ryan didn't hear. His full attention was fixed on the man in front of him.

'Get back,' shouted Hughes.

145

Ryan took a step closer.

Hughes swung the Viking up to his shoulder, peering down the barrel.

'Go on, then, if you're going to do it,' Ryan said quietly.

Fire.

'One more step,' Hughes gasped, his breath coming in shallow, rapid gasps.

Ryan took that one step.

'Come on, then, pull the fucking trigger,' he urged.

Do me a favour. Help me out.

'I'll kill you,' Hughes told him.

Be my fucking guest.

Ryan was still moving forward.

'I swear to Christ . . .'

'Then fucking shoot,' roared Ryan, seeing the uncertainty flash behind Hughes' eyes. The shotgun wavered in the air slightly. 'Pull the trigger,' he urged. 'Come on, you gutless fucker. Do it.'

Please.

There was a loud metallic click as Hughes thumbed back the hammers.

He was shaking now.

'I'll kill you,' he said none too convincingly.

Ryan raised a hand, reaching for the wavering barrels.

One touch on those triggers now and that was it.

Pull them.

'Last warning,' Hughes said, whimpering.

'Fuck you,' snarled Ryan and snaked out a hand.

His fingers closed around the Viking, and with one powerful twist of his wrist he wrenched the weapon from Hughes' grip.

The older man slumped back against the wall, his head lowered, sobbing quietly.

Ryan looked at him contemptuously.

'You gutless bastard,' he snarled, hefting the shotgun.

'You're mad,' Hughes told him.

Ryan held the gun for a moment then spun it round so he was holding the barrels more firmly.

'Why didn't you kill me?' he said. There was a note of anger in his voice.

The private detective lashed out with the butt end of the Viking, driving it hard into Hughes' face, satisfied when he heard the strident crack as it shattered the nasal bone. Blood burst from the smashed appendage, spilling down Hughes' shirt front. He went down in a heap clutching his face.

Crane stepped into the hallway and looked down at Hughes, his face now a bloody mask.

Ryan tossed the shotgun to the bailiff and pushed past him, digging in his pocket for his cigarettes.

'Job done,' he said flatly.

Forty-three

'So it's thirty-two days and still no rain. No need to take your umbrellas out with you today, either, because there's no sign of any break in the weather. Temperatures are expected to remain in the high eighties and . . .'

Vince Kiernan switched off the radio and slumped back on his bed, sweat already running in rivulets down his face. He had the windows in his room open but they brought little respite from the sweltering heat.

In the street outside dustmen were collecting reeking

bags of refuse; the stench of mouldering garbage rose on the warm air to fill his nostrils. He tried to ignore the smell and concentrate on the task in hand.

He ran his index finger down the list of numbers in the personal columns of the magazine, past those he'd already rung or those outside London, searching for new numbers, for the falsely enticing delights promised in the numerous adverts. He jammed the phone between his ear and shoulder and dialled a number that promised a 'stimulating massage by a superb blonde'.

It rang a couple of times and then a chirpy voice announced that she was Jenny's 'lady', but that his masseuse would be five eight, extremely curvaceous (something Kiernan thought to mean overweight) and full of fun.

He hung up before she got to the prices.

As he dialled another number offering 'sensual massage in opulent surroundings', he felt more than a little dispirited. True, his entire time in London searching for his sister had been little more than a catalogue of disappointments, but in the last couple of days the futility of it all had begun to creep up on him. Kiernan wondered if the day would ever come when he would wake up, pack his bags and return home to Dublin, finally defeated.

He shook his head. No, never. Best not to think about it.

The phone was answered and Kiernan listened as the woman told him prices and all the usual crap but there was something else on the line that caught his attention.

There were children's voices in the background. They were playing happily, as far as he could tell.

He gripped the receiver tightly.

'Do you travel?' he asked.

'Where to?' the voice asked.

'Central London,' he told her.

'That's forty pounds plus the taxi fare.'

He hung up.

Glancing at his watch he saw that it was approaching 10.30 a.m. He had time to make a few more calls before he began his daily rounds of London's streets. Some of the prostitutes had come to know his face by now; one or two even spoke to him as he passed on his endless trek.

He dialled another number.

He'd thought about varying the route, but it had become something of a habit with him. He could have walked it blindfolded. Perhaps he should ask the women who spoke to him if they'd seen Jo. Maybe if he showed them her picture it might just spark off something in their memories. Something that would lead him to her. He jammed a cigarette in his mouth and lit it, as much to cover the stench of the rubbish outside in the street as to satisfy the desire to smoke.

He tapped his lighter gently on the phone as he waited for it to be picked up, his eyes scanning the columns for more numbers.

So many to chose from.

The receiver was picked up at the other end.

'I've just seen your advert,' Kiernan said, his eyes flicking over the page, the words well rehearsed from constant repetition. 'Can you give me some details?'

The voice that answered him was Irish.

It took him only a second to realize it was his sister.

149

Forty-four

Kiernan froze.

Was it really Jo's voice?

He gripped the receiver so tightly it threatened to snap in two.

Dare he begin to think that it was her?

Was he mistaken? Was his desire to hear her voice so strong his imagination had now got the better of him?

The voice belonged to an Irish girl.

So what? London was full of Irish girls.

But there was something there that gradually persuaded him that the girl on the other end of the line was the sister for whom he had searched for what seemed an eternity.

The longer she went on, the more certain he was.

He wanted to tell her, to shout to her that it was him.

Jo, it's your brother. I've found you.

But all he could do was listen, dumbstruck. As if the sudden shock had robbed him of his power to speak.

What if you're wrong?

No. He couldn't be wrong. Not after waiting so long. Could God or fate or whoever was to blame for this be so cruel?

There'd been so much disappointment. What if he *was* wrong?

Just tell her. Speak to her.

Vince Kiernan slammed the phone down and sat back staring at it as if it were some venomous reptile.

For what felt like an age he sat motionless in the heat of the room staring at the phone, wanting to pick the receiver up, wondering why he didn't feel the all-embracing elation he'd expected to feel. He felt only anxiety and fear. Fear that, after coming so close, he *could* be wrong.

He dialled again and waited.

Waited.

'Come on,' he whispered, his heart thudding hard against his ribs.

Waited.

'Hello,' he said as the phone was picked up, in as London an accent as he could manage. 'I'd like some information please, I've just seen your advert.'

Let her talk. Listen to her voice. *Be sure*.

She repeated the information she'd given him moments earlier.

Kiernan shifted the phone from one ear to the other.

Jesus Christ, he was sure this time. It *was* Jo.

By a monumental effort of will he managed to remain silent as Jo repeated her well-rehearsed words.

'Would you like to make an appointment?' she asked.

Kiernan shook himself.

'Yes, I would,' he said, trying to sound calm but realizing he was failing miserably. 'As soon as possible.'

'Thursday's the earliest I'm afraid,' she told him. 'I'm going to be away for a couple of days.'

Two fucking days.

Kiernan gritted his teeth.

'Thursday's fine,' he said. 'Do you have an address for me? It only says Finsbury area in the ad.'

She gave him an address.

'How's four o'clock for you?' she wanted to know.

'Great.'

'See you then. It's cash only, by the way,' she added.

She hung up.

Kiernan held the receiver for a long moment before dropping it back onto the cradle. Sweat sheathed his body.

'Fuck,' he whispered, his eyes screwed tightly shut. His breath was coming in gasps, as if he'd just run a mile.

And now?

One part of his mind told him he should go straight over to Finsbury now, find the address and take her away from there. Another part of his mind posed a question he had been trying to avoid until now.

What if she didn't want to leave?

But in her letters to him she had complained how she hated the men she went with.

Hated the men, not the lifestyle.

It was all the same, wasn't it? She would want to leave, wouldn't she?

To be returned to a family who didn't want her? Who had openly disowned her? To be removed from one place of no hope or future to another.

Returning one lost daughter to the bosom of her not so interested family, not a bad attempt, Mr Kiernan. Would you like to come back next week and try for the star prize? Trying to find out how you can make her stop doing it again? The choice is yours.

'Fuck,' he murmured again.

Thursday. Two fucking days away.

He'd find out the truth then. He'd see the sister he'd imagined lost, possibly even dead.

Why then, he asked himself, did he still feel that crushing weight of weary anxiety and the other feeling he could not quite identify?

Was it fear?

Of what? Of what she'd become? Of how she would react to him?

It would be another two days before he found out.

152

Kiernan grabbed the magazine and, with a grunt of anger, hurled it across the room.

Forty-five

Seated in a window booth of Burger King in Coventry Street, Neville could see the hordes of people stream back and forth between Leicester Square and Piccadilly Circus. Many were pouring into the Trocadero across the street, pushing past a man with a billboard which proclaimed:

GOD IS COMING

As he turned Neville saw that the reverse side of the board carried the legend:

ARE YOU PREPARED TO MEET GOD?

Neville smiled to himself and glanced down at his cold cup of coffee.

He looked at his watch. 12.36 p.m.

He pulled the pony-tail from his neck, feeling the sweat there, then got to his feet and crossed to the counter, where two French tourists were trying to work out the difference between a pound coin and a ten-pence piece. They babbled to each other and then to the member of staff serving them, but he seemed unable to help. They finally pushed change towards him and he selected the right amount. The tourists nodded and retreated to a nearby table clutching their hamburgers and chips.

The smell of frying food was overpowering in the fast-food place. The hiss of hundreds of frozen french fries being dumped into hot fat competed with the steady crackle of the insectocutor.

'Coffee, please,' Neville said, digging in his pocket for change.

The assistant scuttled off to return a moment later.

As Neville paid, the assistant said, 'Enjoy your meal,' with practised ease. Neville glanced at him and smiled. He wandered back to his table and sat down, occasionally looking out into the street, scanning the hordes of faces that passed. Where the hell were they all going? None of them seemed to be moving with any purpose, some were pausing to take photos, others were gazing around aimlessly, some tourists were consulting maps.

They were late.

He'd give them until 12.45, then ring Caton who was back at their office in Brewer Street processing orders for the last two videos. The sooner they began shooting the newest effort the better. Stevie Collins' baby was running a temperature. Neville didn't know how much longer it would last. He didn't want the fucking kid to die before it had served its purpose. Besides, it would be a thousand quid down the drain if it did.

He took another sip of his coffee.

The hand that tapped his shoulder was large and powerful and he spun round in his seat.

Paul Thompson smiled down at him.

'How you doing, Don?' the younger man said, seating himself opposite Neville. He was in his early thirties, dressed in a faded black T-shirt with the arms cut off to reveal large biceps. The T-shirt, which hung loosely outside his jeans, bore the slogan:

PURE FUCKIN' ROCK

'Where's Mac?' Neville wanted to know.

'Over there,' Thompson told him, nodding towards the counter.

Neville looked round and saw a squat, thick-set man dressed in a shirt and jeans heading back towards the table carrying a bag full of food.

'You know Mac,' Thompson said, grinning. 'He likes his grub.'

Colin Macardle sat down next to Thompson. Pulling a hamburger from the paper bag, he took a bite and smiled at Neville.

'You're late,' he said.

'Fuck it,' Macardle said, pieces of half-chewed hamburger dropping from his mouth. He grinned even more broadly.

'Where's Eddie?' asked Thompson.

'He's got other business to attend to,' Neville said.

'So what business have *you* got for *us*?' Macardle asked, his heavy Glaswegian accent muffled by the handful of chips he was shoving into his mouth.

'One night's work,' said Neville.

'How much?' Thompson wanted to know.

'Two grand.'

'Each?' asked Macardle, stuffing more chips into his mouth.

'Fuck off,' Neville snorted. 'A grand each is a fucking fortune compared to what you usually get for your little jobs. What's the going rate now? Fifty quid to break someone's leg? A ton if he has to spend a week in hospital? This is a different league, Mac.'

'What have we got to do?' Thompson asked.

Macardle held up a hand.

'We haven't agreed yet,' he snapped.

'You got more urgent business to attend to then, have you?' Neville asked.

There was an uneasy silence between the three men. It was finally broken by Neville.

'Have you got shooters?' he asked.

'What the fuck is this, Don?' Thompson said.

155

'We need a job doing. I'm offering you a grand apiece to do it. What's the big deal?' He looked at the two men seated opposite. 'You either want it or you don't.'

'We'll do it,' Macardle said, shoving hamburger into his mouth. He chuckled. 'For a grand you must want someone hurt pretty bad. Do you want us to shoot the cunt?' He laughed.

Neville didn't speak.

'Money up front,' said Macardle.

'Half before, half when the job's done,' Neville told him.

'Would we fuck you over?' Macardle asked, sounding hurt.

'I'm not going to give you the chance, Mac,' Neville told him.

All three men laughed.

'When do you want the job done?' Thompson enquired.

'I'll give you all the details. Come to our office in Brewer Street. We'll sort out the money then, too.'

'Done,' said Macardle, smiling.

Neville nodded, reaching across to take a chip. He sat back in his seat, smiling.

Forty-six

There was building work in progress on the office block opposite. Joseph Finlay stood in shirt sleeves in his own office, watching as workmen moved hastily back and forth over the scaffolding with the assurance of monkeys on climbing frames. The men were sheathed in sweat from their exertions; Finlay was thankful for the air-conditioning that kept his own place cool. He watched as two workmen tipped barrowloads of rubble into a large chute, seeing it hurtle into a skip fifty or sixty feet below. Dust from the shattered concrete rose in the cloying air, motes of brick dust floating about like rusty cinders.

Apart from his own building, most of the other properties in Furnival Street, off High Holborn, were undergoing renovation or modernization of some description.

Finlay paced back and forth in front of the large window, lost in his own thoughts.

A polite cough from behind him reminded him where he was. He turned and looked at his secretary, who was sitting with her pad on her knee looking expectantly at him. She was drawing small circles on the corner of the pad with her pen while she waited. Finlay regarded her indifferently for a moment and she lowered her gaze.

She was a pretty girl in her early twenties who'd worked for Finlay since leaving school five years earlier, working her way up to her current position of personal assistant. She crossed and uncrossed her legs as she waited patiently for him to continue.

'Where did I get to?' he asked distractedly.

She read back what she had transcribed so far, stumbling once over her own shorthand.

Finlay considered the words for a moment then continued dictating.

'In view of the present situation,' he said, slowly and deliberately.

His secretary scribbled away in an effort to keep pace with him.

'. . . I would suggest that you seek legal advice before embarking on any such scheme . . .'

He moved back to the window.

So Nick Ryan was ill, was he?

The news had not caused him the grief it had evidently caused Kim. Upon her return from her ex-husband's office the previous evening she had been distraught when she'd told Finlay that Ryan was very ill. She hadn't been specific as to the ailment and Finlay hadn't asked. Probably something to do with drink, he'd surmised. Ryan drank like a bloody fish.

'. . . There are many pitfalls that can be avoided by undertaking . . .' He was struggling for the words he wanted. 'By following the . . .' Again he was struggling, annoyed with himself for not being able to think straight.

Christ, it was all Kim had spoken about since she'd returned from Ryan's office. His illness. How bad he looked. Finlay had done his best to show some interest initially but his mock concern had rapidly disappeared to be replaced by a smouldering resentment. She wasn't married to the bloody man any more.

'. . . The . . . er . . .'

'Guidelines?' his secretary offered.

'I know what I'm trying to say, Helen,' he snapped, rounding on her angrily. 'Or perhaps you'd rather write the letter for me. Perhaps you feel you're more capable. Is that it?'

'I'm sorry, Mr Finlay,' she said, her cheeks colouring.

'Just write what I tell you to write,' he snapped, turning back towards the window.

Something else bothered Finlay about this business with Ryan's illness, whatever the hell it was. Kim had said that Ryan might need her help, that he had no one else to turn to. Finlay didn't want her going back and forth to the private detective. He already suspected she thought more of her ex-husband than she admitted. If she began to pity him, that pity might turn into something more.

'. . . By following the guidelines described in my earlier letter, dated 23rd of this month, I feel that you will see the sense of considering this venture more carefully.' He coughed. 'New paragraph.'

Finlay had been relieved that Kelly didn't know of her father's illness. It was bad enough having Kim wandering around the house worrying about the bloody man without burdening Kelly with the knowledge, too.

What if he had called her today? What if she was with him now? Ryan could easily have called the house.

Helen Whiteside sat waiting for her boss to continue. She was tempted to tap her pen against her pad in an effort to shock him from his thoughts, but then she thought better of it. She crossed her legs, pulling down the hem of her skirt so it covered more of her thigh.

Finlay was pacing up and down now, his gaze fixed out of the window.

Helen Whiteside exhaled but not so deeply as to be heard.

What if Kim was with Ryan now?

'We'll finish this later,' Finlay snapped, inclined his head towards the office door. His secretary got to her feet.

'Do you want me to type up what you've dictated so far?' she asked.

'Forget it,' he rasped. 'We'll finish later, I just said that.'

She nodded and turned to go.

He sat down behind his desk and drummed on it with his fingers.

Kim had said that she was going out with Kelly, he remembered.

Perhaps they were both with Ryan.

He clenched his fists.

For interminable seconds he stared at the small console on his desk, his mind racing.

She might be at home. If she was, he could ask her if she'd spoken to Ryan that day.

He shot out a hand and flicked one of the switches in front of him.

'Helen, get my wife on the phone,' he snapped. 'Now.'

And then he thought, *Why am I wasting my time worrying about Kim? What am I going to do about Neville?*

Forty-seven

'Is something wrong, Mum?'

The words shocked Kim Finlay from her distracted gazing out of the car window. She looked across at her daughter and smiled.

'Sorry, I was miles away, wasn't I?' she said, gripping the wheel of the Peugeot.

'You've been miles away for most of the day,' Kelly reminded her as they waited for the stream of traffic to move. 'You haven't said much.'

'You should be grateful,' Kim joked, trying to sound happier than she actually was. 'You're usually complaining I talk too much.'

The traffic in Knightsbridge was heavy; the car could only creep along. Kim glanced around at the other drivers similarly trapped. Most had the windows of their vehicles rolled down, preferring the choking exhaust fumes to the cloying heat. There wasn't a breath of air but what there was felt as if it was being pumped straight from a furnace. Kim ran a hand through her hair and felt perspiration on her forehead.

Kelly toyed with the laces of her trainers, peering around her at the other cars and at the shoppers thronging the pavements.

'Were you thinking about Dad?' she said finally.

Kim looked round with concern.

'Who? Joe?' she asked.

'Joe's not my dad. Not my *real* dad,' Kelly reminded her.

'I wish you wouldn't talk like that, Kelly,' Kim said wearily.

'But it's true, he isn't.'

'He does his best for you. He tries.'

'I know that, but he still isn't my real dad, is he?'

Kim edged the car forward, trying to prevent a black Ferrari which was pulling out from a side turning nosing in front of her. The driver glared at her, as if he thought his vehicle entitled him to some kind of consideration. Kim smiled to herself when she saw that none of the cars following would let him out either.

'I heard the two of you arguing again the other day,' said Kelly. 'Was that about Dad, too?'

'You shouldn't have been listening,' Kim joked, but it didn't lighten the tension between them.

'Joe doesn't like Dad, does he?'

Kim didn't answer.

Should she mention Ryan's illness?

No, he had specially asked her not to.

Kim swallowed hard. And what was she supposed to do when he finally died? Make up some story? Kelly would have to know then. She wanted so badly to tell Kelly, if only to share the knowledge with someone else. It was a terrible burden, being forced to endure the certainty that her ex-husband was dying. Yet she could not bring herself to pass on the burden to her daughter, too. Why should they both suffer?

'When can I see Dad again?' Kelly wanted to know.

161

'That's up to him,' Kim told her. 'You know what he's like. He's very busy.'

'He always was. He always will be, I suppose.'

Not *always*, thought Kim.

Tell her now. She has a right to know.

She felt so bloody helpless caught in the middle. She was torn between her loyalty to her ex-husband and her concern for her daughter. She understood why he didn't want the girl to know of his illness, but he didn't appreciate how painful it was having to lie to her. He had no idea how much she hated lying to their daughter. There was no other way of looking at it. Kim would be forced to live a lie until Ryan was dead. She wondered if hiding the truth that way was really protecting Kelly, or merely making things worse when the time came to tell her about his death.

Questions. Decisions.

The car ahead braked quickly and Kim banged her hooter, gesticulating angrily at the driver, who sat there apparently unperturbed.

Kelly chuckled.

'What are you laughing at?' Kim asked, smiling.

'You,' Kelly told her. 'You don't usually get worked up when you're driving.' The idea of her mother becoming a demon driver seemed to have amused her.

Kim reached across and grabbed her waist, tickling her.

She looked at her daughter and felt as if she wanted to sweep her into her arms.

And tell her the truth?

The streams of traffic rolled slowly on.

It was past six in the evening by the time Kim finally swung the Peugeot into the driveway of the house. The journey from Central London had been a tortuous one and she could feel the beginnings of a headache gnawing at the base of her skull.

She and Kelly unloaded the shopping and carried it inside, Kim muttering to herself when she realized she'd left her car keys in the ignition. She wandered out to the car, taking deep breaths as she reached the driveway. In the stillness of the early evening she could hear the drone of a rotary mower as someone cut their lawn. A dog was barking; she heard children shouting. The noise carried on the humid air. She took the keys from the ignition and locked the car, then turned and headed back towards the house.

She didn't notice the battered blue Cavalier parked across the street.

Inside, the driver smiled and nudged his companion, who also looked across towards Kim and the house.

Colin Macardle nodded.

Forty-eight

The afternoon had dragged on interminably; Joseph Finlay had found it impossible to concentrate on anything. His already frayed temper had been ravaged further by his secretary's inability to reach his wife on the phone on three separate occasions earlier in the day. There had been no answer from the house.

Finlay vaguely recollected Kim mentioning her and Kelly going out shopping; she could have taken Kelly to see her sick father.

Bastard.

If Kelly knew of the illness it would only bring her

163

closer to Ryan.

Finlay sat tapping his pen against the blotter on his desk, one eye on the clock perched on the mantelpiece. There were photos of Kim and Kelly there, too, smiling out at him contentedly. He clenched his fists and rose, walking across to the window. The scaffolding was devoid of workers now. They'd left more than an hour ago. Finlay could see little sense in delaying at his office much longer himself. He pulled on his jacket and reached for his briefcase, anxious to be home, even more anxious to find out where Kim had been all day. He told himself that he would remain calm when he asked her, that he would believe what she told him. He promised himself he would not ask her whether or not she had seen Ryan that afternoon, but he knew the temptation would be strong.

He was about to leave when the phone rang.

Finlay muttered something under his breath then crossed to his desk and snatched up the receiver, watching the winking red light go out as he did.

'What is it, Helen?'

'There's a call for you, Mr Finlay. The gentleman says it's *very* important,' his secretary announced.

'Tell him to call back tomorrow,' Finlay snapped.

There was a moment's silence, then the secretary spoke again.

'He says he has to speak to you, Mr Finlay.'

'Who is it, for Christ's sake? he snapped irritably.

'His name is Neville. He said he's a business associate of yours.'

Finlay felt the breath catch in his throat. He swallowed with some difficulty.

'Put him on,' he said quietly and sat down behind his desk.

There was a crackle of static as the call was transferred.

'Hello,' Finlay said.

164

'Joe, how are you doing?' Neville asked conversationally.

'Cut the crap, Neville, what the hell do you want?'

'It's about our little discussion of the other night,' Neville told him. 'You know, you expressed some dissatisfaction about the videos.'

'Get to the point.'

'Well, I discussed it with my partner and we're both agreed on one thing.'

'Which is?'

'That you can take a fucking jump. We're not moving, Finlay.'

'I warned you . . .'

Neville cut him short.

'Don't threaten me, you cunt. Fuck your warnings. What are you going to do? Go to the police?' He chuckled.

'I told you what I'd do,' Finlay reminded him. 'I'll throw you out of the building. I'll call Charles Thornton now and tell him he can buy it. You're finished, Neville.'

'No, Finlay, not me. You think you can just walk away from this? You start throwing your fucking weight around and expect us to take it? Well, fuck you. I've had enough of your shit. We're going on, and we'll do it rent-free. How does no fucking percentage at all sound to you?'

'You're out of that building, Neville.'

'Try moving me. What are you going to do? Ask your friend Mr Thornton to get us out? Don't forget, he makes even more money out of our little home movies than *you* do. Do you think he's going to give that up?'

'He wants that building for his restaurant and he wants it badly. He'll make ten times the money from a restaurant than he would from flogging your video-tapes, so don't try and threaten me, Neville. I'll give you until tomorrow to get out. Then I'm having you thrown out.'

'Try it,' Neville said challengingly. 'You're not in a position to threaten or to bargain, Finlay.'

'We'll see,' he said and slammed the phone down.

Forty-nine

7.36 p.m.

Kim looked at the clock on the kitchen wall, wondering how much longer Joe was going to be. He was usually home by seven, although if he had meetings she was lucky to see him before nine on some evenings. Strange, though; he usually phoned if he was going to be late.

Across the table from her Kelly was picking disinterestedly at her food.

'If you don't want it then leave it,' said Kim, raising her eyebrows.

Kelly smiled.

'I think I ate too much in McDonalds this afternoon,' she confessed.

'How many hamburgers did you have? Five or six?' Kim said, smiling.

'Mum, I only had one. A Big Mac and large fries,' Kelly reminded her.

'Yes. And a milkshake *and* two apple pies and some chocolate cake when we stopped for a coffee this afternoon. No wonder you can't eat your dinner. When you get older you won't want to *look* at chocolate cake,

166

let alone eat it. You'll be too worried about your figure!'

'When I get older, Mum,' Kelly chuckled. 'What, as old as *you*?'

Kim raised a hand in mock anger, relieved to see her daughter laughing again. It was a marked contrast to the solemnity of their afternoon out, some of which, she realized, was due to her own preoccupation with Ryan's illness.

'You can't eat that,' said Kim, nodding towards the plate of half-eaten lasagne, 'but I bet you'll eat ice-cream if it's offered.'

Kelly grinned and nodded.

As Kim swung herself off the bench and headed across the large kitchen towards the fridge, Kelly also got to her feet and switched on the portable TV on the work-top opposite. She flicked through the channels until she found the one she wanted. There was a soap opera on. There always seemed to be a soap opera on somewhere, thought Kim, glancing round at the set.

'You know Joe doesn't like the TV on while we're eating,' said Kim, returning with a bowl of ice-cream and pushing it in front of her daughter.

'Joe's not here, though, is he?' said Kelly, disdainfully.

No, he's not.

Kim glanced up at the wall clock again.

It was strange he hadn't phoned.

She was in the process of dropping a scoop of ice-cream into her own bowl when she heard the doorbell ring.

'Turn that down, Kelly,' she said, scurrying across the kitchen towards the hall, wondering who it could be. Finlay, perhaps? He might have forgotten his keys.

She pulled the kitchen door shut behind her and wandered across to the front door, peering through the spy-hole before she opened it.

She could see no one standing there. Whoever was outside must be standing to one side of the door. Either that or it was kids mucking about.

She slid the chain off and opened the door.

The figure seemed to appear from nowhere. It loomed before her like a spectre.

Despite the heat of the night, the man was wearing a jacket. But it was not that which caused Kim to freeze. It was his appearance.

His face was distorted grotesquely.

The flesh looked dark grey, his nose was squashed and pulled towards his left cheek; his eyes, deep set, glistened like a dead fish's.

The shocking mask was simple but horribly effective.

'Step back inside the house,' a heavy Glaswegian voice told her. 'Move.'

She wanted to shout out, bellow a warning to Kelly, but the man reached inside his jacket and she understood why he wore the heavy garment.

The shotgun had been sawn off so that the entire fearsome weapon was less than twelve inches long, including the filed-down stock.

The barrels looked massive as Colin Macardle pointed them at her face. When he spoke, his voice was low.

'You scream and I'll blow your fucking head off.'

Fifty

He heard voices as he entered the hallway of the house but it took Joseph Finlay a moment or two to realize they were coming from the kitchen, and another second to ascertain that their source was the television. He frowned. It wasn't like Kim to watch TV in there. Also, Kelly's bedroom was directly above. The noise might wake her if she was sleeping.

Finlay glanced at his watch and saw that it was almost nine o'clock. The drive from London had been tortuous. A lorry had overturned and blocked one part of the Fulham Road, causing delays of up to an hour and a half. Like Finlay, other motorists had attempted to take alternate routes, with the result that all the arterial roads within a ten mile radius of the accident were also blocked. He felt the beginnings of a headache as he headed across the hall to the kitchen.

He pushed open the kitchen door and walked in.

The room was empty.

He crossed to the set and turned it off, then spun round and headed for the dining-room.

Empty.

He crossed to the sitting-room and peered in. They were probably both sitting in there, watching the larger TV; they might well have forgotten they'd left the portable on. They . . .

The sitting-room was empty, too.

Finlay muttered something under his breath. Kim

wouldn't have popped out for something at this late hour. All the local shops shut at six. Even the small supermarkets closed at eight. Besides, he'd noticed her car in the drive as he'd parked. Just to be thorough, he pushed open the door of the room opposite the sitting-room. It was about twelve feet square and contained a desk and chair, some filing cabinets, a fax machine and a phone. On the occasions he had to bring work home with him, Finlay used it as an office. He knew as he peered into the darkened room that there was no reason for Kim to be in there, but he wanted to check anyway.

He closed the door and began to climb the staircase, feeling uneasy.

The doors that faced him as he reached the landing were all closed. The house was silent. Boards creaked protestingly under his weight as he crossed to the door of Kelly's bedroom and opened it.

There was no sign of the girl.

Posters of pop stars stared blankly back at him from her walls.

Finlay swallowed hard, aware now that there was something very wrong.

As he reached the door to his bedroom he saw a dirty mark on the carpet, as if messy feet had trodden there.

His heart thudding hard, he pushed the door open.

Kim was lying on her back on the bed, her legs and arms firmly tied with what looked like the cord from a bathrobe. There was a flannel stuffed into her mouth, secured there by a towel that had been tied tightly around her face. Her face was tear-stained, her eyes red-rimmed and bulging. There was a nasty bruise above her right eye.

Finlay rushed across to her and pulled the gag from her mouth, helping her to release the cord round her ankles and wrists.

'Kelly,' she gasped, frantically. 'They took Kelly.'

'Who?' he said, grabbing her. 'Who took her?'

She tried to shake loose of his grip, tried to grab the phone on the bedside table, but Finlay gripped her arm.

'Get off me,' she hissed. 'We've got to call the police.'

Still he held her, gazing into her red-rimmed eyes.

'Who took her?' he snapped. 'Tell me what happened.'

'There isn't time,' Kim blurted. 'They might have killed her already. Let me use the phone.' She made another grab for it.

'Kim, calm down. You have to tell me what happened.'

'My daughter's been kidnapped. How much more do you need to know? Every second you waste they could kill her. Get out of my way.'

She pushed past him and snatched at the phone, but even as her hand closed over the receiver it suddenly rang.

Kim jumped back and it was Finlay who snatched up the phone.

'Hello,' he said.

Silence.

'Who's there?' he repeated.

'You've got a nice house,' the voice said. He recognized it immediately as Neville's. 'So we're told.'

Finlay could only grip the receiver helplessly, his knuckles whitening.

Kim looked on helplessly.

'You've got a nice daughter, too,' Neville continued. 'Pretty kid.' He chuckled. 'She'll be popular with the boys when she's a bit older. Or maybe she won't have to wait too much longer.'

'What do you want?' Finlay said, his voice a harsh croak.

'I want to do some business.'

'Just let me have my daughter back then we'll talk.'

'What am I? Fucking stupid? Now you listen to me,

171

Finlay. We've got the kid and we're keeping the kid until you agree to what we want. If I were you I wouldn't call in the police. I wouldn't even think about it. For a couple of reasons. First, if I even get a sniff that the Law know we've got your daughter you'll be collecting her in paper bags. Secondly, I think they might be interested to know of our little business partnership, don't you? It wouldn't look too good if the Law or anyone else found out about your involvement with us, would it? Whatever would your wife say?' Neville chuckled.

Kim moved closer, trying to hear what was being said. Finlay held up a hand to keep her back.

'What do you want me to do?' he said meekly.

'Nothing. We'll be in touch to talk about that business I mentioned.'

'How do I know you aren't bluffing? Kelly might be dead already.' He swallowed hard.

'Yeah, she might. You'll just have to trust me, won't you?' Neville told him.

'I want to speak to her. Now.'

'Don't make demands, Finlay. You're not in a position to do that.'

'Then there's no deal. Let me speak to her or I won't believe she's alive.'

'I don't know whether to admire your nerve or pity your stupidity,' Neville told him. There was a long silence then he spoke again. 'The kid's alive. Listen.'

Finlay heard voices, harsh voices.

Then:

'Help me, Mum.'

Kim heard the words too and tears began to flow freely down her face.

'Help me, please.'

Then the high pitched sound of Kelly's entreaties was replaced by Neville's harsh voice again.

'Satisfied?' he grunted.

'If you hurt her . . .' Finlay began but the sentence trailed off.

'You'll fucking *what*?' Neville snarled challengingly. 'Just do what you're told. Be at your office in the morning. I'll be in touch again but, like I said, Finlay. One sniff of a copper and the kid comes back in fucking pieces.'

Fifty-one

'We *can't* call the police, don't you understand?' Finlay snapped, turning away from Kim and pouring himself a brandy. 'If we do they'll kill her.'

'How do we know they won't kill her anyway?' Kim wanted to know.

Finlay ran a hand through his hair.

'We've got no choice,' he shouted.

Kim sat motionless on the sofa, her legs drawn up beneath her. She was clutching a handkerchief which was sodden from her tears. Now she shifted it nervously from one hand to the other, gazing blankly ahead of her.

'What if she's already dead?' she said quietly.

'I heard her voice,' Finlay reminded her. 'So did you. She's not dead. We've got to believe that they won't kill her.'

'And if we raise our hopes and they do?'

Her words hung in the air.

Finlay took a large swallow from the brandy balloon, feeling the liquid burn its way to his stomach.

Jesus, he felt so helpless.

Helpless and angry. His rage was directed both at himself for ever getting mixed up with a man like Neville but mainly at Neville himself.

What was the bastard playing at?

Kidnapping? It didn't seem like his game.

'The man who came here,' Finlay said. 'What did he look like?'

Kim shrugged.

'He was wearing a stocking mask,' she said. 'I didn't get a good look at the one in the car, either. What does it matter?'

'Was he tall, short, dark, fair?'

'I told you, Joe, I don't know.'

'You must have got a glance at him?'

'He was wearing a stocking over his head,' she said, exasperated. 'How many more times?'

Finlay downed what was left in his glass and poured himself another.

'Getting drunk isn't going to help Kelly, is it?' Kim said acidly.

'I'm not getting drunk,' he snapped. 'Besides, what do you expect me to do? I was told to wait, to let them call me tomorrow. That's just what I'm going to do.'

'They'll kill her, Joe, I *know* it,' Kim said, wiping her eyes.

'Not if we co-operate with them.'

'But we don't even know what they want.'

'That's why I have to speak to them tomorrow. To find out what they want.'

'It'll be money,' she said flatly. 'You're rich. Why else would they have taken her?'

Finlay paused for a moment but did not look at her. Perhaps he was afraid she would see something in his eyes.

Guilt?

He wondered if this was how the parents of the children killed in Neville and Caton's videos had felt when their youngsters first left home. Did they feel this sense of desolation? Of helplessness? Of anger? He suspected they did. And the fear. But Finlay knew only too well that he had more reason to be afraid. Whatever the outcome, whether Kelly was returned safely to them or killed (and that was one thing he *dared* not consider) then he risked exposure. His connections with Neville and Caton would be revealed. Then what? Financial ruin? Prison? He exhaled deeply and crossed to the sofa where he sat down beside Kim, sliding his arms around her.

She pulled him close to her, crying softly as she rested her head on his shoulder.

'What can we do?' she said, tears soaking into his shirt.

Finlay held her tight.

'Wait,' he said. 'All we can do is wait.'

Fifty-two

The parcel was about seven inches long and four inches wide, enclosed in brown paper and sellotape. Finlay's name was written on it in black marker pen. Just his name and office address.

'It arrived a couple of minutes ago, Mr Finlay,' his secretary told him, handing over the small package.

He snatched it from her and glanced up at her.

'How did it arrive?' he wanted to know. 'Post? Courier?'

'A man came into the reception and left it. I went and fetched it.'

'You didn't get a look at him?'

She looked puzzled.

'No, he'd already gone,' she told him.

Finlay nodded.

'You can go,' he said and began fumbling on his desk for the letter opener, using the sharp edge to cut through the sellotape wound thickly around the parcel. Despite the air-conditioning in the office, he felt beads of perspiration form on his forehead as he struggled with the parcel, finally pulling the wrapping free, tossing it to one side in the rubbish bin.

He sat staring blankly at the video cassette for a moment, turning it over in his hands.

It was unmarked. No labels. Nothing.

Then he saw a small corner of paper sticking out from inside one of the spools. He pulled it out and found that it was, in fact, a sheet of paper about six inches square, folded so many times hardly a centimetre of it was uncreased. He unfolded it and spread it out on his desk, scanning the words written there, also in marker pen:

ONE MILLION POUNDS OTHERWISE THE KID IS DEAD. WAIT FOR US TO CONTACT YOU. REMEMBER NO POLICE

Finlay swallowed hard and re-read the note, then turned his attention to the video cassette, turning it in his hands as if unsure what to do with it. He had a VCR rigged up in one corner of the office, connected to a small, fourteen-inch TV. He got to his feet, walked across the office and turned both machines on, sliding the video into place. He picked up the remote control and wandered back to his desk. Perching on one corner of it, he jabbed the 'Play' button.

There was hissing on the soundtrack and a blank screen. He stabbed the 'Fast Forward' until he had some semblance of picture, then pressed 'Play' again. The picture began to unfold before his eyes.

A bare floor, but clean. Bare walls, too. In the room there was only one piece of furniture. On the bed, held down by several leather straps, a piece of masking tape across her mouth, lay Kelly. She was naked.

'Oh God,' whispered Finlay as he watched two men approach her, one from either side. 'Oh, my God. No.'

The men were also naked, sporting large erections. One was masturbating.

To his horror Finlay saw that the other man was holding a baby.

'Oh, Jesus,' he murmured, transfixed by the screen.

The baby couldn't be more than six weeks old, he guessed.

But his eyes were riveted to the body of Kelly as she strained helplessly against the straps, her head thrashing from side to side as the man who was masturbating – both he and his companion wore black leather hoods – pushed his penis close to her face.

Finlay wanted to turn the tape off, to wrench it from the machine and hurl it away. Smash it into a thousand pieces. But he sat mesmerized, a mouse watching a snake.

He saw the other man put the baby on the bed beside

Kelly. Then he, too, began rubbing his penis.

As the two men ejaculated, almost simultaneously, Finlay finally crushed the 'Stop' button, hurling the remote control across the office. He spun round, feeling the vomit clawing its way up from his stomach. By a monumental effort of will he managed to retain it. He stood against the desk, his back to the blank screen, his breath coming in gasps. He closed his eyes but the images he'd just witnessed on the screen seemed to flash before him. He put a hand to his heavy stomach and rubbed gently, wishing that the feelings would subside but unable to force the images from his brain. He shook his head, staggered back to the other side of his desk and sat down heavily. The ransom note stared up at him.

NO POLICE

His head was spinning. His stomach churned.

He sat gaping at the blank screen of the television set for what seemed like an eternity, unable or unwilling to move. Then, finally, he got to his feet and walked slowly across the room to retrieve the remote.

Once safely back behind his desk he pressed the 'Play' button again, watching with the same mesmerized horror. But this time he could not bear to watch the action at normal speed. He kept the 'Fast Forward' button depressed, his hand gripping the control so tightly he threatened to snap it in two.

What he saw before him, flying past at four times the normal speed, was beyond anything he could have imagined in his most depraved and warped nightmares.

Kelly untied.

Kelly and the baby.

Kelly held by one of the men while the other . . .

He lowered his gaze momentarily.

Kelly.

Kelly.

He switched it off, jabbed 'Re-wind' and sat back in his

seat, sweat sheathing his entire body. Finally he dropped the remote, and looked at the note again.

NO POLICE

He put both hands to his face and felt the moisture there. His head still spun. His stomach still somersaulted.

ONE MILLION POUNDS

He allowed his head to flop back on his shoulders, his eyes turned heavenward. For long moments he stayed immobile then he leant forward, looking first at the TV screen then at the phone.

'Kelly,' he whispered.

NO POLICE

He fumbled in one of his desk drawers and pulled out his filofax, flipping through it until he found a number.

Picking up the receiver he glanced at the blank screen, his mind filled with the images he'd seen.

As he dialled he noticed his hand was shaking.

Part Two

'Never trust anyone as far as you can spit and
even then, be careful.'

Anon

'People always turn away, from the eyes of a
stranger.
Afraid to know, what lies behind the stare.'

Queensryche

Fifty-three

'Well, well, well. I never thought I'd see the day said Ryan, opening the door. He smiled thinly and stepped aside, ushering Joseph Finlay inside, noticing the sweat on his face and arms. The heat of the day had contributed to his condition but walking up five flights of stairs certainly hadn't helped, either.

Finlay wandered into the office, looking round at the desk, the filing cabinets, the leather chairs and sofa and the books that lined one wall. There was a VCR hooked up to a television in one corner of the room.

'Do you want a drink?' Ryan asked, crossing to the small kitchenette. 'Tea, coffee? Something stronger?'

'I'll have a brandy if you've got one,' Finlay said, sitting down opposite Ryan's desk.

The private detective raised an eyebrow, nodded and disappeared into the other room, emerging a moment later with a glass. He blew the dust off it, set it down on the desk in front of Finlay and poured him a large measure of Courvoisier. Then he sat down behind the desk and gazed across at the property developer.

Finlay saw two bottles of pills on his desk. As he watched, Ryan took two, swallowing them with a mouthful of water. He ran his index finger around the rim of his glass, glancing at Finlay.

'Kim told me you were ill,' Finlay said, sipping his brandy.

Ryan nodded.

That was fair enough. Terminal cancer was about as ill as you could get.

'She didn't say what it was. Nothing serious, I hope,' Finlay continued.

'Let's cut the shit, Finlay,' Ryan said flatly. 'You didn't come here to check up on my health. What do you want? You didn't say on the phone. Only that you needed to see me.' He raised his eyebrows, quizzically. '*Needed*?'

'In a professional capacity,' Finlay told him.

'Don't tell me; you think Kim's having an affair and you want me to tail her, right?' Ryan said, smiling.

'This is serious, Ryan,' snapped Finlay, reaching for his jacket. He pulled the ransom note from his inside pocket and the video from another.

Ryan watched, bemused, as the other man pushed the two items across the desk. He opened out the note and scanned it, his brow furrowing.

'What the fuck is this?' he muttered.

'It's Kelly. She was taken from the house last night.' His voice cracked.

'What do you mean, "taken"?' Ryan said through clenched teeth.

'Kidnapped. Do I have to spell it out?'

'What about Kim?'

'She's okay. They didn't hurt her.'

'Jesus Christ,' snarled Ryan. 'What the fuck have you done about this? Do the police know?'

'The kidnappers said that if any police were involved, they'd kill Kelly.'

'When did you speak to them?'

'Last night.'

'Where was she snatched from?'

'The house. God knows where they've taken her.' Finlay said.

Maybe the house in Cavendish Square?

It was a thought he dared not voice.

Ryan pressed both hands together in front of his face in an attitude of prayer.

'They sent this,' said Finlay, prodding the video tape. 'It arrived at my office this afternoon.'

Ryan picked the tape up and looked at Finlay questioningly.

'Look at it,' he urged. 'I *can't*. Not again.'

Ryan got to his feet and crossed to the VCR, switching both it and the television on. He pressed the 'Play' button and watched as the images sped by.

Finlay lowered his head, unable to look at the screen.

Ryan watched transfixed, his expression indifferent at first, but the knot of muscles at the side of his jaw were pulsing angrily. As the video continued he dropped to his knees before the screen, as if worshipping at an electronic shrine. His eyes never left the images, the outlines of the figures reflected in the glazed mirrors of his eyes. He felt tears forming. Anger building. Anger unlike anything he'd ever known before.

He finally hit the 'Stop' button and sat back on his haunches, his breath coming in short gasps.

'Does Kim know about this?' he asked quietly, his head bowed.

'No,' Finlay informed him. 'Only about the ransom note. I didn't want her to see that,' he gestured towards the tape. 'It would destroy her.'

Ryan took the tape from the machine, gripping it in his fist so tightly he threatened to shatter it.

'Dirty fucking scum,' he hissed, his body quivering. He closed his eyes tightly, as if to wipe away the images he'd just seen, but they stayed as clear as if they'd been burned onto his retina. He slammed the tape down onto his desk so hard his glass of water spilled.

Finlay looked at him.

'Will you help me?' he said.

'What do you mean?'

'I want you to find Kelly. Find her, Ryan. Help her.'

'This ransom,' he prodded the note. 'They didn't say when they wanted the money?'

Finlay shook his head.

'They said they'd be in touch. It says that in the note.'

'I know what it says in the fucking note,' snarled Ryan. 'I can read.' He began pacing the office floor slowly.

Finlay sipped his brandy.

'Do you think they'll kill her?' he asked quietly.

'Without a doubt, if you don't pay up when they tell you. Can you get hold of that sort of money if it comes to the crunch?' Ryan wanted to know.

'It won't be easy, but I think so. Hopefully you'll have found them by then.'

'If I find them.'

'What the hell do you mean? She's *your* daughter, Ryan. Do you want them to kill her?' Finlay snapped.

Ryan spun round, glaring at Finlay.

'Yeah, you're right, she's *my* daughter.' There was a heavy silence between the two men, finally broken when Ryan spoke again. 'Leave the tape with me. Let me think about it.'

'What is there to think about?' Finlay snapped. 'Your daughter is in danger. The longer you spend thinking, the more danger you put her in.'

'Get out,' Ryan said, opening the office door. 'I'll call you.'

Finlay hesitated a moment then got to his feet and headed for the door, pausing there. They locked stares for long seconds, then he walked out. Ryan pushed the door shut behind him. He turned and headed back towards his desk, snatching up the video in the process.

He jammed the tape into the machine and stepped back.

Why the hell would anyone want to kidnap his daughter? He exhaled deeply, feeling a twinge of pain in his chest.

He looked down at the ransom note.

Then back at the VCR.

Reluctantly, he pressed the 'Play' button.

Fifty-four

He couldn't remember the last time he'd cried.

Even when he'd been told that he had just six months to live, he hadn't felt the tears of self-pity and fear he had expected. Only a feeling of empty desolation.

But now, as he sat in his darkened office, eyes fixed to the TV screen, Nick Ryan felt tears running down his cheeks.

He took a hefty swig of the vodka he'd poured himself, swallowing a couple of pain-killers, too, when the discomfort began to mount. He drew in several deep breaths and he felt pain. The pain seemed inconsequential, unworthy of consideration compared to what he was watching on the screen.

The pain his daughter was being forced to endure before his very eyes. That pain and humiliation repeated every time he rewound the tape and watched it again, now through a haze of tears.

Every time he looked as closely as he could at the room, searching for any clue as to its whereabouts, anything that might enable him to recognize it or its occupants, but both of the bastards wore black masks. One had tattoos. A dagger on his right shoulder. A snake on his left.

The other had red hair, some of it visible beneath the mask.

As Ryan watched them, his gaze was drawn hypnotically to the baby lying beside his daughter. He would look at the baby and then at his daughter's face contorted in fear and pain. Ryan clenched his fists, squeezing one so tightly around his glass it seemed it might break.

He watched as one of the men ejaculated onto his daughter's face.

Fucking bastard.

The man with the tattoos lifted the baby and moved it closer to Kelly's face, rubbing its tiny body over her face, sliding it through the semen.

Ryan squeezed the glass more tightly.

Tears flooded down his face.

He saw Kelly writhing helplessly on the bed.

Let her go.

Saw the other red-headed man wipe his penis across her stomach.

His hand crunched the glass with ease.

It smashed in his grip, lumps of the crystal slicing into the palm of his hand, gouging into the flesh. Blood burst from the ragged cuts, spurting onto the desk. Ryan hardly felt it. He hurled the broken glass away. Looking down at his injured hand, he noticed a large shard protruding from the base of his thumb. He pulled it free and tossed it aside contemptuously, his eyes turning back to the screen.

Back to the two men. To the baby.

To his daughter.

He got to his feet and switched off the VCR, then

snatched up the phone, his injured hand hanging at his side. He jammed the receiver between his ear and his shoulder and jabbed out digits.

It rang only twice before being picked up.

He recognized the voice immediately.

'Finlay,' he said sharply, blood dripping steadily from his gashed palm. 'I'll find Kelly.'

'Good,' said Finlay.

'And now I want to speak to Kim,' Ryan said flatly.

There was a moment's silence at the other end.

'Did you hear me?' Ryan said, more forcefully.

Another moment and she was there.

'Nick, please find her,' Kim blurted, her voice cracking.

'I'll find her,' he said, 'And the fuckers who took her. I swear it.'

'Just be careful. Please,' she urged. 'There's no telling what they might do. Not just to Kelly, to you as well. Please be careful.'

'They won't hurt her, Kim,' he said with a certain amount of assurance.

There was a long silence, finally broken by Ryan.

'I love you, Kim,' he said softly.

'I know,' she said.

Then she was gone.

Ryan crossed to the cabinet in the corner and unlocked it. Ignoring the pain from his cut hand he took both the guns from the container and carried them back to his desk, laying them side by side. The 9mm Automatic and the .357.

Ryan knew the men he was going up against were dangerous.

He was banking on it.

But he had nothing to fear from them. What could they do to him? Shoot him?

He hoped so.

Better a death like that than a long lingering death by cancer.

Jesus, he was almost looking forward to catching up with them. And when he did he'd make the fuckers pay. He would make them feel pain unlike anything they could have imagined. But he had to save his daughter first. And, to do that, he had to find her.

Fifty-five

It was the seventh shop that morning; they had begun to take on a weary familiarity after number four. By the time Ryan walked into Lovecave on Beak Street, he felt he was suffering from déja vu.

All the shops seemed to be decorated in the same putrid pastel colours: blue, pink or yellow. All of them seemed to carry the same kind of magazine and video. He was even convinced he'd seen the same customers in two or three of them.

Soho was filled with shops like these, turds floating in the sea of filth this part of London had become. But what the hell, everyone had to earn a living somehow. And there was certainly a good living to be made out of pornography. Most of the strip clubs had shops attached to them; Ryan had already been into one. But with the time not quite approaching eleven in the morning, most of the clip-joint book shops weren't even open yet. Their staff and their customers lived a kind of nocturnal existence, only emerging during the hours of darkness to ply their trade within the confines of darkened rooms. Men frequenting the establishments also seemed more at home in the absence of daylight.

Ryan had left his office at about 9.15 am. and begun his trek walking round the area close by his own place. Up Greek Street to Soho Square, across to Dean Street and then down as far as St Anne's Court, before moving over to Wardour Street.

Throughout his journey he'd ventured into selected bookshops and video sellers, browsing through their stacks of printed material but always claiming he couldn't find what he sought. A quick word with the assistant and he'd be shown through into a back room where 'harder' material was available. In one shop in Wardour Street, when he'd mentioned his interest in videos featuring children, he'd been practically thrown out. The Manager hurled a magazine at him as he left. Ryan had noticed that it bore a photo of a pregnant woman, her breasts oozing milk, being fondled by two men. A strange kind of weapon with which to express outrage, Ryan had thought, cries of 'sick fucker' ringing in his ears.

Two other shops, Adult Delight in Dean Street and Paradise Showroom in Greek Street, had been more helpful.

Ryan had shown them the video, surprised when they had offered imported gear which was as strong. He'd asked to see it. He'd been told that it was a shop, not a fucking preview theatre, but they said that the youngsters involved were no more than five years old, sometimes younger. Imported from Holland, it was reckoned to be the strongest stuff available. Ryan had said he'd think about it and made his exit.

Now, as he walked into Lovecave, he looked around, pushing the plastic streamers that passed for a door out of his way.

The place was large, the walls lined with shelves.

Every one was piled high with magazines, most of which were in cellophane. There were several spinners in the middle of the shop which held a selection of paperbacks, also wrapped in cellophane, and more shelves accommodated some larger format, thicker books or manuals. They, too, were sealed. Not much fun for the casual browser in here, thought Ryan, glancing around.

The one member of staff he could see on duty was seated at the far end of the shop by a till on a raised platform that resembled a pulpit. The man was in his mid-thirties, his hair long and curly. He wore a T-shirt with the sleeves cut out to reveal powerful arms. He paid Ryan only fleeting attention, more concerned, it appeared, with reading his newspaper and dipping biscuits into his steaming mug of tea.

It was warm inside the shop, the only air-conditioning being in the form of a noisy fan droning loudly by the door. Ryan glanced at the two other customers in the shop, middle-aged men peering avidly at magazines which were not sealed up. Neither of them looked at him as he sidled up alongside, casting appraising eyes over the magazines on display.

The floor was bare lino, badly in need of a clean. The whole place smelled of body odour but Ryan couldn't be sure if it was the building or the customers. Ryan moved towards the assistant, who looked up only briefly from his paper, dipping another biscuit into his tea, cursing when it broke and flopped into the steaming fluid. He set about fishing it out with a spoon.

To the rear of the shop a red neon arrow pointed downwards. The tip of the arrow touched a sign announcing:

VIDEOS DOWNSTAIRS

Ryan pushed his way through another beaded curtain and almost tripped on the dimly lit stairway. He recovered his balance and descended the flight into the basement.

The lighting here was more subdued, not so much for the comfort of patrons, he thought, as to hide the profusion of filthy marks covering the threadbare carpet. There was the familiar musky smell of damp and body odour.

A radio was blaring from one corner of the room. It sounded like Madonna. Ryan looked quickly around at the endless rows of boxes on display. There were many imported films.

MEGA TITS caught Ryan's eye. It was on the shelf next to BLACK SHAVERS and LIEBESSPIELE (Love Games). Ryan was grateful for the translation. He passed by LUSTFUL POSITIONS and NEW PUSSY and headed slowly towards the assistant who was checking what looked like an invoice, leaning over a glass counter which badly needed cleaning.

The private detective studied the man; he was in his early thirties, dressed in jeans and T-shirt. His hair was long, his face burdened by a heavy forehead which made it look as if he wore a perpetual frown. He looked up as he saw Ryan standing there.

'Can I help you, mate?' he said, smiling.

'I'm looking for something,' Ryan told him. 'You don't seem to have it.'

The assistant looked surprised.

'Like what?' he wanted to know.

'You got any stuff with kids in?' Ryan asked.

The assistant eyed him suspiciously, running appraising eyes over the private detective.

'What sort of stuff?'

'I just said, with kids in. Young kids. Twelve, maybe younger.'

'Have you had stuff from us before?'

'No, but I wondered if you had anything like this.'

Ryan took the video cassette from his carrier bag and passed it across the counter.

The other man looked first at the tape, then at Ryan.

'If you're with the old Bill . . .'

Ryan cut him short.

'Do I look like a fucking copper?' he said challengingly.

'Just because you haven't got a tit on your head doesn't mean you ain't filth,' the assistant told him.

'Have a look at it,' Ryan told him, pushing the cassette towards him again. 'I want some stuff like this.'

There was a TV and video recorder on the end of the counter, the lights on the electronic clock flashing repeatedly. The assistant took the tape and inserted it, pressing the appropriate buttons.

Ryan gritted his teeth as the all too familiar pictures came into view. He lowered his gaze.

'Fuck me,' murmured the assistant. 'This is good stuff. Where did you get hold of it?'

'A mate gave it to me,' he lied.

'Good picture quality, too. Do you know where *he* got it?'

'I wondered if he might have got it here,' Ryan ventured.

The assistant shook his head, his eyes never leaving the screen.

'We get pretty wild stuff, but not usually like this. I've got stuff out the back with kids as young as four or five. Was it that kind of thing you were after?' He stroked his chin thoughtfully. 'The girl in this must be about ten or eleven.'

Ryan clenched his fists by his sides.

'Not very often you see babies, though. Your mate must have paid a fortune for it. Something like this would usually set you back a ton, at least. We get a fair amount from Germany and Holland, but this isn't imported.' He nodded towards the screen.

'How can you tell?' Ryan asked.

'The picture quality's too good. It's very sharp. Most of the imported stuff is shot on 8mm and then transferred to video; that's why the pictures lose their quality. Especially by the time they've run a couple of hundred copies off. This one looks like it was shot direct onto video.'

'Have you ever seen stuff like this before?' Ryan asked. 'That wasn't imported?'

'Only a couple of times. There's a geezer in Finsbury who does a lot of kids fuck movies. We call them Jellybaby movies.' He chuckled. 'He's about the only bloke I know who specializes just in using kids.'

'Do you reckon he'd deal direct with me?' Ryan asked, his heart thumping against his ribs.

'I don't see why not. He might check you out first, make sure you're kosher, make sure you're not with the fucking vice-squad or something, but it's worth a try. Do you want his address?'

'Thanks,' Ryan said, nodding.

The assistant scribbled something down on a piece of paper and handed it to the private detective. He took it and read it aloud.

'Raymond Howells. 35A Margery Street, Finsbury.'

'It's off King's Cross Road, almost opposite Mount Pleasant Post Office,' the assistant added helpfully.

Ryan nodded.

'Can I have my film back?' he said, motioning towards the video.

The assistant ejected the tape and handed it to him.

Ryan took it, turned and headed for the stairs, the piece of paper tucked into his pocket.

As he reached the top of the stairs he glanced back at the assistant, who was watching him. He waited until Ryan was out of sight before reaching for the phone.

Fifty-six

The pavement felt warm beneath the soles of his trainers. Vince Kiernan ran a hand across his forehead, wiping the sweat away. He noticed his hand was shaking slightly. Why, when he was so close to the end of his quest, did he feel so deflated? With any luck, in a few moments he would see his sister for the first time in five months. He should feel elated. All he did feel was a gnawing worry.

What if she wasn't here?

What if she wouldn't go with him?

Kiernan tried to force the doubts from his mind.

He checked his watch.

3.56 p.m.

The appointment was at four. So he was early; what did it matter?

It had taken him a while to find the place. The train journey from Hammersmith itself had seemed to take an eternity. Then he found himself walking through areas which had, over the past few weeks, become all too familiar to him. Yet he still had trouble finding the house. The girl on the phone two days earlier . . . *Jo?* . . . had given him this address; even now, looking up at the red-bricked building, Kiernan felt the sense of desolation building even more strongly. What if she'd given him a false address?

Why should she? She didn't know who he was or what he wanted. The girl who'd answered the phone had assumed he was just another punter.

Stop worrying about it and get on with it.

A little further down the street there were a few kids kicking a football around and yelling loudly, kicking it back and forth across the road, ignoring the cars which periodically passed. If any drivers pressed their hooters they were met by a stream of abuse. One car slowed down, the driver gesticulating angrily at the children as the ball bounced off his bonnet. They moved away from the car shouting, one of them spitting on the back of the car as it pulled away.

Kiernan looked up at the house and saw that two of the dirty windows were boarded up. Elsewhere curtains were drawn, to obscure the view, or the glass was simply so filthy it appeared opaque. The young Irishman peered at the ground floor windows, trying to catch signs of movement within, but there appeared to be none. Once more, the idea that he'd been given a false address surfaced in his mind and refused to budge.

A set of rusted iron railings guarded a narrow flight of stone steps that led down to a basement flat.

Kiernan pushed the gate open, hearing it creak protestingly, and descended, peering at the number by the door. He checked it against the address he'd been given two days earlier.

His hand quivering slightly, Vince Kiernan pressed the buzzer of 35A Margery Street.

Fifty-seven

Three times he pressed the buzzer.

Each time no one answered.

He swallowed hard, his worst fears growing.

What if she wasn't here?

What if there was no one here?

He cupped one hand over his eyes and pressed his face to the window, trying to see inside.

The dirty glass and the gloom beyond made it impossible. He pressed the buzzer of 35A again, coughing as the stench of rotting food assailed his nostrils. Two dustbins were crammed into the small space between the bottom of the stone steps and the front door; one of them overflowed with rubbish rotting in the heat. Kiernan wrinkled his nose. From down the street he could hear the kids still kicking their ball about, the noise interrupted every now and then by the banging of a hooter. He gave up on the buzzer and banged hard on the door.

Still no answer.

Kiernan kicked at it angrily, sweat soaking into his shirt as the sun beat down.

'Shit,' he hissed, his initial anger giving way as the door opened a fraction, swinging back on hinges that hadn't tasted oil for years.

A damp, fusty smell wafted out to join the rancid odour of decaying food but Kiernan ignored it, nosing inside the open door a foot or two, peering through the gloom. He blinked hard as he stepped inside, his eyes slowly becoming accustomed to the dingy hallway.

There were three doors leading off it. The floor was covered by a threadbare carpet; the walls were bare, but for some cracked and peeling yellow paint. The three doors were in a similar state of disrepair.

It was cooler inside. Kiernan was grateful for that, at least. He wiped his face with his handkerchief and approached the first door.

It swung open as he pushed it and he looked through into a small bedroom. He stepped inside, again struck by the smell of damp; dark mould crept up two walls. He half expected to see mushrooms growing on the skirting boards, themselves cracked. The bed had been made up. The sheets were dirty; the only light in the room was provided by a bare bulb which hung from the centre of the ceiling. He was surprised, when he flicked the switch, to find that it worked.

Besides the bed there was only a dressing table and a small wardrobe in the room. The mirror had been removed from the dressing table and the doors of the wardrobe hung open. The ashtray on the corner of the dressing table was full of dog ends. There was lipstick on one or two. The remains of a spliff had been stubbed out. The place didn't seem quite as derelict as it had first appeared. It had been inhabited recently, he guessed. Probably squatters, the Irishman told himself.

Kiernan moved back into the hallway, the conviction growing in him that he had been cheated. Jo wasn't here. Neither Jo nor anyone else.

He pushed the next door more forcefully and it swung back, cracking against the wall behind.

This second room was even smaller, cramped and diminished by the absence of light. It was a fifteen by fifteen box, the walls dull and grey in the gloom. Kiernan flicked at the light switch, but this time there was no brightness. The bulb had been removed.

He leant against the wall, feeling the perspiration soaking into his shirt. The young Irishman closed his eyes and exhaled wearily, gripped by a combination of crushing disappointment and anger.

Where the fuck was Jo?

He had the right address. This was the one she'd given him.

What the fucking hell was going on?

He was still wondering when the front door buzzer sounded.

Fifty-eight

When the buzzer was pressed a second time, Kiernan shook himself and scurried back into the first room he'd entered.

He slipped inside and pressed up against the wall behind the door, waiting.

The buzzer was pressed again. Whoever was outside this time kept their finger on the button. The strident sound lanced through Kiernan's ears and he gritted his teeth, waiting for the noise to die away. It did so abruptly as the buzzer was released. He heard the front door creak as it was opened and then tentative footsteps on the hall floor.

Moving closer.

Perhaps he'd been wrong; perhaps the place wasn't uninhabited.

Maybe it was Jo.

His heart began to race faster.

The footsteps came closer. Although he knew he was hidden from view behind the door, he pressed himself ever more tightly to the wall, as if to melt into the damp brickwork.

The footsteps hesitated at the threshold.

He could hear soft breathing in the heavy, cloying silence.

It was all Kiernan could do to slow his own breathing to make it even.

The door was pushed a fraction and the figure moved inside.

He frowned as he saw her.

Saw the skinny frame, the long, bleached hair.

Surely this couldn't be . . .

'Jo,' he said, taking a step forward.

The girl spun round, her eyes wide with surprise. She stepped back as she saw him, her mouth dropping open. She almost fell over a piece of rucked-up carpet, teetering on her stilettos.

'Who the fuck are you?' asked Stevie Collins, her eyes wide but filled with suspicion.

Kiernan frowned.

'I could ask you the same thing,' he said. 'What are you doing here?'

'I'm looking for someone.'

'Who?'

He took a step closer and she moved further from him apprehensively. He was a powerfully built man, his hair and eyes wild, his face unshaven.

'Who are you looking for?' he repeated.

'Are you a copper?' There was a note of contempt in her voice.

'I might be,' he told her. 'What difference would it make to you if I was?'

She raised one arm to brush hair from her face and Kiernan saw the dark marks and bruising in the crook of her right elbow. The track marks.

'Fucking junkie,' he said dismissively.

They locked stares for a moment.

'So,' she continued, '*are* you a copper or not?'

Kiernan shook his head.

'You looking for Ray?' she asked. 'I haven't seen you here before.'

'Who's Ray?'

'The guy who lives here. Or *lived* here.'

'Who else lived here?' he asked, fumbling in his pocket for something.

'Tell me who you are first,' she demanded.

'My name's Kiernan. Vince Kiernan.'

'You're Irish.'

'You're quick,' he added sarcastically.

'Fuck off.'

'Maybe I will. But not with you. Now tell me what you're doing here. This place looks derelict. It's empty.'

'It wasn't until a couple of days ago.'

'What happened?'

'The police raided a house near here. They do that every now and then, just to prove they're making an effort.' There was scorn in her voice. 'Ray thought it was safer to move his operation.'

'Move it to where?'

'How the hell do I know? If I knew where he was I wouldn't have come here looking for him, would I?'

'Who is this Ray you keep talking about? What's his full name?'

'Ray Howells. He's a friend of mine.'

Kiernan shook his head and smiled thinly.

'What is he? Your supplier or your pimp?' he said acidly.

'Why should I tell you?'

Kiernan stepped towards her quickly, seizing her left arm in a vice-like grip, pulling her close towards him.

She could see the anger in his eyes, could hear it in his voice.

'Because if you don't tell me I'm going to break your fucking arms,' he rasped, gripping her other arm too, pulling them out straight to reveal more puncture marks in the other limb. The veins looked black beneath her pale skin, hiding there like limp worms.

'Get off me,' she squealed.

'You tell me who Ray Howells is. Now.'

'I did tell you, you Irish prick. He's a friend of mine.' She struggled to pull loose from his grip but Kiernan kept hold of her. He suddenly pushed her away, advancing on her as she fell to the floor in a corner.

'Stay away from me,' she shouted.

'Was *she* a friend of yours too?' Kiernan snapped, pushing Jo's bus pass towards Stevie, allowing her to see the picture of his sister. 'Have you ever seen this girl?'

Stevie glanced at the picture, then up at Kiernan.

'Look at it,' he snapped.

She did.

'I've seen her,' she said more quietly. 'She used to live here.'

'Do you know her name?'

'I can't remember, I . . .'

He cut her short.

'Try,' he urged angrily.

'Look, I said I know her, right? I just can't remember at the moment. She lived here with Ray and a couple of other girls. I stayed here, too, for a while. I knew her quite well.'

'If you're fucking me around, I'll break your neck,' he hissed.

'I'm telling you the truth, you bastard,' she snapped. 'Her name was Jo.' She stabbed an index finger at the picture; the fingernail was bitten down to the quick. 'Jo.

That's right, isn't it?'

Kiernan swallowed hard.

'Isn't it?' Stevie demanded.

He nodded slowly and stepped back.

'Why is she so fucking important to you, anyway?' Stevie hauled herself to her feet.

Kiernan looked at the photo in the bus pass. The smiling seventeen-year-old. When he spoke again his voice was a hoarse whisper.

'She's my sister.'

The long silence was finally broken by Kiernan.

'How long since you saw her last?' he asked.

Stevie shrugged.

'Like I said, up until a day or two ago she was living here with Ray and a couple of other girls.' She took the bus pass from him and looked more carefully at the photo. 'Yeah, I know Jo. We used to have a lot of the same punters.'

'Was she working for Howells?'

'Both of us were. Us and Christ knows how many more. Not just girls, either. He had guys in his family, too.' She sighed. 'I wish I knew where he was. He's got some stuff for me and I paid him up front.'

'Could Jo be with him?'

'It's possible.'

'Where *might* he have gone?'

'There's a dozen places around London he could be. He'll turn up eventually, when the heat's off. Like I said, the police pull a little stunt every now and then just so people don't start moaning that they never do anything. Every thing'll be back to normal in a day or two. Your sister might turn up then.'

'How well did you know her?'

'We were good mates. I liked her.'

'Did she touch the same shit as you? Drugs, I mean?' he said irritably.

'*Everybody* uses it,' she told him flatly. 'If it's not heroin it's coke or crack. It's the only way to get through life.'

'And Howells gets it for you?' Kiernan said.

'He can get anything. I've even seen him get hold of ice. He can get stuff no one else can get. Idiot pills, morphine, Dr Godfrey's, Space base. Even China White.'

'What a man,' said Kiernan caustically.

There was another long silence; this time it was broken by Stevie.

'We made a film together, me and Jo. Just the two of us and four or five blokes,' she told him. 'Ray arranged it all.'

'Film?' said Kiernan, looking a little vague.

'Ray said he knew some blokes who wanted girls for some video work. Just suck-and-fuck movies. You know the kind of thing. We did about four of them. They paid us a few quid.'

'How long ago was that?'

'Five weeks, maybe a bit more.'

'Jo was into porno films?' he said, not really wanting to hear the answer.

'She needed the money, like I did. It's better than tossing some old bastard off behind King's Cross for a fiver. One of the blokes was quite horny.' She giggled.

'Shit,' murmured Kiernan, leaning back against the wall.

As he did, he saw the door swing open.

He turned, wondering what was happening, his eyes drawn to the figure in the doorway.

Stevie saw the newcomer too but, like Kiernan, she was looking not at the intruder's face, but at the gun he held.

The barrel was levelled at them.

Fifty-nine

For a second Stevie considered screaming, but she contented herself with moving a step backwards, her eyes never leaving the barrel.

Kiernan remained motionless, his gaze alternating between the gaping barrel of the .357 and the eyes of the man who held it.

Nick Ryan coughed and winced at the pain in his chest. But he kept the gun steady, one thumb on the hammer, ready to pull it back.

'Who are you?' asked Stevie, her voice low.

'An interested passer-by,' said Ryan, his face impassive. 'It seems we have something in common.' He glanced at Kiernan. 'Raymond Howells. I'm looking for him, too.'

'How do you know *I* want him?' Kiernan asked, his eyes flicking nervously towards the pistol.

'I know quite a lot of things,' Ryan said. 'I've been standing out in that hallway for the last five minutes listening to your conversation.'

'How did you get in?' Stevie asked.

'Same way as you two. Through the front door.' He motioned with the .357, a sharp gesture, at Kiernan. 'Move back.'

Kiernan did as he was told.

'What the fuck is going on here?' he asked.

'That's what I was hoping to find out,' Ryan

announced. 'Drugs, porn movies, prostitution. This one's got everything, hasn't it? Oh, not forgetting runaway sisters.'

Kiernan regarded him warily, the perspiration beading on his forehead.

'What do you know about my sister?' he asked irritably.

'Only what I overheard,' Ryan told him, smiling thinly. 'Perhaps you'd like to tell me a little bit more.'

'Why should I?'

'I'm holding a fucking gun on you, for one thing. How much more incentive do you need?' Ryan snapped.

'I've been looking for her for the last five months.' He shrugged. 'At least, she's been missing for the last five months. She ran away from home.'

'Where's home?' Ryan wanted to know.

'Ireland.'

'You surprise me,' the private detective said acidly. 'I would have put money on Yorkshire.'

'What kind of fucking comedian are you?' snapped Kiernan.

'The kind with a gun who'll blow your head off if you don't shut it.' He looked at Stevie. 'What's *your* story?'

'You were listening at the door; didn't you hear it?' she said defiantly.

Ryan smiled.

'I've heard of tarts with hearts,' he said. 'What are you? A tart with a trap. Just tell me who you are and what you're doing here.'

'My name's Stevie Collins,' she said. 'I'm looking for Ray Howells, he . . .'

Ryan cut her short.

'He sold you some drugs and now he's fucked off with the money or rather he *promised* you some drugs and he's fucked off with the money. Right?'

'Ten out of ten,' she said sardonically.

'Vince Kiernan and Stevie Collins,' Ryan said, looking at each of them in turn.

'You know *our* names,' snapped Kiernan. 'Who the fuck are you?'

'Ryan. I'm a private detective.'

'And I'm the fucking Pope,' Kiernan snorted.

Ryan pulled some ID from his pocket, a business card, and threw it towards Kiernan.

'Then read that, Your Holiness,' he said, watching the young Irishman snatch up the card and scan it.

He shrugged and glanced once more at the gun then at the private detective.

'Happy now?' said Ryan.

'You never said why you wanted to see Ray,' Stevie reminded him.

'Business,' Ryan lied. 'He's got a product I'm interested in. As a matter of fact, you might be able to help.' He glanced at Kiernan. 'Both of you.'

Ryan stepped back towards the door, the gun still aimed at the other two.

'Move it,' he said. 'You're coming with me.'

'Why should we?' Kiernan demanded.

Ryan thumbed back the hammer of the .357 and aimed it at the Irishman's kneecap.

'Because it's better than learning to walk with a fucking stick,' he rasped. 'Come on.'

'Where are we going?' Stevie asked, walking out cautiously.

'You wouldn't want me to tell you and spoil the surprise, would you?' Ryan said, pushing Kiernan out of the room too.

The Irishman turned and clenched his fists.

Ryan raised the pistol to within inches of his head.

'I wouldn't,' he said quietly.

Kiernan stalked out behind Stevie, both of them heading down the hall and towards the stone steps that led up to street level.

'Kiernan,' said Ryan as they reached the top of the stairs. 'Take these.' He tossed him the keys of the Ford Sapphire which was parked beside the kerb. 'You drive. You *can* drive, can't you?'

Kiernan held the keys up and nodded.

'What if I refuse?' he said.

'I'll kill you,' Ryan said. Then, looking at Stevie:

'That goes for you too. Either of you fuck me around and I'll blow your heads off. Now get in the car. I'll give you directions.'

'I want to know where we're going,' Stevie protested.

'Shut up and get in,' Ryan snapped. 'There's something I want you to see. Both of you.'

Sixty

'Jesus Christ.'

Vince Kiernan's muffled exclamation of revulsion seemed to hang in the heavy air of Ryan's office.

The private detective sat at his desk, a drink cradled in one hand, a cigarette in the other. He had his head lowered, his back turned to the video screen on the other side of the room.

Kiernan and Stevie sat on the worn leather sofa under the window watching the images. Stevie seemed relatively unmoved by it all. Kiernan looked on with his face twisted into a grimace.

Was this what Jo had been involved in?

Ryan downed another large measure of vodka and

refilled his glass. He couldn't bring himself to watch the antics on the screen, couldn't force himself to look at what was being done to his daughter. As if the very thought were causing him pain he winced and touched his chest. With the vodka to wash them down he took two of the tablets and sat back in his seat, eyes closed but aware of everything that was happening on the tape.

The .357 was back in its holster now and had been since they'd entered the office about twenty minutes earlier. Both Kiernan and Stevie had seemed uneasy, even after the weapon had been put away, but Ryan preferred it like that. He wanted them off their guard, unsure what his next move would be. He needed them as allies; the fear factor might prove to be his ultimate weapon.

The tape came to an end. He reached for the remote control to switch the machine off.

'Where the fuck did you get that?' Kiernan said, his face pale.

Ryan ignored the question.

'Is that the kind of film you were making?' he asked Stevie.

She sat almost motionless, still staring at the blank screen. She shook her head almost imperceptibly.

'There were only blokes and girls,' she said quietly.

'Was it always the same girls?' Ryan asked.

'No. Ray would use new girls for every film if they asked him to get them.'

'Who are "they"?' he wanted to know.

'The people he worked with. We never saw them. We only ever acted in the films.'

'You and my sister?' Kiernan interjected.

She nodded.

'It wasn't that bad,' she said, her gaze still fixed on the screen. 'We got well paid.'

'And I bet Howells took most of that, didn't he?' Ryan snapped.

She nodded again.

'He looked after us; he gave us somewhere to live. He took care of us. It was only fair,' she said softly.

'And he got you the drugs you needed, too?' Ryan said.

'Was my sister on drugs?' Kiernan wanted to know.

'I told you, everybody was. Everybody *is*. You have to get through somehow. Jo and I were stoned when we made those films. If you've got five blokes all trying to stick their cocks in your mouth one after the other then it's better to be stoned.'

'How well did you know the girls who made the other films?' Ryan asked her. 'You and Jo weren't in every one, were you?'

She shook her head slowly and, for the first time, Ryan saw that her eyes were moist. As he watched a tear trickled slowly down her cheek.

'Ray said we were *his* girls,' she said, smiling thinly. 'He said we looked good on screen.'

Kiernan clenched his fists.

'He told us we were beautiful,' she continued, tears still trickling down her face.

'Where did he get the other girls, Stevie?' Ryan wanted to know.

'The streets,' she told him. 'Anywhere.'

Kiernan looked across at the private detective, who was watching Stevie intently.

'Do you recognize the girl in *that* film?' he said, his voice cracking slightly.

'She's very young. I've never seen a girl as young as that in one of the films before. She can't be more than about twelve or thirteen.' She wiped a tear away.

Very young.

'I don't recognize *her*,' said Stevie. 'Just the baby.'

Ryan looked surprised.

'How come?' he said.

'Because it was mine.'

211

Sixty-one

For long moments the room was silent, as if the awful truth of Stevie's words were slowly sinking in. It was Kiernan who broke the silence.

'You sold your baby?' he said. 'Sold it to be used in a fucking film like that?'

'What the hell was I supposed to do?' she snarled, wiping tears away. 'I had no money. I couldn't look after the kid. I needed money.'

'For drugs?' Kiernan said.

'Yeah, for drugs. I had to have them. Right?' she rasped.

'So you sold your own fucking child just so you could pay for shit to stick in your arms?' he said derisively.

'Don't come over all sanctimonious with me. You fucking people are all the same. You sit in your nice cosy houses, living your nice cosy lives, looking down on people like me.'

'What the hell are we supposed to do? Use you as role models? Do you want sympathy?'

'I don't need your fucking sympathy,' she hissed. 'You don't know what it's like on the streets. When you've got nowhere to go but an empty house, no one to care for you, no way of making money. No future.'

'You threw your own fucking future down the drain when you started taking that shit,' Kiernan said.

'And your sister didn't? Why do you think *she* started? Why do you think she ran away from home in the first place?'

'You don't know why,' Kiernan said.

'I lived with her, remember? I talked to her. You wanted to find her.' She smiled bitterly. 'And what were you going to do when you did? Take her back to her loving family? How do you know she would even go with you?'

Kiernan didn't answer.

'Who did you sell the child to?' Ryan wanted to know.

'Two guys. I forget their names,' she said.

'Try and remember,' he said, his gaze on her unwavering.

'I can't,' she protested.

'Who set it up?'

'Ray did. When he found out I was pregnant he went mad. He knocked me about.' She shrugged. 'Still, it was my own fault. I forgot to take my pill.'

'I thought you lot used condoms with punters,' Ryan said.

'It wasn't a punter's baby, it was Ray's,' she told him. 'He said I couldn't stay with him if I was pregnant. If I was pregnant I couldn't work, well, not for much money anyway. All I could do after the seventh month was suck cocks or do hand jobs. It wasn't bringing in enough money.'

'Whose idea was it to sell the kid when it was born?' Ryan asked.

'Ray said that he knew of some blokes who wanted a baby for a film they were making. He said he'd done business with them before. I needed money, too, for my stuff.' She rubbed her arm self-consciously, as if to wipe away the track marks.

'So Howells set up the sale with these blokes?' Ryan continued.

She nodded.

'One thousand quid,' she told him.

'What were their names?' the private detective pressed her.

'I told you, I can't remember.'

'Think,' Ryan said, puffing on his cigarette.

She wiped her eyes again.

'Clayton or something like that,' she mumbled. 'Clayton and . . . Neville.' She nodded. 'That was one of them. Neville. Don Neville.' She looked pleased with herself.

'Don Neville,' Ryan murmured, writing the name on a piece of paper. 'It'll do for a start. So Ray Howells supplied the kids for Neville and Neville made the films, right?'

She nodded.

'Then I have to find Neville *and* Howells,' the private detective mused. 'I need your help, Stevie. You're the only one who knows what they both look like. Help me find them.'

'Are you mad?' she grunted. 'Either of them would kill me if they found out I was helping to put them away.'

'I didn't say anything about putting them away. I need to find them. I've been hired to track down the girl in that film.' He swallowed hard.

My daughter.

'The only way I can do that is by finding these men and the quickest way to do that is with your help.'

'No,' she said. 'They'd kill me.'

'You've got a choice, then. Get your shit from another dealer and risk filling yourself full of poison, risk Neville or Howells killing you or risk me doing it instead. I'll tell you now, I'm going to find them and you're going to help me. If you don't, I'll do things to you that fucking scumbag Howells never even thought of.' He held her in his cold stare. 'I'll pay you.'

'How much?'

'Two hundred when I find Howells,' he told her.

'Three hundred. Half now,' she demanded.

'You're in no position to bargain, Stevie. Three hundred. But only after I've got Howells. Deal?'

'Deal,' she said.

'I'll help, too,' Kiernan said.

'I don't need your help,' Ryan told him.

'You need all the fucking help you can get, especially if you have to rely on some drugged-up tart to track this scumbag down,' the Irishman said.

'Fuck off, you pig-eyed . . .' she began.

'Shut it,' snapped Kiernan. Then, to Ryan:

'My sister is out there somewhere. I've been looking for her too long now to give up. If I help you find Howells I've got a chance of finding *her* too.'

Ryan sat back in his chair, his fingertips pressed together, his expression blank.

'I'm going to find her, Ryan,' the Irishman said. 'We might as well work together. Besides, the only way you're going to stop me is to shoot me.'

Ryan leant forward.

'All right,' he said. 'You're on. But you fuck up once and I *will* shoot you.'

Sixty-two

'How many more times do I have to say it? We can't tell *anyone*.'

Joseph Finlay shifted his position in his seat and rubbed his temples with the tips of his index fingers.

'If the media even get a sniff of this they'll be all over us. I can't afford that kind of exposure, Kim. You have to understand that. I've been rushing around for the last two days raising the money and the banks are beginning to wonder why.'

'All I understand is that my daughter has been kidnapped,' Kim said angrily. 'She could be dead by now for all we know.'

'And you think going to the papers is going to get her back? I was told that no one was to be told, especially not the police. Do you want them to kill her? Because that's what they'll do.'

'What are we supposed to do? Sit around waiting for someone to arrive and tell us they've found her body?' Kim blurted.

'Ryan will find her. Have faith in the man; he *was* your husband, after all. I thought you believed in him,' Finlay said, a note of scorn in his voice. 'He's supposed to be good at his job. He'll find her.'

'How much longer before the ransom deadline is up?' Kim asked.

'There is no deadline as yet. They said they'd ring again to give me more instructions.'

Finlay clasped his hands across his stomach, squeezing his fingers together.

He hadn't heard from Neville for more than twenty-four hours now.

What was the bastard playing at?

More to the point, he hadn't heard from Ryan either.

He pulled himself to his feet and crossed to the drinks cabinet, where he poured himself a large Scotch and downed most of it in one swallow. He tipped more into another glass, added a splash of soda and handed it to Kim. She merely shook her head and put the glass on the coffee table beside her.

'We can't hide forever, Joe,' she said quietly. 'People are going to start asking where Kelly is.'

'Like who?' he demanded.

216

'The people who live around here. Her school. Her friends.'

'She's only been gone two days. She's on her school holidays. If anyone asks, tell them she's gone to stay with relatives,' he said, dismissively.

'Just like that?' Kim said acidly.

'Well, what the hell do you expect me to say?' he snapped. 'I told you, we can't tell anyone. For Kelly's sake.'

'And for yours.'

'What's that supposed to mean?'

'You said you couldn't afford that kind of exposure. *You* couldn't afford it. Whose life is in danger here, Joe? Yours or Kelly's? What damage could it do to *you*?'

'It would damage my reputation, my standing amongst my colleagues. I don't want every detail of my fucking life dredged up and plastered across every stinking tabloid newspaper in the country. Can you even begin to imagine what that would do to my business?'

'That's all that matters to you, isn't it? Your business. As long as *you're* not embarrassed or inconvenienced you couldn't give a damn about Kelly.'

'That's not true, Kim, and you know it.'

'Do I? I thought I knew you but now I'm not so sure.'

'Meaning?'

'She's my daughter, Joe. I just want her back.'

'She's my daughter, too,' he said none too convincingly.

'But you want her back for different reasons. You want her back so you don't have to worry about newspapers prying into your business. What's so important that you need to hide from them anyway, Joe? What's your big secret?' She looked at him accusingly and saw his expression change fleetingly to one of concern.

She couldn't know of his connections with Neville.

'There *are* no secrets,' he lied.

217

'And when it's over and we do get her back, please God. What then? What if Nick finds her and brings her back? Do you think you can just sweep it under the carpet? What do you plan on saying to Kelly? "I know you've been kidnapped but if you could just keep quiet about it things will be much better"?' There was anger in her voice and something else which sounded like contempt. 'You think she's going to get over it that easily? God alone knows what it will do to her, even if she gets through it alive. We don't know what the bastards who've got her have done to her.'

I could tell you, thought Finlay, gritting his teeth.

'This business isn't just going to go away, Joe, no matter how much you want it to,' she reminded him.

'Perhaps you should be thinking about getting her back first before you start deciding how psychologically scarred she's going to be,' Finlay said, a touch of sarcasm in his voice. 'And whether we *do* get her back is down to Ryan, so you'd better hope he's as good at his job as he thinks he is.'

She glared at him, her eyes filled with anger.

Or hatred?

An image of her ex-husband flashed into her mind. She found her thoughts turning to him, to the awful truth he'd told her about his illness. His death.

Six months.

She shuddered.

Her daughter *and* her ex-husband.

It seemed just a matter of time before they were both dead.

And she had no way of knowing which of them would be the first.

Kim glanced across to the other side of the room and the photo of Kelly smiled back at her.

Sixty-three

The child had been dead for nearly twenty-four hours.

The body was rigid, most of the fingers and toes already rigored; some of the extremities were beginning to blacken. The flesh looked waxen and bloodless. The eyes were closed, as if in sleep, but one lid was slightly open revealing the dull, lifeless eye beneath.

Don Neville looked down at the body indifferently.

'We'll have to get rid of it,' Edward Caton offered, his gaze also drawn to the body. 'It's going to start to smell in this fucking weather.' He wiped a hand across his face and wiped the sweat off on his jeans.

'Do you want us to take care of it?' said Neville, turning away to face the third occupant of the room. 'Or will you handle it?'

The third figure nodded.

'You'll do it?' Caton echoed.

The figure nodded again.

Both men smiled.

'You could try the Thames this time,' Caton chuckled, looking down at the body again. He wrinkled his nose.

He crossed to the window and pushed it open, allowing in something approximating fresh air which drifted in from Carnaby Street. It was preferable to the stench of human putrefaction, though.

The flat was above a large shop which had, at one time, sold martial arts equipment. There were entrances both in Carnaby Street itself and also through a rear door in Ganton Street. It was that door through which Neville, Caton and the third occupant of the room had entered less than an hour ago.

The flat itself was divided into four rooms, all of them small. A sitting-room, a kitchen, a bathroom and what had once been a bedroom. There was still a bed in it, or a mattress at least, stained and damp. The sitting-room was furnished with two wooden chairs and a table. The windows had been boarded up, several slats pulled free to allow light into the derelict dwelling. In the kitchen the sink was cracked and brown. It smelled of cat's piss and damp. There was a three-year-old calendar hanging on one wall, the pages curling and faded.

The heat inside the flat was almost overpowering, unrelieved by Caton opening the one window that hadn't been boarded up. The glass was filthy, caked thickly enough with filth to prevent anyone seeing inside.

The dying rays of the sun glinted on shop windows below, reflecting off them in a blood red haze. Carnaby Street itself was empty now. Gone were the shoppers, the tourists and the curious who thronged it during business hours. As Caton glanced out he saw only two young men walking along, laughing as they chatted.

'I want it out of here as soon as possible,' Neville said. 'If anyone comes up here they're going to wonder what the fucking smell is.'

'Who's going to come up here?' Caton wanted to know. 'How could they get in?'

'Same way we did. *Break* in,' Neville told him.

He watched as a spider scuttled across the floor, climbed over one tiny, outstretched, rigored hand then ran on to disappear into the shadows. Caton made a move to stamp on it.

'Leave it,' said Neville. 'It's bad luck to kill a spider.'

Caton chuckled.

Neville wandered into the bedroom. The other two followed him as he stood by the mattress, looking down.

'We'll get rid of the body, then call Finlay again,' he said.

'How long you going to give him to come up with the money?' Caton wanted to know.

'Forty-eight hours, tops,' Neville said. He knelt beside the mattress, pulling something from his jeans pocket. The other two saw that it was a flick-knife. He pressed the release catch on the blade and the familiar swish-click sound filled the room as the steel was released, springing upright at his touch. He turned the blade over in his hand, looking down at the mattress.

Tied to it by three lengths of thick hemp was Kelly.

There was masking tape across her mouth and, but for a sheet draped over her, she was naked. Her eyes were swollen and puffy from constant weeping.

'Your fucking old man had better pay up,' said Neville, pressing the blade against her cheek. 'Otherwise he's going to be getting another tape through the post. And this time he'll be able to see what we do to you with this fucking knife.'

Kelly tried to turn her head away but Neville held her chin.

Caton smiled.

The third occupant of the room looked on indifferently.

Sixty-four

'That's it, there,' said Stevie Collins, pointing towards the large, red-bricked building in Ossulston Street. 'That's the hostel.'

Ryan lit up a cigarette and dangled it out of his side window, gazing intently at the building Stevie had indicated.

Three storeys tall, almost Victorian in appearance, it had been given a paint job and a new roof but it still looked dirty and forbidding.

'How long were you there?' Ryan wanted to know.

'Three months. That was the longest time any of us were allowed to stay. It's a short-stay hostel. Three months and you're out,' she explained.

'How many kids are there in there?' Ryan asked, sucking on his cigarette.

'There are usually about sixty or seventy, perhaps more. All of us were about the same age, fifteen up to about twenty-five.'

'Is that where you met Jo?' Kiernan asked.

Stevie nodded.

Ryan stroked his chin thoughtfully, his gaze never leaving the building. He watched as two or three people left. All of them were young. They wandered down the street into the Euston Road, two of them disappearing into a small café on the corner. He waited a moment longer then reached across to the glove compartment of the Sapphire, pulling out his camera. He raised it and clicked off four shots of the hostel before replacing it.

'Who runs it?' Ryan asked. 'Who should I speak to there?'

'I think her name was Emma something-or-other. Emma Powell, that's it,' Stevie said, smiling, pleased with herself.

'What are you going to do?' Kiernan wanted to know.

'I'm going to speak to this Miss Powell to find out what she can tell me.' He looked at Stevie. 'Did she ever see Howells?'

'He used to hang around the hostel a lot, but I don't think she knew him,' Stevie said.

'What do you mean, he used to hang around a lot?' Ryan enquired.

'He knew the girls and the blokes coming out of the hostel had nowhere to go. He knew they'd have no money or friends. He used to talk to us, tell us he could find us somewhere to live, get us work.'

'And you believed him?' Kiernan said indignantly.

'So did your fucking sister,' Stevie hissed. 'That was how we met him. Jo and I were having a cup of coffee in a café near here one day and Ray came in and started chatting to us. He said he knew we lived at the hostel. He asked us what we were going to do when we left. He said he could help us.'

'Considerate bastard, isn't he?' chided Kiernan.

'Did you know of any other girls who went to work for him?' Ryan said.

'He told us that lots of girls had left the hostel and gone with him, that he'd helped them,' she informed him. 'We needed someone to rely on, somewhere to go.'

'Someone to get your fucking drugs for you,' Kiernan interjected.

'Fuck off,' snapped Stevie. She looked at Ryan: 'Can't you tell him to shut up?'

'Let her speak, Kiernan,' the private detective said,

223

his eyes still on the entrance to the hostel. Two young girls went in.

The Irishman sat back in his seat, gazing out of the side window.

'Anyway,' Stevie continued, 'when Jo and I left the hostel we went to find Ray. He'd given us an address.'

'And he got you into prostitution and porn movies,' Ryan said flatly, sucking on his cigarette.

Stevie nodded.

'At least it was money,' she added as an afterthought.

'And I bet *he* took most of that, didn't he?' Ryan said.

'He said he was entitled to it for finding us work. You know, like a sort of agent's fee.'

Kiernan laughed mockingly.

'Regular little entrepreneur, wasn't he?' he said.

'Did Neville ever get mixed up in this? Did *he* ever hang around here?' asked Ryan.

Stevie shook her head.

'Ray used to pick up the kids who left the hostel. He was like the middle-man. Besides, Neville had nothing to do with Ray's everyday business.'

'Selling drugs and running a stable of pros,' Ryan said. He dropped his cigarette end and started up the car.

'What the hell are you doing? I thought you were going to talk to the woman who runs the place?' said Kiernan.

'I am, but later,' Ryan told him. 'And while I do that you two can find Howells.'

'How the fuck are we supposed to do that?' Kiernan said.

'Stevie knows where he hangs out,' Ryan reminded him, pulling away. 'Check everywhere he might be hiding. You'll find him somewhere. Even the biggest turds float sometimes. He'll turn up.'

'What do we do if we find him?' Kiernan asked.

'Ring me. I'll give you instructions where you can get hold of me.' As they passed the hostel he slowed down slightly, peering towards the building once again. Then he sped off.

'Do you think Howells is supplying the kids for Neville's videos?' Kiernan wondered aloud.

Ryan inhaled, held the breath then let it out slowly.

'I wouldn't bet against it,' he said quietly. 'Where do you want me to drop you off?'

Sixty-five

Charles Thornton sat behind his desk watching the bubbles in the Perrier water rise to the top of the glass. It was an expensive glass and Thornton handled it with the care it deserved, holding it delicately between his thumb and forefinger by the stem.

Seated on the Chesterfield opposite sat Frank Price and James Houghton. They too held glasses, although Price was more concerned with the papers spread out on his briefcase. That, in turn, was propped on his lap like a makeshift table; he was running one index finger down a column of figures, apparently lost in thought.

Houghton, a year or two older, pulled at his tie, feeling the heat despite the air-conditioning inside the luxury apartment. He was a big man; his body looked as if it had been poured into his dark blue suit.

Over at the far side of the room stood Phillip Alexander, arms folded, gazing out of the large picture window onto Craven Hill Mews. He could see

Thornton's Mercedes parked below; his driver, Colin Moran, stood beside the impressive vehicle smoking. Alexander envied him. He was dying for a smoke but Thornton wouldn't allow it inside the apartment. He took a sip of his ice-cold beer, careful to replace the glass on the coaster provided.

'Well, Frank, what do you say?' Thornton asked. 'What do we do about Finlay? I've given him nearly two weeks, like I said I would, and I've heard nothing from him. I've called the bastard and he hasn't even had the fucking decency to return my calls.'

'The decision is yours in the end, Charlie. I'm only your accountant,' Price said.

'So can I afford to buy him out?' Thornton wanted to know.

'Well, you're not short of money, Charlie, you don't need *me* to tell you that, but the problem is, you can't buy him out if he won't sell.'

'I offered him whatever he wanted for that fucking place in Cavendish Square,' hissed Thornton. 'He still wasn't interested.'

'If *he* won't move, we'll have to move *him*,' Houghton offered.

'Yeah, I know that, Jim, but it's not that easy,' Thornton said, taking a sip of his mineral water.

'Can't he have an accident?' Alexander interjected.

The other men laughed.

'If he goes for a walk under a bus, that leaves me free to move in on the building, but Finlay's a powerful bloke and I don't mean in the same sense as myself.' He smiled self-satisfactorily. 'The only reason I've stayed friendly with him for so long is for his contacts.'

'Fuck his contacts,' said Houghton. 'If he takes a dive under the number 14, who's going to know it's got anything to do with you?'

'No, no, you're missing the point,' said Thornton.

'Killing him isn't a problem, but he's made things easy over the last few years. He's smoothed the way, if you like.'

'So find someone else to take his place,' Price said. '*Buy* another property developer.'

The other men laughed.

'How much do I stand to make if I take over that building, Frank?' Thornton wanted to know.

'On these projected figures, and remember I can only make an educated guess, nothing's concrete,' the accountant reminded him, 'you stand to make two million or more in the first eighteen months. Pre-tax.'

'Tax? What the fuck's that?' said Thornton, grinning.

The sound of laughter filled the room.

'So that settles it then, right?' Houghton said. 'Finlay's history. When do you want him taken out?'

'I'll give him a couple more days,' Thornton said.

'Why? He's fucked you around long enough already,' Houghton said.

'I'll speak to him again, see what he says. If he still says no then you can get rid of him. Right?' Thornton raised his glass and his men followed suit. The gang boss was smiling. 'Cheers.'

Sixty-six

The place looked horribly familiar to Kiernan.

Maxims in Dean Street boasted a MALE AND FEMALE BED SHOW on its hoardings. He knew different; he'd been inside the place during his search for Jo. They waited until there were six people down-stairs before the 'show' began. He'd sat there one day himself for more than an hour as two or three people had drifted in and out, finally tiring of the wait and the oppressive atmosphere of the place. He doubted if Maxims ever put on a show; he doubted six people would be *stupid* enough to sit for *long* enough in the grubby shithole to witness it.

Now, as he stood outside, he grabbed Stevie by the arm and pulled her back.

'What are we doing here?' he said.

'Ryan said to check out all the places Ray used to go, didn't he?' she said. 'He used to be friendly with the manager of this place. He could be here.' She looked at him and smiled, mockingly. 'Why, too shy to go in?'

He pushed her gently, following her inside.

'Hello, Jed, is Dickie about?' she said happily, smiling at the doorman who sat behind a small counter reading a newspaper. The doorman looked suspiciously at Kiernan; for a moment the young Irishman wondered if he might have recognised him from his earlier visit. He reasoned to himself it was highly unlikely, and even if he did, so what?

Stevie leant on the counter gazing at the doorman, who finally managed to look at her and force a thin smile.

'We haven't seen you here for a while,' he said. The words were spoken slowly and, it seemed, with effort. It was the kind of voice Kiernan usually associated with pissheads or half-wits. Looking at the doorman he was inclined to think it was the latter.

'Can you get Dickie for me?' she said.

'Dickie ain't here,' she was told.

'When will he be back?'

'In about three months, unless he gets time off for good behaviour.'

'Shit,' murmured Stevie.

'What did you want him for, anyway?' the doorman enquired.

'I wondered if he'd seen Ray lately. You know, Ray Howells.'

'Your pimp?' He laughed to himself. 'No, he ain't been in either.' He looked at Kiernan again. 'Who's that, your boyfriend?'

'No, I'm her father,' said Kiernan scornfully.

'What?' the doorman said menacingly, taking a step towards Kiernan. 'How long you been a fucking comedian?'

'About as long as you've been stopping buses with your head,' Kiernan replied, making for the door. 'Come on,' he said to Stevie, 'let's get out of here. It'll be feeding-time soon.'

He led the way back out onto the baking pavement, wiping his face with his handkerchief.

Stevie slipped off her light jacket and slung it over her shoulder, sweat forming rings beneath her arms, darkening the red T-shirt she wore. She pulled the sleeves down as she saw a policeman wandering past.

'Afraid he'll see your little tattoos?' said Kiernan acidly, jabbing at her arms.

'Fuck off,' she snapped.

'Where to now?' he said. 'What other exotic places did Howells frequent?'

'There's an amusement arcade just off Leicester Square,' she told him. 'We'll try there.'

'How do you know he hasn't left London altogether?' asked Kiernan as they headed towards Shaftesbury Avenue.

'He wouldn't,' Stevie assured him. 'This sort of thing's happened loads of times before. He'll be around somewhere, just laying low until things blow over.'

'Did *you* get Jo hooked on drugs or was it Howells?' asked Kiernan, looking down at her, as they crossed the main road.

'It was her own choice,' Stevie told him. 'No one forced her.'

'Bollocks.'

Stevie ignored him, gazing straight ahead.

'Was it heroin?' he continued.

'I don't know what she was on,' Stevie said wearily. 'Come on, we go down here,' she added, turning right into Chinatown. 'It's her life, you know. Did it ever strike you she might be perfectly happy doing what she's doing? Why did she run away in the first place? If she was that happy at home, she wouldn't have come here, would she?' She reached into her handbag and took out a packet of Silk Cut, stopping to light one up. 'Did you ever think she might not want her *big* brother to rescue her? Why couldn't you just leave her alone?'

'Because I care about her,' Kiernan said quietly.

'Well, maybe she doesn't care about you,' Stevie said, looking at him.

'What the hell do you know about caring?' Kiernan snapped. 'I doubt if anyone would *want* to find *you*, would they?'

She didn't answer, merely puffed on her cigarette and looked over his shoulder.

'Why did you run away in the first place?' he pressed.

'It's none of your business.'

'Whatever kind of life you left behind must have been better than this.'

Stevie laughed bitterly.

'No,' she said, her voice quivering. 'There are worse ways to live, believe me.'

She wiped her eye hurriedly with the back of her hand, anxious to hide the tears. She smudged her thick mascara and it left a dark mark on her cheek. 'Shit,' she murmured, moving to a shop window to check her reflection. She tried to rub the mark away with her

230

fingers but it only spread more.

Kiernan nudged her, handing her his handkerchief.

'Here,' he said.

She took it, wet one tip with her tongue and wiped away the mark. Then she pushed the linen square back into his hand.

'We'd better get on,' she said, moving down the narrow alley towards Charing Cross Road.

'So?' he said quizzically, catching up with her, 'what was so bad that you had to run away?'

'I told you, it's none of your business,' she said, angry with herself for showing emotion.

'I was just trying to help,' he said. 'If you don't want to talk about it . . .'

'I don't,' she said with an air of finality, turning right and striding ahead through the crowds. Kiernan, bulkier, had to step into the street, avoiding oncoming taxis, in order to find the room to speed up and reach her side. By the time he had done so, they were at the doors of the Hippodrome.

Sixty-seven

Nick Ryan wiped sweat from his forehead and gazed at the pad in front of him. On it were written three names:

Emma Powell

Don Neville

Raymond Howells

He drew a bracket around Howells' and Neville's names and added a question mark.

Howells dealt in child pornography, that much he knew from speaking to the assistant in the sex shop the other day. He also ran a stable of very young prostitutes.

Stevie said that he had enticed several former residents of the Ossulston Street hostel to work for him, including her and Kiernan's sister. He also knew that those same youngsters were supplied for porno videos made by Neville.

How then did Kelly come to be in a video which could have been made by . . .

By whom?

Kelly had been kidnapped.

Why had she been kidnapped?

Because Finlay had money.

But why use her in such a vile way, in such a monstrous video?

No reason. No link.

'Shit,' he snapped, bringing his hand down hard on the desk top.

No link.

And yet . . .

There was something nagging at the back of his mind. Stuck there like the last few chords of a song which stayed, unwanted, in the brain.

Howells promised the homeless kids who left the hostel somewhere to go, Ryan thought. Told them they could rely on him.

When you're homeless you take help from anyone.

Homeless.

Runaways.

No one cared about them.

So no one would miss them.

Ryan stroked his chin, feeling how hot his skin was.

No families.

No one to trace them.

Nobody gave a shit about kids who slept rough on the streets of London or any other big city.

Nobody but Raymond Howells and Don Neville?

Ryan smiled thinly.

HOMELESS. He wrote the word on the other edge of the pad, drumming the fingers of his free hand on the wood.

Homeless.

Untraceable.

The private detective reached for the phone, punching out digits with the end of his pen. He kept looking at his pad as he listened to the ringing.

Homeless and living rough.

The phone was picked up at the other end.

'New Scotland Yard,' said the voice. 'Can I help you?'

'I'd like to speak to Detective Constable Peter Trent, please,' Ryan said, still gazing at his pad.

The line went dead for a moment, only the hiss of static burbling away in his ear. Then he heard a different ringing tone.

He waited.

Something in the back of his mind . . .

And waited.

'Come on,' he murmured.

'Hello,' the voice at the other end finally said.

'DC Trent, please,' Ryan said.

'Who's calling?' the voice asked.

'Just tell him it's a friend,' Ryan said cryptically.

There was a moment of silence on the other end then Ryan heard movement, muffled voices; the taker of the call had obviously put his hand over the mouthpiece.

A moment later he heard a familiar voice.

'DC Trent. Who's this, please?'

Ryan smiled.

'You took your fucking time, didn't you?' he said.

'Who *is* this?'

233

'A blast from the past,' Ryan said, grinning.

Give it another six months and it could be a rave from the grave, he thought, his smile fading.

'Jesus Christ,' said Trent.

'Not quite, but then you never were very good with voices, were you, Pete?'

'Nick Ryan?'

'Is there another one?'

'What the fuck do you want?' Trent chuckled.

'Your help, Pete,' the private detective told him.

'A rich and famous private detective wants *my* help? I'm honoured,' Trent joked.

'Just shut up and listen, will you?'

'That's no way to talk to your old partner, is it? Getting touchy in your old age?' chided Trent.

'How many years did we work together? Six?'

'It seemed like longer,' Trent told him, laughing.

'If you don't shut up it'll be six years before this fucking conversation ends,' Ryan told him. 'Just listen to me. This case you're working on, the one with the murdered kids, the runaways. What kind of progress are you making?'

Trent sighed.

'You know I can't talk about that, Nick. What the hell's wrong with you?'

'I need some information, Pete. It could be important to both of us.'

'What are you working on?'

'That's not important at the moment. What *is* important is that you get me some information.'

'Wait a minute,' Trent said. 'I'm transferring this call to my office.'

Ryan heard a click and a buzz and waited a moment longer until he heard the phone picked up again.

'I couldn't talk,' Trent told him.

'Yeah, that's the problem with New Scotland Yard,

isn't it? Bloody place is always swarming with coppers. Now listen, Pete, this case you're on. According to the papers, you haven't got fuck all to go on, apart from the fact that all the kids were runaways, right?'

'What did you ring for? To tell me something I already know?' Trent muttered. 'Because if you did . . .'

'I need their names,' the private detective said flatly.

'What?' Trent blurted, incredulous.

'I need the names of the six murdered kids.'

'No way, Nick. I can't give out information like that. You know the rules.'

'Fuck the rules.'

'What do you *know*? How are you tied in with this case?'

'I might not be, I don't know. But I have to have the names of those kids.' His tone softened a little. 'Look, if I find out anything I'll tip you off. Perhaps if *you* crack the case instead of Baxter they'll promote you. Then you can have the fucking job *I* should have had.'

'I won't have any job at all if someone finds out I disclosed information to an outsider,' Trent told him.

'I'm not an outsider, Pete.'

'You are now. You have been since you resigned.'

'And you know *why* I resigned.'

'It doesn't make any difference why, Nick. I still can't give you that information.'

'We were partners,' Ryan reminded him. 'More than that, we were friends.'

'Don't try to give me the loyalty bullshit, Nick.'

'There's something else too, Pete. You owe me and you know what I'm talking about.'

There was a heavy silence on the other end.

'If it wasn't for me you'd be dead now,' Ryan continued. 'I saved your life.'

'Look, Nick . . .'

Ryan cut him short.

'You don't need reminding, do you, Pete?' The private detective continued acidly. 'Four years ago in Chinatown? That little shit we were after for carving up a Triad leader, the one who came at you with a meat cleaver. The one you never even saw. The one who would have split you in half if I hadn't stepped in. Remember?'

'Yeah,' rasped Trent, 'I remember.'

'You owe me, Pete. You said it at the time. Well, now I'm calling in that favour. Give me the names of those six kids.'

'You bastard,' hissed Trent angrily. 'You were always a shithouse, Nick, but . . .'

'The names, Pete,' Ryan interrupted.

There was another long silence at the end of the phone. Ryan pressed the receiver to his ear, wondering for a moment if Trent had hung up on him. When the policeman spoke again his voice was low.

'Give me thirty minutes,' he said. 'I'll call you back.'

Sixty-eight

The profusion of sounds inside the amusement arcade combined to form a deafening cacophony. Music blared from speakers mounted high on the walls; the constant buzz of chatter, the electronic burblings of the machines and the periodic rattle of change all combined to create an unearthly din.

The Crystal Rooms in New Coventry Street were busy. Vince Kiernan found himself checking out the faces as he followed Stevie through the maze of fruit machines and electronic games.

Most of the occupants of the arcade were in their late teens or early twenties; some were much younger. Their faces were lit by the multi-coloured lights which flashed so brilliantly as they played. Their eyes seemed blank; the only signs of life were the flickering colours that danced endlessly before them.

Had Jo spent her spare time in a place like this, he wondered?

He bumped into two young lads, barely eighteen, playing one of the electronic games. The first of them, a youth with pitted skin and a dirty Dead Kennedy's T-shirt, shot him an angry glance. TOO DRUNK TO FUCK his T-shirt proclaimed.

Kiernan held the youngster's glassy stare for a moment before looking briefly at his companion, a girl about a year younger whose hair needed washing. She also looked at Kiernan angrily, moving closer to the youth.

The young Irishman moved on, seeing that Stevie was heading for a change booth up ahead.

The woman inside, intent on her magazine, gave her only a cursory glance as she approached.

There was a large, black man dressed in jeans and a polo shirt leaning against the side of the booth. He stepped forward as he saw Stevie approaching.

She smiled up at him but received no response. He merely looked her up and down; he did the same to Kiernan.

'Do you know Ray Howells?' Stevie said, forced to raise her voice over the music.

Neither the large man nor the woman in the booth spoke.

Kiernan stepped forward.

'Ray Howells,' he repeated irritably. 'Do you know him?'

'I heard what she said,' the large man told him.

'So do you know him?' the Irishman continued.

'Are you friends of his?' the woman in the booth asked, eyeing them both suspiciously.

'I've been looking for him all over. He usually spends some time in here,' Stevie explained.

Kiernan stepped forward again but Stevie held out a hand to push him back.

'Your friend's a little eager, isn't he?' said the woman in the booth, glancing at Kiernan.

'Have you seen him?' Stevie asked.

'Who's asking for him?' the black man wanted to know.

'My name's Stevie Collins. If he comes in, ask him to get in touch with me, will you? I work with him. He'll know where to reach me. Tell him it's important.'

She took a piece of paper from her handbag and scribbled her name on it, pushing it across the counter to the woman in the booth. She took it and looked at it.

'Thanks,' said Stevie, turning and tugging at Kiernan's sleeve in an effort to make him follow her.

The woman in the booth waited until they were out of sight, then turned to the large black man. He shrugged.

She screwed the piece of paper up into a ball and tossed it into the rubbish-bin beside her.

Stevie emerged out onto the pavement outside and turned angrily towards Kiernan.

'I told you I'd handle this,' she said. 'What the hell were you doing, sticking your nose in?'

'They knew more than they were letting on,' snarled Kiernan.

'And they might have told us if they hadn't thought you were a fucking copper,' she said, walking away from him.

Kiernan grabbed her arm and spun her round,

ignoring the three or four passers-by who watched the little fracas.

'What makes you so sure they thought I was a copper?' he demanded.

'Because you were too pushy,' she told him, shaking free of his grip. 'Just leave it to me next time.'

'I've left it to you so far and we're no nearer to finding Howells.'

'So look for him your fucking self. Perhaps you think you know these streets better than I do.'

He shook his head.

'I've only *walked* them. You've *worked* them.'

'Then leave it to me to find him. If we don't find Howells, you've no chance of finding Jo. Perhaps you'd better think about that before you go sticking your oar in next time.'

They glared at each other, the temperature around them matching their blazing tempers.

'Lead on, then,' Kiernan said acidly. 'Let's see where your expert knowledge takes us next.'

Stevie shook her head and spun round, walking back towards Charing Cross Road.

'No wonder Jo ran away from home if she had you going on at her all the time,' she said.

'*I* wasn't the reason she left,' Kiernan snapped.

'You surprise me.'

'And I'm the only one who's cared enough to come looking for her. I don't see anyone searching for *you*.'

'I wouldn't want them to.' She rounded on him. 'Especially if they were like you. If I knew *you* were looking for me I think I'd have left for another fucking *planet*.'

She pushed her way through the crowd, turning left then left again into Leicester Square tube station.

'Where are we going now?' Kiernan asked, following her down the stairs.

'He used to hang out in a snooker hall in Pentonville Road. We'll try there. We can get a tube to King's Cross from here, then walk.'

'Great,' murmured the Irishman.

'You want to find her, don't you?' Stevie snapped. 'You want your little sister back?'

'And you want Howells?'

'Fucking right I do.'

'You don't care about Jo, do you?'

'Why should I? She's *your* sister. All I care about is getting the money Ryan promised me. You want your sister, I want the money and the only way we're going to get what we want is by working together. Like it or not and believe me, I hate it as much as you.'

'I doubt it,' Kiernan snapped.

'Fuck off,' she rasped.

They headed for the ticket machines.

Sixty-nine

Ryan looked at his watch, then at the clock on the wall, to verify that both timepieces showed the same configuration.

They did.

He paced the office, puffing agitatedly on a cigarette, his gaze constantly drawn to the phone.

He paused by the video in the corner of the office; the tape was still propped on top of it. *That* tape.

Thoughts of Kelly flooded into his mind, swiftly followed, he was alarmed to discover, by the images on the tape. He blinked hard, as if to wipe them away. He wanted her to stay in his mind as the happy, smiling young girl he knew and loved so well, not the perverted plaything of the two scumbags in the film.

Ryan felt a twinge of pain in his chest. This time, instead of subsiding after a moment or two, it grew more intense. So much so that he was forced to sit down. After a minute he clambered to his feet and crossed to his desk, sliding open one drawer, taking out a small bottle of white fluid and the spoon alongside it. Controlling his shaking hands he poured first one, then two measures of morphine, swallowing it quickly, sucking on his cigarette to banish the flavour. And, sure enough, the pain began to subside. He replaced the bottle in the drawer and closed it, shutting away the cure as easily as the morphine had shut away his pain.

Until the next time, anyway.

He turned again and looked at the video, trying not to think of Kelly strapped to that bed but unable to banish the thoughts. Perhaps somewhere inside him he wanted to cling to them, repugnant though they might be. Yet in that revulsion was one of his reasons for carrying on.

The desire to catch up with the men who had subjected his daughter to such obscenities was growing.

It was swelling inside him as surely as the cancer. His desire for revenge was becoming almost intolerable. Christ, he wanted them to suffer as she had suffered.

And he wanted them to end *his* suffering.

They wouldn't hand her back without a fight. That had always been his hope. He didn't want her handed back; he wanted to be forced to take her from them. To confront them. To precipitate the violence that would end his life before the disease inside him ate him away.

What if her kidnappers didn't want to fight?

What if they handed his daughter back willingly?

Ryan would not let them. He would *make* them fight.

Make *them* release him from his agony.

He sought something in death he had never had in life.

He sought honour.

Ryan's philosophical musings were interrupted by the ringing of the phone.

He waited a moment or two, glanced at his watch then picked up the receiver.

'Ryan Investigations,' he said.

'Just shut up and listen,' Trent told him angrily. 'Have you got a pen there?'

Ryan smiled, reaching for a biro and a pad on his desk.

'Go ahead, Pete,' he said.

'The names of the kids you want are as follows: Alison Cole. Matthew Jarvis. Carla Sexton. Claire Cottrell. John Molloy and . . .'

'Wait a minute. Spell Cottrell,' siad the private detective, writing furiously.

Trent sucked in an angry breath and did so.

'Got it. And the last one?' Ryan enquired.

'Maria Jenkins. Got that?'

'Yes, thanks for your help, Pete.'

'All right, Nick. Now, listen! You get anything on this case, anything at all, I want it. You come to me first, understand? I don't want you messing it about.'

And the DC slammed the phone down.

Ryan replaced the receiver, pulled the sheet of paper from the pad and folded it, slipping it into his pocket. He lit up another cigarette and headed out of the office.

He guessed it would take him about thirty minutes to drive to Ossulston Street hostel.

Seventy

The King's Cross Snooker Club in Pentonville Road stood next door to the Scala Cinema. Both buildings looked as if they badly needed renovating.

The sign hanging over the door of the club showed a black, a white and a red ball; the paint was peeling away from all three. As Kiernan pushed open the black doors that marked the entrance to the club, more paint fell away in tiny, cinder-like flakes.

He and Stevie found themselves at the bottom of a long narrow stairwell which led up to a cramped landing. The wooden steps creaked protestingly as the two newcomers climbed. A single unshaded bulb lit the stairwell, casting thick shadows. Kiernan glanced up at it, seeing motes of dust floating in the dull glow it gave off. In places on the wall, mostly in felt-tip pen, phone numbers and occasionally names had been written, some of them faded.

'What's that?' Kiernan asked. 'The local Yellow Pages?'

Stevie ignored him and kept climbing.

'Where's your number?' the Irishman added.

She glared at him and shook her head.

'How do I know you're not protecting him?' he asked, looking back at her. 'We could be trekking round London for days trying to find the bastard.'

'Why should I protect him?' she demanded. 'He ran

243

off with my money. Besides, I can think of better things to do than wander round London with *you*.'

They reached the landing and were confronted by a small glass-fronted booth that looked like a cinema cash desk. Inside, a heavy-set man seemed to have been wedged. He ran appraising eyes over them both, his gaze lingering for a moment on Stevie.

'Two, please,' said Kiernan.

'Are you a member?' the man asked. He smoothed down one side of his thin moustache.

'No, I just want a couple of games,' Kiernan said, smiling.

Moustache smiled too.

'Five quid an hour,' he said. He looked at Stevie again. 'But, er, no women, I'm afraid. Sorry, love.'

She sighed irritably.

'That's the rules, I'm afraid.' Moustache told her apologetically. 'If it was up to me I'd let you in, but it's not up to me so I can't.'

Stevie pulled Kiernan to one side and lowered her voice.

'You can't go in there on your own,' she said. 'If Ray's in there you wouldn't recognize him, anyway. We might as well go.'

'I'll recognize him if you describe him for me,' Kiernan told her.

'Five quid an hour, mate,' Moustache reminded him.

Kiernan dug in his pocket and pushed a ten-pound note across the desk.

He received a small yellow ticket in return.

'What does Howells look like?' Kiernan demanded.

Stevie looked at Moustache, who was pushing the money into a drawer, then turned back to Kiernan.

'He's about five ten, slim. He usually wears a track suit and trainers. He's got hair to his collar but it's shaved at the sides over his ears. He wears a gold earring in his left ear.'

'Is that it?'

'What else do you want to know?' she said, exasperated. 'His shoe size?'

'Keep your voice down,' Kiernan said, holding her gaze. 'Now, where will I meet you when I come out of here?'

'There's a café over the road; you'll see it as soon as you come out. I'll wait there for you.'

He nodded and turned to go inside.

'Kiernan, what are you going to do if he's in there?' she asked.

'I'll give it an hour. If he's not in here, I'll come and meet you. If he is here, or if he does arrive, I'll keep my eye on him, make sure he doesn't leave.'

'And how do you propose to do that?'

'Let me worry about that,' Kiernan told her and turned away, pushing open the door that led through into the snooker hall itself.

Stevie retreated down the stairs, glancing at her watch.

It was 3.05 p.m.

Seventy-one

Nick Ryan stood at the bottom of the short flight of steps and looked up at the entrance to Ossulston Street Hostel. He took the cigarette from his mouth, grinding it out under his foot, then made his way towards the door.

As he reached it he found his way blocked by a slim girl with dark hair and a sallow complexion. She looked at him quizzically as she opened the door to let him in.

He nodded a greeting to her, glancing down to see that she was barefoot.

Suzi Gray pushed a hand through her hair and studied the private detective with her cold grey eyes.

'I wonder if you could help me,' he said.

'That depends what you want,' she told him.

Ryan looked more intently at her, realizing that she was obviously considerably younger than her appearance. There were lines around her cheeks and eyes that really had no right to be present in one so young.

'I'm looking for someone called Emma Powell,' he announced. 'She runs the place, doesn't she?'

'Are you with the police?' Suzi wanted to know.

Ryan grinned.

'Why, do I look like a copper?'

She didn't answer.

'As a matter of fact, I'm looking for someone,' he told her. 'I'm looking for my son, Roger. Roger Grant. Do you know him?'

Suzi shook her head.

'Well, I had a letter from him saying he'd been staying here, and mentioning this Miss Powell. I'd like to see her if I can.'

'So go and see her,' Suzi said.

'Is she free?'

'I just live here,' Suzi told him. 'I'm not her secretary. I can take you to her office, though.'

'You're so kind,' Ryan said, with a hint of sarcasm.

He followed Suzi as she turned and headed back up the corridor, leading him up a flight of steps to the first floor.

As they walked he glanced around him, peering into open doors, spotting other residents of the hostel. They were all young. He doubted if any of them were older than twenty-five. In one room two youths sat on a bed talking and smoking. In another he saw a young girl reading. She glanced across at him as he passed and smiled thinly.

A fat girl in an out-of-date punk outfit passed them in the corridor and Suzi spoke to her. The girl looked at Ryan, then disappeared.

'Here,' Suzi said, indicating a door with a frosted glass panel. 'This is Emma's office.'

She turned and walked away.

'Thanks for your help,' Ryan said, knocking hard.

A voice from inside told him to come in and he obeyed, stepping into the small, warm office, closing the door behind him.

Emma Powell looked bemused as she saw him and put down her pen, ignoring the work she'd been doing.

'Can I help you?' she said.

'I was hoping you might be able to help me. Miss Powell. It is Miss Powell, isn't it? Emma Powell?' Ryan said.

She nodded.

'Have we met?' she asked.

'No,' he said, smiling. He crossed to a chair in front of her desk. 'My name is Grant,' he lied, extending a hand. 'Stuart Grant.' She shook the offered hand and invited him to sit down.

'I'm looking for my son,' he told her as convincingly as he could. 'I have reason to believe he spent some time here.'

'And what was his name?' she asked.

'Roger Grant. He was sixteen. He's been missing for more than eight months now.'

'And what makes you think he stayed here, Mr Grant?'

'He wrote to me to tell me where he was up until

247

about two months ago. He mentioned this place. He mentioned you, too. That's how I knew where to come.' Ryan rubbed his forehead in mock concern, pleased with his own charade. He rarely looked at Emma who was constantly studying him, making her own appraisals.

'I don't recall the name, Mr Grant. I can't remember your son. Are you sure you have the right hostel?'

'Definitely. Mind you, I can understand you not remembering individual faces. You must see hundreds during the course of a year.'

'Yes, I do.'

'It's a pity you can't do more for them.'

'Meaning what?'

'Well, throwing them back on the streets again after three months doesn't help much, does it?'

'I don't throw them back on the street as you put it, Mr Grant. I have no choice. This hostel is a short-stay hostel. No one is allowed to stay here for longer than three months. If you're looking for someone to blame, blame the government.'

Touchy.

'So you say you can't remember my son?' he continued. 'You keep files, don't you? You could check and see if he stayed here.'

'I told you, his name doesn't ring a bell,' Emma said defensively.

'You also told me that you see hundreds of runaways a year. I can understand you not remembering every single one. Perhaps if you checked . . .'

'I'm very busy, Mr Grant,' she said.

'Too busy to check for *one* name?'

'Look, my files are private. Besides which, I have no proof of who you are. You could be anyone who's wandered in off the streets. I'm supposed to protect the youngsters who live here. They're in my care. They

248

trust me. I can't pull out a file just because a total
stranger walks in, claiming his son once spent some
time here. How do I know you're Roger's father? You
haven't even shown me any identification.'

Ryan smiled to himself.

Very efficient.

'No, you're quite right,' he said. 'I'm sorry for being
so rude. It's just that I'm worried. I've been looking for a
long time; this is virtually my last resort.'

She eyed him suspiciously across the desk, turning
her pen over and over in her hand.

'My son mentioned a man called Raymond Howells
in one of his letters,' he lied. 'Do you know anyone of
that name? My son said this man used to come into the
hostel sometimes.'

Ryan watched for any sign of recognition in her eyes
but he saw only steely defiance.

'The only people who come into this hostel, Mr
Grant, are the residents and myself and my staff. Unless
this Mr Howells was a resident here at the same time as
your son, I don't know what you're talking about.'

'My son said he was a drug pusher,' Ryan said flatly.

'This is ridiculous,' Emma said indignantly.

'My son said he used to try and bribe the young girls
here into working for him. He was a pimp, too, you
see,' Ryan continued, still watching for some reaction.

All she did was look at him blankly.

'Howells, how shall I put it, secured the *services* of
several boys and girls who lived here. He enticed them
into working the streets for him. How much do you
know about that?'

'I don't know anything about that at all,' she said. 'All
I do know is I'm beginning to doubt you *are* who you
say you are, Mr Grant, and if you don't leave here soon
I'll have to call the police.'

'I'm here to make honest enquiries about my son,' he

continued. 'I want to find him and all you can do is question my motives.'

Ryan watched Emma's face intently.

'He also mentioned someone called Don Neville,' the private detective added.

A flicker.

He saw her swallow hard.

'Mr Grant, I think you ought to go,' she told him. 'I don't remember your son. I don't think I can help you. Now, unless you show me some identification, I'm going to have to ask you to leave. If you won't leave I'll call the police.'

She moved her hand towards the phone and rested it on the receiver.

Ryan didn't move.

Seventy-two

The only light inside the snooker club seemed to be coming from the huge overhead rectangular devices which were suspended a few feet above each table. The lamps gave off a dull glow, enough to light the table and about a foot or so around it. Each table looked like a little island of luminescence in a sea of gloom.

Kiernan could see figures moving around the tables, could hear the clack of a snooker ball on ball. There were low mumblings every now and then, but apart from that the place was relatively silent.

There was a counter on a raised platform to his left which served hot drinks, canned drinks and spirits.

Two or three men sat alone around the makeshift bar. One watched him intently as he ordered an orange juice. His gaze moved swiftly from face to darkened face, but as far as he could tell there was no sign of Raymond Howells as yet.

There were twelve tables in the first floor room but only three were occupied, the games being played in virtual silence. A single rotary fan turned in the centre of the ceiling, the whoosh of the blades sounding like a muffled helicopter rotor. The fan did little to alleviate the stifling heat. As the barman returned and pushed Kiernan's orange juice towards him, beads of perspiration on the other man's forearm glistened in the dull light behind the bar.

On the walls of the room hung posters of snooker players both old and new. Joe Davis. Jimmy White. Ray Reardon. Alex Higgins.

'I played him once, you know.'

The voice startled the young Irishman. When he turned, a man a few years older than himself was nodding towards the picture of Alex Higgins.

'He played an exhibition match here and I played him,' the man explained. 'Bloody near beat him, too.'

Kiernan nodded and sipped at his drink, his eyes still roving.

Every now and then he glanced at the door, as if expecting Howells to walk in.

What if the bastard had changed his appearance somehow?

What if the description Stevie had given him was wrong?

He sipped at his drink and tried to push the thoughts from his mind.

She thought her watch had stopped. It seemed that every time Stevie Collins looked at the timepiece the

251

hands were in the same position. She raised it to her ear and heard the ticking. It wasn't her watch at fault. It was as if time itself had frozen.

She shifted position on the plastic chair, gazing out of the café window across the street at the snooker club, hardly lowering her watchful stare even to sip at her 7UP.

Perhaps Howells was already inside.

She looked at her watch and saw that it was 3.23.

There were only three other people in the café. An old woman was sipping at a cup of tea and two men were chatting, the sports page of a newspaper laid out before them.

A middle-aged woman with large thighs and very bad varicose veins mopped tables and collected dirty cups. She passed Stevie twice, glancing at her quizzically.

The young girl sipped her drink and kept her eyes on the entrance to the club.

A number of men passed by but none that she recognized.

She scratched absent-mindedly at one of the track marks on her arm, picking a scab free and tossing it into the ashtray where a number of butts already lay. She lit another cigarette and glanced again at her watch.

3.26.

'Fancy a game?'

Kiernan looked at the man on his left and exhaled wearily.

'I said, do you fancy a game?' the man repeated, nodding towards the tables. 'We can have a fiver on it to make it more interesting, if you like.'

'Yeah, okay,' Kiernan said, putting down his drink.

He went and selected a cue from the rack. The other man opened up a small wooden box and took out two halves of a cue which he began screwing together.

252

'This used to belong to my old man,' he announced. 'He was a fucking good player. It was the only thing the old bastard ever gave me in his life, but it's a good cue.'

Kiernan nodded and began racking the balls up.

'My name's Courtney, by the way. Tim Courtney,' the man announced.

'Vince Kiernan.'

'I haven't seen you in here before. You're not local, are you?' Courtney said.

'No. I came in looking for someone, as a matter of fact.'

But there's no sign of the bastard yet.

'Well, this'll pass the time while you're waiting, won't it?' Courtney exclaimed. 'Let's see your money.'

'What?'

'A fiver, we said.' He dug out a five-pound note and put it on the next table. Kiernan did the same. 'You break,' Courtney said, chalking his cue.

Kiernan took a final look at the door and made his first shot.

As the cue ball came to a stop near the top cushion he stepped back. One of the other men at the bar was watching him. Kiernan tried to ignore him.

Where the hell was Howells?

She froze, the glass mid-way between her lips and the table.

Peering through the window of the café, Stevie was certain.

Raymond Howells tossed a cigarette butt away, then made his way into the entrance of the snooker club.

There were two other men with him. One she recognised, a thick-necked individual with a multi-coloured shirt flapping open to reveal his torso. His black skin looked like polished ebony in the blazing sunlight. Carl Masters stood a couple of inches taller than Howells. The other man, whom she didn't recognise, was slightly shorter and wearing a football shirt, red and blue stripes with the word Tulip on it. There was a dark stain down his back.

She watched the three of them disappear into the doorway. Her breath came in gasps.

Stevie looked round frantically.

She had to warn Kiernan.

But how?

Even if there was a phone in the café she didn't know the number of the snooker hall and . . .

A phone.

Ryan had told them to call him if they found Howells. She had his number written on a piece of paper in her purse. She quickly rummaged through it, finding the scrap. She noticed there were two numbers on it; one was his car-phone.

Stevie got to her feet and hurried across to the counter.

'Is there a phone in here?' she asked the large woman with the varicose veins.

'Not in here, love,' the woman told her. 'There's one in the pub over there.' She nodded towards the building facing the café.

Stevie turned and ran towards the pub.

'They'll be shut now. They're a bit old-fashioned over there,' the woman called after her.

Stevie didn't hear.

It wasn't until she reached the pub that she found it was, indeed, closed.

Seventy-three

'I told you before, Mr Grant,' said Emma Powell irritably. 'I have the welfare of the youngsters in my care to consider. I can't allow anyone to look through my files.'

'It's the welfare of my son that *I'm* worried about,' the private detective said, satisfied with his own insincerity. He didn't think she suspected anything untoward. A worried parent was bound to be a little irrational, weren't they?

Experience had taught him that much.

'So you don't know anyone by the name of Howells or Neville?' he persisted.

'No.'

'If you won't allow me to see your files, would you mind if I spoke to some of the other youngsters who are staying here?' he asked.

'You say your son was here two months ago, perhaps longer,' she said. 'It's unlikely any of the residents at the hostel now would have been here at the time your son supposedly was. I would appreciate it if you just left, Mr Grant. There are other hostels where you can check.'

'Well, I hope they're more helpful than you've been,' said Ryan, with suitably melodramatic indignation. He got to his feet and looked down at her. 'I've read in the papers of that series of murders of runaways, Miss Powell. I just hope my son isn't next.'

'Goodbye, Mr Grant,' Emma said flatly.

He turned and headed for the door, slamming it behind him in mock anger.

Emma stared at the closed door for a moment, the vein on her temple pulsing angrily. As she heard his footsteps receding away down the corridor, she sat back in her chair and exhaled deeply.

What she didn't realize was that Ryan had turned right instead of left out of her office when he left. Instead of heading towards the steps which would lead him to the ground floor and out, he had darted off the other way, past two or three closed doors.

He had spotted the fire alarm further up the corridor before he'd entered; now he looked quickly back and forth to ensure the corridor was empty and, with a powerful blow, drove his hand against the glass of the alarm.

The impact was enough to shatter it. The strident ringing of alarm bells filled the building.

Ryan stepped back, inside one of the doors, hoping there was no one inside.

He was lucky.

As the bells continued to shatter the stillness he eased the door open a fraction, just enough to see Emma Powell's office.

It was only a second before she came hurtling out, heading straight for the stairs, shouting words he couldn't quite make out. Others were hurrying from the other rooms, too. With the clanging bells ringing in their ears, their only thought was to reach the safety of the street.

Ryan slipped across the corridor and into Emma Powell's office. Beneath him and around him he could hear the sound of running feet; of shouting, too.

He knew he would have to work fast.

He slid open the top drawer of the filing cabinet

behind Emma's desk, simultaneously digging into his pocket for a piece of paper. On it were written the names of the six runaways murdered in the last few months. He looked at the first name.

ALISON COLE

It matched the name on one of the files.

He checked the next one:

CLAIRE COTTRELL

That also matched.

MATTHEW JARVIS

Check.

He slid open the second drawer.

It was then that he heard movement outside the door.

Seventy-four

Stevie tugged frantically at the pub doors but found they were locked.

She gasped in disappointment and began hammering on them, not stopping until a face appeared from within. The man looked angrily at her, raised his watch and tapped the face.

'We're closed,' he said, his voice muffled by the glass.

'I have to use your phone,' she called back. 'Please, it's an emergency.'

'We're closed,' the man repeated.

I heard you the first time, you fucking idiot.

Stevie banged on the door again, her face contorted by anger and frustration.

'Please,' she shouted. Passers-by gaped at her. 'Open up. I have to use the phone now. Please.'

Anxious to prevent her shattering the glass in the door, the landlord reluctantly set about unfastening it. Stevie stood back a pace, hearing bolts being pulled back. As the door was finally opened a fraction she barged in, nearly knocking the man over.

'What the fuck are you doing?' he snarled. 'I told you, we're closed.'

'I've got to use your phone. *Please*.'

He regarded her silently for a moment, then jabbed a finger towards a corner of the bar. She saw the pay-phone and scurried across to it, picking up the receiver, feeding coins into the machine. She stabbed out the numbers frantically and waited.

As the ringing continued she tried to control her breathing.

'Pick it up,' she said under her breath.

She heard a click, then the answer machine in Ryan's office cut in.

'Shit,' she hissed and pulled down hard on the cradle. She pulled the piece of paper from her bag and tried the car-phone number.

It rang twice then a metallic voice announced;

'The vodaphone number you have reached is not in use. Please try again.'

She slammed the receiver down, found more change and tried again.

First the office.

Nothing.

Then the car-phone.

No answer.

'Where are you?' she gasped exasperatedly.

'Right,' said the landlord, advancing on her. 'That's enough. Come on, out.' He hooked a thumb towards the door.

'No, please,' she protested. 'I have to make this call. Please.'

'I'll give you five minutes,' he said with finality. 'Then you're out. Got it?'

She nodded and dialled again.

He was just as she'd described him.

Vince Kiernan looked up as he heard the club door open and he saw Raymond Howells walk in, flanked by a black man and a man in a football shirt.

Howells was wearing a loose fitting T-shirt and track suit bottoms which bore the England team's crest. He was thinner than Kiernan had imagined. The unusual thing about him, he noticed, was how big his hands were, disproportionately large for his frame. His hair was indeed shaved over his ears, making it look as if he had a pointed head.

The gold earring dangled from his left ear. Kiernan noticed that it was in the shape of a sword.

For a while the young Irishman stood by the table, his gaze rivetted on Howells as he moved across to the bar with his companions.

So this was the man he'd waited so long to find? The man who might know the whereabouts of his sister. This pimp, this pusher, this ponce. Kiernan closed his fists around the cue until his knuckles turned white, gripping the wooden shaft like a club. His first instinct was to take the cue and smash it across Howells' head. To shatter the wood then use the sharp points on him, drive them beneath his flesh. Pierce his body with them until he told him where Jo was, until he admitted how he had abused her and got her hooked on drugs and . . .

He knew he could not do that.

Not yet.

All he could do was stand helplessly by, not quite sure what to do. Helpless in his rage.

'Your shot,' said Courtney, nodding towards the table.

When Kiernan didn't answer, his companion saw where his gaze was directed.

Howells was laughing and joking with the barman and with the two men.

'Do you know him?' Courtney asked.

Kiernan shook his head.

'I thought he was the one you were waiting for. You've been staring at him ever since he walked in,' Courtney said.

The young Irishman tore his gaze away from the pimp.

'Do you know who he is?' Courtney continued as Kiernan tried to line up his shot.

'He just looked familiar that's all,' said Kiernan, trying to dismiss his obvious interest.

Courtney looked on, unimpressed. He glanced across at Howells, then at Kiernan again.

Who the fuck was this guy?

Undercover copper, maybe?

Courtney leant against the next table, watching the young Irishman.

Wondering.

Seventy-five

As Ryan heard the door handle turn he dropped down behind Emma Powell's desk, one of the files still gripped in his hand, the sound of the fire alarm drumming in his ears.

The door opened a fraction and he was vaguely

aware of someone peering in, presumably to check that the office was empty. A second later the door was closed and he heard footsteps echoing away down the corridor.

He got to his feet, perspiration beading on his forehead as he shoved one file back into the drawer and looked for the next one.

It would only be a matter of time before they discovered that there was no fire; but, as he found the file, he knew he only needed moments.

Ryan grabbed it and looked at the name, checking it against the list he had.

MARIA JENKINS

He remembered the name from the newspaper articles he'd read. She'd been the most recent of the runaways to die.

He worked swiftly and efficiently, blotting out the strident ringing of the alarm bells, concentrating only on the files in front of him.

JOHN MOLLOY

That name, too, was on his list.

As was the last one.

CARLA SEXTON.

'Jesus,' he murmured under his breath, slamming the drawers shut. As he turned away from the cabinet, a thought struck him. He pulled open the top drawer and ran his finger along the manilla files.

It was there.

STEPHANIE COLLINS

He licked his lips.

Stevie.

From the second drawer he found the other file.

JOSEPHINE KIERNAN.

Ryan slotted both files back into place, then headed for the door, slipping out into the corridor and heading down the stairs.

As he reached the ground floor he saw figures still dashing in and out of rooms. Some were heading out of the main door, where he could see a dozen or more of them gathered.

Ryan glanced to his left and right and saw that one of the rooms was empty. He slipped inside and crossed to the window, sliding it upwards far enough to enable him to crawl through. He hauled himself over the sill and dropped the two or three feet to the ground. He found himself in a narrow alleyway that ran alongside the hostel. Moving unhurriedly, he walked along it and emerged into Ossulston Street itself. To his right he could see the group of hostel residents gathered on the pavement.

By now they would have figured out there was no fire. That didn't matter to him. He'd seen what he wanted to see.

Every single runaway killed in the last few months had spent some time in the hostel.

There were dozens of them all over London; it had to be more than a coincidence that this one home should have been temporary shelter to all six victims.

He headed back to his car and slid behind the wheel.

Emma Powell saw him as the Sapphire pulled away. Her eyes narrowed in anger. She knew what he'd done, realized that he had probably managed to get a look at the files she had been at pains to keep from him.

She hurried back into the building, up the stairs to her office. The filing cabinets were still open; one of the files stuck up out of place in an otherwise immaculately kept arrangement.

It was the file belonging to Stevie Collins.

If the mysterious Mr Grant was looking for his son, she reasoned, why was he so interested in Stevie's file?

As the alarm bells were shut off and peace descended again Emma picked up her phone, ensuring first that the office door was closed.

In fact, before she dialled, she locked it.

This was one call she didn't want *anyone* walking in on.

Seventy-six

'Come on, for Christ's sake.'

Stevie Collins pressed the phone more tightly to her ear, listening to the constant ringing from the car-phone.

She finally slammed her fingers down on the cradle.

'You've got one more minute, then you're out,' the pub landlord reminded her, leaning against the bar.

'All right, all right,' she said exasperatedly, dialling again, this time to Ryan's office.

As soon as she heard the answer machine begin she hung up.

'Where the hell are you?' she breathed.

She tried the car-phone again. Then the office.

'Come on, for fuck's sake,' the landlord said irritably. 'If you're not off that phone in thirty seconds I'm chucking you out.'

'Look, this call is an emergency,' she said.

'Yeah, they always are,' he said, unimpressed.

She waited a second or two then pressed the digits again, glancing across the street towards the snooker hall.

She wondered what Kiernan was doing inside there. How long Howells would stay.

There was no answer from Ryan's car-phone, just

that infernal metallic voice telling her the number was not available at present.

She tried the office and got the machine again.

Stevie was beginning to realize that it was too late.

Her fingers were hurting from pressing the digits so often but she kept trying, knowing deep down that time had virtually run out.

Courtney sent the black ball into the centre pocket and stood back triumphantly.

'Game to me,' he said, grinning. 'And my tenner too, I think.' He scooped up the two five-pound notes from the next table and pocketed them.

Kiernan looked across the room at the table on the far side where Howells and his companions were racking up balls for their own game.

At least if they were playing, he thought, it would keep Howells in one place; perhaps long enough to alert Ryan.

Kiernan knew he had no choice but to watch Howells until the bastard moved, until he left the snooker club. Even if it meant stopping there until late at night he knew he had to stay on his tail. Now he'd found him he didn't intend letting him slip away.

He just hoped Stevie had seen the pimp enter and had called Ryan.

When the club door opened he turned, hoping to see the private detective. To his disappointment it was the man with the moustache from the cash desk outside. He got himself a can of cold drink from behind the bar and retreated back out of the room.

Kiernan licked his lips and tasted sweat.

Just hold on. Stay with Howells.

'Do you fancy another frame?' Kiernan asked. 'Make it a tenner each this time?'

Courtney smiled and nodded.

'Why not? I'll take your money if you want me to. Set the balls up, I'm going to have a piss.'

As his companion disappeared, Kiernan began fishing the balls out of the pockets and placing them in position.

His eyes were drawn hypnotically towards Howells but he kept his head low, anxious that the pimp shouldn't spot him.

Just keep playing, you fucker. I'm not letting you out of my sight.

With the balls set up, he waited for Courtney to return.

Waited and watched.

At last.

The phone rang almost as soon as he picked it up and Ryan flicked it on, reaching for the handset.

'Ryan.'

'Who's that?' he said, disorientated.

'It's Stevie. Where the hell have you been? I've been trying for ages.'

'All right, take it easy,' he said, noticing the urgency in her voice.

'We've found him,' she blurted. 'Howells. We've found him.'

Ryan sat up in his seat; even the stab of pain in his chest was forgotten as the news sank in.

'Where are you?' he wanted to know.

'I'm in a pub . . .'

He heard a series of high-pitched beeps.

'Oh, Jesus Christ,' he heard her say.

'Stevie.'

'Howells is . . .'

The line went dead.

She'd run out of change.

Seventy-seven

'Right, that's it,' said the landlord, advancing towards her. 'Out. I said five minutes. You've made your call, now shift your arse.'

'I ran out of fucking change,' Stevie blurted. 'Please, I've got to complete this call. It's a matter of life and death. Just ten pence, that's all I want.'

He shook his head, dug in his pocket and found a twenty-pence piece.

'Here,' he said, tossing it to her. 'Have a party.'

Stevie caught it with one hand and immediately pushed it into the phone, dialling frantically.

Try as he might, Kiernan could not keep his mind on the game and he found himself behind once again.

Courtney moved slowly but purposefully around the table potting balls, murmuring approvingly to himself in the process.

Kiernan's attention was focused equally on his opponent and on Howells who was standing watching as his colleague in the football shirt potted balls.

Without realizing it, the young Irishman was staring at Howells.

The pimp noticed.

For interminable seconds across the dimly lit hall they gazed at each other. Then Howells turned to his black companion and said something. He too looked across at Kiernan and nodded. Howells leant closer to speak again.

What if they'd realized who he was? Kiernan thought in a moment of blind panic.

How could they know?

The black man put down his cue and began walking across the hall towards Kiernan.

Now what?

Kiernan felt his heart thudding madly against his ribs as he drew nearer.

'Your shot,' said Courtney, but Kiernan seemed uninterested in the game any longer.

The man was still advancing.

'Come on,' Courtney pressed.

Then he saw that the Irishman was staring at Howells.

'Do you fancy that fucking geezer or what?' he asked, scornfully. 'You've been watching him ever since he came in.'

The black man was a matter of yards away now.

Kiernan moved around the table, gripping the cue, ready to use it as a weapon if necessary.

'Do you know him or not?' Courtney persisted, prodding Kiernan in the back. 'Is he the one you came in here to meet? Because if he is, then go and play with *him*. I wanted a decent game.'

The black man was at the far end of the table now, his eyes fixing the Irishman in an unyielding stare.

'Either take the fucking shot or let's call it a day here and now,' Courtney said. 'I'll take your tenner and . . .'

Kiernan turned and glared at his opponent.

The black man passed by, giving Kiernan a cursory glance. He headed towards the toilets.

Kiernan let out a sigh of audible relief and bent down to take his shot. He put a red into one of the top pockets, looking round as he got up, stealing a glance at Howells then towards the toilets.

He wondered how long it would be before the black man emerged.

She kept one eye on the rapidly disappearing units as she spoke to Ryan.

They clicked away with alarming speed.

'Howells is in a snooker club in the Pentonville Road,' Stevie said, noticing that the units had already flickered down to sixteen. She knew she had to speak fast. 'It's right next door to the Scala Cinema.'

'Where's Kieran?' Ryan wanted to know.

'He's in there, too. He's keeping an eye on Howells.'

Twelve units left.

'He's got a couple of mates with him, Ryan.'

'Do you know them?'

'One of them. A big black guy called Masters.'

Eight units to go.

'Do you know where this bloody club is?' Stevie said.

Six units.

'Yeah, you just hang on. I'll be there in ten minutes.'

He hung up.

Seventy-eight

She saw the Sapphire approaching, saw Ryan glancing agitatedly left and right looking for somewhere to park. There was a barrier of traffic cones across the road opposite and Stevie ran over, dodging between the other cars, pulling two or three of the cones aside.

Ryan shot across the street, cutting in front of the other traffic. A chorus of hooters greeted his manoeuvre but the private detective ignored them, stepping on the brake and bringing the car to a skidding halt. The engine was still running as he slid out from behind the wheel. Only as he clambered out did he turn it off and pull the keys from the ignition.

'How long's Howells been in there?' he asked, striding towards the snooker club.

'About half an hour,' Stevie said, having to run to keep up with him.

'You're sure it's him?'

'Positive.'

As they passed the front entrance of the Scala Cinema a tall, skinny youth with a faded black T-shirt pushed through the door and pointed at Ryan's car.

'You can't park that there,' he said.

'Fuck off,' Ryan hissed, glaring at the youth, who hesitated then stepped back inside the cinema.

Ryan's shirt was flapping as he walked; he was careful to ensure it didn't blow open wide enough to reveal the holster around his waist. Nestled in it was the 9mm Automatic.

He reached the door of the club and almost sprinted up the wooden steps. Stevie struggled to keep up.

'You say he's got two mates with him?' he said.

'I only recognized one of them, though. I've seen him around a few times . . .' She allowed the sentence to trail off, realizing Ryan wasn't listening.

They had reached the top of the stairs now and Ryan moved straight towards the door.

'Hold on, mate,' said the man with the moustache, pulling himself out of his cash desk and blocking the private detective's path. 'I've got to see your membership. You can't just go walking in there and you,' he looked at Stevie, 'I've told you once there's no women allowed, right?'

Ryan looked straight at the man, his eyes blazing.

269

'Your membership . . .' Moustache said.

'Here's my fucking membership,' snapped Ryan, pulling the Automatic from its holster.

He pressed it up under the other man's chin, forcing him back against the door and then through it.

It swung back on its hinges and Ryan, Moustache and Stevie all stumbled in.

Kiernan looked up, a smile flickering briefly on his lips as he saw the private detective.

Everyone else froze.

Ryan pushed Moustache away and the big man stumbled and fell against the bar.

'Fuck,' hissed Raymond Howells. 'The Law.'

Then he saw Stevie.

'There he is,' she shouted to Ryan, pointing at the pimp.

Howells yelled in anger and hurled his cue at Ryan, making him duck. As he did, Moustache suddenly decided to be a hero.

The big man flung himself at Ryan, crashing into him, knocking him against the door. The gun fell from his hand but Stevie snatched it up, watching as Ryan drove a flailing arm out, catching Moustache in the face.

Howells saw his chance.

'Let's get out of here,' he shouted and he and his two companions bolted for the door.

Kiernan stepped in front of them, twisting the snooker cue in his hand, gripping the thinner end.

He swung the cue like a club, the heavy end smacking hard into the face of the black man.

It connected with such force that the cue snapped, leaving the Irishman clutching the thick end.

Masters went down like a stone, clutching his face, blood pouring through his fingers from his broken nose.

'You cunt,' roared the other man, hurling himself at Kiernan.

270

They crashed against one of the tables, rolling over it, scattering the balls.

Kiernan felt the cue slip from his hand. Strong fingers gripped his throat as the man in the football shirt lifted his head a few inches and slammed it back against the slate bed of the table.

Kiernan thought he was going to black out from the impact, but he reached out frantically for something to defend himself with and his hand closed over one of the snooker balls.

Using all his strength he brought the ball up and smashed it into the temple of his assailant.

The man fell backwards, cracking his head on the overhead lamp, which began to swing crazily.

Kiernan rolled off the table and drove a kick into the ribs of his fallen attacker, smiling as he heard the crack of breaking bone.

Ryan grabbed Moustache by the front of the shirt and headbutted him, catching him above the right eye, splitting the soft skin.

The big man fell back, blood pouring down his face.

'Ryan,' Kiernan bellowed, pointing at Howells who had almost reached the door.

The pimp tried to side-step the private detective's lunge but failed and both of them fell to the floor, Ryan recovering first, driving a fist into the face of his opponent.

The blow split Howells' bottom lip and blood burst from the fleshy flap. Ryan scraped his knuckles on the other man's teeth but kept a firm hold on him, gripping his T-shirt, hauling him to his feet.

Kiernan turned to see the black man rising, one hand still covering his face. He was teetering uncertainly and the Irishman took advantage of his plight, kicking him hard between the legs. The man howled in pain and went down again, rolling over to lie beside his companion in the football shirt who was gasping for breath, clutching his side in an effort to relieve the pain of his cracked ribs.

Stevie handed Ryan his gun and he jammed the Automatic into Howells' face, pushing him out of the door towards the stairs.

Kiernan sprinted across to join them, looking back at the three fallen men.

As they reached the top of the stairs Howells tried to squirm free of Ryan's grip.

'You're going down those stairs, you little ponce,' Ryan hissed, pressing the barrel hard against the pimp's cheek. 'You either walk down or you go down head first, it makes no fucking odds to me. Got it?'

'You can't fucking do this,' Howells snarled defiantly.

'And who's going to stop me?' the private detective snapped.

'You fucking grassed me up, you slag,' Howells shouted at Stevie.

'Just walk, shithead,' Ryan said, pushing him towards the stairs, keeping a firm grip on his T-shirt. 'Save the conversation for later.'

'I'm saying fuck-all to you,' Howells told him. 'I want my solicitor.'

'Just walk, while you still can.' The private detective glanced at Kiernan. 'Keep your eye on the top of the stairs. Just make sure none of this half-wit's mates decide to try and rescue him.'

Kiernan nodded, moving slowly down the steps behind them, his eyes fixed on the door.

Only when they reached the pavement did he move up alongside Ryan.

They walked to the car.

'You drive,' Ryan said to Kiernan, pushing Howells into the back seat and climbing in after him. He tossed the ignition key to the Irishman, who started the car.

Stevie slid into the passenger seat.

'Where to?' Kiernan wanted to know.

'Just drive,' Ryan told him. 'I want to talk to our friend, Mr Howells.'

Seventy-nine

'Who the fuck are you, anyway? If you're a copper, you'll never make anything stick. What are you going to do? Use that fucking slag as a witness? Was she the one who grassed in the first place?'

Raymond Howells spat out the words, the vein in his temple throbbing madly. He looked alternately at Ryan and Stevie, saving his most venomous words and looks for the girl. She sat with one arm draped over the back of the passenger seat, looking at him.

'You fucking bitch,' he rasped.

'Why don't you shut up?' said Ryan wearily.

'You'll never make anything stick, you . . .'

'I'll stick your head through that fucking window if you don't shut it.'

'Tell me who you are. If you ain't with the Law, then who sent you?' Howells went on. 'You won't get away with this. I've got friends, you know, you . . .'

Ryan shot out a hand and gripped Howells' T-shirt, pulling him across the back seat so that his face was only an inch or two away.

'That's enough,' he hissed. 'Now shut your mouth and listen, for a change. I want you to answer some questions. If you do, I'll let you go. If not,' he drew the

273

Automatic and shoved it hard into Howell's groin. 'If not, I'm going to blow your bollocks off. Got it? I tried to keep it as simple as I could, you fucking half-wit. Now you listen to me. Do you know a man called Don Neville?'

Some of Howell's bravado disappeared as he felt the gun crushing against his testicles. He swallowed hard, trying to look unconcerned.

'Maybe,' he said warily.

Ryan pressed the gun harder against his groin.

'Either you do or you don't,' he snapped. 'Now, unless you want a nine-millimetre vasectomy, you'd better tell me. Do you know Don Neville?'

'Yeah, I know him. Who told you? That slag?' He jabbed an accusatory finger towards Stevie.

'You worked with him,' Ryan said. The words were a statement, not a question. 'Supplied him with girls and boys to make his videos, didn't you?'

'Look, I'm not saying anything until you tell me who you are,' Howells said.

'What difference does it make?' Ryan snapped.

'I want to know who you are.'

'I'm the bloke who's holding a gun against your bollocks. Good enough? Now, how long have you been working with Neville?'

'Why don't you just ask *her*? She'll tell you,' Howells said angrily.

'I'm asking *you*, scumbag. How long have you been working with Neville?'

'I'm not saying. I don't work *with* him, anyway. Yeah, I did supply some kids for his videos. She was one of them. She never fucking complained when she got paid for getting fucked up the arse by three blokes, though, did you?' His anger was again directed at Stevie. 'It was good enough to get you what you really wanted, wasn't it? The shit to stick in your fucking arms.'

274

'I never saw that money anyway, you bastard. You took it,' Stevie said angrily. 'Just like you took the last lot I gave you.'

'So Stevie was in Neville's videos, right?' Ryan interrupted. 'What about a girl called Jo? An Irish girl. Do you remember her?'

Kiernan's ears pricked up as he drove.

'Why should I remember some mick tart?' he wanted to know.

Kiernan glanced at him in the rear-view mirror.

'She was my fucking sister, you bastard,' he snarled. 'If you've hurt her, I'll kill you.'

'I haven't touched her,' Howells said indifferently.

'When did you last see her?' Kiernan asked.

'A couple of days ago,' Howells told him. 'Who cares?'

'Was she okay?'

'What am I? A fucking doctor? She was walking about. What more do you want?'

'Kiernan, head for Brompton cemetery,' Ryan said, spotting a road sign.

'Why the fuck are you taking me there?' Howells asked.

'Who said we were?' Ryan asked.

'Then where are you taking me?' the pimp demanded.

'Just somewhere quiet so we can have a chat,' Ryan said, looking deeply into Howells' eyes. 'And believe me, you *are* going to talk to me, sunshine.'

Eighty

Her mind was spinning. Images and thoughts tumbled through it. Kim Finlay found she was unable to concentrate on anything for more than a few seconds, unable to focus. She gazed blankly at the TV screen but saw nothing; the images made little or no sense. In fact if someone had sneaked into the room and removed the set Kim probably wouldn't have noticed. The images were *inside* her head.

Kelly.

Ryan.

The thought that she could lose her daughter and her first husband so close together was almost intolerable, too horrific to contemplate. Yet it was a thought she found herself confronted with time and time again as she sat motionless on the sofa.

Ryan was dying. That much was certain.

The shock of that was bad enough, but to know that her only daughter might also soon be dead, by violent means, was more than she could take.

Ryan had not contacted them since he'd begun his search for Kelly. She told herself it was because he wanted to wait until he'd found her safe and well before he announced the news. Perhaps he'd even turn up at the house with her. The other side of her mind, the side that insisted on confronting her with logic, told her he had not been in contact because he had no information. Why *tell* them his search had been fruitless when the absence of communication was testament to that?

Kim exhaled deeply and rubbed her face with both hands, feeling totally numb.

Finlay sat across the room from her, slumped in an armchair, a drink in his hand. He'd drunk a lot that evening; a little too much for Kim's liking, but she could understand. He was under as much stress as she was. But when she looked at him and saw that his expression, too, was blank, she might have expected the images tumbling through his mind to be the same as those which plagued hers.

They were not.

Joseph Finlay was thinking about Kelly, but he was also thinking about Don Neville and Edward Caton.

And the tape.

That tape.

Ryan had *that* tape. But who was to say Neville hadn't made copies? Who was to say that, after all this was over, he wouldn't still sell it? More to the point, what guarantee did Finlay have that, when he paid the ransom as he must surely do, Kelly would be released safely?

He had seen what had been done to her on *that* tape.

What state of mind could he expect to find her in?

If Neville had succeeded once with blackmail, what was to prevent him trying it again?

Secrets.

They filled his mind. Tormented him.

He got to his feet and wandered out of the room, heading for the lavatory.

When the phone rang, Kim picked it up.

It could be Ryan, ringing to say that he'd found Kim, that she was safe and he was bringing her home.

It wasn't.

'I want to speak to Joseph Finlay,' the voice said briskly.

She knew instinctively that this voice belonged to the man who held her daughter.

'Who is this?' she asked, her voice quivering.

'Is Finlay there?'

'He's just popped out. He'll only be a second.'

'If you're trying to keep me talking so the police can get a trace on this line you're wasting your time, Mrs Finlay,' Neville said. 'And if there are police listening in, you're putting your daughter's life at risk. I told your fucking husband he wasn't to contact the police.'

'No one's listening and we haven't been to the police,' Kim said quickly. 'I swear it.'

'You tell your husband I'll ring back.'

'You'd better not hurt my daughter, you bastard,' Kim said defiantly.

Neville chuckled.

'Perhaps you'd better ask your husband *why* this happened, Mrs Finlay,' Neville said and hung up.

Kim sat there for a long moment, the phone still pressed to her head, only the drone of a dial tone in her ear.

She still had the receiver in her hand when Finlay walked back into the room.

'Who was that?' he asked anxiously.

She dropped the phone back onto the cradle.

'The man's who's got Kelly,' she said flatly. 'He's ringing back. He wanted to speak to you.'

'What about?' Finlay demanded, his brow furrowing.

'I don't know, Joe. You'd probably have more idea than me.'

'What the hell is that supposed to mean?'

'He said I should ask you *why* Kelly was kidnapped. Why would he say that? Why would you know?'

'The bastard's playing games with you, Kim. It's not enough for that kind to realize the misery they cause, they have to hear it too. They enjoy it.'

278

'Who are they, Joe?'

'How the bloody hell should *I* know?' Finlay snapped with undue defensiveness. 'I told you, that kind of person, they . . . it's a game to them. A psychological game.' He picked up his drink and drained what was left in the glass, wiping his mouth with the back of his hand. 'If Ryan got his bloody finger out and found some leads this could all be over with.'

'Don't blame Nick,' she said irritably.

The phone rang again.

This time Finlay picked it up, his hand shaking.

'Yes,' he barked.

'Just listen to me, Finlay,' said Neville. 'This has gone on long enough. I'm sick of waiting for the fucking money. I want it by midnight tomorrow night, got that?'

'And Kelly . . .'

'Just shut up and listen. You pay up and you get the kid back. Bring the money to Forty-three Carnaby Street tomorrow night. We'll make the exchange then. Midnight. If you're one minute late then the kid is dead. And don't forget, come alone. If I so much as suspect you've got someone with you the deal's off and you can use some of that fucking money to go towards your daughter's funeral. Understand?'

Finlay swallowed hard.

'Understand?' Neville hissed.

'Yes, you bastard, I understand.'

'Midnight tomorrow night and we'll complete this little bit of business.' Neville chuckled. 'Don't forget what I told you. Come alone. If I see anyone else but you I'll do my magic trick for you.'

'What are you talking about?'

'I'll turn your fucking daughter into dog meat.'

He hung up.

Eighty-one

The noise of the crowd was deafening, even at that distance. Coupled with the rattle of passing tube trains the spot in Brompton cemetery where Kiernan stopped the car was anything *but* peaceful.

It was ideal.

The floodlights of Chelsea Football Club's Stamford Bridge stadium shone brightly, illuminating the dusky sky, while thousands of supporters roared encouragement.

As Ryan stepped out of the car the roar seemed to diminish; he assumed one of the visiting Liverpool players had the ball. But his thoughts were not of football as he moved away from the car and motioned for Howells to follow him.

Kiernan and Stevie were already out of the Sapphire and standing close by, watching as the pimp eased himself uneasily out of the vehicle and glared at each of them in turn, his most venomous look reserved for Stevie. Some of Howells' bravado had disappeared, however. His eyes still darted back and forth angrily but there was fear behind them.

'Why the fuck have you brought me here?' he said.

'I want you to tell me about Neville,' Ryan said calmly. He lit up a cigarette and drew hard on it.

'I told you all I'm going to tell you,' the pimp said.

'Yeah, so you said,' Ryan reminded him. He took a step forward so that he was barely a foot away from the pimp, who recoiled slightly. 'Now I want to know when was the last time you saw him?'

'I haven't seen him for months.'

'When was the last time you supplied him with kids for one of his videos?' Ryan persisted.

'I told you, I haven't seen him,' Howells insisted.

The movement was so swift it took Kiernan and Stevie by surprise.

Ryan swung the Automatic upwards and slammed it into the side of Howells' head, opening a cut on his temple. As the pimp went down heavily, Ryan grabbed him by the T-shirt with one hand, sliding the 9mm into his belt at the same time.

Using two hands he raised Howells up and slammed the back of his head against the back door of the car.

There was a dull thud. The pimp moaned; his head felt as if it were about to burst.

'How long since you saw Neville?' Ryan snapped.

There was a series of loud roars from the direction of Stamford Bridge.

'I haven't seen him,' burbled Howells, blood running down his face.

Ryan pulled open the rear door and jammed Howells' left hand between the frame and the chassis.

Kiernan, realizing what he was about to do, looked at the private detective in astonishment.

'How much did he pay you for the kids?' Ryan snapped.

'He didn't pay me . . .'

Ryan kicked the door.

It crashed shut, crushing Howells' hand, bones splintering under the impact. Two knuckles were pulped; the fingers bent into bloodied lumps.

Howells screamed in agony.

He tried to pull his hand away, but Ryan held it there and glared into his eyes. They were filled with tears and bulging madly.

'Talk to me, you cunt,' he hissed angrily at the pimp. 'How much did he pay you to supply the kids?'

Howells didn't answer. The pain from his pulverized left hand seemed to have crept up his arm until it felt as if the entire limb was on fire. The appendage was numb; only the pain made him aware it was still attached to his wrist. He tried to pull away but Ryan kept a firm grip on him, twisting him round so that he was staring into his face.

'You got kids from the Ossulston Street hostel, didn't you?' the private detective snarled.

Howells opened his mouth to speak but no words would come out, only sobs of pain.

Ryan slammed the door on his hand again.

Howells' caterwaul of agony was swallowed by a massive roar from the Chelsea fans.

The pimp's hand now looked as if it had been dipped in blood. Kiernan could see pieces of shattered bone sticking through the pulped mess of lacerated flesh.

'You got kids from the hostel, didn't you?' Ryan snarled.

Howells was sobbing now, tears of pain rolling down his cheeks.

'Didn't you?' bellowed Ryan, kicking the door shut again.

As the door shut for the third time on his crushed hand, it looked as if Howells was going to pass out. Ryan grabbed him, slapping his face hard to keep him conscious, denying him the oblivion of a blackout.

'Didn't you?' he repeated.

'Yes,' Howells screamed, blood from his pulped hand running down the side of the car.

Ryan looked across at Kiernan and Stevie and saw the Irishman nod imperceptibly.

'How much did Neville pay you for the kids you supplied him with?' the private detective continued.

Howells was slumped on one side, his hand dangling uselessly by his thigh, blood oozing from several lacerations.

'How much?' Ryan persisted.

'I can't tell you,' Howells wailed.

Ryan shut his right hand in the door.

As he dragged it open the pimp fell face down on the earth, his body motionless.

'Get up, you fucker,' snarled Ryan, placing one foot perilously close to the injured left hand.

Howells didn't move.

Ryan kicked him hard in the side.

The pimp rolled over; his body was racked by sobs.

'Please,' he blubbered.

'Please what?' Ryan hissed. 'Please don't hurt you? Don't hurt you the way you hurt those kids you sold to Neville?'

'I didn't know what he was going to do to them, I fucking swear it,' Howells cried.

'Liar,' said Ryan and stamped on his shattered left hand. He kept his foot there, twisting the heel, not letting Howells get up.

There was another roar from Stamford Bridge.

'Ryan, for Christ's sake,' Kiernan said, stepping forward.

The private detective glared at his companion.

'What?' he snarled. 'Didn't you want me to hurt him? Remember, Kiernan, this is the bastard who used your sister. She could be dead because of this piece of shit.'

Dead, like my daughter.

'How much did he pay you?' Ryan demanded.

'A hundred for each one,' Howells whimpered, both his hands now little more than crimson lumps.

'When was the last time you saw Neville?' Ryan continued.

'I'm not sure,' Howells sobbed.

Ryan brought his foot crashing down on the pimp's outstretched left hand with such force the nail of his middle finger came off.

'When?' Ryan shouted.

'About three months ago,' Howells screamed.

'Fucking liar. When?'

'Three months ago! Jesus fucking Christ, I swear it,' Howells said, the pain now intolerable.

'Where?' Ryan demanded.

'I can't remember, honest to God. If I could, I'd tell you. I haven't seen him for three months at least. I've told you all I know, I fucking swear it.'

'Where does he make the videos?' Kiernan interjected.

'I don't know that either,' Howells blubbered. 'I just got him the kids. On the last film he said he didn't need me. He'd found somebody else to get them for him, he said. I haven't seen the cunt since.'

Ryan looked at Kiernan, bemused.

Someone else to get the kids for him.

'Who was getting him the kids?' the private detective asked.

'He didn't tell me.'

Ryan stepped back. The pimp was curled up in a foetal position, rocking himself gently, his pulped hands held out like bloodied trophies.

'How long is it since you worked for Neville?' Ryan said to Stevie.

'About three months,' she confirmed.

'So the bastard's telling the truth. Maybe Neville's *was* getting the kids from someone else. What we've got to find out is *who*.'

He held out his hand towards Kiernan.

'Give me the car keys,' he said.

'What about him?' Kiernan said, nodding towards Howells.

'He's told us all he knows,' Ryan said with certainty. 'He's served his purpose.'

The private detective drew the Automatic from his belt and aimed it at Howells who, even through his pain, looked up in terror, trying to drag himself backwards on what were little more than pulverized bleeding stumps.

'You can't,' he sobbed. 'Please.'

'I don't think you'll be missed,' Ryan snarled. 'What's one less piece of dog shit on the pavement?'

He pulled the trigger.

The hammer slammed down on an empty chamber.

Three things happened simultaneously.

There was a massive roar from Stamford Bridge that seemed to fill the night.

Raymond Howells filled his pants.

Then he fainted.

He lay still on the earth.

Kiernan exhaled deeply.

'When did you take the magazine out?' the Irishman asked.

'As I got out of the car,' Ryan said, sliding behind the steering wheel.

He glanced round to see Stevie going through the pockets of the unconscious Howells. She scurried back to the car brandishing a couple of twenty-pound notes, which she stuffed into her handbag.

'At least I got *some* of my money back,' she said cheerfully.

Ryan looked blankly at her then started the engine, guiding the car along the cemetery's narrow tarmac tracks until he reached the main gate.

As he waited to turn left into Fulham Road he glanced first one way, then the other. He caught sight of some slicks of Howells' blood on the rear door. He ignored it and drove on, heading back into the West End.

Eighty-two

The suite Charles Thornton used as offices consisted of four rooms situated over The Emperor Club in Dover Street. It was the largest of the casinos Thornton owned; it was especially close to his heart because it was the first such establishment he had ever purchased. It seemed an eternity since he'd taken over the licence from the previous owner, albeit with a campaign of intimidation the Krays would have been proud of. But the club was his and now he sat in the opulent splendour of the largest room, the one he used as his personal office, sipping a glass of mineral water and gazing across the room at a huge panoramic painting depicting the Circus Maximus. Thornton smiled to himself. His admiration for the Roman way of life, the power and the organization, had prompted him to name the club after the ancient civilization's leaders. He saw himself as something of a modern-day Caesar, conquering where necessary, consolidating, bargaining and generally ruling the largest underworld empire in London. Most of what he dealt with *was* legitimate; to the outside world Charles Thornton represented the face, and an acceptable one too, of successful business.

Now this successful businessman, who had personally been responsible for at least three killings and indirectly responsible for many more, sat brushing specks of dust from his polished desk, glancing now and then at his own reflection in the gleaming sheen.

'Are you sure I can't get you a drink?' he said, smiling.

Joseph Finlay shifted in his seat and shook his head.

'I told you, Charles,' he said. 'This isn't really a social call.'

Thornton smiled again.

'Well, if it's *that* important, perhaps we'd better get on with things.'

Finlay looked round to see Phillip Alexander standing by the door.

'I wanted to talk in private,' Finlay said.

'I trust the people who work for me, Joe. You can speak in front of Phil.'

'In private,' Finlay said, unimpressed.

Thornton's smile faded. He looked at Alexander and nodded towards the door.

'Just wait outside for a bit, Phil,' he said and the other man left.

Finlay waited until he heard the door close before he spoke.

'I need something from you, Charles. It's important.' He swallowed hard.

Thornton raised his eyebrows quizzically.

'I guessed it must be for you to come here,' he said.

'I don't know how to say this.' He lowered his gaze momentarily. 'I want someone . . . taken care of. I need you to . . . dispose of someone for me, or however you put it in your business.'

'My *business*. What's that supposed to mean?'

'You know bloody well what I mean. All this . . .' He made a sweeping gesture, designed to encompass the entire room. 'You didn't get it by using your business acumen, did you?'

Thornton regarded him coldly.

'You're a crook, Charles. A gangster. Let's not beat around the bush. We've known each other too long for that.'

'Yeah, let's *not* beat around the bush,' Thornton echoed angrily. 'You call me a gangster, a crook. What does that make you? Don't try to come across all fucking virginal with me, Finlay. You're dirtier than *I* am. It's just that you try to hide behind your credentials, behind your nice cosy little family.' He glared at the property developer. 'Like the man said, Finlay, we're just part of the same hypocrisy.'

'I want someone killed,' Finlay said flatly. 'A hit. I'm willing to pay for it.'

'Well, well, well,' Thornton said sardonically. 'Mr Upstanding Himself.'

'I said I'd pay. Will you do it?'

'Why is it so important to you?'

'I can't say. Listen, Thornton, you're the only one who can help me now. Either you'll do it or you won't but I'll pay you whatever you want.'

Thornton could hear the desperation in the other man's voice. He considered him carefully.

'Who's the bunny?' he wanted to know. 'Who's giving you so much grief you want them *hit*?' He emphasized the word scornfully.

'There are three of them.'

'Three? Jesus, what *have* you been up to, Joey boy?'

'This is no joke. Will you do it or not?'

Thornton stroked a hand over his hair and sat back in his seat.

'It's going to cost you, Finlay,' he said slowly.

'I told you, I don't care how much I have to pay. Money's no object.'

'And money's not what I want. You're right, it's going to cost you but not cash.' He tapped the desk top gently. 'I want that building in Cavendish Square. The one you've been sitting on all this fucking time. That's my price, Finlay.'

'You can have it,' he said unhesitatingly.

288

Thornton narrowed his eyes, suspicious of the other man.

'Two weeks ago you'd have shit glass rather than sold me that building. Why the change of heart?' he wanted to know.

'I told you, I need you to do this job for me and I don't care what it takes. If it's going to cost me the building, that's fair enough.'

'Write it down,' said Thornton, pushing a piece of paper and pen towards the other man.

'What are you talking about?'

'Put it in writing that the building is mine. I want it on paper. We'll get it done properly later, but I want assurances from you.'

Finlay hesitated.

'Do it, Joe,' Thornton insisted. 'Just something simple will do. I, Joseph Finlay, hereby declare that as of today's date,' he looked at his wristwatch to verify what it was, 'agree to sell Number Seven Cavendish Square to Charles Thornton. This agreement to be effective as of noon today.' He checked his watch again. 'That's in about ten minutes' time.'

Finlay gripped the pen until the tip of his finger hurt but then he began to write. Finally he handed the paper to Thornton.

'Sign it,' Thornton told him, pushing it back.

He did so.

'Satisfied?' Finlay said irritably.

Thornton smiled and nodded.

'The building's yours. Will you do the job for me?' Finlay persisted.

Thornton got to his feet, taking the piece of paper with him. He crossed to a small wall safe which he proceeded to open, placing the folded paper inside.

He took out something Finlay couldn't see until he laid it on the desk before him.

The metal glinted under the lights.

'Ruger .45 revolver,' said Thornton. 'You can load those in it.' He tossed a box of shells onto the desk beside the pistol.

'What the hell are you talking about?' Finlay said, suddenly anxious.

'I'm not sanctioning a hit on your behalf, Finlay. You want the fucking job done, do it yourself.'

'We made a deal,' Finlay said angrily.

'You should know not to trust *me*, Joe. After all, I'm a gangster according to you.' His smile vanished rapidly. 'But I've got better things to do than send my men chasing around blowing away some arseholes who've upset you. What do you think this is, the fucking Godfather?' He glared at Finlay. 'Now get out. Our meeting's over.'

'You bastard,' hissed Finlay, reaching for the gun.

He gripped it and pointed it at Thornton, who merely shook his head.

'Get out of here, Joe, or I'll stick that gun so far up your arse you'll be able to load it through your nose,' he hissed. Then he shouted, 'Phil.'

The door opened and Alexander entered.

'Make sure *Mr* Finlay leaves the building, will you, Phil?' Thornton said.

Finlay picked up the gun and ammo and dropped them into his jacket pockets.

'You don't want to be walking around the streets like that, you know, Joe,' he said, grinning.

Finlay glared at him.

'I ought to kill *you*,' he hissed.

'I wouldn't recommend you try. By the way, who *are* you going to kill?'

'What fucking business is it of yours?' snarled Finlay.

'They might be friends of mine,' Thornton said, grinning.

'Their names are Neville and Caton.'

Thornton frowned and shot a glance at Alexander. He merely shrugged.

What the fuck was going on here?

'And the third one?' Thornton asked, his smile replaced by a look of bemusement.

'He's a private detective,' said Finlay. 'His name's Ryan.'

Eighty-three

'I can't see what good this is going to do,' Stevie said.

Ryan tapped gently on the steering wheel, waiting for the lights to turn green.

The private detective didn't answer at first; his attention was drawn to the young woman driving the car in the next lane. It was an XR3i, with its top down. The woman was wearing a pair of denim shorts and a halter-neck top that barely restrained her breasts. She brushed the hair away from her face, re-adjusting her Ray-Bans. Then she glanced in Ryan's direction and realized he was looking at her.

He smiled. She smiled back.

Sit on this, Ryan thought.

While you still can.

He closed his eyes tightly for a second. When he opened them again the girl had gone. The lights were green and someone behind was banging their hooter. He drove on, trying to ignore the pain in his chest. He'd taken a double dose of morphine that morning but he still felt discomfort.

Was the end coming more quickly than he'd expected?

He gripped the wheel tightly, catching a brief glimpse of his haggard reflection in the rear-view mirror.

'I said, I can't see what good this is going to do,' Stevie repeated.

'I heard you,' he said, the words almost lost as the car entered the Euston Road underpass. The sound of so much traffic reverberated around them; the stink of exhaust fumes became even stronger. Only when the car eventually emerged into daylight again did Ryan speak.

'I want you to have a look at the files in Emma Powell's office,' he told her, 'to see if you recognise any of the kids there. She's got pictures of most of them in the files.'

'And how the hell are we going to get into her office? She's not going to invite us in and make us a cup of tea while we look, is she?'

'Did she always keep the files locked away?'

'How the hell do I know?'

'You stayed at the bloody place; you must know how she ran it.'

'I wasn't really interested in how the place was run. It was somewhere to live, that was it. I didn't give two fucks about how it was run.'

'More interested in the charming Mr Howells, were you?'

'You're starting to sound like Kiernan, now. He never stops digging at me. It's my fucking life and I can do what I like with it.'

'It makes no odds to me at all what you do with your life, Stevie. I just need your help. I'm paying for your fucking help, in fact.'

'Yeah, that reminds me. You owe me money. You said you'd pay me when we found Howells. Well, we found him. I helped you find him. You owe me.'

'You'll get it, don't worry,' Ryan snapped. 'It's not

going to break your back to do one more thing for me. I'll give you another hundred quid if you're *that* fucking desperate.'

She took a comb from her handbag and began running it through her hair.

'What are you going to spend it on when you get it?' Ryan asked. 'Drugs?'

'Is it important? Why the hell are you and Kiernan always preaching? Have a look at yourself in the mirror before you start trying to run my life for me.'

'How well did you know Kiernan's sister?' Ryan asked.

'We were friends. We used to work the same beat, we had the same punters.'

'And the same pimp,' he said. 'Where do you think she could have gone?'

'London's a big place, Ryan, you don't need me to tell you that.' Stevie shrugged. 'Paddington. The Strand. Any of the other meat racks. It's difficult to say. I reckon he'll be lucky if he finds her, though. I mean, it's like trying to find a needle in a haystack, isn't it? Besides, I don't think he's realised she might not want to go home even if he does find her. She must have left home for a reason to begin with.'

'And you? Why did you leave?' the private detective wanted to know.

Stevie swallowed hard and turned her head to look out of the window.

'I was pregnant,' she said flatly.

'Did your parents want you to get rid of the baby?'

'My father did. My mother didn't know, or didn't care either way.'

'So you left?'

She nodded.

'My father gave me the money for the abortion. He didn't want me to have it, you see.' She smiled bitterly. 'He didn't want anyone to find out it was his.'

When Ryan glanced at her, he saw that there were tears in her eyes.

'That's right, I was being fucked by my own father,' she said, looking at him. 'It started when I was eleven. I got pregnant when I was fifteen. He tried to blame it on someone else, but I knew it was his. I left home just before my sixteenth birthday and came to London. Two days after I arrived I had a miscarriage.' She shrugged involuntarily. 'I've never seen so much blood. The hospital said I was lucky I didn't die.' She looked down at her hands. 'Put it down to experience, eh?' There was contempt in her voice.

He swung the car into Ossulston Street, looking for a parking space close to the hostel.

Stevie glanced towards the building, seeing no movement on the steps that led up to the main door.

Ryan drove past once, still looking for somewhere to park.

'Ryan, look,' Stevie said suddenly, jabbing his arm.

He followed her pointing finger.

Emma Powell had emerged from the hostel. She looked to her right and left and then set off down the street towards Euston Road.

'She looks like she's in a hurry,' Ryan mused, observing her short, agitated steps. Every few yards she would break into a run.

Ryan turned the car in the middle of the street, narrowly avoiding an Astra parked on his left, and headed off down the thoroughfare.

'What are you doing?' Stevie asked.

'I want to know where she's going,' he said, his eyes never leaving Emma as she hurried along.

'What about the files?'

'They can wait.'

As they waited, Emma looked at her watch and quickened her step.

'Do you think she's late for an appointment?' Ryan said.

A pedestrian moved to step in front of his car and Ryan blasted a warning on the hooter, not wanting to lose sight of Emma.

She headed down Euston Road.

'What if she's just going to get a sandwich?' Stevie asked.

'Then I'll have been wasting my fucking time following her, won't I?' Ryan replied.

Emma was finally turning into the gateway that led to the main entrance of St Pancras Station.

Ryan raised his eyebrows in surprise and guided the car up the ramp in front of the station, ignoring the taxi that was almost on his rear bumper. The private detective kept his eyes on Emma.

'What the hell is she doing?' he murmured.

Heading for the entrance, she was checking her watch again.

She broke into a slight run when she saw the person she had come to meet.

The man was leaning against the red brickwork of the station facade. As he caught sight of Emma he smiled broadly and walked towards her.

Ryan watched as they embraced, holding each other before kissing passionately.

'Well, well,' he said, smiling. 'I wonder who the boyfriend is?'

Stevie gazed intently at Emma and her companion as they stood close, arms around one another.

'And during work hours, too,' Ryan said with mock reproach. Stevie was still staring at the couple, her eyes unblinking. He lit up a cigarette.

'Do you know that geezer?' he asked.

Stevie nodded.

'*That's* Don Neville.'

Eighty-four

There was a steady stream of people moving both into and out of St Pancras and Neville guided Emma away from the irregular procession, pulling her closer to him. She kissed his cheek and he smiled at her, tilting her head up and looking into her eyes.

'What's wrong?' he asked, smiling. 'Why were you so anxious to see me?'

'Are you complaining?' she said.

He shook his head and snaked an arm around her waist.

'Let's go in and get a drink,' he suggested.

'I can't stop, Don,' she told him. 'I've got to get back to the hostel. I had to speak to you, though.'

'What's on your mind? I know you well enough after ten months to know that something's bothering you. What is it?'

She sighed.

'There was someone round at the hostel,' she told him. 'He said he was looking for his son. I forget his name. He wanted to check my files, everything.'

'Did you let him?'

'Of course I didn't.'

'So what's your problem?'

'He was asking questions, Don. He asked if I knew Ray Howells.'

'So what? So he's heard Howells' name. A lot of people know the little prick. That's no big deal.'

'What if he was a policeman?'

'If he'd been with the Law he'd have looked through your fucking files whether you wanted him to or not. And even if he had looked, so what? What would he have found?'

'There are files on the six kids who've been killed.'

'So what? That doesn't necessarily link you to them. Let the Law come looking and asking questions if they want to.'

'That's easy for you to say; you're not the one who'd have to face them. I'm not sure I could, either.'

'What does that mean, Emma?'

'It means I've had enough, Don. I can't do it any more. I can't carry on giving you the names of kids leaving the hostel. I can't carry on sorting out the ones with no families so you can use them in your films. I want out.'

Neville eyed her suspiciously for a moment.

'It's only a matter of time before the police pick up a lead and then they'll find you. They'll find both of us. And then what?'

'You're asking me to stop making the films, is that it?' he said sharply. 'You're asking me to stop selling them, to give up all the money it brings in?'

'You've killed six. How many more will there be?'

'What is this? An attack of conscience?' He laughed bitterly. 'It's a little late for that, isn't it, Emma? A bit late to try and get out? You're in as deep as me,' he snapped, grabbing her wrist and pulling her closer. 'You supplied us with the names of the kids from your hostel. You *gave* us those kids. And don't tell me different. You knew what my business was. You agreed to help. You got rid of that dead baby for me, don't forget *that*, too. You're as much a part of this as me or Eddie Caton.' He released her wrist. There were white marks where the pressure of his grip had caused

297

indentations. Emma rubbed the marks gently and looked at Neville.

'I won't go to jail, Don,' she said quietly. 'I can't.'

'No one's going to jail,' he told her. 'Because no one's going to get caught. Understand?'

She lowered her head but Neville held her chin gently and looked into her eyes.

'No one is going to jail,' he repeated.

She touched his hand gently.

'You love me, don't you?' he asked.

She nodded.

'Then trust me.'

He pulled her to him and kissed her again, their bodies pressed tightly together.

What the fuck do I do?

Ryan sat helplessly in the car, one hand unconsciously brushing against the butt of the Automatic. How easy it would be to haul Neville into the car now, to force him to lead the way to Kelly.

Kelly.

'Are you *sure* that's him?' Ryan asked, his eyes never leaving the couple.

'Positive,' Stevie confirmed. 'He always wore his hair in a pony-tail. I'd recognize him anywhere.'

Ryan chewed his bottom lip thoughtfully.

What the fuck do I do?

The car-phone rang and Ryan snatched it up.

'Yeah,' he barked.

'Ryan, it's Kiernan,' said the voice at the other end.

'What do you want?' the private detective snapped. 'I've got Neville standing in front of me right now.'

'Jesus Christ. What are you going to do?'

'I wish I knew. What's so important?'

'You told me to stay here and monitor the phone until you got back, right?'

'I know what I told you to do,' Ryan snapped. 'Get to the point.'

'There was a phone call a few minutes ago from some guy called Finlay. Joseph Finlay. He said he had to speak to you urgently.'

'What did he say?' Ryan demanded.

'I didn't take the message myself, it's on the answering machine.'

'Where the fuck were you? That's what I left you in my office for, to take the calls.'

'Even *I* have to piss, Ryan,' Kiernan said angrily. 'The fucking message is here, anyway. I think you should hear it. Finlay mentioned Kelly.'

Ryan hung up and immediately started the engine, guiding the Sapphire out of the station car park and back towards Euston Road.

'What the hell are you doing, Ryan?' Stevie said, watching Neville and Emma disappear through the rear window. 'I thought you wanted to talk to Neville.'

'I'll talk to him,' he said quietly, glancing into the rear-view mirror at the man with the pony-tail. For now, all he was concerned with was getting back to his office.

He had to hear the message.

Eighty-five

'Ryan. Ryan, if you're there pick up the phone. All right, listen. This is Joseph Finlay. I know where Kelly is. The kidnappers rang me. I've got to give them the money tonight. I

need your help. I'll be at your office by eleven-thirty. Ring me at my office if you need to, you know the number.'

Ryan pressed the 'Review' button on the machine and sat staring blankly at it as the tape rewound. He pressed 'Play' and listened for the third time.

Kiernan sat on one edge of the desk; Stevie was perched on the end of the sofa. Neither of them spoke. The Irishman was watching Ryan's face. Stevie puffed agitatedly on a cigarette.

'It's over,' Ryan said finally, getting to his feet.

'What's over?' Kiernan asked.

'Our little working relationship,' said the private detective, pouring himself a drink. 'This *ménâge à trois.'* He smiled humourlessly. 'You, me and Stevie. It's finished. I don't need you any more. You can go.'

'As easy as that?' said Kiernan.

'As easy as that,' Ryan told him, downing a large measure of whisky.

'Bollocks,' snapped the Irishman. 'I came looking for my sister and I'm going to find her. You said that if we found Howells he might lead us to Neville, and if we found Neville we might find my sister. Well, I'm not giving up now. I've come too far for that. I'm not going home without her. I'm not leaving, Ryan. I'll come with you tonight if I have to. Anything.'

'Very touching,' said the private detective, taking another large swallow. 'What about you, Stevie?'

She shrugged.

'I agreed to stay until you found Howells,' she said. 'You said you'd pay me if I helped you find him. I helped you.' She raised her eyebrows expectantly.

'Quite right,' Ryan said, crossing to his desk. He slid open one of the drawers and took out what looked like a small strong-box. Using a tiny key on his key ring he opened the box and took out two wads of notes. He tossed first one then the other to Stevie, who caught them.

300

'There's a hundred and fifty in each one,' he told her. 'That was the deal, wasn't it? Three hundred notes when we found Howells. It's all there.. Count it, if you like.'

She pushed the money into her handbag.

'I trust you,' she said, smiling thinly.

'Never trust anyone,' Ryan said sardonically.

Stevie got to her feet and moved towards the door, hesitating when she reached it.

'Thanks for the money,' she said quietly.

'A deal's a deal,' he said.

'You're really going to walk out?' Kiernan asked. 'Just take the money and fuck off?'

'What do you expect me to do?' she protested.

'I didn't expect *anything* from you,' the Irishman told her scathingly. 'Three hundred quid should buy a lot of drugs. I hope you're happy.'

'I hope you find your sister,' Stevie said, one hand resting on the doorknob.

Kiernan turned his back on her.

'When you do, perhaps you should ask her what makes *her* happy,' she added. Then, to Ryan:

'See you around.'

And she was gone.

'Fucking slag,' rasped Kiernan.

'She did her bit,' Ryan said quietly, draining the last drops from his glass. He looked up at Kiernan. 'So you want to be a fucking hero, Kiernan?'

'I just want to find my sister, right?' he said.

'Very noble.'

'I'm sick of your fucking attitude, Ryan,' the Irishman snapped. 'I offered to help you.'

'I didn't ask, did I?'

'This isn't just for your benefit, it's for mine.'

'You don't know what you're getting yourself into. Things have changed now, Kiernan. It isn't a case of

301

wandering around Soho or King's Cross hoping you'll spot her now, you know. You're close. And the closer you get, the more dangerous it gets. Are you ready for *that*?'

Kiernan nodded.

Ryan tossed him his keys.

'That cabinet over there.' He motioned to the other side of the room. 'Use the small brass key to open it.'

Kiernan did as he was instructed.

He saw the .357 lying there.

'Take it,' Ryan told him.

The Irishman reached for the pistol.

'You might need it,' Ryan said cryptically. 'Have you ever fired a gun before?'

'No.'

'Let's hope you haven't after tonight.' He fixed the Irishman in an unblinking stare. 'You could die, Kiernan.'

'Everybody dies, Ryan.'

The private detective began to laugh, a bitter hollow sound.

'Tell me about it,' he said flatly.

Eighty-six

He reached out to touch the piles of money, running his fingertips gently over the stacks of notes bound with elastic bands. Finlay swallowed hard and then closed the briefcase, snapping it shut. He exhaled deeply and turned to study his full-length reflection in the bedroom mirror. There were beads of sweat on his forehead and his skin was waxen, like a Madame Tussaud's effigy.

'Let me come with you.'

Kim was sitting on the edge of the bed, looking alternately at her husband and at the case.

Finlay shook his head.

'It's too dangerous,' he said. 'Besides, they said I had to be alone.'

'They said no police, didn't they?' she insisted.

'Kim, I have to go alone,' he snapped, nervousness getting the better of him.

There was a long silence, which was broken finally by Kim.

'What if she's already dead?' Her voice was almost inaudible.

'She won't be,' Finlay told her, his assurance doing nothing to relieve her concern.

'You sound very sure of that, Joe.'

'Look, we're doing what they told us to do,' he said, agitated. 'I'm taking them the money. The police haven't been informed. We've followed their instructions. There's no reason why they should kill her. I just give them the money and they hand Kelly over to me.'

'And it's as simple as that?' she said sardonically. She was pulling distractedly at the corner of the duvet. When she looked up at him he could see the tears in her eyes.

'She'll be okay,' Finlay said, wishing he believed his own assurances.

Kim merely nodded.

He looked at his watch; his hand was shaking.

'I'd better go,' he said, picking up the briefcase. 'I've got to meet Ryan soon.'

'Don't let her get hurt, Joe, please,' Kim said, a single tear rolling down her cheek.

He paused in the bedroom doorway, thought about

going back to her. Thought about kissing her. Instead he headed out onto the landing and down the stairs.

Kim sat on the edge of the bed until she heard the front door close behind him. Then she wandered out onto the landing, crossing to the window that overlooked the driveway. She watched Finlay place the briefcase on the passenger seat and slide behind the wheel of the Jag. He started the engine then pulled away, disappearing into the night.

Kim looked at her watch.

It was 9.36 p.m.

Finlay also checked the time on the dashboard clock.

It should take him about an hour to get to Ryan's office.

As he shifted in his seat he felt the bulk of the Ruger .45 pressing against his side, secreted beneath his jacket. Kim had not known he was carrying it. He had spare shells in his pocket, should he need them.

He reached down with one hand and touched the butt of the pistol.

He had to be sure he could reach it quickly enough when the time came.

Edward Caton worked the slide on the Ithaca Automatic shotgun, chambering a round. The Deerslayer, as the weapon was affectionately nick-named, felt comfortingly heavy in his grasp. He sat at the battered wooden table thumbing shells into the breech, working the slide every now and then.

Opposite him Don Neville was thumbing .44 calibre shells into the magazine of his Desert Eagle. When the magazine was full he slammed it into the butt of the pistol and worked the slide, flicking on the safety catch before jamming the weapon into his belt.

In the top of one boot nestled a Bowie knife. The thick curved blade glinted in the dull light as he pulled it free.

He ran a thumb over the razor-sharp edge, like a surgeon about to perform an operation. Satisfied, he slid the knife back into his boot and pulled his jeans down to cover the hilt of the blade.

He glanced at his watch.

'Do you think he'll try to fuck us over?' said Caton, putting the shotgun on the table and picking up the snub nose .38 that lay there. He began pushing bullets into the chambers.

'I wouldn't put it past him,' said Neville. 'Even though he knows we'll kill the kid if he does.' He ran a hand through his hair, pulling his pony-tail away from the back of his neck. 'I'll tell you one thing, he won't come alone.'

Caton looked at his companion quizzically.

'I know that bastard,' Neville continued. 'He thinks he's so fucking clever.' He smiled thinly.

'He wouldn't dare,' Caton said.

'If he's *coming* mob-handed then we'll *meet* him mob-handed,' Neville said. 'Get on the blower. Call Macardle and Thompson, tell them to get over here straight away. And tell them to bring shooters.' His eyes narrowed. 'I'll show that fucker.'

He looked at his watch again.

10.16.

Eighty-seven

Vince Kiernan turned the gun over in his hand, feeling the weight of the .357, seeing the office lights glint on the chrome of its frame.

It was already loaded, with six heavy grain shells pushed into the chambers.

'Have you ever killed anyone?' Kiernan asked, glancing at Ryan, who was gazing out of the office window at the lights of Charing Cross Road.

The private detective sucked hard on his cigarette and blew out a long stream of smoke.

'Yes,' he said without turning round. 'But not with a gun.'

Kiernan put the pistol down and looked intently at him.

'When I was a policeman,' Ryan told him.

'I didn't know you'd been a policeman.'

'There isn't much about me you *do* know, is there?'

Like the fact I've got fucking cancer.

'What happened?' Kiernan asked.

'There'd been a hit-and-run accident in Camden. Some drunken bastard had ploughed into a bus queue and killed a woman and one of her kids. We tracked him down and I went in to arrest him. He ran for it. He couldn't have been much older than you. I chased him up onto the roof of the tower block where he lived.' Ryan shrugged. 'He went over the top. Twenty-five storeys, straight down.'

'You pushed him?' Kiernan asked, quietly.

'That's what the official report said.' Ryan sucked in a deep breath, wincing as he felt the pain in his chest. 'I was at the bus stop where he hit the woman and kid minutes after it happened. She was only young, twenty-two or twenty-three. The kid was pretty, too. It was difficult to tell after he'd run over her, of course. The car broke her neck and her back, fractured her skull in six places. When one of his wheels went over her arm it tore off a hand. The kid was about three. We found pieces of its brain in the treads of his tyres.'

Kiernan swallowed hard.

'So did you kill him or not?' he persisted.

'Did he fall or was he pushed?' Ryan chuckled. He looked at Kiernan. 'He wanted to give himself up. He bottled it when he realized he had nowhere else to run. All I could see was that dead woman and kid. Then he started bleating about how it wasn't his fault. I threw the cunt over the safety rail. I watched as he fell, watched him hit the concrete.' He took a last drag on his cigarette then lit another. 'Best thing for him.'

A heavy silence descended.

Kiernan watched the private detective glance at his watch. Smoke surrounded him like a bluish mist.

The buzzer on the voice-com sounded and Ryan crossed to it.

'Yeah, who is it?' he said.

'Finlay.'

'Come up,' said Ryan and jabbed a button on the panel.

By the time Joseph Finlay had walked up the five flights of steps to Ryan's office he was sweating like a pig. As he reached the door he paused, pulling his handkerchief out of his pocket to wipe his brow. He also checked that the Ruger was hidden from view.

307

He found Ryan waiting for him. Even in the dull light of the office he could see how white the private detective looked. Kim hadn't been specific about the nature of Ryan's illness but he certainly looked rough.

As he glanced round the office Kiernan emerged from the kitchenette area sipping at a glass of water.

'Who the hell is he?' snapped Finlay.

'He's coming with us,' Ryan said. 'His name's Vince Kiernan.' He turned to the young Irishman. 'Kiernan, this is Joseph Finlay.'

'No way, Ryan. It was supposed to be just you and me,' Finlay said irritably.

'Well, now it's not,' Ryan told him. 'We might need all the help we can get.'

'How do you know you can trust him?' Finlay protested.

'Why *shouldn't* he trust me?' Kiernan snapped.

'I trust him more than I trust *you*. He's coming with us, so get used to it.'

'If they see anyone with me, they'll kill Kelly. You know that,' Finlay said.

'They're not going to see anyone,' Ryan hissed.

'If she dies, Ryan, I'm holding you responsible,' Finlay told him.

'Open the case,' Ryan told him.

Finlay lifted it onto the desk and flipped it open, revealing the money inside.

'Jesus, how much is there?' Kiernan said.

'One million,' Finlay told him, shutting the case again. But Ryan opened it and pulled out one of the wads, flicking through it.

'What are you doing?' Finlay asked angrily.

'Just making sure you haven't decided to be a fucking smart-arse,' Ryan told him. 'You know, a fifty at the top of each pile and a fifty at the bottom but nothing but newspaper or blank paper in between. You can bet your arse *they'll* check.'

'It's all there,' Finlay snapped. Grabbing the money back and dropping it into the briefcase, he snapped the lid shut.

Ryan looked at his watch.

'We'd better go,' he said and reached for the Automatic hanging in its shoulder holster on the back of a chair. He strapped it on, watching as Kiernan did the same.

'Remember,' Ryan said to the Irishman, 'if you do have to use that don't jerk the trigger. If you're close enough to what you're shooting at you should be able to hit it. That'll put a hole in a brick wall at fifteen feet.'

'Guns?' said Finlay with mock consternation.

'They're kidnappers,' said Ryan mockingly, 'not fucking lollipop men. You take care of the money and let me worry about the rest of it. They might not be too keen on your walking out of there, Finlay, whether you've paid them off or not.'

Kiernan fastened the strap on the shoulder holster and closed his jacket over it.

'All right?' Ryan asked.

He nodded.

Ryan winced as he felt a stab of pain. He turned away so that the others couldn't see his discomfort. He opened the desk drawer and stared down at the bottle of morphine.

He shut the drawer again, gritting his teeth against the pain.

'Come on,' he said, looking at his watch.

It was 11.16.

Eighty-eight

'The cunt isn't coming,' Colin Macardle said, puffing at his roll-up, spitting a piece of tobacco onto the dusty floor. He was standing against the wall of what had once been the sitting-room in the flat above Forty-three Carnaby Street. A Viking double-barrelled shotgun was propped on his shoulder.

In the kitchen Paul Thompson was pacing back and forth in the gloomy glow cast by the paraffin lights, peering at the filthy room. He seemed fascinated by the cracked sink. A large earwig dragged itself out of the plughole and scurried across the filthy china.

A 9mm Browning Hi-Power was stuck in Thompson's belt.

He moved through into the tiny bathroom, urinating gushingly into a lavatory that had long ago ceased to contain any water. When he'd finished he peered into the bedroom beyond.

Still covered by a sheet, still tied securely to the reeking mattress lay Kelly. Her eyes were closed.

Thompson stared at her for a moment and then walked back into the living-room where the other three men were gathered.

'I think the kid's asleep,' Thompson said, sitting down on a rickety wooden chair.

'I said, he's not coming,' Macardle repeated.

Neville looked at his watch.

11.43.

'He'll be here,' he said sternly.

'And we have to sit around like pricks waiting for him?' the Scot muttered.

'It's nearly time,' Neville insisted. 'He'll *be* here.'

'What do we do after he's delivered the money, Don?' Caton asked.

'Kill him *and* the kid,' Neville said flatly. Then a thin smile touched his lips. 'Perhaps we should film it.' He laughed.

The picture had been taken about two years ago. Kelly was dressed in a blue dress, her hair plaited.

Kim ran her fingers gently over the glass, over the image of her daughter. She shuddered.

Despite the warmth of the room she felt cold – the chill came from within. It seemed to grow inside her like a freezing tumour.

Like Nick's?

She found her thoughts turning to her ex-husband. Suddenly they were tumbling through her mind at dizzying speed.

Ryan.

Kelly.

The kidnapping.

The phone calls.

Kim held the photo to her breast as she might hold a sobbing child.

As she would hold Kelly.

She prayed that she might have that joy again but still the iciness grew within her, spreading through her veins like a virus.

She glanced at the clock on the mantelpiece; the seconds were ticking away as the deadline drew closer.

She tried to imagine what Finlay was doing now, but all she could think about was Kelly.

And she wept.

'We'll give you two minutes, then we'll follow,' said Ryan, looking down Carnaby Street.

It was empty at such a late hour; only a shadowy figure lay in the nest of cardboard he'd pulled around him in a shop doorway halfway down the thoroughfare.

Pieces of paper drifted on the warm breeze like strange tumbleweeds. Ryan felt like humming the theme to 'The Good, The Bad and the Ugly'.

He put a hand to his chest as he felt more pain, but he forced it away and jabbed the watch-face again, ensuring that the other two men did the same.

'Two minutes?' Finlay said, swallowing hard.

He could feel the gun jammed into his trousers digging into his side.

Kiernan also checked his watch.

Finlay set off, his pace brisk, his steps even.

Both men watched him, hidden in a doorway across the street. They saw him hesitate as he reached the main door of number forty-three. He pushed it and found it was stuck. After a light bump with his shoulder it swung open.

Finlay disappeared inside.

Other eyes had seen him enter.

'Finlay's inside,' said Edward Caton, leaning back from the window that looked out onto Carnaby Street.

'Is he alone?' Neville asked.

'I can't see anyone else,' Caton said, squinting into the gloom. He turned and smiled broadly.

'Party time,' Neville said. He too was smiling.

He worked the pump action of the Ithaca.

Eighty-nine

The dust was so thick it stuck to his shoes, muffling his footsteps. Small clouds rose with each footfall as Finlay made his way slowly through what had once been a shop.

The wooden floor was littered with rubbish. Waste paper and empty tin cans were scattered everywhere, covered by a fine film of dust.

In the gloom, Finlay peered upwards. Plaster had fallen from the ceiling in a number of places, here and there in lumps. It crackled when he stepped on it; the sound reverberated within the hollow shell.

Shelves had been pulled off the wall and lay strewn around in the jigsaw of neglect. Even their metal brackets had fallen or been torn free of the wall. Several pieces of timber seemed to have dropped from the panelled ceiling.

Nearly blind in the enveloping gloom, Finlay moved as cautiously as he could but the floor was like a huge booby trap. He managed to remain on his feet only by shooting out a hand to steady himself against a wall. Muttering under his breath he moved on, picking up the briefcase which had fallen from his grasp. It was coated in dust, too, but he gave it only a perfunctory wipe; the dust stuck to his hand.

Ahead of him on the left was a door he assumed led to the back of the shop.

He paused before opening it, stepping through to find himself at the bottom of a narrow flight of stairs.

Dull light leaked down from the top of the steps. As he stood gazing up, Finlay saw a figure appear above him.

Edward Caton was holding the .38 on him.

'Come up,' he said.

Finlay began to climb.

From the same side of Carnaby Street, invisible to any prying eyes that might be watching from the window of number Forty-three, Ryan scurried from one shop doorway to another. He beckoned Kiernan to follow him. The Irishman's heart thudded hard against his ribs.

The private detective pushed open the main door, relieved when it didn't squeak. He moved into the cloying darkness followed by Kiernan, who looked round at the neglect and decay. The place smelt of cats' piss. Or rats, he thought, scanning the floor for any signs of movement.

Picking their way over the debris, the two men moved with infinite slowness through the shop towards the far end.

There was creaking from above them. Ryan held up a hand to halt Kiernan's progress.

They stood motionless for interminable seconds, frozen like statues; they even held the breath in their lungs.

Kiernan saw Ryan slip the Automatic from its holster, then he advanced again.

There were more creaks from above, then voices. They were impossible to distinguish, even in the silence.

The door ahead was slightly ajar. The feeblest of light rays trickled through the crack like water through a split container.

The private detective moved towards the door, edging it open a fraction more, trying to hear the voices more clearly.

Kiernan watched his face intently, his heart thudding hard against his ribs.

Ryan heard Finlay's voice, then another man's, and another's.

There was laughter. Muted, bitter.

He peered towards the ceiling.

'How many do you think?' Kiernan whispered nervously.

Ryan shrugged.

'Three, four. It's difficult to tell.'

He heard more creaking from above, louder this time and he motioned Kiernan away from the door.

Someone was coming down the stairs.

Ninety

'It didn't have to come to this, you know,' said Neville, holding the Ithaca in one hand, the barrel levelled at Finlay's chest.

'Just let me see my daughter,' said Finlay sharply.

'Get the kid, Paul,' Neville said to Thompson, his eyes never leaving Finlay.

Thompson headed for the bedroom.

'Put the money down on the table,' Neville said, nodding towards the briefcase.

'Not until I've seen Kelly,' Finlay said defiantly. He

looked at Caton, who still held the .38, then back at Neville. Behind him Macardle was heading down the stairs.

'Put the case on the table,' Neville said.

'No,' Finlay insisted, feeling the Ruger pressing against his side.

His mind was spinning.

Even if he managed to get the gun clear in time, how the hell was he going to take out four men without them killing him first? He'd never even fired a gun before.

Thompson returned from the bedroom, clutching Kelly. She was bound and gagged; tears streamed down her face.

'Let her go,' Finlay said, his voice cracking.

'The money,' Neville insisted.

Finlay dumped the briefcase heavily on the table, flipped it open and took a wad of notes out, hurling it at Neville.

'Now let her go,' he shouted.

Neville picked up the money and held it beneath his nose, inhaling gently, smiling.

'Cut her loose,' he said to Thompson, who began untying the girl.

He pulled the gag from her mouth.

'Help me, please,' she sobbed.

'It's going to be okay, sweetheart,' Finlay said.

'Touching, isn't it?' Neville said to Caton.

'You bastard,' Finlay snarled.

Should he pull the gun now?

'Let her go,' Finlay rasped.

'We'll count this first,' Neville said, and laid the shotgun on the table top.

Now?

Finlay's breath was coming in gasps.

Where the hell was Ryan?

As the sound of footsteps grew louder on the other side of the door, Ryan eased the 9mm Automatic into the firing position, level with the head height of anyone who might step through the door.

Kiernan thought about drawing his own gun, but as he stepped back he tripped and stumbled over a piece of thick wood.

Ryan shot him an angry glance.

The footsteps drew nearer.

The door opened and Macardle stepped into the shop.

For what seemed like an eternity everything froze, then Macardle opened his mouth to shout a warning.

Kiernan moved with lightning speed, grabbing the piece of wood he'd tripped on, swinging it up like a club.

He swung it with incredible force, driving it into Macardle's face. The impact shattered the bridge of his nose.

The Scot let out a low choking sound and dropped to his knees. The shotgun fell from his grasp.

Kiernan brought the lump of wood down again, this time across the top of his head.

The blow fractured his skull, almost splitting the parietal bone.

He fell forward at Kiernan's feet, arms stretched out on either side of him as if in supplication.

'Come on,' shouted Ryan and they both dashed up the stairs.

As he reached the top he heard just three words:

'Kill the kid.'

Ninety-one

Ryan heard someone shouting, but barely realized the roars came from his own throat.

He flung himself up the last two steps and into the room, the Automatic already levelled.

In one brief split second he saw everything in the room with amazing clarity, as if his mind had become a camera, the image imprinted there fleetingly.

Immediately in front of him was Finlay, standing close to an old wooden table.

On the other side of the table he saw the man he knew as Don Neville and, beside him, Edward Caton.

To his right, in a doorway, stood Paul Thompson.

He had one arm around Kelly's throat.

It was her scream that seemed to signal the beginning of the explosion.

'Dad,' she shrieked.

Ryan spun round, firing twice, high to avoid Kelly. The first shot missed, blasted plaster from the wall, but the second struck Thompson in the face, powering into his jaw just below his lower lip. Teeth and bone were driven back by the impact and Thompson's head snapped backwards as if jerked from behind as the bullet caught him. Blood and fragments of bone sprayed Kelly, who fell forward, still screaming.

Finlay threw himself to one side, deafened by the thunderous discharge of the pistol in such a small room. The sound was eclipsed a second later as Neville swung the Ithaca up to his shoulder and fired.

The stock slammed back against the collar bone as the shotgun spat out its lethal load.

Hurtling up the steps behind Ryan, Kiernan crashed into him, knocking him to one side.

Luckily the collision took him out of the path of the shotgun's blast. The massive eruption blew a huge hole in the wall behind.

Cursing, Neville worked the slide and fired again, the second blast ripping a crater in the floor.

The sound of firearms in such a small area was monstrous; they were all deafened by the thunderous retorts. Everything seemed to happen in slow motion.

Ryan fired again, scrambling forward on his knees.

The slide pumped back and forth, spent shell-cases flying high into the air.

Another shot blasted out part of a light socket; the next missed Caton by inches.

Caton swung the .38 round and fired back.

Kiernan howled in pain as a bullet cut through his left calf; it felt as if his leg was on fire. He rolled over, blood spilling from the wound, leaving a slick behind him.

He hauled the .357 free and fired twice, shouting in pain and fear, his bellows drowned by the massive discharge. The pistol bucked in his hand, the stock slamming against him with numbing power.

Two shots thudded into the wall beside Caton, who had not noticed Kelly scrambling out from beneath Thompson's body. She ran through the kitchen towards the bathroom.

Ryan was on his knees now, firing, his breath rasping in his lungs and throat, his mouth dry. The stench of cordite filled his nostrils.

Neville kicked the table over to give himself some cover.

The briefcase and its expensive load went flying,

money scattering everywhere as the table thudded over onto its side.

A bullet ripped through the wood and grazed Neville's cheek.

'Jesus,' he shouted, rising to fire again.

'Come on,' screamed Ryan.

Fucking kill me, you cunt.

Finlay was crawling across the room towards the door, past the injured Kiernan who was trying to haul himself upright.

Caton fired twice with the .38.

The handgun retort was drowned by the massive blast of the shotgun.

Finlay screamed in agony as a bullet blasted off his right middle finger.

The digit was severed by the high velocity slug; he saw it skid across the floor.

Pain immediately enveloped his arm and blood poured from his hand.

Kiernan tried to steady the .357 but it pulled low.

More by luck than judgement he caught Caton in the left hip.

Travelling at over 1,450 feet a second the bullet shattered Caton's pelvis, blasting away a huge portion of bone before exiting upwards through the lowest lumbar vertebrae. A spray of blood and pulverized bone exploded with the bullet. Caton dropped like a stone, the gun falling from his hand, his body paralysed.

Kiernan tried to put another in him, but as he was aiming Neville swung the Ithaca around and fired.

The blast hit him in the chest, ripping through ribs and one lung, puncturing the fleshy bag like a balloon. Blood burst from the wound, the exit discharge carrying lumps of greyish-pink tissue with it which spattered the wall behind the Irishman. He went down in a heap, still clutching the gun.

Ryan saw him fall and fired again at the table Neville was using as cover. Pieces of wood were blasted away. One of the bullets skewed wide, taking off most of Caton's nose and a portion of the side of his head.

Kiernan was slumped against a wall, his body quivering madly. He looked down to see a dark urine stain on the front of his jeans. Blood from his wounds was flowing rapidly from his body; his left side felt as if someone had pulled it open with red hot tongs. He could see portions of shattered rib gleaming whitely amid the pulped mess of flesh and lung. When he tried to breathe it felt as if his chest were being crushed. He tried to speak but the blood, rising in his throat, only let out a liquid gurgle.

He saw Finlay pull the Ruger free of his belt and wave it aimlessly in the air, pulling the trigger to send a bullet harmlessly into the ceiling.

Neville hurled the table over again, trying to knock down Ryan, then the man with the pony-tail hurled himself towards the kitchen in pursuit of Kelly.

Ryan fell backwards, firing all the time, until the slide shot back signalling an empty magazine. He pulled another from his pocket, slammed it into the butt and worked the slide, getting off two more shots but missing with both.

He rose.

As he did Kiernan saw movement on his other side.

At the top of the stairs.

His face a bloodied mess, Macardle swayed there for precious seconds, the sawn-off shotgun levelled at Ryan.

Kiernan could only utter his warning in liquid sounds.

Macardle pulled both triggers simultaneously.

The massive blast hit Ryan in the back, destroying both kidneys, ripping a hole in his back large enough to get two hands in. He pitched forward, blood spilling from the gaping wound.

Kiernan raised the .357, so close to Macardle the muzzle was touching the Scot's leg.

The bullet blew his right kneecap off, splitting the patella and the tibia, almost severing the limb.

He crashed to the ground, facing Kiernan, looking up at him in pain, his mouth open.

Kiernan pushed the .357 into Macardle's mouth; the steel cracked his teeth. Then he fired.

The bullet took off nearly all the back of the Scot's head. Blood, brain and bone were blasted into the wooden floor as the bullet erupted from his cranium, the entire head looking as if someone had placed an explosive charge inside it. Kiernan was splashed with blood and viscera but it was hard to tell to whom it belonged. The room had been transformed into a slaughterhouse.

Deafened by gunshots, blinded by muzzle flashes and choked by cordite and smoke, the survivors smelled the stench of blood and death.

Ryan was lying face down, his spine visible through the wound in his back, tendrils of flesh hanging from the extremities like bloodied confetti.

Caton and Thompson were dead.

Kiernan felt very cold. Tears were forming in his eyes as he sat slumped against the wall. He told himself it was from the pain, but in fact there was little pain, even from the wound in his chest. Every time he tried to breathe the wind hissed through the ruptured lung. He saw Finlay holding the Ruger with one hand, his other arm hanging uselessly at his side, the middle finger blown off. The hand looked as if it had been dipped in red paint.

Kiernan looked down at what was left of Macadle's head and noticed that his eyes were open.

He had a speck of plaster on the iris of his left eye.

Kiernan wondered why something like that should attract his attention.

It was his last thought.

Finlay crawled past the dead Irishman, heading for the kitchen.

Money was scattered everywhere, great wads of it, soaked in blood.

He saw a figure in the doorway. Two figures.

Neville had hold of Kelly by the hair. In his other hand he held the Bowie knife; it was pressed against her throat.

'Finlay,' Neville rasped. 'I'm going to cut her fucking head off.'

Ninety-two

'Let her go.'

The words were gargled through blood.

Ryan felt it spilling over his lips as he struggled to force them out, holding the gun on Neville.

The private detective could hardly feel his legs but he managed to haul himself around on his side so that he was facing Neville.

'Forget it,' Neville snarled. 'She's fucking dead, anyway. Even if you shoot me I'll still have time to cut her throat.'

'Let her go,' Ryan croaked again, the gun wavering in his grip.

Neville knew he only had to wait a moment or two

longer and Ryan would be dead.

Finlay took a step towards him.

'Back off,' Neville said, his attention drawn to the other man.

Finlay kept coming.

'I told you,' Neville shrieked, his eyes blazing. 'I'll fucking kill her.'

Finlay raised the gun.

Ryan gritted his teeth and held the man with the pony-tail in his sights. Fuck, he felt cold.

Fuck. Fuck. Fuck.

This is what you wanted.

But he had to know Kelly was safe.

Before . . .

Finlay stepped closer, the Ruger levelled.

'Last warning, cunt,' Neville snarled, spittle spilling onto his lips.

'Do it,' Ryan urged. 'Finlay, do it.'

'Now she dies,' hissed Neville.

Finlay fired twice.

He shot Ryan both times in the back. One bullet passed through the fleshy part of his side; the other cracked his collar bone as it exited.

Neville looked on, aghast, his jaw dropping.

Kelly screamed.

The shrill exhaltation and the shock of what Finlay had just done made Neville lower the knife.

Kelly fell forward, free of his grip, away from the blade.

Finlay, glassy-eyed, raised the Ruger and, from less than two feet away, shot Neville.

The first bullet hit him in the stomach, puncturing his abdomen, macerating a huge portion of his lower intestine. The second struck him in the right eye, drilling the socket empty and bursting from the back of his skull like a rocket, sending blood and brain splattering up the wall in a sticky red flux. He fell backwards, the knife falling from his grasp.

'Why did you shoot my dad?' Kelly sobbed, crawling across to the body of Ryan. 'Why?'

'I'm sorry, Kelly,' said Finlay, his face splashed with blood, his hand dripping crimson. He looked ashen. 'I had to.'

'Oh, Dad, no,' she sobbed over Ryan.

'I wish you hadn't seen it,' Finlay whispered, and raised the Ruger again.

He was straddling Kelly, the barrel touching the top of her head.

'I do wish you hadn't seen it,' he said again, his voice cracking.

He thumbed back the hammer.

Ryan heard the sound as if it came from a million miles away. As he opened his eyes he saw everything through a red haze.

He saw Kelly bending over him.

And Finlay straddling her, the gun pointing at her head.

He saw Neville's discarded knife lying so close.

So close.

He mouthed her name as he closed his fingers around the hilt.

Finlay pulled the trigger.

The hammer slammed down on an empty chamber.

Ryan drove the knife upwards with all the power he could muster.

The blade tore through the material of Finlay's trousers, plunging on and upwards, shearing through his scrotum, slicing one testicle in half and carving away the penis as it thudded into his stomach from below.

Finlay let out a high-pitched scream and tried to pull the blade free but Ryan kept hold of the hilt, ignoring the blood that cascaded onto his hand and face. He twisted it, driving it deeper, the churning knife slicing the other testicle free. Propelled by a thick spurt of blood it hit the floor with a wet plop, together with a portion of the severed penis.

Finlay was still shrieking as he fell back, finally allowed to fall as Ryan released the knife.

Blood was spreading out in a massive pool around him; some of it lapped against Ryan as he lay in a foetal position on the floor.

The screams diminished slowly. Now Ryan could hear another sound.

It was the high-pitched, strident wail of sirens.

Coming closer.

Kelly was bent over his body now, crying uncontrollably.

'Oh, Dad, please,' she sobbed.

He raised one bloodied hand and touched her cheek. Tears filling his eyes.

'I love you,' she wept.

He couldn't speak the words but he mouthed them, his lips curling upwards.

'No,' Kelly shouted helplessly. 'Don't die.'

She shook him, as if to bully him into clinging onto life.

The sirens were drawing nearer.

Kelly touched his face, her body trembling.

'I love you, Dad,' she whispered.

Nick Ryan was smiling.